the dirty ANGELS TRILOGY

the dirty ANGELS TRILOGY

THE COMPLETE BOX SET

KARINA HALLE

ALSO BY KARINA HALLE

Contemporary Romance Novels
Love, in English
Love, in Spanish
Where Sea Meets Sky (from Atria Books)
Racing the Sun (from Atria Books)
Before the Dawn (from Atria Books)
Bright Midnight (from Atria Books)
The Pact
The Offer
The Play
The Lie
The Debt (Fall 2016)

Romantic Suspense Novels
Sins and Needles (The Artists Trilogy #1)
On Every Street (An Artists Trilogy Novella #0.5)
Shooting Scars (The Artists Trilogy #2)
Bold Tricks (The Artists Trilogy #3)
Dirty Angels
Dirty Deeds
Dirty Promises

Paranormal/Horror Romance Novels
The Devil's Metal (Devils #1)
The Devil's Reprise (Devils #2)
Donners of the Dead
Darkhouse (Experiment in Terror #1)
Red Fox (EIT #2)
The Benson (EIT #2.5)
Dead Sky Morning (EIT #3)
Lying Season (EIT #4)
On Demon Wings (EIT #5)
Old Blood (EIT #5.5)
The Dex-Files (EIT #5.7)
Into the Hollow (EIT #6)
And With Madness Comes the Light (EIT #6.5)
Come Alive (EIT #7)
Ashes to Ashes (EIT #8)
Dust to Dust (EIT #9)

First box set edition published by
Metal Blonde Books July 2016

Cover design by Hang Le Designs
Edited by Kara Maclinczak
Metal Blonde Books
P.O. Box 845
Point Roberts, WA
98281 USA
Manufactured in the USA
For more information about the series and author visit:
http://authorkarinahalle.com/

ISBN: 1535422971
ISBN-13: 9781535422970

dirty
ANGELS

A NOTE FROM THE AUTHOR

Thank you for wanting to read Dirty Angels. Please note that the following book deals with the life within the drug cartels of Mexico and as such, it depicts many brutal acts and events that most people wish to believe don't happen – but they do. As a writer, I tried to stay as true to the real life dealings of the Mexican drug cartels and consulted such books as El Sicario, The Last Narco, and Midnight in Mexico. As a result, the book contains situations that are not suitable for all readers, whether you are 18+ or not.

TRIGGER WARNING: If you are sensitive to scenes that include or allude to rape, domestic violence, abuse and torture, please do not read this book. While Dirty Angels is fiction, it strives to be as realistic as possible to the world of Mexican drug cartels and the mentioned scenes do occur and frequently. Otherwise, please note the book contains a lot of explicit *and* unprotected sex, erotic material, violence, and bad language.

For Scott MacKenzie, from Karina MacKenzie.

If the narcos want something, they will get it one way or another. And as far as the women are concerned, there is a saying: "If I want you, I will have you, for better or worse. If I can't have you one way, I'll have you another way. And if I can't have you, no one will have you, that will be the end of you, and there you will be buried. Simple."

—*El Sicario: The Autobiography of the Mexican Assassin*

Despair and Deception, Love's ugly little twins
Came a-knocking on my door, I let them in
Darling, you're the punishment for all my former sins
I let love in

—*I Let Love In*, Nick Cave & the Bad Seeds

PROLOGUE

I was running.

I didn't know where, all I knew was that I had to keep going, one foot in front of the other. The wet grass brushed against my bare legs and I wished I'd planned my escape a little bit more. After a month of dwelling on it, toying with the idea, then finally committing, you think I would have escaped my husband's house with something more than shorts, a blouse, and a wallet. At least I was wearing running shoes.

There hadn't been any time. I was already outside when I saw my husband's boring guests arrive. I didn't mean to be. I was supposed to be in my room putting on my dress and making myself look oh so lovely. I'd been looking forward to them coming over for the last few days – they'd break up the daily monotony of a woman captive to her narco husband, a slave to the golden palace.

I'd only gone outside, out the kitchen door, to get flowers for the centerpiece. The maid had brought these expensive blossoms from in town, but I wanted the gardenias that grew at the front fence and created a hedge along the line. When the guest's Mercedes rolled in through the gates, I froze in place and watched as they parked and strolled up to the door. The night sky was minutes away from engulfing us.

After Salvador answered with that big phony smile of his and ushered them inside, I took in the deepest breath I could. I couldn't think. I couldn't chance changing my mind. I needed to act, and act now.

I grabbed a few sparse blossoms off the hedge and walked over to Juan Diego at the front gate. I knocked on the glass of his booth, making him jump in surprise as he'd just started to read his tabloid, and told him I was going outside along the hedge to get more flowers. He was reluctant—he had orders to keep me inside, though Salvador always insisted it was to protect me from everyone else. But there was never anyone to protect me against Salvador.

I waved my flowers at him and put my hand on my hip. I had only been the wife of Salvador for two months, but I was going to use that while I could. I needed to act like I owned authority, even if I didn't. Juan Diego was a kind man, and he was in no power to deny the wife of Mexico's largest drug cartel access to her favorite flowers.

The flowers my mama used to put in my hair every Sunday.

He waved me through with a warm smile, and I returned in kind, acting a role, pretending I wasn't trembling on the inside. I slowly walked along the hedge, plucking the flowers, my hands filled with fragrant white petals. I eyed the cameras that were stationed around the outer edge, knowing I didn't look suspicious to Rico, the surveillance guy inside, but if Salvador caught sight of me on the cameras, outside the compound, he would lose his shit.

There was no time. It was now or never.

I had to run. I had to try.

So I did.

Where the hedge started to blend in to the surrounding jungle and the clipped front lawn became unruly and unkempt, I dropped the flowers at my feet and ran into the darkness. I had studied our land—his land, it was always his land—time and time again, and all I knew was to avoid the roads. If I headed down behind the house, I'd come across the river that was too deep and wide to cross, and if I went across the road I'd be heading into the backyards of our neighbors who were as guarded as we were. I had to keep running north, through the trees, through the twilight.

I just had to keep running.

I ran for a good twenty minutes straight, my body coasting on adrenaline and the endurance I had built while working out in the home gym every day. I fell a few times, my hands always taking the brunt of the fall before the ground could take out the rest of me. I always got back up. There was no time for pain. I felt it, but it was almost a relief to have. After what Salvador had done to me, I could take a lot.

I ran and ran and ran, tripping over roots, dodging the trees in the weak moonlight that filtered through the trees, until the river suddenly cut across in front of me. I had no idea where I was, and I could see a few more stars than usual without the city lights. Somewhere in the trees a bird called out.

I thought about my parents, the people I was most worried about. Actually, the only people on this earth who mattered to me. I worried about Salvador finding out that I had run, I worried that he would kill them. But as brash as he was, he wouldn't do anything until he knew the facts. At least, I hoped that would be the case. The plan was for me to call my friend Camila and get her to take care of them – before he could.

Looking around me, I made my way to the river's edge and contemplated going across. It wasn't as wide here and didn't look to be as deep, with the tops of a few boulders poking their way through the current. I wondered if Juan Diego had alerted Salvador about what happened. I wondered if Rico had been watching when I disappeared from the cameras. I wondered how much time I had before they found me.

A branch snapped behind me. Even though that was the only sound I heard, I knew it belonged to a person who was probably wincing very loudly at his mistake. You couldn't afford to make mistakes in Mexico.

I quickly jumped from the shore and into the river, the cold water coming up to my mid-thighs and catching me by surprise. I gasped loudly and was momentarily frozen from the shock. Then I heard a fervent rustling behind me and knew I had to keep going or I'd die.

Or worse. With Salvador there was always worse.

The current rushing up against me was strong, and my sneakers slid against the sand and pebbles under my feet, but I made myself move, made myself push through the river, the other side so close. I kept going, my legs turning to ice, my eyes focused on the dry land, my arms stretched out as if I could reach it that way.

I heard a splash behind me. I would not turn around. I would not give up.

I cried out in frustration, lunging forward to reach the sand, as if that would save me in the end. But there was no saving me.

Suddenly thick, rough arms went around my waist, lifting me up out of the water. I heard another splash, nearly drowned out by my cries, and everything went black as a bag was placed over my head. My arms were yanked back behind me so fast that I thought they were being pulled out of the sockets. I screamed in pain, my breath hot inside the bag that felt like it was already starting to drown me.

Another pair of hands went for my legs. I started kicking wildly, hoping that the current would catch the person off-balance, but within seconds my legs were wrapped with rope and I was being led out of the river like a pig on a stick, a man holding up either end of me.

"Two minutes," someone said, a man's voice that I didn't recognize. Despite the bag that made everything sound muffled, he sounded like he was from the east coast.

"Are you sure?" asked the other man, his voice low and baritone, and close to my ear, the one who gripped my hands behind my back.

"I'm never wrong, hey."

"All right, Este. Let's not go down this path again. We have the bitch, let's go."

I swallowed hard, my stomach sick, a swirling pool of knots. This wasn't Salvador. These weren't his men. This was someone else, and even though I was running away from him, it was always better with the devil you know.

I was suddenly jerked downward, my back arching, and I cried out again. I cried out for Salvador as a last resort.

"Salvador!" I screamed through the bag, the heat rising up to my cheeks. "Help me!"

A fist came down on my cheekbone, my face exploding in stars of pain.

"Easy now, Franco" said Este, and the fist didn't come again. My lips throbbed, my mouth filled with blood, and I knew better than to try and cry out once more.

The men, Este and Franco, carried me away, their pace quickening. I only heard their breathing, fast and shallow, and the sound of the earth beneath their quiet feet. I could smell Franco's greasy breath, so close to my head. Every time I thought I might be able to move out of their hands and make an escape, their grip tightened around me even more.

I was going to die. There was no doubt about that now. Not at the hands of Salvador. In the hands of some unknown fate. These men, they were taking me somewhere. There was a reason I wasn't dead yet—death was the dessert.

I took in a deep breath, my mind beginning to swim laps in a dark pool. I wished these men had just killed me. My parents had money now because of my marriage. That was the whole point of it all. That was the point of everything—to give them a better life in their ailing years than I ever had growing up. If I died, I would die with peace in my heart knowing they were okay. It was the only thing that made my life worthwhile.

I must have lost consciousness due to lack of air because suddenly my head slammed back against something hard, and I fell over onto a cold slab. An engine whirred, the smell of exhaust seeping through. I was in a car—no, the back of a van—being taken somewhere. That dessert again.

I was in and out for the next while until the van jerked to a stop. I heard the back doors open, and before I could move, there were hands on me again, three pairs this time. They pulled me out of the van so fast that I cracked my head on the door frame. I heard Este apologize under his breath but that was it. Strong fingers seared into my arms and waist, and I was yanked forward across what felt like well-kept grass. For a split second I thought I wrong, and I was actually back at home. For that second I had hope, hope to just keep living, while before I only had the hope to live under my own terms. Now it was all about survival, instinct trumping reality.

The moment I heard a door open and I was shuffled down a staircase, the damp and musty smell permeating my nostrils,

I knew I wasn't back at home. We didn't have a basement. Salvador had rooms for torture in other houses, but not ours. At least, no rooms that I could ever see.

My mind began to race, flipping through thoughts and images I had been subjected to ever since I married Salvador. Who had taken me? Salvador had the Sinaloa state military and the police at his command, so it wasn't them. It was another cartel or one of his old associates trying to usurp the boss. He had told me from the beginning that there were men out there who wanted me, who would do anything to have me—to take me, torture me, hold me for ransom, then torture me some more.

The wife of the jackal is the greatest card you can play in this game.

I was thrown down onto a chair, my hands and feet immediately unbound, and then tied back to the arms and legs before I could struggle. I thought about screaming again but the side of my face still throbbed with the violence. Este had warned Franco off, but I knew cartel men; I knew them too well, and I knew that courtesy never extended very far.

I started to shake uncontrollably and my whole body rocking with the spasm while hot tears pooled in my eyes. But I refused to let them fall. I knew what was coming next. The bag would come off my head. The bags would go on theirs. The camera would turn on.

I didn't want the world to see me afraid. I had been afraid for too long.

"Is everything ready?" Este asked.

"It's all set up," I heard someone say, another male voice, heavy footsteps coming toward me. I tensed up, sensing Franco and Este and some other figure on all sides of me, and the other person, the one who had just spoken, who stopped a few feet away. I wondered if there were more than four people in the room and decided there must be. I could almost *feel* someone else's eyes, hear their breath, read their silence.

"How drugged is she?" the unknown voice asked.

There was a pause. Then Este said, "Not badly. She's somewhat coherent."

"You didn't gag her?"

"No, but she shut up when she needed to."

"It's lucky she was out there."

"Yes. It was."

Who were these men? Which cartel? Salvador had so many enemies and so many alliances that harbored grudges, you could never be sure who was looking for some way to ground traction. But even though I knew my fate was most likely death, it all depended on who I was with. Who had me. Some men were more deplorable than others. Now that the famous gringo Travis Raines was dead, Salvador himself was probably the worst of them all.

Though there was one cartel, one man, who I'd been told could give my husband a run for his money. He was famous for slicing the heads, hands, and feet off of people and littering them in streets all over the country.

There was a strange moment of silence and I concentrated hard, trying to hear more than the obvious. They were all waiting. Waiting for the order. Waiting for the man in charge to speak.

He did.

It came from the left of me. His voice was cool, calm, and collected. I didn't have to see to know who had taken me. The man I'd heard so much about. The man I'd been taught to fear.

"Gentleman," he said, and I could almost feel his infamous eyes on my body, "remove the bag."

There was a rustle and my face was immediately met with cool air that seized my lungs and bright lights that blinded me. I scrunched up my face, afraid to look, to see. Now it was all so real and I wanted to stay in the dark.

"Who did this?"

Suddenly, cool hands were at my swollen cheek and I flinched.

"Who did this?" my captor repeated, an edge to his level voice, his cigar-laced breath on my face.

"Sorry," Franco mumbled. "It was the only way to quiet her."

A heavy pause filled the room like dead weight. Finally the fingers came away from my skin, and my body relaxed momentarily. The man was in my face, the spicy scent of tea emanating off of him.

"Look at me, Luisa Reyes."

Chavez, I thought to myself. *I will always be Luisa Chavez.*

"Darling, aren't you curious to know where you are?"

"My name is Luisa *Chavez*," I said. I opened my eyes to see golden ones staring right back at me. It was like looking at an eagle. "And I know where I am. I know who you are. You are Javier Bernal."

He raised his brow in amusement and nodded. I'd seen his picture before, on the news. There was only one, and that was his mugshot, but even in that photo his eyes made an impression on you. They saw right into your depths and made you question yourself. He was one of the men that Salvador feared, even though Salvador had more power. He was the one I had been told to watch out for, the supposed reason why I'd always been locked in the compound or escorted by the local police to go shopping.

And yet here I was, tied to a chair in a cold, leaking basement with nothing in it except five cartel members, a video camera, and a knife that lay on top of a stool in front of me.

All of that for nothing. I could escape Salvador but I could never escape the cartels.

I had asked for this fate.

"You know why you're here," Javier said with deliberation, straightening up in his sharp black suit. He walked over to the stool, picked up the knife, and glanced at me over his shoulder. "Don't you?"

I could only breathe. I wanted to look at the others, at Este, at Franco, at the two other mystery men, but I was frozen in his gaze like a deer in headlights.

"What is the knife for?" I asked, my throat painfully dry.

"You'll find out after," he said. "It is for your husband. For your Salvador." He stepped to the side and waved his arm at the camera. "And this is also for him."

He eyed someone over my shoulder and gave a sharp nod. I heard a rip from behind and a piece of duct tape was placed over my mouth. I squirmed helplessly and the lights in the basement dimmed. The men stepped to the side while Javier went behind the video camera. A white light came off the front of it and bathed me in an eerie glow.

Javier cleared his throat, his face covered in shadow, and said loudly, projecting to the camera, "This is Luisa Reyes, former beauty queen of the Baja State and property of Salvador Reyes. Salvador, we have your wife and we have a long list of demands, demands which I know you can meet. I expect full cooperation in this matter or she dies in the next seven days. If she's lucky. I'll give you some time to think about what you're willing to give up for her. Then we'll be contacting you. Goodbye."

The light on the camera switched off, but the rest of the room remained dim.

"I hope your husband checks his emails often. It would be a shame to have to put this on YouTube."

There was a smirk on his face at that as he slowly walked toward me, the knife glinting in his hand. His eyes burned through the shadows then grew somber.

He held up the knife. "I think it's only going to hurt the first time."

My eyes focused on the silver of the blade, but the terror inside me grew too strong, and my urge to breathe through the duct tape became too difficult. My lungs seized in panic, pulsing dots appearing in my vision. I felt a hand on my collarbone, gripping the edge of my blouse, and then everything went black.

CHAPTER ONE

Three months earlier

"Excuse me, miss?"

I sighed and took a moment to compose myself before I slowly turned around, reminding myself to respond in English.

"Yes?"

The man and his buddies were staring at me with that stupid ogling look they had the whole time they were here. I was happy when they finally asked for the bill, just wanting them out of the bar and back to their drunken tourist festivities or whatever the white men got up to in this damned city of Cabo San Lucas. But it seemed I wasn't free yet.

The guy who called me, the most obnoxious of the group, wagged his brows at me and nodded at a spot behind me.

"You dropped something."

I opened my mouth to say something but shut it. I looked down at my feet, then behind me. My pencil was on the ground. Not that I ever needed it to remember orders anymore.

"Thanks," I said, and bent down to pick it up. Immediately the guys snorted and I quickly snapped back up. Of course they'd wanted me to pick it up—my uniform at Cabo Cocktails consisted of the shortest skirt ever.

I ignored them, not even bothering to turn around again, and made my way back to the bar. I slammed my bill holder on the counter and eyed the receipt. The little jerks hadn't even tipped me. Not that it was customary in Mexico, but with Americans in a tourist town, you always expected it.

"Stiffed again?" said Camila.

I looked over at her as she snapped the cap off of two bottles of beer. As usual, my colleague had an impish smirk on her pixie-like face. She always got the tips, maybe because she was always smiling.

"Yeah," I said, wiping the sweat off my brow. The fan beat overhead but it was always a bit too hot in the bar, didn't matter what time of the year it was. I turned around and eyed the boys who were still at the table, laughing and occasionally looking my way. "Those assholes over there."

"You know, if you just joke with them and smile sometimes, they'd probably tip you more," she said innocently, putting her beers on a tray.

I put my hand on my hip. "The minute I smile or play nice with them is the minute they take advantage of me. I don't want to give them the wrong idea."

"Luisa, I'm really starting to think you're afraid of men."

That bothered me a bit. "So? Aren't you?"

She rolled her eyes. "I'm a lesbian because I like pussy, not because men scare me." And with that she took the beers over to her waiting table.

I pressed my hand on the back of my neck, trying to alleviate the constant strain I felt there. It was nearly eleven o' clock at night, and I had been on my feet for twelve hours. I had three more hours of this before I could go home, which meant a forty-minute drive to San Jose del Cabo where I lived with my parents.

Which reminded me. My mother's birthday was tomorrow and I knew she deserved something special. We didn't have much money—I was the breadwinner at the house since my father suffered from early onset Alzheimer's and my mother was blind. She was healthy otherwise, but neither she nor my father could work, which meant everything fell on me. It was a lot for a twenty-three year old but I'd been working since I was a child; even when my father was able to hold a job it was never a high paying one. I was used to poverty and I was used to hard work.

I just could never get used to being treated like a piece of meat. I could never get used to the constant fear. And working at Cabo Cocktails, working for my boss, Bruno Corchado, meant I'd been dealing with those two things since I was twenty.

And now, because the only way I could get my mother a gift tomorrow would be to ask for an advance on my paycheck, I was walking right into the lion's den.

I took a deep breath, looked around to see if any new patrons had come in, and when I saw they hadn't, I straightened my shirt, pulling it up around my cleavage, and walked around the corner to Bruno's office.

I gave three quick raps on it and stood back. I hadn't seen him much today so I wasn't sure what kind of mood he was in. I was hoping for generous and disinterested but knew that was pressing my luck a little bit. At this time of night he was usually drunk and a jackass. Or a lecherous pervert.

I swallowed hard as I heard him bark, "Come in!"

I opened the door and poked my head in. "Bruno?" I asked.

He was sitting at his desk, a row of empty beer bottles beside him, going over the ledger. He looked at me with red eyes, his head swaying from side to side, and I immediately knew I'd made a mistake. "Luisa. My beauty queen. Come on in." He nodded at the door. "And shut that behind you."

My heart rate started to pick up. I'd been in this exact situation too many times and knew this was going to end very badly. Still, I needed this favor. I did as he asked, the door shutting like a cell door, and walked two steps toward him, hoping I could keep my distance.

Bruno wasn't a bad looking guy. He was in his late thirties, an apparent family man, though he never wore his ring at work and told every waitress that his marriage was open. We'd never seen his wife, or his children for that matter—we weren't even sure if they lived in the city, and none of us cared enough to ask. Many men operated businesses elsewhere and only visited their families on the weekends.

But just because he wasn't bad looking, didn't mean he wasn't bad.

"What is it, Miss Los Cabos?" he asked, stroking his chin and looking me up and down with drunken eyes. "You know, I was Googling you the other night and I found a picture of you winning that beauty queen contest. What were you, eighteen? Your tits were higher back then."

I bit down on my tongue to stop me from saying something that would probably get me fired. Work in the waitressing industry in Cabo was hard these days and not easy to come by. Damned economy in America meant the tourists weren't coming here as much.

I ignored his remark and ignored that his eyes were still fixed on my breasts. I licked my lips quickly and said, "I was wondering if I could ask a favor."

He raised his brows and gave me a sloppy grin, teeth gleaming with opportunity. "Well, well, well. What is it this time? Time off to take your dad to the hospital again? Something wrong with your mother?"

I dug my nails into the palm of my hand. "No. But it does involve my mother. It's her birthday tomorrow and I would like to get her a gift. I was wondering if I could get an advance on my wages. Two hundred pesos."

He laughed. "What are you buying for your mother for two hundred pesos? She's blind, isn't she?"

It took everything I had to keep it together. "It's a Kobo. An e-reader. A used one. I can buy audiobooks for her on it. She doesn't like Braille so much anymore with her arthritis."

"Well aren't you just the perfect daughter. You must be the apple of her eye."

His choice of words wasn't lost on me. "They've given so much to me over the years just to keep food on the table. It's the least I can do in return."

He stared at me for a few heavy moments before picking up his beer and having a long swig of it. "And what will you do for me in return?"

This was what I feared. I looked him straight in the eye and said, "You can have my word that I'll pay you back. Dock it out of my paycheck."

He grinned, though there was only malice in his eyes. "Oh, you'll pay me back. I know you will. I will take it from you before you have a chance. But I mean, what are you going to do for me to thank me for being such a wonderful and generous boss?"

I took in a deep breath. I didn't have much choice but I still had a choice. "I don't know. What did you have in mind? An extra shift?"

Bruno snorted and got out of his chair. He wasn't a tall man, but I was only 5'2" and he still towered over me. His eyes became lazy with lust and a bit of spittle dripped out of the corner of his mouth. "Not an extra shift. Tell me, Luisa, why is it that every single woman here, except for the dyke, has been with me and you haven't?"

It felt like a piece of dry toast was lodged in my throat. "Because you're not my type."

He raised his brow then nodded as if this whole thing was an elaborate joke. "I'm starting to think you don't have a type, Luisa. That you just like to be a tease. I see you every day, walking around in that outfit, flashing those legs and ass, showing those tits. You're fucking beautiful and you know it. But you don't fuck."

"This is the uniform you gave me."

"And yet you wear it better than any of those other girls. The men all come here to look at you. They want you. And you're such a stuck-up bitch that you can't even pretend to be nice. If you did, you wouldn't be here asking me for money. You'd be paying for everything with your tips. And your tits."

"This was a mistake," I said, feeling dizzy. I turned around, ready to leave. He reached out and grabbed my arm, his fingers digging into it.

"It is a mistake to leave," he said, pulling me close to him. He smelled like beer and chili, and it made my stomach roll. "I promise to give you your money, you just have to give me something." He read the fear on my face. "Don't worry, I'm not going to hurt you. I just want to see what others do not. I want to feel you."

I didn't know what to do. He dug his nails into mine and then he pushed me back. "Take off your shirt."

I opened my mouth to say no. I had to say no. In the past he had grabbed my ass, rubbed his erection against me, had kissed me briefly on the mouth, and made an attempt to grope my breasts. But he'd never told me to take my shirt off. This was too much, and yet I thought, I felt, if I could just do it and go to some other place in my head, I would be okay. I wouldn't be a whore. I would still be a virgin. I would still be pure and intact.

I could be all that and be a good daughter. I could ease the guilt of my mother staying at home, essentially alone, because my father was often a million miles away and didn't know who she was.

So I pulled my low-cut T-shirt over my head and stood there before my boss, the fluorescent light flickering behind him and making everything look that much worse. I stared at him straight in the eyes while he leered at my thin cotton bra.

"Well," I said. "Now you're seeing what no one except for me and my parents and my doctor have seen. Is that all?"

He looked so dumbfounded that it was almost laughable. Granted, I knew I had a good body, but I worked hard at it by going for my 5K jogs every morning. But I wasn't any different from any other girl. My breasts were still breasts.

Bruno managed to close his mouth. "Your bra. Take off your bra."

I could tell this was non-negotiable.

You're not here, you're not here, you're not here, I chanted to myself while I reached around my back and undid the clasp. I took it off, my breasts free, and held the bra in my hands.

He whistled. "I feel privileged."

"Funny how I don't feel the same."

He gave me a sharp look. "You're not done yet."

I gulped while he walked up to me. I wanted to close my eyes, but I couldn't be afraid. I didn't want him to think he was winning. I looked straight at him while his greasy hands went to my breasts, cupping them. I sucked in my breath while he ran his thumbs over my nipples, and I felt relief that they were reluctant to harden. The last thing I needed him to think was that this was turning me on. The reality was that I wanted to vomit, and if it happened, I wanted it to be all over him, just so he'd know how disgusting I thought he was.

He leaned in close, and for a second I thought he was going to kiss me. But he whispered in my ear, "I should have asked for more."

I suppressed a shudder, holding my breath while I waited for his next move. To my utter relief, he took his hands away and stepped back.

"You may make yourself decent again," he said nonchalantly. "To be honest, I expected your breasts to be a little bit bigger. I guess the shirt makes it look like you have more than you have. Again, that would come in handy if you actually cared about tips."

I knew my breasts were just big enough for my frame, but I didn't dare say anything while he sat back down at his desk and started removing pesos from his wallet. I put on my bra and shirt in record speed and tried to remind myself that my loss of dignity was worth whatever happiness I could buy my mother.

He gave me the money, holding on to my hand for a little too long, before he said, "Don't say I don't do you any favors. But if you ever ask for one again, expect more involvement from your side. Nothing in life is free. You of all people should know this."

I nodded, thanking him curtly and yanked the money out of his slimy grasp. As I turned and left his office, back into the heat, satellite TV and drunken cries of the bar, I made a vow that at the first chance to leave this place, the first promise of a better life, I would take it.

I didn't even have to wait that long.

CHAPTER TWO

The next morning I woke up early and went for my jog around the neighborhood. The house I rented for me and my parents was just outside of the airport. All day long it was nothing but the unrelenting sun and the sound of airplanes. Dust coated everything, and I was convinced if anyone did a scan of my lungs they'd find a sandcastle in there. But it was cheap and cheap was all I could afford. Plus, we did have a lot of privacy which was great for when my father had one of his episodes, and the house was big enough so that there was a bedroom for each of us. That was more than we had when I was growing up.

I usually jogged just after dawn when the air was still relatively cool. After my shower I got breakfast ready and woke my parents. I was lucky that most mornings my father was still my father. He knew my name, he knew where we were, and he smoked his pipe with his left hand. It was during the day that he would falter. If I wasn't home, like I hadn't been yesterday, my mother had to deal with it all by herself. Her blindness wasn't even a disability at that point since she knew quite well how to handle herself. I just knew how hard it was to have to control Papa, to calm him, to make him understand he was loved and with loved ones. One day I could afford a nurse to take care of him, but that day always seemed so far away.

That morning I made breakfast with my special fried potatoes and peppers with goat cheese that I only brought out on special occasions, and brought the breakfast with a gardenia in a vase to my mother. She wouldn't see it, but the smell always lifted her spirits. When she and my father were both well fed and well caffeinated, I got in my car, a beat-up old Toyota with windows that didn't roll up, went out into the town of San Jose del Cabo and bought the Kobo device I'd had my eye on at one of the local pawnshops.

The woman who normally worked there wasn't on duty, but a young man was, and he tried to jack up the price at the last minute. I tried out what Camila had recommended—smiling more, acting flirty—and even though I felt a bit silly doing it, it actually worked. I got it for a lot less, leaving me enough cash left over to pay the library fees I owed and get a bottle of cheap sparkling wine for my mother.

"You shouldn't have," my mother said as I handed the e-reader over to her. Her mouth was set in a stern line, but I could tell from the way she was handling the device, like it was precious gold, that she already loved it more than she could say. She was a proud woman in every sense of the word, and if it wasn't for the empty look in her pupils, you wouldn't know she was blind. She always stood very tall, neck long, her dark hair pulled off her face with only a few strands of grey coming in at the corners.

"Well, Mama, it's your birthday and I have," I said, brushing back her hair. I looked over at my father who was watching us with a wry smile on his face, a few crumbs caught in his greying beard.

"You're a good woman, Luisa," Papa said. I gestured to his beard and he wiped the crumbs off. He continued, "But you shouldn't be spending so much on your mother and I."

"Are you jealous, Papa?" I asked wryly, getting up and pouring them both another cup of coffee. "I'm sure she will let you use it when she's not." He quickly put his warm hand over mine and looked at me with gentle eyes, the kind of look that made my heart bleed when I realized how close I was to losing this man.

"I always like it when you read to me," he said. "I am happy with that. When you were younger you used to make up stories. Crazy little stories about trolls and goblins and princesses with swords. Do you remember that?"

I couldn't recall any particular stories, but when I was younger and we didn't have enough money for toys, I would make up stories instead. I always liked the darker ones, the scarier ones, the ones with the villains and the ugliest creatures—those were the most like real life. Fairytales and happily-ever-afters were for people in other countries.

I kissed him on his forehead. "I remember you telling me to stop telling them, that I was scaring you."

Suddenly the Kobo started speaking and my mother jumped in her seat, letting out a nervous laugh. "Woo, *this* scared me."

I went over to her, picked it up, and pressed pause. Though the Baja state was often behind in the times, the local library did have an e-reader program where you could borrow e-books and audiobooks for free. Now that my library fees were all settled, I had borrowed a range of crime thrillers for her to listen to.

I left the house later feeling relatively happy. I hated the fact that I had to go back to work and face Bruno again, but knowing that my parents were full from lunch, my mom was listening to her books for the first time, and my father seemed stronger than normal, it was enough to get me by. Sometimes, when I took the car onto the highway that led me to Cabo San Lucas and the sea air came through the open windows just right, it was enough to bring a smile to my face. In those moments I always lived outside of my reality, outside my head, and was just a child of the earth, an element like the sun and water.

When I finally got to work—traffic being especially heavy today—I was relieved to find the bar half-empty and Bruno nowhere in sight.

"Where is everyone?" I asked Camila at the till before I headed to the washroom to change from my sundress to the dreaded uniform.

She shrugged, her long earrings rattling lightly. "Just one of those days. Bruno went out and I don't think he's coming back. Anita should be coming on the floor any minute. Dylan and Augustin are in the kitchen."

Thank god. I didn't want to see Bruno and remember his eyes on my body, his grimy hands on my breasts. I got changed and started my shift feeling a million times lighter.

For the first hour I only had two tables—one was an older gentleman with a bowtie who was more than content to sit alone in the corner and nurse his martini, while the other was three giggling girls. They looked to be around my age, maybe younger, but had the newest fashions and those carefree smiles that only belonged to girls who never knew what struggle was, who had the world at their fingertips and the appetite to make it work for them. Part of me hated them, my insides writhing with jealousy, even though I knew it was very wrong. I tried to be a good person, to do right, but sometimes it was hard not to feel how hopeless it all was.

But I was nice to the girls, and they tipped me quite well, and I made a note not to be so judgemental. I was filling up a bottle of hot sauce behind the bar when I heard someone clear their throat.

I turned to see a man staring at me. At least he looked like he was staring at me—he was wearing sunglasses inside.

"Can I help you?" I asked, remembering to smile.

The man didn't return the smile. With a deathly pale face and an all-black suit on his skinny, tall frame, he looked like an agent of death. "I'm here with a friend of mine," he said, voice completely monotone. "We would like you to be our server."

I looked over his shoulder to see a table nearest the patio occupied by a large man, his back to me. Camila was walking past him, giving me an I-don't-know look. "That's usually Camila's area..." I started.

"We don't care. My friend would like you to be our server. We will make sure you are treated justly and tipped generously."

I swallowed uneasily. Why was this guy wearing shades now anyway?

"All right," I said carefully. "I'll be with you in a minute. Will you be having food?"

The man nodded and then went back to the table. I quickly waved Camila over while their backs were turned to me.

"Who are they?" I whispered, pulling her close.

"I don't know. They just sat down and said they wanted you to serve them. I said they'd have to ask you."

"He's weird. He's wearing shades inside. And it's nighttime."

"The other guy is too," she said. "In fact, the other guy looks familiar and not in a good way."

The skin at the back of my neck prickled. "Familiar like he comes in here sometimes?"

Camila looked me dead in the eyes. "Familiar like I've seen his face on the news. But with the glasses, it's hard to tell."

I straightened up and looked back at them. The man who had spoken to me was watching me with an impassive look on his face, his hands folded in front of him like he'd been waiting awhile. The other man, the one that Camila said looked familiar, was sitting there rigidly, but I still couldn't see his face.

I grabbed the menus and Camila squeezed my hand for good luck. I walked carefully over to them, reminding myself that these men probably just wanted a hot waitress to attend to them, that they didn't have to want anything else, and that I would be tipped for my efforts.

I stopped in front of the table and smiled. "Hello, my name is Luisa. I'll be your server tonight."

The other man looked up at me and my breath caught in my throat. Camila was right. He did look familiar. Though his wide aviator sunglasses covered up his eyes, there was no mistaking the overly thick mustache peppered with grey or the mullet-like swoop of hair on his head. His face was scarred in places, with both scratches and pockmarks, and had that slightly bloated look that middle-aged men got. Though his clothes were simple—faded blue jeans and a western shirt over his beer paunch—they didn't hide the immense power and notoriety this man had.

He was none other than Salvador Reyes, one of the most feared and well-documented cartel leaders in the country. And he was sitting in my bar, asking me to serve him.

I kept the smile plastered on my face while invisible fingers trailed ice down my back. This could not be a good thing. This wasn't even his area; he controlled most of Sinaloa. Aside from Tijuana, most of the Baja Peninsula was relatively untouched by the cartels and the impending drug violence.

Untouched until now.

I was vaguely aware that both men were staring at me through their sunglasses, their faces grave and unmoving. I quickly placed the menus down on the table like they were hot to touch and launched into my specials. "Nachos are half price as are the buckets of Tecate," I said, nervously tripping over the words.

The man I thought was Salvador picked up the menu and glanced at it briefly. The other man didn't even look.

Finally Salvador smiled. It was nothing if not creepy. "Top shelf tequila, two shots. And the nachos. Please, Luisa."

I nodded and quickly trotted back to the kitchen to place my order with Dylan. I felt something at my back and whirled around to see Camila staring at me expectantly.

"Well? Do you know what I mean?"

I nodded, trying to stay calm. "He does look familiar. But I don't know how. They seem harmless."

The funny thing was that I felt like if I told Camila it was Salvador, the infamous drug lord, things would take a turn for the worse. Right now he was in the bar, with his friend, probably his right hand man—*the one who lives with the jackal*—and no one seemed to notice him or care. This was good. This man had the power to murder everyone in here if he wanted to and completely get away with it. To him and to many others, he had a right to rape me in the back room and I could never press charges, or he could rape me in front of everyone, and no one—not even Camila—would ever dare say anything. This man was above the law, as so many men in Mexico were, and the less attention that was brought to that fact, the better.

For my sake and the sake of everyone around me, I had to pretend that I didn't know who this man was.

I went over to the bar and poured a special edition of Patron that we only had for high rollers, my hands shaking so badly that the tequila spilled over the edges and I had to mop it up with a washcloth, then took the shots over to the table. I thanked Jesus that I had worn my ballet flats to work today instead of the ridiculous heels that Bruno often made us wear.

The men were conversing with each other, voices low, and I stood back for a few moments to let them finish before I placed the shots in front of them.

"Here is a special edition of Patron." *For the patron*, I finished in my head.

"You didn't get one for yourself," Salvador said, smiling again. He did have very white teeth, probably all fake. Even though I had seen his picture on the news and in the paper on occasion, I'd always imagined his teeth would be gold.

"I can't drink at work," I told him, forcing confidence into my voice and trying out that smile again.

"That is nonsense. What do you think this is, America? Of course you can drink at work," he said. "I don't see your boss anywhere and I promise I won't tell." There was a teasing quality to his voice, the kind that people used when they were flirting, but the concept of Salvador flirting was a hard thing to swallow. I was reminded about how wrong this situation was.

"I'll go have a shot for you after work," I said.

"And when is that?" he asked. He still hadn't had the drink yet. "When do you get off work?"

Damn it.

"When the bar closes, at three a.m." I tried to sound nonchalant, adding an extra hour.

"Then we shall wait here until you are done with your shift. And we will have the shot then. Isn't that right, friend?" he said, looking across the table. The pale man nodded but didn't say anything.

"I don't think that sounds like a lot of fun," I said, the words coming out of my mouth before I could stop them. Salvador stared at me, his thick greying brows knitted together but I still continued. "I mean, there are better bars here in Cabo. This one is pretty boring—I should know, I work here." I attempted a smile again. I felt like I was slipping. "Are you two just here on business or…?"

Salvador stared at me for a few long moments—moments that had me cursing in my head—before running his stubby fingers over his mustache, his gold rings glinting. "We are not here on business. We are here to relax. Have a little fun. Enjoy the beach." He picked up the glass of Patron. "And we're here to get drunk. And I don't think you have any right to tell us where we can do that. If we want to get drunk here, if we want to wait until three in the morning for you to get off your shift, we can do that. And we will do that."

At that, both he and the other man slammed back their shots.

I gulped and squeaked out a "sorry" and then turned to leave.

"Oh, Luisa," Salvador called, stopping me in mid-step. "Do come back here. We aren't finished with you."

I closed my eyes, trying to find my inner strength, willing myself to stay calm, before I went back to him.

"Yes?" I asked.

"I have a few questions for you. If you answer them truthfully, I will not wait for you until you are done with your shift. I will leave now and leave you a lovely tip for your cooperation. If you lie to me, I will not tip you. I will instead wait for you. And then hopefully you will learn to be honest with me—at three in the morning. You understand?"

"Yes," I said, barely audible. My knees started to shake.

"Good," he said. He rubbed again at his mustache, seemingly in thought, then asked, "Where do you live?"

"In San Jose del Cabo."

Please, please, please don't ask for my address, I thought.

"Ah. And who do you live with?"

"M-my mother and father."

"No husband."

"No."

"Children?"

I shook my head.

"Boyfriend?"

"No, just my mother and father. I don't have a boyfriend."

I knew that's what he wanted to hear. His smile became very sly.

"Good girl. Boyfriends are useless. You need a husband—a man, not a boy."

I didn't say anything to that. My mouth was drying up.

He went on, looking around, "Is this your only job?"

"Yes."

"How long have you been working here?"

"Three years."

"How old are you?"

"Twenty-three."

"Are you happy?"

I frowned at him, taken off-guard. "What?"

"I asked if you were happy. Are you happy?"

"Are *you* happy?" I retorted.

He raised his brows. "Yes. Of course. I have everything I could ever want…almost."

He wanted me to comment on the *almost* part, I could tell. But I steeled myself against curiosity.

"How nice. Well, I am poor and I work this job to take care of my parents, who are sick. I have always been poor and I have always worked hard. I am not happy." I was slightly amazed at the honesty that was coming out of my mouth, things I didn't even admit to myself.

"Do you ever get in trouble for talking back?" he asked, and for a moment I thought I was in big trouble. Then he shook his head. "It doesn't matter, you can be trained out of that. So you're not happy. But you're so beautiful, Luisa. Beautiful enough to bring me in here, to make me want to talk to you, to make me want to know more about you."

"Beauty means nothing," I said.

"Ah, but you've won pageants before, prizes that have given you money."

My heart jump-started. "How did you know that?"

"I know many things," he went on, "and I want *many* things. Final question: are you a virgin?"

My cheeks immediately grew hot. "That is none of your business."

He grinned like a crocodile. "I'm afraid it is my business. Whether you like it or not, you are my business now. You can tell me the truth or I can wait until three in the morning and I'll find out for myself. Oh, and don't act like you're going to call the police over this. You know exactly who I am and you know exactly what I can do."

I felt like I was seconds away from fainting, the fear was so great. But somehow I managed to say, "Yes, I am a virgin."

He nodded in sleazy satisfaction. "I thought as much. Perhaps that is why you're so unhappy."

He looked to the other man who brought out his wallet. He placed $500 on the table.

My mouth dropped open at the wad of money just sitting there while Salvador and the man got out of the booth. I quickly backed out of the way.

"You can eat the nachos," Salvador said, hiking up his jeans and looking me over. "You look like you could use a bit more weight in those thighs. I wouldn't want to hurt you...much."

Then Salvador and the man left the bar. One moment they were here and I was caught in the most frightening conversation of my life, the next minute they were gone. I stood there for a long time, trying to wrap my head around what had happened. Then I realized that they had gone, for real, and there was a huge amount of money on the table waiting for me.

I quickly scooped it up and stuffed it down my shirt before anyone could see. Then I tried to go back to work, but every hour I was looking over my shoulder in fear that the drug lord would come back.

He didn't come back that night. Not even when I finished my shift.

But he did come back the next day.

And the next.

And the next.

And the next.

Until I learned not to fear him as much.

Until he made me an offer I couldn't refuse.

CHAPTER THREE

"Luisa you've barely touched your food," my mother said. I looked up from my plate to her blank stare, always wondering how she could sense such things. It must have been motherly instinct.

"I'm just not very hungry," I admitted, pushing the chicken around on my plate, my head and heart heavy as if someone had opened my mouth and poured sand inside me.

She slowly placed her fork down and sighed. "You haven't been yourself for the last few weeks. Is there something you need to talk about? Is it work?"

I glanced at my father. He was eating away, apparently content. I knew he wasn't really here right now—when my father was one hundred per cent himself, he was very intuitive and a straight shooter. I could rarely keep things from him either.

"It's not work," I said slowly, knowing that I was going to have tell them. I just didn't know how. They wouldn't see it the way I saw it. I wondered how much I could hide from them.

"Mama, papa," I said. I cleared my throat and straightened up in my chair. Even though my mother couldn't see me, I felt her looking. Only my dad remained lost in lost thoughts, and for once I was okay that he would have no reaction. "I met a man."

"Oh?" my mother asked, her interest piqued by the foreign subject. "Who is he? Where did you meet him? Do you like him?"

"I met him at work," I said, skirting the other questions and shoving a piece of stewed tomato in my mouth. I chewed slowly, planning my words. "He took an interest in me. He is very wealthy and has promised me the world."

Her face fell slightly. "I see." She paused, pushing her plate away from her. "I am not surprised, Luisa. You are a beautiful, intelligent woman. I am only surprised that this is the first man you have talked about to us."

Here it came. "That is because it is serious. He has asked to marry me."

The room stilled, choking on silence and the oppressive heat. My heart throbbed with fear from just hearing those words out loud.

It was the cold, hard truth; Salvador Reyes had asked me to marry him.

I couldn't read my mother's expression at all. She was in shock, that was for sure, but whether she was happy, sad, angry or suspicious, I didn't know. Finally she said, "When did this happen?"

"A few days ago," I told her. He had come into the bar every day, sometimes with David, that creepy crony of his who always wore his shades inside. A few times, though, it was just Salvador. I never had any doubt that there was an army of people stationed all around, so we were never really alone, but it was during those times that he would ask me to have dinner with him, even if I was in the middle of the shift. At this point, Bruno knew who he was and what was going on, and he had to allow me as many breaks as I wanted. Salvador controlled the entire bar from the moment he stepped into it until the moment he left.

And he controlled me.

The curious thing, however, was that each day I grew more comfortable with his presence. It wasn't that I was less scared or intimidated by him. It was just that I got used to the fear. The fear of Salvador, of what he wanted from me, of what he would do next, became as soft and easy as my favorite blanket. And because he was the scariest of them all, I no longer feared anyone else but him. Bruno, he was nothing in comparison. My terrors had become consolidated into one greasy, mustached man with a beer gut and bad hair. A man who ruled such a violent part of the world and who would now rule mine.

Because, when he asked me the other day, when I had finished my shift early and he insisted I walk down to the marina with him, I knew I had to say yes.

If I was being honest with myself, there was a part of me that could have swooned at the proposal. When Salvador got down on one knee and took my hand in his, his palms sweaty, his fingers large and fat, I tricked my mind and heart into momentarily believing that Salvador knew me, cared for me, loved me. Of course, he only wanted me to look good at his side and that was it. Well, that and be in his bed. What else could there be after just a few weeks?

So I said yes and tried to believe I meant it. If I said no, I would be killed. There was no doubt about that. No woman turned down Salvador Reyes, not for a date, not for marriage.

"I will treat you like a princess," he had said to me, a stupid, lopsided grin on his pockmarked face. "And you will have everything you ever wanted. You'll be richer than the President."

And that's when I found the tiny shred of hope to cling to. By marrying the country's most notorious drug lord, a man who had politicians and police under his thumb, a man with more money than he probably knew what to do with, I would be buying myself safety from everyone but him, and I would be buying me and my parents a life we would never get to experience otherwise. I would no longer have to work for Bruno. I could have my mother and father taken care of and their every whim catered to.

It was at that thought that I was finally able to give Salvador a genuine smile. He responded by kissing me for the first time, his mustache tickling my upper lip. I wished it could have meant something to me, but all I could do was concentrate on the two competing feelings in my chest: relief.

And dread.

"Did you say yes?" my mother asked quietly, snapping me back to reality, to the kitchen table with the one wobbly leg, to the overhead fan that did nothing to disperse the hot air, to my father's kind but desolate eyes as he stared curiously at my mother, perhaps seeing her for the first time today.

I nodded and dabbed at my mouth with the napkin. "I did. It is for the best, Mama, you will see."

She gave me a funny look. "You act as if marriage is a bargain you have to make." When I didn't say anything, she went on. "So what is the bargain here?"

"He has a lot of money, I told you. He will take care of me and I can take proper care of you." I quickly reached across the table and put my hand on hers. "Mama, please, this is a good thing."

"Then why can't I hear it in your voice? You are anything but happy."

"I am happy," I said. "I will be happy. In time. It's all so new and..."

"And so who is this man who you suddenly agreed to marry?"

"You don't really know him," I said carefully. "But he has a lot of power and a lot of influence."

"And what does he do?" she asked, her voice taking on a strange steely quality. She knew that no wealth in our country came honestly.

There was nothing for me to do but tell the truth. The truth would hurt her, but it would also keep her safe.

"His name is Salvador," I said. "And he is in charge of a cartel."

My mother's mouth dropped open while my father muttered the first words I'd heard from him all evening. "Salvador Reyes," he said, musing over it. "He is a bad, bad man." Of course he could forget his own wife and daughter sometimes, but a notorious drug lord lived in every memory.

"Luisa," she said breathlessly. "You can't be serious."

I gave her a tight smile. "Unfortunately, I am."

"Salvador Reyes. The Sal? The drug lord? The jackal?" She shook her head and folded her hands in her lap. "No. No, I refuse to believe this."

"But it is the truth."

"But why? Why here? Why *you?*"

"I wish I could say, Mama. I don't know. He thinks I am beautiful and worthy of a better life." *He thinks I am worthy of his bed.*

She snorted caustically. "A better life? Who does he think he is? Has he been here? We are not living in squalor, Luisa. We have everything that we need right here."

"No, we don't!" I yelled, surprised by the ferocity in my voice. "Every day I struggle to get by, for you, for Papa. And it's still not enough."

She rubbed her lips together, taken aback. I could see the wash of shame on her face and I immediately regretted losing my temper.

"I'm sorry," I said quickly. "You know I've done everything to take care of the both of you and I'll do whatever I can to keep doing so. This is an opportunity—"

"This is a death sentence," she muttered.

Her words sent cold waves down my spine. I swallowed hard. "No," I said, though I didn't believe it myself. "He can protect me. I will go and live with him in a mansion in Culiacán. I will be safe, safer than anyone in the country. And you will be safe too. I will make sure that you and Papa are taken care of, you can live with us on the compound or stay here, in some place really nice. I will do whatever it takes. I am doing this for you."

She just shook her head, a few strands of her greying hair coming loose around her face. "This is wrong. You deserve to marry a man for love, not money."

"Maybe I can learn to love him. Maybe he can learn to love me."

Her mouth twisted into a sad smile. "Oh, Luisa, I know you are not that naïve! He is a drug lord. They do not know how to love a fellow human being. They only love money and they only love death. He will never love you. He will have other women on the side. You will never be able to leave. You will become a prisoner of his life."

Is it any different than being a prisoner to this life? I thought to myself. I sighed. "You know I have no choice. Whether I'll love him or not, whether he'll love me or not, you know I can't say no."

"There are always choices, my daughter. God gave you free will to make them."

"Then I am choosing to die later instead of dying now."

I thought my mother would admonish me for talking so fatalistically, but she understood. There was nothing easy or right about this situation, so there was nothing left for me to do but try and make the best of it.

"You deserve so much more," she finally said, staring at nothing.

I looked pointedly at her and my father. "As do the both of you. And now, we shall have more. Let's just ignore the cost for now."

She nodded and went back to her food, picking aimlessly at the chicken that had grown cold. Now that she knew of the weight on my shoulders, she didn't have an appetite either.

...

The next day I had my final shift at the bar. My mother thought I was crazy, but Papa had instilled such a good work ethic in me that it was hard to shake. Despite everything Bruno had done to me over the years, he had provided me with a job and the means to take care of my parents, and I couldn't just leave without warning. The moment Salvador had asked me to marry him and told me he would be taking care of me from now on, I gave Bruno one week's notice.

I have to admit, it was a bit sad to say goodbye. As I stood behind the bar and looked over the people in the booths, laughing over drinks, I forgot about all the times I was treated like dirt by customers and forgot about being afraid of Bruno's advances. I only remembered the comfort and security, as false as it had been. Faced with the infinite unknown of my new life, the job had seemed so simple and safe.

"I'm going to miss you," Camila said after she'd hugged me for the millionth time that day. She held me by my shoulders and leaned in, her eyes inquisitive as they searched mine. "And I'm going to worry about you, you know."

I nodded, trying to keep my posture straight, my face falsely confident. "Don't worry about me. I am better off."

She frowned, and her eyes flitted over to Bruno who was standing by the entrance and hitting on the hostess. "Perhaps so. But as obnoxious and disgusting as Bruno can be, he is not Salvador Reyes."

"Don't worry about me," I repeated, looking her hard in the eyes.

She smiled softly and squeezed my shoulders before letting go. "Then I won't."

The rest of the shift went smoothly, with the staff and Bruno giving me a small slice of cake at the end. We all did shots to honor my departure, and Bruno gave me a very proper, very professional handshake, wishing me well in the future. As much as I wanted to spit in his face and take advantage of his newfound respect for me, I played polite and silently hoped that one day karma would come knocking at his door.

It was around nine o' clock when my last day was finally over. I walked out the door and made it about halfway down the block, squeezing through throngs of slow tourists, before a black town car pulled up to the curb.

"Miss Chavez." David stepped out of the passenger side and gestured to the back door, those sunglasses ever present on his skinny face. "Would you get in the car, please?"

My heart thumped loudly. "Of course," I said, trying to keep my voice steady. I hadn't planned on seeing him or Salvador today.

I opened the door and got in the backseat. To my surprise it was empty. My limbs were heavy with dread.

"Where are we going?" I asked David as he quickly sped away from the curb.

"To see Salvador," he said simply.

"I parked just around the corner from work," I said feebly, looking behind me as it all got lost in the traffic.

"I will return you to your car after," he said, not looking at me in the mirror. "Salvador has a few things he needs to discuss with you."

He could have added, "Don't be afraid," but he didn't. I'd probably always be afraid when Salvador wanted to talk with me whether we were married or not.

After about twenty minutes, we were coasting up the dry, cactus-strewn hills outside of the city. David pulled the car over, and in a minute the door opened and Salvador stepped in. He was wearing jeans and a grey, sweat-stained T-shirt that was covered in a layer of dust.

"Turn up the air conditioning," he barked at David as he closed the door and the car pulled onto the road.

Salvador sat across from me and pushed his shades to the top of his head. He was sweaty and his eyes were extra puffy, perhaps from drinking too much. For a split second I wondered if I could marry this man, let alone share his bed. There was just nothing to attract me to him. If he had a good personality, it might have been different. But he didn't have that, not even when he was faking it.

"I am sorry, princess," he said, still overly polite with me. "I'm afraid I cannot stick around Los Cabos any longer. It is no longer safe."

Well, you were kind of flaunting that you were here, I thought to myself but didn't dare say.

He reached into the back of his pants and pulled out a small, cloth wallet. He took my hands in his and placed it in them. "Here. This is one thousand American dollars. It's enough to take care of you for the next month, just as I promised. But it's not enough to buy you a new life, if that's what you're thinking."

I opened my mouth to protest, fear coursing through me.

He shook his head. "I am only joking," he said, though I could tell from the cold, wicked glint to his eyes that he wasn't. "But in one month, I will be back for you. We will have our wedding less than a week after that. Don't worry about the dress, I will pick that out for you as well."

I could only stare dumbly at him. "We'll be getting married in a month..."

"More or less," he said. "I thought you'd be happier."

I forced a smile on my face and leaned over, placing my hand on his clammy arm. I swallowed my revulsion. I played my part. "I am happy. Very happy. I am just surprised and sad that you are leaving me for so long."

He smiled at that, his bushy mustache twitching up, droplets of sweat gathering in it. "You will survive. You have until now. And after we are married, you will always be at my side. You will never be alone again."

Those words rang through my head as I later drove back home, toward my mother and father, the fat wallet on the seat beside me. I had one month to enjoy my life as it was before it would change for good.

CHAPTER FOUR

Javier

The whore was beautiful.

Then again, Este usually did have good taste in women, if not in fashion. I watched as she walked uneasily down the cobblestone driveway, heading toward the guards at the gate, heading toward freedom. She reminded me of a spindly-legged fawn, her high heels a poor match for the uneven ground, and for one brief moment I felt sorry for her. Pity, even. Such a pretty thing selling her body for riches that never came. She only got money, but that was never what the whore really wanted. What she really wanted, she would never, ever get.

She was better off dead.

And at that thought, the twinge of pity was gone.

I watched as she approached the gate. Though the two guards were facing forward, their eyes hidden by sunglasses, I could tell they were exchanging a look, wondering who was going to kill her first. Orders were orders.

They didn't need to debate for long. A shot rang out, a bullet to the back of her head, and the whore fell to the ground slowly, as if she had just grown too tired to stand. Blood began to flow from her head.

I craned my neck, mildly curious to see who had done it. I couldn't see anyone but the guards, which meant it had to have been Franco. It had turned into a hobby for him lately, as if he discovered he had a taste for being a sniper, but it was better the whores than anyone else at the compound.

Somewhere I knew my gardener, Carlos, was cursing himself. Franco never disposed of the bodies, and it would be Carlos's job once again to do something with her, wash away the red mess from the hot stones. Naturally, he would never complain to me, or someone else would have to clean up his own blood.

There was a knock at the door behind me. I kept my hands behind my back, my eyes glued to the blood that was pouring out of her head, a hypnotic, moving painting.

"Come in," I said. I didn't have to turn around to know it was Este. "What was the whore's name?" I asked, still staring at the growing crimson pond.

The door clicked softly and I felt him step into the room. "Laura," he said. "She could fuck like no one's business, hey. You should have tried her. You know I don't mind sharing."

I ignored him. "Don't you think it's a bit, oh, I don't know…crude, to have the whores leave this way?" I asked him. "Wouldn't it be better to kill them in bed?"

I heard him snort. "No, *that* would be crude. We might as well let them have that bit of hope that they'll make it out alive, don't you think? Besides, this is more sporting. It's hunting. Hunting is elegant."

I nodded. I supposed he was right. It wasn't very sporting otherwise. I watched as Carlos came scurrying toward the body and started to drag Laura away. I never asked what he did with the bodies, but as long as I never saw them again, it didn't really matter. Out of sight, out of mind.

I turned around and eyed Este. "I suppose in a perfect world, we wouldn't have to kill them at all."

He smirked and leaned on my desk. "Well, look at you getting all soft."

I raised my brow. "It's just a shame that you can't buy silence anymore."

He shrugged. "One whore talks and then you get fuckers at your door. We all need to get laid, well at least I do." A wry look came across his face at that. "There really is no other solution."

"I suppose not," I said, and sat down at my desk. I adjusted my watch and stared up at him expectantly. "So, why are you here? Showing off your terrible taste in shoes? Are those made of cardboard?"

He peered down at his feet. As usual the man looked like he'd rolled out of the California surf with his T-shirt, board shorts, and terrible Birkenstocks. Not the image the cartel had at all, but there was no talking style into him. Believe me, I had tried.

He placed a large envelope down on the desk. "Got the email from Martin just a few minutes ago and had these printed out for you."

I stared at the envelope for a beat before laying my fingers on it and sliding it toward me. A quiver of anticipation ran up my arms and I did my best to quell it.

"I didn't respond," Este went on. "He mentioned that the location of the wedding changed at the last minute yesterday, but he was still able to get everything done. I printed out the email. It's in there too."

I nodded and slowly opened the flap.

"Should I get anything more from him?"

I shook my head and slid the papers out of the envelope and onto the desk. "No, it doesn't matter. Martin is dead."

I glanced up to see Este staring at me with a stunned expression. "So soon?"

"Yes," I said absently, looking back to the paper in my hands. I skimmed the printed out email.

"What a shame, I liked the guy."

"I didn't," I said. "But he got the job done and that's all that matters."

"Kind of like the whores."

I pursed my lips. "Mmmm," I conceded. From the email, Martin had done the job well. He had observed Salvador Reyes and his bride from a few days before the wedding and gotten photographs during the ceremony. "But killing women is always so ugly, isn't it?"

"You see," Este said, crossing his arms, "right there, that sort of shit surprises me. You know, considering your issues with women and all that."

I shot him a piercing look. "I don't have issues."

"No," he said slowly with an easy smile on his lips, knowing all too much. "Of course not."

It was those moments that I hated Esteban Mendoza. Hated that he was my right hand man, hated that he was the closest person to me, even though that never amounted to much. I hated that it would hurt me so to kill him.

"Martin would have talked," I said to him. "Much like the whores. He did well. Don't worry, his wife and children will be taken care of."

Este raised his brows.

"With money," I supplied quickly. "They will be fine without their father, who was stupid enough to get involved with us to begin with. I'm not cruel."

"Well, you're not shooting whores," he said. "And I'm not worried. You know I rarely worry about you."

"How touching," I said wryly.

He walked around the desk and stood behind me, looking over my shoulder. I hated when he did that. "I'm interested in what you think," he said.

"About what?"

"About *her*," he said while I slid a photograph out of the pile. "Mrs. Reyes."

It was black and white and printed on paper, making it less sharp than a photograph, but it did the job. It was a picture of a woman in a white strapless wedding dress, very fluffy and extravagant from the waist down. Her hands were clasped demurely at her front, her face caught in a nervous smile.

She was extremely beautiful but that was to be expected. The country's most flagrant excuse for a drug kingpin would never marry anyone less than stunning, and this woman, Luisa, fit the bill. But despite her body, with her round, perky tits and elegant neck, her long dark hair and classic face, there was another layer to her that immediately got me hard. It was this look in her eyes. They were so pure and soft, giving her radiance that seemed to leap off the page.

I wanted nothing more than to have her on her knees, have her fix those round, angelic eyes on me and watch as I pinned her down and came right into them. I would take her purity and make her see the world for what it really was—a hot, sticky mess at the end of my dick.

"I bet she'd be a tight little fuck," Este leered over my shoulder.

I shot him a disgusted look. "She's not a whore, Este," I chided him.

"Not to you," he said, as I looked at the next picture of her, now with Salvador at her side.

"I mean it," I said, my eyes drawn to her again and again. "No one is touching her. Not you, not Franco."

"I give you my promise," Este said. "But Franco can barely control himself around the whores."

"No one is touching her," I repeated. "She will be our hostage. She is collateral. No one is laying a hand on her."

"Except for you, I assume."

She almost seemed too good to even touch. I couldn't wait to break her down. "She is very valuable," I admitted.

I flipped through a couple more photographs and grew harder at each one. I wished Este would just fucking leave so I could deal with it. I almost wished Laura was still alive so I could flip her over and come all over her back. I never fucked the women around here, but that didn't mean I didn't use them.

"You know," Este said, his lazy voice starting to grate on me. "If Martin had been there close enough to spy on them, close enough to photograph, why didn't you just get him to put a bullet in Salvador's head? Especially if Martin was going to die anyway."

I eyed him warily, disappointed that he could be so rash. "Because life is a game and we're all just trading cards. We play the right hand to get ahead." I studied the smiling, ignorant face of Sal as he stared at his bride. "Death stops the game. It's too final, too inflexible. Death is viciously stubborn."

When Este didn't say anything, I looked up to see a dull gleam in his eyes. I sighed and pinched the bridge of my nose, annoyed at his ineptitude. "What good would killing Salvador do? Right? David Guirez or whoever, anyone, someone, they would step in and take over faster than you can shit after your coffee, and nothing will have changed. Look at Travis Raines.

The moment he died, I was able to slither on through to the top, to right here, right now."

"Only because you killed Travis," he noted. "More or less."

"We killed Travis," I corrected him. "Anyway, the point is that the dead make lousy deals. If we want the shipping lane, we have to force him to give it to us. Killing him does nothing. Taking his new bride, now that will do something."

"You sound so sure," Este said, walking around the desk.

"I have no reason not to be sure," I said. "They are newlyweds. He needs her, he wants her. We will get her soon, before he gets bored of her cherry ass. Sal has pride. We all do. It is our weakness. I know that enough about myself to know it about others."

He smoothed his hand over the scruff on his chin and gave me a smooth nod. "All right."

I stared at a photo of them at the altar, a lavish outdoor ceremony. He was staring at her with that pride I was talking about. And she was staring at him with a look that was all too familiar to me.

"She doesn't love him, though," I commented, almost to myself.

"How can you tell?" he asked, taking a step closer and peering at the photos again.

I shrugged. "I just can. She doesn't."

"So is she marrying him for money then?"

I took the papers and sorted them until they were neat and evenly stacked before slipping them back into the envelope. "Probably. Does it matter?"

"No. So when do we act?"

"Soon," I said, putting the envelope in the first drawer. I knew I'd be taking it out again after he left. "But we'll do it slowly. Start with recon first, perhaps see if we can track down Derek to help us with this."

Este gave me an odd look. "Derek...we haven't talked to him since he...I'm not sure he's even in Mexico anymore."

"Perhaps not," I said. I wasn't too worried. Derek Conway was an American ex-military man, an assassin for hire. He had been contracted to us during some of our more important moments. In fact, the last time I saw him was three years ago. He'd put a bullet through Travis Raines' head. Ordered by me, of course. Then he screwed us over, but I couldn't fault him for that. He would be loyal to whoever paid him the most.

But he wasn't the only man at my disposal. Since I had taken over the cartel, I had a whole legion of men to do my dirty work, the best of the best. For the next month or so, I wanted someone who would be sleek and loyal. Kidnapping the wife of Mexico's largest drug lord wasn't going to be a walk in the park, but with the right people, it wouldn't be impossible.

Perhaps I was just being overconfident, but it had only served me well in the past.

I gave Este a levelling stare. "I'm putting this in your hands. Can you handle it?"

"When haven't I?"

"Oh, I don't know. I sent you to Hawaii once to finish a job but you ended up fucking some suicidal surfer chick instead."

"I still got the job done. What's the difference if I get action at the same time?"

I rolled my eyes at his crassness and gave him a slight, dismissive wave. "Go put this all together. And don't disappoint me."

"Funny," he mused. "I'm not sure what it's like to *not* disappoint you." Then he turned and left the office, shutting the door behind him.

I got up and walked over to the window. The driveway was wet where Carlos must have watered it down, and the body of Laura was gone, the blood all washed away. It was like nothing ugly ever happened. I took in the mountains, the violently green foliage that stretched beyond the property and melded into the cliffs of The Devil's Backbone. Sometimes I wondered if there was someone out there plotting something in the way I was plotting for Salvador. I usually decided there was. You didn't run a cartel without having an army of people out there wanting to kill you. After all, I used to be a solider in that very army. I just never dwelled on it—I moved through each day thinking that I was better off alive, a card that kept the game going.

I also clung to the archaic, and perhaps slightly naïve belief that everything happened for a reason. I hadn't cheated death so many times, I hadn't had my heart ripped out, my soul lost, my family murdered, my future trampled all for nothing. I was put away in an American prison for three months, and thanks to the grace of God and friends in high places, I miraculously walked away and back into Mexico where I was able to jump back in to the cartel that had rightfully become mine. All of that, all of those miracles, all of that grace, hadn't happened for no reason.

My destiny was constantly being rewritten and it would continue to be until it was fulfilled. Until I was at the top of the world and I had everything I'd ever wanted at my feet. Until I could crush everything with none of the mercy that was bestowed upon me.

I went over to the wet bar, and with some pleasure, pushed back the curved top of the old-fashioned globe that revealed the bottles of alcohol beneath. The bar used to be Travis's, something he had picked up at an antique store in Mississippi where I had worked for him back in the simple times. I'd always admired it, the vintage elegance, of a time when men were really men and when they got up in the morning they showed up for the world.

I poured myself a glass of old Scotch, opting for that instead of my usual tequila, and went back over to the desk. I sat down and gently brought the photographs of Luisa out of the drawer. I felt a foreign pang of indignity as I looked them over again, as if someone was watching me, judging me, for something I shouldn't have been doing. But I needed to look at her. I needed to study her. I needed to know the exquisite creature I would be bringing into this house. I needed to know the woman I would destroy through and through before I handed her back to Salvador.

I needed to ask her soft, radiant, pixelated face for forgiveness for what I was about to do.

She would soon be sorry she ever married Salvador Reyes.

CHAPTER FIVE

Luisa

"You look nervous," the makeup artist said to me as she dusted a light coating of glimmering blush across my cheekbones. "Don't be. You look beautiful."

She had a singsong quality to her voice that would have soothed any bride-to-be, but there was no soothing me. If I got up and looked out the window, I would have seen the plaza below absolutely filled with people here to see me and Salvador get married. I would have also felt, though not seen, the countless snipers that were lined up to take out anyone who might have... interfered. That should have made me feel better, safer, but it didn't. I felt I was only safe until the moment I said "I do." After that, I was just a rat scurrying through the desert, the hawk biding its time from above.

"And you said your parents are here," she went on, her voice quicker now, trying to get me to talk, to say something. I'd been more or less silent the whole time. Perhaps she was nervous too. She knew who I was marrying, after all.

"Yes, they are here," I said, my throat feeling strangely raw.

"They must be so proud," she said, tilting my chin up with her fingers in order to line my lips with precision.

"They don't normally travel," I said by way of explanation, barely moving my lips. My parents weren't so much proud as they were scared out of their minds. My father hadn't been himself for days now, and it was only by luck that he was calm and under control. Luck, or perhaps some medication my mother borrowed from a friend of hers. My mother herself was rigid and unyielding, trying hard to be happy for me but failing at it. For the first time in my life, I could hardly stand to be around her. She only reminded me of what I was giving up and giving in to.

"Where do they live?" she asked.

"In San Jose del Cabo," I said.

"They won't be joining you with your husband?"

I shook my head and then smiled apologetically when I realized it messed up her work. "They wanted to stay where their friends were. It's too…inconvenient for them to be living with me and Salvador." Not to mention that with Salvador's help, I was able to buy them a beautiful new home close to a retirement center and hospital. Both my parents had a full-time caregiver now, a tough but lovely woman named Penelope, and they had their activities and their friends. It happened fast, and we were all still adjusting to the change. I did what I could to ease the guilt since I couldn't live with them anymore, but it was so much better than them risking their lives to live with us in Culiacán. Though they were out of my reach, I felt they were much safer in the Baja.

"Well, perhaps that is for the best," she said, giving me a quiet smile. "Nothing ruins a marriage like in-laws."

I returned the look, and to my relief, she finished up my face in silence.

The wedding ceremony itself went a lot smoother than I thought. The three glasses of champagne I nicked off a waiter certainly helped. It was quite elaborate with the priest and our vows and the endless sea of people watching our every move. But I did my part, acted in the play, and did my best to pretend I was the blushing bride eager to be wedded to her powerful husband. I could only hope that my face would not betray me and show the world just how terrified I was.

The moment he slipped the ring on my finger—a big, blinding diamond that cost more than most people would earn in their life—and we said our vows, I knew I should have wept with power. I was the wife of the jackal, nearly the most powerful man in the country. But while others would see power resting on my shoulders, I knew deep down the cape was an illusion.

And it didn't take very long to find out how fake it was.

For our honeymoon, Salvador and I headed to the coast to a quiet little village that was completely under his jurisdiction, where he had a massive beachfront property. I barely had any time to say goodbye to my mother and father, my hands still clasping theirs, holding on for dear life, as I was ushered away from the ceremony, flowers in my hair, and into the waiting limousine.

It was bulletproof. But I was not.

Salvador and I sat in the back, the only inhabitants, while I craned my neck around and watched as my parents disappeared from sight, two frail frames against the relentless sun.

"That was rude of me," I said, even though I knew it was best to keep my mouth shut. I wished my voice wasn't shaking. "To just leave them like that." It was more than rude; it frightened me more than anything else to have them out of my reach, so fast and so soon.

Salvador turned in his seat to face me. He looked almost handsome in his tuxedo, his hair slicked back, his mustache trimmed. His eyes though, they always betrayed him. They were frazzled, sparking, like bad wiring.

"You're my wife now," he said with a grin that was far too wicked to be genuine. "You no longer answer to your parents, you answer to me."

I swallowed uneasily, trying to decide on whether to wear defiance or pleading compliance on my face. It was a split-second decision and defiance won out.

It got me a smack across the face.

I took a few moments, my newly ringed hand on my cheek, trying to soothe the throbbing. I stared at Salvador in dumb shock. I knew that everything had been for show so far, I just had no idea it would turn to the truth so fast.

"You answer to me," he repeated, his eyes growing thinner and hard as steel. "That means no talking back."

I opened my mouth and he immediately backhanded me again, harder this time, enough that I saw lights flashing behind my eyes, my teeth biting down on my tongue as the back of my head hit the seat rest. I tried not to panic, tried my hardest to remain composed all while wanting to cry out from the pain. The fear was greater than I'd ever known.

After a moment, I straightened up in my seat, inching away from him. He only leered at me, as if the whole thing was one giant joke. Perhaps it was.

"When I say no talking back," he said, running his fingers over his mustache, "I mean it, like I mean everything I say. We can have a nice, happy marriage if you learn to behave. I will still give you the world and you will want for nothing. But there are rules that you will have to follow. Nothing is free in this life, do you understand?"

I nodded, not daring to speak.

Suddenly he shot forward and was in my face, a vein throbbing at his temple. "I said, do you understand!?" he screamed, spittle flying onto me.

I shut my eyes tight, as if it would make him go away. I felt like the life was being drained out of me with every second that I spent in that limo, that this was the start of a slow and painful death. And I had willingly walked into it.

You're doing this for your parents, I told myself, trying to draw myself inward to where it was dark, warm, and safe. *Remember that. Remember whose happiness you are buying.*

"Look at me," Salvador said, his voice quiet now, though I could feel his hot breath on my skin. "You have to look at me when I'm talking to you. That is one of the rules." He grabbed my chin and squeezed hard enough to make my eyes flutter open. I stared at him blankly, not wanting to really see him. My husband.

"The other rule," he went on, softer now, "is that you will not talk back. You will also be loyal and you will not stray. You will not even look at other men. For your own protection, you will not be allowed to have any friends that I do not choose for you. You will not be able to leave the house on your own. You will always stay thin and beautiful, with a big smile for everyone you meet. And you will not deny me my rights as a husband." He licked his lips as he said that. "Now. Do. You. Under. Stand?"

I did understand. The life of Luisa Chavez was really and truly over.

There was only Luisa Reyes now.

And she was about to live a life of pain.

...

Salvador took my virginity in the back of that limo, minutes before we even reached the beach house. It happened quickly, and for that I was glad. It didn't lessen the pain—the horrible, ripping pain—but it meant I didn't have to suffer the humiliation of my first time for too long.

He wasn't kind, he wasn't gentle, he wasn't generous. If that's what sex was, I wondered how anyone could enjoy it. He treated my body like a piece of meat, a slice of property. I had no claim to it, and that's what he wanted to show me, again and again and again. I had no say, no rights. I was his, whether I wanted to be or not, and he would have me anytime he wanted. My own feelings and desires didn't matter.

I didn't want to the second time. I was sore, oh so sore, and trying to sleep in, afraid to face him and my first morning as his wife. But Salvador didn't believe in the word *no*. It didn't matter how many times I said it, if I struggled...in fact, he liked it when I did. He'd strip his bloated, ugly body naked and force himself on me and into me with a grin on his face that not even his mother could love.

If he even *had* a mother. I couldn't imagine anyone ever raising him. When I tried to picture him as a young boy, I knew there would have been no innocence in his heart. He'd have been the one to put firecrackers in dogs' mouths, to take the fights in the playground too far, to spit in his grandmother's food. I tried to think about these things, trying to figure out how one becomes such a vile, hateful thing, while he violated me from the inside out.

It wasn't enough that I was clearly in pain and vulnerable while this happened—if I struggled in the least, he would assert his dominance in other ways.

"Mrs. Reyes," the housekeeper called out from the balcony behind me. I was sitting on the beach, the warm Pacific lapping at my feet and soaking the ends of my dress. I'd been sitting there for hours, and I knew she was calling me in for lunch. But I couldn't eat even if I tried.

I ignored her and stared down at my arms, at the marks and bruises up and down them, ugly purples and yellows from the last few days, so bright in the daylight. For a split second there was so much terror filling up my chest like ice water that I thought about running straight into the ocean and trying to swim until I drowned.

But that would be nearly impossible. To the left of me, standing half-hidden in the palms, was one set of guards, watching the property and watching me. I couldn't see who was to my right, further down the beach, but I did know that they wouldn't let me drown.

They wouldn't let me escape.

We'd been on our honeymoon for one week. I never once got the opportunity to speak to my parents on the phone. I never once got to leave the property, not even if I was escorted. Salvador was only around at night and in the mornings when he would systematically beat me and rape me. One time, he made me perform a lewd act on David, his second in command, and when I didn't want to do it, he put a gun to my head. Part of me was tempted to keep refusing, just so he could pull the trigger, but I knew he never would. I'd only been his wife for a few days, and there was a lifetime of enjoyment still left for him.

"Mrs. Reyes," the housekeeper repeated. "Lunch is served. Mr. Reyes would like to eat with you."

So he was in the house today. Lucky me. It took all of my strength not to yell back at her and tell her that I was Luisa Chavez first and Luisa Reyes second, and that Salvador could go fuck himself. But now I was learning how to play the game. I got punished either way, but the safer I played it, the smaller the punishment I got. I'd learned not to talk back to Salvador after the limo ride, I'd learned not to refuse him the morning after, and I'd learned never to question him after what he made me do to David. I'd learned a lot in such a short time.

The reluctant education of the narco-wife.

I sighed and got to my feet, absently brushing the sand off my dress. My hair billowed around me like a dark scarf, caught in the cool breeze off the ocean. I closed my eyes and imagined, just for one moment, what it would be like not to live in fear. To actually feel happiness and love from a man. My heart practically shuddered from the realization that I'd never, ever have that for as long as Salvador Reyes lived.

As I walked back to the beach house with a heavy heart, I tried to think about my parents and how they were better off. I tried to think about how I was better off, not having to slave every day for someone like Bruno, how I'd never have to worry about how to make ends meet.

The fact was, I wasn't better off at all, and neither were my parents. I'd take Bruno and his busy hands, the long hours on my feet, the fear of never being able to give my parents what they deserved—I'd take all of that and hang on to it tight if I could. If only I could have realized that what I had wasn't so bad after all and if I could have gone back in time to take it back, I would. I gave everything I had away, just for a shot to have more.

Of course, there was the fact that I never really had a choice. That I could not have said no to Salvador. But as my mother said, we always have choices. And I was starting to think that in the grand scheme of things, perhaps I had made the wrong one.

The lesser of two evils was actually the greatest.

CHAPTER SIX

Javier

"So finally I meet *the* Javier Bernal." The man sat down across from me, a cigarette bobbing out of his lazy mouth. I wasted no time in snapping it out of his lips and breaking it in half, tossing it to the ground beside us.

He stared at me, dumbfounded for only a second, which I appreciated. A man who can get over things quickly is a man you want on your side.

"No smoking," I said, my eyes boring into his as I jerked my chin at the sign on the wall. The bar couldn't give two shits if people smoked or not, the sign was only there for legal reasons. But that wasn't the point. The man needed to know the score. I'd heard a lot about this Juanito, though there was no point in committing his name to memory. I only needed him for his intel, and the less I had to know, the better.

He nodded, that easy smile still there, if not faltering. That was good too. You needed to bounce back, but you also needed to stay afraid of the ones in charge.

He needed to stay afraid of me.

"Can I still drink?" he asked, raising his bottle of beer.

Ah, and he had a sense of humor. This made him easier to deal with, even like—too bad a sense of humor wouldn't save him in the end. I've killed some of the funniest fuckers I've ever met. They had me laughing even with their heads on the ground.

"Of course," I said to him and raised my glass of tequila. "To new beginnings."

We drank as some ballad from a Mexican pop idol played in the background. This bar was one of the few bars in the area where I could go and relax and not have to worry about watered down booze or uncouth patrons. The owners were paid handsomely by me, as were all law officials in the town and the state of Durango. I had no fear of a rival cartel coming in and blowing my head off, and I had no fear of the Mexican Attorney General coming in and trying to take me away. As much as I hated to admit it, without siphoning Salvador Reyes' Ephedra shipping lane and adding more routes for opium, cocaine, and marijuana, I really wasn't the guy they were after. Naturally, with more power and influence came the danger of being public enemy number one. Right now, Salvador Reyes was the most wanted criminal and drug lord in the country. Not that the police or anyone were doing anything to stop him.

As for me, I had more to fear from rivals than from authorities. I wasn't clean by any means—I couldn't ever step foot in the United States again, for example. The last time I was there, I was arrested for drug trafficking. It was a minor mix-up, I wasn't actually trafficking any drugs, just trying to trade a hostage to get ahead, but there was bloodshed and the feds got involved. Apparently they have nothing better to do up there than to worry about us Mexicans.

However, having enough money and knowing enough people who work for the DEA gets you a free ride in the states, so long as you promise to send them information on your enemies from time to time and swear to never set foot in the country again. And so that's what I did. Paid the right people and made my promises, and I was free to go, three months later.

Those three months though (while Esteban was taking care of my affairs and the cartel I had taken from Travis Raines) had cost me a lot. I should have been on my home soil and expanding; instead I was behind bars. The prisons in America were nothing like the ones in Mexico. It could have been a vacation for some, though perhaps I was treated so well because my dollar went further in the cells. There is so much power and influence in money and drugs that it makes me wonder why anyone would bother going straight. To save face? No, that is ludicrous. Your face never looks better than when you've got a gun in your hand and money under your ass.

I suppose I should have been grateful that I was only in prison for such a short time and I walked away unharmed with only a new smoking habit to add to my regrets.

At that thought, I fished a cigarette from my slim gold case and placed it in my mouth.

Juanito frowned at me. "The rules…" he said feebly.

I struck the match along the side of the wood table, then lit the cigarette and slowly blew smoke in his face. "The rules don't apply to me. Never have, never will." I placated him with a smile. "Now, let's talk business, shall we?"

He nodded and relaxed a bit on his stool, eager to get started. Another good sign. It said he was confident in his job.

"What I need from you, Juanito," I said, continuing to stare at him, "is to perform your job like it's the last job you'll ever do."

His smile went crooked. "Will it be the last job I ever do?"

I suppose my reputation preceded me. I puffed on the cigarette, in no hurry to answer him, until he had to look away from my stare. "You'll be paid enough so you never need to work again, if that is what you mean."

He swallowed hard, and I could sense his leg bouncing restlessly under the table. "There are rumors, you know."

"About me?" I asked simply.

More nervous gestures. "Yes."

"Are they about how large my dick is?"

Relief washed over his face, and he managed a laugh. "Not really."

"Too bad. It's true, you know. About my dick."

He didn't seem too impressed. He spun the bottle of beer around in his hands. "They say you end up killing most people who do jobs for you."

I shrugged. "So?"

"Is it true?"

I tapped the cigarette and let it ash onto the floor. "It's not a lie. Look, if I promise not to kill you, will that ease your worries?"

His forehead scrunched up, unsure of what way to take me.

"I keep my promises," I added. "Just so you know."

"Well, that will help," he said.

"Then it's settled. You do your job, I'll pay you a lot of money and I won't kill you either." I signalled the bartender to pour me another drink, then went back to staring Juanito down. "So, before you start jacking up my bar tab, tell me your plans."

Now that his worries were eased, he was able to clearly explain exactly what he had to offer. Juanito had done some work with Esteban while I was in prison. Este was the technical guy who could hack into accounts, security systems—hell I think he'd even done some fucked up wizardry with satellite cameras before. But Este was needed at my side, for counsel and for my own protection. Juanito would infiltrate the Reyes compound as best he could, spying on Salvador and Luisa's routine for a week or two before reporting back with concrete intel. I had no doubt that Salvador had his new wife watched, but as the days went on, I also had no doubt that one of them would slip up. When that happened, we would make sure it happened again.

Then we would take her.

Juanito, at first glance, didn't look like the kind of man best suited for the job. Aside from his nervous mannerisms, he had a wiry build and a young face with round cheeks. But I knew better than to judge a book by its cover. All you needed to know about a man was in his eyes, and in Juanito's I could see the confidence in his skill. That sold me.

It also made me stop regretting my promise not to kill him—perhaps he would come in handy in the future.

"When will you start?" I asked as I nodded my thanks to the bartender who placed another glass of tequila in front of me.

"Tomorrow," he said matter-of-factly. "I can be in Culiacán by noon. By tomorrow evening, I promise you I'll know what house they are staying at and where. I've got connections there."

I raised my brows. "Who doesn't," I muttered, and then swallowed my drink. I cleared my throat. "Well, Juanito. I guess that's it."

"And you're not going to kill me?"

"My promise is my promise," I told him solemnly as I made the sign of the cross over my heart. He probably didn't believe me, but when he realized he wasn't dead yet, he would. I gestured to the door with a flick of my wrist. "You better be on your way. Este will pay you your deposit tonight. You'll get the rest after you deliver Luisa Reyes."

He licked his lips eagerly and got off the stool. "Fifty thousand American dollars."

I nodded with a tight smile. The longer I was in the business, the less I liked spending money. People like Salvador and other narcos, they wasted it on lavish bullshit. I liked the finest things in life, but anything better than the finest was just gratuitous.

But in order to get ahead, you needed a loss leader. Luisa was my loss leader.

I stuck my hand out and Juanito stared at it in surprise before he shook it. Call me old-fashioned but a deal was not a deal unless you shook on it. There was still a code among men in this business.

His eyes widened as I squeezed his hand and pulled him slightly towards me. I lowered my voice, my eyes fixed on his, and said, "But just so we're clear, if you fail, if you do not bring me the girl, I will hunt you down and skin you alive. I have a couple of pigs that get fat on human jerky, and I make *them* promises, too. Do you understand me?"

He blinked a few times, nodding quickly.

I let go of him and leaned back, raising my glass in the air. "Well then, cheers."

"Right. Cheers." He awkwardly took a sip of his beer, then wiped his hands on his shirt, and took off out of the bar and into the black night.

I sighed and finished my drink before pulling out another cigarette. At least Juanito would be putting in one hundred and ten percent now. Any boss worth their salt knew how to best motivate their employees and I was no different.

...

We had good news from Juanito a week later. He'd located the Reyes compound and had started infiltrating their security system, taking it slowly, so that no one would even know something was amiss. He did nothing but observe Luisa day in and day out, not exactly the toughest part of the job. At least it wasn't when you had something as easy on the eyes as she was.

A week later, he suggested we start getting ready to move. The perfect opportunity would eventually present itself, but we couldn't do a thing unless we were set up and primed for action. That meant a lot of waiting in the trees, scouring neighboring houses, and hiding in unmarked vans. It all took patience, but luckily I had grown to be a very patient man. I could chase something for years before I felt the need to catch up with it.

While Este and Franco went to Culiacán to join Juanito in the operation, I used two of my bodyguards, Tito and Toni, to help me set up the safe house. We needed the location to make our demands and to keep Luisa for the first few days or at least until Salvador gave in. When we were all done, I'd return to The Devil's Backbone a smarter man, and Luisa would return to her husband, perhaps a bit more broken than when she'd left.

I'd also included The Doctor as part of my arsenal. The Doctor was, yes, an actual physician and very shrewd. Though nearing his late sixties, he had been an integral part of Travis Raines' cartel and now he was a key figure in mine. He knew a lot, especially about the kidnapping side of the business. In Mexico, taking hostages and demanding ransom was as ordinary a job as operating a food cart. The Doctor had been involved in many of them over his lifetime and was the best of the best.

He was also supremely skilled at torture—another good reason to have him around. In some ways, with his knowledge and his groomed, elegant appearance, The Doctor would have made a superior assistant instead of Este. But as much as I respected The Doctor, there was something about him that reminded me of my father, and for that reason I didn't want him around me all day long. The dead were better off dead.

It wasn't long after we headed off to the safe house that I got the call from our driver, The Chicken. He reported that Este and

Franco had captured "the girl," and they, Juanito included, were heading right back to us.

I hung up the phone and grinned stupidly at The Doctor, who had been standing beside me in the modest kitchen where he had been frying shrimp and rice for our dinner. There was something kind of nice about operating out of the safe house—it was basic and simple, like camping for kingpins.

I immediately smoked a cigar, both in celebration and in anticipation. I hadn't been this excited and anxious about something since...well, since a very long time ago. But that memory needed to stay in the deserts of California, where it belonged. The new memory was upon me, and I could practically smell it. I could practically smell *her*.

Luisa Reyes.

She was mine.

After we made quick work of the cigar and the meal, The Doctor and I headed down into the basement to get everything set up for her arrival. We had the chair and the ropes, and chains if we needed them. We had the digital camera set up and ready to record our ransom note which would then be uploaded and emailed directly to Salvador's account, thanks to Este's expertise. We even had bottles of water and carafes of hot tea and coffee—for us, of course. I liked for my men to be hydrated and have a clear head at our most crucial times, and this was most definitely one of those times.

With the safe house being much closer to Salvador's compound, The Doctor and I only had to wait a few hours for them to arrive. We drank our tea and discussed local politics to pass the time and smoked another cigar—anything to calm the nerves. I didn't even know why I was so nervous; it was very unlike me. If things went wrong with our hostage, it wasn't that big of a deal. She'd die and that would be that. There would always be another card to play.

I suppose, if I was being honest with myself, I wanted more than just to get the shipping lane into the Baja, the one Salvador controlled. I wanted to humiliate him, to prove that I was as big of a player as he was. All my life I struggled to get ahead and be the best, but my personal best no longer mattered. Each step

I took, the higher and higher I went, the more power I had, it never satisfied me. I wanted more, always more.

I wanted Salvador to fear me, to be looking over his shoulder for me. Perhaps he already did—I'd been known to commit some unsavory and highly publicized acts over the years—but I wanted him to feel that fear firsthand. And what fear is greater than the fear of feeling stupid?

I got up from my seat and picked up a knife I had placed on the table earlier.

"Is that for show?" The Doctor asked, raising a neatly trimmed white eyebrow. He sipped his tea carefully.

I shook my head. "No. It will be put to use. Every day."

"On the girl?"

I nodded. "Yes. On her. One letter a day. When she goes back to Salvador in a week, I want him to see my name on her back."

He crossed his legs and gave me small smile. "You're getting more twisted and snarled the older you get. Like a root over the years. Are you sure you're only thirty-five?"

I managed a grin. "I'll take that as a compliment. And I'm only thirty-two."

"Wouldn't know it." He shrugged with one shoulder. "Guess Salvador might not want his wife after you give her back with your name carved into her. Ever think of that?"

I let my fingers slide around the blade. "That's not my problem, is it?" I picked up a nearby stool and placed it in front of Luisa's empty chair. I put the knife on top of it with reverence. "As long as I get what I want, what Salvador does with his wife afterward is none of my business."

"And your indifference is what will get you far in this world."

"Indifference," I said with a dry laugh. "I've heard worse."

At that I heard the faint sound of a car a door slamming shut. There were two ways into the basement—one from inside the house and the other leading to the driveway. My eyes flew over to the latter just as the door opened. Feet appeared first on the steps, followed by long legs. Este. Behind him were Juanito and Franco, holding on to the girl.

In person, Luisa Reyes was a lot smaller and more delicate than I imagined. She looked like I could pick her up and carry her in the palm of my hand, the same hand that I could so easily crush her with. Her legs were bare, short, and splattered in mud, but they had soft curves that I wanted to run my hands over. Her hips were full, her waist tiny, even in a loose blouse that was achingly low-cut over her perfect breasts. I couldn't see her face because of the black canvas bag they had placed over her head, so I focused instead on her collarbone. I wanted to nip it with my teeth.

I bit down on my lip instead.

I needed a moment to get back in the game.

They took her over to the chair and immediately bound her hands behind it. I watched, trying to steady my breathing, and took in every detail of her that I could. The more I could deduce about her character, the better. Her shorts were jean cut-offs, her shoes were Adidas runners. She had on no jewelry. She wasn't at all what a typical narco-wife looked like. She looked… normal.

I had to make sure that wouldn't be a problem for me.

I nodded at The Doctor who got the ball rolling. He walked over to the video camera on the tripod and lined it up with Luisa's hooded figure.

"Is everything ready?" Este asked him.

"It's all set up," he said, and walked toward Luisa, peering down at her. "How drugged is she?"

"Not badly," Este said, shooting me a nervous glance. I didn't like that glance. "She's somewhat coherent."

"You didn't gag her?"

"No, but she shut up when she needed to."

"It's lucky she was out there."

"Yes. It was," The Doctor said. There was a pause and everyone looked at me.

Waiting.

I took in a deep breath through my nose.

"Gentleman," I announced as I slowly walked toward her, "remove the bag."

Este leaned over her and quickly pulled it off her head.

She immediately put her face to the side, her eyes shut tight, trying to avoid my gaze or perhaps the overhead light. All it did was highlight a red and purple bruise that marred her beautiful cheek.

A curious bit of rage simmered in my stomach. "Who did this?" I asked, my hands going for her ruined face while my eyes immediately went to Franco. "Who did this?" I repeated. Luisa flinched under my touch, perhaps from pain, perhaps from revulsion. She still didn't look at me.

"Sorry," Franco mumbled, not sorry at all. "It was the only way to quiet her."

I sucked in my breath and tried to bury the fire inside. The man was such a sorry excuse for a human being. He got the job done, but he often went overboard while doing it. He was a messy, sloppy fuck with beady eyes that showed what little intelligence he had in his thick skull. If Luisa was going to suffer any pain—and she would—it would not be at the hands of this brute, a man who had no finesse in his actions, no respect for violence. It would be from me. I was the one in charge of her.

When I was calm and air was flowing through my lungs with ease, I took my hands off her soft, swollen skin and bent down in front of her. Now I wanted her to see me. She couldn't avoid this forever.

"Look at me, Luisa Reyes." She didn't move, didn't open her eyes. Her chest heaved, but I kept my eyes on hers. "Darling, aren't you curious as to where you are?"

For a moment there I started to wonder if I had the wrong girl. With the bruise and the pain in her wincing expression, I wondered if I'd captured a woman who was already broken. There was no challenge in that, only pity.

"My name is Luisa *Chavez*," she said. She straightened her head and her eyes flew open, staring right at me. "And I know where I am. I know who you are. You are Javier Bernal."

I had nothing to worry about. She was not broken at all. Those deep brown eyes burned with strength.

I raised my brow and nodded, exceedingly pleased and terribly turned on. The fact that she knew my name made my dick twitch.

"You know why you're here," I said, straightening up. I walked over to the stool, eager to begin, and glanced at her over my shoulder. "Don't you?"

She was staring at me, a bit of fear coming off of her, making her look even younger. My god her lips looked so full and juicy as they quivered before me.

"What is the knife for?" she croaked.

"You'll find out after," I said. "It is for your husband. For your Salvador." I stepped to the side and waved my arm at the camera. "And this is also for him."

I eyed The Doctor who was standing behind her now, duct tape in hand. He quickly ripped off a piece and placed it over those lips while Este dimmed the lights in the room. I went behind the video camera and focused the light on her. She looked like a ghost, lit up against the darkness. So hauntingly dramatic.

I cleared my throat and hit record on the camera. "This is Luisa Reyes," I said, making sure my words were clear enough for the recording. "Former beauty queen of the Baja State and property of Salvador Reyes. Salvador, we have your wife, and we have a long list of demands—demands which I know you can meet. I expect full cooperation in this matter or she dies in the next seven days. If she's lucky. I'll give you some time to think about what you're willing to give up for her. Then we'll be contacting you. Goodbye."

At that, I switched off the camera light and hit stop. The room remained dim. It was romantic.

"I hope your husband checks his emails often," I told her, picking up the knife. "It would be a shame to have to put this on YouTube."

I walked over to her and then held up the knife, making sure she could see it well. "I think it's only going to hurt the first time," I said truthfully, hoping that would make her feel better about what was going to happen. It was the only courtesy I could offer.

While Franco held her still, I ordered Este to rip apart her blouse and push her down, exposing her back. That's when she passed out, her chin down to her chest, her shoulders slumping.

In an instant, The Doctor had a syringe in his hand, filled with lidocaine, ready to be injected into her heart. "Shall I keep her awake?"

I quickly shook my head. "No. I'll grant her this mercy." After all, she never asked for this. I guess it wouldn't hurt the first time after all.

Only the second.

With careful precision I carved the letter J into her shoulder blade. It bled, bright crimson on her creamy skin, but only a little—the cut was deep enough to leave a light scar but not so deep to cause damage.

I wasn't a savage.

CHAPTER SEVEN

Luisa

When I woke up, I could have sworn for one moment I was back at my old house in San Jose del Cabo. Something about the way the light slanted in through the window and onto my face.

For that one little moment I was happy again.

It only took me a second though to realize that I couldn't have been farther from home. The events from last night came flooding into my mind like rancid garbage. I'd finally done it. I'd finally escaped.

And I'd only gotten a few minutes away before I was captured.

By Javier Bernal.

I groaned quietly, afraid that I wasn't alone, and opened my eyes wider, trying to take in what I could. To my surprise, I wasn't locked up in some cage in the dingy basement. Instead I was lying under the thin covers of a soft bed in what looked like a bedroom. There was one bare window from which the light streamed through, and through a door I got a glimpse of a dark bathroom. The rest of the room was empty, the walls covered with faded, yellowing wallpaper.

Once I realized I was alone, I slowly sat up in the bed. I was wearing a man's linen shirt that smelled like spicy tea. The smell hit me like a hammer and I suddenly wished I was naked. To be undressed was one thing, but the fact that I was dressed again was another, something far more intimate than I wanted to think about.

Suddenly the image of a blade flashed through my mind. I gasped, and in a panic, started feeling over every inch of my body, making sure everything was intact.

As far as I could tell, I was in one piece. But when I moved, the shirt stretched over my back and made my skin sting. I felt along my shoulder blade and winced. There was a curved cut there, just in that one spot. Why? What were they trying to do?

I stared down at my hands, turning them over, studying them. I needed to ground myself, to bring myself into this new reality. These were my hands and I was still Luisa Chavez. I was free from Salvador but imprisoned by another danger.

And yet, as I sat there on that bed in that small room with the sunlit walls, in some house in some location I'd probably never learn, I didn't feel any fear. I had no idea what they were going to do to me. Perhaps I should have been more afraid. I was just...sad. Sad that my life had to go this way, sad that I could never catch a break. Sad that I'd probably never see my parents again.

I swallowed painfully. I knew Javier would kill me. That was what he did, just as it was what Sal did. There was no difference between the men in that regard. I knew that Sal would never do what Javier was going to ask of him; I wasn't important enough to negotiate for. He'd just find another woman to rape, another woman to hit, to kick, to beat on a daily basis.

The last seven weeks had been pure, unadulterated hell. Now I was in another hell, but this time around I couldn't find the energy to dance with fear.

But, perhaps I could find the energy to escape once again. I looked around the room, searching for cameras. Salvador had cameras in every room of our house, and I had no doubt that Javier or one of his men were watching my every move. Still, I couldn't see them, though that didn't mean they weren't there.

I carefully got out of bed, feeling sore all over, and checked out the bathroom. It was plain, just a toilet and sink and one roll of toilet paper. I walked over to the window. There wasn't anything except forest for miles. It looked a lot like the woods surrounding Salvador's, which made me wonder if we were still in the Sierra Madre Occidental. Thought it was blindingly sunny, there were dark grey clouds hanging above distant green peaks.

There was a knock at the door and I quickly spun around. My instincts told me to cover myself up—the linen shirt barely covered my underwear—and to grab the nearest weapon. There was nothing I could do for either of those. I was practically indecent and completely defenseless.

The knock came again, followed by the sound of the door being unlocked. Why didn't they just come inside the room, why put up the faux-polite pretenses? If they were doing it to confuse me, it was working.

I waited, my breath in my mouth, and watched the doorknob. When nothing happened, I swallowed my courage and walked toward the door. With my hand on the knob I waited a beat before flinging the door open.

Standing on the other side was a man holding a tray of food and a pot of coffee. I recognized him from last night, I think his name was Esteban. The one who didn't hit me in the face, though possibly the one who carved something into my back.

He smiled at me, a lopsided grin that made him look innocent even though he was anything but. His hair had a bit of a curl to it, brown with lighter streaks, which reminded me of some of the surfer hippies we had in Los Cabos. He was even dressed like them—board shorts and a wife-beater tank top that showed off his muscles. The only thing that reminded me of his line of business was the scarring on the side of his face. However, it didn't make him ugly, just dangerous. It kept me on my toes.

I eyed the tray in his hand with suspicion. "What is this?"

"Your breakfast," he said, nodding down at it. "Tortilla, eggs, salsa, fresh mango juice. Coffee."

"All laced with drugs to knock me out," I said, not trusting him for a second.

His smile straightened out, looking playfully amused. "You're free to do whatever you want with the food. Eat it, don't eat, we really don't care. We just want to make sure we're a good host."

I could have laughed until I realized he was serious. "You want to be a good host? Let me go free then." I looked down the hallway and noticed a man stationed at the end of it, standing guard. For a moment I thought I could throw the food in Este's face, perhaps smash the coffee pot into the other cheek and scar that one up too. But I wouldn't get far. Where there was one guard there were more guards.

"I'm afraid we can't let you go until Salvador pays the ransom," Esteban said. "That's how these things work."

"Too bad for you he'll never pay any amount for me," I told him.

At that Esteban looked completely surprised. The look vanished when he said, "It's not money we are after. We have more than enough. We want a certain shipping lane going into the Baja."

I gave him an incredulous look and shook my head slightly. Was he for real? They had absolutely no idea about me and Salvador's relationship. They were going to have a rude awakening when they realized he wasn't going to give them anything. And I was going to die.

When I didn't say anything he gestured to the room behind me. "May I come in?"

"If I say no, will you do something about it?"

He frowned. "You're a bit of a feisty one, aren't you? You do realize what has happened to you, don't you? Javier Bernal is not a nice man and you're his prisoner."

"I'm being treated fairly well for a prisoner," I countered.

He raised his brows. "We like to extend some courtesies when we can. So I take it you don't want your food?"

"You and your food can go fuck yourself," I said, feeling a rush of hot blood go through me. I wasn't used to swearing or talking back. If it was possible, my newfound fearlessness scared me.

I was so certain that Esteban was going to throw the coffee in my face or strike me, force me into the room and brutalize me. But that never came.

He only gave me a stiff smile. "I'm only trying to make things more comfortable for you. The others aren't as nice as me." His look darkened. "But I can be the bad guy if you want me to."

I believed him. Underneath the boyish demeanour I saw depth that held anger and malicious intent, a bitterness that marred his true nature. Perhaps the darkness wasn't for me, but it was there. I had seen that same look on Salvador, only he wore his depravity on the surface. While I had no doubt that Esteban was probably considered the good guy in this whole operation, I told myself to never think he was on my side.

Without taking my eyes off of his, I slowly stepped back into the room and shut the door in his face. I stood there, waiting on the other side of it, until I heard a shuffle and the door being locked.

I breathed out a long sigh of relief that rocked through me until I felt like I was too heavy to stand. I leaned back against the door and slowly slid down it until I was sitting on the floor. I rested my head back and stared at the window, at the sun that was still shining through.

I was going to spend my last days in this room unless Salvador came through. But even that would mean a return to a horrible life. There was no winning this game.

The only thing I had to hold on to was my sense of self. I had let Sal ruin me, day by day, piece by piece. I wouldn't let that happen here. They could try and carve me up, they could rape me, torture me, try and confuse me with hospitality, but they would not get to me. They would not break my soul. They would not see my pain.

And at that, a single tear leaked out and ran down my cheek. I swallowed and willed myself to stop. That was for my father and mother who I tried so hard to do right by. That was the only time I would cry from now until my death.

They would never reach the deepest parts of me.

...

I woke up to the sound of the door being unlocked. I had fallen asleep sitting on the floor, my head slumped to the side, my neck aching. It was twilight now and the sun was long gone.

The door suddenly opened, pushing against my back. Whoever this was, the whole knocking courtesy didn't extend to them. I quickly rolled out of the way and got to a crouch just as someone stepped in.

In the dim light, I couldn't make out who it was, but I knew right away. He stared down at me, and I could see his eyes glinting against his shadowy face.

"What are you doing down there?" Javier asked in a silky smooth voice.

I didn't say anything, I didn't move.

He shut the door behind him and cocked his head at me. Even in the low light I could feel his eyes, feel him studying me. "I heard you weren't too interested in eating today. Este says you told him to go fuck himself. I wish I could have seen that."

When I didn't say anything, he took a step toward me and held out his hand. "Get up," he said, waiting. His posture stiffened and his voice lowered. "I said get up. I don't like to repeat myself."

It was only then that I noticed he was holding something in his other hand. Two things, it looked like. A folded-up rope and a knife. I waited for the pang of fear to hit me. It was subtle and I didn't let it show. I also didn't obey him.

He quickly reached down and grabbed me by the arm, yanking me up to him until I was pressed against his chest, crushing the front of his suit jacket.

"You're a light little thing, aren't you?" he asked in a bemused voice, his breath smelling faintly of cinnamon and tobacco. "Delicate and easy to break."

We'd see about that.

I acted instinctually. With my free hand I jabbed my palm into his nose. He yelped in surprise, maybe even in pain, and momentarily let go of me. That's all I needed.

I pushed past him and went for the door. I put my hands on the knob and turned, pulling it toward me. There was a wonderful feeling of freedom for just that one moment where the door opened and the light from the hallway spilled in. The feeling of power that came from fighting back.

Nothing in my life had felt as good as my hand connecting with his face.

But the feeling was fleeting. All at once the door slammed shut and Javier was behind me, the rope going around my chest. He hauled me backward into him so that he was holding me tight from behind.

"Don't you know it turns me on when you fight back?" he whispered in my ear, his voice ragged. "Though it turns me on when you don't fight back, too. I guess you can't win." He sniffed. "I think you bloodied my nose."

"Then I guess you'll have to bloody my face," I taunted him, my veins on fire with the strange adrenaline that was running through me.

He sucked in his breath. "No, my darling. I would never do that to your face. Just your back. I have a lot of respect for beautiful things, you know. They are usually the most dangerous."

Oh, how I wished I could be dangerous to him, to anyone.

"You know, Luisa," he said, holding me tighter now. I could feel his erection pressing into my ass. "We're going to be doing this dance with each other until we give you back to your husband. You could make things easier on yourself. I don't like to play rough with you."

"No," I said quietly. "You just want to cut me up."

"I'm merely branding you," he said. "Don't make it sound so ugly." He lifted his arm so that the knife was shining in front of my face. I could almost see my warped reflection staring back at me. "My penmanship with a knife is very delicate. A hard-earned skill. If your husband's name was Javier, I think you would be quite pleased with the finished result."

The man was completely crazy. He planned to carve his name in my back, as if he was doing me a favor.

"Come on," he said, and quickly wrapped the rope around me so my arms were held tight to my sides. He made a few knots and then shuffled me over to the bed before he pushed me onto it, face down. I turned my head to breathe and he pressed down on the side of it, to keep me in place. "Now stay."

He straddled me, legs on either side of my waist, and his hands stroked softly along the back of my neck until he grabbed my collar. "My shirt looks good on you," he commented. "But it looks better off." He reached underneath me, grabbing me by my collarbone, and ripped the shirt open before pushing it to the side and sliding most of it off until one shoulder was bare.

"He's not going to want me when he sees what you've done," I managed to say.

"He's not going to see what I've done until I have what I want. What your marriage can and cannot handle is not my problem and none of my business."

"You're disgusting."

"I'm many things but disgusting isn't one of them."

"You're sick."

"Well, there's no argument there. Good or bad, there is great power in knowing who you are and owning it. So, tell me, my beauty queen...who are you?"

He leaned down so those blazing eyes of his were visible to mine.

"No one you will ever know," I told him, relieved at how strong I sounded.

"We shall see about that."

He adjusted himself on my back, and I felt him press the dull side of the blade into my shoulder. The cold threatened to make me shiver, but I suppressed it.

"You know what I am going to do to you and yet you are not afraid. Why is that?" His voice was lower now, wispy like smoke.

He wouldn't be interested in the truth. "Why do you want me to be afraid?"

Silence thickened the room. He didn't answer. I knew now that I had spurred him on to try and do his worst. It would hurt me dearly, but as long as I never showed it, never gave in, I would be the one who would win in the end. I could beat Javier Bernal at his own twisted game.

"There are some things in life you should be afraid of," he finally said.

"Like you?"

His eyes burned into me but I didn't look away. He straightened up and turned the knife over. He dug the blade in, and it pierced me with a sharp, nauseating blast of pain. "Like me," he said quietly.

I bit down on my lip as he carved the A right beside the still tender J. I didn't know what his penmanship looked like, nor did I care, but he was very quick, I had to give him that. He could have drawn it out a lot longer. The pain was sharp but brief.

"Now that that's done for today," he said, his voice still soft as he removed the knife, "can I get you anything?"

It was as if my back wasn't bleeding from his torture. I didn't even know what to say so I didn't say anything. I just pressed my teeth together and prayed he would go away.

"You really should eat something," he said, still straddling me. "I happen to be a good cook." He waited, and when he didn't get a response, he leaned down and gently blew on my fresh wound. "I can get you fresh clothes, I have a whole selection put aside for you. Perhaps they will be a bit long, I had no idea how short you were."

I kept my mouth shut and my face emotionless, giving him nothing. But inside, I couldn't quite comprehend what a psychopath this man was. He and Salvador were so much the same and yet so different.

"All right," he said, straightening up. "If you wish to be stubborn, then I'll leave you." He gracefully eased himself off of me, and I heard him walk over to the door and open it. "I'll see you tomorrow, Luisa Reyes."

The door shut behind him and I could hear it being locked. It was only then that I realized he'd left me on the bed, still tied up and unable to move my arms.

I spent all of two seconds trying to figure out how to free myself before the pain and exhaustion overtook me and pulled me off to sleep.

CHAPTER EIGHT

Javier

"Need a sparring partner?"

I hadn't even noticed that Este was behind me, but my right hook never faltered and it delivered the blow head on. The heavyweight bag swung and I stepped out of the way, wiping the sweat from my brow as I looked to him standing in the doorway. They all called me self-indulgent when I insisted all the safe houses be equipped with a small gym and heavyweight bags, but if I wasn't staying in shape by boxing, I wasn't myself.

"Do you remember the last time I sparred with you?" I asked him, grabbing a bottle of water and having a sip.

He shrugged, trying to act like he wasn't embarrassed. Este always had this way of trying to prove something to me, to one-up me. The last time we had a sparring session, he turned it into a full-fledged fight. Naturally, I knocked him down with just a blow. All my training hadn't been for nothing. I had hoped I knocked his ego down, too, but that wasn't the case.

He pointed at me and wiggled his fingers. "Were you sparring with someone else? Your nose looks more crooked than normal."

I raised my brow. "You were right about her being feisty."

He smiled. "I see. But I guess you still got your way."

"When don't I?"

He casually jammed his hands in the pockets of his cargo shorts. "Oh, I can think of a few times."

That was enough. "What do you want, Este?" I asked pointedly.

He nodded, smiling to himself, knowing he got to me for just that one second. "I was going to go check on the girl, bring her some breakfast. Just letting you know that Doc's cooked up a feast. Do you think it's too soon to let her eat with us?"

I grabbed a towel and started wiping the sweat off my arms and chest. "I'd like to see if you can convince her to eat, let alone eat with us. But you never know—I did leave her in a rather vulnerable position."

He frowned and sighed, leaning against the doorway. "I don't think she realizes what a vulnerable position she's actually in."

"I was being literal, but I agree," I told him, stretching my arms above my head. "So she really thinks that Salvador won't give a shit about her life?"

"I've been checking my phone, my emails all morning," he said. "There's nothing from him yet."

"Maybe he hasn't seen the video yet." I went over to the bench and picked up my watch that I removed only for boxing. I didn't like the way my wrist looked without it. I quickly strapped it on and felt an immediate sense of relief when it covered up the tattoo that resided on my veins.

"Javi, he's seen it. I can tell."

"Then he's waiting for us to tell him what we want. He's not a stupid man, not entirely. He won't act rash right away."

"I hope you're right," he said. "Otherwise, this was a lot of effort for nothing."

I glared at him. "That's not for you to ever question or worry about."

He raised his palm at me. "It's all cool, hey."

I gave him a disgusted look. Everything was always so fucking cool to him, like the cartel was one big frat party where he could coast along, screwing chicks and trying to be the big man on campus. He took all the wrong things seriously.

I watched as he left the room, and then I turned back to the bag. Despite the watch being on my wrist, I started punching again, harder. I hated to admit it, but there was this tiny thread of doubt that Este had placed in my head, wriggling around like a maggot.

Even if Salvador didn't love his wife, he still had pride, and that was what I was banking on. I could only hope that his pride was worth part of his empire. I had built my own empire—or siphoned it, depending on who you asked—and I knew how much it was worth to me. But my pride, my image, was worth just as much.

Then there was the other piece in the game, the lovely, stubborn Luisa who so bravely dared to defy me last night. After I had left her tied on the bed, it took all my willpower not to go in there and make her see how serious I was. She hadn't been afraid—she didn't even make a sound when the blade cut her beautiful skin—and it was driving me mad. I couldn't tell if she just didn't realize the danger she was in, or she just didn't care. If it was the latter, that made her more dangerous than I wanted to admit. She needed to appreciate the art of violence, the beauty in fear, the fragility of her own life.

I had to make her care. If all went well, I only had her for four more days, and in that time I would make her care, make her cry, make her realize just who I was and what I could do to her.

...

Luisa

I'm not sure how I slept the whole night through with my arms bound to my sides, face down on the bed, but I did. I didn't wake until I heard knocking at my door. I knew who it was—Esteban knocked, Javier didn't—and hoped that he would just go away. But I guess his politeness didn't extend that far.

The door opened and I heard Esteban say, "Wow, he wasn't kidding."

It closed behind him and he walked over until I felt him hovering over me. I stiffened, wondering what would come next.

Esteban placed his hand on the small of my back. "Would you like me to untie you?"

Again, I didn't answer. I didn't want to beg or ask for anything.

"Well, I'm going to," he said. He started undoing the rope and soon it loosened my arms falling beside me, my muscles screaming from the pain.

"You know I'm not going to hurt you," he murmured. "Let me help you up."

He reached for me, but with what strength I had, I sat up and swatted him away.

"Don't you touch me," I scowled.

He raised his palms at me. "All right. Just trying to help."

"Somehow I doubt that," I said, sliding the shirt back to normal and making sure I was decent.

He nodded at it. "I have something here for you."

I looked down at his hands and noticed him carrying a piece of fabric in hot pink.

"It's a dress," he said. "You know, if you don't feel like wearing Javier's shirt for the rest of the week. Or, you know, you can go naked. If you want." He gave me a cocky grin and I wished I could do the same to his face as I had done to Javier's. I just wasn't sure I had the strength. My arms felt weak from being tied all night and I was absolutely starving.

When I didn't move or say anything, he threw the dress on my lap. "Put it on," he said. "I promise to turn around. I won't look."

"I don't care if you do look," I told him, raising my chin. I didn't want to do a single thing Esteban or anyone told me to do, but I also wanted to get out of this shirt.

He raised his brows but slowly turned around anyway.

I quickly slipped off the shirt, wincing as it brushed against the cuts on my back, and pulled on the dress. It was strapless and had a smocked bust and waist that conformed to my body perfectly. To what little credit Esteban had, he didn't turn around for quite some time.

"You look very fresh," he commented, looking me over. There was a strange look in his eyes that I couldn't quite place. It was as if he were devious, but at the same time, it wasn't lustful or sexual. "Are you ready to eat, or do you still want to be stubborn about it?"

I wanted to say yes to both those questions. "I'm fine."

"I'm afraid you don't have a choice, hey," he said. Before I could move, he reached over and grabbed my arm, yanking me straight out of bed. My wrist twisted painfully, and his fingers pressed into me with startling ferocity; enough that I couldn't help the yelp that escaped from my lips.

"You're hurting me," I managed to say, staring up at him, at the highlighted hair that fell in his hazel eyes.

"You're being an idiot," he said back, smiling, the scars looking unsettling on his face. "Now come on. You're having breakfast with us and you're going to behave. A big smile for the boss."

He let go and grabbed my upper arm, not as tightly as before, but I obviously wouldn't be escaping. He led me out of the room and down the carpeted hallway to a set of stairs where a guard was standing watch. I stared at the guard while he took me past. He winked at me in response.

Downstairs the house was a bit more modern. Light pierced through the slats in the blinds. I noticed all the windows were covered, and the furniture in the living room was bare yet still tastefully decorated. I'd never been in Salvador's torture houses, but I assumed they weren't as nice as this. It could almost be a middle-class home if only I didn't know its purpose.

"Right in here," Este said, leading me through a doorway and into a black-and-white tiled kitchen that smelled of fried pork. At a round table sat an older man with grey, slicked back hair and a mustache. He was dressed all in white and was wearing small round glasses as he looked over the newspaper. He didn't even glance up at me.

Beside him, sipping on a mug of tea and staring at me with vague surprise, was Javier. This was the first time I was able to get a good look at him in daylight. He was wearing a white dress shirt with the top few buttons undone. A gold watch glinted from his wrist while his elbows rested on the table.

In some ways Javier was an unusual looking man. He wasn't movie star handsome—or even *Telemundo* handsome. His mouth was a little too wide, his nose was a bit crooked, perhaps a tad puffy from last night. He wasn't terribly tall, and his body was sleek with an athletic build, not as muscled as Esteban. But he had sensual lips, dark, expressive brows, and high cheekbones. His hair was dark, shiny and thick enough to make any man or woman envious, a shaggy and slightly long cut. Then there were his eyes, that stark, golden gaze that cut you from the inside out. You couldn't help but get sucked into them, swirling into whatever darkness lurked below. They were relentless, terrifying, and oddly beautiful, just like the man himself.

Javier took his eyes off of me and fixed them on Esteban. "I wasn't expecting her."

Esteban let go of my arm and nudged me toward the table. "She wanted to come. I told you I could convince her."

I swallowed hard as Javier looked back at me, searching my face. I wasn't sure why Esteban lied—he had certainly not convinced me of anything—but I wasn't about to call attention to it either.

"Well then," Javier said, nodding at the empty seat across from him. "Sit down. Eat Este's breakfast."

I didn't want to move, but Esteban nudged me again, harder this time, until I practically fell into the chair. The mugs and glasses of juice on the table rattled, spilling over slightly, and Javier briefly shot Esteban a deadly look, though I couldn't tell if it was for my unceremonious treatment or the spilled drinks. Most likely the latter.

"I got her to wear the dress too," Este added, standing behind me and resting his hands on the back of my chair.

Javier's gaze slid over my body before resting on my face, looking remotely suspicious. "So I see. I hope you like it, Luisa. If you don't, there's more where it came from."

I could only stare blankly at him, too overwhelmed by the situation.

"Oh, and where are my manners?" He looked over at the grey-haired man. "Luisa, this is The Doctor. Doc, this is our dear houseguest, Luisa Reyes."

The Doctor eyed me dryly before turning back to the paper. "Yes, I met her the other night."

"Ah, but the other night was so...chaotic, don't you think?" Javier folded his hands in front of him. "Perhaps proper introductions are still needed. You know who I am, so you say.

The man behind you is Esteban Mendoza. Another partner of ours, Franco, is running errands. I'm afraid you don't want to get on his bad side—again." He gestured to my cheek which was still tender, thanks to the hit it took the other night. I'd made a note not to look at my reflection in the bathroom mirror, but I knew it was deeply bruised.

"There are a few more people you'll see milling about, but their names aren't important. They won't have much to do with you unless you make trouble for yourself. It seems as if that's something you like to do—I recommend you don't. We don't want to do any harm to you. That said, we're not completely against it either."

I snorted and gave him the most disgusted look I could muster.

It made him smile, cunning and cruel. "So you know how to find humor in life. That will go a long way, my darling. But you should also know when I'm serious. We've given the demands to your husband. The ball is in his court."

I couldn't help the smirk that sneaked angrily across my face. "He'll never make a deal with you. You'll see."

"I think you underestimate your worth," Javier said earnestly.

"And I think you overestimate my husband," I said. "You would have been better off just killing him instead of taking me. That was your biggest mistake."

His jaw flexed very lightly, as if he were biting something back.

"There was no mistake," he said carefully. He paused. "So you would have preferred we kill your dear Salvador?"

"If you killed him, I wouldn't be here right now, wearing a whore's dress and being forced to eat your shitty food."

A genuine smile spread across Javier's face, lighting his eyes up like citron stones. There was a beauty to it that shocked me, making me momentarily forget who I was dealing with.

He laughed, nodding his head. "You are something, aren't you? You know, by the time you leave, I think the two of us will get to know each other very well. I might even end up liking you."

I didn't return the smile. *No, you won't*, I thought. *Because I won't give you what you want.*

It was all for show now, all of this, the banter, the pretenses that this could be a cordial experience. It didn't fool me for a second. After all, there was a V that needed to be carved into my back.

"I'll have you know," The Doctor said, slowly getting to his feet, "that the food is only shitty when Este is cooking."

"Hey," Este said from behind me, sounding hurt.

The smile suddenly departed Javier's face. He looked to Este and The Doctor. "Do you mind giving us some privacy? Luisa and I need to talk. Alone."

I felt Esteban hesitate at my back, but he and The Doctor left the room by way of the kitchen door. Sunlight, heat, and birdsong streamed inside for a moment. I breathed in deeply, trying both to find my courage to face Javier alone again and to take in the smell of the surrounding mountains. It smelled clean, like sunbaked leaves and dry air. It reminded me that life was going on outside this house, and that it could be beautiful.

"What are you thinking?" Javier asked me in a low voice, sounding genuinely interested.

I would not let him in. I looked at him point blank. "About how you're going to kill me."

He raised his brow. "And how do you think I'm going to kill you?"

I shrugged, pretending that even talking about it didn't scare me. "You'll probably slice my head off. That's what Salvador does...when he's in a good mood."

He stared at me intently. "It wouldn't be the first time for me. But the blood is starting to be a real pain to clean up."

"Then how will you do it?"

His brow furrowed. "You really think I'm going to kill you?"

"If Salvador doesn't give you want you want, then yes. But before that, you'll start sending him my body parts. My fingers and toes first. Perhaps my ears. A tit."

He leaned back in his chair and shook his head, looking disturbed. "You are a morbid little woman."

"I didn't used to be. Then I became the wife of a drug lord."

He licked his lips, looking me over. "You're very good at pretending not to be afraid. But I am very good at seeking the truth in people. You can't go far in this business without becoming somewhat of a mind reader." He folded his hands behind his head, looking utterly casual. "And I can sense your fear, buried beneath all your bravado. I can smell it."

I ignored him and looked up at his wrist. His watch had moved over an inch and I could see the word "wish" tattooed beneath it in English.

"What does your tattoo mean?" I asked.

His face froze for a moment then relaxed. "It's English."

"I know how to read English," I told him. "I worked at a bar in Cabo San Lucas for the last three years."

Oh damn, big mistake. He didn't need to know anything else about me.

"So I heard," he said. When he noted my expression he added, "Don't look so surprised. I had people researching you for some time. I know a lot of things about you, Luisa Reyes."

"I'd rather you call me Chavez," I told him. "The Reyes name means nothing to me."

"Apparently. So why did you marry him then? Money?"

"What does the tattoo mean? You tell me something, I'll tell you something."

He pursed his lips for a moment and then nodded sharply. "All right. The tattoo is for a Nine Inch Nails' song. I got it when I was young and stupid and living in America."

That couldn't be all there was to the story, but his face was completely unreadable.

"So you married him for money?" he asked.

"Yes." I nodded. There was no chance of me telling him the real reason. As long as my parents were alive, this monster would never know about them. "He took an interest in me, and of course I said yes to him."

"Of course," he said slowly, a hint of disappointment on his brow. "Well, Luisa, I hope it was worth your life."

My heart thumped uncomfortably. "I thought you said you weren't going to kill me."

He gave me a small smile. "I never said that. I only asked why you thought I was. If Salvador does not comply, we probably will have to start sending him little pieces of you. Or we may just chop your head right off and send him that."

It was hard to ignore the fear now. I don't know why it suddenly felt so real. I guess sitting across from him, looking at Javier Bernal, made it hard to ignore. Still, I straightened up in my seat. "You'll have all that blood to clean up."

He shrugged lazily. "True, but that's what Este is for, after all." Suddenly the look in his eyes darkened. "You like him, don't you?"

I frowned, totally confused. "Like him?"

He gave me a dismissive wave and got out of his chair. I could see now he had on dark blue jeans with a hand-tooled leather belt. That, combined with his pristine white shirt, made him seem so elegantly casual.

So elegantly dangerous.

"It doesn't matter," he said, coming around the table. "Get up. Take off your dress."

I blinked at him. "What?"

He kicked at the leg of the chair, moving me back a few inches. "Do it. Please. Or I will do it for you. Would you like that?" He reached out for me and I balked from his touch. "Because I think I would."

I didn't know what to do. I felt frozen, stuck to the chair, unable to move.

He didn't wait for me. He quickly reached down and put his hands around my waist, lifting me straight out of the chair. He was deceptively strong, and he placed me on my feet with grace, as if we were a figure skating pair.

He held me close to him, hands still cupped around my waist, staring down at me like he was trying to hypnotize me with his eyes. "You are my enigma," he said gruffly. "But I never leave anything unsolved."

Before I could say anything to that, he pulled the dress right over my head and tossed it on the ground behind him. There I was, standing stark naked in his kitchen, still dirty from my escape. I felt like the dirt was in every corner of my soul while I stood there and he looked me over with an unmeasurable smile.

He stepped back and I did what I could to cover myself. He quickly swatted my arms away. "No, no, Luisa. You just stand right there until I tell you otherwise." He slowly walked to the side of me, pushing the table out of the way. "You were a beauty queen, this should be nothing but second nature to you."

"I was never a whore," I managed to say, keeping my eyes focused on a blank spot on the wall. I wondered if Esteban and The Doctor knew what was going on, wondered if one of Javier's guards would come sauntering in here. I tried to push the memories of Salvador and the humiliating things he had made me do out of my head. It was all I could do to stay strong.

"You're right," he said softly, stopping behind me. "I can see you were never a whore. Your purity shines through you. It's intoxicating." I felt him step closer, his breath at the back of my neck. He breathed in. "More intoxicating than the finest liquor." He breathed out, slowly, blowing a few strands of hair. "And this is why I refuse to believe that Salvador won't give me what I want, not for as long as I have you."

I closed my eyes, knowing I couldn't change his mind, not now.

He pressed close to me.

"I will break you," he whispered in my ear, his breath hot. He ran his hands down my sides, then reached around my breasts, finding the nipples. I steeled myself against him, not allowing myself to feel anything. Though his touch was soft and gentle, his intentions were not. The intentions of men never were.

I swallowed hard and said as steadily as I could muster, "Then do your worst. And you will see that the worst has already been done."

He sucked in his breath, just for a moment. Then he said, "Is that so?"

"You've only stripped me naked."

"Are you asking for more?" he asked softly, his lips now at my other ear, my nipples finally starting to pucker under the rhythmic teasing of his thumbs. My body was responding in a way it shouldn't, in a way I never thought possible. "I'm not done with your back, you know. There are more letters in my name."

One of his hands traced the letters J and A. I winced from even that light pressure on the wounds but quickly buried the pain. Thankfully, his fingers didn't linger there. His hands began to drift down my bare back. They swept over my ass, sliding his finger underneath my cheeks, in the soft spot where they met the thigh. It nearly tickled me and brought out a low groan from him.

I'm not here, I'm not here, I'm not here, I chanted to myself.

Javier walked around me, keeping his hands at my waist, until his face was right in front of mine. I opened my eyes to see that perpetual smirk twisting the ends of his lips. "I am far from done with you, Miss Chavez, the beauty queen."

He then crouched down, his hands sliding down my hips, the sides of my thighs. His touch was so gentle and so deceiving. I sucked in my breath, doing what I could to ignore the goose bumps of pleasure.

"You're doing this for revenge," I said, staring down at him, refusing to look away, refusing my body's betrayal.

He smirked and started running his hands up my inner thighs. "On Salvador? Well, I suppose that is pretty obvious, my beauty."

"No," I told him. "This is your revenge on women." His hands paused at that, gripping my skin. "Because a woman broke *you*."

His eyes slowly trailed up to mine, simmering in a golden fury that belied his cold exterior. He straightened up, and that look of anger, of pain...was gone. The hypnotizing, handsome mask was back.

"I don't know what you are referring to," he said with ease.

I couldn't help but smirk right back at him. I had found his sore spot. Someone had broken his heart. "No. Perhaps you don't." The tattoo had tipped me off. If it really had just been about a band, I would never have seen that look of fear pass through his eyes. Now I was thrilled I had something to go on, some way to get to him. "Perhaps you don't want to talk about it."

"There is nothing to talk about." This time he said it a little too easily. His voice grew husky. "Now, give me your hands."

He grasped both my wrists and brought them behind my back. Before I could look over my shoulder, I felt them being bound together with rope. Did he keep a length of rope on him at all times? Probably. That and a knife.

"Get on your knees," he commanded.

"Here?" I asked, my breath catching in my throat.

"Yes," he said. He leaned in and said into my ear, "Here. Now."

I wondered what would happen if I refused. One moment he acted as if he would never hurt me, the next moment there was this dark malice in his soul, the part of him that chopped people's heads off.

Either way, the only choice I had was to be as unaffected as possible. So I did as he said. I dropped to my knees, carefully, with my hands bound behind me.

"Good. Now put your face on the floor. Keep your gorgeous ass in the air."

I complied, leaning over until my cheek was pressed against the cold tiles. I couldn't have felt more vulnerable, more humiliated, if I tried.

And it seemed like Javier was a person to try. I heard him unzip his jeans, the sound seeming to echo off the kitchen walls, so simple and so terrifying.

I squeezed my eyes shut and braced myself. As I had done with Salvador or whatever man he'd made me have sex with, I removed a part of myself from the situation. I swallowed the fear and the feelings, and I became a blank slate, a void that wouldn't feel any pain, wouldn't process any emotion.

Javier could do his worst. I was ready for him. Ready to feel nothing.

But the pain never came. I didn't know if this was part of the game, but he never touched me. Was he waiting to pounce when I least expected it? Was he taking his time?

I opened my eyes, and though I didn't dare look over my shoulder, I caught sight of him in my peripheral. He was standing there, right behind me. But he wasn't just standing there. He was moving ever so slightly.

I heard a small moan escape from his lips and finally realized what he was doing—he was pleasuring himself.

I felt a jolt of revulsion mingled with perverse curiosity. A part of me wanted a better look, wanted to see him in the act. Another part of me—the better part—wanted to pretend none of this was happening.

So I closed my eyes again and tried to pretend I wasn't there, but I could hear his palm sliding up and down on himself, skin on skin, his breath as it hitched in pleasure. I couldn't shut it out of my mind. The more worked up he got, the more it teased me, taunting me to look. I could barely imagine a man like Javier wrapped up in the vulnerability of release, and yet it was happening right behind me. It was happening because of me.

And yet he hadn't laid a finger on me, not yet. He was getting off on just the sight of me, the bare sight of me before him. I didn't know whether to feel humiliated or flattered.

He is only making fun of you, I told myself. *Just because he's not forcing himself on you doesn't make him any different from Salvador.*

Then how come I was tricking myself into thinking this was...better?

"You're so complicit," I heard him moan from behind me, his voice low, rough, caught up in his own passion. "So good. Why do I feel there's a bad girl in you that needs to come out?"

I didn't say anything. The sound of his breathing, his stroking, intensified.

"Perhaps if I come all over your beautiful back," he whispered, pausing to catch his breath. "Come onto my letters. Rub myself into your skin, into your blood. Will the bad girl come out? Will I awaken the true Luisa?" He let out a deep groan that reverberated into my bones. "We'll see, won't we, my darling?"

At that he sucked in his breath and groaned even louder. "Fuck," he cried out, gasping over the words. "Fuck."

Hot fluid spurted onto my back, making me flinch, catching me by surprise. For a moment I could only hear his heavy breathing and I waited, not knowing how literal he was going to be.

I heard his zipper go back up and felt his shadow looming over me.

"I look good on your skin," he murmured. He pressed his hands on my back and began to rub the sticky fluid into my back, into the wound. I bit my lip and held back a cry as it stung like crazy, making my eyes water.

"Finally," he whispered, and I could feel his yellow eyes observing me closely. But he didn't say anything else. He kept rubbing until my skin had absorbed all of him, just as he wanted. He then undid the rope around my wrists and stepped back.

I put my hands on the ground, and he walked around so I was facing his leather boots. He crouched down until we were almost eye to eye and he held up my dress in his hands.

"Thank you," he said with a small smile, his eyes glazed with lazy exaltation. Then he grabbed me by my arms and hoisted me to my feet. Quickly, he slipped the dress on over my head and pulled it down until I was covered again. "You're free to go," he said.

I stared at him in surprise which brought out another smile from him.

"To your room, of course," he said. Suddenly, he was turning around and snapping his fingers. "Tito," he barked, and the guard who had winked at me earlier appeared in the kitchen doorway. "Take her to her room."

I felt my cheeks flare from embarrassment—had the man seen the whole thing? If he had, Javier definitely didn't care who saw him come all over me.

Javier reached down to the table and handed me the plate of uneaten food that had been for Esteban. "Almost forgot your breakfast."

And at that he turned around and walked down the hall, disappearing into one of the rooms.

I stared at him, bewildered, clutching the plate of food in my hand.

Tito pointed the way toward the staircase, gesturing as if he were being polite. I barely took in his youthful but menacing appearance before I walked numbly up the stairs and back into my room. He shut the door behind me, locking it, and I was left alone again, with food that I didn't want but needed, and thoughts that I didn't need but wanted.

CHAPTER NINE

Luisa

When the sun rose the next morning, I was so tired I felt like I'd been drugged. I hadn't been—I just hadn't slept at all. The fact that I couldn't be on my back, on the fresh V that Javier had carved on it late last night, didn't help either. But mainly it was the nightmares that plagued me at every turn.

I'd never been the type of girl to fear the dark—when I was young, I loved for my father to tell me scary and thrilling stories. But now they were no longer stories, they were real, and every time I woke up from a nightmare, I was faced with a reality that was no better.

In some strange way, being alone made it worse. It's not that I wanted Javier's company, but I had to admit that when he was in the room with me, even when he was branding me and inflicting pain, it took my thoughts away from their darkest places. He distracted me. Even when he asked me questions about my past, questions I tried to dance around, it was still a distraction.

I would have thought that having someone nightmare-inducing with me would have made things worse, but it didn't. Because my nightmares weren't about Javier. They weren't about what he was going to do to me. They weren't about the fact that I could die in a few days at his hands.

My nightmares were about Salvador. They were about not what happened if he told Javier they had no deal—they were about what happened if he traded for me back.

What would happen to me if at the end of the week, I was set free and picked up by Salvador's men? If I was brought back to the house? If Salvador saw how Javier had claimed me as his? I knew what the man was capable of, and it scared me to think of what else could happen—not only to me, but to my parents. Salvador was sick beyond comprehension, and I had a feeling that I had only seen the tip of the iceberg.

I think Javier even sensed that I didn't want him to leave. When he was done carving the V, I started asking him questions. About his family, about his own past. He waited in the dark, thinking, perhaps about my angle. Why I was curious. Then he told me that I could have answers at another time.

Then he left, locking me in the room, locking me in with the nightmares that would never end.

I suppose the lack of sleep showed on my face, because when Esteban came into the room in the morning, he did a double take as I lay there on the bed, staring dumbly at the wall.

"Rough night?" he asked, a careful tone to his voice.

I didn't have the energy to be amused at his apparent concern.

He put the breakfast tray down beside him and walked to the end of the bed. He playfully grabbed my foot. It made me jump, withdrawing my knees to my chest as my attention snapped to him.

"So you are alive," he said, taking his hand back. "Glad to see it. I brought you breakfast."

I glared at him. I'd refused dinner last night and thought I could pretend not to be hungry, but my stomach growled in protest.

"Tell you what," Esteban said, noting my expression. "How about we make today a little bit better for you?"

"Better for me," I spat out. "How about you stop pretending that you're doing me favors? Don't think for one second that I haven't forgotten why I'm here."

"Just eat your breakfast. I'll come back with some new clothes for you. I think you've earned it. Then we'll go for a walk. Doesn't that sound nice, hey." He grinned at me and then left the room, locking the door behind him.

I waited a bit, trying to ignore the food, but my resolve could not overpower my stomach. I scarfed down the tortilla and eggs and a large cup of coffee. I never knew when I'd need my strength.

I'd just finished when Esteban came back into the room, carrying a woven bag full of clothes. He tossed it on the bed. "For you," he said, bending down to pick up the empty plate. "Take a shower, get dressed. I'll be back here in thirty minutes whether you're ready or not."

I eyed the clothes spilling out of the bag. "Where did these come from?"

"Long story," he said. "Let's just say Javier can be sentimental."

I wanted to hear this story—I had no idea that someone like Javier could possess that emotion. When he'd gone again, I pulled out an aqua skirt that was so long on my short frame it would fit me as a dress instead. I went into the bathroom and ran the shower. As the room filled up with steam, I couldn't remember the last time I had been clean. It had to have been at Salvador's, the night I ran away, yet I never felt clean when I was his wife. He filled my life with dirt.

Of course, I technically still was his wife. But the word had never meant anything to me.

I stayed in the shower for so long, letting the hot water strip me down, wishing for my worries and nightmares to be carried down the drain, that I was surprised when there was a knock at my door. I could hear Esteban in my room, and I quickly dried myself and slipped into the dress, my wet hair cascading down my back.

I paused in the doorway of the bathroom as Esteban looked at me and smiled.

"You look ravishing," he said.

His compliment bounced right off me. I didn't understand how I could look ravishing with no makeup and wet hair and a bruised face, and I wasn't falling for it. Men thought women were so easy, that they could tell us how beautiful and thin we were, and we'd excuse them for whatever they'd done or were about to do. Until I met a man that saw past all of that, saw me for me, compliments meant nothing.

I nearly smirked to myself. There was no chance of that happening anymore. I'd either die here, surrounded by drug lords, or live with Salvador. All my chances of love and happiness with a man had gone out the window the moment Salvador stepped into Cabo Cocktails.

"Care to join me?" he asked, holding his arm out, as if he were some gentleman.

I stared at it and then at him. "Where?"

He shrugged. "I told you. A walk. I thought it might be good for you to get some fresh air."

"Oh, and you're so concerned about my well-being?"

Another shrug. "I'm not a monster," he said.

"No. Just a chump."

He frowned and I knew I was pushing my luck with him. I stifled a wave of apprehension that coursed through me.

"You know," he said slowly, his gaze intensifying, "I may be the only friend you have here. I might be the difference between life and death for you...or losing your little toe or your whole leg."

I wasn't sure if I believed that. Even though Esteban was Javier's right-hand man and business partner, I don't think he had the power he thought he did. It seemed that he constantly wanted to call the shots with Javier but wasn't quite there. If I were Javier, I'd keep a close eye on him.

"Friends don't threaten each other," I told him.

The darkness on his brow eased up. "I guess not. Well. Come on then."

He gestured for me to grab his arm again. I ignored him but slipped on my running shoes just the same. The truth was, I wanted, needed, to get outside and breathe fresh air and feel the world again. I felt like I was losing perspective of the value of life.

We walked out into the hallway, me in front of him, and were just about to head down the stairs when the guard who was stationed at the end of the hall stepped out in front of us. At least, I thought he was a guard, at first. But from the way he blocked the stairs, arms crossed, with a menacing twitch to his face, I could tell he was more than just a guard.

He leered at me in a way that made my skin feel sick.

This was Franco, the man responsible for the bruise on my face. I could just tell.

"Where are you going?" Franco asked Esteban, though he was staring at me.

"None of your business, Franco," he said. He gestured for him to get out of the way but Franco wouldn't budge.

"Planning on running away with the hostage?" he asked. He had a stupid look in his eyes, but in this world, it was the stupid people you had to fear. Too much testosterone and too little brains were a dangerous combination. I had no doubt that if Esteban wasn't there, I would be in big trouble. It didn't help that Franco was a huge guy with muscles that pulsed grotesquely.

"I just want to feel her hair," he said, licking his lips as if I was a steak. "The whores have such rough hair."

He reached out and made a fist in it. I gasped but couldn't move or else his grip would yank a huge chunk out.

"So you've felt it now," Esteban said, sounding tired. "Kindly move out of the way. We're just going for a walk."

Franco gave my hair a small tug, enough to make me gasp again. Then he grinned and let go.

"Sure thing," he said, chuckling to himself and moved aside to let us pass.

Esteban quickly led me past him. We were halfway down the stairs when I heard Franco whisper after me, "Much better than a whore's."

I shivered even as Esteban took me out of the house and into the bright sunshine.

"Don't pay any attention to Franco," he said to me. "He's a bit messed up in the head."

"I can see that," I said, my heart rate returning to normal as the fresh air filled my lungs and the heat hit my skin. The house was located at the end of a rocky road. There was a simple dirt driveway leading out and long, overgrown grass that stretched toward a decrepit wooden fence and miles of forest beyond that. No neighbors, no nothing.

"You shouldn't be afraid of him," he went on as we walked together. "Or maybe you should."

I swallowed. "I'm not afraid."

"You know, I met a girl like you once," he told me as we walked down the driveway, ochre dirt rising up in the still air. I was barely listening to him. I was taking in every sight, every opportunity. There were no guards out here which I thought was curious. Franco, thank god, had decided not to trail us, and all the rest of the guards seemed to be inside the house, perhaps with Javier.

"You met a girl like me once," I repeated absently. "How nice."

"Yes," he said. "About a year ago. I was in Hawaii. I saved her from drowning. I saved her from a lot of things, including herself."

"What a hero," I said dryly. "You must think you're such a nice guy."

He nodded. "I do. For the most part. But she was like you because she no longer cared about life. She was more or less suicidal."

I stopped and glared at him. "I am not suicidal," I hissed.

He shrugged. "You don't seem to care much about anything. Javier is right...he thinks you're unbreakable."

"Just because he can't break me doesn't mean I'm suicidal," I told him. "What kind of sick man wants to break a woman anyway?"

"I don't know. You married one of them, didn't you?"

"I married a demon, not a man."

"Well, I guess Javier's not exactly a demon."

"No such thing as a sentimental demon?" I asked. "Tell me about the clothes. This skirt, this dress...whose is it?"

He gave me an inquisitive look. Our path continued down the rough road, birds calling from the towering lush trees. "Why are you so interested?"

Now it was my turn to shrug. I didn't know why. I guess I felt that the little bit of information I could get about Javier, the more I'd have to work with, to use against him when needed.

"I'm making conversation," I said.

"Right. Well, if you care so much, the clothes belong to an ex-girlfriend of his."

I snorted lightly out my nose. "Girlfriend? I would have thought Javier only used whores. Who else could be interested in him?"

I felt Esteban studying me closely. Of course on the outside I could see why any woman would be interested in Javier Bernal. He was beautiful to look at, and I was sure he could be charming when he wanted to be. He also had money and power. But any woman worth her salt would run once she realized what kind of a depraved psychopath he was. The idea of him having an ex-girlfriend, one to get sentimental over, confused me.

"*She* was interested in him," he said, "a very long time ago. When they were young and stupid, I guess. But she was also a con artist."

I nodded. "I see." She was just as bad as he was, then. That explained some. "What was her name?"

He frowned. "Ellie. Why?"

"Just curious. Mexican?"

"American."

"And she broke his heart? Or did he break hers?"

He pursed his lips. "Both. He broke hers and she broke his. And then she broke his again."

"So she won."

"Something like that."

I smiled to myself. "Good." I hoped the bastard suffered.

"It was good," Esteban admitted. "I liked the woman, but she never would have joined his side, never would have had the confidence you need in this business."

We slowed and he turned me around so we were walking back to the house again.

"You need confidence to be a good torturer, kidnapper, murderer?"

"You need confidence in yourself, to never question who you are."

I nodded. "Maybe you all need to question yourselves more often."

He gave me a funny look, as if I were the one who was crazy.

I stopped, noticing my shoe was untied. We were almost back at the yard, and I could see Javier stepping out of the house with Franco milling around in the doorway. Javier was staring in our direction.

Bending down, I tied my shoe and eyed the pile of rocks we were beside, the result of someone clearing this road a very long time ago. Javier and the guards were far off. It was only Esteban and I out here. I made a split-second decision.

I tied my shoelaces then quickly grabbed the nearest rock. I swivelled and leaped up, my arm overextending, as I smashed the rock into Esteban's face. Because I was so much shorter, I got more of his jaw instead of his temple, but it was enough to make him yelp, holding on to his face as he staggered backward, barely able to stand up.

I didn't check to see if he was going down. I turned on my heel and started bolting toward the trees. I didn't know what the rest of my plan was, but I knew I had to get away while I could. Esteban said I was suicidal, just because I didn't show fear. But I was the opposite of suicidal. I loved the life—the free life I once had—and I would do anything to get that back.

I was almost at the trees, at the freedom they represented, when I heard a small pop, like a gun going off. The next thing I knew my body was stiffening, and I lost all function to move as my nerves fired in a burst of strange, buzzing pain. I fell straight down to the ground, I think I was screaming, as my muscles vibrated nonstop.

I heard someone, Javier I think, yell "What the fuck are you doing?" and then the vibrations and pain stopped. Just like that. And then I was out cold.

CHAPTER TEN

Javier

"What the fuck are you doing?" I bellowed at Este and started sprinting down the driveway toward them.

One moment I was about to berate Este for taking Luisa out of the house, the next moment she had bashed his face in and was making a run for it before he took out a motherfucking Taser gun and fired on her. I don't even know when the fuck he got the Taser, I thought I left that back home.

He looked over at me in surprise though he was still firing the gun, the wires connected to Luisa's fallen, twitching body twenty feet away. I yanked it out of his hands and immediately the electricity stopped jolting through the wires.

"She tried to get away," Este said unapologetically.

"I can see that," I sniped at him. I looked at her, now motionless on the ground. "Jesus Christ."

I ran over to her, dislodging the cartridge from the gun and tossing it to the ground. I crouched down beside her and gently put my hand on her neck, shaking her back and forth. "Luisa?" I said.

There was no answer or movement from her, but I could see her breathing in and out, which was a relief. I removed the darts from her back, blood trickling out of the holes. It looked so cheap and brutal below my letters.

I turned and glared over at Esteban who was watching me from a distance. "You're a fuck, you know that? What if you accidently killed her? The Taser isn't supposed to knock her out, just bring her down. And why the fuck did you put yourself in this position in the first place? You were supposed to give her breakfast, give her clothes, and that was it."

He shrugged. "I wasn't worried, Javi. I figured she may try something but thought I'd let her see who she's dealing with here. If she ran, I'd Tase her. She'd learn not to do it again."

"*I'm* who she's dealing with here," I said, the anger simmering in my blood. "Not you. She's not yours to touch, not yours to go on walks with, and not yours to fucking brutalize."

He laughed. "I think Luisa was right. Maybe you should question yourself more often. You should hear the shit that comes out of your mouth."

I wished I could reuse Taser cartridges because there's no doubt I'd be delivering all those volts right to his miniscule balls. I sucked in a deep breath and tried to regain my cool. There was no point losing it here and now.

"Why don't you get the fuck out of here," I told him. "Go check on Juanito. Perhaps he has word from Salvador."

Esteban hesitated, as if he was going to argue with me, but his brain kicked into gear and he turned and walked back toward the house with his wide-legged, frat boy stroll. Fucking degenerate.

I looked down at Luisa, realizing she was wearing the skirt I gave her as a dress. The color was stunning on her smooth, tan skin; her long hair was extra shiny in the sunshine, cascading into the earth around her. I reached over and ran a strand through my fingers—soft and wet, probably just out of the shower. Now she was dirty again.

The sight of her lying unconscious and broken should have made me smile. It should have soothed something inside of me. After all, this was what I wanted. But it wasn't the same. This was unplanned and without merit. She may have looked weak, but I still did nothing to break her. If she were conscious, she'd be fighting me with her body and heart and mind.

I'd come to appreciate the fight in her.

I picked her up under her arms and hauled her to her feet, her head hanging down, creating a curtain of hair that masked her face. It took little effort to scoop her up, one arm under her arms, the other under her knees. I carried her back toward the house, and her head rolled back, exposing her fine collarbone, her fragile neck, her beautiful, sleeping features.

She really was light as air in my arms, just this helpless, submissive creature. As I approached the door where Franco was standing watch, I felt a pulse of possessiveness run through me. It wasn't just that while she was here, I thought she was mine. I also felt like I needed to protect her. If I didn't, no one would. Esteban had Tasered her without care, and Franco was staring at her with such ugly lust that I made a mental note to never let her near him. I knew his appetite for destruction was large and unceremonious.

"What happened to her?" Franco said, licking his lips as he looked her over. "Este looked pissed off."

He reached over and grabbed a few strands of her hair. I automatically stopped walking and shot him a steady, deadly look.

"Don't touch her," I said, my tone both hard and calm. "Don't you *ever* touch her. Do you understand?"

Franco slowly brought his eyes to mine. They were mildly defiant for a moment as a snarl appeared on his face. Then it melted into a sloppy smile. "Sure thing, boss."

I went inside and took her to her room, kicking the door shut behind us, and laid her down on the bed on her back. I wasn't about to leave her, not with her being unconscious. I had never been Tasered before, but I knew that sometimes there were complications. Sometimes people died. I had the Taser gun for torture, for the purpose of pain. After all, we shoot to kill in Mexico, and if we want to stop someone, a bullet works pretty well. A Taser though, that doesn't kill...that *prolongs*. But I had no idea of the effects of a Taser on a woman.

The morning light was streaming in through the window, illuminating her like an angel, but a dirty one. Feeling strangely remorseful, I brushed some of the dust off of her. I ran my hands over her legs, her hips, across her stomach, her breasts, her chest, her arms. I rubbed the earth from her face, carefully running my thumb along her cheekbones, her skin so devastatingly soft. Though I needed to wake her up to make sure she was okay, I also wanted her to keep sleeping. I went to the end of the bed and pulled off her shoes, letting them fall to the floor, then put a pillow under her head. I stood there for a few minutes, just taking in the sight of her, my sleeping beauty.

The impulses that sporadically ran through me were hard to fight. I wanted to keep feeling her, that effortless glide of my palms against her skin. I wanted to caress her breasts, lick at her nipples, make her wet with my fingers. I wanted to take out my cock and rub the head against her slightly open lips. Then I wanted to flip her over and finish carving my name. Today I would do the I.

But I wanted her awake for all of it. It would be wrong otherwise.

I must have stood there for an hour, having this fight between my body and my mind, before she finally stirred. Her head moved to the side and she let out a small moan, stretching her limbs for a second. I sucked in my breath in anticipation as her eyes slowly blinked open, staring at the ceiling.

She carefully lifted her head and looked straight at me, having sensed I was there. Disappointment was etched into her face.

"You didn't quite get away," I said in a low voice.

She stared at me for a beat or two before looking down at her body in alarm, her hands smoothing over the dress.

"I didn't touch you," I told her, examining my fingernails, making sure they were clean. "Don't worry."

"Then what are you doing?"

"Watching you sleep."

"I wasn't sleeping," she said. "I was knocked out."

I grimaced. "Yes. That was Este. He had a Taser. But you tried to run." I flicked my eyes to her. "Sorry."

"Sorry? You're actually sorry I was Tasered?" There was a bite to her voice. The fight was back, and it was making me hard.

I gave her a soothing smile. "I am. I had no wish to see that happen." I paused. "What did it feel like?"

She glared at me. "Like when you hit your funny bone, but more intense and all over your body until you think you're going to die."

"That sounds terrible."

"It was," she seethed.

I took steps closer so I was leaning right over her, my eyes fixed on hers. They were so impossibly lush and dark, I nearly felt a little lost. I cleared my throat. "So next time, maybe don't try to run. At least not around Este."

She stared up at me and swallowed—I could see her throat bobbing. So delicate. "What if I try and run from you?"

"You won't want to run from me. You don't want to know what happens when I catch up with you."

I watched her closely, waiting for fear, waiting for ambivalence, waiting for apathy. But I saw nothing in her except this fire that burned deep within her eyes. I wanted to taste that fire on my lips, I wanted to fuck it with my dick. I wanted to feel it in every way I could. I wanted to bring the fire out of her.

But she kept it inside, out of reach. She was utterly fascinating because she was not broken and refused to break. No matter how hard I tried, she refused to break.

Though I wasn't done with her yet.

"I'll come back for you later," I said to her, and turned to leave the room. I heard her breathe a sigh of relief in my wake and I couldn't help but smile. At least the sight of me leaving meant something to her.

...

For the rest of the day, Este acted like he had this giant chip on his shoulder. Of course he did. He always did. He was usually better at hiding it under that surfer boy persona. It was enough that I hesitated after dinner when he asked if I wanted him to bring Luisa her food. At least he did ask—his manners hadn't all gone to shit.

When he'd come back to the kitchen, The Doctor and I had lit up our cigars. We kept the kitchen door open, the screen keeping out the mosquitoes, and watched the breeze pull our smoke outside. It was a hot night, sticky, and I was feeling all out of sorts. I felt as if I was starting to lose my control of the situation.

The fact was, we hadn't heard from Salvador. Juanito had left earlier in the day, on a mission to Culiacán to gather information. People talked. He'd know right away if Luisa's disappearance was gossip or not. Este had been scanning websites for any mention of Luisa being taken, in either casual blogs or newspapers, but so far there had been nothing. It was as if she wasn't upstairs in that room and we weren't here figuring out what to do with her.

"How did it go?" I asked Este between puffs. I let the smoke fall out of my mouth and watched it drift away to the door.

"She's eating," he said. "She's kind of being a bitch."

The Doctor snorted with mild amusement.

I narrowed my eyes briefly at Este. "She has every right to be a bitch."

Este grinned at me and pulled out a chair and sat down. "Well, look at Mr. Bernal empathizing with his own captive."

"Don't mistake understanding for empathy, my friend," I replied.

"Don't mistake collateral for something you can keep," he said. "Once Sal does the deal, back she goes."

"Javier is not an idiot," The Doctor said thoughtfully as he blew smoke through his nose. "She goes back when Sal comes through. If he doesn't come through, she dies. Slowly. And painfully. Until our point has been made." He gave me a pointed glance. "Isn't that right?"

"Of course." I nodded quickly. "Of course."

"Anything less than that," The Doctor went on, "and well, news travels fast, doesn't it? No cartel that has gotten this far has ever shown that kind of weakness. We're all about preserving the empire. Javier's empire." He gave me a kind smile, the type that an elder would bestow on someone younger that they were proud of. Only I knew the type of man The Doctor was. He didn't have a lot of kindness for me, just tolerance. I doubted you could become so revered in the art of torture and negotiations and still have a kind bone in your body.

It was at that moment that I realized what we all must have looked like. A bunch of sharks sitting around a table, giving each other our razorblade grins and winking with black eyes. If we stopped eating, stopped swimming, we died.

"There is no question of what will happen to Luisa if Salvador doesn't come through," I said, leaning back in my chair. "But I do believe Salvador will come through."

"Why don't we make another video?" Este suggested with a wag of his eyebrows. "A warning."

"Yes," said The Doctor. "That couldn't hurt, could it?"

It wouldn't hurt us, no.

I gave him a quick smile and tapped my fingers on the table. "I thought standard procedure was to do that if the ransom was being negotiated or the kidnappers weren't being taken seriously. Not if he just hasn't responded."

"Oh, Javier," he said. "You're an odd duck with this code of honor and following procedures. You're a fucking drug lord. You can do whatever the hell you want to do, there is no rulebook. There is no honor. Not here." He looked at Este. "Tomorrow would work."

"It has to be tomorrow," Este said. "Or we're running out of time. Tonight would be best."

I felt as if the room had started to tilt. I placed both my palms flat on the table and pressed down, trying to steady myself. "Hold on. Let's not rush into this. We have to plan this perfectly."

"You and your planning," Este scoffed. "I say we go upstairs and smack her around a bit."

"Losing an appendage is always more effective," The Doctor added. "I know the right cuts to make."

My chest tightened. I wasn't sure why my body was reacting this way. "No," I said. "No one is doing anything to her except for me. This is my operation and she is my prisoner."

"So, then you do it," Este said. "But we have to act fast. Why not start tonight? I can get everything set up in a minute." He stood up, pushing back his chair and stared down at me. "Or are empathy and understanding confusing themselves again?"

"Sit the fuck down," I sneered at him, pointing at his seat. "Or have you forgotten your place?"

Our eyes locked in a deadly stare until he finally looked away. He always looked away. He sat back down but his attitude never cleared up. "Have you forgotten *your* place?"

I was fast with a knife. Always was. Before Este could register it, I pulled the knife out of my boot under the table and threw it at him with an easy flick of my wrist. I heard him scream and knew it had lodged itself into his shin.

He kept yelling and fell off his chair to the floor. I got up and walked over to him. The knife hadn't gone in very far. I tapped the end of the knife with my boot, driving it a bit further into his leg. Este let out a bloodcurdling scream that only made me grin.

"You're a fuck," I said as I leaned over him. His face was contorted in pain but his eyes could see me. "This is your place, right here on the fucking floor. I'd piss on you if I could, but I'm a bit too turned on at the moment." I straightened up and gave The Doctor a warning look. I was about to turn around, but then I reached down and plucked the knife out of his leg. "Forgot, I'll be needing this," I said over his scream.

I took it over to the sink, rinsed it off, and dried it on a faded washcloth and looked back at The Doctor. "Let's leave Este out of this one, shall we? Though I'm sure his screaming would come in handy. What a fucking pussy."

He nodded, his brows frozen on his forehead. Seemed I had the ability to surprise him, too. I think I showed them to not ever question how the fuck I did my job.

Together we left Este writhing on the floor and went to get the video camera before bringing it up to Luisa's room. I don't know why I felt the need to knock, but I did. She would be expecting me, but not the camera, and not The Doctor.

Good thing she wasn't in a position where she should ever expect anything.

I unlocked the door and flicked on the lights when I entered.

Luisa was sitting on the bed, her knees drawn to her chest, hands wrapped around her legs. She was in a pair of jeans and a grey tank top that had belonged to someone else, looking like any young woman out there. Except she wasn't just any young woman. She was beautiful. She was mine. And she was going to bleed for her husband.

"We're mixing things up," I told her, raising the knife in the air as The Doctor shut the door behind him. "The Doctor is going to set up the video and film our little nightly interlude."

"Why?" she asked softly. "Did Sal not want to negotiate?"

"Your husband hasn't responded at all. We hope this will be seen. And I'll come join you in the video, just so he can see who has you, in case he hasn't realized how fucking serious I am."

Was that fear I saw in her eyes, or was the light playing tricks on me? I walked over to her and pointed at the bed with the knife. "Lie on your stomach."

She didn't move. "Are you going to let him see what you're carving into me?"

I shook my head. "On the off chance that my name would forever taint you for him, no, I won't let him see. All he will see is that you will be in a lot of pain."

She smiled at me, wicked, her eyes smug. "We'll see about that."

I wanted to ignore that, but the fact was, she had never given me any reaction before. I needed her to react this time. Otherwise it looked like I wasn't doing anything to her. I would have to drive the knife in deeper, and as much as I hated to admit it, I wasn't looking forward to that.

I gestured to the bed again. "Lie down, *now.*"

She did as she was told, and I winced inwardly at the crusted marks on her back where the Taser probes had gone in. She had a hell of a day and it was about to get worse.

I looked to The Doctor. He was watching me, bemused. "Are you ready?" I asked, annoyed by his look.

"Yes," he said, getting behind the camera. "The light isn't very good but it's all ready to go. Aren't you going to tie her up?"

I looked at her. "She's not going anywhere."

"No," he conceded. "But if you don't, it looks like she's complying with you. Letting you. Not exactly the kind of message you want to send to Salvador. She also doesn't look the slightest bit afraid. I think you need to fix that."

I didn't like being told what to do, but he was right. She looked at me, waiting. I smiled back, wolfish, as I took the rope out of my pocket. There was just enough for her wrists, and it wasn't very strong, but it would do for this situation.

Grabbing her hands, I quickly tied them behind her back. Then I got on the bed and straddled her.

I leaned down so my lips were at her ear. "I'm going to hurt you more than normal," I told her. "You'll react this time. If not for me, for the camera."

She fixed her eye on me, head to the side. "Why? So Salvador will trade with you? I don't want to go back. It's a worse hell than here."

Something in my gut sunk like a stone. I inhaled sharply and said, "This isn't about what you want." I looked up at The Doctor who was watching her curiously.

"Interesting," he said in that slow voice of his. "But Luisa, he is right. It's not about you. It's about us. And it's about other people you may care about."

At that her head lifted up to look at him.

The corner of his lips twitched at her attention. "You do have parents. They were at your wedding. If Salvador doesn't think you're in danger, if he thinks you'd rather die at the hands of a rival cartel than come home, what do you think he's going to do to your parents?"

I felt her body stiffen beneath me, as if it had just crossed her mind. So this was what she cared most about. Her parents. It killed me that The Doctor knew this and I didn't.

"Just something to think about, anyway," The Doctor finished. "I'm about to hit record. Are you speaking to the camera, Javier?"

I nodded, shaking myself into the role, and pressed the knife down on her back, ready to make the slash for the I. I waited for The Doctor's cue, then looked up at the camera.

"Salvador, we're a bit disappointed that you haven't reached out to negotiate the safe return of your wife. My suggestion to you is to at least respond to us, otherwise you won't be getting Luisa back in one piece." I grabbed her hair and yanked her head back so he could see her face. To my surprise, she let out a cry of pain. I really had hurt her.

The Doctor was smiling behind the camera at her reaction, and I had no choice but to smile as well. Only difference was, mine was fake.

"You have a very lovely wife," I went on to say. "Very beautiful. It would be a shame to ignore this because you didn't think we were serious. I am very serious. You have two days to contact us. After that, she becomes property of my cartel. And I'm sure you know what that means. This is just the start." I pressed the tip of the blade into her skin. Instead of feeling the thrill I normally felt, I felt my guts twist. But I persevered through the frivolous sentiment and dug the knife in sharply, an inch deep.

She let out a scream. I didn't know if it was because of the pain or the thought of losing her parents. It was what we wanted though. I slowly dragged the blade down, rivers of crimson pooling around the metal and spilling down her back and onto the bedspread. She screamed again until The Doctor told us we were done.

Then her screaming stopped. She was breathing heavily beneath me, the blood pouring freely, but she wasn't even whimpering.

The Doctor shook his head slightly and said, "I'll go upload this and check on Este. There's been too much blood tonight, even for someone like me."

He gathered up the camera and left the room. Once we were alone, I felt completely flustered, a feeling that was foreign and terrible. I untied her wrists then got off of her and stared at the blood for a moment before going and getting a towel from the bathroom. I pressed it down on her back and she flinched under my touch.

"Are you okay?" I asked.

She didn't say anything.

I kept pressure on the towel and watched as the red monopolized the white. "It is a fairly deep cut this time. Ugly. I don't like to make ugly marks."

I expected her to tell me off. I wanted her to tell me off. But she gave me nothing, as usual. It was frustrating beyond belief.

"Interesting thing about your parents," I told her, searching for that spark.

Her muscles tightened beneath my hand and she looked like she was holding her breath.

My heart danced. There it was. "I had no idea they meant so much to you," I went on. "Of course, I don't know anything about them at all, but I'm sure I could find out their names and addresses tomorrow if I wanted to. I'm assuming they weren't living with you and Salvador. No, my guess is they are back in Los Cabos, completely unprotected." I leaned in closer. "You know, my darling, most daughters don't leave their parents behind to go off and marry a drug lord."

She suddenly sat up, hair in her face, her eyes blazing with fury. I kept the towel pressed against her wound, keeping her close to me. Fuck me, I wanted to put my tongue in her mouth and feel that anger. I wanted to take her fury right here on the bed, let the blood wash over the both of us.

"You don't know anything about me and my parents," she hissed at me. "So don't even try."

I grabbed her arm and pulled her even closer so she was almost pressed up against me. "Oh, I'll try. Tell me then how it went? Girl ditches her proud mama and papa for a chance to marry the man of her dreams and become a narco-wife? Bet you regret that little fancy of yours, don't you?"

She raised her other hand to smack me, but I was quick. I dropped the towel and snatched her by the wrist. I forced her down on her back, holding her hands above her head and pinning her to the bed. She struggled but not for long as I climbed on top of her.

I stared down at her and couldn't help but smile. She'd be so easy to fuck right now, but I wanted to fuck that pretty little head of hers even more, see what was inside.

"You don't know anything!" she said. "I was a good daughter. I did this all for them. This was all for them. If I married Salvador, I could pay for someone to take care of them. They're ill and I struggled every fucking day to provide for them, to make sure they were fed and happy, and it was never a guarantee. I did everything I could to give them the best life I could. We grew up poor but they made sacrifices for me. I had to make sacrifices for them. My life was the biggest sacrifice. So I married him because he asked me, and I knew I could give my parents the life that they deserved. I never expected love, I never expected anything good except knowing that they were going to be okay."

She wasn't quite crying, but her eyes were wet. I frowned, a strain of compassion running through me for this strong little woman. She didn't feel sorry for herself, she rarely got angry, and yet she'd been handed the shit card in life, just as I had.

"You care that much about your parents?" I asked, aware that I was crushing her. "You'd marry Sal just for their happiness? Though I don't see how any parent could be happy with you marrying *that* man."

Her brows knitted together as she stared up at me. "Don't you care about your parents?"

"My parents are dead," I said simply.

"Oh. I'm sorry." And the curious thing, I could see she was.

"I'm not," I said, not wanting her pity. "Family gets you killed."

She shook her head. "That is not the Mexican way. Family is everything."

"Then perhaps that is what is wrong with Mexico."

"That's a terrible thing to say."

True. "And I am a terrible person," I told her glibly.

"Yes," she agreed. "You are. But that is nothing to be proud of."

"And yet here I am, lying on top of you, full of pride for all the terrible things I do. I worked hard to be this way. It's not easy to have confidence in who you are, to say fuck it, the world thinks I am a monster because I *am* a monster. And I don't care."

She bit her lip and I wanted to do the same. "You're not a monster."

"Just a terrible person, then."

"Yes. There is a difference. I lived with a monster. I know what that feels like."

I gave her a wry grin and lowered my face so it was just inches away from hers. This close, I could see flecks of gold in the mahogany of her eyes. "Does it feel like a knife in your back?"

She blinked, taken aback, realizing the truth. Monster, terrible person, it didn't matter. I wasn't so different from her husband. I was just another man playing the game.

And it had to stay that way.

I got off of her and pulled her to the edge of the bed so she was in a sitting position. I turned her back so I could see the wound. The pressure of being pressed against the bedspread had stifled the bleeding a bit, but now her bed was soaked with blood. "I'll get you new sheets."

She stared at me with a dull expression. "Don't bother. I kind of like it."

I raised my brow at her. She was nothing if not always keeping me on my toes. "I think the bleeding has stopped. The Doctor may have to give you stitches tomorrow."

She gave her head a nearly imperceptible shake. "You're giving a hostage stitches because of the torture you inflicted on them?"

She had a point. A good one.

I couldn't care about that. I couldn't care about her pain or her well-being or her past or her feelings. I was holding her for ransom, using her body and life to get what I wanted. I couldn't care about any of that.

And yet, I think I did.

CHAPTER ELEVEN

Luisa

I woke up in incredible pain, my back feeling like it was on fire. Memories from the night before came flooding into my brain, first a trickle, then a dam unleashed. My attempted escape from Esteban, the Taser shocking me, waking up with Javier watching over me with an unpredictable look in his eyes, Esteban's half-hearted apology with dinner, then Javier coming back with The Doctor and filming his branding for Salvador.

Javier had hurt me, really hurt me this time, but I did whatever I could to keep that hurt buried. That was until my parents were brought into it and the whole reality came smashing down on me. This was no longer about me—my parents' lives were at stake. It was a cold desolate feeling knowing that what I wanted—freedom—I could never have. When I was with Salvador, my parents were safe. When I wasn't with him…they would be cut off or worse. As much as every instinct in my body was telling me to never go back, to be glad that Salvador wasn't giving in to their demands, I knew that my selfishness would cost everything.

So when Javier told me to react for the camera, I was reacting to more than just the brutal, deep cut he carved into my back. I was reacting to the fact that I would never ever win, no matter what I did. I was reacting to the unfairness of it all, of my very existence.

And somewhere on that bed, as a drug lord knifed his name into my back, I found the thread of anger that I'd hidden from for so long. It was starting to unravel, slowly, like a snake. I nearly welcomed it. I almost invited it to stay. I suppose it was enough to just know it was there, to know I had a wicked part of me that was mad, that wanted more than what was given to me and everything that was taken away.

That morning, I spent the hours locked in my head. Every time there was a knock at the door, I was both relieved and disappointed that it wasn't Javier. In some ways, I wanted to talk to him. He had made me open up about my family, about my life, and now I was itching to get the same kind of information from him. There was something so traumatic about the night before that I felt even he was affected by it. That was a silly thing to think, of course. He was a man used to torture on a much worse, much larger scale. But even so, some part of me felt like last night was a first for him, in whatever way that was. Maybe because as he dug that blade in on the side of my spine, I could feel the hesitation in it, like he didn't want to hurt me to that extreme. I wanted to know why.

Why would this man hesitate for even a second when he had so much at stake?

I know what my mind wanted to think. It wanted to think that perhaps this man found me special, that he would change his ways because he saw me for me. But I knew that wasn't true, and every time the thought entered my head, I felt sick because of it, because something in me wanted to entertain it. But I'd given up those fantastical notions a very long time ago. Fantasies were for young girls who had no idea how the real world worked.

The last time I remember thinking that perhaps I was special and interesting and would one day capture the attention of a man was right after I had won my first pageant. There was a boy who worked at the restaurant, a line cook, who was only there for a few months. I could tell he liked and wanted me, and I wanted the same, but I was too afraid. So I locked myself in my mind, in daydreams about a better life, and I did that until he left. After that, there was no one else. There was nothing else. Because the truth was, as beautiful as some people said I was, it had done nothing for me but bring me pain. It didn't end the threat of poverty and the constant struggle, and it didn't prevent my father from losing himself.

You're an idiot, I told myself after Esteban left, the lunch tray lying on the floor. *Get your head back in the game, this is about survival.*

And I was right. But even though it was a game, I wondered if I was playing it right. Javier was drawn to me in some form, and though I couldn't figure out what form that was, he still seemed to take special interest in me. I needed to figure out how to make that work to my advantage. Javier was my only way out of here, I knew that much. Forget Esteban, his power seemed weak at best, and the others seemed ready to throw me to the dogs at first chance. As much as I hated to think it, Javier was the one person who could save me.

I just didn't know how.

...

Javier

"Good news," Este said, limping into the makeshift office I had at the safe house. The door didn't close properly, which cut my privacy down to zero and apparently other people's manners as well.

I sighed and snapped my laptop shut, looking up at him with dry interest. I'd been having a hard time believing in good news lately. Luisa had become this ticking time bomb in my life, her presence and predicament penetrating my thoughts, whether I was away from her or not. No matter where I was in this house, I couldn't escape her.

"Don't look so happy," Este said, and flashed me that cheesy dumbfuck grin of his.

"Give me a reason to be happy, then," I said, gesturing to the worn office chair on the other side of the desk. It didn't help me get into the right frame of mind when I felt like I was setting up camp in a derelict's house. Este had assured me the furnishings in the safe house were classy, but then again, he wouldn't know classy if it took a shit right in front of him.

He sat down and I exhaled hard through my nose. He was complying, which was good. It meant there were no hard feelings about the knife. Well, I'm sure he hated me as he usually did, but at least he was showing respect now. Sometimes subtle violence is all you needed to keep a man in line.

"I just heard from Juanito. He says that though everything is being kept from the media, Salvador knows we have Luisa, has seen both videos, and is currently thinking of a strategy."

I raised my brow. "Strategy?" I wasn't sure if that was good or bad. A year ago we had tried to strike a deal with an informant for the Tijuana Cartel. He tried to strategize. We turned our assassin—*sicario*—on him instead of the narco we were after. That's what happened to people who tried to outthink us.

Unfortunately, I was no longer so sure that we were holding all the cards. We only had one, a queen, and I was starting to think she was worth more to me than to Salvador.

Este shrugged. "I wasn't sure. My call with him was brief. But it seems to me like Salvador is ready to make a deal. Perhaps we can't get the Ephedra coming in from China, but maybe he'll give us coke from Colombia."

A pang of anger ran through me. "We already have that. We want *more*."

He didn't look too concerned when he tried to cross his legs; instead he winced from the pain in his shin. Good. "Well then we'll have more coke. It's better than nothing."

He was right, but it did nothing to make me happy. If I wanted more coke shipments, we could have easily gone east, after the Gulf Cartel in Veracruz. I just didn't like the idea of returning to that city, what used to be the disputed territory of Travis Raines, a city that held filthy memories. I took Luisa because I wanted something I never had—an opportunity for new power from a new source.

"Come on, Javi," Este said. "If it makes you feel any better, I'm in a lot of pain."

I frowned. "You don't seem like it."

"Well, what good is The Doctor if he can't get you high all the time? Poppies, Javi, from the very mountains we're in, possibly from the very farms owned by Salvador. When in Rome..."

I could tell Este wasn't that high on morphine, otherwise he'd be floating, but I made a note to speak with The Doctor after this. Pain was a lesson, and besides that, we all needed to have clear heads. That was why I had such a low tolerance for drug use. I'm sure it was ironic to many, considering my empire was built on the drug trade, but I'd been burned too many times by past employees whose addiction not only fucked them up but made them mutinous.

As for me, I almost never partook in it. After prison there was a period where I understood how drugs made a preferable reality for some people. It was one of my few moments of weakness, but even then I found strength in it. Discovering how dependent people got, how the right drugs could bury every broken heart and heal shattered pride, made me realize that in some ways, the cartels were doing the world a favor. We were giving people an escape from their sorry existences.

I tapped my fingers on the desk, my gaze directed out the window and at the sunlight trying to break through the clouds. "I suppose the bright side is that we'll hear from him in two days."

"How many letters do you have left?" Este asked.

"Today is E. Tomorrow is R."

"And then we say goodbye."

"Yes." I cleared my throat. "Then this is all over."

"I can't tell if you're sad it's ending because you're enjoying the torture, or...other reasons."

I shot him a sharp look. "What do you think?"

He smiled and got up carefully. "I don't think anything. You could say I've learned."

"Keep it that way."

I glared, and he nodded his head, leaving the room while trying to stifle his limp. Once he was gone and I was left in peace, I flipped my laptop open and stared at it. It was a picture of Luisa, the ones that Martin had taken at the wedding. It felt so much safer for me now to admire her from afar, even though I knew she was in the room above my head, even though I knew I would have to return tonight, knife in hand and face her once again.

...

After dinner, I decided to be the one to take up Luisa's food. I told The Doctor to ease up on the morphine for Este, and I volunteered to make dinner. I'd always been somewhat of a good cook, and was curious to see if Luisa would notice. Franco had even been sent into the local village to buy tomatillos, lime, and corn.

I paused at her door, taking in a deep breath. Out of the corner of my eye, I could see the guard down by the stairs trying not to watch me, and I automatically stood up straighter. I quickly knocked and waited but a few seconds before I knocked again.

I heard nothing from her, not a "fuck off" or a cry to go away. It was dark out, evening, and she must have known it was me and what I was there to do. Her silence compelled me to open the door.

The room was dark, and from what I could see, she wasn't in the bed. I quickly shut the door behind me and switched on the light, ready to be ambushed. She wasn't anywhere, but the bathroom door was closed. I couldn't hear her which made my heart pulse with worry. I racked my brain, trying to think if there was anything around here that she could hurt herself with.

But there was only me.

I slowly placed the tray on the bedside table. "Luisa?" I asked softly.

No answer.

I walked over to the bathroom door and rapped on it with my knuckles, saying her name again, hiding the urgency in my voice. Knowing the door had no lock, I turned the knob and slowly opened it.

The bathroom mirror was fogged up with steam, obscuring my reflection. Luisa's clothes were scattered on the ground. She was in the bathtub, lying there, fully naked and exposed. Her hair pooled around her like octopus ink.

I expected her to cover up, to glare at me, but she did nothing but stare forward, her eyes fixed on the beads of condensation that ran down the edge of the tub. I could do nothing but stare at her naked form, the way her nipples poked above the still water, how beautifully vulnerable she looked. I liked that.

Naturally, so did my dick. It strained against my zipper, and for once I tried to ignore it.

"I brought you dinner," I said, once I was able to gather some of my wits.

"You sounded concerned," she said, her voice chilled on ice, her eyes avoiding mine.

"I was," I admitted as I stepped closer to her. I crouched down so I was at her level, one of my hands on the rim of the bathtub. "I was afraid something had happened to my greatest asset. Without you, I have nothing to trade."

A small smile tugged at the corner of her lips. "Right. Well I'm alive, as you can see."

I noticed the way she was laying there, her head taking off most of the pressure from her back. "Are you in pain?"

The smile vanished but she said nothing. I knew she was.

"Lean forward," I told her.

"Why?"

"I want to admire my handiwork."

She finally looked over at me and my eyes locked with hers. "You'd rather admire your handiwork than admire my body?"

I swallowed hard but managed to give her an easy smile. "I can do both. Your back is just as beautiful as the rest of you. Perhaps even more so."

But that was a lie. I knew it as soon as she leaned forward. I reached over and lifted her dark, heavy wet hair from her back, placing it over one shoulder. Her back looked ugly now, the Taser wounds plus that deep gash of the I all ragged and crude, her flesh flayed and puffy from the water.

She looked so small and pure and helpless in the bath, those letters such a contrast, that I was hit with an unwelcome jolt of shame. It nearly knocked me off balance and I found myself gripping the edge of the bathtub harder than I wanted to.

Unfortunately, she noticed that too. Her eyes flew to my hand.

I had to remedy this right away. She was just a woman, a woman of no consequence. I didn't know her and she didn't know me. She never *would* know me. She'd be dead or gone in two days' time—having feelings of shame or remorse over what I'd done and was about to do was useless, ridiculous, and dangerous. So fucking dangerous.

"You almost took my breath away," I told her, giving her my most leering smile. "Such beauty in such pain."

"I am in no pain," she said. "If you've come to give me another letter, shoot another video, then do it. Don't pretend you're here under the guise of giving me dinner."

I took a long, sweet look at her body and let the sight of her cause a spike in my cravings. "Perhaps I am here for other things."

I waited to see fear in her eyes but there was none. There was something else though, something I'd only seen once or twice in her face, hovering around the surface. It was curiosity. For good or for bad, it was as if she was interested in seeing just what else I could do to her. Or perhaps, for her.

She looked away, breaking our heated gaze, and hugged her knees tighter to her chest. "Well, if you are here for other things, then do them."

I clucked my tongue. "You are a strange one, Luisa. You should know better by now than to tempt the devil." I reached forward and traced an invisible E on her back with my finger. She flinched at my touch but still let me do it. I wondered now what else she would let me do. I wondered if I reached my hands into the bath and stroked her breasts, if she'd surrender like last time. Or would she fight back? Or would she welcome it, want it?

I could bet she'd never come before, never had an orgasm. I found myself savoring the thought of giving her both pain *and* pleasure.

I traced an invisible R, imagining the finished product, telling myself it would look beautiful. Then I trailed my fingers over to her shoulder and down her arm into the warm bathwater. I gently caressed her nipple, as if by accident, and watched her closely for her reaction. Her nipple reacted exquisitely.

She closed her eyes, and in turn I closed mine, taking in the rich, sweet smell of her wet skin, listening to her breath catch and release.

"Did you like that?" I whispered.

I could hear her swallow hard. "I'm just waiting for the knife," she said softly.

My eyes snapped open and I stared at her. Of course she couldn't find anything pleasurable when there was blood to be drawn.

"And you shall get it," I said quickly. I retracted my hand and waved the bathwater away while I got to my feet. "Especially now since Salvador is working out a strategy to get you back."

She jolted, as if suddenly shocked, the water splashing around her. She stared up at me with horror, horror that wasn't meant for me. "You heard from Sal?"

"In a manner of speaking," I said slowly. I reached for the bath towel and held it out for her. "Come on out of the bath."

"I'd rather you do it here."

I frowned. "Your flesh is extra tender. It may hurt more."

"And I'd rather sit in a pool of my own blood." Though she said this with a hardened voice, her chest was rising and falling rapidly and she was nearly shaking. The night before I had seen how she reacted to going back to Salvador, but I hadn't quite realized it was that bad. I had to wonder what the fuck had been done to her.

And then I had to stop myself. It would only make this harder.

"Very well," I said. I folded the towel and placed it neatly on the sink, then whisked the knife out of my boot. "You sure you don't want to have your dinner first? I made it. Fresh produce from town and everything."

"I prefer the blade," she said. Then she leaned forward even further, gathering her hair tight to her side, making sure her back was completely clear. What I was doing had no effect on her, it was as if she wanted it. I was getting further and further away from breaking her and deeper and deeper into something else, something more troubling.

I leaned over her, and with one hand at her small, delicate neck to steady myself, I began to cut the E. I didn't do it nearly as deep as the I and it took much longer. I kept hesitating, something I knew she was recognizing, but it couldn't be helped. When it was finally over and the last cut was made, I watched the blood run down her back, like it was crying crimson tears, and the water around her waist became tinged with pink.

Before I knew what I was doing, I placed my lips on the wound, tasting the salt of her blood, the purity of her veins. I wanted to soothe the damage I had just created and feel the vitality of her existence pulse beneath my skin.

To her credit, she didn't flinch. She let me kiss her back and take my time doing so. She let me be a vampire, high on her blood and after her soul.

"I wanted to break you," I murmured against the blood. "I wanted to destroy you, ruin you. But you would not break. You will not break. Why won't you?" My last words were barely a whisper.

She pulled away from me and looked at me over her shoulder, her eyes expressionless even as they gazed at my red-stained lips.

"Give me back to Salvador," she said, looking deeply at me, "and I promise you, you'll never be able to piece me together again."

I could see that she was right. The truth felt like a tiny sliver in my heart.

I swallowed the feeling down and straightened up. I gestured to the towel. "Dry yourself off. Your dinner is getting cold. I'll be waiting out there to make sure it doesn't go to waste."

I left her in the bathroom and closed the door behind me. Once I was alone in the room, I put my hands over my face and breathed in deeply, trying to get a grip. Things were happening and unravelling at a breakneck pace and I had absolutely everything on the line. Whatever fucked up...*feelings* I was having for Luisa weren't real; they couldn't be. Feelings never got you anywhere, only instinct did. And my instinct was telling me to run, to distance myself, to get ready to pull the plug on her because either way, even with my name on her back, she wasn't mine. She was either Salvador's or she was dead, and in the end, they were the same thing.

It didn't take long for Luisa to emerge from the bathroom, wrapped in a towel, looking angelic and breathtaking. She stared at me curiously, and I wondered what she could see on my face, if anything. I couldn't let her see anymore.

She walked over to the bed and sat down on the edge of it, eyeing her cold food with little interest. I knew better than to try and make her eat it. In fact, the best course of action was just for me to go.

"I'll be seeing you tomorrow," I told her brusquely as I turned on my heel and headed for the door. I wondered what she'd think about my hasty departure, then I had to remind myself that I couldn't care.

"Why do you want to break me so badly?" she asked quietly, just as my hand went to the doorknob.

I paused and thought about the truth. Without looking back at her I said, "Because I want to destroy beautiful things before they can destroy me."

There was silence to that. But when I opened the door, she let out a low chuckle. I paused and turned around to look at her.

"Wow," she said dryly, her mouth quirked up in an amused smile. "She really did a number on you. Ellie," she added, as if I didn't know who she was talking about. As if there would ever be another *she*.

I slammed the door shut in front of me, wincing at the discomfort that radiated out from my chest. I turned to face her and managed to keep my expression still, my voice flat and cool. "Don't say her name."

Luisa frowned. It felt like a kick to my gut.

"Don't look at me like that either," I added.

"Like what?" she asked.

"Like you pity me." It shamed me to say it.

"But I do pity you, Javier Bernal," she said, her voice dripping with superiority. "I pity you a great deal. Such a cruel, tough man still licking his wounds."

I was across the room and at her bedside in one second. I grabbed her arm and yanked her close to me until my lips were grazing her earlobe. "The only wounds I've licked," I whispered harshly, "are yours."

Then I released her from my grip and got the fuck out of there before further damage could be done.

CHAPTER TWELVE

Luisa

It's funny what time can do to a person. It's funny what a childhood, a few years, a couple of months, a week, can do to a person. My childhood made me believe in the people that loved me, that The Beatles were right and love was all we needed. My few years at the bar made me realize life wasn't fair and that the world was full of cruel people who preyed on the weak. A couple of months of marriage made me see how fucked my life was, how I was trapped in the famed golden prison put forth by the country's narcos, how there would be no escape. And a week as a hostage let me know just how damn fed up I was with every moment of time that had passed before it.

I had changed this past week, in ways I wasn't even able to understand. Without realizing it, I was starting to relate to Javier Bernal instead of fearing him. I saw his desire to make me break and I felt that same desire, to make others break, the ones that hurt me all this time. He was getting his revenge on the woman who had left him, whether it was by becoming more successful or by humiliating and overpowering me. I understood now the vengeance that rocked through him, because the need for it was starting to rock through me. That anger deep in my belly continued to uncoil, threatening to be let loose. I wasn't sure what would happen if I set it free—probably nothing helpful since I was but a woman in a man's game—but if I could have that rare chance to be part of the game, I felt like nothing would be able to stop me.

After he left me in the bedroom, my thoughts kept sweeping over our conversation. I saw he had the ability to hurt, and I saw his even greater ability to lie. While he acted callous and cruel, I could see deep into those golden eyes of his and know when he was hesitant, when he felt bad or ashamed. I could see his feelings, emotions, buried so far beneath his dirt that they almost didn't exist.

But they were there.

The truth was, however, as much as Javier may have felt something over his quest to ruin me, I also knew reality would trump emotion. When tomorrow came and Salvador got in touch with him, I knew that Javier would hand me over. And if he didn't, I knew that he would have to kill me. Oh, I figured he wouldn't do it himself—his emotions wouldn't let that happen. But Este would do it. Or The Doctor. Or Franco. I would be killed, possibly in the most horrific way, because that was the way things went. Whatever Javier might have felt for me, he was no idiot. He was cunning, manipulative, and he had his pride. A lot of pride. Cartel leaders did not let hostages go because of bleeding hearts.

He would have me killed because he had to. Then he would go on with his life, looking for another opportunity to get ahead, to bury the ghosts of his own past. I would be a memory in a week. Some other form of revenge would take my place.

In the other scenario, at least I could keep my parents safe. If Salvador bargained for me, that meant he really wanted me as his wife. To have and to hold and to rape and to abuse, but he'd still have me there, and in turn I would take it and have my parents stay alive. I would put up with whatever I could for as long as I could.

Then, maybe one day, I'd get them far away and safe, before I killed Salvador. I would definitely die in the process, but I would die with a smile on my face.

I fell asleep with those thoughts. When I woke up, I was surprised to see Javier bringing me my breakfast. I thought he would have avoided me again like he did before, but there he was at my door, bringing me a tray of food, like a butler with a taste for blood.

My blood. I remembered the shivery sensation of his lips as they kissed my wounded back, both soothed and revved up by the strange feeling. Now he was standing before me, and I couldn't help but feel my skin thrum like an electric fence.

Javier usually looked elegant but today he was dressed down, as down as one can go. He was wearing black lounge pants that were tight at his hips and loose in the leg, and a damp white tank top that clung to his upper body through sweat. His longish shaggy hair curled at the ends from being wet, his charismatic face covered in a light sheen.

I'd never seen Javier look this worn and raw, though his confidence still shined through, just as that watch never left his wrist. Oh, to be that woman who destroyed him so thoroughly. I found myself envying this Ellie woman and wondering what kind of a man he was with her. Their relationship obviously never began with a knife. He had broken her heart just as she had broken his, which meant at some point there was love to give and love to take. It was nearly impossible to think of this man being capable of love.

But not completely impossible.

He came over to the table and put the tray of food—fruit, this time—down on it. I found myself studying his body, starting to understand how Ellie must have become enraptured with him. If I had met him under other circumstances, perhaps I could have felt the same. It could have just as easily been Javier who waltzed into the bar, looking for a wife, for a conquest.

Then again, that didn't seem like something Javier would do. He would have seen that as too…desperate. He had intelligence, good looks, and charm, whereas Salvador did not.

"What have you been doing?" I asked him after he gave me a dry "good morning."

"Boxing," he said, looking down at himself, as if he had just remembered he was half-dressed.

Was that the truth, or had he wanted me to see him like this? There was something so lithe yet masculine about his body. He was the complete opposite of Salvador in every way, and I couldn't help but admire it, the sharp V of his hip bones as they disappeared into his pants, the taut flatness of his stomach, the firmness of his chest, shoulders, and arms. He looked every bit the boxer, someone who worked hard for his body, who possessed skill that begged to be tested. Since he always moved like a panther or a snake, easy and controlled, I'm not sure why his athleticism surprised me, but it did.

When I looked up at him, his lips were stretched into a wry smile and his eyes sparked with amusement.

"Do you have interest in boxing?" he asked. "Or just in me?"

I quickly looked away, ashamed that he caught me ogling him so blatantly. He must have thought I was quite the fool. Still, my eyes went back to him, this time focused on the tattoos he had on the inside of his biceps. One said Maria. The other said Beatriz and Violetta.

"Who are those women?" I asked cautiously.

His eyes became vindictive slits. "No business of yours."

I ignored him. "People you killed? People you know? Ex-wives?"

He sucked in a deep breath before he sat on the edge of the bed, hands clasped between his thighs, and stared down at the floor with a dreamy look in his eyes. "You know, once I went fishing with my father."

Okay. This was unexpected.

"We were in La Cruz, just north of Nuevo Vallarta. Nice town, you know? Marlin fishing was really big there, still is, I'm sure. My father was a marine mechanic, so we had free use of his clients' boats whenever we wanted. Well, I'd always wanted to go fishing. Hell, I suppose I just wanted to spend time with him since we never ever saw him. Occasionally, he'd give me and my sisters money to get ice cream and candy, but other than that, he was never around. I always questioned that, you see. Even at a young age."

He cleared his throat. I didn't dare move or make a sound in case he stopped talking. I needed to know more.

With a shake of his head, he went on. "I was an idiot when I was a boy. Ignorant. Anyway, we went out. It was a stunning day, calm seas. We didn't go quite far enough to get the big fish—my father said he wanted to be close to shore in case he was needed for something. But it didn't matter, I enjoyed being out there more than anything on earth. He was even kinder to me than normal. I remember he wiped sunscreen on my nose, tousled my hair, you know, like a real father would do. It was the best day that I could ever remember, better than when my neighbor, Simone, showed me her tits. Better than that. And then I ruined everything."

"How?" I found myself asking.

"I asked too many questions," he said, giving me a poignant look. "I asked why my father worked so hard for being a marine mechanic. I asked why he was never home, what he was really doing, if this was really his job. I got a whack across the face. He had never hit me before and he never hit me again, but I'll always remember that feeling. The shock. Then he turned the boat around and we went back home, empty-handed. He didn't say a single word to me for days. Whatever closeness, love, I had felt for that brief time on the water, that was gone forever." He sighed and stared up at the ceiling. "Years later, when I was sixteen, he was shot. See, I had always suspected on some level that my father worked for a cartel. I just never had the proof until he was killed. I figured perhaps he asked too many questions, too."

I felt my heart throb with compassion. He probably didn't deserve it, but my heart knew no different. "What about the rest of your family? You said you had sisters? How many?"

He gave me a sad smile. "I had four sisters, Alana, Marguerite, Violetta and Beatriz. Now I have two. I also had a mother, Maria. Now I have none."

"All related to the cartels?"

"To live and die in Mexico," he said, getting to his feet. "That is the way."

"Violetta, Beatriz, and Maria..." I stated.

"They are the reasons why family gets you killed," he finished, his voice hard. "As does love. And as does asking too many questions. Do you understand?"

I swallowed thickly but nodded.

"Good," he said, flashing me an insincere grin. "Now, since this is your last day in our beautiful safe house, I figured I'd ask you what you wanted to do today."

"Do today?" I repeated incredulously. "Are my choices eat food, get Tasered, or become a human carving board?"

"I was thinking maybe you wanted to do something else for a change."

As strange as it was to think it, the idea of change scared me. Things were bad for me, but I always knew they could be worse. In fact, tomorrow they would most definitely be worse and I was in no hurry to experience that already.

The look in his eyes softened as he held out his hand for mine. "Come with me," he said. "You have nothing to be afraid of."

"Only you," I pointed out.

"Only me."

I wasn't sure why that made me smile, but it did. I was starting to fear I was becoming as sick and twisted as he was. Then I realized that perhaps that was nothing to fear.

I put my hand out and he grasped it, his palm warm and soft, his fingers strong. He pulled me up to my feet, and I realized I was only wearing a long t-shirt and no underwear. I don't know why I was suddenly self-conscious, considering the way I was yesterday, considering I'd had my ass in his face a few days ago, but I was.

"I need to get changed," I said, looking away. He had brought me close to him and I could feel those eyes of his tracing my skin, from my toes to my lips.

"Do you want me to give you a minute?" he asked. "Because I'm afraid I've already seen everything. In every way possible."

I ignored that and pulled away from him, reaching for a pair of shorts, the shorts I had been captured in. I slipped them on, revelling in their familiarity, then knotted the t-shirt above my waist. Like hell I was going to bother with a bra.

"Low maintenance," Javier commented.

"It's easy when you're held hostage. I'm surprised I'm still brushing my teeth."

"Well, you don't want to turn into a savage."

I gave him a funny look. It was times like this that I could almost pretend I wasn't his captive at all, like my fate didn't hang in the balance of tomorrow.

I put on a hard face. "So, where are you taking me? Aren't you going to, well, look more appropriate?"

He shrugged. "We're just going for a ride. Tomorrow is a day for suits. Today is a day to...relax." I tapped my foot and he went on. "I've heard there's a beautiful waterfall here at the end of the road. Apparently you can see the Pacific from the heights. I thought we could go there."

I couldn't figure out just how sincere he was. "You're just going to take me on a car ride?"

"Don't look so concerned," he said. "You won't be able to escape."

I figured that much. He opened the door and we stepped out into the hall. Immediately, the repulsive pig that was Franco was at our side. Javier seemed on edge around him, his eyes burning into him like a warning, while Franco handed over a pair of handcuffs.

Franco then went down the stairs, and Javier slipped one cuff over my wrist and held on to the other one before taking me outside into the sunshine. There was a black SUV—the narcos' car of choice—running in the driveway. Franco climbed into the driver's seat and Javier put us both in the back, making sure the other end of the handcuff was fastened to the handle above the door. There would be no escaping from this vehicle, not unless I wanted to be dragged to my death.

We rode in silence for the first bit, the only sounds the crunch of rock beneath the wheels and my heart pounding loudly in my chest. It was jarring being out in the real world, so much so that I had a hard time taking it all in. It wasn't until Javier put down my window and the fresh mountain air came pouring into my lungs, that I remembered I was alive, even if only a short time. Lush, tropical foliage covered the road on both sides, and birds squawked happily from the trees. It was beautiful outside, and I realized that this was indeed a gift for me.

Yet, I had to wonder who all of this was for. Me? Or for the tiny speck of a conscience I knew he had.

I shifted in my seat and studied him for a moment, sitting there still dressed down in his top and lounge pants, looking more like an ordinary—albeit handsome—man.

"Why are you doing this?" I asked.

He stared out the window for a moment, as if he didn't hear me. "Because it is your last day here, your last day in my presence. I wanted to make it memorable."

"My last day on earth," I said grimly.

He gave me a lopsided smile. "Well, tomorrow you will either be gone..."

"Or I will be dead. It's pretty much the same thing."

He frowned. "I feel like Salvador knows how very precious you are. If I were him, I wouldn't let you go."

"But you're not him."

"No," he said with finality. "I'm not."

"So how are you going to kill me?"

His dark brows shot straight up. "Excuse me?" he asked incredulously.

"I said, how are you going to kill me? I know how most sicarios kill women. Through strangulation. Are you going to choke me?"

He rubbed at his chin, his eyes still bewildered. "Choking belongs in the bedroom, Luisa, and if you stayed around me long enough, you'd find that out for yourself."

I shrugged and looked at the trees rushing past, the way the road climbed and climbed. The air was turning cooler by the moment, the land smelling sweet and earthy. I felt like every sense was turned on, heightened, perhaps because this really was the last day.

"Choking is a horrible way to kill someone," Javier went on, his voice heavy. He placed his hand on mine, and I looked to him in surprise at the gesture. His expression was grave, his lips set in a hard line. "To feel someone's life slip out of your hands is not enjoyable."

"Is any killing enjoyable?" I asked coldly.

He raised his chin. "Yes. Some are."

"So how are you going to kill me?"

His grip tightened on my hand. "Why are you talking about such things?"

"Because it is the truth. Is it Franco here?" I asked, jerking my chin to the monkey driving the SUV. "Will he do it? Lower me into boiling water until the little parts of me burn, until you cut those bits off, until I pass out and you revive me and you do it all over? Will you sprinkle me with acid? Gouge my eyes out, rape me with a burning hot tire iron and leave me in a room to die? Don't think I haven't learned a thing or two about being a narco-wife. I know how your business is conducted." My voice had become higher at the end and I realized how heated I was getting. I needed to calm down.

I took a deep breath and looked away from his face, his face that was still searching mine, seemingly in disbelief.

After a few thick moments passed, the tension in the car mounting, he removed his hand from mine and said, "You will be shot in the head."

A stone dropped into my stomach. The truth.

"I see," I managed to say.

"It is fast and painless. You won't feel a thing. Just hear a loud noise, perhaps some pressure. And then it will all be over."

"Are you going to do it?"

"No," Javier said. "That is not my job."

"I would like you to," I said, looking back at him. "I would like you to pull the trigger."

He frowned, shaking his head slightly. "Why?"

"Because I am your responsibility. And you are the boss. Don't become like Salvador, letting the people below you do your dirty work. Own up to the problems you created. Handle them yourself, like a man." I leaned in closer, close enough that I could see my reflection in his eyes. "I am yours. Act like it."

A faint wash of panic came across his face. "I am not finished with my name."

"Then take me back home and finish me."

Now he was really taken aback. He gestured to Franco and the world outside. "But we haven't reached the waterfall. The view is breathtaking, I—"

"You wanted to make my last day memorable." I cut him off. "Then you should do what I want. I want to go back to the safe house. I want you to finish your job. I want to be done with all of this. I want to be done with you."

I could see Franco eying him in the rearview mirror, unimpressed that I was ordering around his boss. But I didn't care.

Javier watched me for a few beats, a darkness swirling in his eyes. Finally he said to Franco, "Turn around, we've seen enough."

"Yes, boss," he said, now glaring at me. I turned and stared out the window, taking in the sights that I would possibly never see again.

It didn't take long before we were back at the safe house and Javier was taking me up to my room. He practically shoved me in there and quickly locked the door, acting almost like he was mad at me.

I was alone again. But I knew not for long. He wouldn't stand me up, not after what I said to him. He had too much pride.

So I sat down on the bed and waited.

...

Javier came just after nightfall. Perhaps he was a vampire. His shining knife, caught in the moonlight, acted as his dutiful fangs.

He came in the room and flicked on the bedside light, which gave off a dull glow. He was wielding the blade in one hand, still dressed down, but in jeans and a tight white t-shirt. He didn't say anything to me, just stared down at my body. There was a strange emptiness in his eyes, and I had to wonder if he was really here or somewhere else in that peculiar head of his.

We both knew what he was here to do; there was no point discussing it anymore. I no longer feared his knife; I'd grown accustomed to it, just as I'd grown somewhat accustomed to him. I unknotted my shirt and pulled it right over my head, not caring that I was bare-breasted in front of him.

He bit his lip and I could see his chest rise and fall, as if he was trying to catch his breath. But he still motioned for me to turn over. I did as he asked, feeling as if we were doing a well-choreographed dance and this was our final performance.

Javier climbed on the bed, straddling my thighs, his groin pressed against my ass, and I felt that familiar yet still foreign hardness. I wondered why he never tried to have sex with me, particularly since I seemed to turn him on so much. Pleasuring himself onto my back was one thing, but there was a distance to it. I wondered why he had never forced himself on me, why he never tried to get inside me.

I wondered what would happen if he suddenly did. A growing part of me realized that I kind of wanted him to try. I wouldn't fight him off. I wanted to participate, to be involved for once. I wanted to know if it was possible for sex to be different than the cruel, painful game I'd always had to play.

These were dirty thoughts. And yet I couldn't push them away.

I heard him breathing heavily and felt a finger trace the previous letters in his name. He traced them over and over again, as if in a trance, and the knife never once pressed into my back.

"Why are you hesitating?" I asked him softly.

His finger paused. I heard him swallow. Finally he said, his voice sounding rough in the dark, "Because I don't think I can."

My breath caught in my throat. "Why?"

"Because I think your last night should bring you no pain."

"There is no pain, Javier," I assured him. "Not anymore. I want you to finish your name. I am more yours than I am Salvador's."

Silence thickened the room. His erection grew harder, and finally he shifted against me.

"What did you say?" he asked.

"I said I am more yours than I am Salvador's," I repeated, as truthful and sad as it was. "So finish branding me. I want the knife. I want your name."

I think I might want you. You, the man who might pull the trigger.

I felt him lean over me, and the tip of the blade pressed in slightly, not enough to break skin. "Tell me again," he said, "that you want my name on you."

"I want your name. I want it to say Javier. I will wear those scars proudly." *And I will show the world that I survived it all, to the end.*

"Tell me you want me," he said huskily.

I stiffened, wondering if he had somehow learned my thoughts.

"Tell me you want me," he said again, "and I'll do it."

I decided to shed my self-consciousness. "I want you," I whispered. Then I said it again, until it sounded right, until I knew it was true.

Javier dug the blade in one sharp motion. I sucked in my breath, feeling a mix of pleasure with the tingle of pain. He finished the final sections of the R with gusto, his work quick and seamless. I felt the blood begin to pour from the wound. In seconds, he was kissing it, soothing it with his lips and tongue, absorbing the blood. He was so unbelievably tender, even after such an act of cruelty.

I closed my eyes, not wanting him to stop.

He slowly moved his lips away from the wound and began kissing down my spine, his tongue zig-zagging over it. I arched my back toward his mouth, an involuntary reaction from my body, wanting more contact, the wet heat of his lips.

"Do you like that?" he whispered as he paused at the small of my back.

I decided to be honest this time. "Yes," I murmured.

"Tell me you want me again," he said.

"I want you."

His hands slipped around my waist and under my pelvis and began undoing my shorts. "Tell me you're mine."

"I'm yours," I told him, suddenly feeling both turned on and afraid of what was to come, afraid of the unknown, of the change between us. But I didn't want to fear anymore, not tonight.

"Good girl," he said throatily. "Such a good girl." He grabbed the hem of my shorts and quickly yanked them off so my bare ass was exposed. I heard him groan at the sight of me. "A very, *very* good girl," he whispered. "And I'm about to do very, very bad things to you."

He ran his hands up my calves, my thighs, my ass, up the sides of my back all the way to my shoulders where he kissed the wound one more time. Then he reached under me and flipped me over until I was on my back. I winced from the pressure of the bed on my cuts, but he took no notice and pinned my hands above my head with one hand.

He placed his other hand on my neck, squeezing delicately. My eyes widened in surprise.

"The thing about choking," he said slowly, his voice dripping with lust, his eyes glazed with passion, "is both parties have to be ready for it. You, my beauty queen, are not. But I do know what you are ready for. Something to erase all your pain. Something…memorable."

He lifted his hand off my neck and leaned in so close, I was sure he was going to kiss me. My lips parted, wanting it. But instead he went for my ear, licking the lobe, and said gently, "I want you to relax and lie there. When it feels good, you grab my hair and pull hard until you're sure you're hurting me. I look forward to it."

Then he let go of my wrists and started making his way down, kissing my chest, my breasts, his tongue doing smooth circles over my nipples. He bit them and I cried out, from the shock and pain and the warmth that came afterward, a warmth that spread down my core and between my legs, making them spread open.

He kissed and sucked down my stomach, at my belly button, and then headed lower. I tensed up, afraid, but I felt him pause. I lifted my head to see those sharp lustful eyes staring at me with such want, I wasn't sure if he was going to kill me or fuck me.

"Just relax," he murmured, and his eyes never broke away from mine as he passed over my pubic bone and placed himself between my legs, his arms hooking on to each thigh. "I will do all the work." He looked down between my legs, bare and vulnerable. "You have a beautiful pussy, did you know that?"

My cheeks flamed and I chastised myself for feeling so bashful.

His face lowered even further and my body stiffened in response.

"I want to feel your clit throb between my lips," he whispered, his breath sending electricity through my thighs. When I didn't say anything—I couldn't, I was frozen in shock—he lifted his head from between my legs and gave me a curious glance. "You've never had an orgasm before, have you?"

I shook my head.

He grinned with easy carnality. "Do not worry. I'm very good at giving girls an orgasm for the first time. And for every time after that."

Then he placed his mouth on me, and a million volts of electricity ran through me, making me flinch. The feeling slowly melted away though as the wet warmth of his mouth spread all over, and I found myself relaxing into the most foreign sensation that had ever touched my body. His tongue slowly lapped up and down my slit before concentrating on my clit in slow, easy circles. I knew how my body worked, I just never touched myself before, never realized the pleasure that could be had.

I started thinking I was an idiot for not doing so all this time, but soon all thought was being sucked out of me and into his mouth. I was only sensation, this beautiful feeling that his lips were bringing me. I felt my whole body both relax and tense, and I began to raise my hips into his face, craving deeper contact when his tongue became whisper light.

"That's my queen," he said into me, and the vibrations caused me to squirm. "Your pussy tastes seductive, more delicious than milk and honey. I should drink you with my tea in the mornings."

I moaned, not even blushing this time. I just wanted him, needed him, to continue. I found myself reaching for his hair, burying my fingers into his smooth strands and gripping them. I pulled his face further into me and his tongue started to fuck me, entering in and out.

Now I was bucking my hips, craving him, wanting more.

"You're so wet, I'm drowning in you." He groaned. One of his hands left my thighs and he pulled back slightly. Suddenly he put one of his fingers inside me and I found myself trying to clench around it. "You want so much, it's beautiful."

"Just keep going," I said breathlessly, my back arching, my fingers wrapping tighter into his thick hair.

"I'll keep going until you are coming."

"How will I know?"

"Well," he said slowly, and though my head was rolled to the side and I couldn't see him, I knew he was grinning. "It will feel like this."

His tongue started flicking my clit harder just as his finger began to thrust and curl inside of me, pressing against my wall repeatedly. The pressure in my core began to build rapidly, my limbs stiffening, my breath escaping me. I held on to his hair as tight as I could while I felt like my whole body was on pause, that moment before falling when you're in mid-air, when all time stands still, when breath and heartbeat and bloodflow all stops.

It was the most beautifully exquisite torture.

Then everything broke loose. My body became a wave of fire, of pulsating light, of air and heat and explosions that all went off at the same time. I was completely unaware of any sounds I was making—I think I was screaming—and I hadn't realized I was yanking on Javier's hair so hard that I lifted his head right off me.

I lay there, writhing, moaning. It was like being Tasered but only with pleasure. Then, as my eyes stopped rolling back into my head, as I began to catch my breath, I was hit with a second wave.

Only this one was pure emotion. I felt like my heart was light and fluttery, and there was pain and sadness and joy and regret and anger, and every single buried feeling being unearthed. I was beside myself, unsure of how to process what had just happened to my body and what happened to my soul.

And Javier, this horrible man, this narco, my captor, he was right there on the bed beside me, wiping his mouth and gazing at me before tucking my hair behind my ear. I could only stare at him in pure bewilderment, my eyes wide, my mouth open, trying to breathe, to remember who I was and what I was to him.

But I could barely remember any of that. I was feeling a pull to him stronger than anything before. This man was capable of such cruelty and violence, yet he had pleasured me, giving me something I'd never had. Well, the sated look in his hooded eyes told me that he found it nearly as pleasurable himself.

He rested his hand on my cheek, soothingly. "You better get some rest," he said. "Big day tomorrow."

And then more of the real world, of my life, came back, pecking away at the golden wave I was still riding, making my heart slow.

The thing, the crazy thing, was that as much as I didn't want tomorrow to come, I also didn't want him to leave. I wanted him to stay with me. At least until I fell asleep. I needed him, the little comfort he could give me on my last night.

He was staring at me expectedly, like he wanted me to ask him. Or he wanted to ask himself. Maybe we could do something else to pass the time. Maybe I could do something for him. Maybe it wasn't time to say goodnight.

But then he sat up, perched on the end of the bed, and smoothed down his hair. There was another moment where he licked his lips, his eyes flickering, his mind caught in some internal dialogue.

I almost said something. I opened my mouth and almost asked him to stay, as foolish as it was.

He got up and picked up the blade from the other side of the bed, sliding it into his boot.

"Goodnight Luisa," he said, and I knew the moment was over.

I couldn't find the words to say goodnight to him. He gave me a quick, almost grave smile, then left the room, the lock turning loudly behind him.

It was the loneliest sound.

I lay there naked, remembering the feeling I just had moments ago, a feeling I would never get back.

I let a tear fall, my emotions still running rampant in me, and then gratefully drifted off to sleep before the thoughts of his touch could turn into thoughts of his bullets.

CHAPTER THIRTEEN

Javier

I had woken up with the taste of her pussy on my lips. Proof that it hadn't been a dream.

Men who think they have to rape and violate in order to assert their power and control have no idea what they're missing. Real power comes in giving a woman pleasure. Real control is knowing you've taken that woman to another place, another plane of existence, and you're the only one who holds the key. I gave Luisa what she wanted, what she needed, and she would never be the same again.

In some ways, the same went for me.

But today of all days was not the time to dwell on such accomplishments. Today I had to separate my impulses toward Luisa and focus on the big picture, the task at hand.

My empire had so much to gain, so much to lose, and it all rested on one man's feelings toward a beautiful little woman, lying in bed in the room above me. I knew now that Salvador didn't love her—he wouldn't have abused her like he did, she wouldn't have hated him so much, and he wouldn't have let this charade go on for so long. But pride was easily confused with love and I knew how much of that he had. Too much self-love could be utterly destructive. I needed to play that card.

"Javier?" The Doctor asked.

I looked over at him, remembering what was going on. I was sitting down in the shitty little office, The Doctor in the seat across from me, Este and Juanito who had just returned from their travels, standing by the door. Franco was outside in the hall. By Luisa's room I had more guards than normal, just in case she panicked during these final hours.

On the desk was the old-fashioned flip cell phone Salvador would be calling. It couldn't be traced, but we would still destroy it after anyway.

"Yes?" I asked, tapping my cigarette and watching the stem of ash flake into the ashtray.

"How would you like for us to dispose of her?"

It was the way The Doctor said this, so callously, as if we were talking about garbage, that bothered me most of all. Naturally, I couldn't show it.

"I think a bullet to the head would suffice," I said quickly, before puffing back on the smoke. I'd already gone through half a pack that morning.

He cocked a brow at me, the lines in his forehead deepening. "Is that so? Don't you think we have to send a better message than that?"

I narrowed my eyes at his questioning. "What message is there? This isn't a secret killing, we don't have to bury her facedown. We have her, he doesn't obey, we kill her."

"But you know how sweet torture can be," he said with a wistful look on his face. "And it has been too long."

I stared at him, at the white Panama hat on his head that gave him this air of sophistication that hid all his depravity. "And you know I don't like women to be tortured."

"Right," he said slowly. "You think it's ugly."

"It *is* ugly."

"Are you sure it's all women," Este spoke up, "or just Luisa?"

What a fucking shit disturber. I gave him a dull look as I blew a cloud of smoke toward him. "*All* women."

He grinned and crossed his arms. "Interesting. You know, I could have sworn I heard you torturing her last night. There were screams..."

"Would you like another knife in your shin?" I asked. "No? Then shut the fuck up. For now, that is your job. Shutting the fuck up."

"No need to get violent again," The Doctor said, leaning back in his chair. "Not today. It's fine, Javier, if you don't want to torture Luisa. A bullet to the head will work, as long as we can remove her head afterward. And other parts of her. We'll mail it out to Cabo San Lucas, have Juanito here display her just so on the steps of city hall. It's her city, and that city has avoided the violence of the cartels for far too long, don't you think?" He ran a finger over his mustache, smiling at the thought. "Yes, that would send the right message. It will show the world, the whole world, that we don't fuck around."

"Um," Juanito said, speaking for the first time that morning, "wouldn't it also show that Salvador doesn't fuck around? I mean, if I saw a cartel boss' wife's body, I would assume that it was because he didn't negotiate. That his own wife wasn't worth it. That says some seriously fucked up shit right there."

Before I had a chance to run that terrible scenario through my head, the phone rang, causing us all to jump.

I snatched it up before anyone else could. It was a horrid ringtone to boot.

I flipped it open. "Hello."

"I take it this is Javier Bernal." The man's voice was raspy, heavy, like talking was an effort.

"I take it this is Salvador Reyes," I said.

"You're correct. I'm sorry I haven't gotten back to you earlier. You see, it took me some time to figure out who you were." He snorted in through his nose and I heard him spit on the ground. I grimaced. "I'd never heard of Javier Bernal. But one of my friends pointed out that you were the one arrested in California. Rumor has it that you were turned in by a woman, is that right? And now you appear to have my woman."

She's not your woman, I thought, but the thought didn't stick around for long.

"That I do. I have your wife, Luisa. Pretty little thing. You really shouldn't have let her out of your sight."

He grunted. "Have you ever tried to tell a woman what to do? It's not always easy to lay down the law."

His jovial tone was making me troubled.

"You've heard our demands, then," I prompted him. I looked over at The Doctor, Este, and Juanito who were all watching me, on edge.

"I did, I did," he said. He cleared his throat and spat again. "I did. And you must know that I love my wife very much. So very much. But you're asking a great deal from me. The Ephedra lane is a lot of money, a lot of work went in to that. Surely, as one master to another, you can appreciate that. I'll have no problems securing another one, but you get so attached to these kind of *things*." I could practically hear him smiling over the phone. The happier he sounded, the worse the knot in my gut.

He sighed. "How about this. Give me another week. I'll see what I can work out."

Every instinct told me to tell him there was no deal. That I was negotiating here, not him. That I was the one in control. I wanted to tell him that it was over, and I would personally fuck and kill his wife, and then I would hang up the phone. My instincts told me that because that's what they had been trained to do.

But my instincts were pushed to the side. "Fine," I told him. "You have another week exactly. If you don't deliver, we will. Her raped, mutilated body will be on the front page of every newspaper. And perhaps a few toes in your morning cereal. Goodbye."

I quickly snapped the phone shut and pushed it away from me. I hadn't realized I was breathing hard, my chest racing. Everyone was staring at me, seemingly in shock.

"What?" I snapped.

"You negotiated?" The Doctor asked in disapproval. "Javier..."

I pulled a cigarette out from behind my ear. "So what? It's another week. What's another week when we can get what we want instead of nothing at all?"

"You're giving him the upper hand."

"How? How the fuck am I doing that? I have his wife. If he didn't want her back, he wouldn't have asked for an extension." I lit the cigarette angrily then leaned forward in my chair, my eyes blazing into his. "You've done this a million times. Sometimes people can't come up with the money right away. So we work with them. We all know that is how this is done."

"For civilians," he said slowly. "That is how it is done with them. Salvador doesn't need to come up with anything, he has everything. He is playing us."

I shook my head. "No, you are wrong."

"This woman is clouding your brain," he said, getting to his feet. "I should just do us all a favor and kill her right now."

I shot up, leaning across the desk, fury rocketing through me. "You do that and I will kill you." I jabbed my finger at him. "You know I will. I will torture you the same way you torture everyone, and I will smile the whole fucking time."

He stared at me in surprise before his face crumpled into laughter. "You are serious. I like that about you, Javier. I like your edge. So, a word of advice then from your elder—don't lose it."

With that he turned and walked out the door. I looked over at Juanito, wondering if he had any more interesting anecdotes, but he quickly followed in The Doctor's footsteps. Only Este stayed behind. He closed the door behind him and then sat down across from me, putting his hands behind his head.

"Well, that was a doozy," he remarked.

"What did I tell you about shutting the fuck up?"

He nodded, looking away. "Yes, yes, I should do it more often. I'm just curious, Javi."

"About what?" I asked in annoyance. My heart was still racing along, my pulse beating wildly against my watch.

"About what you hope to gain from all of this."

"That's fairly apparent."

"Is it?" he asked as he picked up the cell phone and began to dismantle it. "You know at the end of next week, you'll still have to either kill her or send her on her way. You're delaying the inevitable."

"I'm delaying what I can to get what I want."

He shot me a look. "Look, I want to fuck Luisa just as much as you do. Or perhaps, just as much as you have. Her screams last night were not from being tortured. I'm not that much of an idiot."

I wasn't sure if I should own up to what I did; after all, I was the "master" as Salvador had called me, and that was our right as the master, the boss, to take what we wanted. Or I wasn't sure if I should gloss over the whole thing and pretend nothing happened. I didn't know what would be better for Este to hear. So I said nothing.

He continued, "I also know that another week with her is a mistake."

"How so?"

"It will be harder for you to...say goodbye."

"Then you don't know me very well."

He shrugged and displayed the phone on the desk, now in tiny little pieces. "That's true. I don't really. I should, but I don't. But that doesn't mean I'm not concerned for you."

"And why would you be concerned about my well-being?"

"I dunno. Being a good friend, I guess."

I laughed. "Friend. That's a good one."

His expression grew serious. "This organization means a lot to me, almost as much as it does to you. I just don't want us to be in over our heads. I don't like that Salvador has control back and I don't like that this might leave us looking like assholes." He bit his lip, thinking something over. "Are you still in contact with that chick from the DEA?"

"Lillian Berrellez," I told him. "And I haven't been in contact with her for a while."

"Do you think if things go south with Salvador, we could give her Juanito? He can give her all the intel. They could pinpoint one of his safe houses, one of his mansions. I'm sure with some extra inside info, they could make an arrest, make it happen."

I shook my head. "I am not a snitch, Este. There is still honor among cartels. We don't rat each other out to the Americans."

He snorted, shaking his head like I'd just said the most ridiculous thing. "Oh, come on, Javier. You and your stupid moral code that doesn't exist. There is no honor. How do you think Chapo was caught before Salvador took over? Huh? The cartels put up those wanted posters around the continents, not the Mexican government, and not the American one. This is a new Mexico. There is no code among men because there are no men anymore. Only monsters who sit behind their desks and give orders." At that, he looked at me with a touch of exaggerated disgust.

"You think I'm a monster?" I asked. Funny how Luisa said I wasn't.

"I think you'll get there one day," he said carefully. "If you don't mess up."

He was talking around me and I hated it. I waved my hand at him. "You're starting to bore me, Este. Go and pack everything up."

"Where are we going?"

"Back to my place."

"What about a safe house?"

"I miss nice things."

"You can't bring Luisa there."

"I can do whatever I fucking want," I said, and instinctively reached under the desk for the gun I had put there. Este picked up on it and nodded, quickly leaving the room. He was right. He wasn't that much of an idiot after all.

Once he was gone, I was alone with my thoughts. Then my thoughts became too convoluted for me to wade through. So I got up and went to tell Luisa the news.

As usual, there was no answer to my knock. I opened the door and poked my head in. She was up, staring out the window, wearing that hot pink dress again, her hands behind her back. She didn't look over at me when I came in the room. I was glad. It gave me a few private seconds to appreciate the marvelous things her ass did to my dick. I had another week of this luxury.

"I have news," I said, clearing my throat.

Her shoulders tensed up but she didn't turn around. "Oh? Good or bad?"

"I'm not sure. What would be good news to you?"

"That you'll just let me go free."

I pursed my lips. "Well, that means I have bad news, I'm afraid. Because I can't let that happen."

She didn't say anything to that. I walked over to her and paused at her back. I lifted up her thick, soft hair and placed it gently over her shoulder, and peered at my name underneath. It looked less ugly now that it was done. I began to swirl around in the memory of the night before, the way she begged for me to finish it, to brand her, the way she told me she wanted me. I closed my eyes briefly and took in a deep breath through my nose.

"My name looks good," I said softly.

Her shoulders slumped. "Am I going back to Salvador?" Pure desperation tore through her voice.

"No," I said.

"Are you going to kill me?"

"No."

Finally she turned around and looked at me, puzzlement on her beautiful face. "Did you even hear from him?"

I nodded.

"What did he say then?"

I ran my tongue over my teeth. "Well, we've made a new bargain." Her eyes widened. "He said he needs time to give me what I want. I gave him one more week."

A cynical smile flashed across her lips. "You see. He doesn't want me."

"You sound happy."

"You have no idea what happy sounds like," she sneered, her eyes flashing with bright fire. "I am only relieved, but I am still here and I still face the same fate in a week. You've bought me more time to face my own death. How can I be happy about that?"

I'd be lying to myself if I didn't feel the way my heart pinched from her words.

I stepped closer to her and brushed her hair back over her shoulder. "I think I showed you last night just how easy it can be to pass the time," I said, lowering my voice. "I think you can find happiness in the time I've bought you. Don't you?"

She rubbed her lips together and looked away.

Where was that sexually curious girl from last night? I leaned down and grazed her satiny earlobe with my lips. "You're mine for another week, Luisa. Why not make it count? The tip of my tongue was only the tip of the iceberg. Trust me, you'll want to see—and feel—the rest."

I slipped my hand around the small of her waist, relishing in how large it felt around her, and started kissing down her neck. Her nape was so soft, so seductively fragrant with just her own scent that it took a lot of effort to stay the course, to not throw her down on the bed, rip her dress off, and fuck her brains out.

She relaxed into my touch, into my lips and tongue, but it wasn't long until she pushed me back, her hand on my chest.

"No," she said, her voice uneven as she stared up at me.

I raised my brow. "No?" I removed my hand from her waist and used it to straighten my tie. "All right then."

I turned around and strolled to the middle of the room. I gestured to the clothes scattered everywhere. "I suppose there are more pressing things to deal with. You'll need to pack up everything."

"Why?" she asked, her hand at her heart.

I smiled. "It's no longer wise to stay here. I'm taking you home." She froze and I quickly went on. "Home to my place. No more safe houses, no rented mansions. You're coming to stay with me."

"Is that…safe?"

"My darling, you can't get any safer. I spend what I earn. I have informants at checkpoints outside of my local town who report all new people moving in, people who may be part of rival cartels. I have sicarios patrolling the town, searching for new vehicles, new people that may have gotten past the checkpoints. It's just as controlled as any federal agency. In matters of safety, I spare no expense. The same goes for shoes and liquor."

At that she glanced down at my shoes, perhaps noticing their quality craftsmanship for the first time. And they say women were always first to notice fine clothing.

Then again, Luisa was born poor. Her knowledge of wealth and style was only thrust upon her in the last few months, lost in the mess of abuse and brutality. I could smell that depravity waft in over the phone that morning, the sickness that was Salvador. I kept trying not to think of them together, of the things he must have done to her, but hearing his voice made it all the more real. I started to wonder how the hell I would be able to give her back to him in a week.

"Are you okay?" she asked me.

I blinked, bringing myself back to the scene.

"Yes, fine," I said quickly. "I'll come back in a few. Then we'll be gone."

CHAPTER FOURTEEN

Luisa

It took me a few moments to wrap my head around the new situation. When Javier came into my room, I was certain my world was about to change forever. Either Salvador was making the trade and wanted me back, or Javier would have to shoot me in the head—or at least get someone else to do it. I hadn't been kidding when I said I wanted him to pull the trigger. It only seemed fair, and if I was going to die because of him, he was going to suffer.

To have a week of your life extended was an odd thing. I wasn't sure if I was grateful or not. It was another week of uncertainty, but it was still another week of being alive. A week held chances, surprises, and possibilities—if one was in an optimistic mood. I wasn't, of course. No one in my shoes would be. Though I had to say I felt my knees threaten to give out when Javier started kissing my neck.

That man's lips did things to my skin—shocked me, gently, with warm electricity—and I found myself wanting him to raise his head and bring his lips to mine. I wanted to know what *that* felt like. But I wasn't about to give him the upper hand. As much as I didn't want to say no to him, as much as I fantasized about a repeat of last night, I did say no.

And to his credit, he immediately backed off. Didn't even try to make me feel bad for it. Javier definitely followed his own set of morals and honors, and it was strangely fascinating trying to uncover each one. A whole week of discovery lay before me. I suppose that was the only bright side to everything. That, and the fact that I was still alive.

The only thing that really worried me—other than my outcome in seven days—was the fact that we were leaving the safe house for his compound. I had no doubt that the place was well protected but it couldn't have been a good thing that *I* was going there. I was still considered the enemy, hostage or not. I was Salvador's wife and could return to him, report back to him, spy for him all to re-enact revenge on my cruel captor, Javier Bernal.

It was almost as if Javier was trusting me, though he had no reason to.

And for some reason, that scared me.

It wasn't long until I was "packed." I just shoved all my clothes back into the bag that they came from. I no longer thought of them belonging to someone else, except when I had to hike up the long skirts so they wouldn't drag. They were a part of me, part of this disturbing transition from one life to another. Some of the articles had bloodstains on them that wouldn't come out with soap and water, but I didn't care. I liked the stains, what they meant, what I'd survived.

Esteban came up to my room to get me, limping slightly. I asked him the other day what happened. He wouldn't say, which made me think he was getting too cocky with Javier for his own good. I was glad he had been put in his place.

Unfortunately, he wasn't alone. I could see Franco and a guard leering around outside the door. In Esteban's hands he had a blindfold and handcuffs.

"What's going on?" I asked, trying not to panic.

"You don't like kinky games?" Esteban asked with a smirk, coming toward me.

I instinctively took a step back.

He stopped and gave me a wry look. "Oh, come on, hey. I'm just getting you ready for your journey. You don't think we'd actually let you see where we are taking you."

I suppose he was right. So I was just trading one golden prison for another.

"Now be a good girl," he said. "And we won't have to hurt you."

At that, the old doctor stepped into the room holding out a syringe. Like hell I was going to let them drug me.

"I think I've grown tired of being the good girl," I snarled.

Este frowned, and I took that moment to pick up the lamp beside me and bash it into his head. I got him right on the bruise from where I'd smashed the rock into him. He swore as the glass shattered all around him, but I was already jumping across the bed and going for the other lamp, ready to fight off the doctor.

But when I turned around, Franco was coming into the room and shoving the doctor aside. The dull, mean glint in Franco's eyes and his veiny muscles meant that there was no way I could fight him off, even if I managed to grab a piece of glass and gouge it in his eye. Nothing would stop him.

He lunged for me, his hands hard on my chest, and he pushed me. I flew back against the wall, my head striking it, producing a shower of stars in my vision. Suddenly I felt rough hands grabbing my arms, squeezing them until I thought they would break like twigs, and through the throbbing in my ears I heard people shouting.

The next thing I knew there was a loud bang, a shot, and the blurred vision of Franco began to slip away. His grip on me loosened and now he was swearing his head off in between screams of pain.

I squinted, trying to see past the waves of dizziness and stay upright, and I saw Javier standing in the doorway, a gun in his hand, pointing it right at Franco who had turned around and was yelling at him. I looked down and saw him trying to clutch his foot, blood seeping out of his shoe and onto the floor.

"The next time you touch her," Javier said, his eyes crazed with burning rage, "I will remove the foot I just shot. And your other one. Then your hands," he stepped closer, the gun still trained on him, "and your shriveled cock." He aimed the gun down at Franco's crotch. "And then I'll piss on every single wound. I'll take your head last, so you can see each piece of you disappear, and then I'll piss in your skull. Do you understand?"

Franco didn't. He told him to fuck off.

The room seemed to freeze.

But Javier marched right up to him and pistol whipped Franco across the face, a man twice his size. He whipped him so hard that blood spurted out of his mouth and sprayed onto my arms and chest. I held my breath, so certain that Franco wasn't going to take that. But he did. Power was everything, and Javier had power. He just proved it.

Javier shoved him out of the way and gave me a quick glance of concern before he turned and faced everyone else in the room, a guard at the door, the old doctor with the syringe, Esteban who was holding his head and cursing.

"All I asked of you fucking delinquents was to bring Luisa to me." He glared at the doctor. "I did not ask for her to be drugged. I did not ask for Franco. This should have been an easy process. Now I have another reason why I have to do everything my fucking self if it's going to be done properly." He jerked his chin at Esteban. "Leave the blindfold and the cuffs and everyone get the fuck out of here before I lose my temper again."

The men obeyed with no hesitation and left Javier alone with me.

He sighed and rubbed his hand down his face before he turned to look at me again.

"Did he hurt you?" he asked wearily.

"No worse than you have," I answered.

He nodded. "Good. Because I meant what I said."

"About?"

"About him touching you. I don't want anyone touching you. I won't let it happen. You won't have to worry about that."

"I don't know, you seem like a very touchy feely bunch here," I said humorlessly.

"I'm serious," he said, taking a step closer to me. He ran his hand down the back of my head where it hit the wall, gently cupping it. His eyes bore into mine and I couldn't look away. "I will protect you. I promise, and I keep my promises." He paused, licking his lips. "The only person I won't be able to protect you from is me."

I believed it. And in some messed up way, I was okay with that. I could survive him, his touch, his anger, his passion, because I was starting to understand him. I just couldn't survive anyone else.

"All right," I said slowly, still locked in his gaze. I wondered what they were seeing in me, deep down. There was no way he could look at me like he was, his stare so absolutely penetrating that I felt it in my heart, and not see something. I wanted to know what it was, who I was in his eyes.

But he looked away suddenly, breaking the spell, and pressed his hand to the back of his neck. "I'm afraid I'm still going to have to blindfold you and put you in cuffs. But I promise, you will not leave my side."

I nodded and bit my lip while he picked up the cuffs and the black satin sash from the bed.

I dutifully held out my hands for him. "Do you prefer in front or behind?"

He smiled openly at me, and it was the most shockingly beautiful sight. He looked so damn young, almost angelic. "Oh, my beauty queen, you should know I like it every way possible."

"I meant the handcuffs," I said, though it came out in an uneven whisper. I was still a bit shaken.

He cocked his head at me. "Well, just in case," he said. "The more informed you are, the better off you'll be. Let's take it from behind for today." He quickly walked around me and pulled my arms back, snapping the cuffs over my wrists, which now felt heavy and weighted with the cold metal.

I swallowed the tiny prick of fear that was forming in my throat as he reached around me and placed the blindfold over my eyes. The world went dark, save for a tiny sliver of grey light at the bottom, and he tied it securely behind my head. Now I was one hundred percent powerless and completely in his trust.

I could only pray that he really did keep his promises.

He gently grabbed my upper arm and put his mouth to my ear. "Now I'm going to pick up your bag and take you down the stairs to the car. I'll put you in first, then I will come in right after, and we'll be on our way. If you need us to stop to use the washroom, well, there are plenty of trees. I'll try not to watch you too closely."

I raised my brow, the fabric barely budging from the movement. "How courteous."

I could sense him smiling. "I've been called worse."

...

True to Javier's word, he literally did not leave my side during the excruciatingly long journey to his compound. And, as he had said, he was even there when I had to pee. I was trying to avoid it, but wherever he lived was an eight hour journey, and even I couldn't hold it that long. There's nothing quite like trying to pee in the jungle with a blindfold and handcuffs. I suppose he could have taken the blindfold off for just those moments, but from the sound of his laughter ringing through the trees, I could tell it was funnier this way. To him, that is.

It was near the end of the ride that I found myself falling asleep. I must have dozed off for quite some time, because the car jolting to a stop woke me, and when I raised my head, I realized I had fallen asleep on Javier's shoulder. The feel and smell of him must have been strangely comforting. I felt embarrassed for some reason but said nothing, wondering why he had let me sleep that way.

"We're here," he said in a quiet voice. In the darkness, it washed over me like silk.

I heard the doors open and felt his grasp on my arms as he gently pulled me out of the vehicle. I gulped in the air, still smelling fresh and sweet. Mountainous. It was cool, making my skin erupt in goosebumps. It figured he would have a fortress somewhere up high. I started to miss the dry, hot desert air and sea breezes of Los Cabos. I started to miss a lot of things.

I was brought down a smooth path that felt like cobblestones beneath my shoes, and unfamiliar voices greeted Javier from all sides. I was ushered inside, across a tile floor, then up a long, curving flight of stairs. He took me down a lushly carpeted hall and finally into a room.

The door clicked shut behind me. Locked.

"Where am I?" I asked as he led me across the room. The floor here was tiled but I nearly tripped over a rug. His grip on my arm kept me upright. I expected him to remove the blindfold by now, but he didn't.

"We're in my room," he said. His hands went around my waist, and he picked me up and placed me back down so I was sitting on something lavishly soft, like a fluffy cloud.

His room.

His *bed.*

My pulse began to quicken.

"Don't look so scared," he said. "My room is a very good place to be." He leaned over me and I felt his hands go to the blindfold. I thought he was about to untie it, but his hand slipped down to the back of my neck and he gripped me there.

"I have been dreaming about you in my room," he murmured, his grip massaging my neck. "About what I would do to you if I ever got you here. And here you are."

I had expected to be brought to my own quarters, to be left alone or brought some food. I hadn't expected this. This was taking me completely off-guard, and the handcuffs and blindfold weren't helping at all.

"And what is that?" I somehow managed to get out, though the words felt lodged in my throat.

"Do you want me to tell you," he said, pulling down the front of my dress so my breasts were exposed, my nipples tightening from the air, "or would you rather I show you?"

"I'd rather you tell me," I said warily, even as his lips so softly grazed the tips of my nipples, causing a flood of need spread through me. Now I knew for sure what cards were on the table.

"And I'd rather I show you," he said. Suddenly he was pushing me down on the bed and flipping me over so that I was on my stomach. In one quick motion he pulled my ass up in the air and flipped my dress over my hips. "This has to come off." He pulled my underwear over my cheeks and down my legs, taking his time.

This position felt awfully familiar. "You're going to come all over me," I said.

"No," was his response. I tensed as I felt a hand skim between my legs, sliding up toward where I was becoming increasingly wet and hot. "I'm going to fuck your cunt with my fingers and your ass with my tongue."

It took me a full moment for what he said to register. Then it hit me like a brick.

"What?" I gasped, utterly shocked.

He put one hand on my ass cheek and began to knead it with his fingers. "I've been staring at your perky, firm, heart-shaped ass for too long. I want you to clench around me as you come, I want to experience you from the inside out." He paused long enough to kiss me, slowly, on both cheeks, while one of his fingers slipped inside my opening, his thumb on my clit.

"And what if I say no?" I asked. I swallowed, trying to gather up the desire to say it. But it wasn't there.

"Don't you trust me?"

"Not exactly," I admitted breathlessly. He hit a sweet spot that made my back arch, my eyes clench shut, my body want more of it, so much more. I was surprised at how fast it was betraying me, like an addict after a fix.

"Let me rephrase that," he said. He plunged his finger in further, causing me to release a moan. "Don't you trust that I can make you feel better than I did last night?" He rubbed at me harder, increasing the pressure, making me swell. "Don't you trust that I can make you come so hard, you won't be able to stop yourself from screaming my name?" His tongue teased the top of my crack. "Don't you trust that I can give you things you've only dreamed of?"

I did trust that.

"Well?" he asked.

I nodded my response.

He stopped what he was doing. "I need to hear you say it."

"Yes," I said quickly, eager for him to continue. "I trust you."

"Good," he said soothingly, kneading my skin again.

"Isn't it..." I started, then decided it was too embarrassing to say.

"What?" he asked, his voice rough and low now, like sandpaper.

I bit my lip as the pressure continued to build inside me. *How do I say this?*

"You're a very dirty man."

"Filthy," he corrected me. He smacked my ass lightly, causing me to jump. "Oh, that's just fucking beautiful."

He did it again and again, not enough to hurt but enough to sting. Each time, he licked the place where his handprint would have been. Then, with one hand he gently pried my ass cheeks open. I couldn't help but cringe.

"You need to relax," he whispered. "This won't hurt. And I'm sure you took a bath this morning, didn't you?" I murmured yes in response. "Then you're clean and you have nothing to worry about. As for me, I'd take you anyway I can. It's all exquisite to me."

He was right. He was filthy.

"Relax, Luisa," he said again. "Relax."

And so I tried.

The first contact from his tongue made me shudder. The sensation was so entirely new to me, but what wasn't at this point? Yet his mouth, lips, tongue, were all warm and wet and gentle, and I found my body immediately relaxing into the steady motion. I pushed aside all thoughts about how unpure this was. Purity had done nothing for me anyway. It was better to be dirty. It was better to take what you could. It was better to embrace your lustful, needful, animalistic side because that was the side that *lived*.

I let those languid thoughts roll through me until they were replaced with deep-seated desire. His tongue became more forceful, entering me with an in-and-out motion that matched up with the same rhythm as his thrusting fingers. He was completely fucking me in every way and I was letting him more and more, my body opening up, craving him.

"Oh, god," he said, pulling away slightly. I could feel a trickle of saliva roll down my crack. "You feel like velvet. You taste like sweet cream."

Then his tongue returned again, making my body shiver and rock from the sensations that were blurring my mind and shocking my senses.

At the sound of his fly unzipping and him moaning into my ass, I knew he had started to pleasure himself while pleasuring me. Suddenly I wanted nothing more than to do it for him. I was surprised at my desire—after what I'd been put through, I'd never wanted a cock near me or my mouth. But now I wanted him. I wanted to see him naked, see his cock, see what he looked like, wrap my fingers, lips, tongue around him and give him the same kind of ecstasy he was giving me.

But there was no time for that because he was just as skilled as he was relentless. His mouth and fingers brought me to the edge of a frenzy, the pressure building inside me from so many different sources that it had to give. My arousal splintered, rocketing through my body in hard, violent waves. I cried out, yelling Javier's name, my hands curling into fists behind my back, pulling against the cuffs.

He came too, loud, angry sounding grunts, but I was so far gone I barely heard him. I was swept away on that ship of emotions again, keeping pace with my body that was still spasming into his mouth and hand. I was so overwhelmed by everything rushing to the surface that I found myself sobbing quietly into the bed as the world ebbed and flowed around me.

There was a long pause, then his zipper went back up.

He placed his hand gently on the small of my back. "Luisa," he said, his voice throaty but touched with concern, "are you all right? Did I hurt you?"

I shook my head. "No," I mumbled into the soft bedspread. "I'm fine."

The truth was, I didn't know if I was fine or not. I didn't know anything except I had experienced something so achingly familiar it brought my head back to a moment in my life. What I felt just then was the same thing I used to feel when I drove to work in Cabo San Lucas, when the sea air flew in through my open window and I felt I was more than my reality, as if I were an element like the sun and water. Something simple and whole and everlasting.

I just never imagined that something like sex—or whatever just happened—could make me feel that way. It made me feel like a fucking queen. A rush of anger went through me as I cursed Salvador for nearly ruining me, for tricking me into thinking pleasure was one-sided, that sex was such a horrid, disgusting, cruel act. I could have died with that in my heart, never knowing the truth.

Javier's hands were at my wrists now and I heard him undo the cuffs, carefully taking them off. My arms burned in pain as I tried to bring them forward, and he gently eased me over onto my back, running his hands down my arms calmingly before removing the blindfold from my eyes.

I blinked rapidly at the intrusion of light, my eyelashes wet from the weak tears. I looked up at Javier's face as he leaned over me, his cheeks flushed, his hair messy, his eyes glazed. He smiled shyly and put his hand on my cheek. "My darling. You're going to be my undoing."

...

Javier

She looked so soft and delicate beneath me that I had meant what I said. Her beauty, her very essence, the way she cried out my name as she came around me, they were starting to fray my ends. It was only in that very moment that it didn't frighten me because my own completion was still rippling through my body. If only my cartel could figure out how to export this kind of high.

Granted, I'd much rather have made her come first then thrust myself inside her. My hand was getting a bit tiresome, and I knew how velvety soft and slick she'd feel around my dick. I wanted to shoot my semen high inside her and then watch it all run out between her legs and onto the sheets. She needed to be stained on the inside.

But that wasn't an option. If I fucked her, if I even kissed her, I would lose control of everything I kept chained together. It had happened years and years ago—with Ellie—and I wouldn't, couldn't, let it happen again. I had paid too dearly a price.

Still, the wetness around her eyes, the pretty way her mouth parted as she stared at me, was making it hard, in more ways than one. Even earlier, when she fell asleep with her head on my shoulder, the smell of her hair intoxicating me, I didn't have the courage to make her move. I enjoyed every second of the ride home.

And now, she was here. In my home. Everyone said it was a mistake to bring her here, but I didn't care in the slightest. Their opinions had become so tiresome and predictable. The fact was, she would be safest here. This was my throne. This was where I held all the power and all the control.

It would be nice to have a queen, even if just for a week.

"I'm sorry," she said.

I stared down at her in confusion, tucking a few strands of sex-mussed hair behind her ear. "Why?"

"For doubting you."

I smiled. "Most women do doubt...*that*. But if they're brave enough to be open-minded and own their sexual curiosities, they are greatly rewarded."

Her forehead furrowed slightly and I realized that alluding to other women probably wasn't something she wanted to hear. Oh well, I wasn't going to pretend I hadn't fucked a million women.

I cleared my throat. "Do you want to take a bath or something? I have a large Jacuzzi. I have a lot of things here you may enjoy."

She shook her head. "Am I sleeping here?"

I slowly sat up, distancing myself from her a bit. "No. You have your own room. Down the hall. I can assure you it is much nicer than the shithole you were in before."

She smiled weakly and I helped her into a sitting position. She tugged on her dress, covering up her perfect breasts. "The other place wasn't so bad..."

"Perhaps not to you," I said. "You've only known luxury a short while."

She tilted her head and looked me closer in the eye.

"What?" I asked, alluding to her intrusive gaze.

"Tell me about your sisters," she said. "The ones who are alive."

My face must have fallen because she looked ashamed and quickly said, "I'm sorry. That sounded callous. I meant, tell me about Alana and Marguerite."

I bristled. It wasn't exactly a favorite subject. I wondered why she was digging around. Was she trying to get information to use against me down the line, to hurt the rest of my family? My paranoia still fit me like a glove.

It was a glove that had kept me alive.

"I'm just curious," she said softly, looking away. "Never mind."

"It's fine," I said, smoothing on my mask. The last thing I wanted was for her to know what affected me. "What do you want to know?"

She shrugged. "Where do they live, what do they do, what are they like?"

"Well, they are both very pretty. Twins, you see. Which also makes them major pains in the ass. In the past, we weren't so close, but after Violetta...we became closer. I try and talk to them every month or so. I offer to send them money but they rarely accept it." I shrugged. "It's a good thing, I guess. Alana is a flight attendant in Puerto Vallarta. Marguerite is in New York City."

"Wow."

"I suppose," I said, absently running my hand over the bedding. "It seems so cliché to me, to go live in that city. She fell in love with some filmmaker and I guess he treats her well. I don't know. She comes to visit Alana once in a while, but I am not sure if they are even close anymore."

"Do you love them?"

I shot her a sharp look. "Of course I do. Why would you ask that?"

She didn't say anything. I took the opportunity to turn the tables on her.

"Tell me about your parents."

She gave me a wry smile. "Oh, I see how this works."

"Give and take," I said matter-of-factly. "You should know this by now."

She nodded and her face crumpled a bit as she opened up. "My parents are lovely, loving people. Even though we grew up with nothing, they gave me everything they could. I wasn't an unhappy child. You're not unhappy when you have unconditional love. They made sure I had every opportunity that was available to me, and even though I knew how the other half lived, I didn't want for much. Then," she closed her eyes, "then my father started acting differently. My mother, she's blind, you see, and my father was always able to work enough to support us all, even though I helped out when I could. But now he was forgetting things, slipping into trances. One day I forced him to a doctor and they told us he was developing Alzheimer's." She took a deep breath and turned slightly away from me. "It set in pretty fast. He is—or he was—getting worse by the day. I had plans for university, you know. I was hoping that the money from the pageant I had won and maybe a scholarship would get me to school. But I couldn't do that. I couldn't be that selfish."

I shook my head vigorously, hating her selflessness. "Oh, but you should be, my darling."

"But I'm not," she said sharply. "So I forgot about that and decided to get a full-time job. I was lucky enough to work at Cabo Cocktails for three years. I was able to keep my job with a bit of...luck." A flash of disgust came across her face then vanished. "I took care of my family. I paid for everything. I did everything I could for them, just so they could be happy. I think I made them happy. I pray I made them proud."

I could feel the sadness leaking out from her heart. I couldn't help but be tainted by it.

"And how was your job?" I asked.

She shrugged. "It was a job."

"Was your boss nice?" I asked because I knew the types of men who ran those kinds of places, who hired women who looked as gorgeous as she did.

She pressed her lips together. "Bruno taught me that men were wicked and unkind."

I swallowed a pit of hate. "Did he rape you?"

She shook her head. "No. He didn't. But...he did other things. Not just to me, most of the other girls were...subjected to his advances. But he did seem to have a special fondness for me. I don't know why. Perhaps because he figured I was a virgin."

My blood started pumping hot, my face prickling with heat. "I'm going to bring you his head one day," I told her with one hundred percent conviction.

She gave me a wry look. "It's in the past. It doesn't matter anymore."

I rubbed the back of my neck, feeling the strain build up. "It matters. It all matters. Jesus. Luisa, your life has not been fair. Doesn't that anger you?"

"No," she said earnestly. "What's the point of yelling at the sky, it's not fair, it's not fair? It doesn't change anything."

She didn't seem to understand the power her rage could give her. "But if you get angry enough, it could change everything." Our eyes held each other. "I think I'd like you if you were angry. Very angry."

"Would you like me to start with you?"

I bit my lip, wanting her to unleash on me. It would be gorgeous. "Yes."

She smiled stiffly. "Maybe some other time." She got off the bed, rubbing her arms up and down. I couldn't tell if she was cold or she was bringing life into her tired muscles.

"It's been a long day," I said, feeling strangely awkward. I got up too and adjusted my suit before gesturing to the door. "I'll take you to your room."

She complied and we didn't say a word to each other as I took her by the arm and down the hall. Her eyes took in the photography of world landscapes that I had adorning the walls in gilded frames, noted the various closed doors that all led to guest and employee rooms.

Finally we came to her room, and I led her inside, flicking on the lights. It wasn't exceedingly large, but it had a lovely en suite bathroom with a claw-foot tub and brass fixtures, walls with moldings, and a large four-poster bed, much like mine. An antique desk and chair were placed in front of the bay windows that overlooked the pool and hot tub in the gardens of the backyard. She'd be more impressed when the morning came and she saw the beauty around her more clearly.

I let her go and nodded to her clothes that were already hanging in her closet. I had called ahead and gotten the gardener,

Carlos, to go out and fetch her some brand new ones as well, items that were properly fitted to her body. The man sure sounded embarrassed when I gave him his orders—I'd made him buy undergarments as well.

"If you need anything," I said, walking toward the door, "the phone by your bed is a direct line to my room."

She looked at me blankly, perhaps just overwhelmed. That couldn't be helped. I put my hand on the knob, ready to turn it.

"Wait," she said in a small voice.

I turned to look at her. "Yes?"

She glanced at the bed. "Do you think...do you think maybe you could sleep with me?" I frowned. "Or, or just stay until I fell asleep."

I straightened my shoulders, not allowing myself weakness. "I would if I could."

"But you can," she said, taking a step toward me. "You can do anything. You're the boss."

And a boss still has to answer to himself.

"Goodnight, Luisa," I told her, locking her in her new cell.

CHAPTER FIFTEEN

Javier

I was having a nightmare. I was on the fishing boat with my father, only I wasn't a boy anymore. I was the way I was now, thirty-two and wearing a suit. My father looked old, far too old to be alive, and had a Panama hat on his head. Every fish he reeled in he injected with a syringe, some kind of red poison, and threw them back. Soon, the whole ocean was filled with floating, bloated, dead fish everywhere you could see.

He ended up catching something really big on his line, enough that the whole boat started to tip over. When he finally managed to reel it in, we saw it wasn't a fish at all.

Luisa was hanging on the end of the line, her neck broken. The giant hook was through her throat and blood poured down from the wound, staining her body red. Her eyes were lifeless, like the dead fish that were slowly turning as red as she was.

"What part of her do you want to eat first?" my father asked me with a bloody smile.

I thought I woke up screaming. But it wasn't my screams at all that I was hearing.

They were Luisa's.

In a second I was in my pajama pants, a .38 Super in one hand, and I was running down the dim hallway toward the room I had put her in earlier. I kicked down the door, not even bothering to open it, and to my utter horror, I only saw Luisa's legs on the floor, sticking out from alongside the other side of the bed. Franco's beefy form was over her, his face grinning. I couldn't see what he was doing, but I could guess.

Guesses were good enough for me.

I aimed the gun and shot him in the stomach, wanting the fucker alive. He howled, and before I knew what I was doing, I was running across the room and shoving him off of Luisa and tackling him to the ground. He tried to get up, but I head-butted him, breaking his nose. I pistol-whipped the same spot I did earlier, then quickly frisked the weapons off of him. I tossed them away and rolled his heavy, writhing body to the side. The rage, the living anger I had inside of me, was threatening to completely take over, something I rarely let it do, but I had to take care of Luisa first.

Then there would be no helping me.

I looked to her, my eyes wild, mouth open. She was grabbing her throat and coughing, trying to sit up, both cheeks red and swollen from where he had hit her. Her shirt was up around her breasts, and her underwear was crooked, halfway down her thighs.

Jesus Christ. If I hadn't gotten here in time...

"Luisa," I whispered, reaching for her. She looked at me with fear, total and utter fear, and tried to scoot backward and away from me. The bed and nightstand was blocking her exit.

I raised my palms as I went toward her on my knees. "Luisa, it's okay," I said as calmly as I could. It wasn't easy. "I'm not going to hurt you."

She shook her head, panicking, her hands clawing at the sheets as if she were trying to climb up on the bed. I gently grabbed her arm, but she pulled it away and started shaking uncontrollably, tears streaming down her face.

I was frozen in my own form of panic. I was watching her destruct. I was watching her break. And it hadn't been me who broke her.

"You promised," she gasped between her heaving sobs, crying into the side of the bed. "You promised."

Her words sliced through me like the slickest blade. I had promised. I promised I wouldn't let anyone hurt her. I promised to protect her.

I broke my promise. And by doing so, I ended up breaking her after all.

Suddenly Este was beside me, trying to make a grab for her. I could hear The Doctor behind me, peering over Franco, remarking on my shot, how long it would take for him to die. But I remained there on my knees, stuck in that moment where I finally ruined Luisa. The coldest, blackest rage had a hold on me, and after a while, it was all I could feel.

Fury became my captor. My hands were bound in shame.

Eventually, The Doctor pulled me up to my feet and poured a vial of bitter liquid in my mouth, moving my jaw so I would swallow it. I could barely stand and found myself pitching over but The Doctor held me up. He was saying things but I couldn't hear anything above the blood roaring in my ears. Fragments of my nightmare came rushing back.

"So what are your plans with him?" The Doctor asked. His words found their way into my ear, sinking in for the first time and penetrating the fog.

I looked to him in slow surprise. I was sitting in my chair in my office, The Doctor across from me, smoking a cigar. "Oh, so you're finally here," he said with a nod. "Nice of you to join the real world, Javier."

"Where is Luisa?" I asked thickly, taking in my surroundings, wondering how catatonic I had been.

"Don't worry about her," he said with a flick of his wrist. "She's with Este and Juanito in the kitchen. She's drinking tea. She's a little bruised but she's fine otherwise."

Fine? He hadn't seen her destruction the way I had. That strong, beautiful woman folded over from too many years of fear.

I couldn't stop seeing her eyes.

"Franco didn't get a chance to rape her," The Doctor went on, smiling slyly. "But I still think we should let him suffer, don't you?"

"As much as humanely possible," I said, my jaw clenching. My hands kept opening and closing, making fists. "I want to do everything that I told him I would do."

"Either he wanted to test you or he had a death wish. Regardless, the man is a dumb fool and we don't need dumb fools in our family, now do we?"

I shook my head absently, not really listening. I was already fantasizing about my revenge. I looked over at him. "You can revive him, right, if he dies or passes out?"

He chuckled. "Well, I can't revive him if you remove his head, so save that for last."

"That is the plan."

He got up, a gleeful tone to his voice. "Tell me what tools you need and I'll set things up in my office."

The Doctor's office was in the small guest cottage on the property. It's actually where the Doctor lived. I wanted his torture house to be as far away from me as possible. Screams were so disturbing when you were trying to eat dinner, though now I wished his office wasn't soundproof. I decided I would leave the doors and windows open and let everyone hear exactly what we were doing to Franco.

"I want a saw," I said. "A very rough, strong saw. The kind that really rips flesh and gristle and bone. I want a jar of acid, something to dip toes and fingers and tongues in. I want a cattle prod. I want a red hot poker. My Taser gun."

"I see. Would you also like a rat and a bucket? Medieval torture never goes out of style." He went over to the door. "Franco is unconscious upstairs, but I'll get him down. I stopped the bleeding because I wasn't sure what you wanted to be done with him. He'll be awake and ready for you by the time you come by."

I swallowed hard, the anger continuing its course up and down my body, firing off in electric flames. I was going to make Franco pay. I was going to make him regret he ever looked in her direction. Then I was going to make Luisa see what I do to those who hurt her. I was going to make her look at him. And then she'd know exactly what I'd do for her.

This was all for her.

...

Luisa

The screaming started at four in the morning, about two hours after Franco had attacked me, and continued on well into the afternoon. At first it rattled me, bringing back memories of being at Salvador's and the torture I had to hear, and it kept me from sleeping.

Not that I could sleep at first anyway. I knew Este and Juanito were always around, watching me. I suppose their job now was to protect me since Javier was out exacting torture, but that didn't mean I trusted them. Who would protect me from them? Still, Juanito seemed safe enough, maybe because he was young and reminded me of a boy I grew up with. And to his credit, Este didn't appear to hold any grudges over me attacking him again.

After a while though, I was able to rest, my head on the island in the middle of the chef's kitchen. When I woke up around ten a.m., light streaming in the kitchen, Juanito was serving me tea and toast, the latter which I refused. I had no appetite. It was then that I noticed the screams were still coming from the cottage—the doctor's office—though they were weak now and sporadic. They no longer had an effect on me. I was able to ignore them, and perhaps, if I was honest with myself, I was starting to enjoy them.

Just a little bit.

I had been lying awake in bed, daydreaming about a life I never had, when Franco came and knocked on my door. At first I thought it was Javier, coming to stay the night with me. It was so embarrassing when he turned me down, and I hated myself for being so needy and vulnerable in front of him. I just didn't want to be alone. I had my reasons and my reasons all came true.

Once I saw it was Franco, I screamed. I could see it in his eyes, that vile tar, that blackness, what he had come for. I expected him to lumber toward me with his injured foot, but he was fast. He threw me out of bed and onto the floor, and after he punched me a few times, my cheekbones taking most of the hits, he started strangling me with one hand. With his other hand he squeezed my breasts painfully and started to yank down my underwear.

With Salvador, I had learned to stop fighting back. I learned to stop struggling. He had always told me it was his right as my husband to do whatever he wanted to me and that I had to do whatever he wanted to him. Even if I had been one of his whores, he would probably say the same thing. It was his right simply because he was Salvador Reyes.

But I wasn't going to let Franco rape me, not without a fight. So I struggled. It was all in vain. His grip on my throat was so strong that I felt all the life drain out of me. The edges of my vision grew black as I gasped for breaths that I couldn't take in. I thought I was going to die on that floor, completely helpless while he had his way with me.

The thought of dying like that did something to me. It made me so afraid that I couldn't even function.

When Javier came in and shot Franco and I was free, my first instinct was to get away, to escape. All the formalities and politeness, and yes, lust that Javier seemed to show for me didn't seem to matter anymore. He was supposed to protect me, and I was a fool to believe a lion would ever shelter a lamb, especially from his own pride.

But, of course, there was nowhere for me to go. There was no escape from the golden prison. So Esteban and Juanito took me down into the elaborate, shiny-clean kitchen where they looked me over and took care of my bruises. And as they did so, as the screams of Franco began to ricochet throughout the surrounding jungle, a dark mass against the hazy blue of the pre-dawn sky, my fear began to melt away. It began to change inside me, as if all the chemicals were taking new forms and shapes.

My fear turned into anger. And when I woke up to Franco's waning screams of agony, I let the anger wrap around me like a cloak.

Javier had asked why I wasn't angry enough.

It was because I didn't let myself be.

But now, it was a part of me. The coil had unraveled. And I wasn't letting it go anywhere. Not anymore.

I was halfway through the cup of tropical green tea—judging by the excess amount of boxes in the cupboards, I gathered it was Javier's favorite—when the Devil himself showed up, standing in the hallway.

Javier had never looked worse. His white dress shirt was stained with blood, as were his jeans. He had circles under his eyes, his hair was messy and damp, and his gaze was blank, as if he were sleepwalking, even though he was looking right at me.

"Luisa," he said in a rough, strained voice. "Would you like to see what I've done to him?"

I stared right back at him.

"Yes," I said without hesitation.

He looked taken aback for a moment—perhaps he wasn't expecting me to want this. But I did. I wanted to see what justice looked like. I wanted to see what his anger was capable of.

He glanced briefly at Esteban and Juanito, perhaps delivering wordless orders. I got out of my chair and joined him at his side. We walked down the tiled hallway, past large rooms that held many secrets, until Javier opened the French doors out into the blinding brilliance of the backyard.

The gardens around the lawn and the pool area were absolutely beautiful and impeccably landscaped with the most exotic and colorful flowers you could imagine. There were bushes of red bougainvillea and white gardenia, pink plumeria, blue and purple orchids, magenta and yellow hibiscus, and birds of paradise, all of them expertly blending into the lush green grass and flowerbeds. Hummingbirds and butterflies filled the air, and dragonflies darted above a pond filled with koi fish and floating white lotus.

For a moment I was so stunned by their beauty and elegance, how tenderly cultivated and cared for they were, how seamlessly they seemed to thrive, that I forgot why we were outside. But beyond the dazzling blooms and shining heat of the morning sun, there were cries of pain and a man being tortured, and I was yanked back into reality.

I wanted to say something to Javier, ask about the garden, tell him how gorgeous it was, but now was not the time. As usual, I was caught between beauty and depravity.

I'd be lying if I said I wasn't a bit fearful as we approached the cottage, the door wide open, beckoning us into the darkest places. Javier put his hand at my elbow and gently pulled me to a stop just outside.

"Are you sure you can handle this?" he asked, his eyes focusing on my bruises.

I raised my chin. "Yes. Don't worry about me."

He squinted at that, studying me, perhaps worrying after all.

"Very well," he said. "Come on in."

The first thing I noticed when we stepped inside was the strong smell of ammonia that burned the inside of my nostrils.

The second thing was how spotlessly clean the room was, considering the messy state Javier was in.

The third thing was what made me fall ever so slightly into Javier. His hands went to my shoulders, and he held me up, and I willed myself to stay conscious, to take it all in, even though it was all too horrible to take.

On a metal table in the middle of the doctor's office, lay Franco. He was completely naked—but he wasn't *complete.* His feet and hands were gone, bloody, cauterized stumps in their wake. His genitals had also been removed in a choppy, ragged manner. His torso was covered in hundreds of festering burn marks. Remarkably, he was alive. His head was propped up in a vise-like clamp that pressed down on his head and up on his jaw, his eyes staring at me, dull and milky.

The doctor was standing over him with a syringe poised at his heart, ready to inject him with the drug that would prevent him from losing consciousness. Judging from the amount of needle marks on his chest, this had been done many, many times.

The closest thing I had seen of torture myself was when Salvador was about to perform the "double saw" on an informant. It was enough to see the man, hung naked from his feet, upside down, with the saw positioned between his legs. I knew that was one of the most gruesome torture techniques, and I thanked my lucky stars I had gotten out of there before I saw any blood spill.

What Javier did didn't seem that much better. And because Franco was still alive, I knew it wasn't over yet.

"Take a good look at him," Javier said in my ear. "Look at his face. Look at the monster that he is."

I did. And I didn't just see Franco. I saw Salvador too. I saw Salvador's men. I saw Bruno. I saw all the men who ever wronged me, all the faceless cartel men out there who were wronging women left and right.

And I tried to imagine seeing Javier there, too. After all, he had kidnapped me, tortured me, humiliated me, and in the end, broke his promise to protect me.

But I just couldn't. The man had a hold on me that I couldn't even begin to understand.

"Franco," the doctor said to him. "That over there is Luisa. Do you remember what you did to her? What you wanted to do to her? Javier warned you, did he not? You were a dumb fool for breaking the rules—all along you knew this was the price you'd have to pay." The doctor looked at me, his voice chillingly glib. "Luisa, if you can perhaps give him a smile. It will be the last thing he sees."

I wasn't sure how it was possible, but I managed to plaster a smile on my face. It might have even reached my eyes.

"How beautiful," the doctor commented. Then he reached over, and with two quick twists of a lever on top of the clamp, it tightened around his head. There was a crunch as all the teeth in Franco's jaw shattered, blood pooling out of his mouth and onto his throat, then a faint, wet pop as his eyeballs fell out of his sockets, dangling by their optic nerves.

That was all I needed to see. I turned around, glancing up at Javier who was watching me with an unreadable expression.

"I'm ready to go now," I said quietly.

Javier nodded and looked over me at the doctor. "Keep him alive for a bit longer. Then remove his head. With the knife, not the saw."

"Yes, Javier," the doctor said, a trace of awe in his voice.

I stepped out back into the sunshine and heat and the birds that called out their beautiful song from the nearby trees. Had all that just happened? How did so much ugliness co-exist with this?

"You must be tired," Javier said to me, gently leading me back the way we came, down the groomed gravel path that took us past the pond and gardens and back to the house.

"I'm okay," I said. Truth was, I felt like a million tons of caffeine was moving through me. It must have been the adrenaline. I was amazed I wasn't throwing up.

As we passed by the pond, Javier nodded at the lotus blossoms.

"Those are my favorite, you know," he commented. It was as if everything in the cottage had been a dream.

"The lotus?" I asked. Despite everything, I couldn't help but admire them again. "They are beautiful."

"Yes, they are." He stopped and stared at the flowers for a few moments. "I love the lotus because while growing from mud, it is unstained," he said, as if he were reading something aloud. He glanced at me. "A Chinese scholar once said that. I agree. It represents everything that I am not."

We started walking again. We were almost at the house when I said, "You must feel your soul is dirty then."

He gave me a wry smile. "Oh, my darling. No," he said, opening the French doors for me. "I don't even have a soul."

CHAPTER SIXTEEN

Luisa

For the rest of the day, I was given free rein of the house. I wasn't sure why—maybe Javier was extra confident in his security, or perhaps with Franco gone, he believed I had nothing to fear. I didn't know, but I did take every moment to explore what I could.

Downstairs was a game room with leather couches and a bar. There was a dart board on the wall and a billiard table in the middle. It was styled to look like one of those gentlemen's clubs: lots of dark mahogany, green-glass lamps, and gold fixtures. I stayed in that room for a long time. It was quiet in there, and the heavy curtains blocked out all the light from the outside. I wondered how often Javier used the room, if he came here to escape, have a drink, pull a limited edition hardcover book from the shelves and immerse himself in it. I wondered what kind of a life he had day to day, when he didn't have a hostage in his house.

Hostage. The word was starting to sound foreign. I was still a hostage, his captive, and yet when the word ran through my head, it had no meaning. I wasn't anything anymore...I was just me and I was just here.

After some time, I went to investigate the other rooms on the main floor. There was a small but state-of-the-art gym, some guest bathrooms and bedrooms, a large, immaculate dining room that housed a table that could fit at least twenty people, an open living room with a flatscreen TV built into the wall, and the kitchen.

Upstairs there were more bedrooms, as well as a few doors that didn't open, and one door that I didn't even try.

From that door I could hear Javier's voice on the other side, talking to Esteban. I couldn't make out what they were saying—the door was thick and their voices were muddled—but I knew it must have been Javier's office.

I kept walking past it, not caring what they were saying. They were probably discussing me, about what was to be done with me when the week was over. I wondered if Javier was at all having a dilemma over Salvador's upcoming deal, if he was still planning to shoot me in the head, or if torturing Franco had awakened some kind of appetite.

I wondered if it was scaring him. When I asked him to stay with me last night, I wasn't the only one who had been afraid. For one quick moment, like a burst of lightning, I saw fear in his eyes.

I made sure not to forget it.

Later, I ended up falling asleep on my bed, a science magazine I had snatched from downstairs open on my lap. It was dark out and my stomach was growling. I vaguely remembered Esteban coming into my room and telling me there was dinner for me, but I was so out of it he must have let me keep sleeping. I suppose I had been more exhausted by everything than I thought.

I glanced at my bedside clock. It was eleven p.m. I'd crashed for hours.

I groaned, trying to shake the grogginess out of my head. For a moment I thought about my parents, wondering where they were, if they were still being taken care of. The caretaker made them go to sleep at ten every night, but I knew sometimes my mom stayed up later, listening to her audiobooks.

My heart clenched at the thoughts and I had to willfully force them away, otherwise, I would weaken. There was no time for weakness anymore.

I got up slowly and changed out of my rumpled clothes, and into a camisole and boy shorts that had magically appeared in my dresser drawers. They were lilac and made of the finest silk, fitting my body like they were made for me. I used the washroom, splashed water onto my face and combed back my hair, then opened the door to the hall. To my surprise it opened, which meant I was still allowed to be free. I smiled to myself and quietly padded down the hall. The house was still, and I wondered if I could raid the kitchen for something to eat without waking anybody. Obviously there was a security system set up and cameras everywhere which relayed to a guard somewhere, but I didn't care if they saw me getting a late night snack.

When I passed by Javier's office, I saw his door was open a crack. The light inside was on, spilling faintly into the hall. I thought this odd since everything Javier did seemed to happen behind closed doors.

I paused, listening, and heard the clink of glass. Taking a deep breath, I gently pushed the door open.

There was a click and I saw Javier sitting behind his desk, a gun pointed straight at me.

I froze.

"Oh," he said, his voice sounding odd, "it's just you."

He quickly put the gun away and picked up the glass beside him. Ice cubes rattled in smooth, brown liquid. An antique bar globe was open, a half-empty bottle of scotch taking prominence.

"Sorry," I said breathlessly. My heart was still going a mile a minute from the image of the gun aimed at my head.

He nodded, not looking at me, and waved his glass at the room, scotch spilling over the rim. "Come in then, come into my office. Close the door."

I did so and took two steps into the middle of the room. I pretended to admire how tastefully it was all decorated, but instead I was studying him. Was Javier...drunk?

"I see you've found your new clothes," he said, his eyes feasting on my body, drinking me in like the booze at his lips. "You're gorgeous." He tossed the rest of his swill back and then wiped his hand across his mouth.

Yes. He was drunk.

I swallowed, feeling slightly nervous. I wasn't sure what Javier was like when he was drunk. Bruno became bold and disgusting when he had too much, while all of Salvador's vile actions were magnified. Javier was always so cool, calm and collected. To see him slightly unhinged threw me off.

That said, it was also intriguing. When one was drunk and the other sober, the sober one held all the cards and all the power.

"Are you okay?" I asked.

He tore his eyes from my body and poured himself another glass, nearly getting scotch on his elegant desk. "I'm fine. Why wouldn't I be?"

"You're drunk."

"I'm not," he said as his brows furrowed. "I'm just having scotch."

"Half a bottle of it."

He looked back at the bottle absently. "Oh. I already went through a full one earlier. Men like me must know how to control their liquor."

"Men like you," I mused. I walked over to the desk, completely conscious of the fragile garments I was wearing. I placed my hands on the desk and leaned down, staring at him. "Tell me more about men like you."

He must have caught the cynical tone of my voice because he looked at me sharply. "What do you mean?"

"I mean," I said carefully, wanting to push his buttons but needing to be cautious at the same time, "tell me why a man like you is sitting alone in his office, getting drunk. Don't you have body parts to clean up in your torture chamber? Or is that the hired help's job? You seem to get them to do all your dirty work."

His mouth set firmly, and a muscle ticked along his jaw. "I don't enjoy telling a lady to shut up. But I'm not above it."

"And how do you do that?" I asked, unfazed and unwilling to break away from his simmering stare. "How would you shut me up?"

He ignored that. "Why are you here?" he asked in a measured voice.

"I was just curious as to how my captor was doing. You had such a busy morning, chopping off limbs and such."

Suddenly he was out of his chair and leaning across the desk, his glass of scotch sloshing over. His face was inches from mine. I could see the flecks of brown in his amber irises. If I looked hard enough, I wondered if I could find that soul that he pretended he didn't have.

"Do you think I enjoyed that?" he growled, grinding his teeth. The smell of alcohol and tobacco wafted toward me.

I didn't move. "Yes. I think you did."

"I did it for you."

A smile tugged at my lips. "I think you also did it for you. I think you enjoyed giving Franco what he deserved."

He frowned but didn't back off. "So what if I did? He deserved everything he got. I told him that, I warned him what would happen if he ever touched you again. I never make empty threats."

"Why did you care so much if he touched me?"

He blinked, swallowing hard. "Because you're mine," he said, as if this was common knowledge.

"Because you carved your name in my back?"

He looked at a loss for words. He shook his head briefly. "No."

"Then why?"

He broke away and flopped down in his chair, staring off at a painting on the wall. "You should go back to bed."

"I'm not going anywhere," I told him. I walked around the desk so I was blocking his view. "If you think I'm yours, then you have to deal with me."

"You're becoming a pain in the ass."

"But you like my ass *so* much."

He glared at me. "What are you doing? What do you want from me?"

I went right up to him and hunched over so I was at eye level. He wasn't going to escape me that easily. He was drunk and he was close to breaking.

"I want to know why you're drunk." I cocked my head. "Is it because of me?"

He looked away from my gaze and didn't say anything.

"Is it?" I prodded, my voice rising. "Is it because of me?" I shoved at his shoulders. "Answer me, dammit!"

His eyes widened and I saw that fear in them again as he looked at me. "Yes," he said, barely audible.

"What?"

"I said yes!" he bellowed, grabbing me roughly by my arms as he shot up out of his chair. "Yes, fucking yes, it's all because of you!"

Even though his eyes were enraged, there was a vein pulsing along his throat, and his hold on my arms was tight, I wasn't afraid.

But he was.

"Why?" I asked.

His brows knit together in confusion. "Because I broke a promise. I never break those. That's not *me*."

I stepped closer into him so my chest was nearly against his. His perplexed look deepened. "I don't think you know yourself quite as well as you think you do."

His voice lowered. "Is that right? Well, then you tell me who I am, since you know me so well," he said tauntingly.

I rubbed my lips together, and I saw the way he focused on them hungrily. His breathing was heavy now, like he was fighting to keep himself together. I didn't want him together. I wanted to undo him.

"You're afraid," I whispered.

"Afraid of what?" he asked incredulously.

"Afraid of me."

He snorted in open disbelief. "Ridiculous. You?"

I looked at him more closely, until he was all I could see, and I was all he could see. "Yes. Me. You were afraid to stay with me last night, you're afraid of what you'll have to do at the end of the week, you're afraid to see me as a human fucking being. Afraid, afraid, afraid!" I angrily jabbed my finger into his chest. "You're nothing but a coward!"

His nostrils flared, and for one small breath I worried I made a mistake, that the beast would be unleashed and he would hurt me.

But a different beast was unleashed altogether.

He grabbed my face, his fingers pressing into my jaw, and kissed me so hard that it stole my breath. It was quick and violent and his lips were soft only for a second before he pulled away, breathing hard. He stared at me in thinly veiled shock, as if he couldn't believe he had done that.

My lips tingled from his absence and I tried to regain my footing in our battle.

But I couldn't think and there was no time.

His eyes sharpened with intensity, and suddenly he grabbed me again, this time one hand behind the back of my head and the other around my waist, jerking me toward him. My chest pressed up against his so tightly I could feel the rapid beating of his heart through his shirt and tie.

His lips engulfed mine, hungry, eager and wild. He kissed me deeply, thoroughly. Luxuriously wet. I felt like my feelings were sediment at the bottom of the sea, and he was shaking me loose, stirring me free, until it was swirling around both of us, clouding everything. I kissed him back, my pace easily matching his frenzied one, an appetite unleashed. Our tongues and lips melded like satin and sparks, and the more I got, the more I wanted.

My hands found their way into his hair, and I gripped his thick, silky strands, tugging on them until he whimpered softly into my mouth. He spun me around so I was leaning back against the desk, and I found myself writhing against him, trying to alleviate some of the pressure that was building between my legs.

He pulled away briefly, his eyes heavy-lidded, his mouth wet and parted, and quickly lifted me up in the air, placing me on the edge of the desk. He pulled down my camisole so my breasts were free and tended to them while he started ripping off his tie.

I grabbed the back of his head and yanked him closer to me as his lips encircled my nipple, sucking deeply at one then the other. I felt like I wasn't even myself, or maybe I was myself and I was just waking up. But I wanted things more dearly than I'd ever wanted them before. I didn't even ask for them, I made them happen. Javier was awakening me.

He worked my nipples into hard peaks, flicking them until I was gasping with need. Then he stopped and looked up at me, that wonderful mouth of his grinning at me while he ripped off his shirt. "Is this what you want?" he asked hoarsely before continuing.

"It's what I need," I said, my words punctuated by my own groan.

"Then I'll give you everything," he said. He yanked the camisole over my head and kissed me passionately again, his mouth snaking down my neck, washing me with his tongue as he pushed me back on the desk. My head was resting uncomfortably on a stack of papers but I didn't care.

When his lips got to my stomach, I expected him to pull down the thin, lacy shorts I had on. Only he stepped back. I looked up to see him swiping a letter opener off the desk.

My eyes widened, and before I could say anything, he reached between my legs with the blade and made a quick slash down the center of my shorts. The edge of the metal didn't even come close to grazing my skin.

"I told you it was a hard-earned skill," he said slyly, stabbing the letter opener into the desk so it was sticking straight up. My god, even during foreplay there had to be knives around.

While I marveled over that with a mix of trepidation and excitement, he undid his pants, which only made those emotions double. He brought his cock out into his hands, hard, long, and judging by the look in Javier's eyes, somewhat dangerous. I breathed out slowly as I took in the sight of him. I thought by seeing him naked, he would be vulnerable in my eyes, but he was the complete opposite. His body was a fine-tuned machine and he owned it one hundred percent.

"You do realize," he said huskily, removing his pants, shoes, and socks until he was totally bare, "that once I go down this path with you, this is all I'm going to want, all the time."

"So I better like it then."

He grinned and it did funny things to my heart, just as the sight of his cock was doing funny things to my body. "My beauty queen, you know you'll like it. What you don't know is how much you'll *love* it."

Then his smile vanished and his expression was replaced by greedy lust again. He came forward, spreading my legs wider and climbing on the desk between them. "I'm going to fuck you and fuck you hard. I'll make sure you come, but I've been wanting to do this for a fucking long time and it's going to be rough. Do you understand?"

I nodded. "Yes."

"Yes, Javier."

"Yes, Javier," I said, though I couldn't help but smile.

"That's my good girl," he murmured as he started nibbling on my neck, sending shivers over my skin. His fingers entered the slit he created in my shorts. He slid his thumb over the swell, swirling it around until I let out a guttural moan. "But," he went on, biting my earlobe now, his breath hot, "what I really want is for the bad girl to come out." He paused and moved his face so it was right above mine, our lips inches from each other. "So, if you're feeling particularly...passionate...I invite you to hurt me the best that you can."

Before I could say anything to that, he reached down and wrapped his hand around his cock, positioning himself at my entrance. Instinctively I clenched up, afraid.

He put his hand to my face, his fingers trailing lightly over the bruises. "I'll go in slow," he said, assuring me with his confidence. "If I went in fast, this would be over in a minute."

With my heart in my throat, I nodded, and he slowly pushed himself in. Because I was tense, there was pain, but his movements were steady and controlled, and I soon found myself expanding, letting him inside. I ended up wrapping my legs around his waist.

"Good," he whispered, his eyes shutting in concentration. "Keep your legs and hips up, it will make it easier for you." He exhaled loudly and groaned. "Oh, Jesus, you feel so tight, it's like fucking an angel."

"I'm no angel," I said breathily, letting his width fill me.

"No. You're a queen." At that he thrust himself in, all the way to the hilt. My eyes flew open and I stared up at him while the realization that he was deep inside me hit. I didn't know what I was doing. But it felt so damn good, and so strangely right, that I didn't care.

I had let this man inside me.

It was going to be hard to get rid of him.

"Do I feel good?" he asked me, his impassioned eyes searching mine as he slowly pushed in and out, taking his sweet, torturous time, getting in deeper and deeper.

"Yes," I said, gasping, finding the need to both stare into him and look away. It was so intimate being able to gaze into his hypnotic eyes while he made me feel so alive and electric. "You feel good."

I didn't feel like I was very good at talking during sex but he didn't seem to care. His nostrils flared at that and he grunted. His breath was becoming shorter as were his thrusts into me. "I can make you feel more than good," he said.

He reached down between my legs and started stroking me. Now the pleasure was doubling throughout my body, from the wet swirls of his fingers to the thick fullness of him inside me. I loved watching his shaft drive in and out as he fucked me, loved the way his arms and shoulders rippled from the strain. I couldn't take the bliss anymore. It wasn't long before I was coming, crying out and digging my nails into his back.

"That's it," he grunted, "fucking scar me, mark me, make me bleed."

I dug my nails in further and rode out the wave just as he started picking up the pace. He was an animal. He started fucking me and fucking me hard, as he promised. I held on, even as the desk started to move from his strong, sharp thrusts and my head began to thump against the surface. It was turbulent and rough and half-crazed, and yet I was loving it. I loved watching Javier lose all control because of me.

The power felt incredible.

It wasn't long before he was coming and I made sure to take in every single detail. The way his brows scrunched up, his hair stuck to his sweaty face, and how he closed his eyes, his back arching. His jaw went rigid—every part of him went stiff—right before the violent release that had him groaning loudly and gasping for breath.

He collapsed on top of me, careful not to put his full weight on my body. His cock was still inside and I could feel the wetness start to trickle out of my legs. While he slowly regained his breathing, he propped himself on his elbows on either side of my shoulders and coaxed my hair behind my ears.

Javier was beautiful when he'd just come, when he was still inside me, softening. There was a gentleness to his eyes, an easiness to his smile. This was what I'd wanted to see all this time, just a glimpse of the boy behind the man, and the man behind the monster. He stared at me so tenderly and openly that I knew he had a soul. It didn't mean it wasn't stained and filthy, but it was there.

"So?" he asked, running his thumb over my lips. I could smell myself on his fingers. It was the smell of us together, good and bad, captive and captor.

I cleared my throat. "So," I repeated, finding my voice. My world was still a million spinning colors because of that orgasm.

"So I'm going to pick you up and bring you to my bed," he said simply. "And we're going to do that all over again."

I blinked. "Already?"

His mouth quirked up. "I warned you."

That was true. Still, I thought I'd be heading back to my room to be alone again. Even though that's not what I wanted last night, it was something I needed now. I needed time to separate myself from my hormones and reflect on what had happened with some distance and space. I needed to think about the power I earned and all the ways I needed to keep it, especially now that I knew my sex was his weakness.

But as I let him scoop me up into his arms and carry me, while he was naked, down the hall and into his bedroom, I realized he was my weakness as well.

I had the feeling that we weren't through with ruining each other.

CHAPTER SEVENTEEN

Javier

I woke up with a dry mouth and a pounding headache. I was hung over, something that didn't plague me very often. I rarely got drunk—you couldn't in this business, not when you were at the top.

But yesterday I had been a different man. I had become a man enslaved to shame. Not for what I did to Franco. I felt zero revulsion or regret over torturing that man. Even when he begged me to stop and I took out my dick and pissed on his gaping wounds, I didn't feel bad about that in the slightest.

No, my shame was because of Luisa, because I had failed to protect her and because I had broken my promise. I never made them in vain. I had meant what I said. As strong as she was, I knew there was a fragile casing underneath that could crack under the worst circumstances. All this time I wanted to break her, and the only way that I could have was by doing something I would have never made myself do.

I guess that said something about me, that I had a limit to my ruthlessness. But if I didn't have my own morals and my own code, who would? Someone out there had to lead by example.

I rolled my head over and took in the sight of Luisa sleeping beside me, pretty much hanging off the edge of the bed, her back to me. She was wearing one of my dress shirts, oversized on her petite frame, but I couldn't recall why. Perhaps because it looked fucking hot.

She seemed to be in a deep sleep, her sides rising and falling, her hair spilled around her on the pillowcase. Part of me yearned to reach out and feel it between my fingers, to wake her up by kissing her shoulder. But I had to keep those urges to myself. I was surprised I even let her sleep in my bed and hadn't sent her back to her room.

Memories of fucking her on the desk were followed by several rounds in the bed. That's why I didn't send her away.

In all reality, I made a mistake. A big one. I shouldn't have succumbed to her. I shouldn't have kissed her, shouldn't have fucked her. I knew it was a dangerous road to go on for me, to allow myself to be intimate with her, to be inside her. Watching her come while I was buried deep in her pussy was like a religious experience and it flamed my devotion. It spurred an addiction and made me insatiable for the next hit. It was in my nature to crave sex like I craved water, and I knew too well how cravings could derail even the most solid plans.

I exhaled through my nose, trying to focus on said plan instead of her. There was nothing wrong with a man having sex with a woman at his disposal, provided he would still be able to get rid of her at the end. It was expected of me, in fact, to be using Luisa every way I could. Most captives were treated far worse. The complication came at the end of the week, when she would be gone, one way or another.

But I just couldn't make myself think about that, about the hard choices that lay ahead. I had to believe I would do the best thing for me and my cartel. I would make the right choice, as ruthless as it would be. I had to trust that about myself and then let it go. The dilemma would be dealt with then and only then. Until her days were up and Salvador made his call, I was going to pretend that Luisa was here under different circumstances.

I was going to make the best of her.

Carefully, I eased myself out of bed, not wanting to wake her, and made my way to the bathroom. I flicked on the lights and briefly admired my naked reflection in the mirror. Though I boxed in order to beat any opponent—I'd lost a fight once and never intended that to happen again—I also did it to have my body look as good as possible. Judging from the hungry look in Luisa's eyes last night, it hadn't gone unnoticed.

I brushed my teeth, gargled mouthwash, and decided to run a bath and put on the Jacuzzi jets. My limbs were quite sore, not just from the sex but from the things I did to Franco. Rubbing a clit to completion and sawing off someone's foot seemed to use all the same muscles.

It wasn't long before there was a knock at the bathroom door.

"Yes?" I called out, craning my head to see.

The door opened and Luisa poked her head in. Once she spotted me in the bath, she looked flushed but she didn't leave. "Sorry," she said.

I smiled at her bashfulness. "Don't be sorry." I patted the rim of the tub. "Come over here."

She scurried across the tiles, my linen shirt billowing around her, and planted her perky bum beside me. She looked down into the tub and quickly looked away, a small smile on her lips. For obvious reasons—mainly the sight of her—I was already erect, the tip of my dick poking out of the moving water.

"How did you sleep?" I asked, my wet hand caressing her bare legs. I watched the goosebumps erupt on her flesh.

"Surprisingly well," she said.

"That shouldn't be surprising. I wore you out."

Her eyes went soft and held mine for what felt like an infinite amount of time. "Yes. You did."

I nodded at the water—well, at my erection—and skimmed my hand along the surface. "Come, join me."

She pursed her lips, seeming to think about it, before shaking her head.

I grinned at her. "That was a command, not a suggestion."

Before she could protest, I reached forward, put my arm around her waist, and pulled her down into the water. She cried out, half-laughing, as she plunged in on top of me, water splashing over the side of the tub. My shirt was immediately soaked, but I didn't give a fuck.

"Come here," I whispered, bringing her down on my chest, one hand gripped firmly behind her neck. I loved holding her here, so delicate, so powerless. I stared up at her face, the wet ends of her hair tickling my skin. Bringing her closer, I kissed her softly on the lips, teasing the rim of them with my tongue until she let me in. Even in the morning she tasted delicious.

I cupped her ass and gave it a firm squeeze, grunting a little. I needed to control myself—I was already so turned on, stiff and swollen, that the littlest thing could set me off. I had a reputation to keep.

"Ride me," I told her before I held her lower lip between my teeth and tugged. "Ride my cock. Impale yourself on it."

She raised her brows. It probably didn't sound hot to her but it sounded oh so fucking perfect to me. Sex needed to be a little rough and crude to balance out the elegance. A touch of tasteful violence goes a long way.

I reached down, moving my floating shirttails out of the way, and found her bare pussy. I pressed my fingers against her clit, applying just the right amount of pressure to get her started. Her lids drooped and a lazy smile graced her lips.

"You like that, don't you, my beauty?" I said, keeping my pace consistent as I slid my fingers down through her folds and teased the opening of her cunt. It was so tight, begging me to penetrate it, that I sucked in my breath in anticipation.

She nodded and I thrust a finger inside her, her body stiffening around it before relaxing. "Tell me you like it," I coaxed her.

"I like it," she said throatily, shutting her eyes and embracing the pleasure.

"Do you want my cock inside you?" I whispered, licking the shell of her ear.

She moaned, nodding quickly. "Yes."

"Then ride me like a queen." I put my hands around her hips and scooted her back. She grabbed onto the edge of the tub for support while I held her with one hand and kept my dick rigid with the other. She slowly, carefully, lowered herself onto me. It was excruciatingly deliberate, my balls tightening as my body already begged for release. Such a fickle beast it was.

She let out a breathy moan, her fuckable lips parting, and her head went back, exposing her throat. She felt like a velvet glove around me.

The sight of her riding me, my wet shirt clinging to her breasts, my cock going into her tight pussy, was almost too much to take. I kept a firm grip on her hips, holding her tight, so I was in charge. That was the thing about having a woman on top. They think they're in control, that they've got all the power, but that was never the truth. I was controlling this ride. Every thrust, movement, swivel—it was all mine.

I kept the pace slow, the rhythm easy, as the warm water splashed around us, the jets blasting against our skin. The sounds of our moans and heavy breathing echoed throughout the room, bouncing off the shiny glass and tiles. Just when I knew I couldn't take much more, I sat up slightly while keeping her on me. I put my thumb against her clit and reached around and teased her ass with my index finger.

She inhaled sharply but I merely grinned at her. "Keep the pace," I commanded as my finger pushed in between her cheeks. "I'll bring us both home."

She did, moving her hips continuously while I fingered her rosebud, her muscles contracting around me. From the way she sank deeper into my finger, I knew she was enjoying the stimulation, wanting more. I exhaled carefully, controlling my breathing as best as I could. When I was ready to come, I raised my knees so my hips slanted under her and simultaneously flicked her swollen clit back and forth.

She gasped, her eyes rolling back in her head and began crying out, loud as hell. God, I loved how vocal she was. Her body shuddered, and she clenched hard around my dick until I couldn't hold back. I grabbed her hips and kept her moving as she came until I was letting loose inside of her, coming in torrents.

Nothing in this world ever felt so fucking good.

I kept her rocking back and forth, slowing her gradually as her body grew limp from the exertion. Finally she fell on top of me, her breasts pressed against my chest, and she buried her face just below my ear. I heard her breath even out, felt the warmth of it soothe me. It was quiet and satisfied. It brought me a strange bit of peace, something I hadn't felt for a very long time.

We lay there for a long time, her breathing in my arms, until the jets shut off and we were surrounded by silence.

Silence that was quickly shattered by a knock at my bedroom door.

I covered Luisa's ears with my hands and yelled, "What do you want? I'm busy!"

I heard Este say something muffled and then my bedroom door opened. "I need to speak with you," he said.

"Well stay right the fuck where you are. I'm in the bathroom."

"Doing what?"

Luisa raised her head to give me a look and I let go of her ears. I gave her a sympathetic smile then hollered, "None of your fucking business! Give me a minute."

"I'll be in your office."

I heard my door click shut.

I groaned, straightening up in the tub. "Sorry," I said to her. "Business."

"Right," she said as she leaned back on her heels. "Business."

We exchanged a loaded look. We both knew what the business was.

I could see how our fucking was about to make things a lot more fucking complicated.

I quickly got out of the bath and dried off, wrapping the towel around me. "I'll come right back," I told her as she hoisted herself out so she was sitting on the edge of the tub, staring down at her feet in the water. "And you better be naked, lying on my bed with your ass in the air, waiting for me."

At that, I left her in the bathroom and quickly got dressed. Black silk shirt, black jeans. I hurried out my door, shutting it behind me, and went down the hall to my office.

Este was already sitting in the chair, making it swivel back and forth while he sipped on a Tecate.

"It's still early," I said, nodding at the beer as I came around the desk and sat down.

He took a swig and shrugged. "I've had a hell of a time the last few days."

I cleared my throat and folded my hands neatly on the desk. "Well, I suppose that makes two of us then."

He cocked a brow. "Oh yeah? I suppose all the sex is helping."

My eyes narrowed. He needed to be careful. Out of my peripheral I could see the letter opener sticking straight out of the desk. Then the memories of slamming Luisa on the desk last night began to seep into my brain.

"Oh, you've got it bad," he commented snidely after a moment.

I snapped to attention. "Why did you call me here, Este?"

"For obvious reasons. We need to talk about the girl."

"And why is that? Is she bothering you?" My hackles were going up. I couldn't help it.

"No, not me," he said, finishing the beer and putting it on the desk. I watched as the cold drops of condensation ran down the side, heading straight for the fine finish. I reached over and quickly slid a thin coaster under it before it was too late. My desk had been abused with too much scotch and cum last night as it was.

"Then who?" I asked.

"Well," he said, "she's making you bother me."

"Who told you to speak in riddles, Este?"

He leaned forward and looked me dead in the eye. "I'm afraid you're putting yourself and the cartel in jeopardy."

I sighed and pinched the bridge of my nose. "We have already been over this."

"But now you're fucking her."

"So? I know you fuck things too, on occasion. Whores and your hand."

"I'm worried you've been compromised."

I shook my head in disbelief. "I think you worry about all the wrong things, and I think you forget who you're talking to. Since when does fucking someone compromise anything? It's my damn right to use the hostage any way I please. Don't get all jealous just because I'm not sharing her."

"I'm not jealous," he said. "Not much, anyway." He eyed my half-empty bottle of scotch. "But you were drunk last night, which meant something had gotten under your skin. It wasn't what you did to Franco. It was what he did to her. And if that affected you, a little abuse and attempted rape, how the hell are you going to kill her when this is all over? Or deliver her to Salvador, if that ends up being the case? You won't."

My gaze grew flinty. "Don't tell me what I will or won't do. Remember what you used to say about assuming, how it makes an ass out of you and me. Don't be a fucking ass, even though you're so good at it."

"Funny," he said, slowly getting to his feet. "Anyway, I thought I'd bring it up again. I'd hate for the others to start thinking the same thing."

I got up too, pushing my chair back. "How about you let me worry about that?"

He gave me a self-assured look. "Just don't grow a mangina."

I snarled at him and unzipped my fly, swiftly bringing my dick out into my hands. "Does this look like a mangina to you?"

He blinked and looked away, shielding his face with this hand. "Jesus, Javier. Put that thing away."

I kept my cock out for a moment, stroking it once, before putting it back.

Este peeked through his fingers and lowered his hand when he saw it was safe. What a homophobe.

"Is it always hard," he asked, "or just when you're looking at me?"

"Just when I have a wet cunt in my bedroom, waiting for me to stop talking to you so I can go back and fuck it. What do you have?" I waved at him dismissively. "Why don't you go and enjoy your hand?"

He made a sound of displeasure and started to leave. "One more thing," he said, pausing before he opened the door.

"Yes, what now?" I asked curtly, resisting the urge to roll my eyes.

"Where is Luisa right now?"

I frowned. "I told you. In my room. Waiting to get fucked."

"Alone?" he asked, drawing out the word.

"Yes, *alone*," I said, mimicking him.

"How many guns do you keep in your room, Javi? A nine millimeter under your pillow. Your thirty-eight super in your drawer. An AR-fifteen under your bed. Am I right?"

I didn't say anything although my pulse quickened curiously.

"I'm just saying," Este said gravely. "Be careful when you open your door." He left the room with a morbid look on his face.

Shit.

But Luisa wouldn't shoot me. Would she?

Of course she fucking would, I told myself quickly. *She's still your fucking hostage and she'll do anything to escape.*

I exhaled sharply and picked up my pistol from underneath my desk, quickly checking the chamber. I really fucking hoped I wouldn't have to use this.

I left the office, seeing Este head down the stairs in the opposite direction. Some backup he would be anyway. I gripped the gun in my palm and eased myself down the hall toward my bedroom. I paused outside the door and put my ear to it, listening. I couldn't hear a thing.

Taking in a deep, steadying breath and hoping for the best, I quickly turned the knob, my gun down by my side, and pushed the door open with my shoulder.

Luisa was on her knees on the bed, naked, my 9mm in her hands and aimed right at me.

I automatically had my gun pointed back at her.

The sexiest Mexican standoff I'd ever been involved in.

"What are you doing?" I asked, taking a cautious step toward her, not lowering my gun for a second.

"Leaving," she answered, her eyes hard. She was distracting as all hell, her tits and pussy and that gun. I don't think I'd ever been so turned on so quick and in such an untimely situation.

"It doesn't look like it."

"I'm going to ask you nicely to let me leave, and if you don't, I'll shoot you."

A grin broke out across my face. My god, she couldn't be more perfect.

"If you shot me, you'd kill me," I said, taking another step. "Then who would make you come all the time?"

"My fingers," she said, her double grip on the gun tightening. "And I'd shoot you in the knees. I don't want to kill you. I'm not that bad."

I cocked my head. "No, you're not. But you could be."

Her face remained serious. "Please, Javier. Don't make me do this."

"Don't make *me* do this. You know the minute you shoot me, I'm going to have to shoot you. And I hate to brag, but I'm a terribly good shot, no matter the range. The odds of you hitting me, even from this close, are very low. Have you ever even fired one of those before?"

I could see she was taking aim at a spot right beside my head, perhaps to scare me, perhaps to kill me. "Easy!" I yelled at her quickly. "If you let that gun off, everyone in the house will be up here and I won't be able to protect you from them."

A venomous expression came across her dark eyes. "You didn't protect me before."

"And I have been paying dearly for it," I told her sincerely, taking one more step so I was almost at the foot of the bed. "Luisa, please, put the gun down and let me get back to fucking you."

She shook her head. "I can't. I need to go. I need to make sure my parents are safe and then I'm going to disappear."

"How are you going to do that?"

Her lips pinched together for a moment. "I have a friend, Camila, she's in Cabo. I could call her and—"

"No," I stated, imploring her with my eyes. "You can't. You won't get to her in time, and she won't get to them in time."

"Please just let me go," she said. Her tone was weaker now, as was the look in her eyes. They seemed nearly lost and hopeless.

There was a peculiar hollow feeling in my chest.

"I can't do that," I told her gently. "You know I can't. I must keep you here until I hear from Salvador. If I let you go, it would ruin everything for me." I gave her a pacifying smile. "Besides, don't you know I've grown kind of fond of you?"

She swallowed. "You just want to use my body," she said, her voice dropping slightly as well as the barrel of her gun.

"And I've grown very fond of doing so."

As soon as I said that, I moved quickly. I lunged forward, hitting the gun out of her hands and it went clattering to the floor, then I tackled her into the bed, pinning her arms above her. Her eyes were filled with a mix of anger and desperation as she writhed under me.

I held her arms tighter, my face bearing down on hers. "I can't blame you for trying, Luisa. And I was the fucking fool who was thinking so hard with his dick that I didn't realize I left you alone when I shouldn't have." I lowered my head so my lips lightly grazed hers. "But you know what," I said huskily, "I don't regret any of it. Because that was the hottest fucking thing I've ever seen. And you, my darling, you're really starting to be a queen."

I bit her lip and tugged on it for a moment. "Now, if your adrenaline is pumping like mine is and you're done with gunplay for the day, I say I flip you over and fuck your brains out."

"You can be so heartless," she sneered against my lips, but she didn't turn her face from me.

I sucked her lower lip into my mouth and felt her body respond underneath me. "My dear, you don't need a heart to fuck. Just a big dick." I thrust my erection against her stomach for emphasis and grinned.

Her eyes widened appreciatively.

She was a goner.

CHAPTER EIGHTEEN

Luisa

I thought the days leading up to Salvador's negotiations would take forever. The not knowing, the fear, the anxious anticipation—they all had ways of making the time drag.

Instead, the three days passed by me in a blur of sex and ecstasy. It was naked flesh and intimate fluids, languid limbs and earth-shattering orgasms. It was Javier's eyes in a million different ways: intense during sex and soft after coming, playful while we were in bed and glacial when we were with others. It was the way our bodies melded together that was absolutely captivating, addicting, and strangely freeing.

I started to feel like I knew his body inside and out as he did with mine. I learned what he liked, what he didn't like, what he craved. I knew the things to say that would make him fuck me breathless, and I knew what to say when I really wanted to piss him off.

And all this time, these days of mindless passion, I never had the urge to run again. Maybe fucking me was one way of keeping me under control. Maybe me fucking him was doing the same. I didn't know. But as much as I feared my future, I made myself live in the now. The now was all I had, and I made sure to enjoy every last drop.

I knew very well what Stockholm Syndrome was. I knew it was common. I just didn't think it applied to me. Because the women who fell for their captors that way, it was considered so strange and unusual that it needed a clinical name. It was an issue that could be diagnosed.

The longer I was with Javier, feeling myself stir, my wings stretch and flutter, I felt as if there was something so terribly right about it. When a woman is captured from her home, she is forced to contend with another man, one who wants to bring her harm. When I was captured from my home, I was forced to contend with a man who was better than the one I was taken from. Bad still, of course. Javier was terribly bad. But he wasn't the worst. And when I caught him staring at me sometimes, I could fool myself into thinking that he could possibly be the best.

But Javier himself still remained an enigma to me, despite the feelings I slowly found myself needing from him. For all his grace and tenderness that he sometimes bestowed upon me, there was this shield, this wall up around him that, for all my beauty and blow jobs and sweet conversation, I could not penetrate. He kept himself distanced from me and it made me frustrated and a little mad. Not necessarily because I needed to know what he was thinking, what he felt for me, but because I hadn't done that with myself. The both of us knew something horrible was coming up, and he was the only one who had the strength to protect himself from it.

Me, I knew I was done for. But at least I got to live a little in the process.

At least that's what I kept telling myself.

"What are you doing out here?"

I turned to see Javier strolling toward me, hands casually jammed in his linen pants pockets. I'd only left his side a few hours ago and had come out to sit on the stone bench by the koi pond.

"Feeding the fish," I told him, lifting a few pieces of bread I nicked from the kitchen.

He stopped behind me and gazed out thoughtfully at the lotus. A breeze caught a few strands of his shaggy hair, the sun highlighting the gold in his eyes. Times like this I could pretend I lived here and that there wasn't a horrible world outside the beauty and blooms.

He eyed the bread and ran his hand along his strong jaw in amusement. "You do realize that koi fish need special food."

I shrugged. "I thought they were like your pigs and they'd eat anything." The other day he took me down a path that passed through a clump of trees at the edge of the yard and we ended up at a farm of sorts. He showed me his pigs. I'd learned how Franco's body had been disposed of.

He took a seat next to me. "Not quite."

Somewhere beyond the flowers, the gardener Carlos, a nice little fellow, started up his lawnmower. The sound was so mystifying. It reminded me of the traces of suburbia and normalness I used to see when driving into Cabo San Lucas.

I glanced over at Javier, wondering if he ever found it odd how normal and peaceful his life seemed to be on the outside when it was anything but. I wondered if he orchestrated it that way, to keep all this beauty and elegance around him in order to balance all the bad. I wondered if he had ever come close to making this place even more domestic than it was, if he ever dreamed about having a wife, having children.

"So what happened between you and Ellie?"

He went rigid for a moment before his gaze settled sharply on mine. "Where did that come from?"

"I don't know. I'm curious."

His eyes narrowed suspiciously and he shifted in his seat. "Why are you so focused on my past?"

"Because the past makes you who you are. I want to know why you're this way."

"This way?" he repeated with a wry smile. "Luisa, I hate to break it to you, but I've always been this way."

"Then what happened? Humor me."

He clasped his hands together, his watch jangling.

"In a nutshell," he said with an exasperated sigh, "I was trying to help her get revenge. I was also trying to show her who she really was, or who I still thought she was. In the end, my help did nothing. She'd changed. She played me. She threw me under a bus so she could be with another man, some dumb fuck, and laughed while I was taken away. I'm sure she knew I ended up in prison. I'm sure it only cemented her decision to be *good*. That was all the thanks I got for trying to help." He shook his head, anger simmering in his eyes. "People are so fucking ungrateful."

"So she broke your heart."

He gave me a sidelong glance. "Don't mistake broken pride for a broken heart. No man wants to look like a fool. Because of her, I lost almost everything, and it took years for me to get it all back. That isn't something you can forget overnight."

Now I understood the shield.

A few moments passed us by. One white and orange fish did several laps around the pond, eyeing me hopefully every time he came near. I thought about what Javier said, how he saw something in Ellie that he wanted to bring out of her. Her truth.

Finally I looked to Javier and shyly asked, "Will you help me?"

His brow furrowed delicately. "Help you what?"

"Help me see who *I* really am."

He smirked. "I think you're already finding that out. One day at a time."

"But there are no days after tomorrow," I said, trying to keep my voice as flat as possible.

Tension broke the surface of his face but he reined it in. "I guess you're right. So what are we to do?"

Something, I screamed in my head. *Anything!*

I gulped my thoughts down so they didn't dare escape from my lips. "I don't know."

He eyed Carlos who was now mowing behind a flowering bush then looked back at me. "You do," he said, his heady gaze trailing to my lips. "What we've always done."

He reached for my shoulder and slipped off the strap of my dress with his index finger. His eyes fastened to mine as he gently eased me back so I was lying flat on the bench. In moments, his pants were unzipped, my underwear was pushed to the side, and my leg was straight up against his shoulder. He pushed into me in broad daylight, while the lawnmower whirred in the background and the flowers perfumed the air with their delicate fragrance.

Even though I felt completely exposed to the living, breathing world that whirled around us, I was absolutely captive to the private one between us. When I came, my nails raking down his back and into the loose linen threads of his shirt, I was holding on to more than just him; I was holding on to the day, the moment, the second.

The time where I was queen.

And where I was free.

CHAPTER NINETEEN

Javier

It was the middle of the night when Luisa woke me, just a few hours before dawn, before the day came and I would get Salvador's call.

As usual, she woke me up in the most exquisite way—her naked body pressed against mine, hands in my hair, lips on my chest.

"What time is it?" I groaned, both from lack of sleep and from the way she pushed herself against my dick.

"Does it matter?" she asked softly.

I opened my eyes and made out her features in the waning dark. "No, it doesn't. Not when you're like this."

Her pearly teeth flashed in a gorgeous smile. "Good," she said. She trailed her fingers down the side of my face and that smile slowly vanished. I didn't even have to ask why. I knew why. I knew what was coming. I was doing everything I could to steel my mind against the impossible choices I'd have to make in a few hours.

"Javier," she whispered, my name sounding like heaven. "What are you going to do to me?"

I grinded my jaw, trying to keep it together. "Don't ask me this."

"But you must know."

"But I don't know," I whispered harshly. "I'll know when the time comes."

"Will you promise to be the one to shoot me? Like you said."

"I never said I would do that."

"Will you promise?" she repeated, running her hands into my hair again.

"No," I told her. And I was telling the truth. "I will not shoot you. I will not harm you. I will not kill you. Do you feel any better?"

She shook her head, and I could see how wet her eyes were. A tear drop fell on my chest and the hollowness beneath it grew. "I don't feel better, because I know the others will. Salvador will not want me."

I grabbed her shoulders and shook her. "We don't know that!" I hissed.

"And then so what if he does! Can you let me go? Can you watch me go back to him, to be his wife again?" She pressed her fingers into her tearstain and swirled it around my heart in angry circles. "Is that what you're still capable of?"

Yes. I had to be.

"Luisa," I said carefully, looking into her shining, desperate eyes. "You can't save me."

She smiled, letting out a caustic laugh. "I don't want to save you," she said, bringing her face closer to mine. "I want to *join* you."

I stared at her, completely dazzled by what she had said. Even with everything that I was, she didn't want to change me, she didn't want to save me. Perhaps it was because I was so beyond saving. Either way, she saw who I was and all my filth and she wanted to roll around in it with me.

She had become my equal.

And in the morning she would become nothing.

...

"Did he say when he was calling?" Este asked with a hint of annoyance.

I couldn't even answer him. My eyes were trained on the new flip phone lying on my desk in front of me. It was the exact same scene as the week before, except there was one difference. Este was right. Luisa had compromised me.

It didn't mean I wasn't going to do what I needed to do. But it meant that though I looked annoyed on the surface, I was being crushed underneath.

"Well, Javier told him exactly a week," The Doctor said mildly. He adjusted his hat on his head. "I suppose Salvador could take him literally or not."

"If it's literal then he's already late," Este said. I could feel his eyes on me. "Are you sure Juanito is a good enough guard, Javi?"

I jerked my chin into a nod. They wanted Luisa guarded during this so I sent Juanito to do the job. The man had his flaws, but I knew he wouldn't hurt her and would obey me. Someone like Este couldn't always be trusted. My mind started picking that apart, wondering if perhaps one day I could get rid of Este before he attempted to get rid of me. My mind wanted to think about everything except what was about to happen.

"So what is our course of action if he wants her back?" The Doctor asked. "We shouldn't give her over until everything is absolutely secure. We need proof of the shipping lane. We need physical evidence before we do anything. This might mean holding on to her for a few more days. But I'm sure Javier can handle that, can't you boy?"

I barely heard him. My eyes willed the phone to ring, to get this fucking over with.

And, like God himself was the operator, the phone started dancing, vibrating on the desk. We all watched with bated breath before I snatched it up.

I waited a moment, that one golden moment where everything stayed the same, before I flipped it open.

"Hello," I said into the receiver, relieved at how strong my voice was sounding. I could almost fool myself.

"Javier Bernal," said Salvador, his voice dripping with false formality. "I'm glad you were waiting on my phone call. I almost forgot about it, you see. Nice to know you hadn't."

I pressed my lips together, hard, waiting for him to go on. He didn't.

"No, I hadn't," I said with deliberation. "So what have you decided? Will you deal with me or not?"

There was a pause and the other end of the phone erupted with laughter. It was so loud that I knew The Doctor and Este could hear it. They exchanged a concerned glance with each other.

"Deal?" Salvador spat out when he calmed down. "What was the deal again? An Ephedra lane for my wife? Javier, Javier, Javier. Have you seen my wife? Have you tasted my wife?" His voice grew lower. "If you're anything like me, you have."

I'm not anything like you, I thought bitterly.

"But for her beauty and body," he went on, "do you really think she's worth a shipping lane? You just might be dumber than I thought." He snorted and my chest constricted painfully. "The world is full of naïve, brainless, helpless women like her. I can pick up another one. In fact, I already have. Several. So no, Javier, I will not be making a deal with you." He paused. "Chop her fucking head off."

The line went dead.

Everything inside me went dead. I slowly removed the phone from my ear and stared at it in my hands.

I had been wrong. Luisa had been right. Salvador didn't want her. I kidnapped her in vain. I wasn't getting anything in return.

It seemed fitting for a man who loved to fuck so much that I had royally fucked myself over.

"Javier?" The Doctor asked carefully. "What happened?"

I glanced up, meeting Este's eyes by accident. He immediately grimaced, knowing the look of failure.

"Shit," he swore. "No fucking deal, hey."

The Doctor made a tsking sound, leaning forward on his knees. "That is a shame. A real shame. All the time we wasted. And now we look like fools. Well, the only way we can recover from this, Javier," he said my name sharply so that I would direct my attention to him, "is if we show we don't mess around. And I know you don't. Look what happened to Franco. No idle threats there." He got out of his seat and peered down at me with curiosity. "You know we have to kill her and do it publicly."

I raised one finger to silence him. It was oh so hard to think when you could barely even breathe. "Give me a minute," I managed to say. My brain was working on overdrive, trying to figure out a way to save my pride, save my cartel, and save Luisa at the same time. I barely noticed Este leaving the room.

But I certainly noticed when he came back.

I looked up to see Luisa in the doorway looking beyond frightened, Juanito and Este with tight holds on either side of her. Her eyes flew to mine, and in an instant she knew exactly what was happening.

I'm sorry, I mouthed to her. I didn't know what else to say.

"Ah," The Doctor said, clapping his hands together gleefully. "Just the woman we wanted to see. Luisa, Javier has something very important and troubling that he'd like to tell you. Don't you, Javier?"

I wanted nothing more than to chop *his* fucking head off. My eyes burned into his but he took no notice. He had that look on his face, that dreamy, wistful look that preceded his torturing someone.

I slid my gaze over to her. "Luisa," I said thickly. "I just spoke with your husband. He doesn't want to make a deal. You were right. He wants me to chop your head off instead."

I suppose I could have said that more eloquently.

Her eyes widened for a moment before something passed over them, something that made them grow cold. She was retreating inside herself. I didn't want that to happen. I wanted her to fight back. Her fight would give me courage to do the same.

"I see," she said blankly. "Sometimes it's horrible to be right."

I nodded and looked to the men. "Do you guys mind excusing us? I need a moment with her alone."

The Doctor narrowed his eyes. "Javier, you know you have to do what's right for all of us. As gruesome as it may be."

"Please go," I said, my voice growing harder. "Now."

Juanito, Este, and The Doctor all exchanged a worried look before they reluctantly left the room. As soon as the door shut behind them, I went up to it and locked it before turning to look at Luisa.

We stared at each other for a long moment. There was so much to say and yet so little.

"So this is it," she said.

I shook my head and went over to her, grabbing her face in my hands. "No. This isn't it. I won't let this happen if you won't. Tell me you'll fight this. Promise me."

She stared up at me in the open need to believe. "How can I fight?"

I licked my lips and looked away. "I don't know. The cartel will suffer—I will suffer—if we don't deliver. We all follow through on what we say we're going to do. If we say we're going to kill you, then we have to do it."

"Then find someone else," she cried out, her eyes dancing feverishly. "Go into the village, go and find a woman, a hooker, someone, anyone, anyone that looks like me. Bring her back here and tie her up and film it. Cover up her face in a bag and take her fucking head right off!"

I jerked my chin into my neck. Where had this brutal Luisa come from?

She smiled and shook me. "It will work," she assured me. "Killing another woman instead."

"No," I said, watching her closely. "It won't. They might want proof of your actual head."

"Then let me stay here," she said. "You don't have to kill me. You can tell them no. You're their boss."

"I know I am. But that doesn't help with pride, with image."

"Fuck your pride!" she yelled, her face contorted. "What the fuck has that ever gotten you?"

She didn't understand. "It's gotten me everything," I told her.

She made a sweeping gesture to the room. "All these dear things you love so much," she said sarcastically. "All your fucking flowers and your clothes and your money and the shitheads who work for you."

I rubbed my face in my hands, trying to get a grip, trying to get control back. I felt like I'd lost it many days ago, somewhere deep inside of her. No matter what I chose, I was going to suffer in some way.

"Look," I said carefully, slowly meeting her wild eyes. "If you stay here, even if the cartel can't save face, what do you think happens to your parents? If you run off into the jungle, what do you think will happen to your parents? If we kill some other woman and pretend it's you—what do you think will happen to your parents?" Her face fell and I took a step toward her again. "You're not thinking straight. You're thinking out of survival and instinct, and that's *good* because that means you're finally being selfish. But you've got a pure heart, my darling. You wouldn't be able to be selfish for long. I don't want you living or dying with that kind of regret on your shoulders."

She seemed to think about that for some time, her eyes staring at a blank spot on my shirt. I could almost see the wheels turning inside, that fight to survive and the fight to protect the ones she loved.

I hoped I wasn't included on that list.

When she came to a conclusion it looked like she was wearing the weight of the world on her face. She looked me dead in the eye and said, "I have to go back to Salvador."

I frowned, a bolt of panic going through me. "What? No."

She nodded and raised her chin defiantly. "Yes. It's the only way. I have to go back to him. I have to be his wife again. It's the only way I can live and keep my parents alive at the same time."

I grabbed her by the hand and squeezed hard, hoping to press some sense into her. "But you won't be alive for long," I hissed at her. "You know what that man will do to you. Christ, what happens when he sees my name on your back!"

"You never cared about that before."

"But I do now! You can't do this, this is a death wish for fuck's sake."

"I will do this," she said, her voice growing calmer by the moment, as if she had made peace with the horrible fear. "You'll let me go. Even better, you'll have someone drop me off in Culiacán. I'll wander around until someone spots me. The whole city knows who I am, the whole city is still under my power. I'll tell them what happened—that I knew I was going to be executed. I'll tell them I escaped and that I've come to beg my husband to take me back, that he made the right choice by picking his business, that there are no hard feelings. I will grovel. And to save his own face, to save his own fucking pride, he will take me back into his house." She swallowed. "And I...I will be his wife again. Just as before."

I was angry. So angry that my breath wouldn't leave my lungs. It took all my concentration to calm down, to start breathing in and out of my nose. Why did she have to choose this of all things?

"Luisa, please," I told her, hoping she could see the truth. "You will die. He will take you in on pride but you are nothing to him. Do you hear me? Nothing! You will last a week or two, and then he will kill you. And before that, you know what he's going to do to you. He—" I broke off, unable to finish the sentence. I couldn't even let myself think about it, but it was there, poking around in my brain. The sound of Salvador's voice, the fear I'd seen in Luisa's eyes, the brutality he'd proven he was capable of.

"And I will handle him as I handled him before," she said, almost proud. "This is the only way. At least I can say I gave it a shot. One more shot at life, as pathetic as it may be. And you? You only have to lose your precious pride among your workers here. The rest of the world may laugh at your faulty security, but I'm sure it will be something they'll soon forget. To Mexico, your cartel is still one to be reckoned with and your pride will remain intact. And you, Javier Bernal, will continue on as you had before. In a week, you won't remember me."

But she had to know, had to realize, how hard this was for me, too. If she did though, perhaps she didn't quite care.

"All right," I said, nodding at her. "If this is what you want, I can tell the others the plan. They won't like it, but they won't be able to do anything about it."

"Thank you," she said. She smiled at me with the strength of a million breaking hearts. It was the saddest thing I'd ever seen, and I'd seen a lot of sad things in my lifetime, things that would chase me to the grave.

And that's when I knew, with nothing but a smile, my Luisa, my queen, had broken *me*.

CHAPTER TWENTY

Luisa

I slept alone that night. In fact, I spent most of the day alone as well. After I learned the news and after I had came up with my own horrid plan, Javier told his comrades about what we were to do. They didn't take it well, as I figured. Este was pissed off like a whiny boy and even Juanito gazed upon Javier with an air of disrespect. I had to say, as much as I mocked him for his foolish pride, there was a moment where I felt almost sorry for him.

The Doctor seemed to take it worst of all. In that calm, cynical, monstrous way, he berated Javier in every way he could. He called him weak. Soft. Pussy-whipped. He talked about me as if I wasn't even in the room, but those lewd insults about how well of a fuck I must be, well they meant nothing. All I cared about was putting my plan into action.

And, eventually, that's what happened. Javier lost face among his men but they would protect the cartel as a whole. I would be let go. The next day, Juanito would take me to Culiacán. I would look like I had just escaped from somewhere. I would have a story to tell. And then I would hope for the best.

I knew Javier wasn't happy with my choice—I wasn't happy either. I was actually so scared that I'd grown numb. I didn't let myself think about what might happen to me, I just knew it had to be done. My chances for survival were extremely low. My chances for vile abuse, torment, and torture were extremely high. Either way, I was in for a lot of pain.

But like I had done all week, I put that on the back burner. I tried to appreciate the last day I had in that house that, in the dying sun, became only golden and not a prison at all. I wished I had Javier by my side, but he was ignoring me, avoiding me. I knew it was for the best. I knew that if I was with him, in his bed, that it would make leaving even worse.

It's not even that Javier and I were lovers. We weren't really anything you could explain. What relationship we did have was fucked up beyond reasoning. It made no sense for me to feel more than just attraction to a man like him, and yet I did. I shouldn't have let my emotions excuse the things he'd done, the person he was, but again, I did.

I should have been grateful that he didn't kill me, that it wasn't even an option to him. A week ago, I would have been certain he'd take my head off, and with glee. Now he was willing to take a hit to his ego, not just to resist killing me but to actually let me go. Not to mention actually let me go through with a plan that I, his hostage, had initiated.

And yet I still wished for more. I wanted him to ask me to stay again. I wanted him to protest just a little bit more. There could be other ways around all this. He could go and take my parents somewhere safe and then keep me here as his. I would gladly stay. There might have not been any love in this house, but it was better than a house of hate.

I couldn't find the words. I didn't see the point. It should have been enough that he did, finally, see me as a human being. It's just that being a human being meant I also wanted what I couldn't have.

Him.

The next morning, after a fitful sleep, I was awakened by a knock and Este bringing me my breakfast. He was one of the last people I wanted to see.

"Thought you deserved this in bed, since it's your last meal with us and all," he said, shutting the door behind him with his foot and bringing the tray to the bedside table. He shot me a sidelong glance. "It's only because you're leaving that I can trust you not to bash me over the head with the bowl of fruit or something."

I didn't smile, I merely stared at him.

"No jokes today, hey?" he asked with a shrug. He sat down on the end of the bed, and I instinctively drew my feet toward me. "You know, Luisa, I think we may have gotten off on the wrong foot here. But I just wanted you to know, I like you."

I grimaced. "Is that supposed to be a good thing?"

"It's not anything," Este said. "I can see how Javier is so obsessed with you."

"Obsessed?" This was news to me.

"Don't be too flattered," he said wryly. "Javier gets obsessed easily. Though it doesn't happen very often with women. Considering the way things have gone for him in the past and his devotion to building an empire, I'm actually surprised at the way things have turned out."

"But you're unhappy about it," I said.

"I am. I think he's letting his feelings for you cloud his judgment. But things could be worse."

Feelings for me? I wanted to ask him to elaborate, to tell me more. But I realized how damn inappropriate that was, considering my dire circumstances, and internally chastised my heart for even skipping a beat.

Este studied my face. "Just so you know," he said carefully, a knowing look in his eyes, "his *feelings* for you only mean that he's not killing you. That's all. You can't get much more than that out of him. It's like getting blood from a stone."

"I know," I said quickly. "I never figured otherwise."

He nodded and patted the bed. "Good. Well, I suppose I should be off. I hope all of this is worth it, you know. You could just as easily disappear and get a new identity, a new life, a new everything."

I shook my head. "I couldn't do that. I have a conscience."

"And that *will* be the death of you," he said. "Juanito will come up and get you in an hour. It's a long drive, as you know." He got up and paused, as if remembering something. "Oh, and sorry again about Tasering you."

I stared at him coldly. "Really? I'm still thinking about hitting you in the head with this tray, just because."

He grinned. "I figured as much."

He opened the door.

"Esteban," I called after him. "Could you please send Javier up here?"

His face twisted doubtfully. "I'll try."

The door shut and I waited. When the hour ticked closer, I put on my dress and my running shoes, the only things I would be pretending I escaped in. I would have nothing else. No money, no ID, nothing. I stared at my face in the mirror. I wondered if Salvador would see the horror in my eyes and mistake it for where I had been, not where I was going. I hoped so.

Eventually, five minutes before the sand in the hourglass was up, Javier came to me. He wore a mask of elegance and indifference, his unusually handsome features taking on the appearance of a sculpture. But I had no idea what the artist was trying to say: Here's a man in denial? Here's a man without a soul? Here's a man who will build empires and legacies, whose pride shaped the land? Or here is a man who for once in his life, doesn't know who he is?

Whoever the man at my door was, it was apparent this was the last place he wanted to be.

"You wanted to see me?" he said so formally that it cut worse than his blade.

"You weren't going to come say goodbye?" I asked him. He remained at the door. I remained near the bathroom. Neither of us moved.

"I was," he said, an air of defiance to him. "At the door."

"Oh," I said caustically. "How very kind and proper of you."

"Luisa," he warned.

"So after all you've put me through," I said, folding my arms, "you're just wiping your hands clean and pushing me out the door."

Indignation flared in his eyes. His hands clenched and unclenched, but he managed to keep his voice hard and steady. "This was your choice. You chose this."

"Because it's the only choice I have," I said. "Isn't it?"

Our eyes fastened on each other. I wanted him to come closer. I wanted to see something that wasn't there.

"Can't we go back in time?" I asked, my voice softer now. "When I believed I meant something to you?"

He swallowed and looked away. "You were always my captive. I was always the man holding the knife."

And again that knife was buried straight in me. I took in a sharp breath, willing the pain away. "I suppose I shouldn't be surprised. Esteban said getting feelings out of you was like getting blood from a stone."

"Esteban doesn't know shit," he snapped, glaring at me. "What the hell do you want me to say? Do you think anything I say will make any difference to you? To me? To this fucking situation? Huh?"

"You could tell me not to go."

"I did!" he cried out, marching across the room. He grabbed me by the shoulders, his reddening face in mine. "I told you not to go. I told you there could be another way. You could go free, away from certain fucking death. But you're like this..."

"This what?" I goaded, watching his eyes spark and flame. "What am I?"

"A martyr," he said, spitting out the word. "You wear your nobility like a goddamn crown. I am so sick and tired of it, especially when I know there is a strong, unapologetic woman in there just dying to come out. I've seen her. I've fucked her. I want *that* woman to win."

"That woman will have to live with regret."

"That woman," he said, giving me a shake, "will *live*." His eyes sought the ceiling, trying to compose himself, but when he looked back at me, the fire was still there. The mask had slipped. "I know you love your parents, Luisa. But is their safety—not even guaranteed—worth your own life? Do you really think your parents want you to do this? Do you think this will make them fucking proud? If they're anything like me, they'll be angry as hell. They will live their lives with regret instead. Is that what you want to give them? A dead daughter and a lifetime of fucking sorrow?"

I was stunned. He grabbed my face with both his hands and stared at me with crazed intensity. "Be fucking *selfish*! Save your own life." He let go of me suddenly, turning his back to me, his hand on the back of his neck. "Lord knows I can't save it for you."

I watched his back, the strength of it underneath his navy suit jacket, wondering if it ever got tired of shouldering this world. It seemed all so easy for him to give orders, tell people what to do, and never have to give an ounce of himself.

"You gave me a reason to run," I said to him. "Give me a reason to stay."

He paused and slowly turned to look at me. "Give you a reason to stay?"

"Yes," I said, walking up to him, refusing to break my gaze.

His eyes softened, just for a moment. "What can I say to make you stay?" he asked, his voice barely above a whisper.

"Tell me you love me."

My boldness shocked him more than it shocked me. He stared at me, unhinged and absolutely bewildered, like he didn't understand. "I can't do that," he managed to say.

I had nothing to lose. "You can't because you don't."

He opened his mouth then shut it. He gave a small shake of his head, and then said, almost chagrined, "No. Because I don't know what that is anymore."

I placed my hands on his jacket, running them down his silky lapels. "Well," I said sadly, "it's what you feel for your suits. And your money. And your mansions. And all your power." I looked up at him. "Except you feel it for me."

There was a knock at the door. I reluctantly broke his gaze, his lost and helpless gaze, and looked to see Juanito standing in the doorway.

"So sorry, boss," he said nervously, trying not to look at us. "But it's time to go."

Javier nodded, clearing his throat. "She'll be right there."

Juanito left, and it was just the two of us again, and for the last time.

"I'm sorry," Javier said sincerely, reaching for my face and gently brushing a strand of hair behind my ear. I wasn't sure what he was apologizing for—for not loving me, for Juanito interrupting, for having to say goodbye. Perhaps he was apologizing for that first moment when he decided my life would be worth a shipping lane. It didn't really matter in the end.

"I'm sorry, too," I told him. Then I walked away from his touch and to the door, down the hall, and down the stairs to where Juanito was waiting for me in the foyer.

Waiting to take me home.

I did not look behind me. I did not look back. I kept my head high and conviction straight, even when Juanito placed the bag over my head, so I would still not see the way in and out of this place.

With his help, I got into the SUV that was running outside and told myself, for the umpteenth time that day, that I was doing the right thing.

It began to really worry me then, when the right thing started to feel so very wrong.

...

The drive back to Culiacán was longer than the drive to Javier's. I wasn't sure if it was the mountainous roads or Juanito's driving, or the fact that every mile we passed, my veins filled with ice-cold fear. The fact that I couldn't see didn't help, but a few hours into it, Juanito leaned over and pulled the bag from my head.

I squinted in the afternoon light. We must have been far enough from Javier's that it didn't matter what I saw. I guess I couldn't blame them for thinking that I might have ratted on their whereabouts. That thought made me wonder if perhaps Salvador was going to think I was a rat myself.

But once I entered his doors—if I even got that far—I would never leave them again. Whether I had switched sides or not, it didn't really matter. I knew I would die in that gilded cage.

Night was just falling, the sky turning into a brilliant blend of periwinkle and tangerine that made my soul hurt, when Jaunito pulled the car to the side of the highway. He cut the engine and eyed me expectantly. "Well," he said.

"Well," I said back.

"This is where you get off." He nodded to the dusty shoulder that was riddled with garbage.

"But we aren't even near the city," I protested. "The sign said we had another two hours or so."

"True," he said, "but my orders were to drop you off here. How you get into the city is your own doing. Soon, there will be checkpoints, all from your husband's cartel. They'll be looking at each car. I can't risk being seen with you."

"So then, what do I do?"

"Hitchhike," he said.

"But that's so unsafe," I said. "I could be attacked or raped."

He gave me a melancholy smile. "What do you think's going to happen to you anyway?"

I flinched. The truth stung. "You're turning heartless, just like them," I warned him.

"Occupational hazard, I guess," he said. "It may save your life if you were to turn the same."

At that he nodded at the door, eager for me to leave his charge. I sighed my acceptance and got out. Though I had told Javier I wanted to be bound at the wrists, he assured me it wasn't necessary to make it look like I escaped. I was grateful for that. I needed every ounce of power I could get, even if it was just an illusion.

The minute my feet hit the soil, Juanito pulled away. I watched his red lights until he did a U-turn a few meters away. Then he roared past me, heading back to Javier, back to safety.

I'd never been so envious in my life.

I stood there for a long time, just a black figure against the darkening sky, the passing cars anonymous with their blinding lights, my hair and dress billowing around me in their wake. It wasn't until I summoned the courage to stick my thumb out that one car eventually stopped.

To my utmost relief, it was a middle-aged woman driving. I got in and kept quiet while she scolded me for being out on the highway. I didn't give her much of an explanation as to why I was out there—I was saving that for later—and I kept my face turned away from her so she wouldn't see the faded yellow and blue bruises that still colored my skin from Franco's assault.

She made good company, talking about her newest grandchild and how scandalous it was that he wasn't baptized yet, and how all the neighbors were flapping their lips. I wondered what it must be like to live a totally normal life. To fall in love, get married, have children and grandchildren. To drive to the supermarket and drink instant coffee and watch daytime television and go to church and take every fucking day for granted.

Because of her normality, we sped past the one checkpoint we saw. The armed men didn't even slow us down. We just kept driving through, their eyes trained only for people like Juanito.

When we finally arrived in the city and I asked her to drop me off at one of the busy plazas, I told her she was lucky to have all that she did. She only stared at me in disbelief. Then I thanked her and got out of the car. She drove off, shaking her head and talking to herself, and I wondered if I was going to be news in the morning, and if she'd be flipping through her morning paper and realize just who she had given a ride to.

Now, it was time to play a part, a me from another timeline, a timeline where Javier was the brutal captor and that was it. I closed my eyes, inviting the other persona in: frightened, relieved, jubilant at their escape. I looked around the plaza for someone who would know who I was, who would hear the underground tittering from the Sinaloa Cartel, who would first have to hear my story.

I found a musician—a *narcocorrido* singer—sitting by the side of a fountain, playing murder ballads on his accordion. The man, with his slicked back hair and soulful voice, glanced up at me as I hugged myself in front of him, shivering for show, and he immediately knew who I was. I was sure he had sung many songs about narco wives. Perhaps even one just for me. Sing me a song about Luisa, the one who was taken, the one who wasn't wanted back. The one who found her freedom in another man's bed.

It didn't take long before I was wrapped in a blanket and being escorted into a police vehicle, flashing lights illuminating the plaza in red and blue. A few onlookers were watching, camera phones out, recording my apparent rescue as they would the murders that littered the city.

Once in the vehicle, the officers extra courteous, I was driven in a different direction than I thought we'd go. Then I realized that after my kidnapping, Salvador must have abandoned his old mansion for another one, for security's sake.

It made no difference to me; they all held the same horrors.

Soon we were driving past checkpoints—some operated by other police, some by men with black ski-masks and automatic rifles—and then through the heavily guarded gates of my husband's newest palace.

Once we came to a stop, the police escorted me out of the SUV and straight up the polished steps of Salvador's front door. One officer went to knock but the door was already opening, slowly, ominously, like a scary movie.

Salvador stood on the other side, backlit from the foyer, his ugly face cast in sinister shadow. He stroked along his mustache and gave me a smile that even a crocodile would be ashamed to wear.

"Luisa, my princess," he said cunningly, opening up an arm for me. "Welcome home."

I looked to the police officers, wondering if I had enough strength to turn back, to run, to plead for their help. But they were paid handsomely by my husband, and their job was about indifference to anything but money. There would be no help from them. There would be no help from anyone.

I was on my own.

I gave Salvador a stiff smile as I walked into the house.

He slowly closed the door behind him and shot me a sly look over his shoulder. "This took me by surprise. I must say I never expected to see you again."

"I know," I said, putting on the face of the scared yet sympathetic wife. "And I understand. When I saw I had a chance to escape, I took it. You'd be shocked at how immature Javier's men are. They are nothing like yours."

He smiled briefly at my compliment. "I'm surprised you came back *here*."

"You are my husband," I told him, hoping he bought the sincerity. "Where else would I go?"

He studied me for a moment, his jaw ticking back and forth. "I guess you're right." He took a large step toward me, his cowboy boots echoing on the floor. "It's too bad that you'll soon wish you hadn't."

My face fell. His lit up. "Sometimes," he went on, "you don't know what you've got till it's gone." He chuckled to himself.

"I realized what I had wasn't even worth bargaining for." He shrugged and pulled at his chin as he looked my body up and down. "But that doesn't mean you aren't worth something. Get on your knees."

I opened my mouth in protest and almost said something I'd regret. Talking back to Javier had become a bad habit, one he had encouraged.

"I said on your knees, cunt!" Salvador yelled at me. He grabbed me by my hair and thrust me down to the floor, my knees taking the brunt of the fall. I heard his zipper go down but I couldn't make myself look up.

He made me look. He made a fist at the top of my head and yanked my hair straight up, my nerves exploding in pain. I looked past his rancid cock and right at his face. It was evil incarnate. He shook his head, clucking his tongue. "You hesitated, Luisa, and a woman never hesitates. Looks like I'm going to have to retrain you all over again."

The next thing I knew, his knee came toward my face. There was pain and spots and all the world went black.

CHAPTER TWENTY-ONE

Javier

The saying goes, if you love something, let it go. I always thought it was better to just shoot the damn thing so it'd never go anywhere.

But now I understood. Now that I didn't have a choice.

I suppose I could have said something. I could have told Luisa what she wanted to hear. But that would have been a lie. I didn't love her. I couldn't. That was something that was no longer applicable to the person I'd become. There was no place for it in my life; it didn't fit, it didn't work. Love didn't build empires, it ruined them.

What I felt for Luisa wasn't love. But it was curious. It was something, at least. It was deep and spreading, like a cancer. Yet, instead of only bringing pain, it brought purpose in its sickness. Her lips soothed me, her heart challenged me, her eyes made me bleed. My bed was where we held our exorcisms. She brought me peace. I brought her fire. Now the flame was out—gone forever—and there was a war raging inside me.

I went a full week pretending that nothing had happened. Pretending that nothing was eating me from the inside out. I wore my mask every day. I worked with Este on our next targets, our next hand in this game. A trip to Veracruz was becoming more and more possible. But that city no longer stirred fear in my heart, no longer played on bad memories. Those memories meant nothing to me anymore. There was something so much scarier raging just below my surface.

One night I woke up from a nightmare. I think it was the same as I had before, with my father and I fishing, Luisa on the end of the hook. It was hard to remember; the dream shattered into fragments the moment I woke. But the feeling was there. The unimaginable fear. This was the sickness manifesting itself. This was the war coming. This was what happened to me when I no longer had her to placate me.

And then I realized with certainty that I had been a coward this whole time. I was in my bed, safe and comfortable in the life I had created for myself. I wanted for nothing. And yet she, she was with Salvador. She had been there a week already and I couldn't imagine her state, if she was even still alive. She wanted for *everything.*

I didn't go back to sleep. Even though it was the middle of the night, I slipped a robe around me and left the house. I went to sit by the koi pond, the lotus blossoms looking ghostly in the moonlight. I stared at their white purity until the sun came up. Then, in that glow of dawn, I saw more clearly. The flowers were magnificent, but they weren't as the Chinese scholar had said. There were imperfections on their surface. There were stains. Their beauty didn't come from the fact that they were untainted, their beauty came from their resilience. They were proud to have grown from mud.

Even if my beauty queen was already dead, I knew what I had to do. There would be dire consequences for my actions, but there already were. What was the difference if I stirred up a little more trouble? At this point, it was pretty much expected of me.

Later that day, I told the men I was going away on a business trip to Cabo San Lucas. Este, being my right-hand man and all, insisted he come along for the journey, but I told him I needed to do this alone. I would be safe and I wouldn't be long—two or three days, at most. And if I happened upon the wrong people at the wrong time, then that was that. I knew Este would slide right in and replace me anyway.

I was a nervous flier. It was a quick trip across the water, but it still took a lot of composure to not drink all the alcohol available in first class. There was a man in the row across from me who stared at me like he might have recognized me. I only smiled back. Though this was risky, I also knew that most people would never do or say anything to me. Besides, my face might have been out there once or twice but Salvador was right—I wasn't on anyone's radar.

Though the airport was closer to San Jose del Cabo than it was to San Lucas, that wasn't my first stop. I wasn't lying to Este when I said I had business that needed attending to. This time, I wasn't going to give an order and watch someone else do it. I was going to get my hands very, very dirty.

It was all for her.

And it seemed the more I did for her, the filthier I got.

Once in Cabo, I took a long stroll around the town. I hadn't been here in a long time and was shocked to see how much it had changed. What was once a small marina was jam-packed with million-dollar yachts. Cruise ships hovered offshore while drunk teenagers on jet skis did circles in the azure surf. The beaches were filled with dance music and DJs announcing hourly body shots. The popular bars spouted Top 40 hits and celebrity-owned statuses.

The town had no soul. Perhaps this was good for tourists—indeed it was excellent for Mexico's economy, as were my drugs. But I could never live in a place that catered to the other half. Sure, the town was safe and the drug wars hadn't littered the streets. But where was the real Mexico? Where was the grit beneath the glamour? Where were the proud flowers rising from the mud?

I spent most of the day walking around, taking in everything. Despite all my misgivings toward the resort town, I still enjoyed myself. I was a tourist, just looking at all the sights. I was a man just looking for a bar, a place to get a drink.

And then I found it. It was barely distinguishable from all the other tourist traps.

Cabo Cocktails.

I went in and sat at the bar. Even though it was a hot, sunny day and nearing three o' clock, the bar was fairly empty. There was an old man nursing a beer at the other end of the bar and a couple in a booth. That was it.

The bartender, a cute girl with blondish pixie hair, was quick to serve me.

"A gin and tonic," I told her. "Perfect for a day like today." I gave her the smile that I knew could remove panties.

She smiled back but I could tell I had no true effect on her. She was probably into women.

"No problem," she said, and got to work.

"What's your name?" I asked her while she fished out a can of tonic water.

"Camila," she said, an edge to her voice that told her not to bother asking for more than her name. But I wasn't here for her.

I waited until she served me my drink and told me the price, then I asked what I really wanted to know.

"Camila, I'm wondering if you can help me," I said, smiling again. "You see, there's a girl who used to work here."

Her eyes widened. I wasn't sure what tipped her off I was talking about Luisa; perhaps it was my sharp suit, or maybe she'd been on Camila's mind. "And I'm very worried about her," I went on. "Luisa is her name. Have you spoken to her recently?"

She shook her head, her eyes darting around the bar. "No."

"But she did work here..."

She nodded. She looked to the old man at the end of the bar. I waved at him dismissively. "Don't worry about him. I just have a few questions and I'll be out of your way."

"Who are you?" she asked.

"I'm a friend," I told her. "One of the few that she has these days. So you haven't seen her around here then? She hasn't called you?"

"No. No, I haven't seen or spoken to her since a few days before her wedding."

"To Salvador Reyes."

She swallowed. "Yes. Tell me, is she all right?"

"I really hope so," I said. *I really doubt it.*

I knocked the rest of the drink back, feeling immediately refreshed and energized, and slid the money toward her. "One more thing."

"What?" she asked, a bit of impatience mixed in with her apprehension. I could tell she was a tough girl. No wonder Luisa and she had been friends.

"Is your manager around? I'd like to ask him a few questions about her."

She nodded and jerked her head down the hall. "Bruno. He's in his office, I think. He comes and goes."

I grinned at her. "Perfect."

I waited until she left to go tend to the couple in the booth, then I reached over behind the bar and picked up the knife she used to cut up the lime for my drink.

I caught the man at the end of the bar watching me with mild interest that only tired old men have. I flashed the blade at him and smiled. He shrugged and went back to his beer.

Making sure the blade was hidden from sight, I walked down the hall and paused outside the door that said Bruno Corchado on it. I gripped the knife in my hand, slightly sticky from the lime juice. It would have been better if I had my own, but airplane security wouldn't have let me fly with it in my boot or in my carry-on. Bastards.

I decided not to knock. I opened the door a crack and poked my head in.

"Camila," the man grunted in annoyance until he looked up and saw me. His annoyance deepened. He obviously had no idea who I was. Good.

I shut the door behind me. "Bruno Corchado?"

"Who the fuck are you?"

I shrugged. "I could be a customer coming in with a complaint. Do you talk to all your customers that way?"

He glared at me. It was pitiful. "I can see you're not. What do you want?"

"I wanted to ask you a few questions about your past employee, Luisa Chavez."

He smirked and rolled his eyes. "Haven't you heard? She's Luisa Reyes now."

"Is that right?"

"The bitch married a drug lord," he said. "Salvador Reyes."

I sucked in my breath. "I see. Well, good for her."

He picked his nose and then wiped it under the desk. My lips wrinkled in distaste.

"She was money hungry," he informed me, as if I was suddenly his friend. "She'd always come in here asking for money. Said it was for her parents. I bet it never was. But I don't know what the hell she spent her money on, actually. Not men. Maybe she was into women, too." He gave me a knowing look. "She was always such a prude. Doesn't mean I didn't get to have my fun with her, if you know what I mean."

"I know what you mean," I said, trying hard to keep my voice steady.

Bruno picked up on something anyway. "Aw, shit," he said, straightening himself in his chair. "You're not like a relative of hers or something?"

I cocked my head. "No. Though she does carry my name."

He frowned. I could almost hear the rust in his head as the cogs turned.

"It's on her back," I told him. "Where I carved it."

Before any panic could fully register on Bruno's face, I swiftly flung the blade out. I aimed for his upper neck, but it went straight in the hollow of his throat.

Good enough.

He gasped, wheezing for air, but the air would not come. His hands went for his throat, trying to pull the blade out as the blood began to run down his chest, but he was already too weak to grab the handle. He started to pitch over, falling for the floor. I was at his side before he could.

I grabbed him by his greasy hair, holding him up by the roots.

"No, no, no," I said in a hush, making sure to stare him right in the eye. "This is not over."

I grabbed the knife and quickly yanked it out. Now the blood was gushing from the wound, drenching him in seconds. But as beautiful as the sight was, I had to be careful not to get any on my suit.

With my grip firm in his hair, I leaned over to whisper in his ear, the blade poised at his bloody throat. "You know all those things you tried to do to Luisa," I said. "Well, I did them.

I did them again and again, and she loved it. Maybe because I'm one of the few men who has ever seen her for the queen that she is. All you see her for is her beauty. I see her for *her*, stained and everything." I pressed the blade in harder. "And I see you for everything you are—a sleazy sack of shit."

I slowly, deliberately began to work the blade into his throat. He squirmed and kicked and fought against me, but in his current state, I was stronger. His will to live was pathetic, just like he was.

Eventually he stopped kicking. I kept cutting. When I was finally done, I was covered in a sweat and only a few drops of blood on my shoes and pants. They'd come out with a good wash.

I put his head into the garbage and pulled the bag out, making a knot at the end. I hoped it wouldn't leak through. Then I looked around the office. It was a mess before I came in, piles of paper and empty beer bottles scattered around. The addition of blood and a headless corpse was barely noticeable.

I pushed in the lock on the door and quickly exited, shutting the door behind me. I couldn't see Camila around, which was a shame. If she had asked me what happened, I would have told her Bruno had a headache and didn't want to be disturbed. It was such a good line.

Soon I was out of the bar and strolling down the street again toward my rental car, bag of garbage hoisted over my shoulder. My first order of business was complete. Now it was on to the second.

I had a feeling it was going to be a lot harder.

...

"Excuse me," I asked the aproned-woman who came to the door. "But do Raquel and Armand Chavez live here?"

The women stared at me for a moment, slowly wiping her hands on her apron. I had left Bruno's head in an ice cooler in the trunk, so there should have been nothing too unusual about a smartly-dressed man standing on the steps. "Yes, they live here. Who is asking?"

I breathed out a sigh of quiet relief. So Salvador hadn't killed them yet, which meant that Luisa was probably still alive.

"I'm a friend of their daughter," I told her, smiling as genuinely as possible. "Could you let Raquel know that I wish to speak with her? It's rather important, I'm afraid."

Again she studied me. I had a feeling that Luisa personally hired this woman. She was bold and suspicious, just the kind of person she'd want to protect her parents. If my instincts were right, she probably had a gun very close by and knew how to use it.

"What is your name?" she asked.

"Javier," I told her.

"No last name?"

"Garcia."

"All right, Javier Garcia," she said. "I'll go get Raquel. Please stay here."

The door shut in my face.

I shrugged and took a seat on the bench beside a well-tended rose garden. I admired the flowers while I waited to hear the door open again.

When it did, I swiveled in my seat to see a beautiful, elegant older woman standing there. Her focus was on me, even though I knew she was blind.

"You wish to speak to me about Luisa?" she asked. I could see the caretaker hovering right behind her.

I started to rise but Raquel quickly said, "You stay right where you are. Don't get up. A friend of my daughter's is a friend of mine."

I really hoped she hadn't said that about Sal.

"Your senses are outstanding, Mrs. Chavez," I told her as she came down the two steps and on the path toward me, moving with grace and confidence, not needing any help at all.

She smiled, and I saw Luisa in her face. It did funny things to my gut, rotting it with sadness.

"Thank you," she said, "but this is just life for me. It doesn't need to be so hard."

"No," I said, "I guess not with this. You have a lovely new home." My eyes slid over to the housekeeper who was now leaning against the doorway, openly watching us. "And very watchful help."

"Ah, that's just Penelope," she said, waving her away. "Go back inside, Penelope, I'll be fine. This man is not going to hurt me."

Penelope reluctantly did as she asked, but even so I saw the blinds move and knew she was spying through the window.

"She's very paranoid," I noted, turning back to Raquel. "Is there a reason for that?"

She gave me a small smile. "Yes." But she said no more.

I didn't want to make Raquel paranoid, but I had to ask, "How come you're so sure I'm not going to hurt you?"

She sat down beside me and folded her hands in her lap. "You can read people's faces, can't you? I can read people's souls."

I couldn't help but laugh, but her smile and confidence never wavered.

"Oh, you're serious," I said, feeling slightly ashamed. I covered it up. "Well, I'll have you know I have no soul to read."

Now it was her time to laugh. "Of course you do!" she exclaimed. "You're here right now, aren't you? Now, tell me why, and you'll see that I'm right."

"Why I'm here?"

She nodded gently.

"Mrs. Chavez..."

"Raquel."

"Raquel," I started, "have you heard from your daughter recently?"

She shook her head, her hands trembling just a bit. "No. Not for at least three weeks. Do you know if she's okay?"

I sucked on my lip for a moment. "Truthfully? I don't know anything. But I don't think she is. I think Luisa is in a lot of danger and so are you. Salvador Reyes makes bad men look good."

"I know that," she said in quiet anger.

"And I know that he's no longer interested in keeping her as his wife..." I breathed in and out loudly. "And when that happens, she's as good as dead to him."

She stared up at the sky blankly for a few moments before she said, "What do you need from us?"

"I need to make sure you're safe," I said. "It's all Luisa ever wanted. She cares more about you than she does her own life and her own happiness." It's actually infuriating, I wanted to add. But even I knew when to keep my mouth shut.

"I know," she said, barely audible. Her eyes were watering. I really hoped she didn't start crying in front of me because I would have no idea what to do.

"If you're safe," I told her, "both you and your husband, and away from here, away from where Salvador can find you, then I can go and get Luisa. I can bring her back."

"That's impossible," she said. "Salvador Reyes is the leader of the Sinaloa Cartel."

"He is. And it won't be easy. I'll most likely die in the process. But there is a way to do it. There's always a way."

She seemed to take that in. She wiped away a tear with the back of her hand and nodded her head, as if agreeing to an internal conversation.

"Why are you doing this?" she eventually asked. "What is Luisa to you?"

"She's a friend." It wasn't quite a lie.

"You're in love with her," she stated, a wide smile on her face.

I shot her a look she could not see. "I care about her very much," I corrected her.

"Well," she said, not put off, "if that's good enough for you, that's good enough for me."

"Then you'll let me help you," I said cautiously, feeling like this had gone over easier than expected. I thought there would be a lot of protesting, a lot of yelling, a lot of doors slammed in my face or guns held to my head.

"Of course I will," she said. "And Armand will too."

"And you're trusting me, just like that?"

"Yes. I am. I told you. My senses are sharp, and you, my boy, have a very good soul, even if you choose to believe otherwise."

"I may not be as good as you think."

She smiled and waved at me. "Oh, I don't doubt it. I can smell the blood on you, after all."

I looked down at my pants, at the few dark spots that stood out against the navy blue. "I had some business to take care of," I tried to explain.

"I'm sure you did." I wondered how much exactly this woman thought she knew about me. It was fascinating and troubling all at once. But as long as she was willing to help herself and her daughter, I couldn't care.

"Will Penelope be an issue?" I asked, eying the house again.

"You're not shooting her," Raquel told me, "if that's what you're thinking."

I frowned. She seemed to have a pretty good handle on me after all. "I wasn't," I lied. "But will you be needing her in the future, or will someone else do? I can hire you anyone you want on the other side, but it's too risky to bring Penelope along with us. She's on the cartel's payroll, after all."

"Anyone kind will do," she said. "What do you mean the other side?"

"I can get you and your husband on a private ship leaving from San Jose's marina in thirty minutes. You'll go straight to Puerto Vallarta. There, I'll have someone meet you and help you get settled. You can trust her."

"Who is she?"

"My sister, Alana. She owes me more than a few favors." At least, in my mind she did.

"All right," Raquel said. "I trust you."

I smiled. "Normally you shouldn't, but in this case, I'm glad you do."

I helped her up, even though she didn't need it. Just before I was about to lead her to the door, she reached out and touched my face. She touched my forehead, my nose, my lips, my jaw, feeling delicately at each one.

"You're a striking man, I bet," she finally mused, looking satisfied. "All these parts that shouldn't work together but do."

I raised my brows and she gently took her hand away. "You could just call me handsome. Everyone else does."

Once we were back in the house, I told her to go get Armand and pack up everything important. Penelope started asking questions, panicking. I knew she'd either shoot me or stop them, so I stopped her before she could. It was just a sleeper hold of sorts, something to knock her out long enough until Luisa's parents were safe and on their way to Puerto Vallarta.

I quickly slid the body into the kitchen, making sure she wasn't visible to anyone passing by, and left her a great wad of American hundred dollar bills, knowing that it was worth more than she'd get in a few month's pay. It might buy her silence—there was no way Penelope wanted to own up to being the one who let Luisa's parents escape. It also bought Raquel peace of mind.

Armand was a bit more cantankerous than I thought, and even though he drifted in and out of confusion, he was willing to go wherever Raquel was telling him. Soon I was driving them to the docks and helping them onto a fishing boat that one of my men operated. It paid to have my workers everywhere.

Once on board, Raquel looked up at me and smiled. I'd be lying if I said it didn't creep me out a little, the way she knew where you were, the way she seemed to see into you without seeing you at all.

"Good luck," she said. "I trust that you'll do everything you can."

I nodded. She was right about that.

After I watched them leave, and their ship faded on the horizon, I put in the call to Alana. If she wasn't willing to help out, I had a few people on that end that would. Still, I didn't trust them quite the way I trusted her.

"Hello?" she answered, sounding short of breath. "Javier?"

"Alana," I said. "Is this a bad time?"

"No, no, I was just doing my workout video, it's fine."

I'd forgotten that Alana was a bit of a health nut. I hoped happy endorphins were running amok.

"Yes, well, so here is the thing." I launched right into it, telling her only what she needed to know—mainly that she needed to take care of two ailing parents for a few days. She tried to get out of it, telling me she'd get fired from the airlines for taking time off. I told her I would ensure that not only would she not get fired, but that I'd pay her three times what she'd miss. She told me she wasn't equipped to act as a nurse, and I told her I'd give her money to hire a short-term nurse if needed. I had an answer for everything, and I was very persuasive. I was also an expert in the art of guilt-tripping.

After she reluctantly conceded, she asked, "Who are these people, Javier? Why are you doing this?"

"Their daughter is important to me," is all I said.

"In what way?" she asked suspiciously.

"In ways I don't even understand. Thank you, Alana. I'll be in touch." Then before I almost hung up, I quickly said, "Oh wait. They'll have a cooler with them. There's what looks like a head of lettuce in there. Can you put in your freezer at home? I want it there for safe-keeping."

"*Is* it a head of lettuce?"

"It's something I promised to get." I cleared my throat. "A gift. But for fuck's sake, don't peek at it."

"I wouldn't dare," she said dryly, then hung up.

I sighed and put my phone back in my pocket. I walked away from the turquoise waves and the fishermen, back to the car, back to the airport, back to Mazatlán and back to The Devil's Backbone. When I left again, there'd be no guarantee I was coming back.

CHAPTER TWENTY-TWO

Javier

"You're fucking crazy," Este spat at me, grabbing the ends of his hair and pulling on them. It was surprising to see him acting like a teenage girl, even for him.

"We all know I'm crazy," I agreed. "This should not be new information. It takes crazy to run this business."

"No, Javi," he said, sitting down in his chair in a huff. "What you're talking about isn't running a business, it's *ruining* a business."

I gently pulled at the ends of my shirt, making sure they were even. "And it also has nothing to do with the business. I go in and get her. End of story."

He narrowed his eyes, taking me in for a moment. Then he shook his head. "If you come back dead, that will affect the business."

I gave him a hard look. "And then you'll take over. That is what you've always wanted, isn't it? Me out of the picture."

He scoffed at that. "If I wanted you out of the picture, Javi, I would have made that happen a long time ago."

"No," I said, smiling slowly. "You wouldn't have. You can't. And you know it. No one gives a flying fuck about you because you haven't had to do anything to get where you are except just show up. People respect me. I worked for everything I've got. You'd last a few hours if you were ever to usurp me and you know it."

He rolled his eyes. "Point taken. You don't have to be so mean about it."

"If I wasn't mean, I wouldn't be me." I leaned forward, hoping he saw how serious I was. "And if I wasn't crazy, I wouldn't be me either. I know what I'm doing, Este."

All right, well that was a complete lie. I had no idea what I was doing or if it would work. I was guessing the odds of getting Luisa out—if she was still alive—were fairly high, but the odds of me surviving, or not being hauled off to prison again, were very low. But for once in my life, the odds were worth the risk.

Two days after I returned from Cabo San Lucas, I finally heard from Lillian Berrellez. She had been my absolute last resort, but I was at the point where I could admit that not only did I need special help in getting Luisa back, but I needed to shed a few points from my moral compass.

In old Mexico, the Mexico I aspired to be a part of, the cartels all operated around each other with an air of respect. Bargains were made—I give you something, you give me something. There were no ruthless, pointless killings in the streets. There were no innocents being raped, murdered, tortured. There were no 16-year-old versions of myself being taught to fire AR-15s. There were no gangs of punks running amok and killing people over fifty dollars worth of stolen cocaine.

We did our business to better ourselves and to better the country. We were vicious and violent but elegant and discreet. There was a dance to all of this, one that kept all things flowing in the right direction, a circle that ensured the smartest and brightest would stay on top, not the man with the most guns and the smallest dick.

And in this dance, there was a code. We are born as Mexicans and we die as Mexicans. Our problems stayed our problems. We never get the States involved in our affairs. The DEA, the FBI, the CIA, they were our enemies, and as cartels, we needed to unite against an enemy that thought they knew what was best for us yet had no idea how our business worked. The USA had no right to tell us, citizens of another country, what we could and couldn't do. They didn't live here, they didn't know. They only knew their privileged, fat, wasteful society while they pointed their fleshy fingers at us and blamed Mexico for all their problems.

When I was let out of prison, it was because I struck a deal with the DEA, an agency that was sometimes more corrupt than we were. I had promised to provide intel when it was needed—something I never wanted to do, something that went against my morals. I also paid a shitload of money.

Lillian Berrellez was a young, attractive, saucy woman who was born in San Diego to Mexican parents. I used to have more than a few fantasies about her while we were striking our bargains. She was a tough nut to crack though, completely devoted to her job, though obviously not above a little bribery. Though I had promised her intel, aside from a few things here and there, stuff that was of no use to her, I had never really given her any since my return to Mexico.

And the funny thing was, she never asked. I suppose she knew I would protect my country before I ratted any of my countrymen out, whether they were enemies or not.

But now, I was asking her. I was providing her with everything she needed to know about Salvador Reyes. I was making a bargain with the enemy across the border, all so I had a chance of getting Luisa out of there alive.

Luisa was a woman who never needed saving. But this time, I was afraid she did. It was too bad that I was going to be the one to have to do it.

"I just don't understand," Este went on. "Why Luisa? Do you want to start a family? Have kids until you have a son to carry your name, carry your empire? You're not the only one, Javier. All the narcos want that, all the narcos have that—except for you. But why her? You can find a hot, pretty woman who's a good lay anywhere. You could snatch them up in a second. It would be far less complicated. You don't need to love them to have a family. You just need a willing pussy." He considered his own words. "Or a non-willing pussy, if you're anything like most men."

A few seconds ticked by in silence. I eyed the bottle of scotch I had been imbibing on for the last week, grateful I was putting my days of misery and inertia behind me.

"I just want her," I found myself admitting. "That is all. It's that simple."

He sighed, running his hands through his hair. "Fine. And I know you don't believe me, but I am just looking out for you. It would be a million times easier for all of us if you just forgot about her."

"I've tried. I can't."

"At least let me come with you," he said. "You know if you go alone the DEA will take you. You're playing right into their hands. They'll arrest you."

"Berrellez said I wouldn't be touched," I said. Unless I killed Salvador, I finished in my head. Then she said all bets were off. They wanted that fucker alive. That was going to be the hardest promise to keep.

"And you trust that woman?" Este laughed.

"Not really," I admitted. "They could very well take in Sal and me at the same time. Two major cartel leaders in one raid. Wouldn't that buy them a larger pension and a watch. Headlines all across the country chanting, 'USA, USA!'"

"You do realize I'll probably never see you again."

I smiled quietly. "Bury me by the koi pond. And wait at least a day until you crack open the Cristal."

He chuckled and I added, "Oh, and if I don't make it out and Luisa does and you happen upon her again, promise me two things."

He sighed and crossed his arms. "What?"

"One, that you don't dare lay a finger on her or I will rise from my grave and fuck you up the ass. And don't you think I won't enjoy it—I'll be dead and I'll take any hole I can get. Two, that you tell her to see my sister Alana in Puerto Vallarta."

"And then what? Even I don't know where your sister lives."

And I intend on keeping it that way. "My sister will also be looking for her. I just want her to be aware."

He looked uneasy. "Word about this will get out, you know," he said gravely. "Everyone will know what happened and why you did it. All your enemies will know your weakness—your weakness is women."

"Women?" I repeated, confused by the plural wording.

He nodded. "Yes. Luisa. And your sisters."

"I don't think many know Alana even exists, and Marguerite is safe in the US."

"Fair enough," he said. "I guess you can keep Luisa safe, *if* you get out alive." He got out of his chair, ready to leave. "Any last requests? Any more noses you want cut to spite your own face?"

"Yes," I said, twirling my watch around my wrist. "If you do take over, don't fuck it up. I didn't build an empire to have you come in and destroy it in seconds flat."

"Then don't fuck it up yourself," he said imploringly. "Don't do this. Let Luisa go and save your face, save your empire. Save everything you say you worked so hard to build."

"I told you!" I snapped, frustrated with his inability to understand, though even I was having a hard time understanding myself. "I tried. I just can't let her go. I can't let her die." I composed myself and added softly, avoiding the pity in his face, "I know that makes me a fool..."

"It makes you weak," he corrected me.

I swept a shrewd eye over to him. "Or maybe it makes me strong."

After all, a kingdom was only as good as its ruler, and a king and queen could do more damage together than a king alone.

"It makes you aggravating as all hell," Este said sourly. He sighed. "But you wouldn't be Javier Bernal if you weren't." He left the room.

I poured myself a glass of scotch and wondered if it would be the last scotch I'd ever have. Was Luisa really worth that?

But I knew she was. And if I really wanted to pretend I was still completely selfish, saving Luisa would save me from my own torture, my own demons. Not having her around was hard enough. Her absence ate at me. My dick throbbed for her when my own hand wouldn't do. She had given me something during the short time she was with me, something I never knew I needed. Now it was gone, she was gone, and I'd become captive to the foolish notion that I could get it back.

It wasn't that Luisa completed me—she couldn't be the other half of my so-called soul. But she was all I could ever want, all I could ever need. If I was going to be swallowed by my own dirt one day, I'd rather have her with me, smiling and free.

...

The next day, armed with as much detailed information from Juanito as possible—information I had already forwarded to Berrellez—I headed out on my suicide mission. I made sure I looked good. The finest silk and linen suit I owned. Black leather boots—a 9mm in one and my knife in another. Two .38 Supers in my harness under my jacket. A bulletproof vest under everything else.

I couldn't do anything to protect my head, but at least my hair looked good.

I had Juanito drive me to Mazatlán and drop me off at one of the high-end resorts.

I took my seat at a flashy bar overlooking a glittering blue pool, aviator shades keeping my struggles internal and away from eyes.

"Looking good, Mr. Bernal," a husky voice said from behind me.

I grinned to myself before I turned and shared it with Lillian Berrellez.

I looked her up and down. "You're also looking good, Ms. Berrellez," I said smoothly, in English.

She was a fairly tall woman, nearly my height, with a very tight, curvy build. Her tits were huge and fantastic, and her ass was larger than an aircraft carrier. Her eyes were hooded, her lips gratuitously full, her hair big and light auburn, which somehow worked with her darkly tanned skin. She was wearing a black suit that fit her perfectly.

She smiled, cheeky as always. It was her way of making you think she liked you. I knew the truth—she was tough as nails and didn't like anybody, especially me.

"English?" she asked.

I shrugged. "It's good for me to practice."

"I'm guessing you won't need any practice for what we're about to do."

I gave her a sly look. "I'm not sure who you think I am and what I do all day, but I can assure you that I don't take part in government-operated raids on a daily basis. I'll be more of a fish out of water than you."

"Hey," she said sharply, though her eyes were still playful. "I'll have you know I helped initiate a bust in Culiacán that resulted in thirteen million worth of drugs and cash being seized."

"That was you?" I asked. "Oh, your parents must be so proud."

She glared at me. "Your English needs some work. You're not very good at sarcasm."

I finished up my drink and followed her through the hotel lobby and out to a waiting white SUV with tinted windows. I felt a bit like a lamb being led to the slaughter. I hoped they knew there was a lion underneath all my wool.

I climbed in the back, beside her, and was quickly introduced to her team before the vehicle roared off. There was the driver, Diego, a traitor to my country, obviously, and Greg, a gruff silver-haired dope in his early fifties who didn't say much but obviously had a problem with the fact that Berrellez was sharing the operation with him. He only spoke up when he needed to take control.

While we chugged along the highway heading north to Culiacán, I was filled in on their plan. Naturally, I wasn't given very much to go on. Though I was thanked and told that the intel that Juanito provided was the final puzzle piece that helped them pinpoint where they thought Salvador might be, they gave me no background into how closely they had been watching him, how much they already knew, and how they got all their previous information.

I suppose they could have been doing the exact same thing to me, although I was a smaller fish to fry. Technically I wasn't wanted in the states anymore for anything, but I had a giant rap sheet in Mexico. My government did nothing to enforce it, but I wouldn't be surprised if the DEA tried to take things into their own hands. They'd say capturing Javier Bernal would make America a safer place.

Fucking morons.

But Salvador, Salvador was wanted for a few things in the USA. Cocaine trafficking charges and the murders of several DEA officers and officials were just some things that the DEA wanted to hang him for. The rest of his charges would come via the Mexican Attorney General. I had no doubt that the DEA and the PGR were working together on this, using Mexican soldiers who had no ties to the cartels.

Of course, it was always so hard to tell what side people were on here.

"Did you know that the character of Sinaloa is that of an angel and a devil?" I said to Berrellez as we started getting closer to the city, our vehicle beginning to snare up with traffic. "It was lawless and violent, even before the poppies started growing."

"Thanks for the history lesson, Javier," she said, not taking her gaze from the window. "It's a wonder you aren't from here."

"I merely live nearby. Besides, I'm all devil, no angel."

She raised a brow and looked at me with that perpetual smirk. "Is that right? Tell me again about the woman you are doing this for..."

I pressed my lips together, not wanting to share more about Luisa than I had to. If they weren't going to be so forthcoming with me, I wouldn't with them.

"She's an innocent woman who got taken in against her will," I finally said.

"She looked happy in her wedding photos," she noted.

"She wasn't," I said, my tone flinty. "And you know that whatever Salvador wants, Salvador gets."

"Sounds a bit like Javier Bernal."

"Well, we shall see then, won't we?"

"It's just strange you've taken an interest in his wife. I have a hard time believing you're doing this out of the goodness of your heart."

"Then keep believing that. But once you see her and you look in her eyes, you'll know. And you'll know there was no point in even having this conversation."

"What if she's already dead?" Greg asked from the front seat.

I shot him my most violent look. "If she's already dead, there's no difference. Her eyes will look the same."

It was something I was trying my hardest not to think about. As much as I thought about Luisa, as much as I pictured her beautiful face, her fiery spirit, her pure heart, the way she felt like home when I was inside her, I didn't think about the way she was now. I couldn't even let myself imagine the horrors she must have been going through with Salvador.

For the second time, I felt total shame for carving my name into her back. That would bring her so much pain, much more than the pain I had given her. I hoped she wouldn't be too broken, when and if I found her. I hoped she'd still find that fight inside of her, that courage. I also hoped she wouldn't let her selflessness kill her, especially not for someone like me, who didn't deserve an ounce of it.

I wished I had the guts to realize what she had meant to me, back when I could have changed things. Now it was probably too late.

After a while, we came across our first checkpoint. Considering our vehicle and the fact that Greg, a white man, was in the passenger seat, I was certain we were going to be busted by Salvador's men.

But the masked gunman only waved us through.

"That was easy," I commented, twisting in my seat to watch them stop the car behind us.

"They're on our side," Berrellez said smugly.

"And what side is that?"

"Mexico's. They're your army."

"And Salvador's checkpoints?" I asked, waving at the distance in front of us. I knew there would be a few more and they wouldn't be on "our" side.

"Just trust us," she said.

Yeah fucking right.

But I had no choice. Soon we were pulling off the highway and down a dusty road that seemed to head into nothing but farm fields, rows of eggplant and tomatoes as far as the eye could see. Finally the fields tapered off and we ascended up into a forest, the road starting to wind.

"Where the hell are we going?" I asked. There was a niggling feeling in my gut that perhaps they were planning to off me.

They didn't answer. That didn't help.

Eventually, however, we came to a stop in a wide, mowed field beside a rather large barn. The field was occupied by at least seven black helicopters. Dozens of armed officers with the words DEA emblazoned on their backs were milling around. All of them were wearing goggles and helmets, covered head to toe in protective gear and holding matte black automatic rifles.

"Wow," I commented. "Very professional looking bunch."

"It's the DEA, what did you expect?" she asked, opening her door.

I shrugged. "I thought it stood for Drink Every Afternoon."

She eyed me with impatience. "Come on, get out."

I did so, stepping on to the grass with ease and felt every single pair of goggles turn in my direction. Here I was, Public Enemy Number Two, and completely surrounded. I was tempted to give them all a little wave but figured some hotshot would probably mistake it as a threat and blow my hand off.

"Now I'm going to go change," she said. "Want a gun? They're brand new carbine AR-15s."

I pursed my lips. "Nah. Seems a bit impersonal, don't you agree?"

She stared at me for a few beats. "How about protection?"

I grinned at her. "I don't use protection. Dulls the senses."

"For your body," she said in annoyance.

"I've got a vest underneath and a few pistols. I'll be fine."

"Your funeral," she said before she turned and headed toward the barn.

It wasn't long before she came back looking like a man. Every part of her was covered up in the DEA's armor, the long AR-15 held proudly in her hands. She smiled at me. "Well, I just spoke to the PGR. They have another five helicopters at their location, and they're about to set off. Are you ready?"

"To be thrown out of a helicopter? Not particularly."

She jerked her head toward a helicopter that was just starting up, its blades slowly whirring around. "Let's go."

Just like that, everyone around us started clamoring toward the waiting choppers. I climbed in with Berrellez, Greg, and four other men whose names I didn't know, nor could I tell them apart, and soon we were lifting off into the air. Though I denied an AR-15 and protection, I was still given a headpiece which I could talk to them through, something that was already useful, considering how loud the helicopter was.

"You look nervous," Berrellez said to me.

"I'm not the best flier," I admitted.

"Nothing to do with you being dropped off at the heavily-armed compound of the world's most wanted drug trafficker?"

"No," I lied. It wasn't that I was freaking out. It wasn't even that I was afraid. But there was a thread of apprehension that ran through me, tickling me from time to time. It wasn't often that I was out of my element, and beyond that, beyond the idea of dying fruitlessly, I was worried that I still wouldn't be able to save Luisa in the end.

"Good," she grinned. "I'm not nervous either."

To my surprise, the choppers didn't head toward the city of Culiacán, the hazy mass of roofs and rivers. They headed further inland, into the mountains. It seemed that Salvador had changed it up after we captured Luisa and had moved to another mansion. I had no doubt that the remoteness meant security was even tighter.

"Based on satellite images," she said, pulling out a mobile device and flipping through it, "there's a plot of land both behind the house and down the road by a few meters. We'll go as close to the house as possible. If the PGR aren't already there, we'll be the first on the scene. We'll all head out first, then you follow."

I nodded, understanding but not agreeing.

Suddenly the choppers swooped up, nearly missing a row of trees that protruded from a rapidly rising cliff.

And on the other side of them, settled in the middle of a plateau, was Salvador's house. It was a mansion not too dissimilar to mine, albeit with none of the class or beauty, with a few guards milling about and some stationed at the gates. Naturally, as soon as we started bearing down on the house, they started panicking and shooting at us.

The gunman in the chopper began firing back, taking out as many as he could before the pilot began a quick descent toward the green grass of the backyard.

Not going to lie—my heart was in my throat.

And I had to take every opportunity I could. As soon as Greg slid the doors open and the chopper was making its way past one wing of the house right over a small balcony, I made the sign of the cross, leaped past Berrellez, and jumped out.

Someone tried to grab me at the last minute, maybe it was Berrellez, but gravity had taken hold and I plunged about fifteen feet, landing straight on a glass table. It shattered beneath me and I lay there for a few moments on my back, the wind knocked out of me, staring blankly up at the black chopper blades as it continued on its way. The sound was incredible, hypnotic, until I heard Berrellez squawking in my ear.

"What the hell was that?" she yelled at me through the scratchy earpiece. I quickly rolled over in time to see someone coming to the balcony door. I whipped out my pistol and shot right through it, getting the figure before they could get me.

"You do things your way," I said to her, "I'll do things my way."

"Don't forget the deal. All bets are off if you end up killing him. We need Salvador alive!"

"Yeah, yeah," I said, and switched my earpiece off.

I scrambled to my feet, shrugging the broken glass off of me. Rapid gunfire erupted on the lawn though I couldn't tell who was firing the most and who was already winning.

It didn't matter though. I was after only one thing.

I gripped my gun and stepped through the broken glass door and into a cool, carpeted bedroom of Salvador's house.

Time to find my queen.

CHAPTER TWENTY-THREE

Luisa

At first I thought it was the end of the world. I heard the deep rumble slice through the air, felt it quaking in my bones, shaking the floor of the bathroom I was lying on.

I welcomed the end of the world with open arms. In fact, I think I smiled knowing that death was finally on its way. It had ignored my pleas for far too long.

But then, when I didn't die and the world didn't burn and crash around me, I realized that the sound I was hearing was helicopters. I tried to raise my heavy head to look through the narrow window above the shower. It was glassless now, as was the mirror. Salvador had taken them out after I had stabbed him in the forearm one day with a slice I broke off. It cut my hands up pretty bad and I received a round of electric shock torture for my disobedience, but damn had it felt good.

Through the window I saw a black helicopter fly past, heading right over the house and the sound built up, growing deeper. Then I saw another helicopter and another.

Something was going on. I should have been happy, just having a disruption to the daily monotony. I wasn't sure how long I'd been kept in the bathroom, perhaps ten days, perhaps two weeks? It was hard to remember. My brain wasn't functioning anymore since he stopped feeding me several days ago. I still had water coming out of the bath and the taps and the toilet, just to ensure I wouldn't totally die. If I was dead, how on earth could he torture me? How would he hear me scream?

Salvador hadn't even raped me aside from the first day or two that I had arrived back. I felt like that was purely to assert his dominance, especially after he saw Javier's brand on my back. He wanted to make sure that I belonged to him again. But to my surprise, the sexual attacks stopped soon after.

It was nothing to be relieved about. Salvador's big thing now was to torture me in other ways. I was no longer his wife that he could have every which way he wanted. He no longer *wanted* me. So I was treated like an informant, like a spy, like a hostage. I was locked up in the bathroom somewhere in his house and he would visit me...sometimes once a day, sometimes twice, sometimes once every couple of days, all his ways of keeping me in suspense.

Too bad I had become too numb inside to even care anymore.

The first week, he removed the nails from my pinky toes. While one of his men held me down, he slowly ripped the toenails straight out. I prided myself on not passing out, but boy did I scream. It was just what he wanted. After that, I did my best not to make a sound. I was able to make it through the Tasers, being the old pro that I was already, but when it came to the hot irons he applied against my stomach, well that I could never keep inside.

And while I was able to take the beatings quite well, the other day he took a hammer to my finger. He seemed extra angry, muttering something about my choice in hired help, and I was punished accordingly. I screamed more after he left, when I attempted to bandage my broken index finger to my middle one using a toilet paper roll and strips of the shower curtain I had painstakingly ripped off.

Now I was lying on the cold tiles of the floor, wondering if the end was coming or if the helicopters were only going to bring me more pain. I didn't even have the strength to crawl over to the door and see if I could hear anything.

Not that I needed to. Soon the air was filled with the sound of gunfire coming in all directions. People were no doubt dying. I wanted to smile at that. I wanted the whole world to burn.

I closed my eyes again and lay down my head, envisioning the madness that was going on outside, pretending that the good guys had come—whoever they were—and that Salvador would be caught in the crossfire. I hoped he'd die feeling like a fool.

Minutes passed and more helicopters sounded. More gunfire followed. I wondered what would happen if someone found me. Would they mistake me for being part of the cartel and shoot me on sight? Would they show me mercy? Or did the world hold worse things for me? It didn't seem possible.

Eventually I heard quiet footsteps on the floor outside, and when I opened my eyes, I could see a pair of boots underneath the doorframe, waiting on the other side.

I started smiling before I even knew why.

The door was suddenly kicked open, narrowly missing my face, and I followed the boots up to see a pair of golden eyes staring down at me. Waves of pain and relief swirled in them with startling clarity.

"Luisa," Javier whispered, immediately dropping down to his knees. He looked completely beside himself as his eyes searched my body up and down. He touched my face and I closed my eyes, leaning into the warmth of his palm. He was here. He had come. My beautiful, ruthless king.

"Luisa," he said, gently running his other hand down my side, feeling carefully for anything broken. "Stay with me, darling. I'm getting you out of here. Can you walk?"

I nodded. "I think so," I said, my voice so painfully raw.

He looked at my broken finger, at my toes, at the wounds in my arms and legs from the Taser, at the bruises on my face. The more he searched me over, the more broken he looked. I couldn't let him lose it if I hadn't yet. Now was not the time.

"I'll be fine," I said, trying to get to my feet.

He gripped me by my arms and carefully pulled me up. I wobbled a bit on my feet, dizzy from the lack of food, and fell into his chest. He immediately wrapped his arms around me and held me tight. It took everything I had not to break down crying.

He kissed the top of my head. "I should have never let you leave."

"I never should have left," I said softly. I had regretted it the moment I stepped into the house, the moment I realized that Salvador would probably have my parents killed anyway. For once, I hated how selfless I had been.

"I'm going to kill him," he growled, and I could feel the anger and tension starting to roll through him. "I want to kill him more than I've ever wanted to kill anyone. I want to do everything he did to you to him, but worse. I want him gone." He sighed in frustration. "But I made a promise not to."

That surprised me. "To whom?"

"The DEA," he said. "They're the ones who got me in."

"You made another deal with the Americans?"

He pulled away and stared at me intensely. I had missed his eyes so much, the power inside them, the passion and strength. "I would do anything to get you back. And I did."

"But your cartel," I started.

He shook his head. "It doesn't matter. None of that matters. Only you matter, Luisa, only you." In the distance, the gunfire reigned. He paused. "But it will all be in vain if I don't get you out of here. I'd tell you I need you to be strong, but I can tell you already are."

I managed a smile, refusing to let fear enter my veins anymore. I wouldn't fear with him by my side. We would make the world pay.

"Give me one of your guns," I said, holding out my good hand, which was thankfully my right one.

He grinned at me and reached into his boot, pulling out a handgun and placing it in my hand. "Try not to shoot the guys with DEA on their backs. We might get in trouble."

"Save that for another time?" I said, not really joking either.

He planted a hard kiss on my forehead. "Goddamn it, you're perfect."

He led me out of the bathroom and into the adjoining guest bedroom. We were almost out in the hall when one of Salvador's guards appeared.

Javier pulled me down and shot the man just as another guard appeared. From my position on the ground, I somehow managed to aim the barrel and pull the trigger.

I hit the second man right in the chest, and he stumbled backward against the wall before toppling over on his fallen comrade.

My heart galloped wildly, loudly, and it felt hard to breathe.

I had just killed a man.

Me.

Just like that.

Javier looked down at me in awe before helping me to my feet.

"How did that feel?" he asked in amazement, peering at me closely.

My breathing had returned to normal and the adrenaline was starting to coax through my veins. My flesh tingled all over. I swallowed as I looked at him, sharing his wonder.

"It felt good," I told him honestly and not feeling the tiniest bit ashamed. "Almost like sex."

He shook his head, his nostrils flaring. "Stop that," he said gruffly. "I almost came just from seeing you pull the trigger."

He brought me to the hall, and after checking both ends, we ran down it, heading away from the gunfire that now sounded like it was coming from the foyer. He darted into the room of David, Salvador's asshole assistant, and I could see where he'd already come in. The French door and the table on the balcony were already smashed, David's dead body lying amidst the damage.

I spit on his body as we stepped over the corpse and onto the balcony. In the distance a helicopter was flying and I could see a few of them on the lawn. The grass was littered with bodies, most of them Salvador's men. Bullets still ripped through the air, though I couldn't see the combat.

"We'll go on the roof," Javier told me, staring up at it. "That way one of the helicopters can pick us up and we'll be safer. We can see anyone coming from below and we'll pick them off."

If we stood on the edge of the balcony's railing, there was a small overhang that would be easy to climb up on, at least for him. Escape was so near.

"I don't know if I can pull myself up," I told him, starting to panic a little. "I don't have much strength."

"I'll pull you up," he said confidently. He quickly eased himself onto the railing, balanced himself, and then jumped up onto the ledge, needing to pull himself up a few feet.

And while he was doing that, his back to me, I felt a gun press against my temple and an arm hook around my neck. I dropped my gun in surprise and it went skittering over the balcony edge.

Heavy breathing seeped into my ear.

Fear gripped my heart.

Salvador.

By the time Javier found his footing and was turning around to see what caused the clatter, I was completely under Salvador's control. The look of utter outrage and madness strained Javier's face. I knew he wanted nothing more than to tear Salvador from limb to limb, but that would never happen now.

Now that he had me. Now that he would kill me in front of Javier.

"Javier, Javier, Javier," Salvador said, his voice raspy. "Finally we meet in person. You know, you're a lot smaller than I thought you'd be, even with you way up there."

His chokehold around me tightened and I tried to pry him off with one good hand, giving me a few more inches of breathing room, but the strength just wasn't there. I was slowly losing air.

"Let her go," Javier commanded, his voice steady despite everything. "Do what you want with me, but let her go. You've already hurt her enough."

"Really? I don't think I have," Salvador mused. "Tell me, Javier, when you were fucking her, did she scream for mercy like she does with me? Did you make her bleed too? You must have. Nice carving job, by the way. For an amateur."

Javier swallowed. I could see how hard he was breathing, how difficult it was for him not to whip out his gun and try and shoot Salvador, promise to the DEA or not. But he couldn't, not when I was a hostage once more.

"Let him kill me." I managed to get the words out to Javier. "Let him kill me, just make sure you kill him. Make him suffer."

"Shut up!" Salvador roared in my ear. "I will kill you, but then he's next. He doesn't even have his gun out. Fucking pussy."

The gunfire in the background had started to die down. The helicopter that we had seen in the distance was now long gone. I wondered what side was winning now. I wondered if they'd come and find us only after it was too late. I could only hope that if Javier and I were dead, the DEA would ensure that Salvador suffered, that he would never get out of jail alive, that our deaths wouldn't be for nothing.

"So what do you want, Salvador?" Javier asked, raising his hands. "Why are you doing this? Just shoot her now if that's what you want."

"You're as fucking crazy as she is," Salvador said, sneering. "Don't the two of you have any respect for death? You of all people, Javier, should know the importance of making a show of it. Of making it last. The true torture doesn't come during death—it comes in the moments before. When you know it's about to happen, but you don't quite know when. Just like now."

Javier's chest heaved. I could see his wicked brain working on overdrive, trying to come up with a way to at least save me if not himself. I could also see he had no options to go on. For all the fury he was carrying, I caught the sorrow on his brow. I saw the soft way he was coming to terms with the end.

But that didn't mean I had nothing. Even if it meant us getting shot, I at least had to try for the both of us. I welcomed the end more than he did. I had nothing to lose.

I held Javier's eyes with mine and then slid my gaze over to the partly-healed gash on Salvador's forearm where I had driven in the piece of glass last week. I couldn't reach around with my own arms and touch it, but that didn't mean I was powerless.

When I saw the nearly invisible hint of recognition in Javier's eyes, I knew it was time. I drew upon my reserves of anger, of injustice, of pure unadulterated rage that I had coiling deep inside me. I let those feelings, those hot, swirling, pulsing emotions wrap me up into an uncontrollable tornado that had nowhere else to go. Then I gave it permission to fuel me, to become my strength.

I screamed, a raw, brutal sound that ripped out of my gut and my throat, and used all my power to twist Salvador's forearm toward me. I bit straight into his wound, tasting the blood, loving the blood, relishing the feeling of my teeth plunging in deeper and deeper, tearing through muscle and nerve and causing so much pain.

The next thing I knew Salvador was screaming, caught off-guard by my violence, and Javier took that moment to whip out his gun and shoot.

He aimed for Salvador's shoulder. He got it.

Salvador spun back, out of my teeth and grasp, but not before he took his own gun and fired it at Javier as he fell.

I thought Salvador's aim would be off.

But it wasn't.

He shot Javier right in the head.

I screamed as Javier stumbled slightly then pitched forward off the roof and facedown onto the balcony, the glass bouncing around us from his impact.

With what strength I had, I kicked Salvador's gun off the balcony, then scampered over to Javier, crying, screaming, feeling like my own heart was bleeding, my breath pulled from me. The pain in my chest was so incredibly great, I wasn't sure how I was going to survive it. I wasn't sure if I wanted to.

I fell to my knees beside Javier, afraid to touch, afraid to roll him over. I wouldn't be able to handle what I so deeply feared to see.

But before I could reach out and touch him, he started to stir.

Alive.

"Javier!" I sobbed, my hands going for his head. I brushed away his hair and saw the wound, a long trail of blood on his temple. His eye opened and fixed on me.

"Fuck," he groaned. "Did he get me?"

I burst into the biggest smile and nearly laughed at the intense amount of relief flowing through me. "Get you? I think you were just shot in the head!"

He reached up and gingerly touched the wound. "Oh." He smiled weakly. "It just grazed me. How is my hair?"

I wasn't sure whether to punch him or kiss him.

But before I could do either, I was suddenly picked up by my shoulders from behind and thrown to the side. My head smacked against the floor, making everything spin and swirl nauseatingly, blackness teasing my vision and keeping me down.

I stared helplessly as Salvador launched himself on top of Javier, trying to choke him. Even with his one arm useless, he was a big man, stronger than Javier, and he was able to squeeze his throat tight with just his one hand.

"Look at you," Salvador sneered at him, saliva dripping down into Javier's face. Javier gasped for breath, his skin turning white. "A traitor to Mexico. You brought in the Americans just to take this whore back. You're a pussy. You're soft over a woman. A girl. You'll be known as the drug lord who became oh so good for no good reason."

"I am not good!" Javier managed to roar, the fight coming back in his face. With all he had left, he managed to kick up under Salvador and get his knife free from his boot. He raised the knife above his head, and just as Salvador looked up in surprise, Javier swiftly drove the knife between Salvador's eyes, plunging it all the way in to the handle. "I am just not as bad as you," he spat out.

Salvador froze up, the knife stuck into his brain. It instantly killed him, and Javier quickly rolled out from under his crushing body. He rapidly crawled over to me and felt along the side of my head. "Are you okay?" he asked, his voice cracking.

I swallowed and tried to talk but couldn't. I burst into tears instead.

"Shhhh, Luisa," Javier said soothingly. "I'm alive, you're alive. The fucker is dead. We're okay." He sat down beside me and pulled me into his lap, cradling me while I let everything loose. Anger, pain, shock, sorrow. He let me cry for as long as I needed. And when my tears started to dry, he said something that made me cry more, only from happiness.

"You should know that I have your parents," he whispered into the top of my head. "They're safe with my sister in Puerto Vallarta."

Even though Javier had never told me he loved me, I still had never known such love. I couldn't thank him enough, couldn't get over how absolutely selfless he had been, and all for me.

We sat like that together, me gathering strength in his arms, until a few DEA agents burst onto the balcony with their guns blazing. One of them I didn't even know was a woman until she took off her helmet and shook out her hair. She stared down at Salvador's body in dismay.

"Honestly, it was self-defense," Javier protested at her disapproving glare before she could say anything.

"But I bet you still enjoyed every moment of it," she said.

He smiled. "Of course I did."

And I did too.

I could tell Javier was nervous though, about what the DEA might do with him since Salvador was dead and he'd broken the one condition. But by the time the medics arrived by helicopter and had treated his head wound and splintered up my broken fingers and applied antibiotic creams to my body, we were told we'd be free to go anyway.

"He may not be alive," the woman, whom I learned was Lillian Berrellez, said, "but at least we were able to dismantle the Sinaloa Cartel. That's not too shabby."

No, it certainly wasn't. Even though there was a cartel that was ready to take its place: Javier's.

The DEA knew that, too. But for now, we were shaking hands and agreeing to walk away from each other.

I knew Berrellez would be back though. And if I was still by Javier's side at that time, I'd be making sure she didn't get far.

In this business, you didn't build empires by being good. And though I'd never truly be able to forget the person I was and could never fully eradicate my morals, I was looking forward to being bad.

I was looking forward to getting dirty.

Very, very dirty.

CHAPTER TWENTY-FOUR

Javier

It was the next day when Berrellez finally dropped us off in Mazatlán. Luisa and I were tired, wounded, and sore, but we were together and the DEA was letting us go free. For now, at least. But that was enough for us. We had each other and we were going home, back to my compound where I would surely scare the shit out of Esteban with my untimely return from the dead.

But even though that was the plan, that wasn't the only plan I'd made. Truth be told, I wasn't sure what the next step was. I felt as if I were being pulled by different hands, and though I knew which one felt right, I no longer knew what *was* right. Perhaps I had never known the difference. Perhaps there was no right or wrong anymore, not in this life.

Once Berrellez left, I took Luisa by her good hand and led her out onto the beach. Like usual on the coast, it was a blindingly beautiful day, the heat stunted by the cool Pacific. We weaved our way through thatched umbrellas, fat tourists on towels, and vendors hawking their cheap shit, until I found a more secluded place away from the hustle and bustle of bloated indulgence.

We sat down in the warm sand and I made a mental promise to myself to try and escape to the beach more often. It was nice to leave the controlled comforts of home and step into the chaos. I really had been making too many of my men do the work when I should have been doing it myself. Even though it was risky, it was a lot more fun to get my hands dirty.

"I was thinking that this weekend we could make the trip down to Puerto Vallarta," I told her. "To see Alana and your parents."

She beamed at me, her cheeks looking so cute I wanted to fucking bite them. "Oh, that would be wonderful."

"I even have a special present for you there," I said.

"Ooooh," she cooed, clapping excitedly. "What is it?"

"It's a surprise." Boy, was it ever. There weren't many men who'd deliver your lecherous ex-boss's head to you. Then again, there weren't many men like me.

While she sipped a Corona that I bought from a ten-year-old kid with a cooler, I pulled out two passports from my inner pocket and threw them down on the sand.

She eyed them with curiosity. "Where did you get Canadian passports?"

"They're ours," I told her.

She planted her beer in the sand and picked up the nearest passport, flipping it open. There was a picture of a woman that looked almost like her, just a few years older and with different hair, both things that could be easily faked. "Christine Estevez?" she said, reading it. "Who is this?"

I shrugged. "Who knows? It's legit though. I didn't have a photo of you so I had to obtain an actual passport through one of my channels." I flipped open the other passport and pointed at my unsmiling picture, not so different from the actual mug shot I had upon my arrest in the States. "Mine, however, is completely forged. You can't buy anything better though. It will pass all the tests again and again, so as long as you can remember who you are. I have birth certificates and driver's licenses, too."

"Javier Garcia," she read off of mine. "I think I like Javier Bernal better."

"Of course," I said, straightening my collar. "He is the best."

She bit her lip, thinking. "So why do we have these? Are we going to Canada? I think I have an uncle there, maybe we could go visit him."

"Darling," I said to her, pulling her to me. I ran my thumb over her lips then ran it over mine, tasting the beer. "We can go anywhere you want to go. And for as long as you want. We don't ever have to return."

She frowned, shaking her head. "I don't understand. What are you talking about?"

I took in a deep breath, my heart beating hard against my ribs. I'd rehearsed this a few times in my head already. For something this serious, this life-changing, I couldn't chance saying the wrong thing. "I risked everything to get you, Luisa. There's no way I can risk losing you again. You say the word, and we can run. Tell me to do it and I'll do it. I'll give all of this up. We can be free out there, out of danger. We can leave all of this behind."

"We can't run away, Javier," she said slowly.

"Yes, we can. We can do anything we want to do."

She smiled patiently and gently kissed my lips. "No, my love, we can't," she said, cupping my face in her hands. "You can never run away from yourself, you'll just go in a circle. There is no escape from this life because this is *your* life and you are what you are. And there is *nothing* wrong with that."

Her words sunk into me like the sweetest blade. Even so. "I can't lose you," I told her, feeling the truth in my bones.

"You won't lose me. I'll gladly live this life with you. I feel that it's what I was meant to do. To be your queen and rule by your side."

I rubbed my lips together, trying not to smile at her beautiful phrase. "It's an ugly life."

She shrugged. "I know. And it's all I've ever known. But at least now I'll have enough power to mask the ugliness."

I grinned. My heart could have burst. "You'll have all the power. You'll have everything."

"And yet all I want is you."

"You have me, my black heart and my dirty soul."

I grabbed her and kissed her forcefully, unable to hold anything back. She'd never tasted better. The smell of sun on her skin, the cool ocean spray, the idea of her ruling by my side, with all her good and all her bad—all of it made my heart spin and my dick throb mercilessly.

"I don't think I've ever wanted you more." I groaned into her mouth, falling back into the sand and bringing her down with me. I pulled her on top of me, gripping her legs so she was straddling my waist. My tongue eagerly plunged into her mouth again and again, stirring the flames that I wasn't able to hold back. I'd dreamt about this for days and days.

"We can always get a hotel room," she said against my mouth, and from the way her breath hitched, I knew she was just as turned on as I was. I could still get her hot in seconds flat.

"Fuck that," I said. I reached between her legs and under her skirt. I pushed her underwear aside and grinned at how wet she was. "My queen, we aren't going anywhere."

She moaned, her eyes fluttering. "But there are people on the beach. We'll get arrested."

"Is that so?" I asked, knowing I'd never be arrested in Mexico for anything.

"People will see."

"Tourists will see," I told her, licking her ear. "And let them see. Let them go back home and think that Mexico is a fun place." I bit her neck hard, relishing the feeling of her skin between my teeth. She shivered, loving it.

"I don't know," she said breathlessly, her back arching. I thrust my fingers into her with one hand while unzipping my fly with the other. It was a losing battle on her behalf.

"Look," I said, stifling a groan, "are you a Mexi-can or a Mexi-can't?"

She laughed, throaty and hot. "Quoting movies now? You're bad."

"You love that I'm bad."

She smiled serenely at me. "You know I do." Then her mouth twisted into an "o" as I took my swollen dick out and eased it into her. She was so exquisitely tight, so silky, so perfect. It didn't matter if we were fucking in public and in the broad daylight on the beaches of Mazatlán, or in the confines of my bed, she was everything I needed, everything I wanted.

"Take me home, my queen," I whispered to her. Finally she relaxed, sitting back, and I plunged deep inside of her. We both cried out from the pleasure and pain. It was impossible not to.

I gripped her hips and moved her back and forth in slow, subtle swivels. We were barely moving but that didn't mean I wasn't feeling everything, everywhere.

It wasn't long until the yearning I had felt for her, the fear of losing her, the intense sun behind her back, the blue sky and the passing people murmuring their disapproval and admiration, built up to a thunderous climax. I came hard into her, making sure her clit was well fed at the same time. While she clenched around me, squeezing me dry, she called me her king.

I don't think the words had ever sounded so right.

...

After our escapades on the beach, I went and got a rental car that I would never be returning, and we headed off on the highway that lead to Durango. It would have been a shorter trip home but my sexual appetite had been reawakened by all the violence, adrenaline, and the fact that we had almost lost each other. We pulled over twice: once because I craved the taste of her pussy so bad that we ended up going down on each other in the back of the car, the good ol' sixty-nine. The other time, I wanted to be back inside her warmth so she climbed on top of me while I was driving and started riding me that way. I only went about ten feet before I nearly crashed the car. Seemed I was good at most things but fucking and driving at the same time wasn't one of them.

Eventually we made it back home to the compound around sunset. The guards at the gate seemed shocked at my return, but they were smart enough to look happy about it. When it came down to it, there were worse bosses than me.

I parked the car right outside the front doors and looked over at Luisa, sitting serenely in the passenger seat. She seemed to glow.

"This is your home now, you know," I told her.

She smiled. "I know."

"It's your castle."

She leaned over and quickly kissed me. "And it will be a golden one."

We got out of the car just as the front door swung open to Este staring at us, completely dumbfounded. I relished the faint strain of disappointment in his brow. It served him right for me to prove him wrong.

"I don't fucking believe it," he said in quiet awe.

I raised my arms. "The ghost of narcos' past has returned to fuck you up the ass."

He grinned. "Lucky for me, I haven't had time to screw anything up. How the hell did you pull this off, Javi?" He continued to look between the two of us in amazement.

I shrugged. "What can't I pull off?"

I put my hand on the small of Luisa's back and guided her up the stairs. We paused in the doorway, looking Este over. "Esteban Mendoza," I said to him. "Meet your ruler, Luisa Chavez." I leaned into her ear. "You know, he's your employee now. How does that make you feel?"

She grinned at Este before she stared up at me. "Makes me feel like I should keep a Taser gun on me at all times. You know, just in case he misbehaves." She then winked at him and went inside the house.

I laughed at the look of fear in his eyes. I patted him on the shoulder. "She's not kidding either. She killed a man back there. I think she's gotten a taste for it."

We left the bewildered Este out on the steps, and I quickly led her straight up to our bedroom, where I would bring her fire and she would bring me peace, that beautiful peace.

I was her king.

She was my queen.

And we had a fucking empire to rule.

After we were done fucking, of course.

After all, I was still Javier Bernal.

THE END

ACKNOWLEDGEMENTS

Some books are easy to write, others are hard. Dirty Angels has the distinction of being an incredibly easy book to write considering the very hard circumstances I found myself in while writing it.

First of all, I actually came up with the concept of Javier's book back in February of 2013, when I had just finished writing On Every Street. Though I knew he wasn't the man for Ellie at that point, I also knew that I wanted to explore his story later. The man utterly fascinated me—and I knew I wasn't the only one under his spell.

Second of all, I started writing a big chunk of the book back in December of 2013, though the book had to be put on hold for various reasons. Starting and stopping with a book can be extremely difficult, though I was later grateful for this because when I did sit down to finally start writing again…

…I was planning a wedding. Yes, I wrote this book while I planned my wedding and finished it less than a week before the ceremony. I will be editing on my honeymoon. It's just the way things go when you're an author. But had it not been for Javier Fucking Bernal and my love for that crazy sexy psycho, I wouldn't have been able to do it. Somehow, despite all the outside stress, I wasn't stressed at all when writing it. It was easy, it was fun, and I had a blast.

But of course that's not to say that I didn't have help. From my best friend, Kelly St-Laurent, to my parents, Tuuli and Sven, to my husband, Scott MacKenzie, and all my friends who rallied behind me and this book (Sandra Cortez, Kayla Veres, Stephanie Brown, Shawna Vitale, K.A. Tucker, Barbie Bohrman, Ali

Hymer, Lucia Valovcikova, Nina Decker, Laura Moore, Chelcie Holguin, Kara Malinczak, Chastity Jenkins at Rock Star PR), I had a LOAD of help in all directions, and with them this book could *not* have been possible.

Thank you!

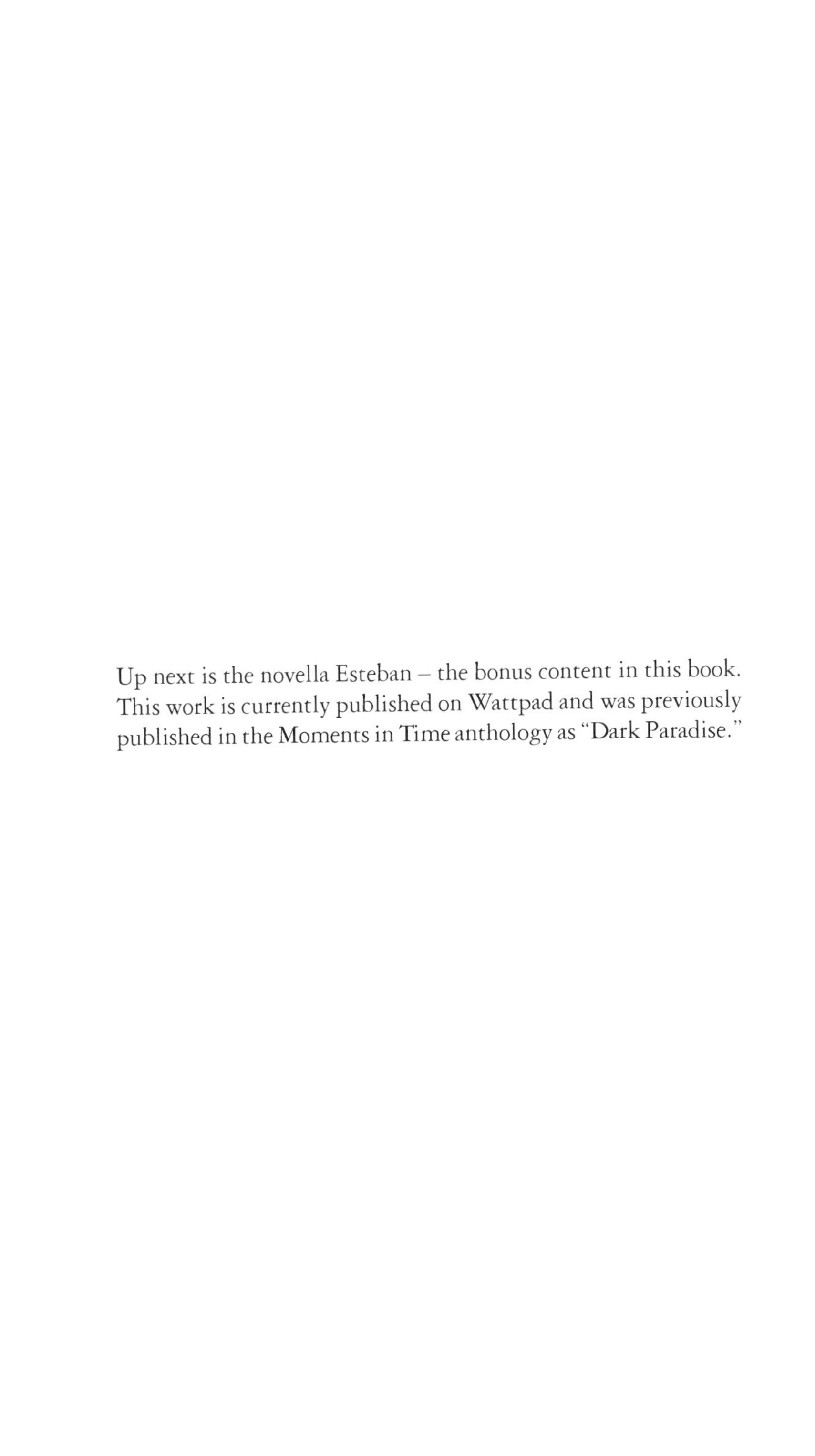

Up next is the novella Esteban – the bonus content in this book. This work is currently published on Wattpad and was previously published in the Moments in Time anthology as "Dark Paradise."

ESTEBAN

A SHORT STORY WITH CHARACTERS FROM THE DIRTY ANGELS TRILOGY

KARINA HALLE

CHAPTER ONE

I knew that the wave was too dangerous. I knew it and that was why I went for it. It came rolling into Hanalei Bay like a brilliant blue shock wave, diamond-studded from the sun, catching the attention of the bored surfers on this otherwise average day. It called to me like a slippery siren, just as it called to them. But instead of watching it pass underneath my dangling legs, like I had done with every surfable wave in the last hour, I decided to answer the call.

I decided it would be a good way to die.

Determined, I lay down on my stomach and began paddling like a madwoman, knowing the liquid beast was barreling up behind me. I could hear some of the territorial surfers out there were yelling, perhaps to get out of their way, perhaps to warn me, but I didn't care. The golden beach spread out in front of me as kids grabbed their bodyboards and fled from the surf, their parents yelling at them to be careful. They knew the dangers, just as I did.

I wasn't a great surfer. But then again, that was the point.

I sucked in my breath, salt dancing on my tongue, and got to my knees as I felt the massive pull of the wave take me and the board back.

My feet found the rough, beaten surface, my legs bracing for balance. The ocean roared beneath me. This wave was what every surfer could ever dream of, their holy grail, their Moby Dick, and I captured it like fireflies in a jar. I could feel the power, the surge, the sea spray, the sun on my skin. I could feel everything, as if I were finally alive and breathing and part of the world.

And yet living was the last thing on my mind.

I rode that wave for a few seconds that stretched out into eternity. Maybe my life flashed before my eyes, or maybe it flashed behind them. One moment I was up, feeling the immense girth of the wave curling up behind me, and the next I was down, a flower crushed in a closing hand. The board was yanked away from me so hard and fast that the cord was ripped off my ankle, and I was pulled in a million directions before the way down was the only way to go. The wave pummeled me until I took in water and gave up nothing in return.

No fight.

My eyes closed, burned by the salt, and my hair whipped around my head like seaweed. With heavy limbs and a heavy heart, I sank.

The ocean took me under, intent on holding me hostage with no ransom.

No one would have bartered for me anyway.

And then a hand reached out for me in the depths, wrapping around my wrist. I didn't know if it was the hand of life or death. But it had me.

Then another hand grabbed my arm and I felt the water around me surge, my body being pulled upward. I opened my eyes into the stinging blue glow, and past the rising bubbles and foam, I caught a glimpse of a man's face. His expression was twisted in turmoil; I suppose from the act of trying to save me. He obviously didn't know how little I'd appreciate it, how little I was worth it.

Suddenly, I was brought up to the surface, the sun and air hitting me just as the water began to rush out of my lungs. I could only cough until my chest ached, the rest of me completely useless as the man towed me toward the shore. My brain switched on and off, processing everything in splices of film:

The man's longish hair sticking to the back of his bare neck.

The gray clouds that hunkered down above the cliffs of the Na Pali coast.

The people on the beach watching my rescue, hands to their mouths, murmurs in the crowd.

The painfully vivid sky as the man laid me down on the beach, cradling the back of my head in his hands.

The man as he stared down at me—his disturbingly scarred face contrasting with his beautiful hazel eyes framed by wet lashes.

The face of a man I knew would be more dangerous than any wave.

And so, with consciousness slipping out of my hands again, I smiled at him, at the danger I recognized within.

And then the new world went black.

...

"Are you sure you don't want us to take you to the hospital?" the EMT asked me for the millionth time.

"I'm fine," I said deliberately. "Though I'm getting a headache from all your questions."

"It's really better if—"

I narrowed my eyes at the clean-cut man, even though it hurt my brain to do so. "I didn't call the ambulance, and I have no intention of riding in one to the hospital all the way in Lihue." I paused, inwardly wincing at what I was about to say. "I'm an artist and I'm uninsured."

He gave me a dry look. "Well, if you're going to continue surfing, perhaps looking into insurance is a good idea." But before I could say anything to that, he snapped up his kit and headed back to the ambulance that was purring behind the public restrooms.

I sighed from my perch on top of the picnic table and ignored the curious looks of the vagrants who were hanging around underneath the shelter, drinking cheap beer. Water from the rains that had passed by a few hours ago was still dripping off the roof, smacking the concrete and sand below with a desolate sound. The looky-loos who had been twittering about me earlier had gone on their sunburned ways back to the sand and surf, and Hanalei Bay looked as it did before I nearly died.

I was back to being alone. Back to being caught in my thoughts. Back to everything I had tried to escape from.

Except now that I'd actually willed myself to give it all up, there was something that pushed at my mind.

Someone.

The man who had saved me.

Just where had he come from and where did he go? When I came to on the beach a few minutes later after I had blacked out yet again, he was gone, and I was stuck looking at the faces of the panicked tourists, one who must have called the ambulance for me. The man, with his scars that crisscrossed the side of his face, and his vibrant eyes that hinted at the depths within, had completely disappeared.

The least he could have done was stick around so I could thank him.

But *would* I have thanked him? Perhaps if I saw the darkness in him, he saw the same darkness in me.

I got off the table and stood on the stiff grass, careful not hurt my ankle. It was especially tender after my board was ripped away from me, but not bad enough to warrant spending the money to get it checked out. I wondered if my board had washed up on the beach somewhere or if it was lost to the waves, then decided to forget about it. I didn't want to spend an extra minute here, knowing that I'd made a fool of myself by almost dying and all that.

I fished my keys out of my board shorts and headed to the Jeep I'd rented during the last two weeks. I had one week left on it before I was supposed to return to the mainland, back to Doug and the life that was drowning me. I swallowed my bitterness at still having to find a way out of all of this.

On the way back to Kilauea, I drove fast—too fast—nearly smashing into a waiting car as I sped over the one-lane Hanalei bridge, stars in my eyes and the war raging on in my mind. It was a miracle I even pulled into the driveway of my rental house in one piece.

The fact is, I wanted to keep driving. I didn't want to come back even to here, the place that should have been the escape from my marriage, from my job that didn't even insure me, and everything. But that was the irony of trying to escape to an island. There was nowhere to go; you just kept going in circles, coming back to where you started.

I went inside to the kitchen and poured myself an extra-large glass of red wine, wishing I hadn't finished the bottle of Scotch the night before. Leaning against the counter, I stared at the backyard, which disappeared into a thicket of hibiscus and gardenia, the azure sea stretching beyond it. I'd stared at the same scene ever since I arrived, willing myself to paint it. There was a papaya tree in the corner, a small fish pond, a hole in the distressed wood fence where brightly colored feral chickens would come through. This should have been paradise—this should have brought me and my art back to life. But it hadn't.

My phone buzzed and vibrated on the counter. I didn't even look at it. I knew I probably had a million missed calls since I headed out surfing, and I knew they were all either from work or from Doug. Work, because I was sure the temp couldn't handle another day under my boss's direction, and Doug because he just had to know where I was. Not because he cared—he stopped caring two years after our wedding—but because the fact that I took off to Kauai by myself was the biggest fuck-you to his renegade ego that I could have done.

I wondered what he would have thought if he knew I'd almost drowned without his permission, what he could have said if I'd come home with a death certificate. Would he genuinely be upset, distraught at losing his wife because he loved me oh so much—or would he just write me off to be with Justine?

I gulped back the rest of the wine and thought about what the gravestone of Lani Morrison would say on it. Here lies a wife? Here lies an artist? Here lies one lost woman who never quite found her way?

I hoped it would be blank and that people could draw their own stories about my life. They'd all be better than the truth, that Lani Morrison died at the age of thirty-three, childless by choice, locked in an unhappy seven-year marriage with a man who'd been in love with someone else for most of it. She lost her parents to a car crash when she was seventeen, found mediocre fame in her twenties for her watercolor paintings, then when her muse, her "spirit" for the art, left her, she had to find work as a part-time assistant in an office selling dishwashers.

May she rest in peace.

Fuck peace.

I slammed down the glass and it shattered on the marble countertop, sending shards everywhere. As I looked down at the mess, I felt acutely overwhelmed for a second, before I decided to let it all go. I plucked the bottle of wine off the counter and headed out into the backyard, where I sat down on the back stoop and proceeded to drink until all the cab sav was gone and I was even more numb than before.

Though not numb enough to prevent my thoughts from going back to the mystery man, my savior. What was it about him that kept stealing my attention? Every time I tried to picture him, I either saw his face under the water, partially obscured by the bubbles rushing past my eyes, or the sun-kissed look of his neck, his wet hair clinging to it as he pulled me to the shore.

I closed my eyes and leaned my head against the back door, the images replaying over and over in my mind until a noise brought me to attention. It sounded like someone was outside the front of my house.

Carefully easing myself up, feeling more than a bit drunk, I made my way through the cool house to the front door. I opened it and had to blink a few times at what I was seeing.

It was my surfboard, leaning against a potted Phoenix palm. I walked over to it and ran my hands down the smooth sides, then looked around. The street was empty except for a lazy cat waddling through the neighbor's grass. Who dropped it off, and more importantly, how the hell did they know where I was staying?

For the first time that day I felt uneasy, my skin prickling with gooseflesh. As empty as I had been, the fact that someone must have followed me to my house to return it to me was a bit unsettling, yet considerate. I took in a steadying breath and picked up the board, about to take it inside, when a piece of paper fluttered to the pavement.

I placed the board back against the palm and scooped up the paper in my hands. In neat cursive handwriting, the note read: "The next time I save you, you'll want me to."

A strange thrill ran through me as I remembered the man with the face of danger.

I wondered if he *really* knew how hard it was to save me.

CHAPTER TWO

I spent the next morning pacing up and down the hallway, trying to figure out what I was going to do with my day. Every now and then I'd wince as my bare feet found yet another slice of glass that I'd missed when I cleaned up the mess from the day before. From time to time I'd stride over to the windows and nervously peer out past the palm fronds, looking for a sign of that man who wanted to save me again.

It was kind of ridiculous, actually, but I was enjoying the suspense, the way my nerves rattled every time a car drove down my street. It gave me a strange sense of focus that had been missing the last few weeks...or months. Or years.

Finally around noon, after I managed to get down a bowl of cereal, I decided I'd had enough. I packed a beach bag, grabbed my board, and got in the Jeep. Though Hanalei was my favorite part of the island, I didn't want to head back there. I knew that the November surf was notoriously wicked on the North Shore, part of the reason why I had wanted to go there in the first place.

But this time, it wasn't really about being saved.

It wasn't about dying either.

I steered the Jeep onto the highway and decided to head southeast to Larsen's Beach. It wasn't the easiest beach to get to—I'd have to travel down a road that would coat the car in the island's infamous red dirt before heading down a dangerously steep path to the beach itself. But if this man really wanted to find me, if he wanted to chase me, to save me, all the way there...he would.

I parked the Jeep at the end of the red road, finding space along a fence of buffalo grass. I wasn't the only person that day with the idea of surfing at Larsen's; about seven other cars were crammed into the same area. Apparently everyone wanted to take advantage of the sunshine and light winds. Maybe some surfers would have been mad that other people would mean they'd be sharing the breaks, but it made me feel safe, as if I were going on a blind date with someone.

Except that I'd seen him before.

I took my time unloading my board and putting on my sneakers for the hike down, constantly looking over my shoulder in hopes of seeing a plume of red dust rising up through the air. Nothing yet. Maybe the man had just been nice in that note. Maybe he had no intention of saving me again.

I pulled my long black hair into a ponytail and headed past the open gate and down the steep, uneven path that went from the very top of the cliff to the golden beach below. I wasn't far along, still near the top, when I decided to take a moment and observe the waves. Steadying myself with my board still under my arm, I climbed onto a few volcanic boulders that were wedged into the cliffside, rising above the tall grass that obscured my view.

Below, the ocean glistened with patches of turquoise where the bottom was sand, and royal blue where it was rocky. The waves crashed on the reef just offshore, and the tiny figures of surfers were already catching the steady swells. You'd think that just looking at the water, imagining myself back out there, would have brought some fear into my chest, but my fear was different now.

The hair rose on the back of my neck.

"Don't jump," a low, accented voice growled.

I gasped and quickly spun around to see a man—my man—standing on the path and watching me. His eyes widened just as mine did. I had turned so fast with the board that I was toppling to the left, my foot trying to find stability and finding none.

I was going over.

Falling.

I cried out, whipping my head back around to see where I was going to end up, what my doom would be. I wasn't fearing death, but the amount of pain before death.

Or endless pain *without* death.

Then, with reflexes like a cat, he was at me, grabbing on to my arm as the ground beneath me turned to air. The surfboard crashed down the cliff but I was hanging on to him, staring up at his face as he pulled me to safety. Again.

"I wasn't going to jump," I said, breathless. Of course I'd be defensive.

"A simple thank-you would have sufficed," the man said. His accent was Mexican, and now that he was standing right beside me, still gripping my arm, I finally had a clear look at him.

He was about six feet tall, with a nicely toned body he wasn't hiding very well under his board shorts and white wifebeater. His skin was this smooth, golden tone that you just wanted to run your fingers over and over again, and played off the strands of bronze in his wavy hair. Those hazel eyes of his were watching closely, and though his dark brows were furrowed with concern, maybe even anger, there was a startling brightness to them.

The scars that lacerated his left cheekbone were ugly as sin, yet there was something almost beautiful about them. They added depth and secrets to a man who was probably in his late twenties. He had a story to tell.

I wondered if I'd be around to hear it.

When I became aware that I was not only staring at him but that he still had a grasp on my arm, I pulled myself away. "You scared me," I explained. "I was watching the waves."

He cocked a brow. "Planning to surf so soon after yesterday?"

I crossed my arms. "It's none of your business what I do. I don't know you."

He smiled prettily. "I'm the man who saved you from a watery grave. I also delivered your board to you. And I believe I might have just saved your life again."

"As I said, you scared me."

He shrugged. "I couldn't be sure, not after yesterday. Hey," he peered over my shoulder, "want me to get your board again?"

I didn't want to look down in case I experienced a bout of vertigo. "It's fine. Maybe it's a sign I should give it up."

He gave me a curious look and then opened his mouth to say something. But he shut it with a smile and then turned around, heading to the path. "If you gave up surfing, how would I keep meeting you like this?"

He trotted down toward the beach. I watched him for a moment before I shook my head and went after him.

"Why are you doing this?" I asked him, carefully following him. Damn, he was quick. "I still don't know you."

"My name's Esteban," he shot over his shoulder. "Now you know me."

"You don't know my name," I called out after him, my knees starting to hurt from the quick descent. Oh God, I hoped he didn't know my name. That would be terrifying.

"I don't," he said without pausing. "But I figure you'll tell me eventually."

"Oh, really?" I called after him. Cocky little bastard. Well, tall bastard. And a savior instead of a bastard. Still...cocky.

When the path almost started to level out, he vaulted off into the wild greenery that clung to the cliffs, his athletic form disappearing. For a moment I couldn't hear anything but the sharp wind that rushed up to me, the cry of mynah birds and the waves crashing on the reef.

Time seemed to slow as I took stock of the situation. I had no idea who this guy was other than he was a pretty hot Latino and his name was Esteban. Yes, he was retrieving my surfboard for me—at least I think he was—and yes, he had saved my life. But he'd also followed me to my rental house and to the beach today. That took some sleuthing and was stretching the boundaries of being a Good Samaritan.

"Got it!"

I whirled around, surprised to see him appearing a few feet down the path, my board under his arm, while he wiped away the loose foliage that was clinging to his hair. He strode over to me proudly and lifted the board out in my direction.

When I reached for it, though, he pulled it back to his chest. "Not until you tell me your name."

I tried not to roll my eyes. "It's Lani."

"Lani? Interesting…short for something?"

Was this really the time and place for small talk? "It's short for Lelani."

"Lelani, hey? Are you Hawaiian? I thought you'd have better surfing skills than that."

"Actually," I said as I wrestled my board out of his grasp, "I have Hawaiian ancestry. My grandparents were from here. But I just like to come here to…"

"Escape life?"

I pursed my lips as I eyed him. Despite the sparkle in his eyes, there was still something odd about him. Though I didn't feel I was in danger, there was still a sense of unpredictability and circumstance that seemed to swirl around us.

"Yes," I said slowly. "To escape life."

He nodded, then asked. "Are you part Japanese?"

"My grandmother was, why?"

He smiled. "No reason other than you're strikingly beautiful. Most mutts are."

Though I was blushing, I had to laugh at the mutt comment. I think it was the first genuine laugh I'd had in a long time. "Well, we can't all be purebreds."

"Oh, senorita," he said cheekily, "I don't know what the hell I am other than the fact that I was born in La Paz, Mexico. One of my aunts has bright blue eyes, like the ocean here, and my half sister is a redhead. I'm probably one of the biggest mutts around. Would explain why all my ex-girlfriends would call me a dog."

I nearly laughed again but I saved it with a smile. It was almost gratuitous after the last few days.

"Well, thank you," I said, moving to walk past him.

"That's it?" He reached out and grabbed the back of my board, pushing it to the side so I had to face him. "You laugh and then you leave?"

I had no idea what to say. It wasn't that I wanted to leave, but I had a hard time processing anything new. I had been so happy to just plod along on this island, keeping quiet and looking for the easy way out.

Esteban cocked his head toward the beach. "Why not try surfing, like you'd planned. The waves look nice." He took a step toward me, and I imagined his eyes were darkening. "Or is that the problem? It's not dangerous enough for you."

My pulse raced as I bit my lip. I noticed beads of sweat on the crest of his forehead, and wondered if they would taste salty on my tongue.

I really needed to go.

"I was watching you, you know," he said. "I was out on the waves, too, though I know you didn't notice. You were just sitting there, watching every wave pass by. For the longest time, I thought maybe you were a total beginner. But even from far away, I could see it in your eyes."

Shocked, I swallowed hard. Though the sun was bright as sin, I felt a chill creeping up my limbs. "What could you see?" I whispered.

"The shadows," he said simply, as if he were making sense. "I have them, too. You have to in my line of work. But you wanted yours to pull you under."

"Look," I said, trying to appear cool and calm, as if he hadn't seen who I was out there. "It was really nice that you saved me and got my board, but I think we have to part ways here. I'm just here on vacation. I like to surf. I like to paint. I'm here to relax and have a good time, like everyone else." I stuck out my hand so I wouldn't look scared. "Good-bye, Esteban."

When I expected him to be put out, he just smiled at me, so pure against the scars. "Esteban Mendoza. I'm staying at the Princeville Saint Regis. If you ever feel like discussing those shadows of yours."

I was about to tell him I wouldn't be doing that, but he just turned around and headed down the path to the beach. From there I watched him trot toward the water's edge and dive into the clear blue water, swimming powerfully out to the reef. He made it past the breakers, disappearing into the foam before appearing out on the horizon, a tiny dot against the navy swells.

I could have sworn he waved good-bye to me. It must have been my imagination.

...

After the beach, I stopped by Foodland to pick up another bottle of Scotch and headed straight back to the house. I poured myself a drink, neat, and took it into the shower with me. I stood in there, washing and washing and washing until I felt raw and real and my skin had turned pruney. I could have stayed in there forever, just living in the warmth.

Oddly enough, it felt like I'd taken a shower for the first time in my life. God, how much of my day was always on autopilot.

When I finally dragged myself out, slipped on my robe, and wound my coarse hair into a braid, I decided to call Doug.

He picked up on the fourth ring. Just like always, he made himself seem too busy for me, yet would get mad if I didn't pick up right away.

"Hello?" His voice was distracted, and I heard the distinctive crinkle of a potato chip bag in the background.

"Hi, sweetie," I said, trying to sound cheery and sober.

A pause. "Nice of you to call me back, *finally*. I was trying to reach you yesterday. Where were you?"

"Surfing."

"Not painting?"

"Not painting," I said with a sigh. "So, how are things?"

Now it was his turn to exhale. He launched into tirade against some of the new clients at his work, the tightness of our purse strings, the lack of opportunities. With each sentence I could feel the stress and frustration pour out from him. He often used me as a venting board, though I assumed it was only on the days that Justine wasn't around.

I let him talk, not putting in a word edgewise, not even when he reminded me that the time I was spending in paradise was costing us money we didn't have, and if I wanted to truly make it worthwhile, I'd need to start painting. I'd need to create. I'd need to make something, and something of myself.

Instead I eventually hung up the phone with a stiff "I love you," and poured myself another glass. I let the drink burn on my tongue as I stared at the easels and blank canvases that were hidden in the shadows of the room.

Those damn shadows. They really were here with me, filtering out through my soul, permeating every inch of my life. Just how long had they been living my life for me?

I finished my drink, then placed it down on the counter with a desolate clink.

I googled the number for the Saint Regis and was put through to one Esteban Mendoza.

CHAPTER THREE

The next morning I woke up to the sound of a motorcycle outside the house. I barely had time to register that I had slept through my alarm when there was a knock at the door.

Fantastic.

I quickly got out of bed and slipped on my pajama pants, all the while thinking it couldn't be Esteban. We had made plans to do something in the morning, but I'd assumed he would have called me first.

On the way to the door, I paused by the mirror and winced at my reflection. My eyes were sleepy and puffy with smudges of mascara underneath, my hair was a mess, and my nipples were poking out of my camisole. Another knock prevented me from trying to fix myself up.

I opened up the door and lo and behold, Esteban was on the other side, a motorcycle parked behind the Jeep.

He looked surprised at my disheveled appearance and couldn't hide the cheekiness in his grin. "I'm sorry," he said. "I thought we said noon."

I wiped underneath my eyes and crossed my arms over my chest the minute his eyes rested on my breasts.

"You said you'd call me first."

He shrugged, taking my body in, his gaze trailing from my tired face all the way to my bare toes. I felt like I was being dissected. Couldn't say a tiny part of me didn't enjoy it. I couldn't remember the last time Doug looked at me like that. I couldn't remember the last time I wanted him—or anyone—to mentally undress me.

"I'm sorry," he said more sincerely this time. "I should have called." He looked at his watch. "It's eleven thirty...want me to come back?"

I sighed. He was already here, and I didn't feel right about turning him away. Luckily I never took too long in getting dressed, so I invited him inside. He said he'd put on a pot of coffee while I got ready. I picked up my clothes for the day, hoping I wouldn't have to ride his motorcycle, and went into the bathroom to do my face.

The only problem with the vacation rental—and it wasn't a problem when you were alone—was that it was extremely *un*soundproof. While I washed my face and put on the barest touches of makeup, I could hear him puttering around in the kitchen. It was an odd feeling having a stranger in the house, doing domestic things while I was in another room. Of course he could have been casing the joint, stealing my camera and the few pieces of jewelry I had brought with me, but I didn't feel that was the case with him.

Then again, other than his name, I didn't know Esteban Mendoza at all.

When I came out of the bathroom I found him standing on the back steps, two cups of coffee in hand, admiring a pair of chickens that were strutting around the backyard. He shot me a winning smile and handed me my cup of coffee like we were old friends.

He nodded at it. "It's black. There was no milk and sugar in the house, so I figured you liked it dark."

I couldn't tell if that was sexual innuendo about his deeply bronzed skin, but I tried not to dwell on it.

I took the hot mug from him, our fingertips brushing against each other. The brief contact caused my face to grow hot, something I didn't quite understand. I was never shy—introverted, but not shy—but this man made me feel like an awkward teenager again.

"Thank you," I said, tucking a strand of hair behind my ear.

He watched my movements like a hawk and just before his attention became too intense, he smiled. His dimples were such a contradiction to his scars. I had this terrible urge to reach out and touch them, to stroke his face and find out what shadows followed him.

Instead I cleared my throat and said, "Thanks for taking my call last night. I was..."

"I know," he said, taking such a large gulp of coffee that I winced, imagining it must have burned going down. "You don't have to explain why. I told you why. I'm just glad you called." He gestured to the yard with his free hand. "This is a beautiful spot."

I nodded. "It is."

"You're a painter."

I gave him a sharp look, feeling intruded.

He tilted his head. "I saw your easels. I saw no art, though, so I could only assume. You have the hands of a painter."

I sipped my drink, gathering my thoughts before I said anything. "I do paint. I came here to...but...I just haven't."

"You haven't been inspired."

I snorted and shot him a sideways glance. "If you can't be inspired on the most beautiful island on the planet, there's something wrong with you." My smile quickly faded at my last words. There *was* something wrong with me. Fatally.

"Maybe you're not looking in the right place. Inspiration isn't in your backyard or at the bottom of the ocean. It's somewhere else."

I glanced at him curiously. His face was grave but his eyes bright, shining like the sun.

"Come on," he said, tugging lightly at my arm. "I'll show you."

Minutes later I had finished my coffee and was climbing on the back of his bike. Legally you didn't have to wear helmets here, but he still gave me his to wear. Truth be told, I hated motorcycles—I hated the speed and uncertainty, finding them to be more constrictive than freeing. They also forced intimacy with the person you were riding with. Not only did I have Esteban's helmet on my head, which was damp from sweat, though it was a musky, pleasant smell, but I had to put my arms around his waist. This Harley was definitely not a cushy cruiser.

"Where are we going?" I shouted into his ear as he revved the engine.

"Around," he shouted back at me.

"That's not very helpful!"

"Don't worry, it will help you in the end!"

"How do I know that you're not taking me somewhere to kill me?"

He shot me a lopsided smile. "Because you'd already be dead. Besides…they call me the nice one."

"Who are *they*?"

He didn't answer. He accelerated and we were flying down the road toward the highway. Esteban was a safe driver, though, and didn't go much faster than the speed limit, which on Kauai was stupidly low, yet I still found myself holding on to him for dear life. My God, he had fucking abs of steel, and somehow I felt guilty just touching them.

It took about ten minutes of us heading south before I began to loosen up a bit and reduced my Kung-Fu grip on his T-shirt. I began to appreciate the speed as we picked it up and the road rushed past us. The scenery was breathtaking; to our right were deep-cut green mountains, straight from the scenes of *Jurassic Park*. To the left were the fields of tall grass and small farm stands, red dirt coating the signs while the Pacific sparkled in the distance.

But despite how much I relaxed, the ride—everything—felt dangerous. It wasn't the same type of danger that I'd been courting, though. This danger was more subtle, more menacing. This danger spelled trouble for the life I'd have to go on living.

Eventually we passed through the towns of Kapa'a, Lihue, and Poipu before I realized we were going quite far off the beaten track.

"Where are we going?" I yelled at him.

"You'll see," he said. "You're not afraid of heights, are you?"

I wasn't. But being afraid of a stranger pushing you off from a great height was a different story.

Soon we passed the ramshackle town of Hanapepe and started zooming up toward the mountains, heading inland.

There was only one place for us to go, and I knew where we were going: Waimea Canyon.

It was one of the places I hadn't been before, thanks to its location at the south end of the island. Also, when you're traveling alone, you don't really feel like being a sightseeing tourist.

Eucalyptus trees flew past us as we ascended the mountain road, the foliage becoming greener, the earth redder, the air filling with ethereal mist.

When we zoomed past the most popular lookout over the canyon, I started to get a little nervous.

"Where are we going?" I asked again.

"That view is, how you say, overrated."

We accelerated as we rounded a corner, the colder air snapping against me. I went back to holding on to him for dear life as we passed more and more viewpoints filled with tourists. I started to wonder if this was such a good idea after all. It seemed he was taking me to the end of the road, the end of the line.

That idea hadn't scared me before; it was curious that it was scaring me now.

But eventually when the road did end, it did so at a parking lot with a couple of cars parked and some sightseers milling about. I breathed out a sigh of relief as the bike came to a stop and I was able to get off.

I slipped off the helmet, knowing my hair was probably sticking flat to my head, and Esteban stared at me curiously.

"You seemed a bit scared at the end," he noted.

I swallowed hard and looked away. "Well, I've never been good on bikes."

"It's a good sign to be scared, hey," he said. "When you stop feeling fear, that's when it becomes dangerous. That's when you die."

I resisted the urge to say something, to tell him he didn't know shit. He acted like he knew all this stuff about me, just because he rescued me and saw my "shadows," something we hadn't even touched on yet.

"This is the Puu o Kila Lookout," he said as he lightly touched my elbow and guided me toward an unpaved trail that sloped away from the parking lot. "Not many people know about it. They stop at the one before and never venture on. But this is better."

"And how do you know so much about this island?" I asked him.

"I like to do my research," he said in a low voice, and I followed him as we went down the smooth red banks until suddenly...I was breathless.

There, sprawled out in front of us, was a view like nothing I'd see before. The red dirt sloped off sharply with no guardrail to keep us back, and when the drop ended thousands of yards below, the valley begun. It ran green and wide toward the ocean, the cliffs rising up from it on either side, gouged out by millions of years of rainfall and weather. Though the sun was out, clouds passed through the valley, quickly scooting over our heads, so close at times that I wanted to reach out and touch them.

"Careful." His voice whispered at my neck as he gently put his hand around my waist and pulled me back a step. I looked down at my feet and recoiled with horror when I realized how close I had gotten to the edge. It was almost like I had really been going for the clouds.

"It's okay," he said, leading me away from the edge.

I was shaking; I couldn't help it. Jesus, I had been so close to going over.

"Come on, we can get the same view from up here." He took me to where the path sloped up. We were farther back, but the surreal view was the same. Too bad my heart was still beating so fast, my blood pumping loudly in my ears.

Esteban took his hand off me and I felt a strange chill in its absence. "Are you okay?" he asked, his eyes searching mine.

I nodded. "Yes," I said, licking my lips that were suddenly dry. "I'm fine."

"When women say they're fine, they're usually seconds from throwing their shoe at you."

I cracked a smile, my gaze flitting over to him. "Is this from personal experience?"

He shrugged and tucked his wavy hair behind his ear, the highlights catching the gleam of the sun. "I've pissed off my fair share of women. But it's not my fault they all fall so madly in love."

I laughed. "I think you're full of shit."

"Oh, I am," he said, facing me. "Perhaps that's why they throw the shoes."

We lapsed into silence, our attention turned back to the view. Now that I was calming down and we were farther away from the edge, I was able to take in the view as much as I could. It was like watching a moving painting. There was something so...unbelievable, unnatural about finding such beauty in real life. I felt like I had stepped into my own art.

And that was when it hit me like a kick to the shin.

I was inspired.

The feeling, the itch to paint, to capture the crazy, otherworldly beauty of this place, the rich, thriving greens and the opulent blues and the vista that seemed carved out of time.

"I told you so," Esteban said.

"Told me what?"

"That you were looking in the wrong place."

Thoughtfully, I rubbed the back of my hand across my lips, not sure what to say to that. But he was right. We stood there for a little while longer, not saying anything, and pretty soon the silence was as comfortable as warm flannel.

I thought about the man standing beside me, the relaxed yet intuitive way about him, the way my feelings about him swung from easygoing to vaguely fearful in the blink of an eye. He was handsome as hell, the scars only adding to his rugged appeal.

I needed to know more.

"So you said *they* call you the nice one," I said. "You never said who they were. How do I know I can trust their opinion?"

He scratched at his sideburn and squinted at the sun. "They're my colleagues. Out of all of them, I am the...most civilized. Though I guess that's not saying much, hey."

"What kind of work do you do?"

He shoved his hands in the pockets of his board shorts. "Oh, you know. This and that. I'm usually a tech guy. Sometimes I help out in other areas of the business."

"What business is it?" I asked, and immediately felt stupid for doing so. From his evasive nature, to the darkness, to his very scars, I knew whatever he did, it wasn't working at Target.

"I'll tell you the truth if you tell me the truth," he said without looking at me.

"Okay..." I started, feeling a little bit uneasy. "What do you want to know?"

When he picked up my left hand in his and raised it to eye level, my skin immediately began tingling.

"You're married. Why aren't you wearing your wedding ring?"

My chin jerked down. "How do you know I'm married?"

"Tan line," he said. "You live somewhere where you get a lot of sun, and normally you wear your ring. But here you don't. Why?"

I looked at my hand, at the sun spots and faint lines and a tiny splice of lightened skin where my ring usually was. "I don't know. I was in the water so much, I took the ring off. I guess I haven't put it back on. It's on my dresser."

"I see," he said.

I frowned. "It's true."

"I believe you. I was just curious."

I eyed his bare left hand. "Are you married?"

"Nope," he said with a smile. "I don't think I'm cut out for it."

"I'm glad you know that," I said solemnly as clouds momentarily blocked the sun. "Men aren't cut out for it. But so many think they are."

I knew he could tell I was talking from personal experience, but luckily he let it go. He cleared his throat. "Is that what you wanted to know? If I was available?"

The silky way he said "available" sent a rush of blood through me. "No. What business are you in? I mean, unless you're a CIA agent and you'd have to kill me first."

"I'm Mexican," he said. "The closest thing we have to the CIA *is* the CIA."

I stared at him with impatience until he continued.

"I'm in the import and export business."

I raised a brow. "Of?"

"Drugs."

I froze. He couldn't be serious. Of course he wasn't. If you were involved in importing and exporting drugs, you didn't just tell a stranger that.

And that was when the hairs at the back of my neck danced. He wasn't joking, was he? I stared at him, afraid to see the truth in his eyes, but his scars and that glimmer of burning darkness within told me otherwise.

He was a drug dealer. He was part of a cartel. An actual fucking Mexican drug cartel.

I tried to swallow, feeling like there was a lump in my throat. "Oh," I said stupidly.

"Are you afraid of me now?" he asked with intensity.

I squared my shoulders and looked him in the eye. "No more than I was before."

"I saved your life, you know," he said. "You shouldn't fear someone who won't let you die."

"Why not?" I countered. "They might love granting something and then taking it away."

"Lani," he said, and my name never sounded so sweet. "You don't trust me because you don't trust yourself."

"You know nothing about me."

"I know you're in an unhappy marriage. That you're struggling to find your art again. That you feel this life holds nothing for you anymore, and you think that you're doing your husband and the world a favor if you just...disappeared."

I hated the way he—this stranger, this fucking drug dealer—thought he knew me.

"You're wrong," I lied.

"Then why are you here, with me, now, looking to find those shadows?"

I opened my mouth to speak, but nothing came out. I didn't even know what to say.

Esteban reached out and touched my arm gently. My skin buzzed under his fingers, feeling alive, as if it had been nothing but dead cells before.

"Some fear will kill you," he said. "Some fear will open your eyes. I know all about the difference."

I let out a shaky breath. He was getting under my skin and his occupation didn't help the situation. Still, I found myself asking, "So, what are you doing on Kauai?"

He smiled and removed his hand. "Ah, the million-dollar question. How about I tell you about it over dinner?"

I smiled warily. "Is that code for 'dump my body somewhere afterward'?"

"I told you," he said breezily, clapping his hands together, "that isn't my intention. You took a chance on coming here today, didn't you?"

I looked away, letting the scenery fill my sight. "I did."

"And it was worth it, wasn't it?"

I nodded, still not used to the competing feelings of fear and exhilaration running through me. "It was."

"Come on then," he said, stepping away from me and jerking his head toward the parking lot. The golden strands in his surfer hair caught the sunlight that was piercing through fast-moving clouds. "Let's get you home, get you rested. Maybe when I pick you up tonight, you'll be splattered with paint. That would make me very happy."

That would have made *me* very happy. I followed him to the bike and shot one last glance at the kaleidoscope of greens that tinted the lush cliffs. I couldn't imagine recreating such beauty, but I knew in my heart I was about to try.

CHAPTER FOUR

It wasn't that I didn't think there was something wrong with the scenario. It was more like what *wasn't* wrong with the scenario. Everything that had happened since the day I almost drowned had been nothing but wrong. Never mind my mental state, the thoughts of hopelessness, desperation, and despair. Never mind those shadows that trailed inky fingers over my skin and tried to pull me back under, to let everything go and forget.

There was Esteban, a total stranger, who had admitted to me that he was part of a drug cartel. He had rescued me in ways that were not just lucky but calculated. Nothing was accidental when it came to him. Then there was the fact that I willingly let him whisk me away to a perilous place, all while on the back of a motorcycle. And of course the fact that I had agreed to go to dinner with him.

Perhaps that was the most troubling part of all. I was a married woman—an unhappily married woman, as he so astutely pointed out—but a married one, nonetheless. My marriage vows at this point were no more sacred than my own life, but they still meant something, which in turn meant there was something so very wrong about agreeing to go to dinner with another man.

And yet, despite all these things, all the things that were red flags waving as obnoxiously as a matador's cape, I wasn't worried.

Why?

Because when Esteban came to pick me up later that night, I was in the backyard painting the last rays of the sunset. Streaks of pink, gold, and purple were in the sky and on my canvas and dotted on my white T-shirt. I was touched by color.

"That's beautiful," he commented, surprising me with his presence.

I only briefly looked over my shoulder at him, too afraid to take my eyes off the scene. A few doves cooed in the nearby bushes, and I wished I could add audio to my painting.

"I suppose you just waltzed into my house?" I asked mildly.

"Yes, sorry about that. I knocked a few times, but there was no response. I did tell you seven, didn't I?"

"You did," I said. I dabbed a bit of ochre on the horizon. "But I lost track of time."

"And I'm glad to see it." I heard him walk down the back steps and toward me. The chickens that had been pecking at the ground clucked and ran back through the hole in the fence in a flurry of feathers. I felt him stop right behind my back. "Should I come back later, Lani? Or perhaps, not at all?"

There was an edge, a coldness to his last words, as if he was hurt. It was absurd to think that a member of a drug cartel could feel slighted.

I sighed and carefully rested my paintbrush on the easel's ledge. Then I turned around and brushed my hair out of my eyes with the back of my hand, careful not to get any paint on my face. "I'm sorry," I said and offered him a shy smile. "This light is disappearing anyway. I was about to wrap it up. Give me a few minutes and I'll be ready to go."

He smiled in return, his greenish eyes softening. It was only then that I realized he cleaned up really well. Gone were the board shorts; instead he was wearing gray slacks and a short-sleeved white dress shirt with the first two buttons undone, his skin glowing gold. His hair was tamed by what looked like gel, and he'd shaven. His look was elegant and casual all at the same time, and had it not been for the scarring on his face, that constant reminder of his job, I would have thought he was like any well-dressed man out there.

But he wasn't like everyone else. Wasn't that why I picked up the paintbrush?

True to my word, I washed up quickly until the only traces of paint were lines of lavender caught in my cuticles. Then I touched up my makeup and slipped on a plain yellow shift dress.

I debated on bringing a cardigan, but today was a few degrees warmer than normal, and I knew the evening would be just as balmy. I had no idea if we were going to a fancy restaurant, but this was Kauai and I had to assume that my flip-flops would be tolerated.

I walked out into the kitchen where Esteban was drinking a glass of white wine. I'd told him to help himself; I just didn't think he'd be so literal about it.

"You look beautiful," he said, his gaze raking over me.

I plucked the wineglass from his hands and took a sip. "Thank you." His eyes never left my lips. It should have made me feel uncomfortable, but it didn't. Though I knew if this kept up, the way he was looking at me, it eventually would. "Shall we get going?"

"With those shoes?" he asked, pointing at my Reefs. "You might lose them on the bike."

I smiled wryly and put down the glass, then picked up my purse from the counter. "I'm pretty good at keeping articles of clothing on." He opened his mouth to say something but I went on. "We'll take my Jeep. You just give me directions."

He appraised me for a moment, running his fingers along his dimpled chin. "All right. Nothing wrong with the woman calling the shots."

I rolled my eyes and we headed out to the car.

Though the restaurant ended up being close by, in the Princeville Resort where he was staying, being in a car with Esteban was more challenging than the motorcycle ride. I felt the need to keep the conversation going, but I wasn't sure how. The things I really wanted to talk about seemed inappropriate, and the way he stared at me didn't help either.

"You seem nervous," he said with an elbow propped up, leaning casually against the door.

I raised my brows. "I'm not nervous."

"You keep biting your lip."

"Maybe I'm just hungry."

"You've gotten funnier, you know that?"

I eyed him quickly. "Since when?"

"Since this morning."

"You don't know me very well. I'm often funny."

"Maybe in a past life. In this life, you've been nothing but sad."

When I shot him a look, he smiled. "It's all right, hey? You started painting. That made you happy. That's a start."

I tightened my grip on the wheel. The generic rock from the radio station hummed in the background. I was about to bite my lip but stopped, suddenly conscious.

Then I looked back to the road and cleared my throat. "You make it sound like you had something to do with it."

I could tell he was smiling when he said, "I just wanted you to be inspired. It worked."

"And tonight, is this the same thing?"

"You're awfully suspicious," he said. "I've saved your life, twice, brought back your inspiration for your art, and now I'm about to buy you an extraordinary meal."

"And that's it?"

He laughed. "Sure. That's it. I'll tell you this, though, the meal doesn't have to be the only...," he paused, "*extraordinary* thing to happen tonight."

The silken quality to his words conjured up an image in my mind of me facedown in some swanky hotel room, with him removing my thong, dragging it down my legs with the tip of a 9mm handgun. I don't know why I conjured up that scene, but I found myself blanking on it, heat flushing on my chest and cheeks. I squirmed slightly in my seat.

"Does that interest you?" he said, his voice lower now.

I had to pretend that it didn't, even though my body was currently screaming the opposite.

"Dinner sounds wonderful," I said.

He smiled. "Good, good."

Soon we pulled up to the restaurant, and the valet took the jeep. Esteban held out his arm for me, and I hesitated for a moment before I took it.

The restaurant was beautiful, swanky in this beachy way with low lighting, sand-colored tablecloths, and dark teak furniture. A centerpiece of frangipani floated in a small dish lit by candles.

We were given an amazing seat, right by the edge, where the restaurant was open to the ocean. You could hear the steady roar of waves as they crashed against the cliffs in the darkness below. It was a dramatic and appropriately primal setting for someone like Esteban.

"Are you impressed?" he asked, a wicked curve to his mouth.

I nodded, knowing he must have requested the table especially for me, for *us*. I couldn't fathom why, though. He did know I was married, though he probably figured if it was that important to me, I wouldn't have come. There was nothing innocent or accidental about us being together anymore, not with the way my thoughts were turning toward him anyway, and he knew it.

He knew it and he was using it to his advantage. I wondered if I was there with him because I still felt I owed him. That was what the moral part of me wanted to think. But I was beginning to think that the moral part of me drowned in the ocean all those days ago. My morality was floating with the sharks.

Esteban quickly ordered us two mai tais, telling me that the bar at the restaurant had the best ones (as did every other place on the islands, apparently), and then folded his hands in front of him, a gold ring with a jade stone in it gleaming in the candlelight.

I was thankful for the conversation starter. "That's a lovely ring," I told him, gesturing to it.

He smiled. "Thank you."

Not as forthcoming as I had hoped. "Is that from a significant other?"

He raised a brow to that and then smiled politely at the waiter as our mai tais were delivered. He nodded at the drink. "Try it. Tell me I'm wrong."

He was skirting the question, but okay. I had a sip. Not too sweet, with just enough fruit and rum. It was pretty perfect as far as mai tais went. I started playing with the purple orchid it was served with.

"You are not wrong," I admitted.

"I rarely am."

"Who gave you the ring?"

He admired it on his hand. "Perhaps I bought it."

I shook my head. "No. It's not really your style. You're wearing it out of respect or obligation."

His mouth ticked up as he eyed me steadily. "You're good. You're very good. You should come work with me, hey?"

I kept watching him, waiting for an answer, something about him to hold on to.

He sighed. "It's from my brother."

"Your brother?"

"Yes," he said carefully. "He...has funny ways of showing his affection. I almost died once, you know." His eyes flicked up to me, their green depths glittering. "But I wasn't trying to die."

I ignored that remark. "What happened?"

He shrugged. "Nothing out of the ordinary. A car bomb."

I choked on my drink and started coughing. He leaned over in his seat, concerned, but I waved him away, my hand flapping rapidly.

"I'm fine, I'm fine," I squeaked out when I could. When I finally got myself under control, I was still blinking at him in disbelief. The words couldn't quite settle into my brain. "A car bomb?" I whispered.

He stroked the scars on his face. "Where do you think I got these pretty little souvenirs?"

"Not from a car bomb," I said honestly as I glanced around to make sure no one was listening. The man had said he was part of a drug cartel, but I suppose I never really understood the reality of it. This wasn't some movie, some story. This was real life, a drug lord's life, and somehow I had gotten licked by it, like a hand darting in and out of a candle flame.

"Well, I did. Wrong place, right time. Or maybe not, maybe it's the other way around. It was, in some ways, the best thing that could have happened to me. Becoming so—tainted, physically—hurt my way around some of the women I was used to having, but on the other hand, I was able to stay low and play dead. I let my brother think I was gone. I let Javier think I was gone."

"Who is Javier?"

A darkness came over his eyes. "He is not important right at this minute, not here, with you." He took a sip of his drink. "By pretending I was dead, that I died in that bomb, I was able to get a second chance at life. I had a chance to go…straight, as you would call it. Unfortunately, there are certain types of people cut out for certain types of jobs. I am one of those people. Leaving is impossible. It wasn't long until I came back from the dead." He sighed and twisted the ring around his finger. "When my brother, Alex, found out, he gave me this ring. He said the jade would bless me and protect me, and in some ways, remind me that I was valuable."

He cleared his throat and splayed his long fingers out on the table. "The ring was the nicest thing he'd ever done for me. Soon after that, he went back to pretending I didn't exist. I guess giving me this eased his conscience. Perhaps he was too afraid I would disappear again. In this business, you push your loved ones away. You don't dare invite in the pain. Love is weakness."

"That's sad," I said.

He pursed his lips. "I would have assumed you, of all people, would have agreed."

I stiffened. There he was hitting me deep with things he shouldn't glean from me. He didn't know me. He didn't. He couldn't.

Esteban went on, stirring his drink. "Loving people *is* weak. We've all been taught that. It's the only way to survive in my business. But I am guessing it's the same for everyone. You may lose love to death. You may lose love to another man. Or you may lose love because you lost it somewhere along the way, and you were just too proud to stop and pick it up." He smiled coyly. "So, which way did you lose it?"

I lost it when my husband cheated on me with my best friend. When he continued his affair. And I continue to lose it, every single day. I'll lose it until I'm just an empty sieve.

I didn't say that to Esteban, of course. He already *thought* he knew me—it would be dangerous if he really did.

He wasn't waiting for a response, either. The green in his eyes shone knowingly. He let me keep my cards hidden.

The rest of dinner went well enough. The dinner was phenomenal, and the food—soft, flakey ono over red curry and rice—was a sharp reminder that my taste buds had been sleepwalking until then. The mai tais kept coming, and I felt warmth fill me up from the inside, especially when the conversation lulled and Esteban had taken to staring at me in this absolutely carnal way that just screamed sex.

I was tempted to slip off my flip-flops and slide my bare foot up his pants leg. It would be completely unlike me, completely objectionable and completely wrong. And yet, the sexual tension between us had been mounting, becoming unbearable. The high I got from painting was starting to wear off, and even though I could see the lilac around my fingernails, I wanted something more. Another chance to prove that I was alive, and that I had some spark left in me.

Just before I was about to suggest we take a walk on the beach, his phone rang, playing Darth Vader's theme from *Star Wars*. Okay, that had to be his boss.

He glanced at the screen in annoyance, and his finger hovered above it as he debated whether to answer it. Finally, he shot me an apologetic look. "Sorry, I have to take this," he said, and held it up to his ear.

"Yes?" he said into the phone, polite but brimming with thinly veiled annoyance. He listened, closing his eyes. "I am busy right now. Yes. Having dinner. Why? Fish. Of course I am not alone." A long pause and Esteban's gaze moved to me. "I'm sitting with a very stunning woman. You would like her. No, I will not tell you her name." Another pause. He looked at his watch. "I have fifteen minutes, there is plenty of time."

Time for what?

He sighed. "Must you? Fine." He cleared his throat and reached across the table to give me his phone. "He would like to speak with you."

I raised my brows. "Who? Your boss?"

He nodded, his lips twisting into a grimace.

"Why does he want to talk to me?" I asked, feeling utterly confused and frightened. I stared at the phone, not wanting to take it.

"Please," Esteban said. I could have sworn there was a hint of desperation on his face.

Jesus. Fine, I'd talk to him, the fucking boss of a drug cartel.

I gingerly took the phone from him and stared at the screen. It just said Darth Vader on it. Helpful.

"Hello?"

There was silence.

"Hello?" I said again.

Someone on the other end of the line took a breath. "You have a very pretty voice," a man said. His voice was smooth, glacial, and calm with only the slightest hint of a Mexican accent.

"Thank you?"

"What is your name?" the man asked.

I didn't want to say, now that Esteban wouldn't tell him. "What is *your* name?" I asked. "The phone says you're Darth Vader."

The man on the other end—Darth Vader—laughed. Esteban was staring at me, wide-eyed. Well, if didn't want me to tell his boss that, then he shouldn't have handed me the phone.

"Well," he said when he eventually recovered. "I can be Darth Vader for you, if you want." His voice was as seductive as satin sheets, but I wasn't fooled.

"So, why did you want to speak to me?" I asked, wanting nothing more than to hang up the phone and go back to the tiny slice of paradise that Esteban and I had created.

"I was just curious as to who had captured Este's eye, that is all. I also wanted to verify that he was indeed occupied. Though, from the sounds of it, you don't sound occupied enough."

"We were finishing up dinner when you called. We haven't had a chance," I told him. I didn't elaborate on what. I could tell that was going unsaid.

"What a pity," the man said. "Just so you know, if he gets his job done properly, he'll be leaving the day after tomorrow. So, perhaps you might want to plan around that."

"What is the job?" I couldn't help but ask.

The man chuckled, the sound creamy and rich. "He'd tell you, but he'd probably have to kill you. And I would definitely need to know your name." His voice became serious over that last word, serious enough to send a chill up my spine. This guy was not joking. I heard him inhale, a slow, wicked sound. "May I please speak to Este?"

Yeah, no problem. I didn't say anything, I just quickly handed the phone back to Esteban and told him I was going to the restroom. I felt extremely uneasy after that phone call, and needed to try to get my wits about me.

Inside the swanky bathroom with its polished chrome and gleaming glass sinks, I eyed myself in the mirror. I looked different somehow, like I was a foreigner in my own world. I looked scared but I also looked...pretty. My eyes were clear and bright, my skin flushed and glowing. My hair was glossed back into a smooth ponytail. I didn't think I had done anything different to myself, but maybe it was all in my head. Maybe the art had started to seep into my body.

Maybe I needed another way to get my fill.

I stared at myself for a few moments, running through all the scenarios in my head. There were only two. I would say good-bye to Esteban here. He would do whatever job he had to do—a job I had no business knowing. I would remain in Hawaii, trying to recapture the fire I'd felt earlier in the day. I'd try to find that finicky will to go on, alone. And if I couldn't...well, the ocean was always right there.

Or I could go back to the table. Take Esteban down to the beach. Try to find myself in his touch. And if I went out, I went out with a bang. A fleeting glimpse of the stars and possibility before the shadows came for me.

I'd lost love with my husband. I'd lost love with myself. I wanted to find something, anything, before I lost everything.

CHAPTER FIVE

I went back to the table and saw Esteban standing, waiting for me with his chair pushed in. His phone was nowhere in sight. I quickly grabbed my purse and said, "Where shall we go next?"

His brows quirked up, as if unsure what to do with the question. "The beach?" he suggested. "There's a path by the cliff here."

I smiled. "You know everything, don't you?"

"That's why they call me the smart one."

"I thought they called you the nice one."

"Oh. That, too."

"Who was that on the phone?"

His eyes sought the ceiling. "My boss is Javier. He controls the operation. In fact, he controls pretty much all of Mexico. Well, almost. We're working on a few things."

"Are any of those things the reason you are here?"

He smiled, white teeth against tanned skin. His scars rippled with the movement, so darkly beautiful. He held his arm out for me. "Shall we go to the beach?"

I nodded, my nerves buzzing with possibilities.

We left the restaurant and he led me down the tiki-torch-lit paths past fancy condominiums. The night was beautiful; the stars were out along with a fingernail moon. It was impossibly romantic, impossibly dangerous. The path down the cliff was unlit, and thanks to the dark and the instability of my flip-flops, I was relying on Esteban to keep me safe. I put my trust in someone who probably couldn't be trusted.

And yet, eventually I felt sand beneath my feet. The wild ocean crashed against the beach in waves of ink dotted with silver sparkles, reflections from the moon. A balmy breeze caressed my face like a gentle lover. My whole body rippled with excitement I hadn't felt in years and years and years.

I felt like I was waking up.

We walked along the sand in silence, heading toward the surf. The foam churned steps away from our feet. Esteban was now holding his shoes in his hand and behind his back. He stared out at the dark horizon, breathing in deeply through his nose. The wind pushed his wavy hair off his face.

"What are you thinking?" I asked him softly, though I supposed I had no business to.

He didn't seem to mind. "I am thinking that I am lucky."

"How so?"

He turned to look at me, the moonlight in his gaze. "That I met you. I was not planning on meeting anyone. But here you are."

"But you leave soon."

He nodded once. "I am leaving. And I will go back to Mexico and all I'll have of you will be memories. We won't call each other. We won't write. We won't e-mail. What we have will remain in the Pacific. Where it belongs."

I didn't understand. How was that lucky?

"You're a beautiful woman, Lani. You're talented, smart. You have a lot going for you, which you refuse to see. Maybe you're too stubborn. Or maybe you still don't think you deserve a second chance. But I will leave here having known you and having made you smile. The memories will be good enough for me. I'll find someone else, someone available, someone who is cut out for my lifestyle. And I'll thank you for that."

Where the hell did his confidence come from, the idea that everything would be okay, even in the line of work he was in? I didn't understand it.

He turned his body so he was facing me and put his hand behind my neck, holding me there. His voice lowered. "Sometimes people come into our lives for just a second, just long enough to let us know that hope exists. Will you let me be your hope, if not for just this night?"

I didn't have time to react before he kissed me.

It went deep, deep inside, stoking a fire I never knew had been building.

I heard his shoes drop to the sand as he sank his hands into my hair. They tugged a little bit at the strands, and I cried out into his warm mouth. His tongue was silky and smooth, making me wet. He slid one hand down to my ass, cupping it firmly. I had never felt a need so powerful, and from the way he pressed his hard erection against me, I could tell he felt the same.

Until Darth Vader's theme song filled our ears.

"Shit!" Esteban groaned and pulled away, pulling the phone out of his pocket.

I felt like I should be annoyed, but knew I had no right to. "It's been more than fifteen minutes, hasn't it?"

He nodded and adjusted his pants before turning his back to me, the phone to his ear.

"*Sí*," he said quickly. There was a pause, then he hung up. He slowly turned to face me and a sober smile graced his lips. "I have to go. Now. I am so sorry."

I shook my head. My heart was still beating so fast, and my clit was throbbing like I was going to die without release. But I understood. I took in a deep breath. "It's fine. Go. Go do your job."

"You can get back up the hill?" he said. "I can carry you on my back, but I have to run."

"It's easier to go up than down," I told him reassuringly. "I'll be fine. I'll…talk to you tomorrow?"

"Yes," he said. Then he grabbed my face in his warm hands and kissed me hard. He took off sprinting across the sand. I had no idea where he was going, but whatever he was about to do, it would be something bad, part of a world I would never have to know about.

Once he disappeared up the path and my hormones had calmed down, I turned to look at the ocean. There was a queer hollowness in my chest. Was this it? Was this all there was to my life? Just the waves again, beckoning me to join them, to sink into depths where love couldn't touch me?

I stood there on the private beach, bathed in moonlight, and watched. And waited. Waited for my legs to start moving, to walk into the water and drown.

But I didn't. Because tomorrow was another day. And someone wanted to see me smile.

Though it was dark, it was still paradise.

...

I woke up just after noon, surprised my body would let me sleep that long. After I climbed up the cliff back to the resort and drove home, I didn't know what to do with myself. I went in the shower and didn't come out for a long time. I masturbated, thinking of Esteban, of what we had started but never finished. I had a glass of Scotch, neat. I sat on the back steps and listened to the crickets until I could no longer ignore the hollowness of my chest.

Then I went inside and called Doug. I let it ring and ring and ring. He never answered and I never left a message.

It was four a.m. when I finally fell asleep.

The problem with waking up in the afternoon in Hawaii is that you lose a lot of good painting light. It wasn't as if that was my original plan. My original plan was to call Esteban. But now, after all those dreamless hours, I didn't feel it was the right thing to do. Now I wanted to paint. I wanted to paint until everything that was left in me was on a canvas.

I packed up my easels and paints into the Jeep and took off for the beach. I decided to go for Larsen's Beach again, the red dirt, golden sand, and aquamarine water, the color of dazzling stones, beckoning me to recreate them with my brush.

I stayed there all day. I didn't eat, and I didn't check my phone—I hadn't even brought it with me. It was just me and the ocean and the colors and my hands and the sky and my heart. I went through three different canvases, saving the best view for last as the sun was going down. Exposed coral glinted like obsidian under the dying light, the waves mirrors of gold, the sky a tangerine dream frosted with the darkest, moodiest grays as clouds swarmed on the horizon.

"There's no light left," I heard Esteban say from behind me. I hadn't jumped at his presence. I had half expected him to show up, to find me here one last time.

"For once, I think I am more optimistic than you." I put the paintbrush on the edge of the easel and, totally aware of what a wreck I must have looked like, turned around to look at him.

I gasped. His eye was totally black and his nose looked bloodied.

"What happened to you?" I cried out.

He frowned, confused for a moment. Then he gave me a reassuring nod. "Don't worry about it. Comes with the job."

"What were you doing last night?"

"Not for you to worry about," he said. But I couldn't believe him, because the carefree and casual Esteban was gone. Not counting his battered face, he looked worried.

"But something happened."

"Everything is fine," he said, his voice a little hard. "Let me look at your paintings."

He came over to me, his feet bare, leather motorcycle jacket under his arm, and peered at the canvases. Normally I would have felt self-conscious—they weren't my best work by far. But I was too concerned about him to care.

"Lani," he said earnestly. "It would be a great honor if I could buy one of these pieces from you."

"These?" I asked dubiously. I looked back at them. There had been total joy in their creation, but joy did not always translate into skill. I hadn't painted in a long time. I was rusty, green.

"Yes," he said. "If you don't mind. I know I will have memories of you when I leave tomorrow, but I want more than just that. These will trigger my memories."

I studied him for a moment, knowing he was completely serious. There was no way I would actually let him pay for one, though. "You can choose one. But you don't owe me anything."

"But who doesn't need money," he said.

Me, I thought. There was still a chance I didn't need anything after he left me. The memory of the ringing phone echoed in my ears. It sounded like waves.

"Pick one," I said. "And you'll make me smile."

He grinned at that, a sight that warmed my soul. He put his hand at my waist. I could feel his skin burning through my thin tank top. He peered over my shoulder at the easel, his breath at my ear. "This one. Because it isn't finished." He turned his face so his lips were touching my cheek. "That's what hope is. An unfinished painting."

If I just turned my head, I could meet his lips. I could kiss him and ignite that passion I was trying so hard to bury. But this wasn't a deserted beach. It wasn't nighttime. And if I kissed him now, I would not be able to stop, not until my hands were on his hard body and he was deep inside me.

I swallowed hard, as if bread were stuck in my throat. "Okay," I managed to say. I kept my eyes on the horizon as the sun disappeared behind the gray. "I think we should head back now." He stayed put, those soft lips close, so very close. But eventually he pulled away and nodded.

Esteban helped me back up the red-coated hill and through the tall buffalo grass until we got back to the Jeep. He followed me all the way back to my house, riding his motorcycle right behind me the whole way. I kept stealing glances at him in the rearview mirror. He looked sexy as hell, in control of the road. I remembered when I was on the bike with him, wondering what it was that got me to take such a chance with him.

You still don't know anything about him, I told myself. The only thing you know is that he is a bad man. Bad people like him like to be around bad people like you. Just end it.

I felt the shadows wanting to choke me, to swerve the Jeep over the bridge we were crossing, to hit the guardrail and go tumbling down into the canopies of acacia trees. I saw it happening, the feeling of falling, the crunch of metal, the smash of glass, the world finally going black.

I shook my head and kept my grip tight on the steering wheel, my eyes half on the road and half on Esteban. It felt like it took forever to finally pull up in front of the house. I was such a bundle of nerves, overcome with fear and confusion, that I stayed in the car until he parked his bike and came over to the door, knocking on the window.

He peered at me in concern and said, "Are you all right?" He knocked again and finally I was able to put my hand on the handle and open the door.

I collapsed right into his arms. He didn't say anything, but simply held me close to him. He smelled like coconut and leather.

"You're going to be all right, Lani," he whispered.

He got my keys out of my purse and opened the door to the house, then led me inside. It was dark, quiet. Strangely cold. Or maybe that was just me.

"You're shivering," he said as he carefully took off his jacket. He held it out for me, as if to cover me in it, but then had second thoughts and placed it on the couch instead. "And you're covered in paint. Let's get you warm."

He took me over to the bathroom and led me inside.

CHAPTER SIX

Esteban shut the door and went over to the tiled shower, turning the knobs until the right temperature water came spraying out. He glanced at me over his shoulder. I was standing by the sink, my arms folded across my chest, my mind both blank and racing, like an empty videotape was just looping and looping. I was freezing now, my skin a mix of gooseflesh and paint splatters. My hands were the color of the sun-mirrored sea.

How is there something still so wrong with me?

He approached me like I was a skittish filly, all measured moves and careful glances. He didn't say anything as he slowly moved for my tank top. He grabbed the hem and with the slightest lift of his chin, motioned for me to raise my arms in the air.

With my breath and my heart in my mouth, I did so. He carefully pulled the tank top up until it was over my head. He flung it behind him and it landed on the floor. His hands, wonderfully warm hands, went behind my back to the clasp of my bra. With a swift, easy motion, it came undone and he pulled it away from my body.

He didn't let himself stare at my bare breasts. Instead his eyes remained focused on mine, forever trying to gauge my thoughts, to read me.

I stayed absolutely still as he bent down and started to pull my shorts and underwear off. They slid down my legs with ease and his hands went for the inside of my thighs, lifting my legs to get my clothing out from under them.

Those were tossed across the room, too. But his face and hands slid up my thighs in tandem, the soft grip of his fingers, the hot breath from his mouth. I felt myself blossoming for him, wanting his tongue and his lips, wanting everything. He kept rising, though, leaving me clenching with disappointment.

He gestured to the shower, wanting me to go in.

But I wasn't going in alone. I reached for his shirt and pulled it over his head.

His smile was pure sex. He quickly took off his pants and then before me stood a naked Esteban, a wonderfully sculpted man, like golden honey and bronze.

I wanted to run my fingers up and down his washboard abs, I wanted my mouth to kiss the ridges of his hips, I wanted his erect cock to slide deep inside me.

But Esteban was a man on a mission. He put his hands on my shoulders and slowly turned me around and led me over to the shower that was now steaming up the bathroom.

The shower was redundant at this point—I was already hot. But the water felt amazing on my too-ripe, too-sensitive skin, washing the paint away so we were standing in a swirling pool of sunset colors.

Having this naked man pressed up against me, this beautiful naked man who had shown me so much in the last few days, I needed to do something for him. I dropped to my knees and took his dick in my mouth. It tasted good, felt good to my tongue and lips, the weight heavy in my hands. I wanted to give him some of the pleasure he had given me, even if the pleasure would never really last.

The sad truth was I hadn't given a blow job in a long time. It hadn't been wanted in my household, and I wasn't sure if I was any good at it anymore. But from the way Esteban gripped my hair, I knew he did want it. It was only when I felt his breath quicken, his balls tighten, that he pulled away and groaned for me to stop.

I did so reluctantly, relishing the feel of him. He brought me up to my feet and held me against his heaving chest before he kissed me breathlessly. We kissed through the water, kissed through colors.

When we were both worked up, Esteban turned the shower off, grabbed a few towels from the rack, and led me out into the bedroom. He put the towels on the bed, then lay me back on it, my legs around his neck.

As much as I was craving for him to go down on me, an image kept flashing through my mind. The one I had in the Jeep the other night, the one of him taking off my panties with the barrel of his gun. The idea of a weapon of death so close to me was tantalizing in ways I was too afraid to understand.

"Esteban," I said, panting while his lips trailed up my thigh.

"Yes," he whispered back. "You have a glorious pussy, in case you didn't know."

"Do you know what would make it more glorious," I said, my voice catching in my throat. I was scared to go on with the request, but knew it was something I'd never get to experience again. This was a once-in-a-lifetime chance to feel alive.

My shadows craved it, as did my body, so I came to a compromise.

"Do you have a gun?" I asked.

He paused, and I looked down to see him gazing up at me from between my legs, his brow furrowed. "Yes. Why?"

I bit my lip and laid my head back down on the bed. "Have you ever…used it? On a woman?"

Another pause. Finally he said, "Do you mean, not in the killing way?"

"Have you ever…put it inside someone? And not pulled the trigger."

He swallowed. "No," he said, his voice low, "but that is probably the hottest fucking thing I have ever heard. And I have heard a lot."

"Will you try?" I asked, feeling extraordinarily vulnerable from both my position and the request. It felt so strange to be laying myself so bare, even if it was just sexually.

"You really do have a taste for death, don't you," he said to me as he came up. He kissed me hard, passionately, hungrily, his fingers pulling on my hair until I moaned. Then he abruptly pulled away and went running naked out into the living room. I heard him pick up his leather jacket and when he came back into the bedroom, he had a gun in his hand.

"Don't worry," he said as he promptly emptied the clip and made sure the chamber was empty.

My eyes widened at the sight. "I'm not worried."

"I keep it fairly clean," he said as he brought it over to me, about to get back into position. "More or less."

"I think I've decided I like things dirty."

"You think?" he asked, his voice rougher now, an octave lower.

I could feel him tracing the gun up between my thighs. I clenched, my body yearning for it, for the cold hard metal, for the kiss of danger.

"Perhaps we need lube," Esteban said. Moments later he slipped his fingers over my slit and sucked in his breath. "Or perhaps not. You're so wet, Lani. I could drink you."

"Do it," I moaned. "Lick me with your tongue, fuck me with the gun."

He swore something in Spanish, I don't know what, but it was impassioned. I felt his lips press down on my clit, his tongue snaking out to rub it just as the cold barrel of the gun teased at my entrance. My legs spread for him as he slowly eased the gun into me. I felt myself expanding, the coldness both a shock and a turn-on. My body rippled with pleasure, with excitement, with the thrill. Something so deadly was deep inside me, a thing that had taken lives was now giving ecstasy to mine.

It didn't take long before I was howling, coming hard and fast as Esteban angled the gun to hit my G-spot, and his tongue rubbed my clit until my body broke in waves. I cried out, grabbing his hair, feeling like I was making up for so much lost time, so many lost moments and opportunities. For one brief second I felt impossibly free.

Esteban carefully put the gun on the floor. "That was something I won't forget," he said.

"You did say you wanted memories," I told him once I'd found my voice. It was already hoarse, my lips dry.

"I did," he said. He slipped his arm under my back and flipped me over so I was on my stomach. "But I'm not done. The gun was hot, but what I have...fires better."

I smiled into the towels as he lifted my ass up into the air, straddling me from behind. He took a firm hold of my hips and thrust into me, making me feel impossibly, wonderfully full. It wasn't long until we were both coming together, grunts and cries and sweaty skin on skin. My world danced with colors, rainbows, sunshine.

Rays of light in all this dark.

...

I must have fallen asleep in Esteban's arms because he moved a bit, jostling me awake, and my eyes flew open. It was nighttime, and everything was in shadow.

"Just getting a glass of water," he whispered as he got off the bed. "I'll get you one, too."

With my tilted vision I watched him leave the room, his firm, bare ass barely visible as he stepped out of the dark and into the faded light of the hall, where he disappeared around the corner. I could hear him searching around for glasses.

Suddenly the hairs on the back of my neck stood up. For no reason, I was terrified deep in my very core, the kind of scared you got as a child when you were certain there was a monster in your closet.

I was certain that there was a monster in the closet. I could almost see him standing behind the doors, feel his eyes upon me.

My instincts were going wild, telling me to flee, that something was very wrong.

That was when I realized there wasn't anything in the closet

But there was a breath at my neck.

It happened so fast.

I opened my mouth to scream and a man placed his hand across it, clamping it shut, pressing my lips against my teeth. He told me to shut up, his voice cruel even though I was unable to make a sound, and the smell of stale tobacco filled my nose.

This couldn't be happening.

What was happening?

Surely I had to be dreaming, but this was no dream.

I was ready to fight, ready to kick, ready to go. But when the man pressed the cold, hard end of a gun against the back of my head, I froze.

All hope drained out of me. Esteban was in the kitchen with no idea of what was going on. I wondered who this man was, and if there was just him, or were there others. Was he just a burglar? Or was he involved with Esteban somehow?

The man ripped me off the bed and I let out a muffled cry, my feet trying to find purchase on the floor. The man's arm was very strong and the grip was very tight.

"So he thinks he can just fuck with me," the man whispered, snarling into my ear with an American Southern accent. "That isn't how we play it."

So this wasn't a home invasion. No, this was something much worse.

I watched in horror as Esteban slowly came back into the room. He was holding something in his hand, a small teapot, I think.

"Lani, I decided to make you some tea," he said breezily. "Chamomile."

Suddenly he stopped dead in his tracks. He saw us, taking in the situation in an instant, then he inhaled, his body tensing.

"Put the gun down," Esteban said in a very calm voice. "She has nothing to do with this. Do not hurt her."

"Do not hurt her?" the man yelled, nearly blasting my eardrums out as he sprayed my skin with spit. "I will hurt her, I'll hurt her and make you watch. Then I'll kill her and I'll kill you. Unless you tell me where Natasha is."

"I will tell you if you let Lani go," Esteban said, as if he had been in this exact situation many times before. He was so calm, and I was so scared. "Please, just drop the gun and we can talk."

"I'm not talking to you, I don't trust you."

"I'm naked," Esteban said. "How could I do anything? You obviously have me in a tough situation."

The man pressed the gun harder against my head and I cried out, but the sound was muffled. I was so fucking afraid.

Though it was hard to see Esteban in the shadows, I could see him frowning, the glint of worry on his brow. "I'll tell you where Natasha is if you—"

"No!" the man screamed. "No ifs. You tell me now or she dies. It would feel really good to see her brains splattered on that wall over there."

And in that moment, I saw it. I saw him pulling the trigger, I saw the explosion, the bullet going in, my brains going out. I saw my death, my very violent death, the death I'd been attempting for weeks. It was finally here, but I didn't get to choose this.

Esteban's words echoed in my head, from the time we were at the lookout. *It's a good sign to be scared. When you stop feeling fear, that's when it becomes dangerous. That's when you die.*

And now, I wanted nothing more than to live.

"Fine," Esteban said. He never came closer, just shifted a bit, but despite my horror I noticed something strange about the way he was holding the teapot. His posture was strained and the more I tried to focus on it, trying to make shape out of the shadows, the more I realized there was something wrong about the teapot in general.

Esteban went on. "Natasha was in the wrong place at the wrong time for the second time. The first time was when she tried to take off with our profits when she was just supposed to stay put. The second time was last night, when she sold you out in an attempt for forgiveness. But I don't forgive that easily." His voice sharpened, his body stiffening as he told the man, "Natasha is dead."

The grip on my mouth loosened by a tiny bit. I felt like it was my time to try to do something, to try to fight, while this guy was in shock.

But Esteban didn't leave anything to chance. He moved, quick as lightning, and there was a burst of light and a dull pop of noise.

The man loosened his hand around my mouth, slowly easing away until he fell away to the ground, collapsing in a heap.

I leaped back, falling back on the bed as I tried to get away.

Suddenly Esteban was at my side and he was holding my arms, trying to get me to look at him. It was still dark and I couldn't see him all that well, but I knew enough. There was a dead man at my feet. I'd almost been killed. Esteban somehow shot him with a teapot.

He was talking to me, but I wasn't listening. He shook me. "Lani. Please. Are you okay?"

I nodded absently, trying to find the words to speak. "Who…who was that?"

"It doesn't matter."

"Was he your job? Are you a contract killer?"

He shook his head. "No, I'm not. That's someone else's job, but he's been gone. This wasn't supposed to be this way."

"You killed someone," I said in horror, the realization slowly coming over me.

"I had to," he said. "You would have been killed. Raped and then killed, that's how these people work."

"These people," I repeated. "You are these people."

"Lani…"

"You killed Natasha."

"You don't know who Natasha is. She was no better than he was. There are things about my job that I don't like, but we all take loyalty very seriously. We also take our safety seriously. For ourselves and for others."

He sighed and looked away. "I guess I should have told you. But I was hoping to spare you the knowledge. This man and Natasha, I was supposed to…fix them last night. I'd only gotten Natasha. This man had left. I would have found him tonight…I was supposed to. But then there was you…and I'm a weak fucking man when it comes to you."

I shook my head, trying to understand. I looked at his hands. Up close I could see he was holding a gun with a silencer. Behind him, an empty teapot lay on the ground. "How did you…"

"I told you," he said, "that we take our safety seriously. I had the gun by me all night…after…well, after *we* used it, I loaded it, put on the silencer just in case. There's another gun under your bed. I put this one in the kitchen. There's another one by the door. All hidden, but I knew where they were. You can't be too careful."

"You hid it in a teapot."

"Quick thinking," he said, giving me a smile that didn't belong at a crime scene. "I was naked, I had to improvise as soon as I heard the scuffle."

Thank God for thin walls.

"You're still naked," I whispered, my attention going back to the dead body on the floor. I stared at the man with the bullet hole in his head. My eyes glazed over, unwilling to take him in, to pay attention to details. I didn't want to *see* him, the man who almost killed me, the man I'd seen get killed. I didn't know him, but I'd never had death at my feet.

"What do we do now?" I asked.

"Well," Esteban said as he sat on the bed beside me. "You go make yourself an actual cup of tea and I'll take care of the rest. Lani, this shouldn't have happened to you. You shouldn't have been a part of this. You shouldn't have known. This was my problem, my job, my reason for being here. I fucked up. I got involved with you and I lost my head for a moment. I'm sorry."

I nodded absently. I knew he was sorry. And I was, too. But I knew what I was getting into when I first saw him, when I first learned his name, when I first learned what he did. I knew he was bad and yet I wanted him. I wanted the thrill, to know what it felt to be alive.

And now, I finally had it. Now I had seen death, though not my own.

But it was enough.

I didn't want to die.

CHAPTER SEVEN

"Are you sure you don't want to come with me, see me off?" Esteban said.

We were sitting in my kitchen, drinking coffee as the sun streamed in through the windows. He had just set down his empty mug and was getting out of his seat, making all the big motions that he was about to leave.

Leaving me alone.

I took a sip of the Kona brew and shook my head. I wasn't afraid anymore—not of that. I believed Esteban when he said he'd take care of everything. He'd spent the whole night making sure there wasn't a trace of the incident, while I spent the whole night cowering in a state of shock. I definitely was still in shock, but I was coming around in ways I hadn't anticipated.

I don't know what he did with the body, or where he went for several hours in the dark of night, but I knew a man like him made no mistakes. He was the smart one, the good one.

He'd saved my life again, even if he was the one who invited danger in.

But then again, I was the one who had beckoned the danger the moment I stepped on the plane to Kauai. I had wanted nothing but oblivion, a place beyond death. Black space, dark shadows. I flirted with death so many times, from a mere handshake to full-on penetration. I wanted change in the most dramatic way; I wanted death to take me from my meager, loveless existence.

Until I realized that my existence never had to be empty.

Love was still out there, as were hopes and dreams and everything else I pretended I no longer wanted. Esteban opened my eyes, and he did so by showing me death, the devastating permanence of it. He dealt with death every day in his job, and here I was pretending I knew something about it. Pretending that death was a choice I wanted. It shouldn't have been anyone's choice. Not the choice of the man who tried to kill me, not Esteban's. Not mine.

In the few days I'd known Esteban, he'd schooled me on what life was, and more importantly, what life could be.

Light.

Colors.

Paradise.

I slowly got out of my chair, not wanting to say good-bye. I knew I'd never see him again. He had my painting of golden seas to remind him of me.

I had nothing.

"Lani," he said gently, his eyes swimming with compassion. He pulled me into him and wrapped his arms around me tightly. We held each other for as long as we could. Shallow, silly parts of me wanted to beg to go with him back to Mexico, to be a part of his life. But we knew our lives weren't meant to intertwine that way. They were meant to meld for a sweet moment, nothing more.

He pulled away and kissed me softly on the forehead. "You're valuable," he said as he placed a cold green jade stone in my hands. "Keep painting."

Then he turned and walked away. With my heart prickling, I heard him get on his motorcycle. The familiar roar filled my ears and then he was gone, the sound fading into the bird calls of midmorning.

I sighed, my chest feeling like an anvil had been placed on it. I squeezed the jade in my hand, knowing I'd never let it go. Slowly I turned and went to the back steps and sat down, staring at the paradise in front of me. The chickens pecked at the grass, not caring about my presence. They just...carried on.

And that was when I realized that Esteban hadn't left me with nothing. I gave him a painting, but he gave me *everything*.

I fished my phone out of my pocket and dialed Doug.

I dialed home.

Doug picked up on the second ring.

"Honey?" I said into the phone, my voice soft. Tears were threatening my eyes, my lungs were starting to feel choked, aching for release.

There was a long pause. Finally Doug said, "Lani? What's wrong?"

I couldn't help it. I hadn't heard concern in his voice for as long as I could remember. It was enough to open the floodgates. I cried, tears streaming down my face, and just bawled, everything flowing out of me, my tears taking me to another place.

"Doug, baby," I finally managed to say, gulping hard for air, my lungs screaming. "Doug, I want to come home. I want to live."

There was more silence, maybe just to let me sob, maybe to gather his thoughts and figure out what to say. Then Doug said something I didn't think he would.

"I want you to live, too. I love you."

The tears continued to come.

So much grief, so much sadness, so much betrayal, so much guilt. So much in my life had gone terribly wrong.

And yet there was so much hope.

And value in my hands.

THE END

dirty DEEDS

A NOTE FROM THE AUTHOR

Thank you for wanting to read Dirty Deeds. Though this book is not as dark or disturbing as the previous book in the series, Dirty Angels, it does contain violence, coarse language and sexually explicit scenes. Reader discretion is advised.

Speaking of Dirty Angels, though Dirty Deeds is the second in the series, it can be read as a standalone. The third book in the series, Dirty Promises, can also be read as a standalone (it should be released this summer). While all the stories are connected, I do write them with the mindset that each reader is a new audience unfamiliar with the other books. So, no, you don't need to read the whole trilogy but of course I personally think it's more fun if you do.

ALSO – please note that I have an excerpt from Vince Stark's House of Sin (erotica) and Jenn Cooksey's Landslide (romance) at the end of this novel. I highly encourage you to read them but please note that due to these inclusions at the book, the percentage or pages left in the book will be off and the story will probably end a bit sooner than you anticipate. I like to warn readers ahead of time. Thanks!

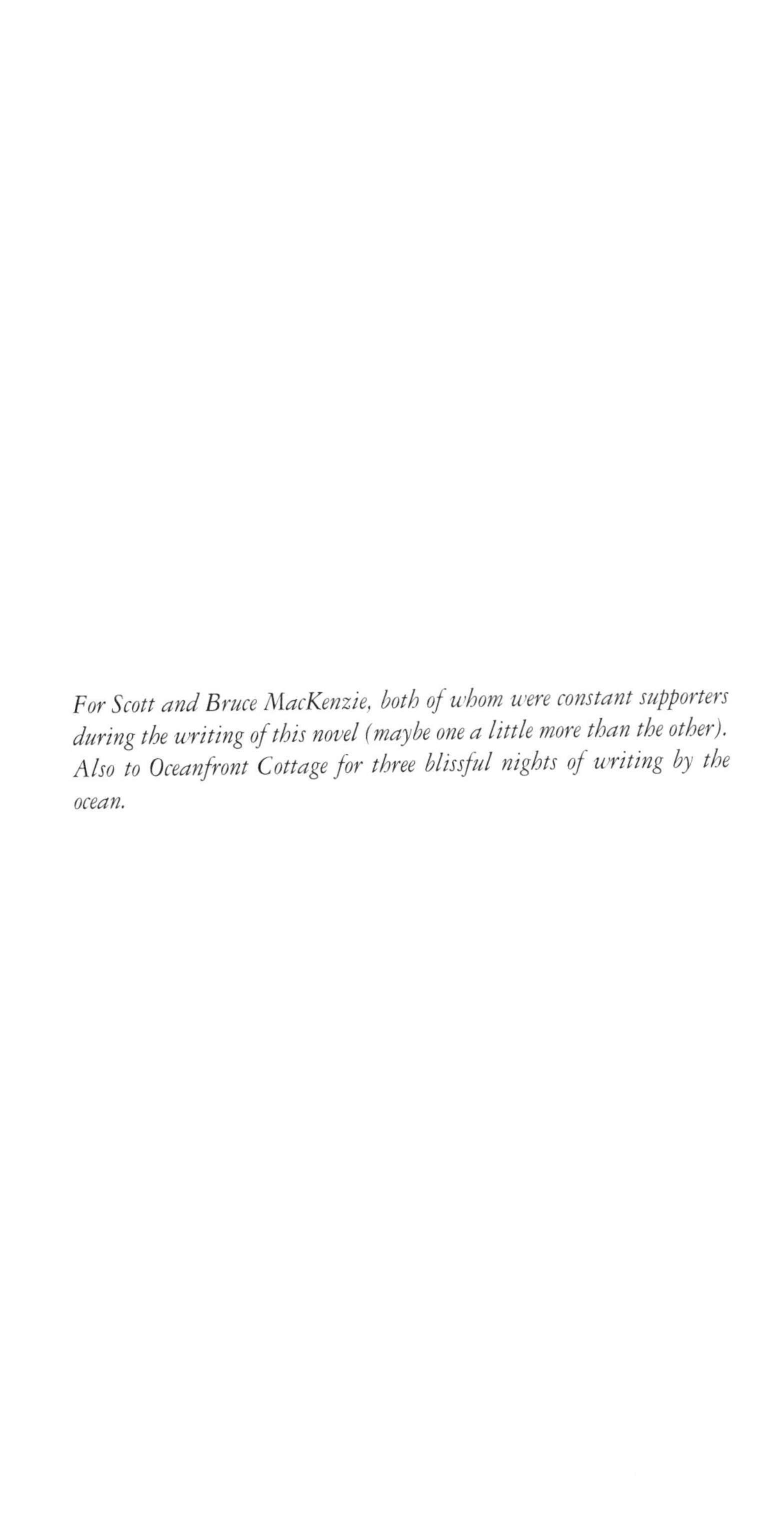

For Scott and Bruce MacKenzie, both of whom were constant supporters during the writing of this novel (maybe one a little more than the other). Also to Oceanfront Cottage for three blissful nights of writing by the ocean.

CHAPTER ONE

The call came at 6:30 a.m. from a voice I recognized but couldn't place. The fact that it sounded familiar was surprising, though. The turnover rate for these guys was exceedingly high. They were shuffled around to different *sicarios* like a game of musical chairs. Sometimes I wondered if the ones giving me the orders—the *narcos* just underneath the bosses—ever lasted more than a few weeks. Did they go on to have long careers doing the dirty work of the *patrons*? Or were they so good at getting the job done that they were employed for a long time, even promoted, just like any assistant manager at McDonald's?

It didn't really matter. I took these calls, I carried out the orders, and I got paid. I was at the bottom of their food chain, but as long as I wasn't tied to just one cartel then I didn't have to worry about long-term security. You didn't want long-term security when working for the *narcos*. You wanted to stay as distant—as freelance—as possible. You wanted a way out, in case you ever had a change of heart.

That was unlikely for me. But I was still a bit of a commitment-phobe. Freedom meant everything, and in this game, freedom meant safety.

The girl next to me in bed moaned at the early intrusion, pulling the pillow over her head. She looked ridiculous considering she was completely naked on top of the sheets. Was it Sarah? Kara? I couldn't recall. She was so drunk last night that I was amazed she even made it to my hotel room. Then again, that's why I was in Cancun. I could pretend to be like everyone else, just another dumb tourist on the beach.

I took the phone into the bathroom and closed the door.

"Yes," I answered, keeping my voice low.

"I have a job for you," the man on the other line said. His English was pretty much perfect but relaxed, almost jovial. Sometimes they gave me orders in Spanish, sometimes in English. I felt like this man was trying to extend a courtesy.

"I assume I've worked for you before," I said.

"For me?" the man asked. "No. For my boss? Yes. Many times. But this has nothing to do with him. Let's just say this is coming from a whole new place."

None of that concerned me. "Tell me about payment."

He chuckled. "Don't you want to hear about the job?"

"It doesn't matter. The price does."

"One hundred thousand dollars, U.S., all cash. Fifty now, fifty upon completion."

That made me pause. My heart kicked up. "That's a lot of money."

"It's an important job," the man said simply.

"And what is the job?"

"It's a woman," he said. "In Puerto Vallarta. She should be very easy to find for someone like you."

"I need a name and I need her photo," I told him. Though the price was quite higher than normal, the man was ignoring the basics. It made me wonder if he had ever done this before. It made me wonder a lot of things.

"I have the first, not the second. As I said, she should be easy to find. You might even be able to Facebook her."

I waited for him to go on.

He cleared his throat. "Her name is Alana Bernal. Twenty-six. Flight attendant for Aeroméxico. I want a bullet in her head and I want it front page news."

Bernal was a very common name, which is probably why it sounded familiar. I wondered what she had done, if anything. Usually when I was sent to kill women, it was because they were involved with a *narco* and had overstayed their welcome. They knew too much. They had loose lips in more ways than one.

I was never really given time to think about it. You weren't with these types of things. There were a few minor alarm bells going off in my head—the high price for someone minor, the greenness in the man's voice—but the price won out in the end. That amount of money could get me away from this business for a long time. I saw a lengthy hiatus on my horizon, one that didn't include fucking drunk chicks on spring break just because I was horny, a hiatus that didn't include bouncing my way from hotel room to hotel room across Mexico, waiting for the next call.

I told the man I agreed to his terms, and we worked out the payment plan. I wouldn't get the other half until she made the news. Considering how rare shootings were in Puerto Vallarta, I had no doubt it would happen. And I would be long gone.

I hung up the phone feeling almost elated. The promise of a new life buried that worm of uneasiness. One more job and then I'd be freer than ever.

I came out of the bathroom to see the chick sitting up in bed and looking extremely nauseous. Once she saw me though, her eyes managed to light up.

"Wow," she said. "You're fucking hot."

I tried to smile, hoping she didn't find me enticing enough to stay. "Thank you."

"Did we have sex last night?"

I stood beside the bed and folded my arms across my chest. Her mouth opened a bit at my muscles. I still had the same physique I had back in the military, and it still got the same reactions from women. They never knew the real me—knew Derek Conway—but at least, with the way I looked, they thought they did. Just another built, tough American boy, a modern G.I. Joe.

They had no idea what I did.

They had no idea who I was.

"No," I told her, "we didn't have sex. You stripped and then you passed out."

She looked surprised. "We still didn't…"

I gave her a dry look. "Sex is only fun when you're awake, babe." I stretched my arms above my head and she stared openly at my stomach, from the waistband on my boxers to my chest. Okay, now it was time for her to go.

I told her I had stuff to do in the morning and needed her to move along. I could tell she wanted to at least take a shower, but I wasn't about to budge.

I had a plane to catch.

...

Alana Bernal was extremely easy to find.

At least for me. She had a Facebook page under Alana B. Her privacy settings were high, but I was still able to see her profile picture, dressed in her Aeroméxico uniform. She had a sweet yet beautiful face. Her eyes were light hazel, almost amber, both stunning and familiar at the same time. They glowed against her golden skin, as did her pearly white teeth. She looked like a lot of fun, and I could imagine all the unwanted attention she got from unruly passengers in the air. She looked like she could handle them with a lot of sass.

Once again I found myself wondering what she had done.

And once again I realized I couldn't care.

That wasn't my business.

Killing her was my business.

I drove to the airport, and for the next two days I began to stalk the employee parking lot, using a different rental car each time. Most of the flight crew I saw looked a bit like her but lacked the certain vitality she had. So I waited in mounting frustration, just wanting this job to be over with.

On day three, just as I was driving past for the forty-second time that morning, I spotted her getting out of a silver Honda, wrestling with her overnight bag. I quickly pulled the car around again and parked at the side of the road, plumes of dust rising up around me. There was nothing but a chain-link fence between us as she began the long walk toward the waiting airport shuttle. Her modest high heels echoed across the lot and she tugged at the hem of her skirt with every other step. Not only was she beautiful, but there was something adorably awkward about her.

What had she done?

No, I couldn't care.

I looked down at the bag in the passenger seat and took out the silencer, quickly screwing it on the gun that I was holding between my legs.

She only had a few seconds of life left before I put the bullet in her heart.

I got out of the car, moving like a ghost, gun down at my side. In three strides I would make it over to the fence where I would take quick aim and shoot. She would go down and I would be gone.

I was one stride away when it happened.

A golden sedan pulled out of a parking space in a hurry and slammed right into Alana, knocking her to the ground. She screamed as she went down, tires screeching to a halt, and people started shouting from the shuttle.

The sedan reversed then sped around Alana's crumpled body, not stopping to check on the woman they had just hit.

I've been in a lot of situations before that smack you square in the face—abrupt and brutal scenes that change the course of the day, the course of a life. They come out of nowhere, but you adapt, you roll with them. You refuse to be shocked. I should have been able to collect myself better than I did.

But seeing that car speeding away toward the parking gates and crashing through them as it fled the scene, well I seemed to lose all logic. Before I knew what I was doing, I was getting back into my car and driving after the hit-and-run sedan.

As I passed the broken gates to the parking lot I could see people—employees—emerging from the shuttle, one of them pointing at me. I had been spotted. Maybe as a witness, maybe as someone that was a part of the crime.

Only it wasn't the crime they thought it was, but the one I didn't get to commit.

I was fucking everything up for myself and I knew it. But seeing that car gun her down then keep going, as if the driver thought they could get away with it, brought back every debilitating moment from Afghanistan. I watched a lot of people get killed before I became the killer.

I would like to tell myself that I was going after them because they fucked up my potentially perfect assassination. That would make more sense than the truth—that I felt like a helpless soldier again, watching the world around him crumble from senseless acts. I was angry, angrier than I had been in a long time.

I'd snapped. I guess I had it coming.

I drove the beat up car I'd rented from a cheap agency right on his ass, following him in heated pursuit. I wasn't thinking, I wasn't even breathing, I was just reacting to some long-forgotten, deep-seated need for vengeance.

The sedan screamed down the road, tires burning on hot asphalt, heading for the highway. I was going to stop him before that. I didn't know what I was going to do after that, but I had an idea.

I pressed the gas pedal down as far as it would go and willed it to catch up, muttering expletives as it shuddered beneath me. The rental car was a pile of shit to look at, but it turned out the engine worked well enough to let me catch up with the sedan that was sputtering erratically, a tire having blown out as it fought for control on the rough road.

I couldn't get a good look at the driver, but through the dust I could see him thrashing around in his seat, panicking at the wheel. He wasn't a professional by any means. Then again, I was supposed to be one and I was trying to kill his fucking ass for no reason at all.

No reason except that it felt one hundred percent right.

His car suddenly shifted right and I took that moment to gun it until my front end clipped his back. The headlights shattered, and with a screech of metal, the car went spinning to a stop.

Before I could comprehend what was going on, I was jumping out of the car, gun at my side, and running to his door. I threw it open and aimed it right at the man's head.

The dust blew around us, and through the haze he looked at me, mouth open, the whites of his eyes shining as they stared at me with fear or shock or regret.

I didn't care which one it was.

He raised his hands, screaming out in Spanish, "It was an accident, please, it was an accident!"

"Who are you?" I asked, my voice more steady than I felt.

"It was an accident," he cried again. For a brief moment he took his frightened eyes off the gun and looked behind him, at the parking lot in the distance and the commotion that was gathering there. Soon they would be heading our way. "Is she all right? Please, please, the girl, is she all right?"

"No," I told him, and pulled the trigger.

Because of the silencer, the sound of his brains and skull splattering on the window—a bright burst of red—was louder than the gun.

I quickly got back in my car and drove away. There was no time to stand around and figure out who the man was, if it was truly an accident or something else. Questions would come later, as they always did, only this time I'd be the one doing the asking.

...

I spent the rest of the day inside my hotel room, cleaning my guns and watching the local Puerto Vallarta news, trying to see if the accident would be mentioned. It was at the end of the segment when they finally reported on it. It was the usual shoddy shot of the serious reporter standing in front of the smashed gates to the parking lot. Alana, as it turns out, wasn't killed or even critically injured. She had been admitted to the nearest hospital. The bigger part of the story was the part that had my hand all over it. It was that someone had caught up with the driver and shot him in the head. The news wasn't sure whether this was a botched hit-and-run or vigilante justice.

I didn't know what to think of it myself. One minute everything was going to plan, the next minute I was putting a bullet in the head of someone else, acting out of pure, untrustworthy instinct. That lack of control scared me. I hadn't responded like that, so loosely, so foolishly, since my wife had been killed.

Regression was not a good thing in this business.

It was just after nightfall when my phone rang. I waited a beat, trying to read my gut before it got compromised by the voice on the phone. My gut was telling me to back out.

"Hello," I answered.

"Hola," the man said in that light tone of his. "I think we may have gotten our wires crossed here. I heard you were the best in the business. I'm a bit confused as to why you killed someone else instead of the woman you were paid to kill."

"No time for pleasantries," I noted.

"No," the man said. "Not when she's in the hospital and you've jeopardized this whole operation."

I cleared my throat. "It was all lined up. Before I was even able to take my shot, she was hit by a fucking car. Everyone saw it. What was I supposed to do, still go through with it with everyone watching me?"

"That still doesn't explain why you shot the driver."

No, not really, I thought.

"I guess I lost my cool," I told him.

"I didn't think that was possible with you."

"Maybe you've heard wrong about me."

"They've called you soulless."

"Maybe I'm getting tired of this game."

"Ah," he said. "The game, but not the money, hey?"

"Maybe money gets you killed in the end."

"No, no," he said. "Money is what gets other people killed. By you." He sighed long and hard, and I tried to picture who this man could be. So, so familiar. And so, so wrong.

"Listen," he went on, "I know things are more complicated now, but the job still has to go through."

"I don't think so."

"No?"

"It's more than complicated. There were witnesses there that could have seen me."

"No one has come forward."

"How would you know that?"

"Don't you worry about it. Just trust me when I tell you that you are clean. The only real complication is the fact that you'll have to get into the hospital. She's being guarded, will be for some time. But I know you've handled dicier situations than that before."

I frowned. "How much *do* you know about me?"

"Enough," was his dry answer. "The price is now two hundred thousand dollars. You can keep that fifty we gave you. This is on top of that."

Fucking hell. Two hundred and fifty thousand dollars would end all my problems forever. But that was way too much money for just a girl, unless she was more than just a girl. She was a death sentence.

Something was terribly fucking wrong here, and I would be an idiot to stick my nose in it for one minute longer.

"No," I told him with steely resolve. "I haven't survived this long to know when there's something more at stake. I'll meet your people somewhere, give you your deposit back if you want, but this is where we part ways."

There was a heavy pause on the line. "Don't be foolish."

"I'm being smart," I told him. "Whatever game this is, I don't want any part of it."

"I suppose raising the price wouldn't help."

"No. This is a job I don't want to touch."

"But you've already had your hand in it," he said, and finally there was an edge to his voice, a warning. "It's too late for you to back out now. You accepted the job, and now you have to finish it."

"You're telling me that the fact that the target was hit by a seemingly random car isn't a warning sign to you? Right before I pulled the trigger? The fact that the dead body of a fucking flight attendant has a two hundred thousand dollar price tag on it? If you want her out so bad, there are plenty of other people you can pay to do your dirty work. This one though, I'm no longer a part of."

More silence. I could hear his breathing. "Have you ever backed out of a job before?"

I swallowed. "No," I said thickly. "I haven't. But there have been jobs that I shouldn't have taken, only I didn't listen to my instincts. I'm listening to them now. This isn't the job for me, and this is where we part ways." I took a deep breath, feeling the monetary sting already. "Just tell me where to meet your people. I'll give you the deposit back, I haven't touched a single bill. I don't want any trouble, we'll just forget it all and move on."

"Oh, you'll be moving on," the man said. "And so will she."

The line went dead.

I stared at my phone for a good minute, feeling absolute dread coursing through me. I was trusting my gut on this one—I had made the right decision, hadn't I?

Within an hour, I was out of the hotel room and booked into one of the swankier all-inclusive resorts close to downtown. I used my fake Canadian passport—Derrin Calway—and credit card. I tossed my phone and got a new one at a street-side kiosk. I still had an email address and a pager number that most people knew, and though many of the cartels didn't possess the same high-tech tracking systems and surveillance the movies would lead you to believe, it never hurt to be careful. I was constantly getting cheap new phones, constantly changing names, constantly on the move.

Most people just called me *The American*. They never really knew my name was Derek, and the ones that did, they assumed it was a fake name. But my name was really the only real thing about me.

I tried to fall asleep that night, but the sound of people partying it up at the sprawling hotel pools was too much for me. Sometimes, only sometimes, the normalcy of the world around me hurt. This was one of those times.

When dawn finally colored the sky tangerine pink, and the only sound was the crashing of the Pacific outside my balcony, I finally fell asleep. My last thought was of Alana, lying on the pavement, her body broken by intent or circumstance.

I wanted to find her.

CHAPTER TWO

Alana

"Alana." I heard a voice cut through the darkness. A firm hand shook my shoulder as the screams and cries started to fade away and only the fear, that deep, desperate fear, was a film left behind.

I blinked slowly, the white light filtering in through my eyelashes. The nightmare was hanging around in the back of my pounding head, and the living nightmare was before me.

Fuck my fucking life. I couldn't believe I got hit by a goddamn car.

"Alana," the voice said again, and I knew it was the nurse, Salma. "Are you all right, dear? You were crying in your sleep."

I brought my eyes over to her without moving my head. I'd gotten pretty good at that over the last few days. If I moved my head at all, I'd be hit with a wave of nausea. The doctors assured me that I probably wouldn't have a concussion, but I didn't believe them. I felt like my brain had been demolished.

The nurse had a kindly face, full-cheeked like a chipmunk. So far she was the only one in the hospital who had been doting on me. The doctors and surgeons were so brusque and professional. I was used to that being with the airlines and all, but it was nice to have someone that acted as if they really cared.

"Sometimes I do that," I said carefully. "I…have nightmares."

She gave me a sympathetic smile. "I can tell." Luckily she didn't press it any further. My childhood wasn't something I liked to talk about.

"How are you feeling, otherwise?" she asked, trying to adjust my pillow. I winced at the movement but was relieved that it didn't hurt as much as it usually did.

"I still get dizzy when I move my head," I told her. "But it's getting better now. Thank god. My arm is really itchy." I looked down to the thickkbandage around my wrist, going from palm to mid-forearm.

"It will get better as your skin gets used to it," Salma said. "You were incredibly lucky, Alana. Not many people walk away from a hit-and-run accident with only a broken ankle and fractured wrist."

"And the bruising and the pain and the head that feels like it is going to explode," I filled in.

"That, too, will go away," she said. "All you need to do is rest."

I swallowed hard. It felt like I had a lump of coal in my throat. "Have they caught the guy yet, the guy who did this to me?"

A funny look passed over her eyes, and I knew she knew something.

"Tell me, please," I told her. "I hate being kept in the dark."

She sighed and cast a quick glance over to the open door leading out into the rest of the hospital. The bed next to me in the semi-private room was thankfully unoccupied the whole time I had been there.

"I haven't talked to the police," she said in a low voice. "It's just what I've been hearing. But the guy who hit you, he's dead."

My eyes widened. "Dead?"

"Someone killed him…he was murdered. Not too far from where you were hit."

"What does that mean?"

She shrugged. "I don't know. I am sure the police will talk to you about it as soon as they can."

My thoughts automatically went to my brother. Javier was protective over me, even more so lately, and this seemed like something he would do.

"How was he killed?" I asked with trepidation.

"He was shot. In the head."

"That's it?"

She shot me a funny look.

I quickly fumbled for my next words. "I mean, that's terrible."

That meant it wasn't Javier. Javier wouldn't just shoot whoever did this to me, he would take them and make them suffer for a very, very long time. My brother might be twisted—as all drug cartel lords are—but family always came first.

"I'm not sure how terrible it is," the nurse said. "This man hit you with his car and took off. Some might say it's his comeuppance."

Some might say all of this was too weird. "I guess I don't have to worry anymore."

She shook her head. "You don't. But there is still a police officer stationed on this floor, for at least tonight. They can't tell whether the hit and run was intentional or not."

"I'd seen that car before," I told her, just as I had told the police. "I got glimpses of the man from time to time. I think he was a mechanic for the airlines."

"That's what they say. No record of criminal history either, but then again it's Mexico, so that doesn't mean much, does it?"

I wanted to shake my head but didn't risk it. "No, it doesn't." I closed my eyes. "When do I get out of here again?"

"The doctor wants you under observation for a few more days. The fact that you are still dizzy isn't good, although that can be a side effect of the pain medication."

"Do you have anything to help me sleep?" I asked, and when I didn't hear her reply, I opened my eyes to look at her pleadingly. What I wanted was something strong enough to knock me out and keep my nightmares at bay. Usually I had them about once a week, but ever since the accident—which happened, what? Four, five days ago?—I had been having them more. Perhaps because for the first time in a very long time I was afraid again.

And perhaps because being here in the hospital made me realize how little I had in my life. My brother hadn't come by to see me yet, but I hadn't called him either, and I hadn't talked to my twin sister Marguerite. Everyone else—my other sisters, my mother, my father, they were all dead. I had no children, no husband, no boyfriend. Nothing. I only had my job and my friends Luz and Dominga.

Salma gave me a conceding smile then left the room. When she came back she was holding two pills and a glass of water.

"This will make you rest for a long time," she said, and gently helped me up so I could take them. The room spun and my head hurt, but I managed to get them down.

It wasn't long until I felt good, sublime, floating on a cloud, and everything went black.

...

It was ten o'clock at night and the hospital was quiet. Luz sat on the corner of my bed while Dominga stationed herself at the door, watching for anyone who might try and stop my escape attempt.

I'd been at the hospital for a week in total and yet the doctor still wanted me to stay for another night or two. I was sick and fucking tired of just lying in bed, watching terrible soap operas and flipping through magazines. Luz and Dominga came to see me when they could, but since Luz was a flight attendant like I was and Dominga was a maid at one of Puerto Vallarta's largest resorts, they couldn't always find the time during visiting hours.

Finally I'd had enough and told them to come and rescue me the first chance they got. Luz had the spare key to my apartment and went in to get me some clothes to leave in and helped me get changed into my dress while we waited for Dominga to finish her shift.

We weren't going far. I couldn't really fathom it in my condition. I was no longer dizzy, but I was still on pain medication, my left forearm was bandaged tightly, and my left foot was in a cast from below the knee down. When I officially left the hospital I would have crutches, but for tonight I would just rely on my friends. The only people I really had.

I had finally called Javier and Marguerite and told them what had happened. Javier said for me to call him as soon as I was discharged, and Marguerite had whined about not having any money to fly down from New York to see me. But the fact was, my only two living family members still weren't here.

"Is the coast clear?" Luz asked, drumming her fingers excitedly on the bed. She had this crazy sparkle in her eyes that she got when she was feeling particularly hyperactive. Luz was tall with long dark hair down to her butt that she almost always wore in a bun, which only added on extra height. She was a force, a powerhouse, and was just as good at putting drunken passengers in their seats as she was at being the life of the party. Luz was a ball of energy and very hard to ignore, and I knew she would get me out of this dull hospital room as if her life depended on it.

Dominga raised her finger to shut her up and kept staring down the hallway. She was about my height, 5'6", but runway-model thin and had this quiet air about her that most people mistook as snobbishness, but I knew it was because she would just rather listen than talk. She also didn't smile much because she hated the gap between her teeth, something we all—especially her husband—found adorable.

Then there was me, Alana Bernal. Sister of one of Mexico's most powerful drug lords. Queen of meaningless one night stands. Flight attendant who couldn't seem to get the routes she wanted.

Forever alone.

And hit by a fucking car.

"Okay, *now*," Dominga said, and Luz immediately got to her feet, helping me off the bed. I had put on a simple black dress that showed off a lot of cleavage—I needed something to distract from the bandages and cast. On my good foot was a sparkly flat sandal for stability and Luz had covered up my body with mounds of concealer to mask all the bruises which were now fading to an ugly yellow purple, like a rotting plum. I definitely didn't look as good as I normally did, but I was still high on pain medication, so at least I felt pretty good.

With all my weight on Luz's shoulder, we hobbled over to the door and looked down the hall both ways. It was totally empty. Thankfully I knew that there were no more policemen stationed on this floor to look after me. They had all been called off once it was ruled out that the hit and run had been a crime but not a deliberate one, and that the man who had shot the assailant had been a vigilante of sorts. At least, that's what the cops had told me. It was hard to know the truth when it came to them.

The three of us scampered down the hall toward the stairwell, away from the nurse's station, and with an awkward, clumsy descent, we made our way down the stairs and out into the hot night.

I nearly collapsed into Luz's arms, bursting into a fit of giggles. I hadn't felt this rebellious since I was a little girl, stealing candy from Violetta. But at that thought, my smile began to falter, as it always did when I thought about my poor sister. She hadn't died long ago.

"Now what?" Luz asked, giving my shoulders a squeeze. She could always tell when I was being held in this violent melancholy and did her best to get me out of it. "What's the plan?"

"I think that was the plan," Dominga said, brushing her hair out of her face. "Get Alana out of the hospital."

"Get Alana a drink," I said quickly. "Did you think I got all dressed up to stand in the parking lot?"

"Are you sure with your medication?" Dominga asked as she eyed me suspiciously.

I waved her away. "I'm fine. Just get me to a bar, get a beer in my belly, get some fucking hot men with big dicks, and I'm happy as can be."

Luz and Dominga exchanged a look above my head. Finally Luz said, "There's a bar down the road, but you know it's going to be filled with hospital workers that may just haul your ass back here, not your usual hot men with big dicks."

"I'll take my chances," I told her, nodding to the road. "Now let's go before someone pulls me back in."

We got in Luz's car and drove a couple of blocks until we saw a bar with a pink and green neon palm tree outside. *Lolita's.* It looked a bit rough around the edges, but the people standing outside smoking seemed like your average Mexican twenty somethings in Puerto Vallarta.

"We can do better," Luz said with a discerning gleam to her eyes. "I'll keep driving."

"I don't think I should go too far from the hospital," I said quietly. "Just in case." Even though I was feeling fine, I was still afraid that a rogue concussion could spring up out of nowhere. I was also afraid that Salma would discover that I had escaped. Lately she hadn't been checking on me until just about one o'clock in the morning, but I felt bad about possibly disappointing her.

Still, freedom felt divine.

"All right," Luz said, and pulled her Toyota into the lot behind the bar.

If there were any nurses celebrating the end of their shift, I didn't see them. As Dominga and Luz helped me into the bar, we were met with smiling, drunk faces and spilled drinks. The music was loud and booming, bass thumping into my bones, and I couldn't help but grin back at the rowdy patrons. I had needed this, badly.

While Luz went to the bar to get us beer, Dominga and I managed to score a booth in the corner. We pushed away the stacks of empty drinks that were left behind and settled in to do some hottie watching. Well, I was the one who was always looking for someone to catch my eye. Dominga took her marriage very seriously and wouldn't even admit whether a guy was hot or not.

"I'll get the next round," I said to Luz as she came back with the beers.

She waved her hand at me dismissively. "You are always buying us drinks, Alana. It's time for us to treat you for a change."

I raised my beer in the middle of the table. "Well, I think I owe you something for your excellent escape plan." I clinked their bottles. "So cheers to that. And thank you."

"And thank you for not dying," Luz said, her features growing stern. "When I saw it on the news..." She trailed off and took a quick sip of her beer. I wasn't used to her acting emotional and it was throwing me off. "I'm just so glad you're okay."

I gave her a look. "I'm not exactly *okay*. I am a bit banged up."

"But you're here now with us," Dominga said. "And that's something."

I nodded. It was true. I really had no right to complain about the fact that I would be off work for at least another month. I was going on disability, but even with the airline funding it, that didn't equal the full amount of pay I would normally receive. I was going to be on a budget for the next month as my bones healed. And because I wouldn't be able to do my yoga or pilates or go for my daily runs, I was going to be bored out of my mind.

But it could have been worse. I know that in my life, the worst possible thing was always lurking in the background, ready to strike.

I turned my attention to the bar. I was ready to be distracted, and a man was usually pretty good for that. Unfortunately there weren't a lot of men here to do a good enough job. I wasn't even that picky, I just wanted someone that made my head turn, my heart skip a few beats, my thighs squeeze together. That didn't mean I never settled for less—I often did, and usually with the wrong man (don't get me started on the pilots I'd had affairs with, always a mistake)—but I still hoped for someone a bit extraordinary.

You would think that with my past and family I would want the safe and mundane, and I guess I craved that in most aspects of my life, but when it came to love, I wanted to be blown off my feet. Hell, I think I just wanted to feel what love was, period.

It looked like I wasn't going to find it here.

"Are you doing okay?" Luz asked, giving me that concerned look again. "Should we take you back?"

"I'm fine," I said before I knocked back the rest of the beer. With the painkillers coursing through my system, it was all hitting me a little fast, but I didn't care.

When they both just stared at me, I rolled my eyes. "I said I'm fine. Really. Hit and run aside, I'm fine."

Luz raised a brow but didn't say anything. I took out a few pesos from my wallet and plunked them down on the table. "I'd go up and buy the next round myself, but I don't exactly feel like crawling on my hands and knees in this place. Do you mind getting me a refill?"

She got up but left my money on the table. It was true, every time we went out I was usually the one paying for their drinks and food and little gifts. It's not that I made more money than them, both Luz and I were paid the same, I just liked to do nice things for them. Who else would I spend my money on?

"Are you really okay?" Dominga asked quietly after a moment.

I gave her a look. "Is this just about the accident or is there something else?"

She rubbed her lips together in thought before saying, "I'm worried about you. About...who did this."

"The police said it was a random event...shit like this happens."

"First of all," she said, "the police can't be trusted. Second, shit like this does happen, but it rarely ends up with the driver being shot in the head. Don't you think that's weird? It has to be connected."

Of course I thought it was weird, but I'd spent the last week in the hospital thinking about it, and I wanted to put it to rest.

"Even if it is connected, the guy who hit me is dead. Don't you think that means someone is looking out for me? If anything." I caught her eye and quickly added, "It's not Javier. Believe me."

Luz and Dominga knew all about my brother. I mean, everyone in Mexico knew about him, but only they knew that we were related. I didn't talk about him much, mainly because I didn't have much to say—Javier kept his life very separate from mine and for good reason. They weren't exactly happy that I was connected to someone so notorious and regarded him with constant suspicion and disdain, even though they had never met him. Though, for all his charm, I think they'd be even more scornful if they had met him.

"So then who?" Dominga went on. "It just can't be an accident. And if it is, why would this other person shoot him? It makes no sense and you are being way too cavalier about all of this."

"I'm not being cavalier," I told her. Suddenly I felt very tired. "I'm worried, very worried. But for tonight, I don't want to be worried."

"Yeah, Dominga," Luz said, giving her the stink-eye as she appeared at the table, placing our drinks down. "Give her a break." Luz grinned at me and slid my beer over. "You've got us both tonight. You're safe. Let loose."

"Oh, so now I'm allowed to let loose?"

She looked me up and down. "You can't get too loose with the way you are."

I took a big gulp of beer, challenged. "We'll see."

An hour later, I was feeling a lot looser. Two more beers had helped with that as well. They also tipped my bladder over to the breaking point.

I pushed back my chair and attempted to stand up, but suddenly Luz was beside me, holding me by the arms.

"Where do you think you're going?" she asked.

"I'm trying to go to the bathroom," I told her. "You don't need to come with me."

The two of them exchanged a look. "I won't go with you into the stall, but you should probably have some help getting across the room."

The bar at this point was completely packed, and people were being rowdy, drunken idiots. I nodded and leaned on her, not willing to risk it on my own. I'd probably be bounced against the wall and stepped on by dancing jackasses.

Eventually we made it to the washroom. It was dirty with wet floors and no paper towels, and had a line of slurring girls with smudged makeup waiting to use the two stalls. Luckily someone took pity on me and let me use it ahead of the line, even though there were a few disgruntled murmurs in the crowd. Even totally beat-up and obviously injured didn't mean I got a free pass.

When I was done, Luz was still in line, so I washed my hands and told her I'd wait outside the bathroom. No way in hell did I want to be in there, especially now as some chick was puking her brains out. I went out into the dark hallway and leaned against the wall. I was drunk, but my body was slowly starting to ache, and I wondered if the pain medication was beginning to wear off.

Suddenly some loud morons rounded the corner from the men's washroom and bumped into me hard. I let out a cry and flew to the side, the ground rushing up to meet my face, when an arm came out of nowhere and caught me.

Before I knew what was happening, I was pulled back up by someone who was very strong. I looked at the large, muscular forearm around me then followed it up to the fitted white t-shirt which belonged to a tall, insanely built guy. His blue eyes were sharp and filled with concern, his jaw wide and stern, his stance fierce.

He was Caucasian. Ripped. And hot as hell.

And he was holding on to me like he wasn't about to let go.

CHAPTER THREE

Derek

It was probably a big mistake. I'd been making nothing but big mistakes since the moment I answered my phone in Cancun. I should have listened to my instincts then, but the goddamn need to escape this life loomed much larger than I thought. I never knew how badly I needed that chance and how much money could buy it until I heard it offered.

But no amount of money, no amount of change, is worth it if you end up dead in the end. If I've learned anything from the people I've killed, it's that.

I was certain that whoever had been on the other line, the one giving the orders, wouldn't let me go so easily. It's not unheard of to back out of a job. Usually the *sicario* gets to keep the deposit and then fucks off somewhere. Usually that *sicario* is not hunted down, but they also aren't used again.

I would definitely have a black mark against me, but that was better than ending up dead. The money, the persistence to have this girl killed even after being hit by a car, the heightened stakes—it wasn't worth it. I'm never told the whole story when it comes to my job. It isn't my business. I carry out the orders for the right price. But when the orders don't add up and things don't make sense, you're a fool if you don't get out of it.

As far as I know, I've never been on anyone's hit list myself. It doesn't work that way. Revenge is never taken on the assassin, but on the one who pays the money, who orders the hit. That's the real bad guy. You still have to watch the ground beneath you for traps, though.

After the phone call and after I woke up the next day from a fitful sleep, I tried to write everything off. If they wanted the deposit back they could get it—the guy knew my email—but if they didn't, I was going to wipe my hands clean of this. Normally I'd get out of dodge as a second safety measure—switching hotels was the first one—but the last place anyone would expect me to stay is Puerto Vallarta.

The truth is, I wanted to see Alana. There was a voice in the back of my head, one that I've been trying to ignore over the years, that told me if she was valuable dead to someone she might be even more valuable alive to someone else. She meant *something,* and those were the people I usually had to kill. No one pays a *sicario* to assassinate the worthless.

For the first time in years, I was intrigued, curious, interested in the world before me. I was fascinated by this mystery woman, this flight attendant with a big smile. Why her? Who was she and what had she done?

And so it was probably a big fucking mistake that I slipped a gun down my cargo shorts before slipping on shades and a wife-beater. I looked like your typical tourist down here to party—no one would look twice at me. Then I headed out the door, taking the bus to the hospital where I knew she was staying.

It's funny how much I stick out like a sore thumb in Mexico. Though I'm as tanned as a motherfucker after being here for so long, I'm obviously not a local. My Spanish is excellent, though I dumb it down more often than not. It's better that way. When you speak the language too well you raise questions, and even though everyone always noticed me, they never noticed what I was doing. That was the big difference.

On the bus, for example, I was just another tourist trying to go somewhere. People looked; an older gentleman gave me a discerning glare, but then they forgot about me. I was different, but not interesting. They would never in a million years know what I really did, how my trigger had, time and time again, changed the course of the cartels, and as a result, the citizens' lives.

Normally, though, I would be cool and calm, but this time I wasn't. On that bus, I was nervous. Just enough to make the palms of my hands damp. I had no fucking idea why I was nervous, except that I was doing something I shouldn't have been.

I didn't *know* what I was doing. And that was a first.

When the bus finally let me off at the hospital, I didn't waste any time. Even without a plan, I knew it was best to keep moving. I waited by the side doors to the building until a nurse went back inside from her smoke break, and then I followed her in. I got looks in the hallway, but again I looked like someone just visiting their sister that had gotten roofied at one of the downtown clubs, or had broken a leg in a parasailing accident.

One doctor ended up stopping me, asking me what I was doing, and after I quickly explained, in English, that I was visiting family, he let me go. When an orderly on the second floor asked me the same, but in Spanish, I answered back in rapid-fire English. That was enough for me to confuse him, and he let me walk past. My size and strength probably had something to do with it as well.

Finally I found her floor. It was a big hospital and slightly chaotic. I used the disorder—the bustling staff, the patients wheeled to and fro, the opening and shutting of doors—to my advantage as I walked down the hall with purpose.

I knew her room because there was a plain-clothed policeman standing outside of it. It wasn't very subtle, but I guess that was the point. To scare away people like myself, people who wanted to harm her.

I still couldn't be certain what she was to me yet, or in what direction I would go.

I slowly walked past and quickly glanced through her open door when the cop wasn't looking. It was a fast look but I had been trained to notice details. I saw her, lying down and all bandaged up with her leg in a cast, a nurse talking over her at a doctor. Even though I could only see a bruised cheekbone, she appeared to be asleep.

I kept walking.

Over the next week, I kept a close eye on her. Sometimes I was parked in a new rental car across the street, watching people come and go. Other times I walked down the hall, stealing glances when I could. Any time someone asked me where I was going, I explained the same story about my sister. To the hospital staff, I was harmless. Frequent, but harmless.

While I watched over her, I toyed with my options. What was I going to do with her? So far there had been no one else around watching and waiting. Not like I had been. Every day it become more and more obvious that the hit and run was just that—no one else was coming by to finish the job.

Unless that meant I was still the only one *on* the job.

Perhaps my clock was still ticking.

The buyer was still waiting.

There was a bit of comfort in that. If they thought I would still go through with it, I was buying her some time. Even though her time consisted of lying in a hospital bed, wondering what had happened.

But after a few days, her spirits lifted. I could hear her laughter in the halls sometimes, so bright and infectious, as her friends visited her. It was always the same women. A pensive looking thing with long hair, and a tall one that was about as subtle as a battering ram.

That was it, though. There was no man—no husband, no boyfriend, no father, no brother. There was no mother. There were those two friends and that was it.

I don't know why I found myself relating to her, this woman I was supposed to kill, but I did. Maybe I always had. Maybe that's why I watched and waited, unsure of what to do, but feeling like I eventually had to do something.

Then one night I saw her and her friends leave the hospital. I ducked down in the car but they weren't even paying attention. I was in the dark, just a shadow, and they were giggling as they helped her into a Toyota. This was the first time I had seen Alana fully dressed since the day I was supposed to kill her. Though she was limping and needed help, she looked beautiful.

That was something else that surprised me. The rush of blood to my heart and my dick. Feelings were rare, unwarranted and unwanted. I swallowed them down like acid.

When their car started, I waited until they left the parking lot and then followed. They didn't go very far. A tacky-looking dive bar a few blocks away pulled them in like a siren.

So, Alana was escaping for a night of drinking. Part of me thought this wasn't very wise and that her friends should know better, not just because of her injuries but because I was there, I was watching, and I was the man who had been hired to kill her. Didn't they know just what kind of danger she was in? The fact that they had no clue made the whole thing even more puzzling.

But part of me was impressed, too. Car accident or no car accident, assassination attempt or no assassination attempt, she wasn't going to let anything hold her back.

I waited in the car outside for an hour, listening to the rhythmic thumps of music and the drunken laughter floating through the humid air, before I decided I'd had enough. I wanted to watch her up close. I wanted to get to the bottom of everything, and that included her.

Once in the bar, I ordered a beer and quickly surveyed the room. It was a riotous mess of people having fun in ways I never really could. Once upon a time, when I was eighteen, before I was deployed, before I lost everything again and again, I had the same sense of naivety and immortality, like the world really wasn't that bad and it was waiting at my feet. I laughed at all my options. Now I was older, and I knew the truth. There were no options. There never were.

The world was bad.

Alana and her friends had secured a table, and were drinking, laughing, and looking like everyone else. I tried to study her as subtly as I could, but from the way she kept looking around the room, I was too afraid to get caught. She wasn't looking around, eyeing people as if they meant to harm her. She was sizing up the men like she wanted to eat them for dinner.

Eventually I removed myself from the bar and went to hide in the shadows. It was safer this way, even though a small part of me was tempted to see her face when she noticed me. I knew the effect I had on most women. That's not even my ego talking, it's just the truth. I don't really take a lot of pleasure in the fact that women seem to gravitate toward me. Being good-looking means nothing. They just want a hard fuck and big muscles. They wouldn't feel the same way if they got to know me.

The more I stared at Alana, the more I was struck by how familiar she looked. I knew that was nothing to ignore—there was a chance that I'd seen her somewhere before. But I couldn't place when or where. Though she looked familiar—it was something about her amber eyes or smile, which alternated between fun and feminine carnality—it was like she possessed this kind of life to her that I know would have made a permanent impression on me if we had happened to meet before.

It was later in the night when she got up to use the washroom. Her friend had to help her navigate the rowdy crowd, and before I knew what I was doing, I was walking after them. I waited by the men's washroom, staring at my phone, pretending to be occupied.

All I could think about was *why*? Why was I doing this? Why didn't I just get the fuck away and go live out the rest of my life? Why was I here? The gun burned against my skin, but I already knew I wasn't going to use it on her.

Then there was movement. I looked up to see her come out of the washroom, alone, and lean back against the wall. She shut her eyes and winced. Time seemed to stretch as we both stood in the dirty hallway. If she looked my way she would catch me staring at her.

Do it, I thought. *Look.*

But she didn't. She seemed like she was in pain. Now she was the accident victim, broken and bruised. Vulnerable.

It was almost enough to make me move toward her. I don't know what I'd say, if I'd even say anything. I just wondered if I could tell who she was by her looking at me, if her gaze would show me why all of this happened. Why I had been sent to kill her.

I barely noticed the two douchebags who barged out of the men's bathroom, bumping against the walls as they passed me, slurring and laughing. I could see they were about to collide with Alana, and before I knew what I was doing, I was there beside her. One guy's shoulder collided with hers and she let out a yelp of pain as she stumbled forward.

My instincts were quick and probably wrong.

I grabbed hold of her arm then quickly brought her up toward me, and from the moment she looked into my eyes, hers wide with shock and pain, I could tell who she was.

A wildcat.

I swallowed hard and immediately forgot about wanting to ram my fists through the two drunk boys' heads. She was staring at me so intently that I knew I could never fade into the background after this. I could never observe her from a distance again. I could never watch from the shadows. From now on, this all had to be out in the open.

"Thank you," she said to me in perfect English, her voice lightly accented. I guess it came with the territory of being a flight attendant.

"You're welcome," I said, immediately relaxing into my role. Without fail, this was the role I'd always fall back into. Dumb tourist jock, Derrin Calway.

However, I failed to relax my fingers. I slowly released them from her arm before I made her uncomfortable.

From the way her lips pouted slightly, I could have sworn she wanted my hands to stay where they were.

A long, heavy moment passed between us as we stared at each other. I tried to take her all in—her hair as it stuck in places to her damp forehead, the faint bruising still evident around her eyes, the stiff way she held her battered limbs, the soft swell of her cleavage—not knowing if I would get the chance again.

Then the door to the bathroom swung open and her tall friend came out. "What a mess in there," the woman said to Alana in Spanish. When she didn't get Alana's attention, her eyes swung over to me.

"Who is this?" she asked, an edge of suspicion to her voice. That actually made me feel relieved. Alana needed protective friends.

"I don't know," Alana mumbled briefly in English. She gave me a crooked smile. "Who are you?"

I tried on an easy grin but I wasn't sure if it was sitting right. I wasn't used to smiling. "Derrin Calway," I told her, extending my hand.

"Alana Bernal," she said, shaking mine. Her palm was hot, her grip firm. Somehow it grounded me. "Thank you for saving me, Mr. Calway. This bar is full of fucking idiots."

She didn't seem apologetic over her language at all. I liked that.

I gave her a nod. "No problem. Bars are always full of them." I eyed her friend. "Tu nombre?" I asked her, butchering the language just enough.

She raised a strong brow. "You speak Spanish," she said dryly. "How impressive. My name is Luz. Where are you from, Derrin?"

"Calgary, Alberta," I answered. "It's in Canada."

"I know where it is," Luz said quickly. "The whole of Puerto Vallarta is full of you Western Canadians."

I shrugged. "What can I say, it's a good place. Your English is very good, by the way."

"We're both flight attendants," Alana said, leaning briefly against her friend in an affectionate way. "We have to know English to deal with drunken white boys."

"Especially those who get too close," Luz added, although this sounded more like a threat. From the way she was staring at me, I had no doubt it was.

Time to play it cool.

"Well, have a good night," I told them both with a quick nod and turned to head back to the bar. I'd only walked a few feet before Alana called out after me.

"Hey!"

My heart stilled. It had been a gamble.

I turned and looked at her inquisitively.

In the dim light it was hard to tell if she was blushing or not. She attempted to walk over to me, but Luz immediately helped her along. "I was wondering if I could buy you a drink."

I feared the smile on my face was actually genuine. "I'd love that. But I'll be buying you a drink. You're the one all bandaged up." I pretended to look around the bar. "What will you have and where are you sitting?"

Alana jerked her head in the direction of their table. "Beer would be great. Any kind. And don't forget Luz here."

"How could I?" I asked playfully before heading toward the bar.

As I walked away I heard Luz mutter something to Alana and Alana say "But did you see his muscles?" in response.

Once at the bar, I put in an order for four Pacificos, knowing there was a chance that her friend at the table would want one too, and took a moment to compose myself. The new plan was working, but I still wasn't sure what the outcome was or why I was really doing it. A tired voice in my head told me to be careful, to bring them drinks, and at the end of the night walk away. Another voice wanted me to keep tabs on her and figure out her importance and how I could make it work to my advantage. Yet another voice told me to take her out back and do away with her like I was supposed to and collect on the rest of the money.

But I didn't want to listen to the voices for once. I wanted to run on instinct, and my instincts were telling me to take this slow and cautious, one step at a time. Eventually the purpose would become clear, like a diamond underneath.

When I brought the beers back, the three of them were looking up at me with wide smiles. Actually, Luz had more of a discerning sneer and the other girl's smile was strained and polite, but Alana's was big and wide. It was the kind of smile that made you stare longer than you should, the kind that made even the deadest men feel alive.

Thankfully I was too dead for even that.

"Here you are, ladies," I said, placing the beers on the table.

"Did you drug them?" Luz asked as she carefully slid the beer toward her.

"Not enough time for that," I told her as I pulled out a seat. "Besides, I know better than to tangle with Mexican girls."

"You got that right," Alana said. She raised her beer toward the middle of the table and said, "Here's to our new Canadian friend." She looked me in the eye, so direct and unnerving that I had to fight the urge to look away.

I clinked the neck of my bottle against theirs, making sure to look all of them in the eye. "And here's to such friendly women in Puerto Vallarta."

And with that, the conversation came relatively easy to us. I found out her other friend was Dominga, a hotel maid, who didn't say much, but was a lot more welcoming than Luz was. When the questions turned to me and what I did and what I was doing here, I told them a bunch of half-truths. My whole life seemed to be built on half-truths.

"Well," I said between sips of my beer. "I used to be in the military."

"The Canadian military?" Luz asked.

"Yes. I was shipped off to Afghanistan. After that...I wasn't sure what I was going to do, so I became a personal trainer. Might as well do the one thing that I was good at."

Alana almost fluttered her eyelashes at that.

Luz folded her arms, not impressed. There was something commendable about her obvious dislike for me.

"And so what are you doing in Mexico?"

I shrugged as casually as possible. "I like it here. The people are friendly. The weather is perfect. The girls are nice." I flashed Alana a smile. "I wish I could stay longer."

"How long are you here for?" Alana asked.

"It depends if I have something to stay for." I was really laying it on thick now. "I was going to spend a few weeks here in Puerto Vallarta, I was thinking of maybe buying a condo here, a vacation home or something, so I wanted to really get to know the city. Maybe I'll be here a month if it suits me."

Alana gave me a half smile. "Well, this town may seem like a dream come true to tourists, I'm sure, but it has its bad side too."

I jerk my chin at her. "When you say bad side, does it have something to with what happened to you?" I hadn't asked her earlier about her appearance; I wasn't really sure what to say.

She pursed her lips, thinking it over. "Yes. I was in a car accident."

"Oh no," I said, hoping my shock was coming across as genuine. I at least knew my concern was. "What happened?"

She paused. "It was a hit and run. I got hit, he ran."

"Shit."

"Yeah it was shit."

"Did they catch the guy?"

She nodded. "They found him." But then her lips clamped together, signaling that the conversation was over. Interesting how she didn't divulge any further. I wondered if she just didn't want to get into it with a stranger—it wouldn't be easy to talk about how the man who hit you ended up shot in the head—or if she just didn't know. Both were possible.

"When are you getting out of the hospital?"

Luz fastened her eyes on me. "How did you know she was still in the hospital?"

Fuck.

I lifted one shoulder. "I just assumed. Her arm still has the tape from where the IV goes in."

They all looked down at Alana's arm. Sure enough, over her vein in the crook of her elbow, the clear sticker remained.

"Playing hooky?" I asked, turning the question on them.

She blushed then coquettishly bit her lip. "Promise not to tell anyone?"

I made the sign of the cross over my heart. "Hope to die."

Her brows furrowed for half a second before she eased back into her sex kitten grin. I wondered what that was about. She cleared her throat. "They said any day now. It's what they keep telling me."

"Well, I'm no doctor, but if you're well enough to be out at a bar accepting drinks from strange Canadians, then you're well enough to be out of the hospital."

"I agree," she said, raising her beer. "Let's all drink to that."

We all raised our beers and clinked again. I held eye contact with her the whole time, trying to read her while trying to tell her something. Mainly that I was a good guy. That I could be trusted.

Even though, at the heart of it all, those were both lies.

We sat there for another half hour until it became apparent that the mention of the hospital had taken the wind out of their sails. Dominga kept eyeing the clock on her phone and Luz monitored Alana's alcohol intake. All the while, Alana was trying to talk with me, asking me question after question. It was a good thing I came prepared and I knew my fake history as if it were my own. It was a lot easier that way. Some days I even lied to myself about what once was.

"Well, I think we should get Alana back to the hospital before she gets in trouble," Luz said as she and Dominga got to their feet.

I rose too, hoping to help Alana out of her chair. "If anyone gives you any trouble, you report them to me," I told her with a wink.

"I will," she said, then gave a resigned sigh as Luz darted over to help, beating me to it. Then the two of them started arguing in Spanish, Alana saying she wanted to stay and talk to me, Luz telling her there were other boys when she's good and ready for them. For some reason, what Luz said rankled me, and I had no idea why. Jealousy was not my thing. Caring wasn't either. Couldn't have one without the other sometimes.

I walked with them as far as the door—walking them to their car seemed borderline stalkerish—but just as they were about to leave, Alana leaned into me and whispered in my ear, "So if someone does give me trouble, like a mean old nurse, how am I going to get a hold of you?"

This was unexpected. Alana was flirty and forward from what I'd seen so far, but I didn't think this would continue beyond tonight. I don't know what I really thought would happen after, but it wasn't her basically asking for my number.

Little warning flags started going off. They weren't as bold or urgent as the ones I'd gotten when dealing with her arranged assassination, but they were telling me my life would be a lot easier if I let Alana Bernal go and I went on with my sorry little life.

But I guess my sorry little life felt like it was missing something.

Stupidity, perhaps.

So I told Alana where I was staying and the room number. And when her friends helped her hobble away into the dark parking lot, she shot me a look over her shoulder that told me I was in for it.

If only she knew.

CHAPTER FOUR

Alana

I could not get that man out of my head. For once, instead of thinking about pain and injustice, I was thinking about a 6'2" man with tree trunk arms, caveman shoulders, and the most sculpted, masculine face I'd ever seen. His wide, strong jaw, straight nose, slicing cheekbones, and piercing blue eyes became my drug of choice to keep the aches at bay. Even his buzz-cut showed off a perfectly-shaped head.

But of course when I told Luz this, I was met with a scowl.

We were sitting in my apartment, having hot chocolate. I sprinkled a bit of cayenne pepper onto mine, liking the burn more and more these days. Making hot chocolate—or any beverage, really—was about the extent of what I could do around the apartment. Luz had to come over and help me clean since I couldn't move my body very well.

"Perfectly-shaped head," she repeated with a sound of disgust. "Will you listen to yourself?"

"Maybe he has a perfectly-shaped dick too," I teased her, though somehow I knew he did. Men like him had to.

"Alana, please get a hold of your hormones. Goodness, woman, you've been out of the hospital for three days now. You think you'd forget about it and get back to your life."

I folded my arms across my chest even though I winced as I did so. "Maybe my life isn't so fun anymore."

She tried to give me a sympathetic look but failed at it. That little bit of Luz hardness showed through her dark eyes.

"Look, it's just temporary. All of this. Every day you're getting better. The doctors told you so."

"Every day is another day away from my job. Luz, you knew that was my life. *Is* my life."

"Well, did you ever think that perhaps this accident was God's way of showing you what's important?"

I rolled my eyes. "Don't start with that God crap." Though it didn't seem like it, Luz was a pretty earnest church-goer. That's par for the course in Mexico but sometimes she comes across as preachy. And by preachy, I mean bossy, because that's the Luz way.

"It's not crap. Don't say that," she chided before taking a hearty sip of her drink. "Besides, I think I'm right. Why not take this time to reflect a little?"

I snorted. Like hell I'd want to reflect on anything except the massive, gorgeous white dude I'd met the other night. Derrin Calway.

I guessed Luz caught the dreamy look in my eyes because she said, "You still haven't called him, by the way. So if you're going to get all smitten kitten on me, you should at least do something about it instead of pining away here like some forties American housewife whose husband is off to war."

I gave her a look. "First I'm all hormonal, now I'm a forties housewife. Make up your mind, you're slipping a little."

But truthfully, she was right. After I saw him at the bar and he told me he was in room 1600 at the Puerto Vallarta Sands Hotel, I had every intention of contacting him. But then I got back to the hospital, was caught as I was sneaking into the room, and got lectured by the night nurse Salma, and then again the next day by the day nurse, and finally was discharged by a very disapproving doctor (apparently news around the hospital traveled fast), and I kind of lost my nerve.

As much as I fantasied about Derrin and his thick forearms and strong hands, as much as I wanted someone like that to take my mind off of things, I was too scared to follow up on it. Normally I didn't have a problem with chasing a man, but then again, normally I didn't have to. But Derrin...I felt like he would have let me walk out that door and out of his life. That's usually how guys on vacation are. They don't bother pursuing anything beyond one night, and if one night doesn't even happen you're pretty much out of luck.

Besides, what would he really do with a cripple like myself? Throw me against the wall and fuck me crazy in my condition? No, I didn't think so. I didn't even know how I'd go down to see him, not without someone like Luz driving me, and I didn't see a chance in hell of that happening. Luz was always a bit suspicious of the men in my life and seemed especially suspicious of everyone since the accident. I couldn't really blame her. I needed to borrow some of that suspicion myself.

But maybe I didn't have to go to Derrin. Maybe he could come to me, at least halfway. I'd never know unless I picked up my phone and gave the hotel a call. Hell, there was even a chance that he'd already checked out and left. Or maybe there never *was* a Derrin Calway, and it was a decoy to throw me off the scent. Stranger things have happened.

Luz was staring at me with a perfectly raised brow and reading my mind again. "Look, either you call the gringo or you forget about it. If you're choosing to forget about it, then let's start now. How about we add some rum to the hot chocolate?"

Now she was speaking my language. But I wasn't choosing to forget.

I picked my cell phone off the table and waved it at her. "If I call him, if we make plans, can you help me get to him?"

Her eyes sought the ceiling for an exaggerated minute, but she managed a thin, stubborn smile. "Fine. As long as it doesn't interfere with work, I'll be your chaperone."

"Oh, you are so not being my chaperone," I warned her as I Googled the number for the hotel. "Let's just call you a chauffeur."

"Great."

I dialed the number and put the phone to my ear while I shot her an overly sweet smile. "You're a doll."

She stuck her tongue out at me.

While the phone rang on the other end, my heartrate doubled. I had no idea how nervous I was until the front desk agent answered, and I fumbled over my words. Meanwhile, Luz was looking at me like I'd lost my damn mind.

The clerk paused over the name, and for a minute I thought maybe he had given me a fake name. But then he corrected himself and told me he'd ring Mr. Calway.

My chest tightened, all my functions pausing while I was on hold.

Then Derrin answered. "Hello?"

His voice was even raspier on the phone—he almost sounded dirty. I was focusing so much on that, that I didn't realize he was waiting for me to respond.

"Hello?" he said again, his voice harder this time, almost panicked, and that spurred my lips into flapping.

"Uh, hola!" I blurted out while I heard a sigh of relief come through the phone. Better relief than regret. "Derrin, it's Alana. We met at the bar the other night. I was the one—"

"All bandaged up," he filled in. "Yes, I remember. Glad you called. I was starting to think I'd never get a chance to tell you how beautiful you looked in a cast."

Wow. He was a lot smoother than I remembered.

"Well this cast are, what is the English word, *hindering*. Definitely hindering me. I could barely use the phone until today." A bit of a lie but I enjoyed provoking the damsel in distress reaction in men.

"Then I'm honored you chose to call me."

There was a pause and I thought he'd go on, but the line went silent instead. Okay, maybe this was just a tad bit awkward. Guess I was going to be the one doing all the talking. Actually, when I thought back to the other night at the bar, I did all the talking then, too. I thought maybe it was because I was drunk—I often rattled people's ears off—but maybe Derrin was the strong, silent type. I could definitely work with that.

"So, um, I was wondering," I started, realizing I didn't have any idea at all what to say next. I looked over at Luz for help. She picked up the mug and mimed drinking it.

"Uh," I continued, "I know you're not in town for long, but I thought we could grab a coffee somewhere. I bet you're sick of all the tourist places and I know some really good ones. You know, local flavor."

"As a matter of fact, I am sick of the tourist shit. But I don't want you to travel too far in your condition. Why don't I come to you?"

I eyed Luz again who was looking resigned, like she knew she was at my bidding no matter what. Personally, I wouldn't have minded bringing Derrin back here, but there was a small, instinctual part of me that insisted that I meet him in public. As much as I liked to have fun, I rarely met men at my house. There was something a bit foolish about that.

"We can meet halfway," I told him. "There's a really good café by Nuevo Vallarta. Do you know how to get there? The buses run there every half an hour or so."

When he told me yes, I gave him more extensive directions before Luz cleared her throat with a very well-placed, "Ahem."

I looked at her expectantly before remembering that it had to go around her schedule. Luckily she had tomorrow afternoon free and wasn't flying out until the evening, so as long as I was back at home by dinnertime, it would be fine.

After I hung up with Derrin, I said to her, "Jeez, I guess you might as well call me Cinderella."

"It's for the best," Luz said. "This will prevent you from sleeping with him. Though if you ask me, I have no idea how you're going to manage that in the near future with the way you look."

"Hey, I look just fine. Besides, my one hand and mouth work great."

She gave another disgusted snort, waving me away. "Okay now, that's enough." She pursed her lips. "I don't know if I trust you with this boy, Alana."

"Why? You think I'm going to break his heart?"

She frowned for a moment and a serious look came across her eyes. "No, I don't think so. I think he's going to break yours."

"That'll be the day," I told her. I'd never fallen in love before. I never did those big relationships with big feelings. My life was all get in and get out and have fun along the way. That's the only thing that was safe.

She shook her head slightly and tapped her blood red nails against the clay mug. "I've got a feeling about this one."

Seeing her so serious always made me pay more attention. Still, I tried to shrug it off.

"You say that about everyone who's not from Mexico. Racist," I joked.

She glared at me. "This one is different. He's..."

"Hot," I supplied, before she could fill me with paranoia. "Built as fuck. Nice. Mysterious."

"Yes," she said, leaning forward. "Mysterious. And sometimes that's not a good thing. Sometimes people are mysterious because they have something to hide."

"We only just met him. I think it's a bit too soon to be making these assumptions. Besides, I'm the one going after him here."

She seemed to consider that before polishing off the rest of her drink. As she delicately wiped at the chocolate above her lip, she shrugged.

"You're right. But just be careful, that's all I'm saying. I'm not going to stop worrying about you for a long time, you know that, right? Dominga and I...we're going to be your little watch dogs, whether you like it or not. Not until this," she waved her nails at my brokenness, "is just a memory. Until then, everyone is a suspect."

"Are you sure you weren't supposed to be a detective instead of a flight attendant?"

"When you're stuck thirty five thousand feet in the air with a bunch of idiots, you become really adept at reading people. You should try it sometime."

Even though Luz and I rarely flew together—airline crew was a lot more spread out than most people think—when we did, she was always the "bad cop" of the cabin while I was the good one. She'd be the one cutting people off from the liquor while I was giving free drinks to the well-behaved passengers.

Later as I was lying alone in bed, trying to ignore the aches and pains that were spreading through my bones and wanting to avoid taking any more pills, I thought about what she'd said. Maybe I did need to be more suspicious of everyone. My whole life seemed geared to make me that way, hard and jaded. Perhaps I needed to start thinking more like my brother.

My only fear about that, of course, was that if I started thinking like him, I might become like him. And there's nothing scarier than that.

I shivered at the thought and pulled the covers over me, despite the thick humid air that settled in my room, remembering the last time Javier had involved me in his business. I had picked up his wife Luisa's parents from the docks, them having come over on a private boat all the way from the Baja. I took them into my apartment, which operated as a kind of safe house until Javier and Luisa came to get them. It was a nail-biting, paranoid two weeks, made even worse when I discovered the thing he wanted me to take out of a cooler and put in the freezer was actually a human head.

Yeah. A human head, not a fucking frozen thing of lettuce like I'd assumed. I wanted to take scalding hot showers for weeks after that.

Surprisingly, there was still a bit of a dull ache inside me. Not because of the accident, but because of Javier. Though we spoke on the phone the other day, briefly, he still hadn't come down to see me. I wondered if I told him that I was scared if he'd visit or at least say something comforting. But I put up a brave front with him, and I guess he did the same with me.

...

I was a young child, trying to sleep. It was impossible. On one side of me was Marguerite, who had this way of snoring like she was a purring cat. Some might find it cute, but when you're trying to get rest for the night, it was annoying as hell. On the other side of me was Violetta, who always curled up under my arms like a doll. Even though our mama was lovely, she was hardworking, especially with Father gone. Sometimes she just didn't have the time to give Violetta—who was the youngest—any attention. For whatever reason, that usually fell on me.

We had two beds in our tiny room. It was supposed to be me and Marguerite, the twins, on one, and Violetta and Beatriz on the other. But as Beatriz got older, she wanted her own space, so the three of us ended up sharing. Mama had her own room, of course, and Javier didn't really have a room. When he was younger, there used to be a cot pushed between our beds, but now Javier slept on the couch. Even as a child, I'm not sure that he really slept at all.

He didn't that night, and it saved our lives. All of our lives, except my mother's. But in my dreams, sometimes I was the one that died instead. I'm not even sure I'd call it a nightmare, because despite the dark and the terror and that horror, there was something about death that I welcomed. Every now and then, as I hid in the closet with my siblings and that door opened, the guns pointed at our heads, I didn't scream or cry as the *sicarios* gunned us down. I smiled. I wanted it. I wanted peace, that safety that comes with death. Once death takes you, nothing can hurt you ever again.

Death takes away your life. But it also takes away your fear.

When I woke up from the dream covered in sweat, I was disappointed to see the room was still dark. There was something so dreadful about waking from a nightmare in the middle of the night, with the adrenaline still coursing through your veins, only to see you have half a world of darkness, to go. Suffice it to say, I couldn't go back to sleep. Even though I sometimes wanted death in my dreams, I didn't when I was awake. When I was awake, I was governed by fear, through and through.

I carefully pulled my covers back up since they were usually kicked off as I thrashed in the throes of my dreams. I stared up at the ceiling, my body still sore and aching. Maybe that's why I was so attracted to Derrin. He looked like the sort of man who could protect me, who could take care of me. He was a soldier. Those were the type who never showed fear, who never ran from anything. For the most part they were honest and noble and brave.

I stayed awake like that for a while longer, accepting the fact that I wouldn't fall back asleep, thinking of him. I thought about him to the point where I was sure I was obsessing—which wasn't new for me—but I let myself do it without judgment. It was a distraction and a most welcome one.

At some point I fell back asleep.

CHAPTER FIVE

Alana

"That's what you're wearing?" Luz asked as I opened the front door to her.

I looked down at myself. I was wearing cut-off jean shorts and a faded yellow tee with a vintage Coca Cola slogan on it. "What's wrong with it?"

"Nothing," she said adamantly. "It's just that I've never seen you so dressed down and casual before."

"Yes you have."

"But not for a date."

She was right about that. "This isn't a date."

She rolled her eyes. "Goodness, just own up to it. It's a date, sweetheart. Even if it's coffee, in the middle of the day, with no sex, it's a date."

"Says you on the no sex thing."

"Are you really going to fuck him the way you are? At a café?" She gave me a look then shook her head and her lip curled in disgust. "You know what, don't answer that. You've already told me your options."

I grinned at her, quickly setting the alarm, and locked the apartment behind me.

It was a Monday and traffic was crazy congested as usual. I started to fret a bit, wondering if I was going to be late, and how long he would hang around for, or if he thought I was standing him up. The skin beneath my cast began to itch like crazy, and I was flipping open the glove compartment to see if Luz had a pen or something.

"Will you calm down, you crazy girl?" she said, eyeing me out of the corner of her eye while laying on the horn in protest of whatever driver did something stupid up ahead.

"You calm down," I retorted. "My arm is so itchy and you're taking forever."

"I'm taking forever," she repeated, waving at the sea of cars on the highway and at the thick dust that choked the side of the road.

In the distance, the jungle green mountains rose up from the dryness, offering respite. The area around the Bay of Banderas was always an interesting mix of the wild and the urban, the wet and the dry.

"Do you want me to drive over the traffic? Because I totally would, you know, if I had a bigger car."

I sighed, blowing a strand of hair out of my face as the car inched along.

Finally when we reached Nuevo Vallarta, we were already fifteen minutes late. All my sighing and foot tapping (the good foot, of course) couldn't change that fact. I could only hope Derrin would understand.

We parked right outside of the Dos Hombres Café, and Luz helped me out of the car as quickly as she could. From the street, I couldn't really see inside, but it looked like the place was packed as always. It had simple décor, a ton of indoor palm plants, and the best breakfast burritos, banana flan, and spicy mochas that one could hope for.

It seemed we had caught the workweek lunch rush, so it took us awhile to actually get into the café and look around. If I didn't have to lean on Luz—crutches were far too awkward to use than I had thought, and I rarely used them—it would have been easy to do a quick sweep of the place.

But even so, he wasn't there.

"Maybe he's in the washroom," Luz suggested hopefully.

Another heavy exhale escaped my lips. We were too late. Derrin was gone. Although there was a chance that he'd never been here to begin with.

"There you two ladies be," a rough male voice said from behind us, speaking in broken Spanish.

We craned our necks to see Derrin coming toward us holding three hot drinks in his large, capable hands. He was wearing knee-length cargo shorts and a grey wife-beater that showed off every single tanned muscle and plane on his body. I had to make sure my mouth wasn't gaping open.

"Sorry we're late," Luz said, switching to English. "The traffic was really bad."

I found my voice. "Yeah. Sorry. I thought we'd missed you."

He gave me a half-grin, something that made his face change from hard and masculine to soft and boyish. I liked both parts of him.

"Like I would leave so easily. I'm used to everything running on Mexican time by now. *Mañana* and all that."

"Such the typical tourist thing to say," I teased him.

"We only say it because it's true," he said, and handed me my drink. "And you know it. I got you just a plain coffee, by the way. I didn't know if you were lactose intolerant or on a diet or what."

I thanked him, and Luz muttered something along those lines as she took her coffee.

Derrin looked around the café. "It seems there is nowhere to sit."

"There's a park around the corner," I said, but even then I wasn't too keen on the idea of having our date on a park bench surrounded by pigeons. Derrin didn't seem as if he liked it either. His smile sort of froze.

"Oh, look," Luz said, pointing to the corner. "Those people are leaving."

"But there are only two seats," he said.

Luz gave him a look. "Nice try, but you know I'm not staying with you. I agreed to be a chauffeur, not a chaperone." She eyed me, a hint of warning in them. "I'll be back here in three hours. Any change of plans—and I really hope there aren't any—and you text me, okay?"

I nodded. She squeezed my shoulder affectionately, raised her coffee at Derrin as her way of saying goodbye, and then she was gone.

"Come on," he said, stepping closer to me. "Let's get you over there before someone else takes the table." He put his arm around my waist so I put mine around his shoulder. His skin was so taut and so warm that it was hard to hide the shiver that went through me.

"Not a fan of crutches?" he asked as we hobbled between the tables.

I tried to ignore how close his mouth was to my face, and the way his voice shot right through me and right between my legs.

"No. Have you ever had to use them before?"

He nodded. "Yes. Broke my leg in Afghanistan. It's why I was sent home. Tried to use them for about a day until I threw them out the hospital window. It was better to hop around on one foot than to knock over everything you came in contact with."

I wanted to take that moment to ask him more about the war—something I was very curious about, but I knew it wasn't coffee shop kind of talk.

He eased me down into the seat. I was amazed I hadn't spilled half of my coffee during the maneuver. I was frustrated at being so helpless and awkward these days, but I guess it wasn't so bad when you had a man like him helping you.

"So," he said, when he adjusted himself in his seat. He leaned forward on his elbows, his eyes staring warmly at me.

"So," I said right back, my chest fluttering with anxiety. "Tell me about the war."

Ah, fuck. So much for "don't mention the war." *Jesus, Alana, you're a mess*, I scolded myself.

To Derrin's credit, although his brow furrowed, making his eyes seem intense, he didn't seem offended. "All right," he said. "What do you want to know?"

"Well, how about how you broke your leg? Trading hospital stories might be fun." But I regretted it the moment I said it. How could what I went through compare to what he had? A hit and run, as traumatic, scary, and damaging as it was, was nothing compared to honest to god war.

"It was silly, really. We were going down one of the roads—which are nothing more than faded tire tracks in the dirt—when a bomb went off." I gasped and he went on, his voice monotonous. "It caught the front of our transport and flipped us. The driver died—so did another one of us. I broke my leg from the flip. We all broke something, everyone that survived."

I felt like a hand had squeezed my heart. Just the mention of a bomb—the very thing that killed my sister—was a sinister reminder of Violetta's violent death.

"How could you say that was silly?" I whispered.

He exhaled sharply. "Because we should have known better. We should have seen it coming from a mile away. The road hadn't been checked, and we were weren't using due diligence."

"Why not?"

"Because we were young kids. Because we'd seen so much, every day, that after a while you become desensitized. You stop caring. And you think you're invincible. Until it happens to you."

"How old *are* you?"

"Twenty-nine," he said. "This was a long time ago. I use due diligence now."

"But you're no longer in the army."

He shook his head. "No. I'm not. But it doesn't mean life isn't waiting out there to catch you unaware."

I took a long sip of my coffee while I mulled that over. He was sounding a lot like Luz. Perhaps they had more in common than I thought.

"So how old are you?" he asked, seeming to want to change the subject. I couldn't blame him. I was sorry I had brought it up to begin with.

"Twenty-four," I told him. "Going on forty."

He smiled but it didn't reach his eyes. "What makes you say that?"

I shrugged. He may have brought up his battles, but I sure as hell wasn't going to bring up mine. The fastest way to scare a guy off is to tell him your brother is the leader of one of the most powerful drug cartels, and aside from your twin sister, the rest of your family was murdered in related incidents. Violent, messy, disgusting incidents.

"I've always felt older, that's all."

"No boyfriend? No husband?"

I tilted my head and gave him a wry look. "Do you think I'd be out here with you if I had either of those?"

"I don't know," he said, leaning back in his chair. His chest muscles moved smoothly under his tank. "Maybe you're in one of those open relationships. You never know with you Mexicans," he added jokingly.

"Hey," I warned him. "If I wasn't so crippled, I'd reach over and smack you right now."

"Good thing you're a cripple then. You seem to be part wildcat."

I made a clawing motion with my good hand. "You have no idea."

That got a smirk out of him so I turned the tables.

"All right, hotshot," I said to him. "What about you? Girlfriend? Wife?"

His lips twisted sourly, and for a heart-stopping moment I was afraid he actually did have one or the other. But he said, "No, I don't."

Yet there was more to it. I quickly glanced at his hand and didn't see a ring or even the tan line of one. I knew already he didn't wear a wedding ring—it was usually one of the first things I noticed about a man—but I had to double check.

He caught me looking but still didn't say anything.

"Ex-wife?" I asked.

He hesitated, and by doing so was already telling the truth. I think he knew this because he looked down at the coffee in his hand and exhaled.

After a moment's pause—which felt like eternity—he said, "Yes. I was married once."

And it was quite apparent he didn't want to talk about it. But like the bumbling, stubborn fool that I was, I pried further. "Are you divorced?"

There was a barely visible shake to his head. "No. She died."

And once again, I was an idiot. This poor fucking man.

"Shit," I swore. "I'm so sorry. How did she die?"

At that he looked up and stared me dead in the eye. "Car accident," he said, completely emotionless. Somehow, maybe because the way he was staring at me was almost a challenge, like he was calling me out on lying about something, I knew it wasn't the truth. But I guess it didn't really matter. When someone was dead, they were dead.

"I'm sorry," I said, and suddenly it felt like all I'd done so far was apologize. It served me right for bringing up such horrid topics.

"It's not your fault," he said. "It was a long time ago. I was a different person then."

But have you moved on? From the darkness in his eyes, it was hard to tell if he had.

"I'm also sorry I'm not so good on dates," I told him. "Or talking in general. And that *is* my fault."

He managed a smile. "You're direct. I like that about you."

"What else do you like about me?"

"You look very pretty in a cast."

I felt my cheeks flush. "What else?"

"You have the sexiest eyes and lips I've ever seen."

My cheeks grew even hotter. I guess this meant he was into me after all. It was kind of hard to tell with him so far.

I decided to take the plunge. This emotionally wounded soldier boy was strumming all the right chords with me. I leaned forward slightly and looked at him through fluttering lashes.

"After coffee, did you want to come back to my place? Luz could drive the both of us."

No, I couldn't be more forward than that.

He seemed caught off guard. He blinked at me, his body stiffening, and I was so certain he was going to take me up on it. Then his brow softened and he said, "Sorry, I can't."

So, big fat no. Score one for rejection.

"Not into crippled chicks?" I joked, but I knew he could tell I was smarting.

"It's not like that," he assured me quickly. "I'd love to. But I have an appointment with a realtor at four-thirty to see an apartment. You know, I told you the other day I was looking to buy something here."

That was true.

"How about we take a rain check?" he asked. "Better than that, maybe you can come down to the resort I'm at. I'll rid out in a cab to get you. Your friend doesn't even have to be bothered."

Okay, this was soothing the embarrassment a bit. "Okay, when?"

"Tomorrow evening," he said. "I'll take you out for dinner."

"Aren't you staying at an all-inclusive place?" Those hotel restaurants weren't exactly known for their good cuisine.

"Yes, but there's a great little fish restaurant tucked away a few streets over. Looks fancy. It should impress you."

"Little do you know that I'm easily impressed."

"Then that's another thing I like about you."

It wasn't long until our time was up, three hours having flown by in flirty giggles and stories and glances, and Luz was honking her horn from outside the restaurant. I looked over at her and waved, even though I knew she couldn't see in properly.

"Is she always so impatient?" he asked as he got to his feet and came around to my side.

"Yup," I said. He held an arm out for me, his muscles strained, the veins in his thick forearm bulging as I grabbed hold of him. He lifted me to my feet like that, as if I weighed less than air. With ease, he helped me across the café and outside to the car, and I relished every second of his warm skin against mine, his bracing, ocean-like smell. For those few moments, I felt completely protected.

He helped me into the passenger seat then shut the door. I quickly rolled down the window.

"So tomorrow?"

"I'll give you a call in the morning and let you know the time."

I grinned up at him. "See you then."

He nodded and raised his hand.

Luz stepped on the gas and we burned rubber away from the sidewalk.

"Where's the fire?" I asked, glaring at her and trying to put my seatbelt on.

"In your pants, I'm guessing," she said.

"Ha-ha, very mature."

"So I guess you have another date tomorrow?"

"Yes, but don't worry, you don't have to be involved. He's coming in a cab to get me. We're going out for dinner."

"I'm surprised you didn't try to eat him already," she commented dryly as we cruised down the street toward the highway exit.

I bared my teeth at her playfully. "That will come later."

We were silent for a while as she drove, the traffic momentarily lighter, an American pop star singing to some bouncy beat on the radio.

Eventually Luz said, "So how was he?"

"Nice," I told her.

"That's it? Just nice?"

I shrugged, staring out the window while secret butterflies danced in my chest.

"That can't be it. What did you guys talk about? Tell me something about him."

"He grew up in Winnipeg, Manitoba, and was going to go into the NHL for hockey. Then he decided to join the army instead."

"And…?"

"Nothing else," I told her, not wanting to divulge the personal stuff. "We talked about this and that."

"And did you mention your family?"

"Of course I didn't. I talked about the airlines. That's always a safe topic. People always want to know about crazy passengers, or the time you were hit by lightning or the scariest landings."

"And did he want to know?"

"Probably not but I told him anyway."

She laughed, and her eyes darted to the rearview mirror. She frowned. "And do you trust him?"

"Do I trust him?" I repeated. "What does that mean? I barely know him."

"I know." Her eyes were still focused on something behind us. I looked in the side mirrors but couldn't see anything unusual except for cars.

"What do you keep looking at?"

"I don't want to alarm you," she said in a way that made me immediately alarmed, "but I think there is someone following us."

Now I managed to twist in my seat and get a good look behind us. It was hard because the back window was so dusty.

"What is it? What car?"

"There's a white truck two cars behind us. It's been two cars behind us before we even got on the highway."

Now I could see it, the top of the truck poking up above the traffic, but it was too far away for me to get an idea of who was driving it.

"Do you think it's Derrin?" I asked, feeling this incredible sense of dread creep up on me.

"I don't know."

"What are we going to do?"

"Take the next exit," she said determinedly. "If someone is following us, we don't want to lead them straight to your apartment."

Jesus. So much for thinking all my paranoia was put past me.

Luz put her signal on for the next exit, one that led to an outdoor market permanently set up in a parking lot. We both held our breath as we exited the highway, and soon after the truck followed.

Shit. Shit. Shit.

We exchanged a nervous glance.

"It's going to be fine," she told me, though she didn't look like she believed it. For once I found myself wishing I had a gun. I'd always been so against owning a gun, telling myself the minute I had one was the minute I became my brother, but considering everything, it made a lot of sense. Too much sense. Maybe Derrin knew something about them and could help me out. He was a Canadian, but he had been in the army, so he at least knew how to handle one.

Luz kept driving past the market stalls, and finally pulled into a parking spot right beside a bunch of other people. Safety in numbers and all that.

We waited, still as ice and with bated breath as the truck slowly crept past us. There was some older man driving—Mexican—with a thick mustache but no real discernable features. He didn't even look our way and kept driving until he parked further down.

I let out the largest puff of air and nearly laughed from relief. "Luz, you are crazy."

"You thought he was following us too!"

"Only because you told me. Besides, he was following us but not in the way you thought." I shook my head and sank further into the seat, my heartbeat slowing. "I think I've had enough excitement for one day."

"Agreed," Luz said. She started the car and we drove back onto the highway. We never saw the white truck again.

CHAPTER SIX

Derek

Her name was Carmen. She had been the love of my life.

When I first came to Mexico, all those years ago, I wasn't sure what I was looking for. I had grown disillusioned with the American government, destroyed by the war. My leg still hurt from the explosion in Afghanistan, and I hurt somewhere deep inside. It was so needless, so senseless. I had lost too much, we all had, over something that was never meant for our benefit, just to pad the pockets of those in the country that mattered most. I'd seen villages burned, young children dead and torn up on the streets, parents wailing, grandparents dying. All for nothing, not really.

The day the Humvee blew up was the day that everything changed. I guess that's the sort of day that *should* change a person. I was one of the lucky ones—one of my buddies lost both of his legs, another had half his body burned to a gruesome crisp. But I would never consider myself lucky because I was burdened with survivor's guilt. More than that, I was burdened with guilt, pure and simple.

When I returned home to Minnesota and was finally healed, I said goodbye to an ice hockey career—or at least the promise of one—and I said good bye to friends and family. Both of those were easy. My father, a cruel, terrible man, had died while I was overseas. My mother, weak and helpless, couldn't seem to exist without his cruelty. She barely noticed I was gone.

As for my friends, they'd all pulled away once they got to know the new me. I barely spoke. I stopped drinking with them, going out, finding chicks, playing hockey. It was all over. I worked out and hated every single minute I had to be a veteran, a survivor, a pawn.

One day something in me snapped. I'm not sure what it was, maybe someone cut me off driving or perhaps I saw an advertisement for Mexico somewhere. But the next morning my bags were packed. I got in my car and drove for the border.

It took days to get there, and once I crossed over through Texas, time seemed to stop. Though I would never completely fade into the background, there was anonymity here that seemed to shake loose what little soul I had left. I felt free from everything—who I was, where I came from, the baggage I carried.

For a year I bounced around from place to place. I started with the resort towns on the Caribbean side before heading to the ones on the Pacific side. Veracruz, Cancún, Tulum, Mazatlán, Puerto Vallarta, Acapulco. When I got tired of the tourists, I moved inland and stayed in different cities, then towns, then villages. Each place had something special about it, and in each place I met people who seemed to think I was of some use to them.

It wasn't until I started running out of money that I found myself reaching for these people. It was also then when I met Carmen.

I was in a town just south of Manzanillo. It was a small resort town, a bit down at the heels but popular with Mexican tourists, which suited me just fine. I'd met a man once called Carlos, and of all the people I'd met, he not only was the most genuine but also the most ambitious. Though cordial and generous, he was also a realist that made things happen. He had connections—none of which he held lightly—and success in his sights.

When I first met him I was sitting in a bar in a rustic but authentic establishment, sipping tequila, which the bartender gave me on the house for no real reason, and reading a book. Some John Grisham thriller, something to pass the time. I read a lot that first year in Mexico.

Carlos was there with two buddies of his, conducting business in the corner. At least I assumed it was business because when I would look over there, their faces weren't laughing and no one except Carlos was touching their drinks.

Suddenly there was a yelp and a fight broke out. Before I knew what I was doing, I was in the middle of it, holding back a man who sneered like a dog and seemed hell-bent on ripping Carlos's face off with his own veneers.

I don't know why I got involved—instinct, I guess. But after the two gentlemen were escorted out of the bar, Carlos bought me a drink. He wanted to know where I was from and what I was doing there. He wanted to know where I had learned to move like that, if I knew how to handle a gun, if I knew how to fight.

I didn't tell him much beyond the fact that I had been in the American military. He seemed happy with that. He said there was a lot of work here for someone like me, and then he gave me his card, patted me on the back, and left.

I kept in touch with him via email after that, just a few messages here and there. Advice. Where I should go next. Every time he told me I should look him up if I was in the area. And sometimes his area moved around, too.

One day, I was out of money and in the same place that he was.

We met up at a bar, and a casual deal was made. I'd accompany him on a few transactions, sort of like a bodyguard. It was easy work and he paid me well. He trusted me and I trusted him.

But soon I did more than just stand around and give people the stink-eye. I started doing him favors. Nothing terrible, but I knew Carlos was a drug lord and whatever package I was delivering, dropping off, handing over to numerous nondescript people either contained drugs, weapons, money, instructions, or a combination of the four.

And still I did my job.

And when I discovered Carlos's sister was moving back to town, and I first laid eyes on Carmen Hernandez, I realized I had more than this job keeping me in Mexico.

I fell in love and fell in love hard. I don't know if I ever picked myself off the ground.

We married. We made plans. We talked babies.

We had a blissful year together.
And then she was dead.
And I lost the last parts of me that were human.
I think it's too late for me to get them back.

. . .

Alana Bernal was doing something to me and I wasn't sure if I liked it. Actually, if I was being honest with myself, I was loving it, but that reaction in itself spurred on one of the opposite nature. I wasn't used to being excited, to being intrigued, to feeling remotely good. I was used to the coldness inside of me, to the life of monotony and that growing numbness that reached into everything I did.

Change was frightening. Change made you weak. And I didn't want any part of it.

But I wanted part of her. That was a problem.

Of course, when I met her for coffee yesterday, I had to act like I hadn't been following her for days. It wasn't so much that I was interested in what she was doing with her time the moment she was discharged from the hospital—because let's face it, I was—but that I wanted to make sure I hadn't been replaced.

Thankfully, from following her and watching her apartment I came to the same conclusion that I had while watching the hospital. There was no one else still, only me. It was wishful thinking that whoever ordered her assassination had just forgotten about her. They hadn't. Not for the price on her head. They were just biding their time. But there was no one else on the job, not that I could see.

I told myself that's why I was hanging around, that I was watching out for her. And I was. I was curious, and after talking to her over coffee, I was even more confused as to what she could have done in her life to warrant such a thing. Such death. Such money.

As a result, I was more or less honest while answering her questions, hoping that if I opened up a bit she would do the same for me. So far though, that hadn't seemed to be the case.

When she invited me back to her place afterward, my first thought was to obviously say yes, and while my mind was trying to figure out her mystery, my body was responding to her gorgeous face and slim limbs like any hot-blooded male would. Plus there was the chance at some answers, as well as sex, if I got a chance to look at her surroundings.

But I couldn't do it. My instincts were telling me to wait until I was in control of the situation. At her place, there were too many variables. In my hotel room, we were safe.

My plan was pretty simple. I didn't need to impress her, so it seemed, but a little wining and dining wouldn't hurt. The emphasis would be on the wining. I know it's pretty backwoods to get information out of someone by getting them drunk—I've done a hell of a lot worse to get what I needed—but it would still be effective. And, because of the company, somewhat fun.

I couldn't remember the last time fun had ever entered the picture.

I called Alana in the morning, telling her our reservation at Coconut Joe's was at seven and that the cab and I would come get her at six. I thought about using the new rental car I had just picked up but thought better of it. I'd already driven past her place too many times in it.

Even the sound of her voice over the line—how buoyant it was, despite all the shit and pain she still had to be going through—did something peculiar to me. I tried not to dwell on it but it was there, lodged in my chest and growing. I wondered if she was becoming more than a curiosity to me—a mystery to be solved. I wondered if she was someone I was actually starting to care for.

Was it possible to care for someone you didn't know?

God, I hoped not.

The hotel called the cab and made sure the driver agreed on the price and the return trip before we started out. Cabbies are known for ripping you off, and Alana didn't live near the downtown area—and soon I was knocking at the door of her first floor apartment.

That was one thing I didn't like about her living situation. Though the apartment building was fairly new, Mission-style with white paint and a red-tiled roof, it was on the ground floor, opening to a small gravel yard that was accessed through a wrought-iron gate. There were bars on her windows, which was the norm here, but that didn't mean it was hard to get inside. All the apartments also seemed to back into an inner courtyard, probably with a pool, which meant there might be another door and easy access point into her place. It never slipped my mind that while I had been watching the front, someone could have been slipping through the back.

It was taking her a while to get to the door, so I tried to look in through her barred windows to get an idea up close without seeming too suspicious about it. But when the door flung open, I was caught somewhat red-handed.

"Hola," she said, leaning against the doorframe. "Wasn't sure if I was home?"

She looked absolutely stunning in a white halter-neck dress that showed off her perfect breasts, thin waist, and full thighs. I barely even noticed her leg in its cast.

"Just noticing your bars on the windows," I said evenly. I frowned. "Is this a bad neighborhood?"

She smiled at me like I was a little boy. "It's not the best but it's not the worst. Most places worth anything have bars. Mexico has more crime than you would think."

I nodded, not letting on what I knew. "Well then, it's good you're well-protected."

"Yup," she said, placing her clutch purse under one arm and reaching for something against the wall. I heard the electronic beep of buttons being pressed. "I'm all alarmed here. Just in case."

I looked over her shoulder to the back of the apartment, but it looked as if there was no entry from the back. That gave me a bit of peace.

I took her arm and most of her weight, and helped her out of her small yard and to the waiting cab. She smelled like flowers and hot sunshine, and I was tempted to kiss her bare shoulders to see if they tasted like the tropics. As usual, though, I brushed the urges away and kept myself in control.

Once in the back of the cab, she was sitting with her thigh flush against mine. I was somewhat dressed up—dark jeans, white and blue pinstriped dress shirt—and yet I could feel her heat through my clothing. That and her smell, and the way her hair fell across her face, highlighting the coy glimpses of her eyes and smile, was driving me borderline insane. Though we made small chat throughout the ride, my mind was elsewhere, concentrating on keeping that well-earned control I had. I had to focus on the task at hand, which, of course, was her. But not in that way. I needed in deep, for her own safety and my own sanity.

It took a long time to finally get to the restaurant, located in the old town of Puerto Vallarta, despite the driver cutting everyone off along the way. You either drove aggressively around here or you didn't drive at all.

"Thank you," she said to me as I took her arm and helped her out of the cab. When she straightened up, she looked at the place and made an impressed face. "Wow. You know, I've never been here before and I've lived in PV for a long time."

"First time for everything, then."

I picked the place because it looked a bit different from the tourist traps in the downtown area. There wasn't much to the outside except for a tall stone fence topped with green, strangling vines, and flowers that bloomed like white and magenta cotton balls. But what was on the other side of the cast-iron gate was a different story.

I helped her over to the fence and a waiter opened the gate, giving us a hearty welcome to Coconut Joe's. I gave him the reservation name and he led us around tables with ivory-lace tablecloths, past a clear blue pool with koi fish and a waterfall, under dramatic palm fronds, all the way to a table in the back corner with a candle on it. The place wasn't anything too outrageous or stuffy; it was just classy enough.

"Again, wow," Alana said as I helped her into seat. I was starting to like being her nurse. She looked around, her cheeks glowing beautifully in the candlelight. "This is something."

"Something good?" I asked as the server poured us bottled water.

"More than good," she said. "The guys I date never bring me places like this."

Something pinched in my chest. "Oh? They take you to McDonald's?"

She gave me a look. "Most of the men I dated were pilots. They would take me somewhere really snobby and expensive to try and seem better than they were." She took a polite sip of her water and straightened her napkin on her lap. Every day, her pain seemed to be easing, her movements becoming more fluid. "Then the next night they would take some other stupid flight attendant to the same place."

As much as I felt an unjustified hit of jealousy, she was giving me some information, something I could work with.

"So I guess there's a lot of drama in the workplace, huh?" I said casually, eyeing the waiter who was approaching us with menus in hand. In the background "Morena de Mi Corazón" started to play from the speakers. "Spurned lovers and revenge in the air."

She laughed. "No, not really. It was my fault. Rookie mistake to date a pilot, even though I did more than a few times." She looked away, embarrassed. "Most guys I date are a mistake, but no one seems to get hurt."

So that probably ruled out the whole spurned lover angle. Not that I thought an ex-lover could or would attempt to have her taken out for that amount of money. Love made people do crazy fucking things, but that would have been a first in my books. Besides, if she did have an obsessed ex-boyfriend I was sure I'd find out about him sooner or later.

The waiter came by and told us the specials. I ordered for the both of us—seared Ahi—because I'd never done that before, not even with Carmen, and made sure he kept the bottles of wine coming.

She was about three glasses of wine in, giggly and eating her fish with gusto when I started pressing her.

"So do you have any siblings?"

The smile seemed to vanish right off her face. There. I had something there. No matter what her answer was, I'd hit a nail.

"I have a twin sister and a brother," she answered simply.

"Oh? And where do they live? What do they do?"

She relaxed her jaw a bit and took a bite of her rice. "My sister, Marguerite, lives in New York. Goes to film school."

Hmmm. That placed her out of range and a student at that.

"And your brother?"

"He lives around here."

"In Puerto Vallarta?"

She shot me a wary look. "Around here. But he's an asshole and I'd rather not talk about him."

I raised my brow. "An asshole? What makes you say that?"

"I just do," she said stubbornly. Then she sighed. "He just is. Every family has a black sheep, right? Well that's him."

"What's his name?"

She bit her lip and said, "Juan."

I didn't know her well enough to tell if she was lying or not. But I'm not sure why she would lie about her own brother.

I pressed it further. "What does he do?"

"He's in importing and exporting. Trade with America. That sort of thing."

Well, we all knew what that meant down here. Running drugs, like everyone else. Still, that gave me something to go on. Of course the name Juan didn't help me much.

"What's his last name?" I asked, knowing that sometimes the men in Mexico took their mother's maiden names.

"Bardem," she said without hesitation. "Why all the questions?"

I shrugged and leaned back in my seat. "Just want to know more about you."

Her brows knitted together as she eyed me suspiciously. "Maybe so, but you're asking with this look on your face like you're all David Caruso."

"David Caruso?"

"CSI Miami. It's still my favorite. I don't care for the other ones."

"Well, I'm sorry to disappoint you, but I don't have the hair to be David Caruso, nor do I have the sunglasses and quippy one-liners."

She took a sip of her wine but couldn't hide her smile. Good, she was back to trusting me again. I wanted to ask her about her parents, but I thought that would be pushing my luck. Whether she was close with them or not, they were either dead or out of the picture. They had never come to see her in the hospital, and the truth about her brother and sister explained why they hadn't either.

What the hell have you done, Alana? I asked in my head as I stared at her across the table, the light illuminating her in an almost angelic way. *Why would anyone pay me two hundred thousand dollars to have you killed?*

And how the hell would I ever know the answers to those questions without incriminating myself?

To help her relax a little more, I turned our conversation to TV shows since David Caruso had proved to be such a good segue. There was nothing that got the passion flaring in this country like *Telemundo* and poorly translated American dramas.

By the time we had finished two bottles of wine, it was getting late and I had no idea where the evening was going to take us. I had gotten her drunk—a little too drunk—and she was looking wistfully at the area by the pool where couples had started slow-dancing to sad mariachi music.

"Care to dance?" I asked her.

She shot me a sloppy smile. "Yeah right. The way that I am?"

I got out of my chair and held out my hand. "We can make it work, I promise."

She didn't look convinced but let me get her out of the seat anyway. She was extra wobbly on her feet now, particularly since she really only had one foot to stand on, but somehow I managed to help her hobble over to the edge of the dance floor.

We weren't quite in there with the crowd of couples—I had visions of us falling into the pool—but we were close enough to feel like a part of it.

"Here," I told her, peering down into her eyes. "Put your arms around my neck and hold on."

She did as I asked, an impish smile on her lips. Her arms around me felt impossibly good.

"What do I do with my feet?"

"Step on my foot with your good one and keep it there. Wrap your other calf around mine."

"Are you sure about this?"

"Trust me," I implored, and her hold around my neck tightened as she placed her sandaled foot on top of my boot and then hooked her lower leg that had the cast around my other calf.

"I'm not breaking you?"

"Are you kidding? You weigh a hundred pounds soaking wet."

"My thighs and ass weigh more than that," she pointed out.

Taking the opportunity, I slid one of my hands down to the small of her back, my fingers just brushing against the top of her curves. "I can't be the judge of that yet."

She grinned up at me, her cheeks flushing. "Yet, you say."

I returned the smile. "The night is young."

She pressed herself into me. *The night is also hard*, I thought to myself. There was no point hiding it though. I couldn't imagine any straight man who wouldn't get an erection with this woman pressed against them.

Focus, Derek, I told myself.

But maybe it was the muggy night air, or the way we moved together to the slow waltz of a broken-hearted band, or the way she looked at me and the way she felt, so soft and so close, that made me lose focus. Just this once, I wanted to be able to feel something without thinking it through. Just this once, I wanted to feel something more than ice inside me.

Alana was heating me up, one beautiful smile at a time.

We danced for three songs until she rested her forehead against my chest and seemed to doze off for a minute.

"Okay," I whispered into her ear. "Time for bed. Let's go."

I thought that would get a reaction out of her but she pulled away and nodded, her eyes still shut. I couldn't help but grin at her, glad I could do so without her noticing.

I paid for dinner and got us in a cab. It didn't feel right sending her off to her own place. She was drunk and vulnerable, and I wanted her in my sight for the night.

The cab dropped us off at the hotel, and I helped her up to my room.

"You don't mind staying the night?" I asked her as we paused outside my door.

She giggled to herself but didn't say anything.

Once inside, I left her on the couch and went into the bedroom. I had cleaned it up earlier, knowing there was a strong chance I'd bring her back here after dinner. All my guns and weaponry were tucked away, and it looked like the hotel room of your average tourist, albeit one on an extended vacation. In fact, if anything I should have had more stuff than just a duffel bag. I was so used to traveling light.

Once I pulled back the covers for her, I got one of my t-shirts out of a drawer, one I worked out in but was freshly washed, and laid it on the bed. Then I went back into the room where she was dozing and scooped her up in my arms, carrying her to the bed. I gently placed her down on it then held her up while I placed the shirt in her hand.

"Put this on," I told her softly. "I promise not to look."

She looked at me through glassy eyes. "You do it. I'm too tired."

"All right," I said, swallowing hard, and reached behind her neck to untie the straps of her dress.

She watched me closely as I did so, her gaze daring me to meet it. So I did. The straps came loose and the front of her top floated down like tissue paper, exposing her breasts.

Fuck. They were so fucking perfect. Beautifully round with dark rose nipples that tightened in the air. Suddenly all I wanted to do was run my tongue under their soft curve then take the nipple in my mouth and suck until she moaned.

My erection strained against my jeans and my breathing deepened. All the while, Alana kept staring at me, almost asking for it. Her eyes were heavy-lidded, her mouth open and wet. I was so close to kissing her hard, to letting my tongue run down that vulnerable throat and to her breasts.

I took a deep breath and looked away from her for a moment, composing myself. I may be a lot of horrible things but I wasn't about to take advantage of her when she was this drunk, even if she seemed to want it. She couldn't know what she wanted right now.

Before I could think better of it, I took the shirt and motioned for her to raise her arms.

She blinked at me, shocked, I guess, but did as I asked. I slipped my t-shirt on over her head then gestured to the bottom of her dress. "I guess you can keep the rest on," I said.

"Don't you find me attractive?" she asked, slurring her words a bit but still sounding hurt.

I took her good hand and placed it on the bulge in my jeans "I think I do." Then I took her hand away and put my arm around her waist, scooting her back into the bed where I quickly undid the straps on her shoe. "But you're drunk and I'm tired, and it's not going to happen like this."

"But it will happen," she said, her head leaning back into the pillow. She closed her eyes and yawned.

"I'll see you in the morning," I told her. Then I went to the washroom, filled up a glass of water, and left it on her bedside table.

I closed the door just in time to see her dozing off, then I settled onto the couch in the other room. I pulled extra blankets from the closet, the nightly battle against the air con, and tried to get some rest.

No way in hell was sleep coming to me in my state. I took my dick out and jerked off in minutes flat, biting down my cries as I came onto my stomach. I didn't know what relationship I had with Alana right now and my own motives seemed to be changing by the moment, but I knew better than to make her aware I was getting off to her.

Once my heartrate slowed and the hazy warmth of orgasm flooded my limbs, trying to take me down into sleep, my thoughts became clearer.

I needed to focus. I needed to find out why she was a target and who had ordered the hit.

Things couldn't get complicated. I couldn't get involved. There was no way any of this could end happy if I did.

But maybe, just maybe, her staying alive was happy enough. Even if I had to walk at the end to protect my involvement, to protect my truth, maybe if she got through this safely, that would be enough.

I had to protect her.

CHAPTER SEVEN

Alana

I awoke to yelling from the other room. It wasn't the type of yelling that made you jolt out of bed, but the unnerving, haunted yelps of someone having a nightmare. I should know, of all people, what that sounded like.

Because the light was dim and the sky outside the hotel windows was the hazy grey of pre-dawn, I carefully got out of bed, feeling out of sorts. My head was pounding from all the wine at dinner and I felt ridiculous in Derrin's t-shirt with my dress around my ass. My god, had he seen me naked last night?

I shook away the embarrassment, recalling bits and pieces and that sting of rejection yet again and then hopped as delicately as I could over to the door that separated the bedroom from the main room.

I opened it a crack and peered inside. Derrin was on the couch, half-covered by a blanket, and twitching. For a horrible second I thought perhaps he was sick or having a seizure, but then in the grainy light I saw his brows come together in a look of pain and he softly cried out, "Carmen…Carmen."

Carmen? I wondered if that was his ex-wife, the one who had died. Poor guy. He obviously wasn't over her yet. No wonder he wasn't throwing himself at me. Not that I expected him to, but when you've got a drunk naked chick in your bed it's hard not to dwell on it and feel slighted.

I watched him for a moment, unsure of whether to wake him or not, but when his yelps grew deeper and more pained, I couldn't stand it anymore.

I hopped over to him and stood at the foot of the couch.

"Derrin," I called out. "Wake up."

He didn't. I said his name again, louder, then I grabbed his leg, giving it a squeeze. I didn't want to get any closer than that when it came to waking someone from a nightmare.

I chose wisely.

Suddenly he bolted off the couch, practically leaping sideways until he was standing on the ground in a crouch, a gun drawn, his eyes focused stiffly on the blank space in front of him.

Actually there was no gun at all—his hands were empty—but he had made the motion as if he was pulling one out from under his pillow.

Okay then. Maybe he knew more than something about guns.

"Derrin?" I said softly.

He slowly turned his head to look at me, chest heaving, and blinked a few times as he took me in. Then he looked down at the way he was posed and slowly straightened up.

"Sorry, I..." He trailed off and pressed his hand against the back of his thick neck, looking behind him at the couch.

"You were having a nightmare," I told him. "I heard you in the other room. I didn't want to wake you up, but..."

He nodded and licked his lips. "Some nightmare," he said, looking visibly shaken.

"Did it involve guns?" I asked, nodding at his hands that were clenching and unclenching.

He shook his head slightly. "No."

"Did it involve Carmen?"

He looked at me sharply. In the dim light his eyes looked like black holes. It scared me a little, but I stood my ground.

"How did you know?"

I gave him a shy smile, feeling awkward over it all. "You were calling for Carmen."

He sighed and sat down on the couch, his face in his hands.

I gingerly hopped over and sat down beside him. "Want to talk about?" I asked hopefully.

"Not really."

I chewed on my lip for a moment, considering my options. I guess I could tell him the truth about me for once, at least one little slice of the truth. "I have them too, you know."

He cocked his head to the side and peered at me inquisitively. "Really?"

I nodded. "Yup. Usually the same ones, though in the past they were less frequent. Now I get them all the time. Ever since the accident."

"The accident," he repeated.

Shit, I'd forgotten I'd only told him so much about that.

"Yeah. The hit and run. I guess it triggered something."

"That kind of trauma would do it. What do you dream of?"

And here's where things got complicated. I hemmed and hawed about it for a moment then decided to just bite the bullet. Sorry little pun, but there it was. I wasn't about to tell him everything, though.

"It's usually me and my brother and sisters in our house in La Cruz. It's a little town, just north of here on the curve of the bay. We're sometimes in bed and then my brother comes into the room and tells us we all have to hide. Sometimes it starts when I'm already in the closet. Sometimes I'm alone, sometimes it's all of us. Sometimes I'm under a bed. Sometimes I'm out on the street and watching it all happen."

His leg pressed against mine. "What happened?" he asked gently, his voice low. "In the dream."

"Some men come to kill us. They kill my mother. My father is already dead at this point. We're all spared because we were hiding, and the cops come soon after. But in the dream, sometimes we all die."

He frowned, his body stiffening. "What do you mean in the dream you sometimes die? Did this happen in real life?"

I took in a deep breath, trying not to choke up over it. I so rarely talked about it because tears often came after. It's like it wasn't real unless I was saying it out loud, as if my words could conjure it from the air.

"When I was young, yes, it happened. I'll never forget it, even though I've tried. It's like my brain won't let me forget. It keeps bringing it up in my dreams."

"What happened?" His full and rapt attention was on me now, those intense blue eyes pouring over every inch of my face. "I mean, why?"

Here came the hard part. "My father was mixed up in some bad business. I guess they took out my mother for revenge, I don't know. But it left us all orphans. My brother had to step up and take care of us, along with my older sister Beatriz."

"Your brother, Juan," he said.

"Yes." I said hesitantly. Javier's fake name felt wrong.

"And Beatriz. I thought your sister was Marguerite. What happened to Beatriz?"

And here came the can of worms.

"Beatriz died later. So did my other sister Violetta."

"How?" Derrin seemed almost hyperactive over this information. Now I was really scaring the poor guy away.

"They are long stories."

"I have time."

"You're a tourist," I reminded him. "You're leaving soon. You don't have time."

He put his hand on my arm and squeezed lightly. "I've met you. I'm not going anywhere."

There was something so kind and sincere in his voice, in his eyes. This tough soldier who had been through so much, yet he was trying to comfort me.

"They were both murdered. Horribly. Brutally. That's all you need to know."

He frowned as he took that information in. "And your father was the same way?"

"Yes. The cartels shape our lives here. The cartels can take it all away."

I know this was a lot for someone like him to understand. I knew Derrin wasn't naïve—the defensive moves he'd just used springing out of bed told me he was far from that. But Canada didn't have the same problems as we did in Mexico. Neither did the States. Mexico was as backward, corrupt, and Wild West as a second world country could possibly get. The poor were destitute. The rich were rich beyond their wildest dreams. The rest of us struggled in the middle, assured that the only way to get higher was to become like the rest of them. Drugs ruled our lives. It was a fact we had accepted, along with the violence that came with it.

"If most of your family was murdered," he said slowly, deliberately, "wouldn't that mean that you're at risk too? You, your other sister, your brother?"

I grimaced. "Marguerite is safe. My brother...probably safer than I am. And me...well, I can't live my life in fear."

"But you have been, haven't you?" He was staring at me so intently, but I refused to meet his eyes, afraid he might see more than I wanted him to. "The accident," he went on. Exactly what I was afraid of. "When you were hit. There is more to that, isn't there?"

I dipped my chin to my neck and nodded. "I still don't know who hit me. The police think it's someone who worked for the airline. A mechanic. He certainly looked like one I would see. The car might have looked familiar too, but I don't know. They told me it was a hit and run, an accident...and I believe them. I guess. I mean, no one has come after me now. I'm here, aren't I? But the weird—the weirder—thing about it all, is that he's dead. Someone shot him in the head moments after he ran me down. They just caught up to him, stopped him, killed him. And no one can figure that part out. If it was vigilante justice, why hasn't the person come forward?"

"Because the person has blood on his hands," he suggested gravely.

"True. But it doesn't make sense. I've seen some horrific things. I've never heard of someone acting this way. I think it's all related, but I don't know how."

"You could be in danger, Alana," he said.

I rubbed my lips together and sighed. "I know. But I just...I want to ignore it. I want it to go away. I want to pretend it's all over." I looked at him with hope. "This could be all over, couldn't it? If the accident was on purpose, the guy is dead. He's not coming after me again. If it wasn't an accident, then I have a guardian angel out there looking out for me."

"Or maybe the guy botched the job—because it wasn't a fatal hit and he knew it—and someone else was hired to take him out and make sure he didn't leave a trail."

I frowned at him, unease gripping my heart. "There you go, acting all David Caruso again."

He didn't smile. "I'm worried about you."

"I'm worried about *you*."

"Why?"

"Because you're scaring me. And you're a nice Canadian boy. If what you're saying is true, and I have reason to be scared, then I'm a target and you'll be put in danger because of me."

"Don't worry about me," he said. "Don't ever worry about that." He paused. "I know how to take care of myself. And I can take care of you."

Those last words were music to my soul.

Still, I said, "That isn't your job."

"It shouldn't be anyone's job. But I'm making it mine." He brushed a strand of hair off my face and I closed my eyes at the rough brush of his fingers. Damn, he could take care of me all he wanted.

"Now, do you know why you were hit?" he asked, soft enough not to break the spell of his fingers on my face. He ran a thumb under my bottom lip and I nearly lost it.

"No," I said quietly, sucking in my breath.

"Everything that happened to your family didn't happen recently. You have no idea why someone would do this to you now?"

I shook my head. Everything in the past had been done to hurt my father or to hurt Javier. But honestly, I didn't know if that was it. If someone really wanted to make a statement, they would kidnap me, not try and take me out. If they kidnapped me they could get Javier to bend to their will.

I wasn't certain that Javier would do that, however. Sometimes I felt like I wasn't even related to him. Though he always said how important family and loyalty was, sometimes I wondered if he would let me die in the streets if it suited him. Family came second to the cartel, to the drugs, to the money, to the power. It always had. He was just good at fooling people.

"What are you thinking about?" he asked, inching closer to me.

"About all the ways there is to die."

"None of them are going to happen to you."

"You sound so sure." And yet I believed him. At least, I wanted to. I wanted so much from this man. I could feel the intensity burning off of him, infecting me, making me feverish from head to toe.

His face was so close now, his eyes half-closed with lust and focused on my lips.

"Are you going to kiss me?" I whispered.

"Yes," he murmured.

"Are you going to fuck me?"

"Oh yes."

A small, brief smile flashed across his lips and then he leaned forward. The kiss was soft for a moment, just enough time for me to luxuriate in the dreamy fullness of his lips, the way they covered mine, wet and warm and wanting. It pulled me in, stirred something deep inside, like a small candle flame that was growing with each feathery stroke of tongue against tongue, each long, lingering taste.

He pulled his lips away a millimeter to catch his breath and it felt like he was stealing mine.

Then his mouth came back onto my own, hard and fast and urgent. His large hand gripped the back of my neck, the other wrapped around my waist as he tugged me toward him. My nipples immediately went hard, brushing against the inside of the baggy shirt I was wearing. Heat pooled between my legs, throbbing for him already.

Damn, he was good at kissing. Each passionate melding of our lips and tongue was stoking the fire inside until I felt ready to self-combust. I moaned against him, trading in the ability to breathe for the ability to be fucked by his mouth. He was so needing, probing, greedy. I loved it, wanted more, wanted everything.

He slipped his hand under the shirt, finding my breast. He gasped, raspy and deep, as his fingers found my nipples, rubbing over their stiffness.

I loved a bit of foreplay. Making out was a long lost art. But I needed this man inside me, and badly. I'd needed him for a few days now. From the stiff bulge in his boxer briefs, I could tell he felt the same way.

"Fuck me," I whispered as his lips found my neck and sucked there. "Don't be gentle."

He paused for a moment, probably remembering my injuries.

"Don't be gentle," I repeated, my good hand holding the back of his head, his buzz cut both rough and soft against my palm.

"I won't," he mumbled against my neck. Then he pulled away and got up. In a second he got his strong arms under my body and was lifting me up in the air. So effortless. I really felt like I was going to get fucked by a superhero or something. He definitely had that whole Captain America thing going on.

He put me down on the bed and pulled the rest of my dress off as I tried to shimmy out of it. There I was lying naked, legs open on the bed, bare for him to see. And boy, did he seem to see it. He stared down at my body, his eyes roaming over me in such a way that I could feel their heat on my skin.

"You're gorgeous," he said, voice raspy and dripping with lust as he slid his large rough hands down the sides of my body.

"So are you," I said, trying not to feel bashful. That wasn't like me at all. "Take off your clothes. It's not fair that I can't do it myself."

He gave me a cocky grin then pulled his shirt over his head. I propped myself up on my elbows and admired the sight of him undressing between my legs.

His chest was a work of art. Everything about him was a work of art, like a living breathing sculpture of what a real man should look like. His pecs were so hard and wide you could bounce pesos off them, his shoulders broad and muscled, his abs a perfect, grooved six-pack leading down to the flattest stomach imaginable. Most impressive of all were his arms. Obviously I'd been admiring them before, their thick, veiny example of Derrin's brute strength, but now with his shirt off he was the total package. He looked like a killing, fucking machine.

"All of it," I told him, my intentions bold even though my voice was barely above a whisper. I was so fucking eager for him I could hardly stand it.

He kept up that arrogant grin—one very rightly earned—and pulled down his underwear, stepping out of them.

Against the virile strength of his thighs, his erection jutted out like a mast. I had been right when I assumed perfect head equaled perfect dick. This man was all man and definitely didn't use any steroids. His cock was thick, long and dark with want. He even had a nice set of balls that I wanted to wrap my lips around.

He stepped to the edge of the bed and I quickly remembered I had condoms in my purse.

"Condom," I told him. "I haven't been taking my pill properly since the accident."

He nodded, almost looking a bit sheepish for not suggesting it, and went over to the chair and fished a foil packet out of my purse. He ripped it open and slid it on himself, and I couldn't help but bite my lip at the sight.

He came back to the edge of the bed and took a hard hold of my thighs and yanked me toward him.

"I need to be inside you," he said, his voice sliding over me like rough silk. I agreed and wrapped my legs around his firm, tight hips. I winced slightly at the sight of my cast, knowing it couldn't feel too nice against his skin, but he didn't even seem to notice. He positioned the head of his cock at my opening and moaned as his fingers drifted over my slickness. Then he grabbed my thighs even harder, holding them up as he thrust into me.

I gasped from the welcome intrusion, his stiff length as it struck deep. He felt so good inside me, so full, so thick. My fingers grabbed the edges of the blanket, holding on as he pulled in and out, so slowly, so deliciously, and I expanded again and again to take him all in.

"Yes," he hissed as he pumped into me. I stared up at him, at this mammoth man, my legs looking so small in his capable hands. There was a sheen of sweat over his hard body, his muscles flexing as he fucked me harder and harder, his hips swiveling and driving in as deep as he could go. When he was pushed in to the hilt, he paused and then started to rub my clit with his thumb, even though I was so close to coming without it.

He stared down at me as he brought me to orgasm, his eyes filling with lust and want and maddening desire. There was something else in them though, some kind of sadness or loneliness that would have hit me in the heart if he hadn't just pushed me over the edge.

I came violently, my body screaming with the release of it all, the release of everything. I writhed and spasmed, feeling no pain, no weight, no shadows. It was all just light, and I was warm and fuzzy and in an angel's hands. An angel who was coming himself with a few loud grunts and a well-placed, "Fuck, Alana, fuck."

I moaned happily, feeling satisfied like nothing else. That was one hell of a fuck.

He pulled out of me, disposed of the condom, then climbed into bed, pulling me up so I was beside him. I wanted to get up to go to the washroom, to have some water, to wash my face, but before I knew it I was succumbing to his arms once again.

We must have dozed off for a few hours because when I woke up cuddled into him, the sun was shining bright and relentless through the window. I turned to look at him and was surprised to see him staring at me, blinking at the light.

"Hi," I said softly. I couldn't help but smile, and it danced on my lips. I couldn't remember the last time I had woken up with a man beside me. Usually one of us left during the night.

I also couldn't remember feeling this warm and secure before. For once I wasn't waking up with a pit of loneliness inside me.

"Good morning," he said. "Did you sleep well?"

I nodded. "How long was I out for?"

"Hours."

"Did you sleep?"

He smiled stiffly. "I rarely sleep."

Right. The nightmares.

"Listen," he said, adjusting himself on his side and trailing his fingers along my collarbone. "I've been thinking. I think you should stay with me."

I raised my brows. This was new. "What, here?"

"Yeah. Just for the time being."

"You don't trust me?"

He gave me a steady look. "I don't trust anyone, and especially not around you. I told you I wanted to take care of you. I want to protect you. I can't do that when you're injured and living all the way out there by yourself."

"My friends…"

"Your friends are wonderful, but they're busy with their own lives. And they're women. No offense, but unless one of them has some special training up their sleeves, they're going to get hurt in the process. Except for maybe Luz. She seems like she'd be brutal."

I bristled at that. "They'd protect me. You don't know them."

"I know they'd try, and that's admirable. But I'm a strong man and I have military training. I have ways of protecting—real ways. You know these people aren't playing, that this isn't a game. If there's a chance that someone is still out there, wanting you dead, then I have to do what I can to ensure they don't touch you."

"But we don't know that."

"And I'm not willing to chance it. You're off work now, and you obviously need help, even if there wasn't anything going on. Let me do this for you."

I blinked at him. "But why?"

"Well, if you can't already tell, I like being around you. With you. Inside you." He put his hand under my chin and pulled it up so I was looking at him. His gaze was so focused. "Maybe some of this is selfish. I want you for myself."

Butterflies scattered in my stomach.

"Okay," I told him. "I'll stay here. Just for a bit. Until you get tired of me."

"Never," he said, and kissed me.

CHAPTER EIGHT

Derek

Even though Alana had agreed to stay in my hotel room for a while, we still weren't in any rush to get out of bed. In fact, we stayed there all day, only taking a break to have room service.

We were both wrapped in hotel robes after enjoying a shower together. She'd gone down on me in there. She couldn't drop to her knees because of her cast, but the shower seat worked just fine. The woman certainly knew how to fuck with her mouth. She also had this uncanny ability to fuck you with her eyes at the same time.

When Carmen died, everything had changed for me. Her brutal, haunting demise, right in front of me had changed the course of my life. It was all my fault. The two cartels, she never should have been caught in the middle of it. I never should have been involved. They said she was in the wrong place at the wrong time, but I knew it was more than that. Carlos had shown such little compassion for his sister before, the fact that she was there at all during that transaction was a sign. He didn't care who got hurt, who died. Neither did the other side.

She was gunned down in front of my eyes. I can still see her running for me from across the road, the fear so rampant on her delicate face. She was telling me to get out of there while I stood there dumbly with my mouth open. I think I was yelling at her to do the same. I can't really remember. One minute I had been waiting in the car, the next I was trying to reach her. It was all a blur. But I do remember the rose shade of her lipstick, the way her long red and white dress flowed behind her, and how, somehow in that terrible moment, she looked more beautiful than she had on our wedding day.

Then it was all erased by gunfire. Hot blasts. Bullets bouncing off the pavement. Smoke.

Blood.

She was shot on both sides. She was riddled with bullets from her brother, from the people I worked for, and ripped apart by the Gulf Cartel.

She was the first victim. And the only innocent one.

Seconds later, others died. The cartels faced off, both meaning to leave no one alive.

I don't know how I didn't run into the middle of it all, to go to Carmen's lifeless body as she lay face down in the street, the blood pooling around her and creating new abstract patterns on her dress. I knew at that moment I wanted to die. I wanted to join her.

But after everything I'd been through, my survival instincts were stronger than my soul. I removed myself from the scene. I drove back to our house. I packed up everything I had that was important. It all went in a gym bag.

Then I got back in my car and drove.

I drove for days and days, my eyes burning behind the wheel during the day. At night I cried and grieved.

Nearly everyone had died in that battle. Everyone except for Carlos.

It didn't seem fair.

I didn't want anything to do with the Gulf cartel—I blamed them as equally as I blamed Carlos. So I went to the Zetas. I had a few contacts there, and I gave them everything I had on Carlos. Then I offered my own brand of services.

They paid me a large amount of money. The next day I killed Carlos, three shots into his head while he was sleeping in his leather armchair. The maid knew me, and though she was surprised to see me back, she let me in.

I had to kill her, too.

I had blood on my hands. But I didn't care. When Carmen died, I lost the ability to care about anything except blood and vengeance. I became a murderer for the first time. I lost my humanity.

Over the years I moved deeper and deeper into the circuit of cartels. I was loyal to no one except those who paid me the most. I became quick and efficient. There were better *sicarios* out there—there still are—but the cartels seemed to love the fact that I was white. They called me their G.I Joe. They liked that no one paid much attention to me, that no one ever looked for me. They liked that I didn't care for politics or drama or fame. I did the job I was paid to do.

Well, except for that last one.

I was a lone wolf. I operated alone, and I usually went to bed alone. If I was horny, finding a chick to fuck wasn't hard. I always treated them nice enough, but they never got anything from me other than a handful of orgasms.

I certainly never took them out on dates, or ordered room service in the afternoon with them, or invited them to stay in my hotel room for an indefinite amount of time.

I never cared about them, not even a little bit. But I cared about Alana.

She was getting under my skin. She was awakening that dead husk inside of me.

She was becoming my second chance.

I couldn't protect Carmen. But maybe, somehow I could protect her.

I started by getting to know her body thoroughly.

While she sat there cross-legged on the messy bed, sipping on a black coffee, I leaned forward, and with one swift move, I undid the sash around her robe so a bronze line of skin from her chest to her pussy was exposed.

"Smooth move," she commented, putting the coffee down.

I moved the plate of food to the side. "Lie down," I told her.

She raised her brow, inquisitive, but lay back on the duvet. I reached over and pulled her robe to the sides, exposing her more. She was so fucking amazing, a body built from the heavens.

I reached for the small metal pitcher of cream that came with the coffee and held it above her breasts.

"What are you doing?" she asked with a smile.

"I'm going to enjoy you and my breakfast at the same time," I said.

"That sounds a bit greedy."

"That I can be."

I grinned at her then tipped the pitcher so that just a bit of the cream poured out in a single stream, splashing between her breasts. She let out a gasp and a giggle, and my dick twitched hungrily. The sight of the white creamy liquid spilled against her dark skin was hot as fucking hell. I wanted to come right on top of her to add to it, but I ignored my urges for now.

I ran my finger between her breasts and licked it. Then I massaged it over her breasts and nipples before lapping the cream up like a cat.

"That was the appetizer," I told her as I pulled away, my fingers still rubbing the rest of it into her skin. "Now for the main course."

"Are you like this with every woman?" she asked me, and though I could see in her bright eyes that it was a joke, it kind of dug deep.

"No," I said quietly. "Not every woman. Only you. You've been the only one who has mattered in a very long time."

She blinked, perhaps taken aback by my honesty. I certainly was. I flashed her a smile and picked up a jar of honey. "Now, I can stop if you want me to," I said, waving the jar at her.

"Don't you dare stop."

So I didn't. I dipped my finger in the honey and began painting suns all over her skin. That's what she reminded me of, the sun, shining always so bright and bold. The darkness was always behind her, waiting to take her out, but most of the time she was this ball of warmth that seemed to melt everything bad away.

"You better get it all," she said, closing her eyes and moaning as I stroked the honey between her legs. "Or else I'll be left sticky."

"Don't worry about that. I'm going to lick you clean then fuck you hard."

Her eyes flew open, even more aroused now.

I ran my tongue all over the honey art on her body, making sure there was nothing too sticky left, just enjoying the sweet taste of her and the nectar in my mouth. Then I put my head between her legs and lapped up the rest of it, sucking on her sweet folds and teasing the swell of her clit until her moans were so loud and I was drowning in salty sweet.

She came quick and hard, her legs gripping my head and holding on tight while she pulsed beneath my lips and tongue.

"Ay dios mio," she swore as she continued to writhe, breathless and panting. Eventually her legs loosened and I pulled away. She lifted her head up, her eyes glazed, and looked at me. "Wow. Just wow. If that was the main course, what's for desert?"

I grinned at her and opened my robe, my dick like a thick piece of steel. I stroked it once. "This. Served any way you want."

She bit her lip and leaned forward to grab my robe, pulling me down on top of her.

It was a long time before room service could take the tray away.

...

Finally we decided to get a move on things. I got her in a cab and she was off to her apartment to pack up some of her stuff. I would have gone with her to watch over her, but while she was gone I wanted to go get a new rental car.

I dropped off the old one and picked up a black mustang convertible at a new rental agency. It was the sexiest thing they had, and I knew how to drive it well, even if they weren't all that practical for the area. But in terms of a getaway car, it worked. After she told me everything about her family, I had a clearer picture of what I was up against.

While I drove the mustang back to the hotel, I had time to think. Her father had been involved in one of the cartels long ago, and he was killed. Her mother came after. Then her sisters. She, her twin, and her brother were all that remained. I needed to find out more about her sisters, when they had died and how. I knew she didn't want to talk about it, but it was crucial to understanding this. The way they had died could tell you a lot about who was doing the killing. From what it sounded like, the deaths of her parents were a pretty rushed, amateur job. Anyone can storm a house in the night and shoot a woman in bed. That doesn't take any skill at all.

It just didn't make any sense to keep going at someone's family. Unless, of course, there was more to it. And I was sure there was. Either Alana or one of her siblings was still involved in something and hanging with the wrong crowd.

Her brother was the obvious choice, considering he was involved with drugs in some way. But so was everyone. Was her brother part of the same network that her father had been? If so, why would they still bother going after the children?

Unless Alana did something, even if she didn't realize it, or knew something she wasn't supposed to. Though she'd been open last night, she was still playing her cards pretty close to her chest. I had more questions for her, but now that it was out in the open that people could be after her, now that she had admitted her accident might have not been an accident at all, I was confident we would get to the bottom of things, especially now that she would be staying with me.

As soon as I gave the car to the valet, I went up to the room and started rearranging things for her arrival. It was a weird feeling knowing I'd be sharing my space with a woman. Not only on an intimacy level, but because I wasn't sure how much of "Derek" I could show her. She only knew Derrin, and parts of me were hard to hide.

For one, I knew she was a bit suspicious of the way I woke up the other day. I couldn't help it. Normally I was a very light sleeper, except when I was dreaming of Carmen, and instincts always took over. I could be up and ready to shoot or run within seconds.

Obviously I was going to pass it off as military training if it ever came up, but she would want to know how else I was going to protect her and that's where the guns would come in. Time to confess to her that I had a bit of a gun fetish. I didn't need to hide that anymore.

I opened the door to the wardrobe and lifted the wooden bottom off the base. I had pried it off when I first checked in and hid all my guns and weaponry in the hollow base. With the bottom back in place, it looked like an empty wardrobe.

I decided to still hide them there—you never knew what the maids were going to think if they stumbled across them—but I would give Alana a little show of them. It sounded like she could handle it. If I were her, I would have invested in a gun a long time ago.

As for the silencers, the Ace bandages that kept the guns tucked to my waist, the knives, the rope, the CF explosives, the tracking devices, the GHB capsules, the duct tape, blindfolds, and handcuffs—well I wasn't sure if she would buy it if I told her I was into some pretty kinky stuff.

I took out everything but the guns, a four-inch silencer for my .22, and the Ace bandage. I carefully placed them in a small Ziploc bag, and brought them into the washroom. With a small motorized saw I always had with me, I cut away the base of the cabinet underneath the sink and stuck them in there. I placed the bottom over top of it then rearranged towels and extra rolls of toilet paper on top so it wouldn't attract any attention. I cut clean, and any leftover sawdust was cleaned up and flushed away, but even so I had to be meticulous. Guns I could explain. Everything else took me to a psychopathic level.

CHAPTER NINE

Alana

"You've lost your fucking mind, woman," Luz swore at me over the phone.

I was sitting on the balcony of the hotel room, watching the waves roll in. "You've been saying that for ten days now."

"And I'm going to keep saying it until you come back home."

"Do you miss me?"

She sighed. "I just saw you last night."

"Yeah, exactly," I told her. In the distance, over the rippling blue line of the Pacific, I saw a parasailer gliding down toward the boat. Everything was so bright and glittery and carefree in this part of town. I couldn't get enough of it. Staying with Derrin seriously made me consider selling my apartment and buying a place on the shore. Unfortunately, my apartment was owned and paid for by Javier, and I was pretty sure I couldn't do anything without asking him for permission. Sometimes I hated that he treated me more like a delinquent kid than his sister, but I guess it was better than nothing.

"You saw me last night," I repeated to Luz, smearing coconut and lime scented sunscreen on my arms. Though my wrist was pretty much healed, I had a bandage in place, and I was determined not to get any crazy tan lines. "You saw that I was fine. Better than fine. Great."

"That's only because of all the sex."

"You'd be great too if you were getting laid by a soldier."

"Shut up," she told me. "I'm still allowed to worry about you. And I still don't trust him."

I sighed. "I know you don't." I didn't blame Luz. Ever since I'd told her that I was temporarily moving in with Derrin, she was the one who was acting like they'd lost their mind. She told me all the things I already knew myself—that I didn't know him, we'd only just met, I was still vulnerable, etc. But the thing was, I trusted Derrin. I don't know why I did, but I did. He had promised to protect me and I believed him. And then later, when I saw his guns, I believed him even more. He had all the skills he picked up in the war, the affinity and passion for firearms, and the courage and determination unlike anyone I'd met. If anyone was going to get me through this, it would be him.

There was nothing to get through, however. As the days passed and the two of us settled into a routine of drinking, food, and sex (rinse and repeat), and our bond grew stronger and my bones healed, there was nobody out there coming to get me.

We were cautious too. Derrin always had his eye on me, like he was born to have this role. But no one approached us. No one was following us. No one was waiting.

Some days I went down to the pool and had daiquiris, other days I went to the beach, all while Derrin stayed on the balcony watching me. I was right out there in the open, just ripe for the taking. And though the experience had been a bit nerve-wracking, time and time again the only people who bugged me were the hustlers selling their cheap trinkets on the beach. Damn, they were annoying. I'd have thought they'd leave their fellow Mexicans alone but they still seemed to think I needed god-awful cornrows weaved into my head.

A few nights a week I met up with Luz, and sometimes Dominga. Because Dominga worked for a sister chain, she had a few friends working at our hotel, and she told me they were keeping an eye on me too. It was sweet of her; I knew both of my friends were so nervous. But as time ticked on, I was becoming more and more convinced that no one was after me. It was an accident. It was vigilante justice.

Sometimes I almost wished they'd try.

Meanwhile, when I wasn't pondering my potential death, I was falling deeper and deeper for this steely-eyed man with a heart of gold.

It was wrong. I knew it was. I didn't fall for men, and I never fell in love. It's not that I didn't want it but it was never anything I pursued.

But I was falling for Derrin. I wasn't quite there yet, but I was well on my way. That feeling that borders on obsession, where your thoughts and body and heart crave him like water. You're in a blissful, warm haze when he's there and suffering in a dark hollow when he's not. It was made even worse because I knew he was leaving. He wasn't Mexican. He didn't have a job here or a life. He was a visitor on these shores. There was something so incredibly romantic and dramatic about that, the whole affair with a timeline, the impending goodbyes and heartache.

Thankfully I didn't dwell on it too much. I wanted to enjoy the present. The past was brutal and the future was unclear, but the present was brilliant. The present was in the shape of a strong, sexy man.

"I still think you should move back," Luz told me, bringing my focus off the ocean. "You're well on your way to recovery now. I say move back to your place and get a cat for company."

I scrunched up my nose. "Listen, you're the cat lady in our friendship here, not me.'

She sighed loudly. "Fine. But I'm still going to call you every day and see if I can change your mind."

"And I'm going to keep having hot, wild sex with my soldier," I told her. "Looks like I got the better deal out of this."

She grumbled something and hung up.

"Did you just call me your soldier?"

I jumped in my seat, the sunscreen falling to the floor, and looked to the door where Derrin was standing there with a cocky grin on his face.

"Jesus," I said, hand to my chest. "How long have you been standing there?"

"The whole time."

"How did I not hear you?"

"I can be quiet when it suits me." He stepped onto the balcony and bent down to kiss me, soft and slow. He sat down in the other chair. I knew he wouldn't be there for long. I guess I could blame my injuries, but I've always been the kind of person who could just sit for hours and hours and not move a muscle. Maybe it was to make up for the fact that when I was flying I was on my feet all day.

Derrin, on the other hand, had a real problem sitting still. He was always moving. Sometimes I told him to chill out and forced him to sit down with a beer, but twenty minutes seemed to be his absolute max before he was up and doing stuff. The man just had too much energy, though I was happy he was absolutely tireless in bed. The other day we'd fucked six times, including a blow-job in the bathroom of the restaurant where we ate dinner. I couldn't get enough of him and he never seemed to tire. We made quite the team.

"So, Luz still hates me, huh?" he asked.

I gave him a sympathetic look. "She doesn't hate you. She just doesn't know you."

"Well, I tried to get to know her last night."

"It doesn't really help that you don't talk much."

"I do with you."

"Only because I talk your ear off and you're forced to keep up."

He clasped his hands together, leaning forward on his elbow, his hands trailing over the gleaming skin of my legs. "So what do you want to do?"

"About Luz?"

"Today. What do you want to do today?"

There were a bunch of things I wanted to do. Most of them involved his dick. I think he knew this.

"Aside from the usual?"

He nodded and tried to wipe the grin off his face. "Yeah. Want to go check out the market in old town?"

"The one that goes over the bridge? You planning on buying overpriced crap?"

He shrugged. "I'm a tourist, aren't I?"

Don't remind me, I thought.

An hour later we were getting out of a cab on the congested cobblestone streets of old town. We would have taken the rental car—he had gotten a super sexy Mustang—but parking in that area of the city was a total bitch.

Today was no exception. It seemed every tourist, expat, gay lover on vacation, and local was out and about. It gave me a sense of purpose and vitality. I had slipped on a light batik-print sundress for the outing, and even though I now had a walking cast on my leg, at least the doctor had been able to put a black one on so it looked a bit sleeker. Okay, it probably didn't, but it made me feel better. Plus it made it much easier to get around. I didn't have to use crutches or lean on Derrin as I had been doing.

Despite that though, he still grabbed my hand. The intimacy of it all surprised me. It sounded absurd after ten days of fucking and sleeping tangled together and cuddling and kissing, and all of that wonderful stuff. But this simplest gesture was so pure and so proud. As he led me through the crowd to the market stalls, I felt like he was showing me off to the world.

How pathetic was I that this was the first time I'd felt that? That I felt someone was proud to be with me?

I blinked back the hot, sentimental tears that wanted to fall down my face. I didn't want him to know how he was affecting me. He was starting fires in my soul with kindling I thought would never burn.

We walked along for a bit, and I couldn't remember the last time I had felt this happy—if I had ever felt this happy. It was like everything before this moment was a blank slate. Even all the bad, the horrible, the sorrowful things, I felt like they couldn't hurt me anymore. There was just me and Derrin, walking on a hot day through the old town of Puerto Vallarta, taking in the smells of fried tortillas and salty ocean breezes. Mariachi music drifted in from restaurants where tourists were smiling awkwardly, trying to get them to go away.

Eventually we found ourselves in one of them, ordering half-priced margaritas. We dipped warm from the oven chips into fresh green salsa and ate them with juice running down our chins.

With a bit of a day buzz going on, we decided to try and walk back to the hotel. We'd cut through the town on the Malecon then walk north along the beach. If we got tired, we'd walk two steps to the nearest hotel and get a drink. It had all the markings of a perfect day. It *was* the perfect day.

We were walking through the town square, past the iconic church tower, when he squeezed my hand and said, "You know what, Alana?"

"What?" I loved the way his raspy accented voice said my name.

"Back in Minnesota, we have a saying that's pretty applicable right now."

I frowned, puzzled. "Minnesota? Isn't that in the states?"

He blinked then said, "Yes. I played hockey there for a bit. Big hockey state. Lot of Canadians go down there to play."

Made sense. "What is it?"

"I'm sweet on you."

I bit my lip to keep from laughing. "I think that's what Americans in the movies say. Not ex-soldier, hockey-playing Canadians."

He shrugged. "It's true, though."

"Well, I guess I'm sweet on you too," I told him. "You know in Mexico, we have our own saying."

"Go on then," he said with a grin and wrapped his arm around my waist, pulling me toward him. I stepped forward, careful not to put my cast on his toes, and pressed against his chest.

A deafening crack rang out.

I felt wind at my back and something solid hit my cast.

Someone somewhere was screaming. It might have been me.

"Run," Derrin said through gritted teeth, staring up and over my shoulder, his grip on me like a vice.

I turned and followed his line of sight. There was quick movement at the top of the bell tower, then it was gone. I looked down at the space behind me where the ground was split open from a bullet. Pieces of concrete had hit the back of my cast.

I was standing there a second ago.

That bullet was meant for me.

I couldn't even process it. Derrin was pulling me along the square, racing for the cover of trees, while people screamed and scattered in all directions. I tried to run as fast as I could with my cast, but I wasn't cutting it.

Derrin knew that, but did what he could to keep me going. Pigeons took flight as we made our way past the gazebo, where a band had paused and was looking around in horror, and we scampered toward the road.

Another shot rang out, hitting one of the gazebo poles and ricocheting off of it. I would have screamed again if I had any breath left in me.

"We're not going to make it on foot!" he yelled at me. He yanked me behind a tree, leaving me there to tremble like a dog, while he leaped out into the road. A small motorbike was puttering past and he quickly knocked the man off. He fell, crying out as he hit the road, narrowly being hit by an oncoming car. Derrin hopped on the bike, wheeled it around, and drove up the curb beside me.

This all took place in the space of five seconds.

"Get on!" he yelled at me, his eyes blazing. But they weren't afraid. They were determined.

I did as he said, leaning on him and awkwardly trying to get my leg over the back of the bike. The man who owned the bike was getting to his feet, yelling his head off, while another bullet hit the sidewalk. I whipped my head to the square to see two men running for us, guns drawn.

This can't be real. This can't be real.

But it was. Derrin gunned the bike forward, and I quickly wrapped my arms around his waist, holding on for dear life.

Who was that? Who was that? Who was that? I kept wanting to ask, to yell, to scream, but I couldn't. I could only hold on and try to catch my breath. My heart was playing drums in my chest and the city I knew and loved was zipping past me in a blur. In seconds it had turned from a warm safe place to one that wanted me dead.

Why?

We zipped along the street, Derrin handling the bike like it was second nature, dodging pedestrians, overtaking cars, hopping on and off the sidewalk when we had to. All I could do was grip him and try not to fall off. Fear was in every part of me, begging me to pay attention to it, but I couldn't. Once I did, that would be the end of me.

I put fear in a box and managed to look over my shoulder. I thought after all of Derrin's fancy maneuvering that we would have lost whomever it was, but there in the distance I could see two motorbikes. They looked bigger. Faster. And they were gaining ground.

"Shit!" I screamed, finding my voice. It practically tore itself out of my throat.

Derrin quickly looked over his shoulder and only raised an eyebrow at the discovery. The bike went a little bit faster, but only a little.

We swerved to the right, heading down a narrow lane, nearly taking out the patio seating area for a restaurant, while people shouted and yelled at us. The sound of the bike's engine was deafening as it bounced off the close walls then multiplied.

I dared to look behind me again. Through the tangles of hair blowing across my face, I saw the two bikes enter the end of the lane, gunning toward us.

"Faster!" I yelled at Derrin. "They're coming."

"I'm trying!" he growled. "Hold on, put your head down!"

He rounded the corner then jumped the bike up onto the sidewalk where we proceeded to head right through a restaurant. We crashed through a table that went flying to the side, then zig zagged around people, waiters, and tables. Broken glass and dishes soared through the air. I kept my head lowered, pressed against his shoulder blades, my eyes shut tight. I didn't want to see any of this.

Derrin swiftly maneuvered the bike back and forth, and then we were in what sounded like a kitchen and then we were airborne, weightless, and I had no idea where we were going to land. I opened my eyes just after we hit the ground with a jolt, biting down on my tongue by accident. My mouth filled with the taste of pennies.

We had soared over the kitchen's back steps and were now twisting right onto a different road, Calle Santa Barbara, heading up the hill that led to most of the tourist apartments at the south end of town. We had a bit more distance behind us now, but the bike wasn't built for two, especially not someone as heavy as Derrin, and it wasn't made for hills, either.

It sputtered, the air filling with the strong smell of an overworked engine.

"I don't think we're going to make it," I cried into Derrin's neck.

He didn't say anything. We kept driving up the curving road, wheels bouncing over rough cobblestones, then a shot rang out. Then another. They hit the stones beneath us. Derrin jerked the bike to the left and another bullet hit a parked car. They were gaining.

"Keep your head down," he said.

I did as he asked and felt him reach into his shirt. He pulled out a small gun then twisted at the waist. I twisted with him, leaning out of the way. He quickly pulled the trigger and fired two shots, hitting one of the guys. He went flying off the bike and the bike fell to the side, just in time for the other assailant to crash into it.

One bullet hit, two down.

Despite being scared to fucking death and my adrenaline feasting on my veins, I was in awe.

I swallowed hard, trying to think of something to say to him.

"Buen disparo." Nice shot.

His eyes smiled at me before looking to the road in front of us. "I like it when you speak Spanish, babe." Then he looked back again and his eyes were cold.

I turned my head to look. A black SUV was thundering up the road toward us. It wasn't full of tourists out for a Sunday drive.

"Fuck," he swore. "Are you ready to get a little wet?"

I stared at him blankly. "What?"

He whipped the bike to the right, and we went thumping down flights of cement stairs, nearly knocking over an elderly couple climbing them.

"Lo Siento!" I yelled at them before I bit my tongue again. At the top of the stairs, the SUV paused then drove off. I knew the road curved down and met with the one we were about to land on. Sure enough, as soon as we hit the road, the SUV appeared at the end of it, turning toward us. Derrin yanked the bike into a condominium driveway then down a brick path that traced the edge of the building. Trees and bushes reached out for us, snagging our clothes and hair as we whipped through them.

Suddenly it seemed like it was the end of the line. There was a pool, and beyond the pool there was blue sky.

"Hold on!" he yelled back at me.

I couldn't hold on any tighter. I let out a cry as the bike lifted off the ground, bounced on a lawn chair, and then drove off the edge of the patio.

We were flying. I kept my head down but my eyes were open.

A sandy beach passed underneath our feet.

Then next thing I knew we had hit something hard and cold, and my arms were ripped from Derrin's waist. Salt water burned my eyes, filling my lungs and nose, and I tried to breathe, to swim, but I was sinking, drowning. The cast was weighing me down.

Suddenly a strong arm wrapped around me and my head broke the surface.

"Breathe, it's okay," Derrin said, gasping for breath just as I was. "Try and swim, I've got you."

I tried to nod but couldn't. I focused on my breathing and moved my arms and legs as much as possible, but he was doing most of the work. When my eyes eventually stopped burning, I was able to see where we were.

We were in the ocean, a few meters offshore. The handles of the motorcycle were just beginning to disappear into the waves, sinking. Beyond that, sunbathers on the beach gawked while people ran to the edge of the condo's pool area to see where we had fallen. On either side of us there were outcrops of stone and rock where the waves gently crashed. We'd been lucky. We could have landed on those instead and neither of us would be alive.

"Right here," Derrin said as he hauled me up to something. I floated around and saw that we had reached a jet-ski that was bobbing in the shallows, clipped to a buoy. I could barely process it.

He swam around me and tried to hoist me onto the edge of the jet-ski. I don't know how he was able to do it while swimming and unable to touch the bottom, but he was. I grasped for the seat, trying to pull myself up as far as I could without hurting my wrist. The shouts from the shore were softening; there were some splashes and a few people coming into the water, maybe to help us.

I don't know if the fall had knocked something loose in my head or I took in too much saltwater, but I had a hard time focusing. All I knew was that Derrin was getting on the jet-ski. He pulled me up so I was in his lap and then he stabbed something metallic, like a small knife, into the ignition switch before hitting the button. The jet-ski roared to life, and he quickly unclipped it from the anchor before we peeled away from the shore.

I was staring blankly up at the patio where the crowd had gathered when I saw what looked like one of the men who had been chasing us—the guy on the motorbike who had crashed into the one who got shot. He was wearing dark aviator shades, but the length of his mustache was memorable. But when I blinked, trying to get my eyes to focus as we moved further away, the man was gone.

"I think I saw one of the guys," I managed to say before having a coughing fit.

"I know," he said. "Keep holding on."

"Where are we going? How did you start this without a key?"

How did you shoot someone while driving a motorcycle?

Holy fucking shit. He just killed someone back there. It was in self-defense, and I'm glad he did it, but oh my god.

Oh my god.

What was happening?

My breathing was becoming shorter, and it felt like I couldn't breathe.

"Hey, hey," he said, taking his hand off the bar and tilting my head gently so he could look at me. "We're okay. You're okay.

We're going to drive this back to the hotel. It's faster than they are, and we have no reason to think they know where we are staying, okay?"

"How do you know that?"

"They would have killed us earlier."

"They would have killed me. They're after me."

He nodded. "And now they're after me because I shot one of their men. It doesn't matter. We'll go back to the hotel, get in the car, and we're out of here."

"We can't just leave the city!"

"Alana," he warned just as we passed over a large wave, landing hard on the other side. My whole body was starting to ache. I was so battered as it was. "If you want to live, you'll do as I say. And you'll answer my questions honestly, okay?"

If you want to live, you'll do as I say.

"Who are you?" I asked incredulously. He sounded like an action hero. My life had just turned into an action film. None of this could be real. This couldn't be real.

But I had said the same thing about my parents, Violetta, and Beatriz, too.

"An ex-soldier. And I want answers from you."

"What answers? Derrin, I told you everything I know. I don't know who those men were. I've never seen them before. I don't know why they want to kill me."

"How did your sisters die?"

I felt sick. "Oh, come on." I rattled off a few swear words in Spanish.

"Tell me how they died. Tell me exactly how they died."

He suddenly switched off the engine, and we came to a stop, bobbing up and down in the waves. There was no one behind us, and the only thing in front of us were banana boats. I could see our hotel from here, maybe just another two minutes of boating and we'd be on the sand. It didn't feel safe enough, and Derrin knew that.

"I will start the engine when I know the truth."

"Why do you want to know?"

"Because the truth could save us," he said, exasperated, and his jaw began to twitch. I had never seen him so bothered before.

Part of me wanted to savor the fact that for once he wasn't being so cool and calm, but that stoic demeanor of his was probably the thing that kept us alive.

I tried to look over his shoulder, to see if anyone was following us again, but his fingers under my jaw kept me in place.

"How?"

I swallowed hard then coughed up a bit of seawater. I spit it into the ocean and realized there was no use pretending to be a lady around him anymore. Finally I seemed to catch my breath, and I willed myself to feel numb. Luckily, after what had just happened, I was halfway there.

"Violetta died in a car bomb," I said simply. "It exploded with her in it."

"Was it meant for her?"

I bit my lip and looked forward, trying to concentrate on the white sand. So close, so close. "From what I understand it was meant for a few people, maybe not her at all. Wrong place at the wrong time. But she was definitely with the wrong people."

"And Beatriz?"

"She was...it was on the news. She was beheaded. So was her husband. And my niece and..." I sucked in air, trying not to cry. "Nephew. Their bodies were burned, their heads displayed in public."

Derrin squeezed his arms around me tighter but didn't say anything. He didn't have to.

When he finally spoke, though, his voice was a bit cracked. "Who is your brother? Who is he really? Is his name really Juan Bardem?"

"No," I said. "His name is Javier Bernal."

He immediately stiffened. I craned my neck to look at him. He was slack-jawed.

"You've heard of him, haven't you? Of course, everyone here has."

"Yes," he said slowly. "I've heard of him."

"So that's the whole story. Violetta died from a bomb I think was meant for him. Beatriz and her family were tortured and killed and publicly shamed by Travis Raines, some sick fuck drug lord who is now dead himself, courtesy of my brother."

Derrin was staring at me with the most rigid, unblinking eyes, like he couldn't quite process this information. Wheels in his head were spinning.

I knew what was going to happen. He was going to take me to the beach. Then he was going to get the fuck out of there, leaving me to fend for myself. I was more trouble than I was worth. He was probably going to do that already, but telling him that my brother's enemies were probably my enemies really cemented the deal.

I was pretty much a walking dead woman.

And I could barely walk at that.

CHAPTER TEN

Derek

I felt like I'd been slugged in the face.

One sharp blow, blinding light, and then a million little pieces all falling into place like nerves returning home.

Javier Bernal.

I should have seen it coming. Bernal is just such a common last name, I didn't think anything of it. In America it would be like the name Smith. When I Googled Alana for research, I certainly never saw a single article or anything linking her to her brother. But it didn't really matter what I thought because this was the truth and it was hitting me hard. Of all the drug lords I'd worked with over the years, I knew Javier the best. The only admirable thing about him was his tenacity. And his payment. He spared no expense on hiring the best.

I'd seen him rise up the ranks of Travis Raines' cartel, break off on his own, and then take over Travis' cartel in the end, like salmon coming back to spawn.

But Alana was wrong about one thing. It wasn't Javier that killed Travis Raines. I was the one who put the bullet in his head. It was a well-placed sniper shot from the roof that took him out, saved the life of Javier's ex-lover, the con artist Ellie Watt, and put Javier in the driver's seat.

For some sad, sick reason I felt compelled to share this information with Alana. I wanted her to know that the man who tortured her sister—and I did know all the grisly details about that death—was killed by my own hands. I wanted her to know that I had helped get her vengeance, whether I knew it or not.

But it was in the only way I had helped.

I had been hired to kill her and I hadn't.

Which cartel had done it?

I kept my mouth shut. I started the jet-ski up again and drove it to shore. I was wasting precious time trying to figure it all out here. I needed to get in our room and get us packed and on the road in five minutes. That is, of course, if they hadn't already discovered where we were staying. I looked up. No helicopters or small planes in the sky. Behind us there were no boats. Wherever the SUV was, it would be fighting traffic coming down Highway 200. If they didn't know, then we had time.

She was silent the rest of the way back to the beach. I felt a bit bad for making her talk about it after everything we had just gone through—there was no way she'd be able to process that so quickly, either—not a civilian like her.

Then again, she wasn't quite a civilian.

I beached the jet-ski and left it there to the amusement of a few beach bums. They could try and take it if they wanted, but I'd taken my makeshift skeleton key with me. There were few things that it couldn't start.

We quickly hobbled past the pool and into the lobby. I made sure my gun was hidden, tucked away in the bandage against my abs, but I knew I could whip it out at a moment's notice if needed.

A moment's notice would be if we were lucky. It's usually less than that.

After I did a quick sweep of the area and didn't see anyone unusual, I led her over to the elevators, one hand firmly gripped around her arm, the other hand hovering above the hidden gun. I pressed the button then kept her off to the side when the doors opened.

The elevator was empty.

Then I brought her inside and pressed the button for the sixteenth floor.

We stared at ourselves in the mirrors that lined the elevator. Both of us were soaking wet, and though you couldn't tell I had a gun on me, you could tell there was something funny going on underneath my shirt. Her hair was tangled all over her face, dripping down her back, and her dress was clinging to every curve. She might as well be naked. I hated the fact that I was so fucking turned on right now. That was the problem with this job. I was used to the guns, the chases, the violence. It didn't damper anything for me. Sometimes the excitement only fueled desire, except I usually got off by shooting a different gun. She wasn't used to it at all.

When the doors opened, I decided the said gun out. Her eyes widened at the sight of it, even though she knew it had been there, she had felt it when she was holding on to me, when she saw me kill that man.

I wanted her to feel safe, and I wasn't sure what it was going to take for that to happen. It wasn't the sight of a gun.

We moved silently and swiftly down the hall to the room. I immediately plugged up the peephole with my thumb and knocked quickly. I gripped the gun and waited, motioning for her to move back against the wall and out of the way before I put my head against the door.

There was no answer, no sound. I looked down, and knowing I had left the curtains open, I saw no shadow passing by the light coming from under the door. I hadn't expected there to be.

I quickly slipped the keycard out of my pocket and jammed it into the slot. When the lock turned green and the mechanical locks whirred open, I opened the door, crouching down as I followed through, my gun drawn and ready to shoot.

The room was empty.

I stood up then motioned for Alana to come in. She did so like she was walking on eggshells, her arms held stiffly against herself. She seemed to be going into shock.

I told her to stay put then did a quick search of the room. My guns were there, my other stuff was there, and nothing had been searched or tampered with. They hadn't found us. We still had time.

Just not much of it.

"Alana," I said to her, but she didn't look at me. I went over and placed my palms over her upper arms, holding her as I stared at her frozen face. "Alana Bernal." She finally looked up.

"Listen to me, Alana," I said, knowing it was best to keep calling her name. "We're safe for the time being, but we have to leave. I'm giving us a ten minute window and then we're out of here. I'm pretty much already packed—you know I travel light. I'm going to pack up your stuff while you take a shower, okay Alana? Hold on."

I went into the bathroom and brought the gym bag out from underneath the sink. Her blank eyes followed it as I placed it on the couch. Then I took hold of her arm and led her into the bathroom. I ran a hot shower, stripped her dress up over her head until she was just in her bra and underwear, and then I took those off too. She may have turned me on in the elevator, but now it was apparent she was frightened to death—a scared, lost little girl, and that made my protective instincts go into overdrive.

I was going to get her far away from here. Then we were going to solve this.

CHAPTER ELEVEN

Alana

I think it must have been late when I finally stepped out of the fog. That's what I called it, the fog. I guess some might call it shock, but when I looked back at that day, the events between being shot at from the Puerto Vallarta bell tower and being in Derrin's newly rented Camry while he handed me a Coke from the gas station, it was all just a fog, like a grey, hazy mist that never really cleared.

Sometimes I wondered if it really all happened, or if it had been a dream. But my body ached and my limbs were covered with scratches from trees whipping us, and my eyes still burned from the salt.

It had happened. Someone tried to kill me. Actually, a bunch of people tried to kill me, but I had no doubt they were all hired by the same person.

Now Derrin knew the truth, and because he was with me, taking care of me and making sure we were taking all the right steps, I didn't mind that he knew. He was one of the few people on earth now that did. He knew the truth about my sisters, about Javier. And he was still with me. In fact, I think he was the only thing keeping me alive.

"How are you feeling?" he asked gently as he got in the car. "You're looking better."

I took a timid sip of Coke. It wasn't very cold but it was fizzy enough. "I think I'm finally, um, here."

"Good. I missed you."

I eyed him, caught off guard by the sincerity in his voice. I swallowed the drink down, my throat buzzing.

"Where are we?"

Now I was really looking at my surroundings. We were in the parking lot of a gas station beside a highway. It didn't look to be an overly busy one, so I didn't think it was the one that connected Puerto Vallarta to the coastal cities. Though it was dark out, there was a line of orange and purple to the left of us, burning the tops of some mountains. We weren't near the ocean either.

He tapped the GPS. "This thing is telling me we're outside Tulepe, two hours east of Mazatlan."

"I miss the Mustang."

"And I missed that attitude," he said. "But you know we had to take it back. These people have connections everywhere. If there was any chance they might've stumbled across the hotel, our identities would be really easy to find, the valet would fess up, and they'd be looking for the black mustang everywhere. No one looks twice at a Camry."

"And how are we supposed to get away in a hurry?"

"We won't be doing that in a hurry," he said. "We're being extra cautious, extra safe, and staying one step ahead. At this point, they've lost us. If they had found us, we'd be dead. Now we figure out what our next moves are."

"You're awfully good at this."

"I watch a lot of spy movies."

"I don't believe you."

"I was in the army."

"That I know," I said, and went back to sucking on the straw, feeling like a confused little child. Derrin did know a lot, about everything, it seemed. More than the average person should and he definitely wasn't average. But no matter what he really did for a living or what he knew, he was saving my life and I trusted him more than anything.

"Can I call Luz and Dominga?" I asked hopefully.

He shook his head. "No," he said. "Not yet."

"Not ever?"

He sighed and rubbed his hand over his eyes. "I'm tired. Let's get a hotel room."

"Do you think that's safe?"

"For now it is. They don't know who I am."

"How do you know?"

"I just do." He shrugged and thumped his fist against the steering wheel. "You're the bigger problem. But don't worry about that. I know a lot of people here who can get us fake IDs. They don't ask questions, and they don't talk."

"Do any of these people work for the cartels?" I asked suspiciously.

He gave me a look. "Everyone in Mexico works for the cartels in one way or another." He paused. "Isn't that right?"

"No," I told him. "There are a lot of honest people in this country making an honest living." I paused. "In the morning, I want you to take me to see my brother."

He wiggled his jaw uneasily. "That wouldn't be wise."

"Are you scared?" I had a hard time imagining he was scared of anything.

"I'm not scared, but it wouldn't be good. People can't just meet drug lords. It doesn't work that way."

"I'm his sister."

His face turned grave. "You are. And he had more sisters. I'm sorry, but I have no reason to believe that Javier is going to protect you."

That stung even though it was the truth. "He's all I have."

"You have me."

"I don't even really know you." *It just feels like I do. It just feels like I don't need to.*

"And yet I'm still here, saving your tight little ass today. Where was your brother when you were in the hospital? Did he ever come to visit? What about after? Do you think he'll be here for you now?"

The lashes kept coming. My nose felt hot, and I blinked a few times, trying to hide the disappointment. "This time it's his fault," I said.

"It's always been his fault, Alana. You never asked for this."

"It was my father's fault before then."

"And still, you never asked for this. Your father is dead. Your brother is not. You're alive and I'm here with you."

"I need to see Javier."

"Then get him to meet you somewhere. I'm not taking you there, wherever he lives. That's like walking into the lion's den. A gringo like me…he'd never let me out of there alive."

I glared at him. "Oh, he's not that bad."

"I know what he did to Salvador Reyes and his men. I know the way he took over the Sinaloa Cartel, the same way he did with Travis Raines. That made the news back in Canada too. I'm not taking any chances. Tomorrow, you call him from a payphone—I'm sure there's one somewhere, and you tell him what happened, and you tell him to meet you there, where you call him from. Tell him to bring his wife too."

"Luisa?"

He nodded. "Yes. From what I've heard, she keeps things civil."

"I think you've heard wrong. You can't believe everything you read on the internet."

He went on, not hearing me. "I'll be waiting with a gun trained on his head just in case anything goes wrong."

I slapped his leg in protest. "No you won't! Jesus, Derrin, he's my brother. He's not out to get me. He's not the one who ordered the hit. For all I know, he might be behind the vigilante killing."

He shook his head ever so slightly and stared out at the fluorescent lights of the parking lot. In the distance, the sky was completely black now. Only the lone headlights blinded our eyes as they passed.

This was a lonely, lonely place and I was suddenly aware of how alone I was.

But I wasn't, was I?

I stared at Derrin's profile, at the strong, hard features of his face, the way his chin dimple was only visible in a certain light, like now, the way his hair was starting to grow in more, a light brown color. He still had the perfect head. He had the perfect everything.

"Okay," I conceded. "I'll do as you say. But please, don't do anything stupid. None of this forgotten army stuff. If you're suffering from PTSD, and I'm pretty sure you are suffering from a lot of things I might add, this won't be the time to sort it out."

He turned his head and held my gaze. "I'm not going to shoot your brother. Or your sister-in-law. Or you. I just want to keep you safe. And I will, at any cost."

I frowned, studying him further but not finding any other layers beneath his handsome features. "Why are you doing this for me?"

He smiled sadly. "Because I can." He sighed then started the car. "Let's go find ourselves a hotel, drink some beer, and see if we can fuck each other to sleep."

Twenty minutes later we were staying in a rustic but fairly clean motel. No one was drinking. No one was fucking. We were asleep the minute we hit the pillows.

...

The next morning I woke up feeling wooden. My tongue was swollen from where I kept chomping down on it during the motorcycle chase, and every part of me hurt.

But I was alive when I shouldn't be, and I couldn't complain. I'd cheated death more than once. Hell, I'd given it the finger.

Derrin was already up, shirtless with his back to me, staring out the crack of light in the drawn curtains and fiddling with something in his hands.

My god he was a fine man. Even now, or maybe even more so, he was everything I'd ever wanted. Each sculpted muscle in his back, from the dimples near his waistband to the ripples that planed off his spine, spoke of what a tireless, tough, well-oiled machine he was. He was so big and strong, my protector. But it never made the fear go completely away, because when it came down to it, he was an ex-soldier. He wasn't Rambo. He wasn't even David Caruso. He was a Canadian with some muscles, a bit of training, and I suppose a lot of luck. He had determination, and he was much, much smarter than his appearance led you to believe. But he wasn't part of the cartels. He didn't know this game or the way things worked as much as he thought he did.

He was so confident he knew how things were going to go that I started to believe him too. But unless there was something about him that I didn't know (and that wouldn't be surprising) I had to keep my guard up. I couldn't rely on him for everything. I had to go on what I knew.

He didn't know my brother at all, just from what he had heard on the news. And while drug lords usually couldn't be trusted, it didn't mean they were all bad people. Javier *was* bad—he didn't get to where he was without being so—but he wasn't as bad as people thought. He'd certainly never hurt me, let alone purposely put me in jeopardy. Marguerite and I were all he had left, and though I hadn't talked to him a lot lately—he seemed to be increasingly busy, which I understood, considering—we had a good relationship. I helped him out when he needed it, and he helped me financially when I did.

And now I had no doubt he would come through when my life was on the line.

I was thinking that and blinking the fuzzy sleep out of my eyes while Derrin took what was in his hands, the Ace bandage, and began to wrap it around his stomach. After the third pass around, he slipped a small handgun in there then wrapped it again, securing it tightly.

When he turned around he wasn't surprised to see me staring at him. I was starting to think he had eyes in the back of his head.

"What's the plan?" I asked, not wanting to mention the gun. That gun had come in handy.

He slipped on a t-shirt, poured a cup of tarlike coffee in a styrofoam cup, and handed it to me before sitting on the side of the bed. I drew my knees up to my chest and took a sip.

Disgusting. I loved coffee but I wasn't about to drink motor oil. I made a face and handed it back to him.

He held the cup in his hands but didn't drink it, looking ahead at a spot on the wall, totally focused.

"We'll check out of here and go up the road for a bit. Find a big public area, like a mall. Find a payphone there and tell him that you need to meet him right where you are at a certain time. Where does he live?"

"About three hours from here. It's remote but he can get here faster than that. I think he has a helicopter now."

He took in this information. "Okay. We'll give him three hours. Then we find another hotel. Check in, under my name only again, and wait there. With two hours left, we split up. I'll be watching you the whole time."

I rubbed my lips together, feeling so damn nervous. "Then what?"

"What do you mean?"

"What happens to me?"

"I don't know. I guess that depends what you're going to ask of him. Do you want to walk off with him, to his compound? Do you seriously believe you'll be safe there?"

"Of course I'll be safe there. I'd have to be. *He's* safe there."

"Yes," he said with a nod. "It would seem."

"He has people everywhere protecting him, the whole state is behind him. Most of the other states too. He practically owns half the country. I'll be safe with him."

Derrin didn't look convinced and sighed. "You're a free woman. I'll do whatever you want me to do as long as you're certain it needs to be done. But the question is, do you *want* to go with him?"

I pursed my lips and reached for the coffee. Maybe I did need a hit of that stuff.

Twenty minutes later we were on the road and looking for the perfect meeting place. I felt somewhat safe. No one was following us; in reality, how could they be? We had been so careful. Not only did Derrin have the gun strapped to his waist, he also had a knife in his boot and another gun strapped around his leg in a holster.

Yet for all his guns, he didn't seem to be enjoying himself. This wasn't a cops and robbers game to him. It wasn't a game at all. He took this all very, very seriously. As I guess one should when you were being trailed by Mexican assassins. Again I had that feeling that there was far more to Derrin's story than I knew, and I wondered if the truth would ever come out. I wondered if I wanted it to.

While we searched for big, public spaces throughout the dry countryside and graveyards of empty roadside stores, I thought about what I would do. If Javier offered me protection, I would have to go. But that didn't mean I wanted to. To be honest, I didn't at all. Being at his compound wouldn't make me feel safe, even if I was safe. All those bad, bad men walking around, owning the place. I'm sure they would treat me with faux respect, but I'd be the first one thrown under the bus. I could never sleep knowing who those men were, what they orchestrated. Though I'd never been to Javier's place, I had heard the rumors, of the twisted doctor and the torture shed in the back. Prostitutes that were killed in the house after sex, or shot for fun.

Now Javier was married—a quick ceremony somewhere that I hadn't been invited to—but I wasn't too sure that having a woman around was changing him for the better. If anything, I think he was making *her* worse.

I guess I'd find out soon, if Javier wanted anything to do with me at all.

And, of course, at the heart of it, I didn't want to leave Derrin behind. Who knows how long I'd have to hide out, and the direction that my life would take. I wanted my life to go in whatever direction Derrin was heading in.

I was falling in love with this man. Fast and hard, just the way he lived and fucked. I wondered if he would love the same way too.

I wanted to be the woman that healed him.

"Bingo," Derrin said, smacking the dashboard.

I looked to the left and saw a giant, brand new Wal-Mart on the side of the road. The parking lot was packed, and there were a few half-finished office buildings and shops flanking it.

"Wal-Mart?" I said incredulously. "You think Javier is going to come meet me at a Wal-Mart?"

Derrin grinned beautifully. "He'll have no choice."

Soon I was at a payphone located just outside the washrooms. Wal-Mart was a living hell full of bad lighting, sad faces, and screaming children. We had only started getting them everywhere in Mexico a few years ago, but it was like all the American stereotypes followed them down here. This was one of the supercenters that had a McDonald's in it and a produce section that pissed off all our farmers. It reeked of everything I hated.

I dialed Javier's number, not knowing if he would pick up. He wouldn't recognize the number, and my own phone had been in my bag when we drove into the ocean. It was now lost at sea.

"Hello?" someone answered. It wasn't Javier. Could I have gotten the wrong number? He always answered his cell. Unless he had his number changed recently, which was possible.

"Uh, hello. Is Javier there?"

"Who is this?" asked the voice, amused. It didn't seem familiar to me.

I didn't want to tell him anything yet. "Is he there? Is this his phone?"

"I'll tell you what you want to know once you tell me who you are."

"If Javier is there just tell him it's his sister."

Silence. Was it possible this person didn't know he had sisters?

"Hello?" I repeated.

"What's your name?" he asked slowly.

"Alana Bernal."

"I see. And you say you're his sister, hey?"

"Last I checked," I said, getting annoyed now.

"Interesting. Can you hold on a moment?"

"What's your name?" I quickly asked.

"Please hold." I could hear muffled speaking like a hand over a receiver.

After a long minute, Javier answered. "Alana?"

I breathed out a sigh of relief and put my hand against my forehead. "Javier. Thank god."

"Where are you calling from? This isn't your number." He sounded ruffled. He usually sounded as cool as a cucumber.

"Sorry," I told him. "I didn't have a choice. My phone is gone. I'm calling from a payphone."

"Where?" he asked.

"I don't know," I said. "Outside of Durango, I think."

"What the hell are you doing there?"

"I'm in trouble."

For a moment I thought he was going to ask me what I did, maybe scold me for some money problem. "I saw something in the news," he said carefully. "Gunshots in Puerto Vallarta."

I took in a deep breath. "The gunshots were for me."

I heard him inhale sharply. "Are you sure?"

"Yes. We were walking through the square—"

"Who is we?"

"Me and my boyfriend," I said on the spot. I didn't know what else to call Derrin, and I knew if I made him sound more casual than that, Javier would grill me about it.

"Boyfriend? What boyfriend? What's his name?"

"Derrin."

"What the hell kind of name is that?"

"He's Canadian."

"Oh, that figures. Go on."

"We were walking through the square. Someone in the clock tower took a shot at me. We ran, got on a motorbike, and ended up outrunning them."

He didn't say anything for a moment. "Alana, Alana, Alana...if what you're saying is true, you don't just outrun someone who is trying to kill you. Not here. Not you. That's impossible."

"We outran them," I said, raising my voice. "Look, we got away."

"Just like that?"

"Yes. We got back to the hotel room, packed up our shit, and fled."

I heard him groan to himself.

"What?" I asked. "What is it? What do I do?"

"What do you do?"

"Javier...people are after me. Probably the same people who murdered Beatriz."

His voice grew cold. "That was Travis Raines. He is dead."

"And there are others just like him trying to teach you the same lesson. I wasn't hit by a car by accident—that had to be on purpose. And now there were actual bullets aimed at my head."

"Are you sure they weren't for the Canadian? He does have a stupid name."

"Javier, please," I begged him, my voice cracking. "Help me."

He exhaled hard. "Fine. Where should I meet you?"

"I'm at a Wal-Mart."

"Wal-Mart?" he asked incredulously.

"Yes."

He sounded like he'd choked on something. "You can't be serious."

I could feel my face going red. I was fed up. I didn't care who he was, he was still my brother.

"I am serious. Come to the Wal-Mart outside of Durango, or wherever you manage to trace this call to. I'll be sitting on the corner of a water fountain between Wal-Mart and an office building. Bring Luisa."

"Luisa, why?"

"I want to talk to her, too."

I hung up the phone before he could protest anymore then left the madness of the store. As I took the stairs down to the parking garage underneath the main lot, I grumbled to myself. After everything that had happened—the accident, the fact that he heard about the gunshots on the news—he still wasn't acting like this was a big deal. I had almost died several times. Why was that so hard for him to believe? Why didn't he care?

I walked through the garage, which was only half-filled with cars since most people had parked up top, and found the Camry. Derrin was in the driver's seat, his face taut. His eyes quickly flew to me, and he leaned over to open the passenger door.

"How did it go?" he asked as I sat down and closed the door after me.

"It could have gone better," I said, trying not to sound as resentful as I felt. In a petty way, I didn't want Derrin to think he was right about him.

He was watching me, his eyes unreadable yet they seemed to be reading me. "Tell me what he said."

"Well, first of all, he didn't answer. It was some other guy. From the way he questioned me, it was like he didn't know I existed."

This piqued Derrin's interest. "Is that so? Did you get his name?"

"He wouldn't say."

"But he got yours."

"Yes."

"Javier was probably trying to protect you and Marguerite, keep you a secret."

"Well, I kind of went and messed that all up, didn't I?' I scratched angrily at the skin around the top of my cast. I wanted this fucking thing off. "Anyway, Javier told me he heard about the shootings on the news, but obviously he didn't know I was involved. In fact…it really sounded like he didn't believe me."

Derrin only grunted.

"I told him where I was. He wanted me to go meet him somewhere else, but I told him no."

"Good girl."

I managed a smile. "It didn't feel right otherwise."

"Did you mention me?"

I paused. "Yes."

He cocked his head. "And what did you tell him?"

"I told him I had a Canadian boyfriend named Derrin."

"Really? And what did he say to that?"

"Well, he was surprised because I never really have boyfriends. And he thinks you have a stupid name."

"Charming brother you have there."

I shrugged.

"So is that what I am?" he asked, leaning closer to me. His fingers traced the skin on my shoulder and a subtle shiver shot down my spine.

"If you want to be," I said quietly, suddenly feeling shy. So not like myself. What was I, twelve?

He reached out and cupped my face in his hand, his sky blue eyes searching mine, trying to overturn every buried stone. "I want to be. If you'll have me around."

"I've kept you around so far," I joked.

His brow furrowed. "I want to be important to you."

I knew he was being serious—when wasn't Derrin being serious? But my default reaction was always to make a joke when things got too heavy. I had to rein that in, swallow it down, even though I was too afraid to take what he was saying as truth. At some point, Derrin and I would part ways. It would have to be that way. He was just a tourist here in a foreign land. He couldn't live in Mexico forever. Why would he even want to?

"Alana," he said. "No matter what happens with your brother, you have someone here that has your back, all the way to the end."

"To what end?"

"To the end of it all," he said, his voice grave. "And I'm not going to let you go so easily. I want you to figure it out with Javier, see what he knows, see if he can help. But if he has no ideas, if he doesn't seem to care, you'll be better off with me."

"How can you say that?"

"Trust me."

"I want to," I automatically said. I corrected myself. "I *do* trust you."

"You don't. And I don't blame you. But if you stay with me, I can make a better life for you. It doesn't have to be with me, but I can get you out of here."

"How?"

"Come up north with me."

I curled my lip. "Too cold."

"The west coast isn't cold at all, you'd love it," he said. "But if not, then Europe. Some small island in the Caribbean. South America."

It sounded tempting. But the whole thing was absurd. "I barely know you."

"I know. And I barely know you. But this is what's going to keep you alive." Now he was cupping my face with both hands. "Alana, unless the men who are after you are killed, unless the person who wants you dead is found out then taken out, this isn't going to stop. There is a lot of money on your head."

I frowned, feeling icky at that assumption. "How do you know that?"

"I just do."

"Like you know how to kill a person and ride a motorbike at the same time?"

"Yes." His grip tightened, his gaze more intense. I felt like he was going to devour me. "Your life as you've known it is now over."

I swallowed the lump in my throat. "You said that I could talk to Luz—"

"I did say that. And I meant it. But I also said not now. They'll be in danger, too, if they talk to you, so leave them out of it. Send them a postcard from a random place. Alana, you're going to need to say goodbye to the person you were. Alana Bernal ended when she was hit by a car."

I felt like a force field went up around me. I wasn't feeling any of this. It wasn't sinking in. No. This wasn't the way. My brother would fix everything.

I looked away and pulled out of Derrin's grasp. "I need to talk to Javier."

"And you're going to. And I'm going to watch the whole thing," he said, straightening up. He started the car. "Let's go find us a place to stay for the night before he gets here and everything changes."

CHAPTER TWELVE

Derek

Being Derrin Calway was becoming harder and harder. I had messed up once, telling her about Minnesota when I should have said Winnipeg, but I don't think she thought anything of it. Still, it was getting increasingly hard to pretend I was just an ex-soldier. She knew I was something more, and I knew in the future I was going to have to tell her the truth.

The question was, how much truth. It's one thing to say you have experience in "getting shit done" for people. It's another to say you're a professional assassin, one that put a bullet in Travis Raines' head at the request of her brother. And it's another to say you were the vigilante who shot the driver in the head, only after you failed to kill her to begin with.

Where did the truth end and where did I begin?

I'm not sure I'd ever figure it out and not come out more of a shell than I was going in.

I didn't trust her brother at all. I knew Javier enough to know that she did mean something to him, but a man changes when he comes into power and I'd seen him change a lot. I wasn't even expecting him to show up to meet her. He was the man in charge of the seedy underbelly of half the country, he wouldn't want to risk anything by going after his sister.

Then again, there was the chance that his marriage had softened him. That's why I wanted Luisa to be there. Alana would be able to get a better read off of her. She wanted to believe the best of Javier a little too much.

While we drove around looking for a cheap, simple motel that I could pay for in cash, I wondered if Javier could be behind any of this. The man who had called me and ordered her hit definitely hadn't been him. Javier's voice and mannerisms were far too distinctive. But could it have been someone working on his behalf? Perhaps it was the man Alana had talked to on the phone, even though he'd pretended not to know who she was.

Who was Javier's right-hand man these days? Esteban Mendoza. Could it have been him on the phone? I wasn't sure. I never paid too much attention to Este back then because he was a bit of a chump, a surfer dude who didn't do shit but wanted to weasel up the ranks. He was proficient in surveillance and electronics—we were able to do the raid on Raines' house all because of him. But Este didn't seem to have the chops for much more than that.

Then again, being second to Javier meant doing a lot of dirty work. An order was an order. But why would Javier want his own sister assassinated? That's what didn't make any sense at all. I didn't trust him, and with good reason, and I thought if she went off with him it would do her far more harm than good. But I didn't know if he'd want to kill her.

I started thinking that even if she did go off with him, maybe I could put myself back in the picture somehow. Ever since I defected from him after the Raines' takeover years ago and helped Ellie Watt out of Honduras to rescue her father—for a price higher than Javier's of course—I'd never seen Javier again. I couldn't just stroll up to him and ask if he needed any help. Javier held grudges like nobody's business, especially those that concerned his ex-lover, and he'd shoot me on the spot.

I guess the problem now was how far I was willing to go for Alana. She'd said again and again how much we didn't know each other, and she was right every time. But even then, I couldn't stay away. I couldn't from the moment I saw her in the airport parking lot. Just one real look at her and she'd done something to me, stirred something that had been dormant for so long.

I couldn't leave her. I just didn't know how to get her to stay with me.

Eventually we found a nice enough hotel. We had an hour to kill before I drove us back to the Wal-Mart and I wished we had more. On the off chance she left with her brother and I never saw her again, I wanted to remember exactly how she felt to touch, to hold, to kiss, to be deep inside of.

Once we got inside the room, I locked the door, drew the shades, and then pulled her into my arms.

The need to drive my cock inside her suddenly overpowered me, and I grabbed her face, kissing her hard, my hands moving down into her hair, down her back to her ass where I squeezed hard. She let out a cry of pain, but it was good pain from the way she attacked me, hands, lips, teeth everywhere.

I'd never felt so hungry for her. Apparently she felt the same. So much adrenaline, emotion and futility hung in the air, throttling our bones, stirring our blood, making us starved, wild animals.

Death made sex feel much more alive.

I quickly pulled off her shorts and thong and spun her around. I pinned her up against the wall. The bed wouldn't do this time. It was too soft, too comforting, too forgiving. I wanted her raw and real. I wanted to feel the pain with the beauty, the harshness of it all. I wanted to feel all of her.

She wrapped one leg around my waist, her cast on the other hooked around my thigh, and held me close to her as I fumbled with my zipper. Once my dick was free, my pants dropping to my ankles, I wasted no time in guiding the tip into her, just teasing her cleft with her own slickness.

"I need to feel you," she cried, her head back, her hips trying to thrust closer, to get purchase. Her nails dug into my back.

"You'll feel every inch, babe," I groaned, feeling her expanding for my tip, so greedy and hungry, just like me.

"Now, Derrin, *por favor*."

Her cries were my undoing. I thrust into her, so wet, so tight, so damn beautiful. I was meant to be this deep inside of her, pushed in to the hilt, like I could stay here forever, like I was supposed to.

I caught my breath, nearly losing it, and pulled out slowly, relaxing into a rhythm, trying to hold myself in check. She felt so good and I started rubbing her clit with tiny, circular strokes. She started panting, squirming, wanting more.

"Harder," she pleaded. "Keep going."

I bit at her neck and sucked beneath her ear, loving how pushy she was. I kept at it, slow and steady, not ready to give her everything just yet.

"Do you like that?" I whispered, delighting in the primal lust that was spilling out of her mouth in load groans.

I thrust into her deeper, faster, torn between wanting to come and wanting this to go on forever. She held me tighter, her nails sharp and drawing blood as I pounded her, keeping my fingers on her wet clit quick and steady. Her grip around me began to loosen as she came close to the edge.

"Alana," I cried out breathlessly as the pressure reached the breaking point. Everything tightened, from my balls to my abs, before I came hard and poured into her. This was so raw, beautiful, that I could barely hold her up anymore. I felt as my seed spilled into her, something was spilling into me and filling up all the caverns deep inside, the dark and hollow places. They felt brighter now. Warm. Real.

She cried out as she came, loud enough for the room next door to hear. But I didn't care. I didn't care about anything except her. My heart simmered.

I breathed into the hollow of her neck, drowning in her smell, the feel of her as she pulsed around me, the sound of her breathless noises she probably didn't know she was making. I'd never been in so deep. I knew I wouldn't walk away from this woman unscarred.

"Shit," she said, smiling and catching her breath. Her legs began to shake around me, worn from the strain, and I grabbed a hold of her, gently lowering her to the ground. She wiped the sweat from her brow and frowned at the marks her fingernails had made on my shoulder.

"I'm sorry," she said, nodding at them.

"Don't you ever," I told her, brushing her wet hair off her face. Everything about her glowed, so hot, so warm, so larger than life.

"You know what you are?" I asked her, leaning in until my lips grazed the rim of her ear.

"What?"

"Sunshine."

Redemption.

...

Even after the sex and intimacy, the ride back to Wal-Mart was strained. Both of us were locked in our own heads, being eaten by our own fear. My fear—the first real fear I had felt in some time—was that I would never see her again. If I never saw her again, I couldn't protect her. If I couldn't protect her, she would end up dead.

Her fear...well, I could only imagine. I just hoped it was enough to keep her on her toes but not too much that she would panic. Fear can only work for you if you know how to recognize it and use it.

Our plan was relatively simple, yet as we sat back in the parking garage, now a bit more full thanks to after work shoppers pushing their carts back and forth, it seemed daunting. There was a mild sense of chaos here, which usually helped me think but today it wasn't cutting it.

I had my sniper rifle and silencer with me, as well as my .22. I would go up first by the doors at the far end of the parking garage, ones that led up to an empty office building. The doors would be locked but that was never a problem for me. I would then secure a spot in an office on the highest floor. I wouldn't be right at the window overlooking the fountain—that was too obvious—but I'd try to find one further back with a clear shot. Then I would wait. The moment Alana looked like she was in trouble or being taken against her will was the moment I would pull the trigger.

In some ways, it was phenomenally easy to kill Javier this way. He would know that too. But what enemies he had I'm sure were masquerading as his friends. In fact, I knew for certain he had no friends. I assumed he knew that too.

And Javier would probably travel without telling anyone. Maybe Esteban. No one would expect to see him here, so he would be safe. In Culiacán, where he lived, that was a different story. People would expect him there. But here, even though he probably felt inconvenienced by the travel, he was actually fairly safe.

But *I* was here.

"So," Alana started, scratching at the top of her cast nervously.

"So. Are you ready?"

She shook her head, her eyes wide and searching. "What happens if I go with him? If he promises me safety. What happens to us?"

I tried to smile but failed. "I'll be here whenever you need me."

"You'll stay in Mexico?"

"Of course."

"Don't you have to go home?"

"I don't have to go anywhere, Alana."

"What if I want to see you again?"

"You can email me." Even though it was the best way to get a hold of me, it still felt so cold, so wrong, to have our contact with each other go from skin to skin to email.

"Not call?"

"I'll probably get a new phone and number to be safe."

"Oh," she said, looking panicked.

I put my hand on her leg, relishing in the warmth of her skin. "When I get a new phone, I'll email you the number. Any time you want to leave, I'll come and get you. Your brother won't hold you there. Remember, this all has to be your choice and your choice alone."

"But if I choose to go, this is it? I mean, I won't get to see you before?"

I wiggled my jaw back and forth and breathed out through my nose. "It wouldn't be safe for him to see me. I'd rather not, you know, be exposed to a notorious drug lord if I can help it."

She nodded. "I get it. Well, I guess you should probably go take your place."

Something in me seized, but I did what I could to ignore it. "All right. If you don't go with him, if anything, anything at all seems the slightest bit wrong, change your mind. Just get advice. See what your options are. And come back here to the car. I'll meet you and we'll be on our way."

"Derrin," she said, adjusting in her seat to face me. She looked so soulful in that moment that I wished to god she was calling me Derek instead. It would only feel real when she used my real name, knew the real me, everything I was, and still stayed.

But she wasn't staying.

Before I could say anything stupid, I quickly leaned over and grabbed her face in my hands, kissing her hard like I was trying to create an impression on my lips, like she could seep into my skin and stay a permanent reminder. She tasted sweet and felt soft, and that fire inside me was burning away. No matter what, I would protect her.

I pulled away, breathless and surprised to see the moisture in her eyes, tears threatening to overflow. I quickly grabbed the gym bag from the back seat that had the sniper rifle in it, and then left the car, shutting the door behind me. The sound echoed through the garage, lonely and cold.

I didn't look back, but I would see her again. I was on my way to protect her.

CHAPTER THIRTEEN

Alana

I'd never felt so unsafe, so alone, until I watched Derrin walk away from the car and disappear into a stairwell. I don't even know how he managed to break the locked door so seamlessly, so naturally, without causing any attention, but he did. Now I was sitting in the Camry wishing I could keep an eye on the time. A watch would have been nice. A new phone would have been nice.

Sometimes I was hit with the overwhelming reality that my life would never be the same again. Something as simple as losing my phone, all my pictures, my useless contacts, my apps—something so normal as that and I felt like I'd never be able to have a good life again. Just the idea that Luz and Dominga were probably calling it nonstop, calling the hotel, checking up on me, was a wrench in my heart. Dominga's maid friend was probably searching the room on her behalf, panicked at our disappearance.

Provided someone else didn't get to the room first. I could finally see why Derrin didn't want me in contact with them at all. I hated that they had to worry, but they would be the first people my enemies would go after for information. If I knew anything, it was how much they loved to extract the truth from their victims. And when the victims didn't know anything, that made it even worse.

I didn't wipe the tear that rolled down my cheek, but I told myself it would be the last time I cried. It had to be. Javier was meeting me here, at least I hoped, and he would fix everything. He would get me out of this mess.

When I figured I'd spent about an hour in the car, I took in a few deep breaths and finally got up. I walked over to the stairs that led up to the Wal-Mart, my cast echoing as I walked. I was less and less awkward, but the damn cast was a reminder that I was always at a disadvantage, and if I really concentrated I'd realize my ankle was throbbing painfully. All that running yesterday had done a number on it and yet pain was the last thing my brain was processing. It was all fear now.

Once up top, the sun hit my face and cleared a bit of the darkness away. Wal-Mart was busy, full of people living their normal lives, going to their cars with bags full of useless crap. I envied them, the blissful ways they could just continue living in ignorance. None of them could have appreciated how easy they had it. I sure as hell hadn't appreciated it two weeks ago.

I walked past the front of the store, past the vending machines stocked with tamarind and pineapple sodas, past robotic horses that children could ride, and gumball machines. I headed over to the fountain.

It was large and circular, made up of terracotta tile with water flowing into a blue-hued pool with only a few pesos at the bottom. There was a bench in the shade where an old man was dozing, a newspaper and a sandwich beside him, but other than that the place was empty.

I tried to look up at the windows of the office building next door, but knew the sun would be in my eyes if I did—it was late afternoon and close to setting behind it—and if anyone was watching me, they might get suspicious. I just had to believe that Derrin was up there, watching over me.

But what if he wasn't? What if he'd skipped town? It was so hard to know, to trust.

It was possible. Anything was possible. But I had to have faith in him. There were few things left that I could believe in.

I took a seat at the edge of the fountain and waited. I wished I had a book or something to make myself look less obvious, but since I was waiting for someone, it didn't really matter. I stared at the tiny birds that hopped around at my feet, chirping, looking for a handout, then watched the highway beyond the store as it piled up thicker and thicker with traffic heading out of Durango, moving like syrup.

Finally a figure caught my eye. She was short, maybe 5'2", and dressed in a strapless yellow sundress, wearing wedge heels, and holding a Chanel bag under her arm. Long dark hair flowed behind her. Even though she was wearing the world's biggest sunglasses, I could still tell it was Luisa. She had this way about her that made her stand out among the masses, and it wasn't just her beauty, nor the fact that she now dressed impeccably well, like a patron's wife.

Unfortunately, Javier was nowhere to be found. When I first met Luisa, I was witness to the warmth and soul she had as she was reunited with her parents in my apartment, but every other time it was a little less and less. I didn't think she was a bad woman by any means, but there had been a hardness creeping into her heart. I suppose that would naturally happen if you were married to someone like Javier.

She stopped right in front of me and I caught a whiff of honeysuckle perfume. She didn't take off her glasses, and she didn't smile. Instead, she looked around her in all directions, checking out everything, including the empty office building, until it seemed she was satisfied.

"Alana," she finally said and only then did she push her sunglasses on top of her head. She looked beautiful but tired. Her eyes, thankfully, were kind, especially as they focused on my bandaged wrist and cast. "Is that from the car accident?" she asked softly.

I nodded. "Yeah. But I'm almost fully healed. Doesn't hurt at all," I lied.

She smiled stiffly and looked around her again.

"Where is Javier?" I asked.

"Are you alone?"

"Of course."

"Where is your boyfriend?"

"Not here," I told her, then quickly added, "In the car."

"We're not going to get to meet him?"

"Then Javier is here," I said.

She nodded. "He is."

I frowned. "But you were sent to make sure the coast was clear?"

"I wasn't sent." She smiled at me. "He didn't have much say. I wasn't about to let him just waltz out here, and he wasn't going to let me either. But marriage takes compromise." Her smile twisted slightly.

"You don't trust me?"

She cocked her head. "I want to trust you, Alana. But this whole thing is so bizarre. It doesn't sound right. You must understand that."

"You think I'm trying to set Javier up?" I asked, feeling hot and indignant. "He's my brother."

"I know that. And you are part of what little family he has left. But if what you are saying is true, then you could have been followed yourself. The only reason anyone is after you, I'm assuming, of course, is because they are after him in some way. Or it could be someone right in front of your eyes. We would be stupid not to take due diligence on this and we are not stupid."

Wow. She was sounding less like a wife and more like a member of his team.

"So where is he?" I asked, scanning the parking lot.

She slipped her sunglasses back on. "He wants you to come meet him. On his terms."

I stared at her blankly. I couldn't leave this spot, not with Derrin watching.

She held out her hand for me and the diamonds on her rings blazed in the sunshine. "Come along, I'll take you there."

"Where?" I didn't want to take her hand.

"Not here," she said. "You're not afraid of your own brother, are you?"

"Is he afraid of his own sister?"

She raised her brow for a second then jerked her chin in the direction of Wal-Mart. "Come."

I sighed, feeling horrible about this. I wasn't afraid of Javier, but being out of Derrin's watch felt wrong and I knew he was probably freaking out—well, as much as Derrin could freak out—up in the office building. I just hoped he didn't try and take Luisa out.

I grabbed her hand and she helped me to my feet. Once I was up, her grip was surprisingly firm which didn't really sit well with me. It was almost as if I were being escorted somewhere.

Somehow I resisted the urge to look over my shoulder in Derrin's direction and kept walking. Even though Luisa had shorter legs, I still had to hustle to keep pace with the cast on.

"That can't be much fun," she noted as she eyed me again. Her voice was softer now, like she was finally being herself and not the wife of Javier.

"None of this is fun," I told her.

She made an agreeable sound then led me toward the Wal-Mart doors.

"He's in there?"

She nodded as the automatic doors opened for us and we entered the world of mayhem again. I was getting really sick of this store.

"This is as safe a place as any," she said, her voice lowered now.

"How is that possible?"

"Who would ever suspect Javier Bernal would be in a Wal-Mart? No one would even recognize him in here because they wouldn't expect to see him. Hiding in a big SUV? Yes. In here, no."

"So he's unprotected."

She led me down the aisles. "No, he's never unprotected. He's never alone. But take a look around and I bet you could never pick any of our men out."

I briefly glanced around. I saw women pushing strollers, slobby looking men with giant beer bellies and trucker hats, short men wearing cheap dress shirts tucked into high-waisted jeans, a guy who looked like he just got back from surfing, store employees in starchy uniforms. They could be anyone. Or she could be bluffing. I would never know. Neither made me feel safe.

In fact, I didn't even recognize my own brother until we were halfway down the canned food aisle. His back was to me and it looked like he was examining a can of beans or something. But of course as I got closer, I knew it was him without a doubt.

Even from behind, he dressed impeccably. His hair was a bit shorter now and not so shaggy at the back. I think last time I teased him that he was close to having a mullet like the redneck Americans do. He must have taken it to heart. Aside from his hair, he was wearing a crisp suit jacket, dark blue with black pants. He wasn't the tallest man in the world, but he had a way of holding his body that could fool you into thinking he was.

We stopped a few feet behind him, and even though I wanted to say something, I knew Luisa was the one who should.

"I've got her," she said.

Got her? And with those words, the blood in my veins took on an icy touch, like I was hooked up to one of the IVs again.

Javier slowly turned his head to look at me, staring at me inquisitively for a moment. He didn't smile, he didn't say anything, he just studied me like I was some sort of imposter. His eyes were burning with that amber intensity they got when he, well, they were always like that.

Finally he looked down at my cast and up again to my face, tilting his head. "You look like you got hit by a truck."

"It was a car," I reminded him.

He raised his brow then idly checked the gold watch on his wrist. "All right, let's make this quick."

I was a bit stunned. I wasn't sure how I could make any of this quick. I wasn't even sure what was supposed to take place.

"Do you want me to explain again what happened?" I asked. Luisa took her hand out of mine but now was holding my arm by the bicep. I looked at her, slightly aghast, but her attention was on her husband.

"Yes," he said simply. He put the can back on the shelf and slipped his hands into his pockets. "From the start. From when you were hit by the car."

Jesus, this was going to take forever, especially since he already knew most of this. But I knew what he was doing. Javier had a way of sucking the truth out of you just by looking at you. He was discerning once and for all whether I was telling the truth or not. It bothered me that he didn't fully believed me yet, but then again I guess he hadn't survived this long by trusting everyone, including family.

I wondered if I would have to start doing the same thing.

But as I told him everything from the beginning, I could see a softening coming into his eyes. He believed me. He could see the truth.

"So you were walking through the town square when the shots happened?"

I nodded. "Yeah. Obviously we didn't notice them."

His eyes narrowed slightly and he exchanged a look with Luisa. "But if these are trained assassins as they seemed to be, how did you not get hit?"

I shrugged. "I don't know. Derrin pulled me in for a hug or something. The ground behind me exploded. Near miss. Then we ran."

"And how well do you know this Derrin? Not at all, right?"

"I know him enough. He saved my life."

Javier smiled, almost smug. For some reason it reminded me of a snake. "So it would seem he did."

I chose to ignore that. "So what do I do now? They're after me because of you."

His eyes turned cold. "So this is my fault, is it?"

"You know what I mean."

"Oh, I know what you mean," he said coolly. "I have no doubt these people want to send me a message. But more than that, I think they mean to deliver the message themselves."

"What does that mean?" I tried to fold my arms but Luisa held tight.

He tapped his long fingers along the cans on the shelf. Somehow they were always so manicured. He must never have to do any dirty work these days.

"It means that it sounds like whatever has happened to you has been part of a more elaborate scheme, to bring someone you don't know into your life. To make you trust them. To make it seem like your life is in danger."

"It is in danger!" I yelled at him. A shopper passing by gave me a quick look before hurrying away.

"Keep your voice down," Luisa warned me.

"Get your hand off me," I growled right back, ripping my arm out of her grasp.

She took a step back, hands in the air, looking to Javier for his orders. He shook his head slightly then turned his eyes back to me.

"Your life may be, but I have no reason to believe that bullet was ever meant to hit you. Same with the car. Same with the motorcycle chase. These people are fake. They are only making it look like they're after you. How else could you explain that you got away?"

Because Derrin is way more than you think he is, I thought to myself. *Even I don't know what he's capable of.*

At that thought I had to wonder where he was right now. Surely he would have come out of the office and trailed me. He had to be watching, but I was too nervous to look around and see.

"So what," I said, "you think that this is all a ruse for me to trust him?"

He nodded sharply.

"And then what? Wait to kill me?"

"Oh, I'm sure he's going to wait to kill you," he said, so casually that it got under my skin. "But that's not a promise. He's waiting for you to come to me. Like you just have. He wants me to take you in."

I shook my head. "No. No, he's the one who didn't like this idea. He wants me to stay with him, he told me it's not safe for me to go off with you."

He tilted his head, considering. "Well, that may be true. My place is no place for a lady."

Luisa cleared her throat in annoyance. He flashed a disarming smile at her. "Luisa, love, you are no longer a lady. You're a queen."

I wrinkled my nose. "Ugh. Cheesy."

He looked to me, not amused. "Whatever would I do without my sister acting like a brat?"

My mouth dropped open. "I am not acting like a brat! I'm scared, Javier. I thought you would help me." I looked to Luisa. "Or at least you. I saved your parents' life, remember? I held on to them for weeks. Do you think that was easy? We were all scared shitless."

Luisa's face momentarily crumpled. There was still a good, kind woman in there somewhere. She was just getting buried by Javier.

She glanced at him. "We should take her in."

"No," Javier said adamantly. "No. This is very clearly a trap. We would take her with us and he would follow. I have no doubt, Alana, that this man is not who he says he is. He is using you to get to me, to who he really wants."

I placed my face in my hands in frustration before throwing them out to the sides. "So then what? You're going to assume something you know nothing about and you're just going to leave me here? With someone you think aims to hurt you, hurt me?"

He frowned and ran a hand through his hair with a sigh. "Don't be so dramatic, Alana. Of course not. I'm just telling you you're not coming with us. I'll make sure you're safe."

"How?"

He took a step closer to me, eyes boring into mine. He could sure be intimidating, I'd give him that. He slipped his hand into his front pocket and pulled out a business card with his first two fingers. He flicked it out to me.

"This is the number I want you to call from the payphone you used earlier. There will be instructions. Call the moment you see us leave. Then go into the women's washroom and wait. Do not leave for anything."

"But Derrin…" I started.

He gave me a caustic smile. "Obviously he will not know of this. Did you not hear what I just said? He is not your boyfriend, Alana. He is not your friend. He is my enemy. He is your enemy."

"Who is he?" I asked, my voice coming out in a whisper.

"I have no idea," he admitted. "But it doesn't matter, does it?"

But it did. It did so much. And at the heart of it all, I knew Javier was wrong.

Wasn't he?

"We'll be in touch," he said, forcing the business card in my hand. When I made a fist around it, he put his hand on my shoulder. He gave it a squeeze and stared at me intently. "I will take care of you, you got that? The only way I know how."

Before I could be touched by this rare show of affection, his gaze slid to Luisa and he straightened up. "Let's go," he said to her.

She nodded, gave me a small smile, and then the two of them walked quickly down the aisle of canned goods, the king and queen of Mexico.

I watched until they disappeared around the corner and into the mass of shoppers.

I felt like collapsing to the ground. The business card in my hand felt like lead, a choice I had to take.

Unless I took none at all.

I slipped it into my pocket.

I didn't want to believe what he said of Derrin, even though some of it made sense. But of course Javier had never met him. He didn't know him. Neither did I, but I at least felt like I knew something about him. I knew he was sincere, and while he might be lying about some things about his past or who he was, I knew that when he was holding me, kissing me, fucking me, that was all real.

He did care about me. I had to trust that.

The question was, could I trust that more than I could trust my own brother?

I slowly walked down the aisle in a daze. Once I got to the doors, I had the option of going to the payphone or of going downstairs to the Camry to see Derrin. Maybe I even had the option of both.

I was almost at the end of the aisle when I bumped into someone with a small basket full of groceries.

"Sorry," I mumbled, and looked up.

It was the surfer-looking guy I had seen earlier. He had a baseball cap pulled down low over his light brown shoulder-length hair, but when he looked down at me I could see his eyes were a very clear hazel, more green than brown. He might have been handsome if it weren't for an ugly scar on the left side of his face.

I immediately averted my eyes, not wanting to stare, and tried to move past.

"No, I'm sorry," he said.

The way he said it, so gravely, made my skin prickle. I paused and looked over my shoulder at him.

He was smiling at me in a way a stranger shouldn't. I was used to men leering at me, but this was different. Besides, it was creepy when men leered at a girl in a cast, like the fact that I was vulnerable and broken turned them on even more.

"Do I know you?" he asked, frowning insincerely.

I wasn't in the mood for pick-up lines, especially from weirdos.

"No," I said, glaring at him. Then I turned around.

"I think I do," he said quietly.

I swallowed hard. I wanted to keep walking. I needed to keep walking.

"Alana Bernal," he added.

Fuck. FUCK.

I should have ran. I should have just ran. But I slowly pivoted around to face him. There was a chance he was with Javier. Luisa said they were all over the store. This was probably one of his men.

"You know my name," I told him, trying to sound casual, hoping he couldn't hear my voice shake. "I should know your name then."

"You probably do," he said matter-of-factly. His grin widened. "I think many people do. If they don't, they will."

He wasn't going to give me his name.

"Do you work for my brother?"

"I work for no one but myself." He slowly reached into his basket of groceries. I didn't wait to see if he was going to pull out a banana. I knew it was a gun.

I turned and leaped to the left, knocking over a display of gravy powder with my cast, and got behind the end of the aisle before a gunshot went off.

It missed me, but brown gravy powder filled the air. I kept running, thankful that the whole store was erupting into extreme chaos. Everyone was suddenly screaming, shoving, crying, running. I was swept up in the mass of shoppers trying to exit, pushing their carts into everyone and everything.

Whoever the fuck that guy was, he definitely wasn't an assassin for hire. He did a pretty shitty job of trying to take me out. But he still tried to kill me all the same, and I had to get out of this fucking store while I could, if I wasn't trampled to death by the mass pandemonium.

There were no more shots, just screams, but even then I was frantically searching the stampede of people for Derrin, Javier, somebody to help me. I didn't know if the man was still behind me, if anyone saw him with the gun, if he was blending into the crowd or being arrested by store security. I didn't know and I couldn't know. There was no time.

I did what I could to get through the crowd and eventually just let the swarm push me to the bottleneck at the doors, everyone packed in tight. People kept stepping on my cast and swearing, but I didn't feel a thing.

Finally I was outside, and I immediately ran down the stairs as quickly as I could to the underground garage.

Down there, other people were running for their cars. It was just as crazy, people peeling out of spots, swiping parked cars, nearly hitting other shoppers. Then at the end I saw Derrin, running toward me.

My heart swelled with relief at the sight of him. This man would protect me. He would keep me safe.

My brother had to be wrong.

"Alana," he said, grabbing my face with his hands. His eyes looked wild. "What happened?"

"There's someone in the store, he looked like a surfer bum. He tried to talk to me, said my name. He knew who I was, Derrin! Then he pulled out a gun. I ran, he fired once and missed. I don't…" I paused to catch my breath, nearly collapsing into his arms, "I don't think he's an assassin, he didn't have the skill. But he still tried to kill me. No doubt."

"And your brother? Where is Javier?"

"Gone," I said just as the sound of screeching tires filled the air. The chaos was growing.

He grabbed my hand, and that alone filled me with strength. "Come on, let's get out of here while we can."

We ran to the car, Derrin literally sweeping me off my feet as a truck almost backed into me.

We made it into the Camry quickly as the doors were unlocked. It didn't really register as strange, just convenient since we didn't have to fiddle with the keys.

I jumped in and Derrin took the keys from me, sticking them in the ignition.

Suddenly proverbial bells started going off in my head.

A warning.

Instinct.

"No," I said just as Derrin turned the keys.

The car stuttered strangely with a loud grinding sound, refusing to start.

"Stop!" I screamed, and he immediately took his hand away, eyes wide as he looked at me.

"The doors were unlocked," I said quickly, barely able to breathe. "I know I locked the doors as I left."

I'd never seen him look so afraid as the realization dawned on him. If he had tried harder, even pushed the key over just a millimeter more, the car would have exploded.

Someone had put a car bomb inside for us.

Someone already knew we were here.

"We have to run," he said, a twinge of panic in his voice.

I'd never heard that panic before.

I nodded. Fear had a net above my head.

We both jumped out of the car and he ran over to me, grabbing my hand and leading me down the parking lane toward the stairs at the end, going against the flow of traffic and people who were leaving. I guess he figured the fastest way out of here was to just get above ground first.

We were almost at the end when the man appeared, the scarred surfer dude with the gun at the bottom of the stairwell, a throng of people on either side of him.

"Shit!" Derrin yelled, and at the same time I said, "That's him!"

The man smiled when he saw us and began to push people out of his way.

Derrin pulled me to the left, darting between cars and then down the lane on the other side in the opposite direction. Suddenly a man appeared at the end, tall and formidable, a stiff face in a stiff suit. He had a gun at his side.

He wasn't here for Wal-Mart's savings.

He fired at us just as Derrin pulled me behind another car. We fell to the ground beside it, glass shattering around us as I covered my head, leaning back against the rear door.

"Stay here," Derrin commanded, pulling out his gun. He got up into a crouch, both hands on the gun. Even throughout all the violence and mayhem, I had to stare at him in awe for a minute. In his cargo pants and white t-shirt, with his buzz cut, steely eyes, and sheen of sweat on his muscles, he looked every inch the man who was going to get me out of here.

My man.

Then the window on the car beside us exploded, glass raining down on us, and I screamed, forced back into this deadly, and very real, game.

Still in a low crouch, Derrin pivoted around the corner of the back of the car and fired at the person behind us. There were two shots and then nothing. With all the noise around us, I couldn't tell if he had hit the guy.

Then there was another shot in the opposite direction, the bullet zinging off the fender of the car on the other side of us.

Derrin looked at me and jerked his head to the right. "Stay down low, hide behind the cars, and go as fast as you can to the exit ramp. The other guy is down, I'll take this guy."

And with that he suddenly sprang up and fired off a few rounds of carefully aimed shots. He swore, obviously having missed, and looked down at me. He was angry now. "Go, dammit! I've got this."

I shook my head, paralyzed by fear. "My cast, I can't crouch like that."

"Fuck," he swore. "I'm sorry."

Then he quickly fired off two more shots. "Reach for my other gun, it's strapped around my calf," he said.

I could at least do that. I quickly pulled up his pants' leg and took another handgun out of its holster. I held it up to him and he placed the one he was carrying in my hand.

"There are two bullets left, use them wisely," he told me.

The gun didn't feel as heavy as I expected it to, and my fingers wrapped around it like a lifeline. I had no idea how to shoot one of these but I wasn't afraid of it. I would gladly use it to protect our lives.

Derrin quickly dropped to a crouch beside me as he slid the hammer back on the other gun. "The scarface guy is still out there," he said, his voice rough and low. "He's hiding behind the concrete pillar. His aim isn't the best and that's what's saving us right now."

"I'm pretty sure you're what's saving us right now," I said breathlessly.

His lips twisted into a grim smile. "We'll see. We have to make a move or he won't come out and we'll be stuck here."

"Someone has to come and stop him. Security."

"I think security has run with everybody else."

"What about Javier?"

He sighed and quickly wiped the sweat from his brow. "If your brother is still here, he's hiding in his car behind bulletproof glass. I'm sorry, Alana, but he would not come back in here to get you."

I had a feeling that was true. It still hurt though.

"Are you ready?" he asked, leaning in closer. "Go left and left again. You run as low as you can and I'll stay up as your shield, all right? When I yell, we'll dart across the lane and keep going till the end. We'll hit the stairwell to the offices. I can open the door and lock it from the inside. The place is empty. It's our way out." He took in a deep breath. "Ready?"

I managed a nod, my grip tightening on the gun.

"Now," he said, and popped back up. Shots were fired in both directions, but I ran hunched down as low and quickly as possible with my injuries. I could feel Derrin right behind me as I turned left at the hood of the car, running flush along the lane. I couldn't help but scream every time a shot was fired off, whether it was from Derrin or scarface. Everything was so much louder down here, so much deadlier. I felt like a rat caught in a maze with several big cats on the loose.

"Head across!" Derrin yelled, now at my side, though in a second he was pivoting around again to take another shot. I darted across the lane, nearly getting hit by a car that suddenly had to slam on its brakes. The person honked, yelling, but the minute they saw Derrin with the gun, they shut up.

We slipped in between cars, ran across another lane, and then finally reached the door to the office stairwell. I was practically flat against it, Derrin pressing me against the door and shielding me as he quickly stuck a makeshift key into the lock with one hand while aiming his gun behind him with the other.

"Hurry." I couldn't help but whimper. The lock didn't seem as easy for him now as it was earlier. Then he dropped the key which clattered loudly on the concrete.

"Fuck," he swore. He gave me a look like he expected me to drop down and get it, but I couldn't do that quickly with my cast. So he rapidly ducked down, and it was at that moment that I saw scarface appear.

He was dead ahead of us, standing between two cars on the other side of the lane, gun raised and aimed right at me.

There was no time for Derrin to stand back up and protect us.

Before I knew what I was doing, I was aiming the gun at scarface, holding it with shaking hands.

Then I pulled the trigger.

The first shot had a bit of kickback and I missed, so as soon as I could, panic and adrenaline coursing through my veins, I pulled the trigger again just as he was about to pull his.

My gun fired, the last bullet sailing through the air, and suddenly scarface howled, tilting to the side. His own gun went off, but at an angle, the bullet hitting the roof above the lane then bouncing back down to the concrete.

I shot him in the fucking leg.

"We're in!" Derrin yelled, now at the lock again and turning the handle. I was too stunned at what I had done—I'd actually hit the guy!—that I couldn't help but be frozen in place, watching as scarface grabbed a hold of his leg, groaning in pain.

Derrin grabbed my arm and jerked me inside the stairwell, the door quickly closing behind us. He immediately locked it, then turned to look at me, the light dim from only one bulb near the top of the stairs.

"You're full of surprises," he said, looking joyous before kissing me quickly on the lips.

"Must run in the family," I said blankly.

He nodded and said, "Come on, we aren't out of the clear yet. You got his leg, but that's only going to make him angry. Leg wounds are like that."

He grabbed my hand and we jogged up the stairs to the top. I held my breath as Derrin put his hand on the doorknob, but to my relief it opened into an empty marble-tiled office lobby. We ran to the front doors, and suddenly we were outside, bathed in the brilliant orange of a slowly setting sun, the sky periwinkle and sprinkled with early stars.

Derrin led me along the back of the building, away from Wal-Mart and the chaos, toward the back fences of residential properties. He opened a back gate and cut through someone's backyard before we found ourselves on a suburban road.

We stopped by a dark green 80s Nissan that was parked by some shrubs, and Derrin, with just a quick glance around to see if any neighbors were watching, opened the driver's side door. It wasn't even locked.

I guess we were stealing this car. I couldn't even protest at this point. I'd just shot somebody.

I got in, and it took two seconds for Derrin to quickly cross some wires underneath. The car started without a problem, and we were off, bolting down the road in a stolen car before pulling onto the highway and getting lost in a maze of traffic. We headed away from Wal-Mart, which was now covered in a sea of red and blue police lights, and in the direction of our hotel.

"You all right?" he asked me as the sun slipped below the horizon. The car reeked of cigarette smoke, which was giving me a headache. I rolled down my window. I wanted to puke.

"I don't know," I said, my eyes focused on the dying light in the sky. It was the truth. I didn't know if I was all right. I mean, I couldn't be. How could anyone be? But at the moment it was all very numb. My heart was still drumming along in my chest, my pulse and breath racing. I felt wired and alive, but dead at the same time, like everything had happened to someone else and I was just feeling the after effects.

I wasn't as stunned as I was the other day though.

"I'm not about to slip into a coma," I told him. "But I don't think I'm a hundred percent."

He nodded, his grip massaging the wheel. "You're doing good. You're doing real good. We're going to get ourselves to the hotel, get our stuff, and leave. We're going to hole up somewhere with a lot of people, maybe Mazatlán. Find a nice beach hotel and hunker down for a few days. We're going to work through what happened. We're going to fix this."

"I don't think we can fix anything," I said, almost to myself.

"We will," he said with pure confidence. "We've seen the enemy now."

"And he's seen us."

"Alana, he's always seen us."

He was right about that.

It wasn't long before we were at the small hotel, quickly packing up our stuff. We were in and out in minutes.

We threw our bags into the back of the Nissan and drove west.

CHAPTER FOURTEEN

Derek

You can sweat, even in dreams. Always in my dreams.

It was a blindingly hot day, the kind that makes you curse the country to the ground. The sun was so strong, so merciless, that it made you wonder how anyone or anything could survive here at all. It was like living on the sun, and everywhere you looked, the glare burned right through your eyes. On those kinds of days, everyone was partially blind.

I had driven Carlos into town, knowing full well what was going to happen. He was exchanging money with Matice Marquez, one of the most powerful men in the Gulf cartel. I knew the money wasn't real. I also knew the drugs Marquez was passing over weren't real either.

Both sides were screwing each other and they knew it. More than that, they welcomed it. This way, someone could be taken out with good reason. Even though the cartels were beyond the law, some of them still run on an odd set of morals. There was a lot of pride and a lot of honor in the way that transactions were handled, in the way businesses were taken over, in the way people were killed. No one was above a bit of torture, but there had to be a good reason for the torture. They would tell themselves anything to make it seem like they were better than everyone else and still pure in the grace of God.

Bunch of delusional pussies, that's what I had thought at the time. It's what I still thought. But I still didn't think anything of it. If Carlos died, it didn't mean I was going to die with him, and it didn't mean he wouldn't have it coming. Carmen and I had discussed for a while now what we would do if I got out of Carlos' clutches. Originally when I had started working for him, I thought it would be easy to leave. But I got too close, and in getting close, he demanded my loyalty. I would only work for him, forever, or until he let me go. And since being let go usually ended with a bullet in the head, Carmen and I had to bide our time.

When I drove Carlos into town, I didn't expect to see so many people. Not just from the cartel, who were loitering very noticeably on the side of the road outside a barber shop, but all the townsfolk in general seemed to be out and about. I remembered something Carmen had said about some Mexican Saint Day earlier that morning, which seemed to explain why everyone seemed dressed up in their Sunday best, even though it was a Tuesday.

"Stay here," Carlos said without even looking at me. I had parked a few yards away from where this was taking place. There was a gun in the glove compartment that I could use if anything went wrong, but I knew he wanted me to be the getaway car.

I sat there, waiting and watching as more people gathered. They all looked the same—high-waisted pale jeans, cowboy or Timberland boots, pastel dress shirts. Some had hats. Some had lariat ties of skinny leather. Their wrists gleamed with gold watches, and their faces bore large aviator shades that reflected the killer sun.

Suddenly, Carlos and Marquez were meeting. I had only taken my eyes away for a second. The exchange went down in the middle of the street, like an old Western, and just like the damn Old West, guns were already drawn on either side. They weren't visible, but I could see them. I could see the blood in their eyes, even beneath their shades.

Usually at this part in the dream Carmen appeared, as she had done in real life. But this time something was wrong. I could see her from far away, walking over to Carlos. But her hair was different. It wasn't this long black mess of curls, but now this wavy, sun lightened hair. The dress wasn't red and white and long, but black and short.

This time it wasn't Carmen at all.

It was Alana.

And she was about to be gunned down.

Before I knew what I was doing, I was grabbing the gun from the glove compartment and running out of the car.

I screamed her name like a banshee and she froze, a deer in the headlights, all long legs and curves, watching as I ran toward her. Like Carmen, she had no idea what was about to happen. Neither Carlos nor I had ever told Carmen what was going on that day. We liked to keep her in the dark as much as possible. Carlos, I'm sure, because he didn't trust her, and me, well I wanted to protect her as best I could. But this time I couldn't. For reasons I'll never understand, Carmen was there that day. Sometimes I wonder if it was to show her a lesson. Sometimes I wonder if it was to show me a lesson.

In this dream, Alana was just as stunned until she realized what she was caught between. Like Carmen, she started to run toward me, when she should have run away from me. She was running toward me because I was her man, the one she loved, the one she wanted to have children with. I was her safety, her solid ground, and her light. I was supposed to protect her.

Alana ran toward me, arms outstretched, seeking my protection from the big bad world.

And as I failed Carmen, I failed her.

The gunfire erupted like fireworks.

Alana screamed as the bullets tore into her from all sides. And yet she wouldn't fall. She was stronger than that. She ran until there was barely anything left to her, skin hanging off in shreds, blood covering her bullet-ridden body from head to toe. Yet she was still beautiful. Still so beautiful, even in the hands of death.

She collapsed at my feet, clawing at my legs in a vain attempt to reach me, in a vain attempt to live.

I couldn't move. I could only stare at her as she looked at me one last time.

"Te amo," she whispered, blood spilling from her mouth before she collapsed dead.

With a start, I woke up from the dream, covered in sweat. Alana was alive and in my bed in this dark, hot hotel room, sleeping soundly in my arms.

I love you too, I thought.

...

"I like this place," Alana said as she peered through her sunglasses at the hotel in front of us. We'd just arrived in Mazatlán after staying the night at a far-flung roach hotel. We had been driving around the beach hotels looking for something simple yet popular. Not too fancy, not too shabby, but some place where we could lay low for a week. People were obviously looking for us, but now that I knew who was doing the looking, we at least had a chance here.

He wasn't as powerful as I had originally thought. Not yet, anyway. That was probably the whole point of it all.

"Then this is the place," I told her, taking the Nissan down the street and around the corner where I found a place to park. We were going to leave the car here, make sure there was no trace of us inside, and then never see it again. It was too risky. When it came time to leave, we'd just take another car, though from where we were there was always the possibility of taking the ferry across the Sea of Cortez to La Paz, or even a boat. The more options, the better.

We got out of the car with our stuff, and as she smoothed a strand of hair off her delicate face, she said, "How are we going to pay for this hotel? It looks like they'd only accept credit cards."

"You let me worry about that," I told her. "Why don't you go around back and hang out by the pool for a bit, and I'll come get you when I have a room."

She nodded, though she didn't look too convinced, and we crossed the street together.

I had told Alana that we needed to stop being Derrin and Alana for a while, and that paying with plastic was the easiest way to get traced. But whipping out another credit card, in another name—Dean Curran—meant having to explain why I had a fake credit card and ID to begin with. If only she knew how many I actually had.

To be fair though, it was pretty obvious that there was more to me than what I had told her. She knew it, she saw it with her own eyes. Yet she was still staying beside me, still trusting me even though I was living the largest lie. She believed I could protect her and save her, and so far I had.

But it wasn't without luck.

Yesterday when she met Javier, I thought I'd lost her. The moment she walked off with Luisa I was certain she would be put in a black SUV and I would never see her again. But to my surprise, they went into Wal-Mart, which was an unpredictable move on Javier's part. No one would have ever guessed a man like him would set foot in a place like that.

It wasn't easy getting a good look at their meeting. The place was crawling with Javier's men, some of whom I actually recognized and could have recognized me if they'd seen me. If that happened, that could have put Alana's life in more danger, and considering I knew now what Javier and she discussed, I had no doubt that's what would have happened.

So I had to stick to the outskirts and trust that she was going to be okay. I loitered around the outside of the store, the parking lot, the parking garage, trying not to pace, to seem suspicious. I was in the parking garage, about to head to the car to wait in there when I heard the screams and saw the stampede of people.

At first I didn't know what had happened to cause all of this, yet all I could think of was that Alana was dead. I had failed her and had failed myself. There would be no redemption here, no second chance at life or at love. There would be only cold, hard failure and a chain attaching me to a life I could never escape.

But then I saw her face, her beautiful, scared but strong face above the masses, and I knew we would get through this. She was better than I had thought—braver, harder.

She ended up proving it time and time again in that garage. We escaped because of her. Because she shot her killer. She shot the man who had hired me to kill her. She shot the man behind it all. The highest bidder.

Scarface was none other than Javier's right-hand man, Esteban Mendoza. It was something I should have seen coming. I had considered him, of course, but my mistake was in immediately dismissing him. I had greatly underestimated that man. Not necessarily in his skill. The man was certainly no assassin. But I had underestimated his resolve and ambition. This was a man that wanted to destroy Javier one step at a time.

He had patience and he had time, and he knew taking Alana out would accomplish that.

And, I was sure, if it didn't, there would be no harm, no foul. Este would try something else to move up the ranks. The man had always been a weasel and his driving force was pure old-fashioned jealousy. Funny how that's always what it comes down to, isn't it? The envy, the desire to have something, a life, a love, a car, a career, that someone else has that they'll do anything to possess it. I had no doubt that Esteban meant to take over the cartel, not by murder or brute force, but by working the system and making Javier as vulnerable as possible.

My problem now was that Esteban knew I had seen him and recognized him. We had worked together a lot, so it was almost like seeing an old friend, albeit an old friend you never liked and thought was annoying as hell. He knew, as I am sure he did before, that I was helping Alana. I wasn't in it to kill her. He knew very well who he was up against and was going to play his cards accordingly.

The other problem I had was that I couldn't exactly tell Alana this. She didn't know who Esteban was and would have no explanation as to how I would know, unless I came clean. While Javier was a public figure of sorts, Esteban wasn't. He was behind the scenes and someone like "Derrin" would not have recognized him. Even Alana didn't. That was my only option. If I could somehow come clean and tell her most of the truth, it might be enough for her to call her brother and tell him. Javier would have Este's balls in a hog's mouth before the end of the day. He never took betrayal lightly. That was one of the few good things about him.

But then there was yet another problem. What if Este was acting on behalf of Javier? Then none of this would do any good and our plans to get out of the country had just gotten a whole lot more complicated. Este only had a certain amount of power on his own, but Javier practically owned the country.

"Have a nice stay, Mr. Curran," the front desk girl said to me with a big, gap-toothed smile. I snapped out of it, took the room key and credit card back from her, and went to find Alana.

...

"So, how *did* you manage to get this hotel room?"

We'd been staying at the hotel in Mazatlán for five days now, and this was the first time this had come up. I'd known it was coming. There was too much silence humming between us these last few days, too much tension and furtive looks. Sometimes I worried she was pulling away from me. Even the sex was feeling more distant when all I wanted was to feel closer to her.

These secrets and lies were becoming too much to ignore. I could only hope that the little slice of truth I was going to tell her would be enough to satisfy her and heal the rift. Once that was dealt with, we could fully concentrate on our next steps. Now, like we had done in the hotel in Puerto Vallarta, we were stuck in some kind of limbo. We were waiting for something, and I didn't know what. Perhaps this was it. Perhaps we were waiting on my honesty.

We were lying on the bed and she was flipping through the TV channels aimlessly. It was pouring rain outside, which was nice for a change, but it kept us inside instead of at the pool or on the private beach. We never went into the town. We stayed as close to the hotel as possible, not risking it.

"Do you really want to know?" I asked, my hand trailing up and down her thigh, pausing at her cast. I knew she needed to see a doctor soon to get this thing off, and something told me we needed it done sooner rather than later.

She nodded then looked over her shoulder at me. "Do you have a fake credit card?"

"Yup," I told her. "Fake ID, too. Driver's license, passport... you name it."

"Why?"

I shrugged, trying to sound casual. "I got into some bad things..."

"Drugs?"

I shook my head. "No. I made some mistakes with the wrong people, let's put it at that. I have some fake identities to use, depending on where I am."

"Where were the mistakes made?"

"Canada," I said, but it pained me to stick with the original lie.

"Are you a wanted criminal there?"

"You could say that," I told her, and her face fell a bit. "I was a bodyguard for some shady people."

"So that's how you know how to do all that stuff," she mused.

I nodded even though there'd never been a mere bodyguard who could do what I do.

"Anyway," I said quickly, "I wanted out and they wouldn't let me out. I stole some money and ran. I made it down to Mexico and here I am."

She pursed her lips. "This is making sense now. How long have you lived here for?"

"Two years," I told her. Again, lying through my teeth.

She straightened up, swinging her legs out so they were crossed over mine. "And that's the whole truth?" she asked, looking me dead in the eye. "You're Derrin Calway?"

Derek Conway. I'm Derek Conway and I'm a mercenary for hire, a trained assassin for the highest bidder. I was ordered to take you out by Esteban Mendoza, your brother's right-hand man, and I was going to, if only you hadn't been hit by that car.

But I only nodded, cool as ice.

"So all the stuff you have with you, the guns," she said. "And the other stuff."

"Other stuff?"

"I know about your other bag."

I guess I'd been sloppy with that. I tried not to look sheepish. "Oh."

"So the other stuff and everything, are you hoping to become a bodyguard down here? Is that why you have it?"

"Yes," I said. "It's really the only thing I know how to do."

"Were you ever a personal trainer? A soldier?"

"Yes to both those things." Finally, something that wasn't a lie.

She seemed satisfied with that but sadness threaded her brow.

"What is it?" I asked.

"I guess I'm just trying to take it all in," she said. "I'm glad you told me the truth, but it adjusts some things, that's all."

"Please don't let it adjust the way you feel about me. Or the way you think I feel about you." I ran my fingers over her soft cheek. She closed her eyes to my touch as I brushed a strand of hair behind her ear.

"How do you feel about me?" she whispered.

"Like I'd do anything for you," I told her softly. "And I would."

"But what about here," she said, reaching forward and placing her hand on my heart. I swear I could feel it grow in size, hot like the sun, just from her touch. "Do you feel anything here? For me? For anyone?"

From the way she said anyone, I could tell she meant Carmen.

I took in a deep breath. "I do. For you. It's complicated."

She nodded, looking away. "I know it is. I can tell. You don't even know me."

"Stop saying that," I told her, grabbing her hand. "I know you. I *know* you, Alana. I've seen you at your worst and I've seen you at your best. And all I want is more. More you, more everything. I want a chance to have you where we can be free and be us and not have to look over our shoulder." I paused. "I'm just...this is new. It's different. It's beautiful."

"Even though we're on the lam and running for our lives?" she said with a crooked smile.

"Yes, even with that. I would rather this than the life I was living before I met you, and there is no lie in that. Even with death at our door, I've never been happier."

I was shocked to hear those words leave my mouth. I'd never even considered what happiness was, that it was a thing that could still affect me and my life. I thought happiness had died with Carmen, and I guess it had. But now it had come back to life. It was here, it was with Alana. Despite everything, I was happy, and that was fueled by knowing it could only get better. Once we made it out of here, once the coast was clear and we could settle somewhere free from fear, my happiness had no bounds.

"I can't say I'm happy," she said, and for a brief moment it stung. She went on, trying to smile. "I can't say it because it's hard to feel it when I'm worried about so many things. But when I'm with you...when it's just you and me, like this, I think I am. I just feel so much, and I wish we could just enjoy it because I think it would be larger than life. The way I feel about you...it almost overcomes what's happening. And it's something I have never ever had." She looked down at her hands, her cheeks growing pink. There was something so vulnerable about her that took my breath away. "I just want to be born anew, start again. Free from this. I want to do that with you."

I couldn't help but smile. I was going to give her that, everything she wanted from me, if it was the last thing I did.

"We could start by taking this goddamn thing off," I said, bumping my knuckles along the cast.

"How?" she asked, making a face. "Is it safe to go to a doctor here? Maybe they know it's something I'd do and they've got spies out there in all the hospitals."

I wasn't too sure Este could arrange such a large operation, especially without Javier knowing, but I couldn't tell her that.

"I've got two hands," I told her. "They can do a lot of things."

She smirked at me, her eyes sparkling. "Oh, I know that." She bit her lip for a moment. "Could you seriously take it off? Don't you need a saw?"

"Well, since you've already discovered that little bag of mine, I actually have a saw in there. I could cut halfway and then rip the rest off."

Actually, I didn't know that for sure but I was sure going to try.

She was considering this. "And it wouldn't hurt?"

"I will never hurt you," I told her.

Minutes later, she was lying on the bed underneath a bunch of towels, her cast propped up under a couch cushion. Being as precise as possible, I cut a line through the cast on the inside of her leg, from the top beneath her knee all the way to her toes. The saw worked hard, whining loudly as plaster dust rose and a sickly burning smell mingled with the air.

She winced the whole time. I was certain I was going to cut right into her bone, but somehow I managed to do a pretty clean job.

"This might feel funny," I told her as I set the saw to the side and poised my hands at the top of her cast. Near the knee was the closest cut, pretty much all the way through, and I hoped it was enough to get a nice tear going through the whole thing.

"If you could not re-break my bones, that would be great," she said, doing an impression of the boss from *Office Space*, only with a Mexican accent.

I grinned at her. "Uno, dos, tres," I said, and then tried to tear the cast apart with all my might. My muscles strained, my hands wanted to slip, but with a satisfying crack the black cast split open with a puff of dust.

"Oh my god," she exclaimed as she stared down at her leg. "My leg is so hairy."

I looked down and smiled. Her leg looked fine. She barely had a tan line. It looked a bit skinny and weak, but considering this was the second cast, it hadn't stunted her all that much. It wasn't like she'd been even close to following the doctor's orders and not used it all. The girl had been running marathons.

"It looks great." I said, slipping the rest of the cast away. "Sexy, even."

She snorted caustically. "I'll give you sexy." Then she went into the bathroom and ran the shower while I cleaned up the remains of the surgery.

She came out twenty minutes later, smelling like coconut soap and dressed only in a towel.

"Ta-da," she said, leaning against the bathroom doorway, her hips swinging saucily to the side.

"Feel better?" I asked, not bothering to hide my roaming eyes.

"I feel like a new person," she said earnestly, coming over to me. She grabbed the collar of my shirt and pulled me in, kissing me on the lips. "Thank you."

I crouched down and ran my hands over her thighs and calves, both of her legs now bare and smooth and golden. "You're perfect," I told her quietly, running my fingers up the insides of her thighs till they met the silky cleft of her pussy. "In every fucking way."

I tugged at the end of her towel until it fell to the ground, exposing her naked body. I leaned forward onto my knees and grabbed her hard at the back of thighs, where the soft skin curved into the swell of her ass. She shuffled forward, her hands resting on the top of my head, massaging it slightly. I groaned at that and groaned more as I pressed my face between her legs and ran my tongue up the insides of her thighs. She was still so damp and fragrant from the shower, it was like licking raw coconut.

I teased her pussy lips with my tongue first, slowly running it back and forth until I used my fingers to part her further. She groaned, her nails digging into my skull, as I dipped the tip of my tongue in, probing at first then sucking her into my mouth.

"Oh god," she said, her breath hitching. "You're going to make me come if you keep doing that."

You wouldn't see my complaining. I didn't stop. I kept at her with my tongue and mouth, sucking at her swollen little clit until she was coming into me. Her legs nearly gave out but I held on to her, keeping her upright.

"How about we see what we can do with this new leg of yours," I said to her as I pulled my mouth away, wiping it with the back of my hand. As usual, her taste was to die for.

"Oh, I know what I've been waiting to do," she said, still trying to catch her breath. I stood up beside her and grinned proudly at her pink cheeks, her dilated pupils, and sated appearance.

"Is that so?"

"Take your clothes off and lie on your back," she said. "I was never able to do this with the cast on, but you're about to get ridden by a cowgirl."

I did as I was told, stripping quickly and lying back on the bed. My dick had been hard since the moment she came out of the shower, and I held its thickness between my fingers, stroking the length lightly. She fished a condom packet out of the bedside drawer and climbed on top of the bed with a saucy grin.

"Allow me," she said while she slipped the condom on. I bit my lip, grinning at the sight.

When it was on securely, I tried to grab for her gorgeous breasts but she swatted me away. Since she immediately turned around, her ripe, round ass displayed in front of me like a bronzed peach, I couldn't complain much.

She grabbed a hard hold of my hard, wonderfully hard dick, and then while propped up in a half-kneeling position, slowly lowered herself onto me. Fuck me, she was so fucking wet that it was like I was being covered in the tightest sheet of the world's softest silk.

"Fuck. Oh, fuck," I hissed between my teeth as she began to move herself up and down. I reached up and grasped her soft hips, holding her tight, fighting the urge to fucking impale her on me. God she was so fucking good at this.

"Don't stop," I managed to say. She shot me a look over her shoulder and began to lightly stroke my balls as she fucked me.

I'd always been good with my stamina before, but this time I had no power, no control.

"I'm going to come so hard," I moaned.

"Yeah, you fucking are."

That was enough. My balls tensed up as I balanced on that edge between pleasure and oblivion. Then I was over, falling, drowning in a million emotions, a million feelings. This was all so much, and as I pumped my cum hard into her, feeling like I couldn't stop coming if I tried, I realized how in deep I was. Not just physically but in every other way.

I had tried to play it cool with her tonight, to skirt around my real feelings. It wasn't easy to admit out loud that I was falling in love with someone else. It wasn't easy to give yourself over when you didn't even know who you were half the time. It wasn't easy to start again when you had lost so deeply.

But this was beyond what was easy. This wasn't something I had a choice in. I was in love with Alana, and it was going to take every part of me, but with any luck, she would give every part right back. She would give me my humanity.

The next time we talked, I would have to tell her. I could only hope my love was something she wanted.

I hoped our love could survive the lies.

...

The next morning we made our plans. We would stay in Mazatlán two more days, then head up north in a rental car. By then, Esteban shouldn't be looking for us around this area, if he was even looking at all. He would most likely assume we had fled the area, but I liked staying close to the scene of the crime, where they wouldn't expect. We would then take the rental car up to a smaller border crossing going into Arizona, return it there, and catch a bus across. The only problem was that Alana didn't have any ID on her, and it was too risky to call someone like Luz and get them to mail her passport. No doubt her apartment was still being watched and that would only put her friends in danger.

I decided I would email my old friend Gus, someone who owed me a big favor, and see what he could do for her. There were illegal ways into the US that I knew he might help with, too, but we wanted to do everything as legit as possible. Alana wasn't even all that keen on the idea of having a fake identity, but I wanted to at least make sure her last name was changed. If it got out at all anywhere on the news or in DEA channels that she was Javier Bernal's sister, there was a chance she wouldn't be allowed in the US and could even be detained.

While she was out at the pool, determined to tan the shit out of her now free leg, I sent the email to Gus from the free computer in one of the hotel's business stations, mentally crossing my fingers. I hadn't seen the guy since I helped rescue him from Javier's safehouse, all on behalf of Ellie Watt and her boyfriend Camden McQueen, but I hoped he was okay, and most of all, willing to return favors.

I went and grabbed a beer from the bar and came back to the room, glad that no one had taken my spot. I checked my email, thinking maybe Gus had already responded.

There was a new email in my inbox, but it wasn't from Gus.

It was from "A friend" and the subject simply said, "Nice to see you again."

I sucked in my breath. It felt cold in my lungs. I already knew who this was from and what it was about.

I clicked it.

It read:

Hello, Derek, or should I say Hola? You've been living here in the country for so long now, I guess it doesn't really matter.

It was nice to see you last week. You haven't really changed since we last were together, though maybe you've lost a few pounds. Still have that meathead look going for you, though, but I was pleased to see that you knew how to take a shot. Not that you hit me. That was your girlfriend, Alana. Perhaps that explains why you failed to kill her in the first place. Maybe you're not as good as you used to be. Well, you know what they do with old racehorses, don't you? Send them to the glue factory. Yes, I wouldn't mind that happening to you—I'd mail Alana my condolences and use your glue to seal the envelope.

Or perhaps she's the problem. Somewhere between you accepting the job and the money (remember, you still have our deposit), you decided to fall in love with her. Or maybe you fell in love with fucking her. It's all the same, isn't it? I know what it's like. I met a girl once, too, nice thing, had a husband. It wasn't to be but we had our fun. You're having fun now, aren't you? So much younger, different, than that wife you once had. Plus there's that element of danger that gets you all hard. I know all about that. You're fucking the person you were hired to kill. Don't you think that might bite you in the ass one day, like one of those mosquitos you just can't kill? Or maybe not. Maybe this will all blow over. Maybe this will all end and I'll go away. Just like the mosquito does when you fail to kill it.

Only it doesn't, does it? Derek, Derrin, or whatever name you are using right now, I don't think you quite realize what you've done. You think you're helping this poor girl find her freedom, but you're only bringing her to her death. Doesn't she know what kind of person you are? Oh right, she doesn't. Even with Javier's warnings, she still chooses to believe in you, in the person she wishes you were. Sure, you're protecting her right now but you dug her grave the moment you signed on to the job. You may not think you're pulling the trigger anymore but you are. You have been this whole time.

Of course, like last time, I have a backup plan. I was concerned that you wouldn't do the job I hired you to do, and that's why I had the man in the car on hand. His instructions were to hit her if you didn't take the obvious shot then drive away. I would have paid him the remainder of what I owed you.

I suppose the poor soul panicked. That's what I get for hiring the locals. And I really didn't see that vigilante side of you coming out. My, that was like something out of a movie. Well done.

Here's what I want from you. I like you, Derek. That's why I hired you. I knew you were a man who got shit done, and I'd still like to believe that, despite all your hesitations. It's harder now, after all you've done, to still trust you, to trust you're the man you've been building up all these years. But I like to believe the best in people. I'd like to believe that you still can come around and do what you were meant to do.

You have twenty-four hours, Derek. Put the bullet in her head or something much, much worse will befall the both of you. You'll still get your money, after all, I'm the one that's fair here. You'll get to walk away, and then you can decide if you can be a better person. Though I suspect you'll end up right where you started. That's the thing about people like us. The people that do the dirty work, the dirty deeds. We can't really escape what we are meant to do. All we can do is become better at it. In the end, you can be the best by doing your worst. In the end, I can do the same. In fact, I am.

Kill her and kill her now, like you promised to do. It will all be over soon.

All my best,
A friend.

It was from one of those email addresses that was just a bunch of numbers. I was sure that even if I replied, it wouldn't go anywhere. There was nothing to say anyway, nothing that even surprised me about this, except that Esteban was even crazier than I thought he was. Of course there was nothing here to prove he sent it, but I knew. I knew that face, that scar, the laid-back attitude that apparently harbored the world's most dangerous grudge. I should have known the voice, too, from when I first talked to him, but I'd never even imagined him in that position.

The man had ambition. Too bad I couldn't find it admirable. I deleted the email and sat there for a moment, stewing over my options. It was an email and I had opened it. It didn't say anything about where I was. I didn't really think there was a chance he knew where we were, but I couldn't be too sure.

I had twenty-four hours to kill her which meant we had twenty-four hours to get out of here.

We had to do better than that. When Alana got back from the pool, I'd tell her we were leaving tonight, getting a rental car, and heading up north. We'd figure out our steps with Gus from there. We couldn't take any chances here. I didn't know what kind of technology Este had at his fingertips, but if there was even a chance he could trace where the email had been opened, I couldn't take that risk. I'd obviously underestimated him before. I wasn't going to do it again.

I went back up to the room and quickly packed all of our bags. Then I hopped in the shower and tried to think about what to do. I had only been there a minute when I heard someone in the room.

"Alana?" I called out cautiously, sticking my head out of the water.

"Yup!" she called back, her voice muffled. "Hey, why are all the bags packed?"

I quickly jumped out of the shower, dripping all over the floor, and opened the bathroom door. She was wearing a bathrobe over her bikini, holding a margarita in one hand, and staring at the bags with worry.

"I thought we should move on tonight," I told her with what I hoped was an easy smile.

"Why?"

"Better to be unpredictable."

She chewed on her lip for a moment before sighing and taking a huge sip of her drink. "And I was just starting to like it here."

"You'll like San Diego more," I told her. "Trust me."

She smiled at that and I told her I'd be right out.

I got back into the shower and had just rinsed the body wash from me when I thought I heard a knock at the door.

"Alana?" I asked again, turning the taps off and listening.

I heard the front door shut then quickly wrapped a towel around me, heading out into the bedroom.

Alana was standing by the front door, dressed in jeans and a tank top now. She was holding a large envelope in one hand and a stack of what looked like 8x10 photographs in the other. Her hands were shaking.

"Who was that?" I asked, coming over to her. "What is that?"

She looked up at me in absolute horror. After everything we'd been through, I'd never seen that kind of look on her face. It was of utter destruction, of deepest, darkest fears coming true.

"Who are you?" she whispered.

I took a step toward her but she shrieked, "Get away from me!" The sound ripped so loud out of her throat that I froze to the spot.

I raised my hands, everything inside me growing quiet and still, waiting for the blow.

"Alana..."

She held something up.

It was a photograph of me outside the fence to the Aeromexico employee parking lot. My gun was out and aimed in her direction. It was taken from the side and clear as day.

My attempted assassination.

It was all over.

CHAPTER FIFTEEN

Alana

I couldn't believe it. Of all the things that had happened to me recently, this was the one that was about to push me over the edge. This was the one that was spearing me, stabbing me, burning me deep inside. I felt like whatever good things I had inside me were being torched to the ground and in its place only ugly ash could remain.

I was holding in my hands a bunch of photographs that placed Derrin at the scene of my car accident. Worse than that, it placed him there with a gun in his hand. A gun aimed at my fucking head.

When the bellhop knocked at the door and handed me an envelope he said had come for this room, I didn't think anything of it. I thought maybe it was a package for a local tour or coupons for our stay. Maybe even our bill so far.

But when I opened it, I opened a world of lies and betrayal. I opened the end of us.

I couldn't tear my eyes away, even when Derrin came around the corner. Though his name wasn't Derrin, was it? Of course not. Everything, everything had been a lie. My brother was right.

"Who was that?" he asked. I could feel him pause. "What is that?"

I could barely speak. I looked up at him, and I saw someone totally different. I saw someone who wanted to kill me.

"Who are you?" I asked, my voice weak.

Frustration passed over his eyes and he came toward me.

"Get away from me!" I screamed, panicked, ready to keep screaming, to fight for my life.

He stopped where he was and swallowed hard.

"Alana," he said.

I held up the photograph that showed just who he was. Then I held up another. And another. All taken from multiple angles, all showing him parking outside the chain-link fence to the lot, taking out his sniper rifle, the very one he was going to use yesterday, and waiting. There was a shot of me exiting my car. It felt like so long ago, and through the photographs it seemed like fiction but it wasn't; it was truth. I finally had my truth.

"Why?" I cried out, my hands curling over the photographs in anger. "Why didn't you just kill me then?"

"Let me explain."

I gave him a cold smile. "Let you explain? What can you possibly say that would make this better?"

He seemed to think about that for a moment. And a moment was all I needed.

I threw the photos at him, whipped around, and grabbed the door handle. I ripped the door open, about to slide my body out when suddenly it was slammed shut, nearly taking my arm with it, as Derrin, my assassin, shoved his hands against it.

I opened my mouth to scream for help, but his hand went over my mouth, holding tight over my nose as well until I couldn't breathe. I was just sucking his palm to my mouth. He quickly grabbed me from behind and lifted me up, spinning me away from the door.

I tried vainly to fight, to kick, to get out of his grasp. My eyes darted around the room, wondering what I could use as a weapon. There were plenty of guns and even a knife on the dresser. It was a long shot, but if I could break free...

I tried to maneuver my mouth under his hand until it had more mobility, then I chomped hard on the heel of his palm, drawing blood.

He grunted but didn't let go. He pressed his palm harder against my mouth.

"I'm not going to hurt you," he hissed, "but you can hurt me all you want. I'm not letting go, either. I'm going to explain what happened."

I tried to cry out in frustration, his blood now spilling down my chin, but he picked me up then put me down on the bed. I kicked beneath him, trying to knee him in the groin, but his thighs gripped mine like a vice.

"I'm not going to hurt you," he said raggedly as he pushed his hand on my mouth harder, the back of my head being pressed into the pillow. His eyes were wild, crazy. I was afraid of him, I guess as I always should have been. Was he going to rape me? Assault me? Break my neck? I'd found out the truth now, and those who know the truth are always the first to die.

"Alana," he said, his face above mine. I still tried to move but he kept me firmly in place. There was no escape. "Alana, listen to me."

He moved his hand further down my mouth so I could breathe better through my nose. I sucked in air hard, hoping it would give me clarity even though I didn't want to hear what he was going to say.

"My name is Derek Conway," he said, and now, *now* I could see he was being truthful. This was who he was. "I'm from a small town in Minnesota. I grew up playing hockey, had a few chances to make the leagues. Hockey, personal training, those things were my life. Then I decided to join the army. I needed to get away from home, out of the house, out of the life that was slowly killing me. I was shipped out to Afghanistan. Everything I told you about what happened there is true." He paused, his eyes searching mine, beads of sweat dripping off his forehead. I could taste his blood in my mouth. "Are you following?"

I stared at him but didn't give him any other indication that I was.

"I came back home a changed man. I was disillusioned with my country, with everything. I packed up and left it all behind, came down to Mexico so I could start over. And I did. I fell in love with the place, the people. I fell in love with Carmen. I had run out of money and started working for her brother. He was in a fledgling cartel, and I was his bodyguard. It was great at first but then I became more than that. One day there was a showdown of sorts between two cartels. Carmen got caught in the middle. She was gunned down, repeatedly. I saw the whole thing."

His eyes didn't start to water but I could see the pain reflected in them. I knew he wasn't lying about this, but I wasn't about to let this affect me. This man once had a gun to my head. This man had tried to kill me.

"It was like a second war for me. Again, I changed. This time I let it ruin me even further. I became a gun for hire, an assassin, a mercenary. I would do the dirty work for whoever needed it, and I was loyal to whoever paid me the most."

I felt like an idiot. I should have realized this all along. The fact that he was a white American, and one I was stupidly in love with, had thrown me off.

"And I did the work. I did bad things. Very bad things. I killed many people, most who probably deserved it and some who probably didn't. None of it mattered as long as I got paid. A lot of the work I did for your brother, Javier."

My eyes widened, not seeing this coming at all. I was also scared of what he might say.

"When he split from Travis Raines' cartel," he continued, "there was a lot of blood that needed to be shed. A lot of retaliation. Do you understand? For things that were done. What was done to Beatriz and her family was one example."

Oh my god.

"I put the bullet in Travis' head. It was Javier's order, but I carried it out. Justice aside, that allowed Javier to take over the business. After that, it was the last time I saw your brother. I betrayed him by helping his ex-girlfriend, Ellie, and her boyfriend escape the Raines' compound. It was nothing personal, they were paying me well, and my job with Javier was over." He closed his eyes and his body relaxed slightly. I lay still, wondering if I should make a move.

He went on. "After I helped Ellie, her boyfriend, and her father out, I was in Acapulco for a few weeks, trying to figure out what to do with my life. I felt like I had done a good thing in helping them, even with the money, and I wondered if I had the strength to move on. To leave the life behind. To return to the United States and find someone else to love, to marry, to raise a family with. I wanted to escape the death. I wanted to kill the person I had become. My own assassination. But I didn't. I couldn't. I was sucked back in for a few more years. Every day was another slog through purgatory and one step closer to hell."

There was so much breaking inside of Derrin's—Derek's—eyes that it was making it hard to concentrate, to get away. But I needed to, I needed to. The more I heard from him, the harder this would be.

"So I did what I did. One day, I was in Cancún, and I got a call from a man I didn't really recognize. He sounded green, new at the game, though, which made me suspicious. He wanted you dead and for one hundred thousand dollars." I gasped against his palm. "He didn't tell me why. They never do. But I agreed to do it. I agreed to kill you." He licked his lips, his breaths coming heavy now. "But then I saw you. I saw you that day, and…I knew it was wrong. Then you were hit by the car and suddenly the job didn't matter anymore. Only you mattered, Alana, you and justice and making things right. So I drove after the guy who hit you. I made him pull over and I shot him in the head. I killed him because he tried to kill you and get away with it. I was your so-called angel."

But if the car hadn't hit me? If it hadn't hit me, he would have killed me. The image from the photograph was burned into my mind. That was a picture of a man who aimed to kill.

"Obviously I was set up from the beginning, to be the fall guy if anything went wrong. And it did go wrong. I got another call and the man wanted to pay me twice the amount. Two hundred thousand dollars. Said I could even keep the deposit. I told him no, though. It was messy, it was wrong, and I wanted out. He told me there was no out. Not for me…" he looked away, "…and not for you."

I could feel my eyes welling up with tears. Suddenly all the fight had drained out of me. It was all true. All of it.

"Alana, please," he whispered, taking his hand away from my mouth. I couldn't even scream. My mouth curled up as my lungs hardened, the tears choking me deep inside. I couldn't breathe, I couldn't do anything but try and keep the horrible sadness inside.

"Please," he said again. "Don't cry. Don't. I know I messed up. I know you think I'm horrible, and I am a horrible person. I'm a bad man. I'm no better than the worst. But please, please know that I couldn't do it. I couldn't kill you, not for all the money, not for anything. I would never hurt you."

"You lie!" I cried out, a sob ripping out of me. "You're hurting me right now, to the bone!" I turned my head away from him, my eyes shut tight as tears spilled out of them and onto the pillow. I felt so stupid, so foolish, so fucking alone. I was alone again like I always was.

The man I loved was only here because he tried to kill me. The man I loved never loved me at all.

I had nobody now. I never did. Not my brother, not my friends. I was as good as dead.

"Why didn't you kill me?" I sobbed. "Why didn't you kill me?"

"I couldn't," he said, his voice ragged. "I couldn't do it."

"You should have. You should have pulled the trigger and ended this!" I screamed the last part then collapsed into sobs. I felt like my body was being torn apart, my lungs and heart and breath all squeezed by the sorrow that was running so violent and deep.

"Alana," he said, burying his face into my neck. He was shuddering against me, trying to breathe himself. "I fell in love with you."

"Liar!" I yelled.

"No," he said, shaking his head. "No. I'm not lying. I love you. I love you, and I would have told you the truth but I didn't know how. I was too afraid to lose you. Alana, please, I can't lose you."

I put my hands up to his chest and tried to push him off me. "You've already lost me."

"No."

I blinked, trying to look through my blurry vision at him. His own eyes looked blurry too.

"Let me go, whatever your name is."

"It's Derek," he repeated, grabbing my arms and holding me tight. "It's Derek Conway and I am not going to let you go. I'm not going anywhere."

"I'll scream," I warned him, not kidding. "I'll scream and get you thrown in a Mexican jail and then what the fuck are you going to do, huh?"

Panic shone in his eyes, their blue color so hard and cold above me. "Alana, listen to me. You can hate me for lying but don't hate me for loving you."

"I hate you because you tried to fucking kill me!"

"But I didn't!" he roared in my face. "And I've been trying to keep you alive ever since! Do you think it's easy to lie, to worry if the person you love loves you or the lie? Do you think I didn't wrestle with the truth every fucking day? Well I did, when I wasn't trying to figure out how to keep us both alive."

His words meant nothing to me now. None of this meant anything to me. He didn't kill me, but in the end it would still come, whether it was from his gun or someone else's. In the end I would still die alone, in a dark, sharp place.

I was empty, I was nothing.

I needed to leave.

But his hold was strong. "No," he said shaking his head. "I will not let you go. The man who sent you those photos knows where we are. He is Esteban Mendoza, and he's the right-hand man of your brother. I know him, I've worked with him. He's trying to ruin Javier, bit by bit, starting with you. When you're out of the picture, he'll go after Marguerite maybe, or Luisa. But he'll get rid of everyone. He'll do this until Javier is run into the ground."

That got my attention. I was sure I'd heard Javier mention Esteban a few times, but I had never met the guy. If this was true, I had to tell Javier. But Javier would want to know who I'd heard it from, and when that came out...

"Your brother has to know," Derek said. "And we have to get out of here."

"I am, without you."

"Don't be stupid!" he yelled, his face going red. "You won't leave here alive if you do. I promised to protect you."

"Yeah well, promises don't mean anything coming from someone like you!" I yelled back. "A liar. A killer. A murderer." I clamped my eyes shut in frustration. "Shit! Shit!" Even though I didn't trust him, I knew he was right. Someone was setting him up, framing him for exposing the truth. They wanted Derek to get in trouble, for me to not trust him. They wanted to put his ass out there. But whatever way it was worded, someone knew we were here. Whether Esteban was the one behind it or it was a lie that Derek concocted to keep me here, I was fucking screwed.

Then I remembered the business card Javier had given to me. I had one more chance.

I swallowed hard and looked up at Derek with pitiful eyes.

"Please let me go."

He shook his head. "I can't."

"You have to."

"I will protect you to the very end. Alana, I'd lay down my life for you."

I narrowed my eyes at him, feeling sorrow and hatred and bitterness choke out whatever love I might have felt. I had to snuff it out before it hurt me. Love was only dangerous now. Love would get me killed. "Your life means nothing to me," I said.

He looked like I had slapped him. I felt like I had slapped myself too.

But he had to let go of me.

"Let me get away, Derek. If you care about me at all, you'll let me get away."

"I can't do that. Please. I have to save you."

I let out a caustic laugh. "Save me? I think you're still waiting to pull that trigger. Now, let me go or I will scream. And if you try and stop me, I will make you hurt me. You say you don't want to but you will if you don't let me walk out this door right now."

"If you walk, you're as good as dead," he said, but there was a resignation coming over his face. I was wearing him down, ruining him as he once wanted to ruin me.

"Then let me die by choice, and let me die alone," I said. He relented and I managed to quickly slip out from under him.

Actually, I was surprised that he let me go so easily. Perhaps he had been telling the truth all along.

I stood there, breathing hard and watching him on the bed. For once he looked absolutely fragile, this big beast of a man who seemed seconds from breaking down.

But I couldn't care about that. He was an assassin, a liar, and it didn't matter if he had kept me alive this long. I would have to figure out the rest on my own, with someone I could trust.

I grabbed my duffel bag that had fallen off the bed then quickly reached into his, taking out a small handgun. I aimed it at him. "You know I can shoot this thing now."

He swallowed thickly but nodded.

"Let me leave as is and I won't pull the trigger. I won't scream. I won't get you locked away. I know that even though you were hired to kill me, you have protected me so far. You've at least kept me alive." At that my voice started to shake, and so did my hand. I took in a deep breath to steady myself, blinking fast. "I don't wish you any harm." Now my lower lip was trembling. Damn it. "I don't wish you any harm, but I can't be with you anymore. I can't trust you. I'm sorry."

Derek slowly shook his head. "Please, Alana. I'm sorry. I'm sorry."

And, oh god, I could see that he was. Tears spilled down my cheeks. "Let me get away."

He stared at me, his jaw clenched, his whole body tense. Then he nodded. "Okay. Okay. Keep the gun. Use it well, all right? If you can go to—"

"No," I said quickly. "Don't tell me anything. Let me do this on my own. You stay in here for twenty minutes. Don't come out or I will go straight to security, you understand?"

"Yes."

"Goodbye, Derrin. Goodbye, Derek."

He didn't say anything back, he just stared at me like he was watching me die. And I suppose he was.

With the gun still trained on him, I left the room. The door shut behind me with a heavy click and I was out in the hallway. I waited by the door for a moment, prepared for him to come straight after me. But he didn't.

I couldn't chance it. I hurried to the elevator, and once inside, stuck the gun in my bag. Once I hit the lobby, I glanced around for anyone suspicious, anyone who could have sent the photographs, and when I didn't see anyone, I ran over to a courtesy phone by a bunch of couches.

I picked it up and fished the business card out of my jeans. I dialed the number on it as per Javier's instructions, and then I waited.

"Hello," a man answered. He sounded kind of young. "Who is this?"

"Who is this?" I hoped I didn't have to get sucked into another one of these stupid games over the phone. There was absolutely no time for that.

"Juanito," the guy said, and I sighed with relief.

"Juanito, this is Alana Bernal."

"Ah, Alana," Juanito said. "Javier will be happy. He was very worried about you. He thought you were going to call last week."

"Something came up. I need to see him now."

"I will go tell him, can you hold?"

"Yes."

I waited about two nerve-racking minutes while Juanito was gone. I kept looking around the lobby, staring at everyone. People were staring right back at me, probably because I looked scared shitless and my eyes were puffy from crying. But these were just ordinary people. They weren't assassins. And they weren't Derek.

Finally he came back on the line. "Alana, where are you?"

"I'm at the Crowne Plaza in Mazatlán."

"Okay, good," he said. "Hold on." I waited while I could hear him typing in the background. "Listen, I'm going to come pick you up but you have to meet me, all right? Just go to the corner of Marina Mazatlán and Sábalo Cerritos. It's a few blocks away. Stay where you are, around people, in the lobby of the hotel. Don't talk to anyone, don't go with anyone. We'll be there in an hour."

"Okay," I said, feeling panicked all over again. What about Esteban? Was Derek right about that? "Will it be you picking me up?"

"Yes," he said.

"Where is Javier?"

"He's not here right now."

"Okay," I said quietly. "What about Esteban?"

"Esteban?" he asked, sounding surprised. "No, Esteban isn't here. I think he's with Javier. Why?"

"No reason," I said, feeling slightly relieved. "Will you take me straight to Javier?"

"Of course I will, those are my orders. He wants to make sure you are safe and I will do just that. He will be happy to know you have called."

"Okay."

"I'll be driving a white SUV. We'll stop and get you. I'll have men with me to watch over you and make sure you're coming alone. These were Javier's instructions if you were to call. We'll bring you back here and you'll be safe, understand?"

"Yes, I understand."

"Be safe," Juanito said, and hung up.

I sighed, and when I tried to return the phone to the cradle, I dropped it. My hands were shaking. I didn't know if I could wait for an hour in the hotel, even if I was around people, knowing that Derek was upstairs.

He hadn't come for me yet, and to be honest, it worried me. I was torn up inside, knowing deep down that Derek would never harm me, not now, but also knowing he was once paid to. Our relationship, my love for him, was built on lies. How could I be sure that the good, brave man I saw was the real him. What if that was the lie? What if all the wonderful things I saw in his soul were nothing but an illusion and I was duped into it by big muscles and hot sex?

My heart told me it was real. But the heart is what gets people killed. I knew I would die at some point for some reason or another, but I would never let it be over my heart.

I stepped away from the phone and walked out of the lobby and into the sunshine. I decided to wait at the hotel next door instead, which wasn't as nice. Finally when the time was ready, I headed down the street. I was still surprised to see that Derek hadn't followed me, but then again, it had been his livelihood to stay invisible.

There was barely any traffic on the road, so it was quite obvious when the big white SUV came barreling toward me. Aside from some people at the beach across the street, there were no other pedestrians either, so it was quite obvious who I was.

The driver of the SUV rolled down his window. He had a full face, maybe even younger than mine, but I could tell he was a bit of a heavyweight.

"Get in," he said.

"Are you Juanito?"

I think he nodded. He jerked his head at the back door which then popped open. "Get in," he repeated.

I took a deep breath, put all my faith in my brother, and got in the SUV.

There was a man in the back staring out the window, and another man in the passenger seat doing the same.

I gingerly sat down beside him, and he turned to look at me. He had bright brown eyes and a narrow face, almost lupine in its quality.

"Shut the door, if you please," he said to me.

I leaned over and shut it. The locks immediately clicked and the SUV sped away. I studied the guy more closely.

"Are you Juanito?" I asked.

"Put on your seatbelt," he said. "And no, I'm Benny."

"Benny," I repeated. Meanwhile Benny was looking behind him. "Are you sure you weren't followed?"

I didn't know what to say to that. "Well, I'm not sure, but I don't think I was."

"And the man you're with, you told Javier you had a boyfriend. Where is he?"

I shrugged. "I don't know. Not with me. I left him."

"Why?"

"Because I couldn't trust him."

He seemed to mull that over. Then he sat back in his seat and stared out the window again.

Silence choked the car.

I had a bad feeling. My mind was so frazzled and I was so lost that I was doing, moving, acting without thinking. I was operating on panic now, ever since I left Derek. But the bad feelings, well those were instinctual. Those are the feelings you should always listen to. I eyed the bag I brought with me, thinking about the gun inside. If something went wrong, would I have enough time to grab it? Would I even stand a chance against these three men?

"Where's Juanito?" I asked, trying not to sound as nervous as I felt. I nodded at the man in the front seat. He still hadn't turned around, and I couldn't see his face in the mirrors. "Are you Juanito?" I asked him, raising my voice so he knew I was talking to him.

He turned his head just enough for me to see a scar on the side of his cheek, made all the more prominent by the fact that he was smiling.

My blood ran cold.

"No," the man said. "Juanito couldn't be here, so I decided to help him out today with this little chore." He fully turned his head my way, and I found myself looking into the very eyes of the man I had shot. "I'm Esteban. Esteban Mendoza. And I believe we've met before."

Without thinking, I made a move for my bag but Benny was fast. I felt a heavy crack on the back of my neck and the world went dark.

CHAPTER SIXTEEN

Derek

I was a stupid man. A stupid, broken man.

I should have seen it coming. I should have known the lies would be exposed and I would lose her. I just didn't think it would happen now, before she had a chance to be saved. I figured it would happen down the line, maybe a few weeks, maybe months or years, when my heart would be shattered but at least her life wouldn't be.

But I was a fool. Fooled by love, of all things. And now it had cost us everything.

I wanted to stop her from leaving. I tried. But when she started to cry underneath me, it absolutely wrecked whatever resolve I had. That reserve of sorrow, that darkness that hid deep inside her, the one that came out when she cried in her sleep, lost to nightmares that were once real, was taking over. She was ruined and utterly devastated by my lies, by the things I had done and the person I wasn't supposed to be, and while I saw her heart break open before my eyes, mine was doing the same.

There is no pain like heartache. I thought I had forgotten all about it, left in those aimless dusty days after Carmen had died. But it came back with a vengeance, as bright as day. It was merciless and brutal and cut you from the inside out, making it feel like you never had a heart, that you've always just had this cold black space in your chest. You can almost feel the wind whistling through you when it gets really bad, carving through those hollow places.

Losing love is lonely. Losing it because of something you did is deathly.

And to see it happening to the person who had your heart, there's nothing worse than that. We were both hurting, and hurting so badly. So when it came down to it, I had to let her go. I couldn't make her suffer anymore, and to be more selfish, I couldn't bear to witness it.

What I needed, though, was for her to believe me. Believe that after everything, I had her best interests at heart—that I always had. And that we had a common enemy, one that could never be trusted. Esteban would be after her the second she stepped out of here, so even though I knew I couldn't protect her where she could see it, I would still try to protect her all the same.

I would protect her to the end, just like I promised, or die trying.

See, even though I knew that I was a stupid man, blindsided like a fool in love, I had still planned for something. A few days ago when Alana was on the beach, I went through her clothes and made tiny insertions in the inner side of all the cups of her bras, near the underwire. There I placed a tracking device that was hooked up to an app on my phone. The device could be activated remotely, and when I was pleading with her earlier, trying to mend us back together, I noted she was wearing her black bra with her grey tank top.

The moment she left the room, I started tracking her. I tracked the blinking red dot downstairs into the lobby and then to the hotel next door. By then I was already stealing a Mazda around the corner and waiting for her next move.

It was obvious she had been picked up in a car by her speed on the app, and I assumed it was probably bad news. She'd probably called Javier from the lobby and he sent someone to pick her up. My money was that Esteban somehow intercepted or got wind of the call and stepped in. This theory was only confirmed once I saw her location move away from the highway that would lead toward Culiacán and head toward the marina instead.

Though there were a lot of marinas in Mazatlán, as well as ports for ferries and cruise ships, her blinking red dot went all the way to a large yacht club on the south shore near the lighthouse hill.

Even though Javier had a yacht, I would bet all my money she was being taken by Esteban away from Javier's compound. Out on the seas, a lot of things could happen, and considering Este was frustrated now, I feared that whatever he had planned for Alana was far worse than me being hired to shoot her in the head.

And so this became a suicide mission.

I drove the Mazda all the way to the marina in time to see a large superyacht leaving beyond the jetty. I looked through my binoculars and saw that it was indeed Javier's, ironically named Beatriz. The sailboat was massive mega-ketch, a 187-foot, 550-ton Royal Huisman. The two masts stuck high into the sky while the navy body glistened above the waves. I couldn't see any crew on board at all except someone at the controls. That's how I knew it wasn't Javier. He liked to travel with a large crew, complete with their own uniforms. He was the king of flaunting everything he had.

This was an undercover operation. Javier may or may not have known about Este taking the boat, but in the end it didn't really matter. He had, and he was heading out to sea with Javier's sister.

A part of me wanted to throw caution to the wind and tell Javier that Este had her. But aside from the fact that Javier probably wanted me dead and would never believe me, I had no real way of contacting him. I had to do something, and I had to do it now. I was the only one who could save her.

I grabbed my bag and made it through the locked marina door with ease, strolling through as if I had a proper key and I wasn't just good at picking locks. I continued to walk purposefully down the docks until I saw the right boat. I needed something that was fast enough but inconspicuous, like a fishing boat. Mazatlán was such a major fishing town that even the big shots at the marina kept fishing boats docked here.

I carefully looked around, making sure no one was watching, and jumped down into an 18-foot Double Eagle. This one even had the keys tucked inside the nearest cup holder.

It purred to life and I steered it out of the marina with ease.

In the distance, Beatriz was disappearing over the horizon line, heading in the direction of San José del Cabo and the tip of the Baja.

I maintained my speed, not too slow, not too fast, my eyes on the boat and on the blinking red dot on my app.

I eyed the bag on the chair next to me where the C4 was waiting.

I had a boat to blow up.

I had a woman to save.

I had nothing to lose.

CHAPTER SEVENTEEN

Alana

When I woke up, I was sure I had woken up in hell. My head felt like it was on fire. It was hot and pained, and I swore I could hear the crackling of flames somewhere deep inside my skull. I tried to open my eyes but the pain made me wince, and the world seemed to rock back and forth. My head fell back down to the bed.

A bed. I was on a bed somewhere, but where? What had happened?

Images floated into my brain like a cloud of powder settling.

Derek. I had fought with Derek. I had left Derek. Derek broke my heart.

His name was really Derek.

My chest pinched at the thought, my stomach twisting painfully. The grief was there, just below the surface, competing for the space in my aching body. I had to give in to it, just for a moment, just so I could breathe.

I lay back on the bed, staring at the ceiling above me, waiting for the sorrow to swallow me whole. It didn't matter that I didn't know where I was, that my head was a fiery mess, and I feared something vital had been knocked out of me. That the tiny room I was in with its wooden plank ceiling kept moving up and down and up and down. None of that mattered.

It trickled in slowly. The betrayal. The hurt. The anger and the pain. It was like acid rain on my soul, eating away at me in small doses. And then the memories of Derek flooded me like a raging river. The way he looked at me, like he would give up the world to keep me safe, the way he felt when I fell asleep in his arms, and the kind words he whispered when I woke up from a nightmare. He had ended up being so much more than I ever thought he would be to me. So much fucking more. He had ended up being my man, the one I wanted to see through to the very end, the one that made letting go of my old life okay because it meant starting a new one with him.

And now he was gone, and I was here. And even though the lies still hurt and the truth was even worse, I believe he had loved me just as I had loved him. And I loved the real him, the one he was hiding from the world but showing only to me. The lie was a half-truth in the end, and he was never not the man who became my shield against the world.

I shouldn't have left. Even though it was painfully, stupidly obvious now, I knew I shouldn't have left. I was just so hurt and shocked and confused that I couldn't process it around him. But this wasn't some silly breakup or a fight you have when you're tired. It wasn't a reevaluation of a relationship gone wrong, or "time alone to think." I had treated it all like it happened in my normal, everyday life, not my new life where people were waiting to kill me.

I should have sucked up my pride, swallowed my tears, and put that all aside just for the chance to stay alive. Instead I was a total idiot, such a foolish girl, who chose the righteousness of her own heart and feelings over the chance to live another day. This all should have mattered some other time.

Now there was no other time. He was somewhere, and I was here, taken by the man that had hired him to kill me, the man that my brother considered his second-in-command. I was taken by someone who wanted to use me, hurt me, abuse me, and kill me in order to stick it to Javier where it really hurt.

And now he wasn't going to play games anymore. I'd already shot him. I'd already stolen the man he hired to kill me. I'd already made him look like a fool.

He wasn't going to take that lightly.

I was in for a world of suffering.

At that thought, I took in a deep breath and tried to bury the fear. The heartache was still there, but the fear was growing and taking over. Death was one thing to be afraid of, but torture was another. I had no doubt that my death wouldn't come for a very, very long time.

...

I don't know how long I stayed in that room, but it was at about the time I decided I needed to use the washroom that someone came to the door.

There was a polite knock at first and then the door swung open before I could say anything. In the dim light that had been on in the corner of the room, I could see the man's shadowy figure as he loomed in the doorway.

"You're awake," he said. Esteban.

"You're going to kill me."

He chuckled and then stepped into the room, closing the door behind him. The fact that he was backlit from behind and I couldn't see his face properly made it worse. I didn't know where he was looking, yet I could feel his eyes trailing all over my body, sliding over me like an oily rag. I tried not to shudder.

"You're very beautiful," he said, taking a step toward me. He was rolling up his sleeves. "I can see why Derek decided to call the whole thing off."

"Why are you doing this?" I asked, ashamed at how meek my voice sounded.

"Because I can," was his answer. "And not many people can say that."

It was a small room. If he took another step, he would be at the foot of the bed. I tried to shift back, as far away from him as I could go, but the movement made me want to throw up. It was like being hit by the car all over again.

"You're supposed to be my brother's friend," I said.

He let out a large, belly-aching laugh that seemed to shake the whole room. "Oh, that's a rich one, hey? Friend? Beautiful, in this business there are no friends, only enemies you're close with. Do you really think Javier is my friend? He's not. He's my boss. And I'm the little son of a bitch he bosses around." His voice dropped off at the end, dripping with bitterness. "I would have thought you of all people would know what that's like."

I swallowed. "We never really had that kind of relationship."

"And I guess you never will."

I frowned at him. "You're really enjoying this, aren't you?"

He shrugged casually. "I'm not the sadistic one here. You're confusing me with your brother."

"If you're not sadistic, then why am I here?"

He looked around him, and when he turned his head I caught the feverish glint in his eyes. "Who said there was anything sadistic about this? You're on a luxury yacht. Javier's. Have you never been on it before? What a shame. It's a real beauty. Of course, he doesn't know I've taken it for a little spin, and he never will know, but we'll just keep that between you and me." He paused. "Did he tell you he named it after your sister Beatriz? Perhaps his next boat he'll name after you. Something to honor your sorry little memory."

He took a step closer, and as my eyes adjusted I saw a man who didn't really know what he wanted but was going to try and find out anyway. If there was some part of him that truly believed he wasn't sadistic, then I had to find that part and work with it. Maybe I could plead with him, change his mind. It seemed to have worked with Derek, and I hadn't even been aware of it.

"You really are beautiful," he said, his voice lower now. "It's a shame I won't enjoy this as much as you think I will."

Before I could say anything, he was on top of me, pushing me down into the bed with his weight. I screamed and tried to kick, but my head made everything spin, making me weak and disoriented. His hands went for my jeans, trying to rip them off while I thrashed back and forth.

He put his hand over my mouth and leered at me. I stared up at him in utter terror at what was about to happen. I had been in a similar situation with Derek earlier, only Derek's eyes were full of love and a promise that he would never hurt me.

Esteban's eyes were full of bitterness and revenge, and at that moment I knew he would do whatever he had to in order to expel those feelings.

Somehow he got my jeans off, and as I tried to close my legs, he placed his knee between them, keeping them open. I tried to headbutt him but he ducked out of the way, laughing, and his mouth came down on my neck and breasts. His fingers went into my underwear, rough and intrusive and wanting to inflict pain.

"You're so beautiful," he said again with a moan as he undid his fly. "I'm going to fuck the beauty right out of you. Make you as ugly as me. Maybe I'll give you a scar just like mine." His lips came close mine and he stared at me, almost hypnotized. I felt my body going into shock, shutting down, and I was so angry at it for not fighting back. Maybe if I just went numb, I wouldn't feel a thing.

"Such beautiful eyes," he murmured.

At that, I couldn't help but grin. Even he looked surprised by it. "I have Javier's eyes," I told him. "That explains why you want to fuck me so badly. You're in love with him. You want him."

That got his fucking attention. He yanked his fingers away from me and jerked his head back in horror and confusion. "What? You're sick. Fucking sick to think that. That is not true."

I kept smiling, loving that I was getting to him. "It explains everything," I said, practically spitting on him. "Why you're so jealous of him. You want him. You want to fuck me and pretend it's Javier. Well, go on. Get your fucking jollies out. I won't tell anyone."

It was a bold move, a brave move. But I had nothing to lose.

It seemed to be working, too. Esteban was beyond indignant.

He straightened up, shaking his head. "You little bitch."

"It can be our secret." I flashed him a big smile.

His eyes blazed with an inferno. "Fucking whore!" he screamed. Then he punched me square in the jaw. The world exploded into stars and fuzzy colors, and I smelled nothing but blood, felt nothing but pure, unadulterated pain.

"You stupid fucking bitch!" he yelled again, and there was another blow to my face, just above my left cheekbone.

I choked on my cries. In my head I sounded like a dying animal.

Then another at my wrist where it had broken. Then my leg that had been in the cast. Then my ribs and my breasts and every other part of me. Esteban kept hitting and hitting, like he was trying to kill me with his fists.

The last thing I remembered was an electric sound, like something being charged, and a zap of light. My body became paralyzed, and for that brief moment there was no pain. There was no anything. I convulsed and shook into a wonderful respite.

Then he removed the Taser and the pain came back so strong it was like every bone in my body broke at once.

I let out a horrific scream until I couldn't scream anymore.

CHAPTER EIGHTEEN

Derek

I trailed the boat into the night. I was so certain it had been headed straight for Cabo San Lucas, but instead it hooked south where it appeared to stop for the night. Not that there was any place for it to anchor, but the speed of the boat had slowed dramatically, I guess to make navigation at night easier. I doubted anyone on board really knew the first thing about sailing; if they did they would have reefed the sails and had them halfway down during the night.

I kept looking at the app to track Alana. She hadn't moved at all from her one spot. I had this sick feeling she could be dead, but I wasn't going to let myself think about that. I was getting her off that boat whether she was dead or alive.

I would not, could not, fail.

When I got the fishing boat within a football field of the yacht, I switched off the lights and the engine and just let it bob around. The night was dark, providing me with the advantage. Their lights were on and I could see into the boat perfectly. They couldn't see me at all.

It turns out there were more people on the boat than I had expected, but it still wasn't a crew. At the controls in the main cockpit at the very top of the boat was a huge guy that had the kind of bulk that could either be strength or laziness. On the next level down, there was a thinner one with an athletic build, and two women. One of the women was topless, and the other was wearing a bikini. They both appeared to be drugged or coked out of their minds, whores rented for the night. I made a silent prayer for them in my head. They were going to be in the wrong place at the wrong time.

But Esteban and Alana, they were nowhere to be found. Even the cabin downstairs was all dark. I had to ignore that wrench in my gut, the one that wanted me to think about all the sick possibilities.

She's dead! it shouted. *She's broken and bruised, raped within an inch of her life! She'll never be that girl again, the one you love. She's not strong enough.*

I had to ignore it. Ignore, ignore.

She was stronger than that.

I was stronger than that.

I was Derek Conway.

And I would save her.

I waited for a few minutes, taking stock of the scene. Then I took off my shirt and strapped the explosives to my chest with duct tape, the putty molding to my skin. This kind would survive getting wet and would be stable until I stuck the detonator inside. I had to put the detonator in a special waterproof pouch, along with the remote triggering device, and strapped that to me as well.

I slipped the shirt back on, stripped down to my boxer briefs, and took off my boots. I didn't even have a place to put my gun. But guns were so impersonal when it came down to it. If I had the chance to come face to face with Esteban, I wanted to feel his neck breaking between my two hands.

I balanced myself at the edge of the boat, holding the end of the long nylon rope, and dived into the water. I landed with barely a splash and then started doing a fast but silent crawl toward the boat, the end of the rope held between my teeth. If I wanted Alana to get away, she had to have a boat to take her back home, and the Double Eagle would quickly drift away if it wasn't tethered.

Though it was the tropics, the water was cold after a few minutes, and I felt my muscles cramping up. I pushed through it and kept on swimming until I was in the froth of the boat's wake. If the ketch had been going any faster, I wouldn't have been able to catch it.

I reached the small set of stairs at the back and tied the rope around it. Above me was a zodiac, hoisted above the water and ready to be lowered at a moment's notice, but I couldn't count on that to get away.

After I spent a moment catching my breath, I hoisted myself up the rest of the way and ended up on the back deck of the boat. There was a second cockpit here, complete with couches and tables full of spilled champagne, but there was no one around. I waited in the shadows, listening. In the kitchen area on the second flybridge, the party with the hookers was going on. I wanted to go up further than that. I wanted the person at the controls.

Silently I climbed, staying hidden and stealthy until I was at the top level. Turned out one of the women was up here. I could hear her moans. I peered over a seat, and I could see her beside the fat man at the wheel, his dick in her mouth.

Sorry sweetheart. Party's over.

I crept up slowly until I was right behind him. They were both so into it – her eyes were pinched shut – that they wouldn't even notice me if they tried. Without standing up, I slipped my hands over the headrest of the chair, hovering for a second on either side of his head. Then I clamped my hands together and twisted quickly until I heard a crack.

The man's head slumped. I heard a gasp and stood above the woman. She opened her mouth to scream. I drove the edge of my hand into her neck and knocked her out cold. She would die anyway when the ship blew up, but I didn't want to kill her with my hands if I didn't have to.

If I had to, though, that was a different story.

I was about to leave when I had a second thought and searched the dead man's pockets. There were no guns on him but there was a giant pocketknife that could come in handy. I gripped it firmly in my hand then made my way down the side of the boat, slithering out of sight until I was just outside of the kitchen.

The thin man was doing a line of coke with the other woman. He looked like he was going to be a bit more of a problem. Some men fought like unpredictable animals while high, and he looked like the type you didn't want to underestimate. If the fat man had been the muscle, this was the guy who did Este's dirty work. This was how it was passed down in the business. If Este took over Javier's position, this guy would take over Esteban's. Then one day he would betray him in order to rise to the top, and the circle of cartel life would continue.

Unfortunately for them, the circle was stopping here.

I watched the two of them for a moment while scoping out the shadows. Este had to be downstairs with Alana, which made things a lot trickier in the long run, but at least here these two would be easier to deal with.

I decided to go for the woman first. I didn't want to kill if I didn't have to, but she looked as if she liked to scream, in bed and otherwise. I'd take her out first then deal with him.

I moved to the back of the kitchen then slinked inside at a low crouch, hiding behind the island. They were on the white sofas, doing their lines off the coffee table. His back was to me, her face in my direction.

I popped my head up, waiting until she saw me, the recognition appearing in her eyes, then I threw the switchblade. It sailed straight and true through the air then hit her right in the eye socket, lodging itself deep into her brain.

She gurgled and keeled over just as the man was springing to his feet, searching wildly for a gun that didn't seem to be on him.

I leaped up onto the kitchen island, picked up a bottle of wine, and broke the end of it off while he tried to tackle my legs. I jumped up again, out of his grasp, and brought the jagged end of the bottle down on top of his head. It dug into his skin and he yelled, but he was a tough cookie.

I landed on the ground and rolled away to the couch, yanking the knife out of the woman's eye then throwing it at the man, but he was already ducking behind the couch. The knife landed hard into a wood post instead.

I jumped at the man and made a few punches which he blocked, then he tried to knock me off of my feet. I twisted backward and ducked as he came at me, then I plowed forward at an angle until he was slammed over the back of the couch.

While he was falling, I spun around and plucked the knife from the post. This time I wasn't going to throw it; this time I was going to stab him.

The guy quickly balanced himself and picked up the couch cushion right as I came at him, slicing the cushion all the way through, the air exploding into a flurry of feathers. I kept at him until my shoulder was shoving him down, and he landed on his back on the coffee table, the glass shattering.

He managed to pick up one of the shards, and with bleeding fingers, sliced open the side of my arm. I brought my knee down into his groin which bought me a moment of stability before I was able to chop my hand into the side of his elbow on one of the arms that was trying to hold me back.

He cried out, arm buckling, then I put my weight on it until it twisted with a crack underneath.

While he struggled for purchase, I headbutted him until his head cracked against the table again, then I quickly dragged the blade across his throat, opening a gushing wound. His eyes rolled back, his body jerking, trying to fight, to live, but not today.

"I should have known."

Esteban's voice from behind made me leap up and pivot, knife held out in front of me.

Naturally, he was holding a gun. But that didn't mean I would lose.

"Where's Alana?" I asked loudly, hoping she could hear me.

He smirked, and with one hand, brushed his long hair behind his ears. "She's going to be out for a while. I don't think she's as strong as you believe. In fact, she broke much like a flower between my hands."

I swallowed down the rage that threatened to consume me. This is why I was good at what I did. I had to compartmentalize. I had to focus on the task at hand before I could focus on her.

I had to kill Esteban.

Even if he thought he was going to kill me first.

"This works out in my favor, though," he said, coming toward me, the gun still trained on me and just out of reach. He reached for the wall and pressed a button. The back of the boat shuddered and clanked. He was lowering one of the zodiacs into the water. "I'll get to go back to the compound and tell Javier the sad truth. You were hired to assassinate his sister. It worked. And you both perished. Perhaps I even tried to save her life by killing you."

I kept my eyes on him, trying to figure out what to do. If he came just a step closer, there was a small chance I could fly at him and knock the gun out of his hands before he fired. He wasn't a very good shot to begin with.

But he didn't come closer. In fact, he was moving a step backward, and from the way his eyes were focused on my chest, I knew that if he missed he would fire until he didn't.

There was too much pride in him to lose again.

"I hope you've atoned for your sins," he said to me with a small smile. "Sadly, you'll never be redeemed."

He fired the first shot. I was already twisting sideways as he did so, anticipating his move. But the next shot would be too fast for me.

Everything went in slow motion. He grinned. Finger tightened on the trigger.

Then Alana appeared behind him. She looked broken, battered and beaten, and close to death. But she was holding the base of a lamp, holding it above her head.

She brought it down with one brave burst of strength, her bruised features straining from the effort. My heart ached in response.

It shattered on Esteban's head just as he pulled the trigger. The second shot grazed me, hitting the side of my chest and knocking me back to the ground. I lay there for a moment, my ears ringing, trying to go through the checklist of my body to find out how close I was to dying.

Suddenly Alana, with her blood-crusted face, was above me screaming, and I stared up at her. Her hands were feeling around my side, and I managed to sit up and look. There was no blood anywhere. I quickly lifted my shirt. The bullet had nicked the edge of the C4 putty. Contrary to popular belief, the shit did not blow up when hit by a bullet. Thank god.

"You bitch!" Esteban screamed, grabbing his head and trying to get to his feet but failing. His gun had been knocked out of reach.

I got to my feet first and grabbed Alana's arm. "You need to head to the boat. He's lowered one to the water and I have one out there, attached by a rope. Get in it and go, now!"

"What about you?"

"I've got something I want to do," I told her. I grabbed her face, conscious of Este in the background. "Grab a life preserver, too. A jacket, a ring, anything that will keep you afloat and wrap it around you, okay?"

"Derek..."

"Go!" I screamed, and at that she quickly limped away to the back of the boat.

I was going to deal with him once and for all. I picked up the gun but saw there were no bullets left in it. For what I was about to do anyway, I wanted him alive until the very last minute, until it was too late and the heat tore apart his bones. I went over to him and pistol whipped him hard on the side of the head until he fell over to the side, unconscious. Then I quickly took off my shirt, pulled out the C4 and the waterproof box, and stuck a piece of it at the base of the propane stove. I stuck in the detonator and then stuck two more pieces on opposite sides of the bridge. I could hear chains clanging and water sluicing and hoped that Alana was finding her way onto the boat. I was planning to leave with her, but we wouldn't have much time.

I ran down the stairs to the bottom level where the engine room and all the bedrooms were. I wasn't sure if I had carried enough C4 with me—I had never anticipated on using it on a ship, let alone one of this size—but if there was one place that would take well to a boom, it was the engine. I stuck the last pieces all around the block, planted the detonators, and then ran back up the stairs to the second level. I was about to head toward the back, toward where I assumed Alana was, when I looked back at the kitchen.

Esteban had moved. He was nowhere to be seen.

Before I could comprehend that, someone ran at me from behind and I went sailing over the railing. I grabbed the edge of the rail, trying to hold on to that and the remote control trigger at the same time.

Este appeared over the side, blood running down the side of his face, pried the trigger out of my hand, and tried to stab my fingers with a knife.

I let go of the railing before he could cut my fingers off and fell down, down, straight into the water. From that height it had knocked the wind out of me so it took me a moment to act. I quickly kicked up toward the surface and looked around. The Double Eagle was almost on top of me, the current having pushed it close, so I grabbed hold of the side and hauled myself up and over as quickly as I could.

I expected to see Alana on board but there was nothing. In fact, the boat was quickly drifting away from the yacht, the rope having been severed at some point.

Suddenly the air filled with the roar of an engine. I saw the zodiac speed away into the night, a dark shadow at the helm.

Please let Alana be on it, please.

But of course it wasn't.

Another movement caught my eye, and I looked up at the top of the boat. I could see Alana's head bobbing as she ran along the side. She was still on the fucking boat!

"Alana!" I screamed, panic tearing through me. "Jump!"

She disappeared behind part of the bridge but I didn't hear a splash. It looked like she had been about to run down the stairs.

"Alana!" I screamed again. "Please!"

Then my scream was swallowed instantaneously.

There was a burst of light, smoke, a ripple in the air. Then a split second later the whole world exploded. I was knocked flat on my back, my head striking the captain's seat of the fishing boat as I went down. Debris rained down on me but I couldn't even cover myself. I just let the sparks and bits of flaming boat hit me.

Alana.

Alana.

Alana.

Not again.

No, not again.

Somehow, though I don't know how, I managed to sit up. My head felt like it had been filled with gel, my hearing blocked, my eyes stinging. I crawled to the edge of the boat and looked out at the water.

The Beatriz had been broken up into three pieces. At least those three pieces were all that was left of it and were quickly sinking down to the ocean floor. Everything else was just a mess of debris and flaming water. Near the edge of the fishing boat I spotted the fat man's severed arm floating beside a pillow.

Alana.

Alana.

"Alana!" I yelled, my voice catching in my throat. "Alana!"

I yelled and screamed and cried her name over and over and over again. I don't know how long I had been doing it for but after some time it turned to tears. Then more screams. Then a combination of the two.

She didn't survive it.

No one could have survived that.

Este had escaped.

I had escaped.

But Alana was dead.

The job had finally been fulfilled.

She was finally dead.

And it was all my fault.

I had failed Carmen, I had failed Alana. I had failed myself.

Esteban was right.

There was no redemption here.

There never really was.

Not for someone like me.

The ones who do the dirty deeds can never really be washed clean.

I swallowed down the ugliest sorrow I had ever felt in my life. I felt it eat at me as it went through my body, consuming all the love I had, my hopes and fears and dreams. Oh those dreams I had for us. Those wonderful fucking dreams.

I lay back in the boat, staring blankly at the night sky as the fire crackled faintly in the background, and prayed for death.

I prayed for the morning sun to come and bake me, for birds to peck at my flesh and sharks to eat my bones. I prayed to drift off to sea forever, until there was nothing left of me.

I prayed until I fell asleep.

And prayed I would never wake up.

...

In my dreams I saw Alana and Carmen, sitting on a beach and talking to each other. They were so beautiful in the sun, so different yet so much alike. No wonder I was so taken by each of them instantly. They were a breath of fresh air, a force of light and nature.

I walked out of the sea and stopped in front of them, salt water dripping down my body.

They both turned their faces toward me and smiled, happy to see me. It was blinding.

"We are finally free," they said in unison. "You'll be free, too. Free and unafraid."

I woke up to see a brilliant night sky.

But I was afraid.

And that had been a dream.

CHAPTER NINETEEN

Derek

Alana's funeral was held at one o'clock at a cemetery on the outskirts of Puerto Vallarta. It was dangerous for me to go, stupid even, but I had to. I had to take the risk. I had to see with my own eyes and know for myself what the truth really was, even if it was damaging.

So much damage had already been done.

I pulled my cap down over my eyes and made my way through the overgrown brush on the side of the cemetery. Everything was so well-groomed and taken care of for the dead, but the moment the cemetery lines stopped, nature was waiting. It wanted to take back the land, for roots to grow deep and suck life from bones, to bloom from death. The mess, the wildness that suited the graves more than mown lawns and wilting flowers.

I took my binoculars out of my back pocket, crouched down and crept, soundless and smooth through the bush, stopping at the edge. In the distance I could see people gathered for her funeral. There were even more than I had imagined, but Alana had been a popular girl, more so than she once thought. The solid white casket was at the front of the crowd, a priest beside it, reading something out and over the grave faces.

Everyone looked destroyed, and that in turn destroyed me. It was a good thing that Alana couldn't see this—it would hurt to know the pain she was inflicting on the people left behind.

Luz and Dominga were sitting on fold-out chairs near the front, tears running down their faces, hanging on to each other while what seemed like their family members tried to console them. There were a lot of people her age, women mostly, whom I assumed were employees of Aeromexico. And at the very back of the chairs, standing at attention, was Javier.

His face held barely any expression, but what was there was nearly heartbreaking. I was surprised. It's not that I didn't think he cared about his sister—I knew that he did—but after losing so much of his family already, I didn't think it was possible for him to be affected any more. In some ways, I didn't think he had the capacity to really feel.

But the look on his face…it was the most controlled version of utter devastation that I had ever seen. This was going to ruin him.

That had been the plan, hadn't it?

Sure enough, coming up behind Javier, was Esteban, as well as Luisa. Like Javier, they were dressed in black, their expressions strained. There was something about them, though, the way they were walking together out of Javier's sight, Esteban's hand briefly at the small of her back before lifting away, that made me pause. Now that I knew who the villain was, I was starting to see another motive at play. This wasn't over, not by a long shot. Esteban was going to take away everything that mattered to Javier, one step at a time.

Alana's death was the first step. The dominoes would follow.

Luisa was next. But in what context, that I didn't know.

I eyed the surroundings, wondering if anyone else was going to show up, if anyone was watching—anyone like me. But it seemed I was alone. Javier had so much control over the state, but sometimes I wondered if he was almost flaunting it. His power was making him lazy, and that laziness was going to cost him. The man who wanted him out of the picture, the man who was his biggest threat, was standing right beside him, forced to mourn while making eyes at his wife.

I could see how this was all going to go down. Luckily, I wasn't going be around to see it. I had plans to get out the country, to get as far away from all of this as possible. If Esteban was going to slowly take down Javier, win people's trust, and take over the cartel, then it was Javier's fault and no one else's.

I almost felt sorry for him.

It's too bad that Alana and I had been brought into it and ripped apart at the seams. Every fucking day I regretted taking that damn phone call from him. But for all the grief and trouble, I knew that if I hadn't, I never would have met her. I never would have been free of my sins and this life. I never would have found love again, or even happiness. I never would have found my redemption.

Now I was starting over. Alana's death was bringing me a new beginning. Bringing us a new beginning.

I watched as the priest continued his talk, and then people slowly came up to the podium to give their eulogies. I wondered about Alana's sister, Marguerite, and why she wasn't there, but then I realized Javier would never allow that. For her safety, I was sure that Marguerite would never be allowed to step foot in Mexico ever again. The only Bernal sister left.

Surprisingly, Javier came up to speak. He was the last one. People stared at him in shock, having not noticed him in the back, probably still processing the now wildly-known truth that Alana's brother was head of one of the nation's largest drug cartels. It was because of him that she had died.

I couldn't hear what he was saying, and I could only see the side of his face as he addressed the crowd, but it was apparent he was getting choked up over his words. He left it short then disappeared into the back of the crowd again.

The casket was lowered into the ground, and the priest threw dirt.

Alana Bernal, as everyone knew her, was laid to rest.

I swallowed hard, feeling their sadness waft across the graves and penetrate my bones. I had felt that utter horror just a week ago when the explosion first went off. That grief, that fear, that big black hole of hell in your heart—it was still all so real for me. Loss. The world was cruel with what it gave you and what it took away.

I stayed in that spot until it was all over. Until the last people to stand over her grave were her brother, Esteban, and Luisa. I watched as Javier mouthed words to the freshly-turned earth then walked away. I watched as Esteban put his hand on Luisa's shoulder and whispered something to her. Her expression wasn't impressed, but his was as cunning as a wolf. Then they followed behind Javier, Luisa walking quickly to catch up to her husband.

This was a detonation waiting to happen. But it wasn't my problem to worry about. It was Javier's. And I had a new life to lead.

When everyone left, I turned and headed back through the jungle for about a mile until I came to a road where I'd parked the truck, the dirt stirred up by a hot breeze. The houses here were little more than rustic shacks, but the face of the old man staring at me from the overturned bucket on his porch told me they were happy.

That would be me soon. The money I got from Alana's hired assassination—that deposit, it wouldn't last me forever. But the happiest people seemed to be the ones with less to lose.

I waved to the old man, and he waved back, content to smoke his cigarette as chickens pecked at the dirt path, and got in the truck.

I didn't stop driving until I reached Guatemala City in Guatemala. I hadn't been here for a long time. Not since the last time I had been involved with Javier, helping to take down Travis.

I had no wish to stay here, but it was an easy meeting spot.

My blood pumped heatedly in my veins as I handled the busy city streets. The closer I got to the hotel—to the first hiding spot—the more anxious I became. The darkness here, the scattered city lights, thrummed with promises.

The hotel was right downtown, and a rather fancy one at that. It was about being unpredictable, now more than ever. Until the danger was far enough away, we had to be careful—we could never ever let our guard down. Even after death, someone would watch the grave. Someone would always wonder what was.

Was that body lowered into the ground today Alana's? Had there been anything to bury at all?

Someone out there was asking themselves that. Maybe not about to follow up on it, but it would be simmering at the back of their head, waiting for someone to slip up one day. You couldn't tempt fate. We had tempted it enough.

I parked the truck a block away then walked over. I got a few stares as I often did—I'd feel better once my hair started to get long and I looked less like myself—I was always going to be paranoid.

I walked into the hotel, glad I had worn a crisp shirt and tailored pants, my watch glinting under the bronze chandeliers that lined the lobby.

"Hola," I said to the well-padded clerk behind the front desk. "Do you speak English?"

He nodded. "Of course."

"I have a reservation for Dalton Chalmers," I told him, and when he asked for ID, I pulled out an American passport with the name on it, a perfect forgery I had gotten from Gus.

"Someone called earlier, asking for you," the clerk said once he'd run my credit card, also belonging to Dalton Chalmers.

"Oh?" I asked.

"A woman," he said, as if he was telling me a secret.

I guess it kind of was. I managed to smile at him. "Well, well," I said, and the clerk grinned in response.

He gave me the key and I went up to the room, my feet light on the velvety stairs. I felt like I was walking on the moon, the thin metal key with the brass sun pendant heavy in my hand. It had been three days.

It had been too long.

I found my room and stuck the key in the door, opening it to a simple but brightly colored room: polished wood furniture, orange and green bedspread, red walls, a bronze sun with a circular mirror at the center.

It was empty. I knew it would be, but even then my heart sank a little. This was what could have been.

I went and sat on the end of the bed, waiting. There was a marching band in my chest.

Then, a knock at the door.

I took in a deep breath, and for a split second I almost dropped my guard. I made sure my gun was loaded, my safety off, my grip on it firm.

I edged toward the door, wishing there was a peephole of some kind.

I waited, my head gently pressed against the wood, listening. I couldn't hear anything.

"Derek," she said softly.

Dalton, I thought, but at that moment I didn't care that she'd forgotten.

I unlocked the door and eased it open a crack, looking at Alana's face.

She barely looked like herself. Her hair was sleek, shoulder-length and light brown, and laced with shades of sand. She had lots of makeup on to cover the bruises Esteban had left, but it was pretty seamless. She was wearing all black, even carrying herself a bit differently. But that smile—that gorgeous smile—was all hers.

"You made it," I told her, trying to contain myself.

She held her chin at a saucy angle. "I'm a better spy than you thought. I was in the lobby, hiding behind a newspaper, watching you."

"Won't you come in then, Anna," I said, emphasis on her new name. I opened the door wider as I put my gun away.

"Right, Dalton," she said, remembering her mistake from earlier. "I guess I'm not as good of a spy as I thought."

She came inside and walked to the middle of the room, looking around. It took all that I had not to throw her on the bed and bury myself deep inside of her, feeling that she was finally here with me, that she was real, that she was alive.

Alana was alive.

Everyone else thought she was dead.

We had escaped Mexico.

We were starting over.

She set her leather carry-on bag down on the ground. I locked the door and went straight up to her, wrapping one hand around her waist, the other at the back of her head.

"You're like the sun returning to me," I murmured, my grip tightening, so afraid to let go, so happy she was here.

"And you're my big, powerful sky," she said back, her golden eyes trailing to my lips.

I kissed her, so hard I thought I'd bring her pain. But she moaned and melted into my mouth, wanting more.

I gave her more. I gave her everything I had.

I stripped away her clothes like a child on Christmas morning, feasting on her neck, her shoulders and her breasts, while she took off mine. The way she looked at me made me feel like she was seeing me for the first time.

Maybe this was the first time for both of us. The first time born anew. The first time at a second chance.

This time was forever.

I scooped her up in my arms and placed her on the bed, torn between wanting to take this slow, to feel every inch, to make the seconds stretch, and needing to have her quickly and all at once, for this frenzy, these flames, to engulf the both of us.

We compromised. While she was naked beneath me, wet and willing, needy and greedy, I thrust into her. She was tight around me, so beautiful that I had to close my eyes to take it all in. While we skipped the foreplay, I wanted to make sure I could prolong our lovemaking for as long as possible.

I leaned on my elbows on both sides of her head, my fingers disappearing into her smooth hair, my eyes staring deep into hers as I slowly, tantalizingly pulled out. My breath hitched and I buried my face in the soft, warm crook of her neck. She smelled like flowers and fresh air.

"I was afraid I wouldn't see you again," she said, her voice whisper-sweet, caught between moans. "I was afraid..."

"You don't have to be afraid anymore," I told her. I pushed in again to the hilt and she gasped before letting out a strangled cry. I wanted her to believe it. We would always be cautious, but we would never be afraid.

Esteban, Javier, everyone had to believe that Alana had died during the explosion, or she would never really be free.

"I love you," she whispered to me just before she came. Her head went back, her eyes squeezed shut, her back arched, so vulnerable, as if she was offering herself to me.

I took her hungrily. Soon I was coming inside of her, and for once I felt like I wasn't trying to fuck something out of me; instead I felt like I was trying to take something from her. Love. Her soul. Her everything. Whatever it was, it made me better.

It washed me clean.

I pulled out of her and gently pulled her into my arms, kissing the top of her head. Light from the city filtered in through the gauzy lace curtains, creating a kaleidoscope of shadows on the wall.

"Are you going to tell me what happened?" she asked, her voice hushed in the room. "Today. My…my funeral."

I exhaled, kissing her again. "Do you really want to know?"

She nodded against me. "Yes. Did you see Javier? Marguerite?"

"Your brother was there," I told her. "Marguerite wasn't. But I assume that was for her own safety."

"Was he upset?"

"Yes," I said. "He was."

"And Esteban?"

"He was there too. Right by his side. I have no idea how the boat explosion was explained but I'm going to assume that Esteban feigned ignorance over it. The crew he had died. There's nothing to place him there at the scene of it all. Maybe he'll have some damning evidence about me if push comes to shove. We don't know. But I think that's why I was brought in in the first place. He needed someone to take the blame, the fall, just in case. He's trying to overthrow your brother. I wouldn't be surprised if he went after his wife next. And I don't mean in a murderous way."

"Luisa?" she asked, craning her head back to look at me with wide eyes. "Luisa loves Javier. I know this. She would never go for Esteban."

"I'm not saying that she would. But it looked as if that might be the next step. Take out the sister, take over the wife, ruin Javier until he can't rule no more…take over the cartel."

"But why me?"

"Because," I told her gravely, "whether you believe it or not, you mean more to your brother than you think. The man I saw today was a destroyed man. Javier will be changed after this. I could see it."

She closed her eyes and shook her head slightly. "I can't stand him feeling that way, to think that I'm dead."

"But it's the only way. You said so yourself."

"I know," she said, her voice choked up. "I know I did, and it's true. If I show my face, if I even give him a hint that I'm still alive, I'll never be free. Not as long as Esteban is in the picture. I can't risk it. I can't risk us. What we might have."

"What we *will* have," I corrected her.

There was a pause and then she asked, quieter now, "And Luz and Dominga?"

I squeezed her to me. "They were there. They were taking it pretty hard."

She sniffed, and a tear rolled down her cheek before she buried her head into my shoulder. "They were everything to me. I can't imagine how they must be feeling."

"I know," I said.

"It doesn't seem fair. To just let people hurt when they don't have to."

"It's not fair. And it's not fair that you had to leave them too. But I would rather you be alive, living a life that's unfair than be dead and not living at all."

"Maybe one day I can let them know the truth."

"Maybe," I said. "Until that day comes, though, they must believe that the body in the coffin was you."

"Whose body is it anyway?"

"I'm not sure," I admitted. "Someone else. One of the prostitutes on the boat, I'm guessing. Whoever it is, though, it fooled the police, or whoever was hired to be the police that day."

And it had fooled me. When the boat exploded and I saw Esteban disappear into the distance, I really thought Alana was dead. There was no way she would have survived that, and it was all my fault. I was the one who put the bombs there. I had let my emotions get in the way, and in a moment of weakness, I messed up. I should have made sure Esteban was dead before I did anything else, I just wanted him to burn alive so badly.

I had lain back on the zodiac for some time as the debris rained down around me, and smoke and flames filled the air. I was so close to jumping off and letting myself sink to the bottom of the sea with her. So damn close to dying.

But then, in the middle of the cold, dark night, something bumped into the boat repeatedly, and when I finally found the strength to see what it was, I discovered Alana, hanging on to a life preserver in a state of semi-consciousness. She had listened to me in the end, making sure she had something that floated to hold on to, and jumped before the boat exploded.

It was still a miracle, but it was one I would gladly believe in.

"And Esteban escaped into the night, wiping his hands clean of everything," she said bitterly.

"Yes, he did. But so did we."

"Our hands aren't clean."

"No," I smoothed my palm over her head. "But in time they will be."

That night she fell asleep in my arms as Anna Bardem. When we woke up the next morning to a beautiful sunny day, we started our new life together.

EPILOGUE

Utila, Honduras—one year later

Alana (Anna)

It's funny growing up in a place like La Cruz or Puerto Vallarta, a land of sand and palm trees, margaritas and blue waves. It's where so many people come to vacation, to forget their troubles, their cares, their everyday lives. It's paradise.

But it's never been my paradise. Home never really is. At least that's what I had thought. When you have the fucked up childhood that I had, home becomes a scary place, and paradise has no business mixing with fear. While tourists—whether they be Americans, Canadians, even Mexicans—came to Puerto Vallarta and the Bay of Banderas to relax and have fun, I lived their paradise like I was trapped in a cage. A cage built of violence and terror and that looming threat that at any minute, I would be taken from this world in a horrific way, just as it happened to my family.

Throughout all that, though, the years of promoting paradise through Aeromexico, or watching foreigners get drunk on the sandy beaches, I always dreamed of my own slice of heaven. It wouldn't look like Mexico, though. It would never be Mexico.

I had finally found it. *We* had finally found it.

After my fake funeral, Derek and I (I still can't call him Dalton), headed through Guatemala, up to Belize for a bit, and down through Honduras. We were thinking we would head to Costa Rica or Panama, perhaps even set our sights on Chile. We were looking for a place where we could be safe, free, and live a long and happy life, one that didn't rely on large sums of money or guns or lies.

We really meant to keep going, but as we were driving through Honduras—a place where Derek had been before—checking out the beaches, we stumbled across a place that could only be called paradise.

The tiny island of Utila.

There, with its talcum powder beaches, golf-cart transportation, tiny towns, and a vibrant mix of Spanish and English, we were able to put down roots, to find ourselves.

With the money Derek had saved in his account, we bought a beach house on half an acre. It's waterfront with its own dock, and we have a fishing boat. On weekends we use it to go diving—I'm certified now, and of course Derek always was. We also go on fishing trips. In the evenings we grill up the fish on our deck and watch the sun go down on the horizon. Sometimes we even have friends over too—it's easy to make them in a place where everyone is smiling.

During the week, we both have jobs. I work as a barista of sorts at a local café and juice bar. It's really low-key and most of the week it's just me by myself. I get paid in cash, and I'm often tipped quite well. It's nice, honest work and a hell of a lot easier than being a flight attendant.

Derek works as a personal trainer at one of the gyms. Sometimes he drives our golf cart around the island—gas is expensive, roads are narrow, cars are rare—and trains people at their homes. He likes his job a lot. I can see it in his face when he comes home, the feeling that he helped someone today instead of, well, murdering someone.

Of course, no one here knows who we are, what we did. The past is behind us, hidden beneath many layers I hope no one ever uncovers. It's not easy to forget the life I led. I miss Luz and Dominga dearly and often spend my nights staring at the star-filled sky, wishing they could hear my thoughts, saying a little prayer for them. Maybe, somehow, they know I'm still alive.

I miss my brother, too. But more than that, I feel sorry for him. It sounds silly to want to protect someone like him, but I feel like someone has to. He's suffering, I know it, from my death, and he's probably leaning on all the wrong people. But Javier has wronged so many people in his lifetime, perhaps this is just the way the world works. It's unfair, but sometimes it can still be just.

Derek is almost like a different man. Almost. He still gets moody every now and then, becomes quiet and withdrawn. I see this spark in his eyes—they harden and become menacing. I know then to leave him alone. He's atoning for his sins. He's thinking of the wife he once lost because of the violence that controlled him. He's thinking about the war and the things he saw and how futile it was to think he could ever escape it.

But he did escape it. He broke that life, that cycle. He's still a tough man and he can seem emotionless even when I know he's not, but he's a better man.

He's my man. I love him and he loves me. Without a doubt, that man loves me.

"How was your week?" Erin asked me.

I looked over at her, snapping out of my wayward thoughts. We were sitting on the roof deck of our house, watching yet another unbelievable sunset as the sun slipped in an orange and pink path toward the distant shoreline of mainland Honduras.

Erin was one of the first people we'd met on the island. Actually, she was the realtor who sold us the beach house and got us a screaming deal. Though she and her partner George were a bit older than us, we fast became good friends. George and Derek often played golf together, although Derek usually returned from those games embarrassed. For a man with a lot of steely resolve, he seemed to lose his shit when he played golf. I found it adorable.

"It was good. You know, the usual," I told her with a smile, reaching for my wine. Derek and George were downstairs in the kitchen, preparing some fish we'd caught yesterday.

She looked pleased, her freckly cheeks beaming at me, as if she'd been part of our integration. In some ways she had—aside from the house, she'd introduced us to a circle of friends who were fun and easygoing, embracing the island lifestyle.

"I'm so glad, Anna," she said. I still found it jarring every time someone called me by my fake name, but at least I was good at hiding it. It hadn't been the same with Derek. After I'd called him that a few times last year, we decided to just tell everyone that Derek was his middle name and that he was used to that. It's not like Derek Conway really existed out there in any form except for an ex-military soldier who went off the grid.

At least, that's what we hoped.

Soon, Derek and George brought up the platters of steamed fish with lemon dressing, Caribbean rice, and sautéed vegetables that I'd picked from our garden out front. Another bottle of wine was uncorked. Local acoustic music from the bar down the street wafted up over the azaleas and palm trees, catching a ride on the sea breeze.

This was paradise. I was home.

Later that night, Derek and I settled into bed. Well, we didn't so much settle as collapse, drunk and exhausted. The two of us had too much wine at dinner, which, after our guests left, led to hot monkey sex in the kitchen, on the couch, in the shower, before we finally succumbed, wet and sated, to sleep.

It must have been the middle of the night—the moon was working its way across the sky and filtering in through the window in silver beams—when I heard the noise. Despite my aching head, I stiffened immediately, my senses flaring up. Derek was already out of bed and by the door. In the moonlight I could see the gun in his hand.

He motioned for me to stay put, stay quiet, but I couldn't. I never could. As he eased our bedroom door open and eyed the dark hallway, I quietly crept out of bed, holding my breath, afraid that the hardwood floors would creak.

While he stealthily entered the hallway, I brought out my own gun from the bottom dresser drawer. I hadn't looked at it since I put it there the day we moved in. There hadn't been a need.

Now I was afraid that our past had finally caught up to us. We were so careful, but someone else had probably been even more so. We had really started to believe that we'd left all of that behind us, that the people we had once been couldn't touch us anymore.

It was worth it, though. If I hadn't touched the gun for a year, that meant it was worth it. Paradise, Derek, freedom—they were worth everything.

I cautiously followed Derek out the door, seeing him go down the stairs at the end. We had made a plan, an escape route, if things went terribly wrong one day. I was to head to the office at the end of the hallway and go through the sliding glass doors that led to the deck. From there I could go up toward the roof, or down toward the ground.

But even though that was the plan, I couldn't go. I couldn't stand the thought of leaving Derek behind. I knew he could more than take care of himself, but even then, dark, horrific thoughts teased at me. I could almost hear a gunshot going off, imagining Derek gunned down, his life seeping out through his blood while I escaped to freedom. That didn't seem fair, and my life had its own share of injustice.

So I followed him down the teak stairway, even though he was shooting me a hard, intimidating look over his shoulder, telling me to stay put. I wasn't listening.

Now that we were on the main floor, the sound had stopped. Upstairs in the bedroom, it had sounded like someone trying to open a door, or perhaps someone accidently banging into something. There was nothing now.

Then the motion detector outside went on near the back door, which looked out onto the beach. If anyone were to break in, there was no fence or real property line in the back to deter them. Plus it was darker back there, just the garden, sand, and sea, and no one to witness a thing.

I looked at Derek, the cold light showcasing the hard, masculine planes of his face as he edged toward the back door, his hand moving toward the handle. I wanted to yell out for him, to tell him not to open it, to keep us locked in our ignorance, but my voice choked in my throat.

It all happened so fast. Derek took in a deep breath then the door flew open, and he jumped out in a low crouch, gun drawn, eyes focused dead ahead.

There was a terrible thud just out of reach, like something hit the side of the house and then a hoarse, vibrating cry that reminded me of a cornered animal or a dying donkey.

Derek froze, not pulling the trigger. Then his face contorted in shock before breaking out into a smile. What the hell?

"Alana," he said, turning to look at me.

I was already at the door and stepping out beside him.

On the back patio there were two donkeys. One of them was looking mildly surprised at our intrusion, the other one was busy eating out of the compost bin they had knocked over.

Donkeys. Motherfucking donkeys.

I looked at Derek with wide eyes.

We both burst out laughing.

Not just giggles, but full-on, gut-bursting laughs that were sure to wake the neighbors. We keeled over, holding our stomachs, our faces growing red, tears streaming down our cheeks. I nearly fell over.

Meanwhile, the donkeys paid us no attention and went back to eating and occasionally stomping their hooves on the deck.

Derek came over to me, his smile as big as the moon, and pulled me into his arms.

"Talk about paranoid," he said, kissing the top of my head. He let out another laugh. "In all my years, I've never pulled a gun on a donkey before."

"Good thing you didn't shoot first and ask questions later," I said, trying to catch my breath.

"You're right. I guess I'm changing, aren't I, sunshine?"

I smiled at him, my heart feeling so unbelievably full. "You are. But you haven't lost all of yourself."

His brow furrowed. "Hopefully I've kept the sexy parts."

I pinched his side. "You did. And then some."

He put his arm around my shoulder and I leaned my head against his chest as we watched the donkeys for a few moments.

"I wonder who they belong to," I mused.

"Probably wild," he said. "Don't you be getting any ideas."

"The only idea I'm getting is that we may need a fence. Then again, I like that they came here. Wild but not afraid."

"Just like you."

I gave him a grave look. "But I was afraid. Back there, in the house, I was afraid."

His lips twitched into a half-smile. "And yet you still stood by me. It's okay to be afraid, Alana. We'll always be afraid to some degree, I think, and that's a good thing. You need fear to stay sharp. You need fear to keep your wildness in check. But just a little bit. Just enough to feel alive." He paused. "I think we're more alive now than we've ever been. Just this life here, this beautiful little life with you and this island and everything, is all I want for the rest of my life."

Hot tears tickled at my eyes as I was lost in the sincerity of his words, in the confidence in his eyes. I reached up and kissed him sweetly, wanting to remember this moment forever.

A loud bray from one of the donkeys was the only thing to interrupt us.

We waved them goodbye, deciding to clean up after them tomorrow, and went inside, and back to bed.

...

During the week that followed, I felt happier than ever. You'd think that would correspond with feeling lighter, but for some reason I felt weighted down, bloated, irritated, and heavy. It didn't help that I had missed my period, either. Finally I had to bite the bullet and face what could really be going on with me.

So I went to our rinky dink local drugstore, and once I was back at home, took a pregnancy test.

It came out positive.

I wasn't really sure how I would react—waiting for that pink line was so nerve-racking that I had no idea what my thoughts were. But the moment it became true, it became real, I felt a happiness bloom inside me like a flower I'd overlooked.

When I told Derek, his reaction was the same—pure joy. We cried and laughed and did a funny dance around the bedroom. We let the news sink in over and over again, and smiled until we were sure our faces wouldn't crack in two.

No more wine (except a glass on occasion), no more fish. Lots of healthy vegetables and grains. The whole island seemed to know I was knocked up, and it was like I suddenly had a giant family rejoicing with me, a family that seemed hell-bent on making sure my child was raised as happy as can be.

Some days I laid on the roof deck and stared up at the sky, hand on my growing belly, and thought about the future. Now it wouldn't just be Derek and me. We would have someone else in our family.

Someone else to love.

Someone else to run wild with.

Someone else to call home.

THE END

Thank you for reading Dirty Deeds! As you can probably figure out, Dirty Promises focuses on Javier, Luisa, and yes, Esteban in a (very) sexy and suspenseful way. Javier might just lose his mind from years of pent-up grief… he may also lose a lot more than that. But, our charming King has never been one to back down from a fight. Except for that one time, but let's not talk about that. Expect a lot more violence, sex, action and depravity…and a scene you never saw coming, as the series comes to an epic showdown.

Dirty Promises will be self-published by me and released by Headline/Hachette in the UK this summer (Dirty Angels and Dirty Deeds will be in bookstores in the UK territories starting in April, with different covers and prices).

In the meantime, you can keep up with me on Facebook at www.facebook.com/pages/Karina-Halle/140649372629593, Instagram at http://instagram.com/authorhalle and my Newsletter at http://bit.ly/KH-Newsletter (cool giveaways and unique opportunities if you sign up!).

**Keep reading for an excerpt from Vince Stark's upcoming erotica *House of Sin* – about a man with dark desires who brings an innocent girl into the seedy underworld of a sex club. Written by a man and told from the male POV, this book is not for the faint of heart. He holds no punches with his book so if you aren't into dirty, filthy, sometimes dubiously consensual sex (I mean, whoa, I'm talking sexually aggressive men who don't take no for an answer, gimps in leather masks and orgies and whips and drugs that make you want to fuck a gearshift) please skip over the excerpt and/or don't buy the book (his words, not mine).

Following the House of Sin excerpt there is an excerpt for the lovely Jenn Cooksey's heartwarming, tearjerking, witty NA romance *Landslide*. You should buy the book (her words, not mine…just kidding, I think you should buy it too).

dirty
PROMISES

A NOTE FROM THE AUTHOR

Dirty Promises is, with a doubt, the darkest and most disturbing book I've ever written (and the 26th published work of mine, so that says a lot). I cringed. I gasped. I wanted to be sick. There were nights where I cried from what I was writing, not just because of what was happening to the characters, but because it straddled the line between fact and fiction. The Mexican drug wars are far, *far* more brutal than I could ever write and in my extensive research for the books, I found this knowledge hard to handle. And, sadly, what you'll read in this book is nowhere near how shocking the reality can be.

I'm not telling you all this in order to over-hype the book, I'm telling you this so that you will be prepared. This book contains a lot of triggers for people: there is rape. There is adultery. There is abuse. There are many violent, gruesome scenes. Because of this, I would rather have some readers shut the book and say "Oh, that wasn't dark or disturbing at all, that foreword got me expecting something bad" than to have a reader genuinely be hurt or emotionally scarred from a rape scene. I want to protect readers. So please, if you are very sensitive to those topics, pass on this story.

The drug cartel life is not pretty and I have done my best to capture that. They are immoral people who do very bad things. Javier Bernal is an example of that. Whether you've read him all the way from his manipulative, cheating, be-heading days in *On Every Street* or just started with *Dirty Angels*, you'll see that he's never been a good guy. That said, he's never been completely evil, either. The *narcos* aren't always monsters – they are still human and sometimes that human side shines through, albeit in different ways. They do have their own moral codes. Family always comes first, even while it's accepted that *narco* leaders have a slew of mistresses. Certain leaders and cartels are actually revered in some places around the country because the citizens argue that they do more good for the people than bad. El Chapo himself is seen as a Robin Hood figure in some areas of Sinaloa.

But heroes, they are not.

For a list of the books that assisted me in my extensive research of the drug cartels, please see the acknowledgements. I whole-heartedly recommend all of them and think that more people should be aware of just what goes down south of the border.

Now you have some idea of what lies ahead of you. Check your morals at the door, keep an open mind and enjoy the ruin and resurrection of Javier and Luisa Bernal.

Dedicated to the ones with the black hearts and dirty souls.

PROLOGUE

My wife was a liar.

Then again, I was a liar too. Perhaps the greatest liar of them all.

And because of this, I can't blame her for anything that happened. I lied and pretended everything was normal, that there wasn't a problem. Our lives ebbed and flowed in this state of organized chaos, but within that chaos, under the guise of mundane brutality and usual depravity, something was wrong. Yes, the violence kept my teeth sharp and my mind sharper. The two of us sat on our thrones, king and queen, with the kind of ease you'd find from an old married couple on a broken down porch, mosquitos buzzing hungrily at their ears.

But the mosquitos drew more blood each time. One drop here, one suck there. Eventually you'd be hollowed out. It didn't matter how content you were, how little they took. Bloodsuckers never rest until they're full.

I made two mistakes. I pretended everything was fine, that *I*, Javier Bernal, was fine.

I also let the mosquitos get too close.

I let them rob me of everything that mattered most. Two mistakes cost me all that I'd worked for, all that I'd ever loved.

But I was not done yet. There was enough blood in me to keep me alive. And that blood boiled hot, red, rank with revenge.

Rage.

It fueled me.

It whipped me.

It *begged* me.

I would not stop until everything was mine again.

Until the heads rolled on the dusty floor.

CHAPTER ONE

Luisa

The heat made the blood smell worse, like you could sense it thickening in the air. It brought out the sharp tang of copper, mixed with heavy dust.

Blood these days reminded me of my mother. Not that she wasn't alive and relatively well, living with my father in an assisted living center in the quiet suburbs of San Diego. She was fine. She was safe. But I guess it made me aware of how disappointed she would be in me. In the person I had become. The smell of blood did nothing to me anymore. It didn't make me sick. It didn't make me feel anything. I was used to something I never thought I'd get used to.

And more than that, sometimes I liked the smell. Sometimes it meant an enemy was finished and we had lived to survive another day at the top. It was this constant climb and a never-ending struggle to keep our footing, and blood, blood meant victory. Security.

Power.

But I never wanted her to see me now, like this.

The wife of a drug king. The queen of corruption.

She knew all of this, of course. Knew what I did to survive and provide a good life for her, my father, myself. She knew that I fell in love.

But I'm not sure if she knows that I am falling out of love. That I didn't realize the cost of trying to keep it. She didn't know that I had become a monster, that the ways of this life—my new life—were slowly sinking into my soul and turning it putrid and black.

Everything costs something now. In the past, when I was just a lowly waitress in Cabo San Lucas, working for a slimeball boss, I had to pay for the right to make money by putting up with his advances. When I married Salvador Reyes, the most powerful madman in the country, I paid for that choice with my virginity, my dignity, and nearly my life. Now, in order to sit on the throne of the country, on top of money and drugs and guns and blood that paved my way, the cost was my soul.

Sometimes I thought it was the only thing I had left.

The screams in the distance died off. Funny, I actually hadn't noticed them until they stopped. The smell of blood still hung in the air, like invisible smoke that would eventually seep its way into your skin.

I grasped my bottle of wine tightly, as if it were filled with precious gems, and got off the bench at the koi pond. This used to be where Javier and I would sometimes talk, when he was feeling particularly romantic or even philosophical. He hadn't been in any of those moods lately. It was like I barely existed.

Well, there were some things. But I didn't want to think about those, even though I knew where he was going after the torture was over and the last drop of blood was spilled.

I carefully made my way past the lotuses, pausing to admire the elegance they granted such a brutal place, and headed toward the back of the pond where the reeds and palms grew thick. Behind them I was pretty much unnoticeable to the entire compound, a place that was nothing short of a palace, a place that had become my home for the last year and a half. But sometimes I still thought of it as less than a castle and more like a prison. After all, I was brought here as a captive and some memories were hard to forget, no matter how badly I tried to find my footing and rise above it.

A few weeks ago I took a bucket from the gardener's shed and brought it over, flipping it upside down to make a seat. I knew it was silly—I could have had custom made chairs or an outdoor sofa if I wanted. I could have had anything. But I wanted something that was mine and mine alone. A secret. I liked sitting here in the evenings, feeling totally protected from the watchful eyes of my husband, of his right-hand man Esteban, of the lackey Juanito, of anyone who worked for our cartel. By the time I finished a bottle of California pinot noir, I felt like another person in another land. These were the little things in my life that I clung to now.

I sat down on the bucket and took a long swig of wine. Javier got cases of it imported just for me, after I once remarked that I liked it. That was a few months ago, before his sister died and everything changed. Back then, I was Javier's queen. Now I didn't even know who I was. But I knew I didn't like her.

I was scared of myself.

I stayed hidden in my spot until the wine was almost gone and the sun was sinking below the hills to the west. The air was still hot, muggy, like breathing in through a wet cloth. Though I'd gotten used to the smell of blood, I hadn't gotten used to the humidity around Sinaloa. Especially where our compound was, nestled deep in a valley along the Devil's Backbone. Javier liked the cover our location provided – the landscaping blended the house seamlessly into the jungle, but it also trapped the heat and added to the feeling of being closed in. Sometimes I woke up thinking I couldn't breathe, nightmares of suffocation bleeding into reality.

During those times, I'd sit up in bed, breathing hard and covered in sweat. Javier would reach for me, seemingly half asleep, and just hold my hand for a moment. Then he would pull me toward him and I'd be lulled to sleep in his arms. Sometimes he would brush the hair off my face and those burning eyes of his would light me on fire. We'd make love and make promises.

It had been like that for a while – his comfort, his presence… he never denied me anything. I knew I wouldn't be accepted into his life so quickly, not by the members of his cartel. I'd gone from captor to lover in a short amount of time, and then from lover to wife soon after that. But he stood by me, ever so proud. He wouldn't change his mind about me and my place in his life, and he'd slaughter anyone who dared to throw an unkind word my way.

For all his cunning ambition and ruthless ways, Javier Bernal really did love me. He was devoted and as much mine as I was his.

All those promises.

"Luisa." A voice drifted over the brush, causing me to freeze.

Esteban came around the corner and gave me a lopsided smile.

"Here you are," he said lazily.

I took my hand away from my chest, my heart beating like a drum, and looked down at the empty bottle in my hands. I felt utterly stupid, which was probably silly in itself considering this was my property and I could do whatever the damn well I wanted.

I also felt acutely disappointed that there really was no safe place left.

I cleared my throat and sat up straighter, even though looking regal was impossible when you were sitting on top of a damn bucket.

"You found me," I said.

He folded his arms and peered down at me. "Dipping into the pinot again?"

I glared at him. "What's your point?"

He shrugged. "No point. I was looking for you though."

"Why?"

"Do I need a reason?"

Esteban and I didn't always see eye to eye, though it pained me to say that lately it felt like he was the only friend I had. There was always Juanito, who was in his early twenties and an eager *narco*, but I think the boy was scared of me, which I found funny considering we both had to be around the same age. And Javier's chief of security, a big brute of a man named Diego, was as quiet as they came. This was a shame because he was a smart man with a colorful past, and I was certain he had a million stories to tell.

Esteban, however, wasn't quiet and wasn't scared, and was there for me more often than not. Usually I found it annoying, how closely he tried to emulate Javier, how badly he wanted to be him. He'd tell you otherwise, of course, but Esteban was power hungry, bloodthirsty, and jealous beyond comprehension. He wasn't very smart, though. His lackadaisical surfer approach to life wasn't just an act, and no matter how badly he wanted to be in Javier's shoes, he could never, ever become him.

Naturally, I also knew I shouldn't underestimate people, and so with him I practiced more of a keep your friends close, enemies closer sort of relationship. While he could never become the *patron*, the ruler, the king, that didn't mean he wouldn't at some point try.

"I worry about you," he said, crouching down to my level.

I rolled my eyes. "Please."

He looked at the wine bottle. "I know things aren't...well, I know how things are."

I tucked the bottle on the other side of the bucket and gave him a pointed look. His green eyes were observing me a little too carefully, something I found off-putting.

"And what could you know?"

He rubbed his hand across his chin, seeming to think. "Well, I know Javier is uh...well, occupied most nights. I know where he goes and what he does."

A knife sliced right into my heart. I tried to keep a blank face, a mask. *Don't let the mask slip*, I told myself, and took in a quiet breath.

"Oh, is that right?" I asked, and winced once I heard the tremor in my voice.

His gaze softened and I hated the fucking sympathy I could see. Of all people, I didn't want it from him. I didn't want him to feel that he was any better than Javier or any better than me. Yes, I knew, damn it I fucking knew what Javier was doing with those girls, and I knew what happened to the girls after, too. I knew everything, but I wasn't about to let him feel that made him better than us. Javier, for everything that had happened, for the person he'd become, was still my husband.

God, even the word husband pinched deep inside.

"Javier isn't well," I told him before he could say anything else.

He actually laughed. "Not well? That's the understatement of the year."

"It isn't funny," I said quietly.

"No?" He placed one hand on my thigh, peering at me closely. I sucked in my breath. "Then let's not skirt around it. Javier has been compromised. He's damaged in a way that is only going to hurt the business. It's only going to hurt you."

I tried to shrug away from him but his grip on my leg tightened.

"Don't pretend anymore, Luisa," he said in a hush. "You know the truth. Alana's death…he couldn't handle it. That was the straw that broke the camel's back. He's lost nearly all his sisters. His whole family. A man can look strong, but that doesn't make him strong. Perhaps some might find it sentimental that he cares so much about his family after all, but powerful people can't afford to be sentimental. He can't afford to lose himself like this." He shook his head. "No, it's been long enough."

Now I felt I had to come to his defense, something I was used to doing, even in my own head, even against myself. "It's been five months since Alana died," I told him. "People need time to grieve. He's grieving in his own way. He will move on."

"Luisa…"

I suddenly got up, feeling emboldened by the wine, and shoved Este away. "No!" I yelled. "He will move on. I won't give up on him, no matter what he's doing. He'll find his way back to me."

"Will he find his way back to this?" Esteban spread out his arms, gesturing to the property. In the distance a few white parrots flew from the trees.

"He's doing fine," I told him, bringing my voice down. I jerked my head toward the place I liked to call the "torture hut." "What was going on in there? Did he not just weed out an informant? Last week, did he not order that safe house to be blown up? Lado's shipment to be destroyed? He's doing everything he needs to do to protect us, everything. We've never been stronger."

"He's being careless," he said imploringly, taking a step toward me.

"How so?"

He paused, eyes bright. "I guess he didn't tell you."

I swallowed thickly. "What?"

"We might have to move, temporarily."

I blinked at him, not comprehending a word of this. "What the hell are you talking about?"

Esteban licked his lips before taking in a deep breath. "I think Javier should be the one to tell you. It's not my place."

Since when did Esteban ever care if it was his place or not? He was constantly handing out his unwanted opinion.

I reached out and grabbed his arm. His eyes met mine briefly and I saw something in them I didn't want to see right then. Anger...or something smokier than that. Almost sultry.

Quickly I let go and placed my hands on my hips instead. "Cut the bullshit and just tell me. That's why you were looking for me, weren't you? You just love being the bearer of bad news."

He sighed. "You know all about Angel Hernandez?"

Did I ever. Though our cartel, the Sinaloa, was arguably the biggest in Mexico, and Javier had been working on getting the other cartels united, or at least on "friendly" terms under one blanket organization, Angel Ochoa Hernandez remained cagey. He reigned over the Tijuana cartel, and with all of that, he controlled the Tijuana and San Diego border. Which meant he controlled all of the drugs going up in the trucks into America on the I-5. Currently we had to pay him a tariff to let our heroin in through—five percent—which doesn't sound like a lot, but when you're dealing with millions of dollars, it is.

With our cartel getting more successful, that tax becomes a lot of money that is better spent on ourselves. Javier controlled Ciudad Juarez port for cocaine shipments and we had a free pass for Nuevo Laredo because he was close with Jose Fuentes who lorded over that. But Angel was determined to hold on to Tijuana with all that he had, and unless he was taken out of the picture, we'd never have control.

For months, Javier had talked about making it happen, hiring a *sicario* to do the job. The only thing that prevented him was timing, and I guess that strange code of honor he carried with him like a reluctant badge. He would never inform on another cartel, and killing a king of one was nearly as bad. But we knew it was something that would eventually have to be done.

Then Alana was killed and it was forgotten. Though Esteban thought he was giving me bad news, the mere fact that he had mentioned Angel's name meant Javier hadn't let his ambitions go completely.

"What about him? Is he dead?" I asked hopefully.

He shook his head. "No, but Javier thinks he has a plan to ensure it happens."

"And what's so bad about that? You've both talked about this, how it would become necessary at some point."

"What's bad, Luisa, is that he wants to kidnap a PFM agent to do so."

"And how does that help?"

He gave me a look that said it didn't. "Anyway, once we get him, whoever the poor fucker is, we'll be off to one of our ranches in Chihuahua for the usual interrogation tactics. I think it's a fucking terrible idea."

"You'd rather him torture a federal agent here?" I didn't know—and didn't want to know—half the stuff that went down on the compound, but I knew we never brought anyone here that was of much importance. A federal agent on our soil would be asking for a lot of trouble, especially since Javier had zero control over the PFM. Police and local military, yes. They were all bribed handsomely to look the other way. Hell, they protected Javier. But the government was something else entirely, and they could raise a lot of hell if they wanted to.

"I'd rather he not do this at all. There are other ways to gather intelligence. He could leave it up to me."

I raised a brow. Esteban was our intelligence man and the techie, but I knew that Javier was having problems putting trust in him as well. "I'm sure Javier knows what he's doing."

He shook his head slightly, his shaggy, blonde-streaked hair falling over his forehead. "But that's the thing. He doesn't. And we both know it."

He looked back at the house. "Come on, it's getting dark. You should go back inside."

But I didn't want to. I planted my feet firmly. I wanted to stay in the dark. I wanted to stay away from the house. The house that had a room Javier used to fuck whichever whore it was for the night.

My heart clenched at the thought of going inside, crawling into bed, and trying to survive another night of a marriage that was crumbling at the seams. But I knew, eventually, when the stars came out and the mosquitos became too much, I would go inside, as I always did.

"You deserve better, you know," Esteban said so quietly it was almost a whisper, before turning around and heading to the house, his tall form disappearing from sight. It was as if he read my mind, or maybe he was just good at reading me. Maybe I was an open book for the world to see. Everyone except my husband.

CHAPTER TWO

Javier

I was already awake when Luisa woke up gasping for breath. I kept my eyes closed as I felt her sit up, knowing she was panicking because of some nightmare, or maybe because of her cruel reality. I feigned sleep, sleep that never came for me anymore. I had always excelled at deception, at pretending, so this fit me like an old glove.

I kept my breath even and hoped she'd go right back under. That she wouldn't want anything from me. How sick is that? The thought of her touching me filled me with revulsion. Not because I didn't desire her, because I did, now more than ever. I *needed* her. And not because I didn't love her, because I loved her to the best of my ability. Whether that equaled what she deserved or not, I didn't know.

Her touch, however, would spur me on. It would undo me more than I'd already been undone. I was a black, rolling pit of rage and exquisitely honed violence. The last thing I wanted was to unleash that on her. Maybe it was the most selfless thing I'd ever done, giving up sex with my wife out of fear of hurting her.

Or maybe I was just deceiving myself this time. Because it was more than just sex. It was everything.

I wondered how long this could go on before she'd had enough. When she found out about the other women. Could she possibly understand that it was better them than her? Could she forgive me for sparing her the brutality, the depravity?

I had my doubts.

And I didn't want to be forgiven.

Her fingers trailed along my arm and I did everything I could to lie still, to not swallow the knot in my throat. It was easier to play dead.

"Javier?" she whispered, voice soft and disembodied in the dark behind my eyes. Just her voice had the power to shake me loose, even after a year and a half of marriage, but I remained in control. As always.

She said my name again, her fingers clenching my arm. I was a light sleeper and she knew this. If I didn't wake up for her, she'd know I was faking it. What was the difference? Either way she'd be hurt.

I swallowed hard. "What?" I asked, voice hoarse. I still didn't open my eyes. I could see her in my head, the mussed up hair, the want in her dark eyes, an open, full mouth just begging to be put to use.

God, don't fucking tempt me.

I heard her lick her lips, those incredible lips. "I can't sleep," she said.

I can never sleep, I wanted to tell her. *You don't see me trying to wake you up.*

"I *know*, you know," she said quietly.

I sucked in my breath. "Know what?" I asked flatly.

She paused before she said, "About your plans for Angel Hernandez."

Esteban. That asshole. He was like a little fucking girl, always having to tell someone the latest gossip.

"Let me guess, Este told you." I finally opened my eyes and tilted my head to look at her. As I thought, she looked absolutely ravishing in the dim, grainy light, that beautiful combination of aching vulnerability and seething contempt. Her long dark hair flowed over her shoulders in waves, her silky black camisole hugging her curves. It amazed me that after everything, she still went to bed looking like a goddess for me.

I was a lucky son of a bitch in this respect. But currently, that luck wasn't enough. Luck is only valuable when it's across the board. One piece of luck is enough to trick a fool into thinking everything's going to be okay.

I wasn't sure if everything could be okay again. How could it, with Alana gone? How could it, when I was punished for loving someone? Family first. What was next? My wife? Best to cut those ties before it all went to hell.

Luisa was watching me, inspecting me. I didn't know what she saw. I hoped she saw nothing at all, just a blank space where I used to be.

"Yes, he told me," she eventually said, brows drawn together, entirely dissatisfied with whatever it was she saw.

"I was going to tell you," I said, not really caring to make excuses. "When it was all said and done. No need to involve you."

She went rigid as I knew she would. "No need to tell me? Javier, I'm your fucking wife. Your partner. I'm in this as much as you are." She let out a heavy breath. "At least I used to be. Am I not still your queen?"

I didn't say anything. I couldn't.

Her fingers dug into my arm. "Javi…please. I know things have been hard. I know you're sad, angry. I know you're suffering, I—"

"I am not suffering!" I roared, my vision flashing as rage forced me up. I pinned Luisa to the bed. She didn't fight beneath me, but I held her wrists nearly tight enough to break them. "Do you understand?" I seethed, glaring down at her as the adrenaline flooded through me. I shook her once. "Do you?"

She stared back at me, and I recognized the mask she slipped onto her face. We both wore them. "I understand," she said, her voice dull.

I didn't want to let go of her, but I knew I had to or this would turn into something else.

But something in her eyes changed. The mask slipped. She seemed to melt under my grasp.

"Fuck me," she said. It was a command. Her tone was languid, her gaze lush as she stared at me.

I wasn't used to her being so direct and I couldn't pretend that I didn't have an erection already. I slept naked, after all.

"Luisa…" I said, shutting my eyes and trying to compose myself.

"Fuck me hard," she said throatily. "Now." I felt my balls tighten, the blood pulsing in my cock.

I looked at her with intensity. "I will hurt you."

She wasn't deterred. "You've already hurt me, Javier."

"Not in this way."

"Then I want it this way." She squirmed beneath me. "Please. Be rough. Hurt me. Make me bleed. Give me *something*."

There was such breathtaking sorrow in her last words that it nearly shamed me to be as turned on as I was.

"You don't want this," I whispered, feeling myself slowly succumb to her wishes.

"I want everything." She bit her lip then closed her eyes. "Just fuck me. Fuck me up. Give me everything you've got."

She didn't want everything I had. I had given that to the whore earlier. As I fucked her raw, against the wall, tied with barbed wire, I took that same wire and brought it around her neck as she climaxed. She was still coming as the blood ran down her neck. She came until her windpipe was severed in two.

I'd be lying if I said I hadn't meant to kill her. But rage is a funny thing. I guess she had it coming though, no pun intended. Anyone who would willingly let their self be choked with barbed wire wouldn't get very far in life, anyway.

"Please," Luisa pleaded.

I didn't let her beg anymore. I reached down and grabbed her by the hair, my fingers scraping along her scalp, and I yanked her up and over, like she weighed nothing at all. She let out a little yelp and I tightened my grip, pushing her face into the pillow.

I lowered my lips to her ear. "Is this what you want? Tell me now if it's not and I'll leave you alone."

She moved her cheek to the side and said, mumbling against the fabric, "Don't leave me alone."

I took in a deep breath. "I won't leave you."

But my voice was shaking.

So I straddled her, and with one hand fisted in her hair, I pulled her camisole up with the other. She slid her arms out of the straps, obedient, wanting it, and I gathered the delicate fabric around her neck, wrapping it and twisting it around my hand until it was tight. Luisa was no stranger to this kind of bed play, but I knew I was squeezing her throat with enough power to shut it off completely. Luckily, the camisole had a touch of stretch to it.

"You say you want me," I told her gruffly, pulling her head back by the hair, by the throat, until her torso was lifted off the bed, like a mermaid at the bow of a ship. "You say you want to fuck me. But I don't think I am who you're looking for. He hasn't been around for some time."

She sputtered under my grasp, unable to talk. I could hear the breath wheezing out of her and none going back in. For one horrifying, startling moment I had a thought of her wanting to die. That this was her plan. That I'd made her life so miserable lately that this was the only way she thought she had a way out.

But even though I was no longer the man she knew, she was the Luisa that I knew. That I fell in love with. That I married. And that I pushed away.

With surprising strength she reached behind her and wrapped her fingers around my cock. She stroked my length and I felt like a balloon ready to burst. But not this way, not yet.

I let go of the camisole and her hair, shoving her back to the bed, her grip on me becoming free. I quickly reached under the mattress and brought out the large steak knife I kept there. Even though I had guards in the house, military patrolling the grounds, I'd be foolish not to have my own form of protection. I could reach the knife or the gun hooked under the bottom of my bedside table in a second flat.

Quickly placing the knife handle between my teeth, I brought Luisa's hands behind her back and knotted the camisole around them. If she handled me anymore, I'd be coming all over her in seconds. And while I had no problems covering her from head to toe, I hadn't been with my wife for a long time. I wanted to at least have her come first, before I made my mark.

There was something so carnal about having her lie on her stomach beneath me, her face unseen, her hands bound. Helpless. Even in the faint light I could still see the scars on her back where I had carved my name into her flesh, back when she was just a captive, before she was mine. In some ways it felt like yesterday.

I took the knife out of my mouth and held it in one hand while I let my fingertip trail down her spine. She shivered beneath me.

"Do you still want me to make you bleed?" I asked in a hush. My fingers twitched and ached, cycling between wanting to hold back and wanting to make it hurt.

She nodded.

"You need to say it."

"Make me bleed."

I slid my fingers between her soft ass cheeks, ripe like peaches and just as easy to bruise, and stroked around her hole before I dipped down into her cunt. It was already dripping wet, drenched for me. Such a good girl. Such a beautiful queen.

And somehow still my queen. I didn't know for how much longer.

With one swift motion I drew the blade of the knife down one side of her spine.

She cried out, a half scream. It reminded me of so many screams lately, but coming from her it made me pause. My heart thudded in my chest.

I wanted to ask if she was okay, but there was too much energy coursing through me. I quickly slashed another line to match down the other side, feeling that strange relief flow through me. She screamed again, breathing heavily as the blood ran down the sides of her back, pooling on the sheets. Such a shame to ruin such an expensive set but that was a minor price to pay.

"Do you want me to stop?" I murmured as I thrust my wet fingers into her ass and she tightened around me like a vise. "Or should I keep going?"

She took a shaky breath in and out. "Keep going." Despite the obvious pain she was in, she was determined. Stubborn.

I took the knife to her ass cheeks and slowly drew the blade across her skin until it sank in with a satisfying give. It took a second for the blood to rise, and then it was flowing hot and fast down the hills. I lowered my head and licked the blood off of her, the sharp taste of copper and salt satisfying some sort of vampire-ish thirst. When I had lapped up as much as I could, her body tensing now from desire, I moved my tongue inward, where it was sweeter, where it was all her.

A moan rippled through her body and she pushed herself back into me, wanting more. I would give her more. I always did.

I devoured her, every inch, my mouth filling with her desire. I swallowed it deep, wanting to drown in it, remembering how much I missed this, missed her. Her taste was incomparable, the feel of her cunt and her ass beneath my tongue, between my lips, was a drug like no other. In that moment, I could have spent the rest of my life with my face between her folds, just taking in everything that was left of her.

I ended up nipping her clit, hard, between my teeth.

She cried out in surprise, in pain, then in pleasure as I licked the hurt away and she relaxed back into me.

Her breathing became shallow, her skin hotter. She was swelling beneath my touch. She was about to come. I pulled back, gasping for breath and quickly positioned myself. I hadn't meant to go inside her. Being inside Luisa was something I thought of as too much of a risk. The feelings she would bring me.

But at that moment I didn't care.

And when she called out my name, almost panting, "Javier, please," then I *really* didn't care.

I thrust into her, holding her hips in place, relishing how she felt, tight fucking silk. I moaned, my eyes rolling back into my head, a torrent of emotion beginning to swirl in my chest, something more than anger this time.

I swallowed it down and let out a hot breath as I slowly, agonizingly pulled back out of her.

"Is that what you wanted?" I asked her.

She nodded, breathless. "Yes, please."

"You're being very polite, my dear. I have a feeling you're not asking for what you really want. You're not quite…full enough, are you?"

Her head shook once.

I bit my lip until I tasted blood, anticipating what I was about to do. Then I picked up the knife and turned it around. I held the blade with my hands, delicately at first, and slid the plastic handle into her ass. She tensed up, and as I pushed it in deeper, my grip on the blade tightened and blood began to seep from my hands. I barely felt the cut, I only felt her around my cock, that soft, wet sanctuary.

I thrust into her, the knife handle and my equally hard dick, moving in unison as she welcomed it more and more. My movements became faster, I went deeper. I could barely hold on to her hips with one hand, too much blood was spilling from the other, making everything red and wet and hot. It looked like a massacre, and I felt I was losing much more than blood.

I came inside her, hard and long, and I only needed to flick her clit to get her to do the same. She moaned loud, beautiful music to my ears, threatening to undo me. She quaked and shuddered as the orgasm rocked through her, and for a wonderful second I imagined my seed sinking into her, finding purchase. The chance at a child.

But when desire and lust lost their footing and my heartbeat slowed and I was spent, my mind could think clearly again. I could dispose of those feelings that had the power to hurt me in the end.

Family was everything.

Family got you killed.

There would be no child.

There was barely a wife.

I looked down at Luisa, my blood spilled all over her back and mixing with her own. I pulled the knife out of her and shook the remaining drops on her rising back as she caught her breath. I ran my hand down her spine, smooth, blending our blood together. It was the best that I could do, it was the most of me that I could give.

I didn't say anything to her as I got off the bed and went to the en-suite bathroom. I washed my hands in the sink, the cut across my inner fingers not too deep, watching the water swirl down the drain, our blood together. Blood of family. Blood of marriage.

Then I looked at myself in the mirror and was glad to see a man I didn't recognize staring back at me. You couldn't take anything from this man. He had dead eyes.

When I emerged, she was standing naked, vulnerable, beautiful, the sheets and blankets piled at the foot of the bed, white splashed with feathering red. Our eyes met and I saw that need in them. She wanted me to come back to her. Maybe just to put her in the bathtub and wash the horror from her back, take care of her, like I always used to do.

I could only stare back at her, wishing she could see that this was all I had. That we were lucky it hadn't taken a turn for the worse. That her wounds on her back would heal.

Even if the wounds in her heart would not.

She nodded once, reading the futility of it all. She was so good at that, seeing the truth. It made me wonder what she'd seen in me all along.

Did she hate herself for losing her heart to a monster?

"I'll get clean sheets," she said, her voice small. She started for the door, seeming to forget that she was naked and bleeding.

I quickly walked over to her and put my good hand on her shoulder. She looked at it in surprise, the generosity of my touch. "No, you go clean yourself up," I told her. "I'll deal with the bed."

She blinked, then gave me a timid, grateful look.

"Thank you," she said, then walked to the bathroom. I watched her go, her back bloodied, yet she wore it like a cape.

And I knew she was thanking me for more than that. She was thanking me for being intimate with her. She was thanking me for waking up, even if just for a few minutes. Even if I brought her a lot of pain with some of the pleasure.

I hoped I had the strength to never let it happen again.

CHAPTER THREE

Javier

I dreamed about Alana again.

It's always the same fucking dream.

It was the last time I saw her. Wal-Mart of all damn places, just outside of Durango. Figures it would be in a fluorescent-lit hell. She'd met me and Luisa there, looking frightened and vulnerable. Lost. A cast on her leg. She thought her brother could save her. She'd survived an assassination attempt. Two, actually, if you counted her getting hit by a car. And the third attempt, the one that blew her and my boat up, that's the one that got her in the end.

I could have done more for her. Maybe that's why the dream didn't stop. Why I kept seeing her crumpled face, why I kept hearing myself say the last thing I said to her.

"I will take care of you, you got that? The only way I know how."

I would hear those words of mine when I was awake, too. They mocked me.

Because I failed. Because I didn't take her seriously enough. But I never did, did I? The only person I ever took seriously was me.

What I thought at the time was that Alana was a trail straight to me, my compound, my cartel. I assumed that the reason she "survived" so many attempts on her life was because they never meant to kill her, whoever they were. They just wanted to scare her, right into my arms.

And it worked. I brushed her off. Of course I didn't turn her out to the wolves, but I certainly didn't trust the situation, nor her so-called Canadian boyfriend. I needed to get away from her, for my sake, for Luisa's sake. And yes, for her sake, too. Because when I was caught, when I was killed, what would happen to her? As long as I was unattainable—safe—she, in a sense, would be too.

But I was wrong. About everything.

I hadn't heard from her for a week. I thought she was going to call the number I gave her. I thought she would have trusted me to take care of her. But she didn't. And now I couldn't blame her.

I got a phone call at five in the morning from the chief of police in Mazatlán, someone who was already on my payroll. He said there had been an explosion in the Sea of Cortez, and the crew who went out to investigate found wreckage of my mega-ketch, blown to smithereens. Ironically I had named the boat Beatriz, after one of my other deceased sisters.

I had no idea what was happening, and it wasn't until they reviewed security footage from the marina, which showed a group of men, presumably dressed like old sailors, pushing a few wheelbarrows down the docks. One of the men stopped and pulled back a blanket that was lying across the wheelbarrow.

It was Alana's face. She was curled inside, unconscious or already dead.

The man kept his back to the camera, fuzzy grey hair sticking out of his sailor's cap that could have been real, could have been fake, but Alana was kept in full view. The man wanted us to see her.

He wanted me to see her.

The next thing they found was footage of Beatriz sailing out to sea.

Alana was on it.

Two horrible days later, while Luisa and I had hunkered down in Mazatlán, I was approached by the coroner. He had bad news. Alana's remains were found among the wreckage. They ran her through DNA testing and it was a match. They were one hundred percent certain that my sister was dead. And the police had no idea who was behind it. Even when they were paid handsomely by me, they still couldn't come up with any leads, and the police down in Jalisco, where Alana had lived, were worthless as well.

I didn't feel anything at first.

I remembered Luisa gripping my hand.

The breath being knocked out of me.

But it was all rather fitting. I recall thinking, *this figures*. Because it did. Violence, the cartel way of life, had taken my parents from me. My sister Beatriz. My sister Violetta, who I saw explode in a car bomb before my very eyes. Now Alana. The only Bernal left was her twin, Marguerite, who chose to stay as far away from me as possible, who wanted to forget that I was her brother. She lived in New York and had cut all ties with me, not only for her own safety, but because she wanted to pretend I didn't exist. My only family left hated me.

I hated me. Because this had all been my fault. Each death was on my head. From the years as the right-hand man to Travis Raines and his cartel, to overthrowing him, to starting my own, and then to overtaking Salvador Reyes, up, up, up to the top. They all died because I kept climbing.

Family is everything. That is the creed in this country. But that creed gets others killed. And it slowly kills you. Your family is the first thing you'll lose. Your soul will be the last.

Luckily, I didn't have much of either anymore.

I had Luisa, of course. She had become my family, my confidante, my lover, my friend. She had become everything to me, in bed and outside of it. But she was a weakness, my weakness. She was what they would go after next, the last thing I could possibly lose.

Unless I lost her first.

I was keeping her safe, as safe as I could, as safe as anyone could. I had all of Sinaloa under my finger, which meant the police and the military. Guards were outside my door, my compound was patrolled, the hills were watched...I had eyes everywhere. Radios, cell phones, everything was monitored with what the local military had. If anyone was coming, we knew about it.

In reality there were few to fear. America wouldn't touch me, not after I had informed on Salvador to the DEA. I had the Juarez plaza and unity with Nuevo Laredo. After I seized Tijuana, which was still my plan, I would control everything except the Gulf. They were not true Sinaloans, not like me, not like the real *narco* royalty. They were who I had to watch, my only real threat in the end. And they had tried before, only to be thwarted in the process.

But keeping Luisa safe from others also meant keeping her away from me. I couldn't let what happened last night happen again. She couldn't be my own victim. I knew I was hurting her by pushing her away, by keeping her at a distance. But it was for her own good, and mine.

I didn't feel like myself anymore. I knew I wasn't myself. I woke up with this deep-seated need to maim and hurt. To fuck. To make others suffer, as I suffered.

And I knew I had to use this anger, sharpen it like a knife. It would be greater than any weapon.

The only way through was up. To the top. Until I had all of Mexico. Until I was unstoppable.

Until there was nothing left to fear.

...

There was a knock at my office door. I didn't have to ask who it was. It was always Este. Luisa never bothered to knock anymore. She never bothered at all.

"Come in," I said, my voice sounding more tired than I'd like. I didn't want Este to think I wasn't on top of the game. He didn't need to know about my dreams, the sleepless nights. It had been a long day, though, and I supposed I was allowed to look like I'd been working at my desk from dawn until dusk.

The door opened and he stepped in. As usual he looked like a fucking moron in his board shorts and wife-beater. Flip-flops on his feet, like a damn Californian cartoon.

"Lose a bet?" I asked as I briefly looked him over.

"You used that line last week," he said, sitting down across from me on the other side of the desk. He kicked off his flip-flops and crossed his legs at the ankles. My lip curled in disgust, the thought of his dirty feet on my sheepskin rug.

"I'll try to be more original next time," I said dryly, putting my agenda away. I folded my hands in front of me and gave him a pointed look. "Have we found him yet?"

A slow, crooked smile spread across his face. It told me everything I needed to know.

I opened my desk drawer and took out a file folder. Call me old-fashioned but I needed to have most of my intel in my hands as well as on the computer. My brain handled it better that way.

Flipping it open, I took out a picture of Evaristo Martinez Sanchez. He was young, twenty-four, a light-skinned, blue-eyed Mexican. Probably made the ladies go crazy. For a moment I realized he was about Luisa's age and that they would make a good-looking couple. I'm not sure if I was relieved or not when I found my stomach curling with jealousy over the thought.

It was a serious photo, like a mugshot, and in color, probably taken for his government ID. Evaristo was part of the task force for the Policía Federal Ministerial, or PFM, those lovely people our government hired to fight organized crime and people like me. This organization, unlike the AFI before them, were hard to bribe and did things by the book like many of the Americans liked to think themselves did. In other words, they were a pain in my ass and could do serious damage to any cartel, if given the chance. The *federales*, we called them.

Evaristo was ranked up there on the team that watched Angel Hernandez and the Tijuana plaza. He wasn't in charge of the unit—kidnapping the boss would be too risky for me and *federale* bosses would never talk. Stubborn little bastards. That stark loyalty and honor would be useful for my side, if only their morals weren't so fucked up.

But being second in command, Evaristo would know enough, and the more I read up about him, the more I liked him. He came from the barrios of Matamoros, dropping out of school when he was thirteen to become a petty criminal. He screwed up once and made enemies with the wrong people (are there any right people?) which put him in a precarious position at a very young age. Like most youth, he joined the Mexican army because there was nowhere else for him to go. He liked the discipline there and had the willingness to do jobs others wouldn't. He was a quick learner and more than eager. As soon as he was out, the PFM swooped in and recruited him.

The PFM wear masks when they do raids so that people like me don't recognize them. But the internet is a funny thing, and Este knew how to get information. I felt like I knew Evaristo well. Already he reminded me of our Juanito, who was essentially Este's guy Friday now, following him around like a puppy.

I was looking forward to kidnapping him. Torturing him, just a bit, at first anyway. I'm not an animal. Just to see how he handled it. To see if he was as good as the reports from his supervisors said he was.

Naturally, I wanted him to fail. When he failed, he would give me the information I needed to take Angel out. When I took Angel out, I'd take over the plaza. Evaristo would be spared because of my graciousness, and hopefully I wouldn't have inflicted too much damage to his pretty boy face. Or maybe I'd be doing him a favor. Too much pussy can be tiring at times.

I was surprised that Este came through with everything. He opposed my plan at first. Said it was too risky and that our cartel was too good for this. Too elegant. That we didn't need to fall into stereotypical violence that besieged the country, that hiring *sicarios* to take out a lord was beneath us.

I don't think Este knew who I'd become.

But Este leaned over and tapped Evaristo's photo. "He's a sitting duck. Two days. I set up the staged bust and they've got the message. They're on it."

"Just as I asked," I reminded him. He had a habit of trying to take over my ideas, even if he didn't agree with them. Always trying to one up me when he should have known there was no one-upping the *patron*, not when you were a barefoot fool.

"Yes," he said, rather reluctantly. "Should I go and make sure it all goes through?"

What was in motion now was that Este had tipped off someone at the PFM about a safe house location and an impossible amount of cocaine and meth looking to make its way up on a big rig to San Diego. But the safe house was a ruse. We would be there waiting for them. And we'd take out Evaristo as soon as we had the chance. It's hard to hide those blue eyes behind a mask, and at six foot two, he'd stand out among the men like a sore thumb. Of course with something like this, I wasn't involved. Other people did my dirty work for me. I had a growing team of ex-soldiers and cops who could go into any situation and come out alive with the target.

"No," I told him. "Let them do it. You'd just get in the way, tripping over your own sandals, your hair in your eyes like a little girl."

My insults didn't seem to work on Esteban anymore. He jerked his chin at my forehead. "Is your hair thinning a little bit? Must be the stress."

I raised my brow. "So is that all you came to tell me?"

"Is that all?" he repeated incredulously. "I come here to tell you that I orchestrated your plan exactly as *you* wanted, the bait has been taken, and you wonder if that's all?"

"I'm sorry, did you need me to pat you on the back, maybe make you burp a little?"

Este made a disgruntled noise and got out of his chair. "You know what, Javier? You may be the *patron* and this may be *your* cartel, and you may think that you earned it, but there is something other *narcos* do that you don't, and that's treat their brothers with respect."

I blinked at him, actually caught off-guard for once. "This isn't a preschool, Este. I will give you respect if you deserve it."

"And what about your wife?"

A block of ice froze in my chest and my eyes became cold as I glared at him. "What business is it of yours to even mention her?"

I could practically watch him think. He knew the wrong thing would get him in a lot of trouble. And he knew what I'd been up to lately, more than once. Sometimes he helped.

"No business at all," he said after some time. He started for the door, then paused. "Though I should tell you that your *appointment* is here. Should I show her in?"

After his comment, I should have said no. But while it made me think twice about what I was doing, it also made me mad.

Still, maybe this one wouldn't piss me off tonight. It didn't always end in blood.

I nodded at him, and in that moment, I wondered if it made me seem weak. I knew Este was no better when it came to women. Maybe I only thought that because *I* used to be better.

He disappeared down the hall and I quickly checked the clock on the wall. It was already ten p.m. Luisa would be settling down for bed herself.

I was about to call after Este and tell him I'd changed my mind when he appeared at the door with a tall, striking woman. She didn't look like any of the other whores. Though all of them were beautiful, this woman had her nose right in the air, as if she were better than me, better than her whole profession.

I immediately disliked her. Perhaps there would be blood after all.

"This is Judia," Este said.

Judia? Named after a bean?

Este turned to leave but I called out after him. "Actually, Este, you can have her."

He stopped and gave me a funny look. I knew he didn't need my charity in this regard but I thought I'd offer it anyway. Even with the scar down the side of his face and his teenage clothes, Este was a ladykiller.

Then again, so was I.

"No offense, Judia," he said to her before eyeing me, "but I don't need anything you think I can have."

Judia smirked at him. "Am I supposed to be flattered, two men *not* fighting over me? What, are you both gay?"

I had to laugh. I hadn't laughed in a long time and the sound was jarring to my own ears.

"Yes, completely gay," I said, getting out of my chair and walking over to her. "Gayest *patron* that ever was."

She shrugged with one shoulder and looked down at me. "That will make things easier. I don't get off with men who are shorter than me anyway."

Este sucked in his breath. My mouth gaped open slightly. Did this *puta* just have the nerve to make fun of my height?

I nodded at her, unable to keep the smile from stretching across my face, and walked back to the desk. "You're very honest, *Judia*. And daring, really. But I don't think it's a very good career decision to be so choosy, especially with *patrons*."

My fingers slipped under the desk and closed around a wide, wooden handle, the cut on my hand stinging from last night. I wore my smile well.

"You know, I am five foot nine, which is fairly average for a man," I told her, keeping my movements quiet. I may have added an inch. "How tall are you?"

She swallowed hard, seeming nervous for the first time. I've been told my smile can be unnerving if I use it long enough.

"Five foot eleven," she said.

I licked my lips, feeling my blood run hot and wild. "So I only need to take off about three inches or so."

Her eyes widened in a mix of confusion and then horror as I brought the machete out from underneath my desk. I'd been trained for this, to maximize force in a small space. It's all in the legs, in the way you spring. In one smooth motion I swung the machete better than any golf club, swiping across her legs mid-calf.

She screamed as she became an amputee in an instant, blood spilling to the ground as she fell to one side and her severed legs fell to the other. I guess I took off more than three inches, but it was better to overachieve than under.

"There," I said as I peered down at her face, an arc of blood spurting from her legs in time with her fading heartbeat. "Now you are shorter than me. Think you can come now?"

Judia screamed again, but her voice was fading, choked in her throat as shock overtook her. I sighed and stared at the sheepskin rug. First dirty with Este's feet, now this.

"You keep a machete under your desk?" Este asked, looking over my shoulder at it, the long bloody blade still in my hands.

I gave him a look. "Why wouldn't I keep a machete under my desk?" I handed it to him. "Here, put it back and get Juanito to clean this up." I gestured to the soon to be corpse and the bloody mess of an office. "I'm going to bed."

Este tried to take it from my hands but I found my grip tightening. "On second thought, I'll take it with me." I didn't want Este to think he could go on about "respect" again, even though I knew he was thinking it with Juanito having to clean up my mess half the time. Everyone had to pay their dues, though.

I took the machete upstairs, my bodyguard Diego following me down the hall as he always did. I barely noticed him until I was about to go into my bedroom.

"Mrs. Bernal is sleeping in one of the guest bedrooms," he said in his low, baritone voice. He didn't speak much, one of the reasons I liked him. "The one at the end of the hall."

"Oh?" The one that used to be her prison cell. "Did she say why?"

"No sir," Diego said. "She just came up to me to let me know."

As if it would go unnoticed. "All right," I said, straightening up a bit, as if this arrangement was the new normal. "Can you make sure we have someone stationed outside her door as well? Arturo?"

"Of course," he said before he strode off to gather Arturo from one of the barracks on the property, probably interrupting his sleep. Arturo was as equally as trustworthy as Diego but usually worked in the early morning hours. Still, I wouldn't compromise her safety. The chances of someone getting into the house to get at her, or me, were practically nil, but sometimes you couldn't trust the people in your house either. I knew better than to underestimate those closest to me. I knew better but I never let on.

I closed the door behind me and got ready for bed. For all the troubles, this was the first time I'd gone to sleep without her. Perhaps she should have done this a long time ago. Perhaps she was tired of having to go to bed and fall asleep first, such a vulnerable stage of life, all alone.

And now, now I was alone. With those thoughts again. Knowing the dreams were waiting. The ones filled with guilt and grief and regret. The ones that made me a little more scared of myself, a little crazier, day by day.

As I fell asleep, I could still smell the blood I had spilled. It worked as well as a sleeping pill.

CHAPTER FOUR

Esteban

Fucking animal, Esteban Mendoza thought to himself as he surveyed Javier's office. Blood was absolutely everywhere, even on the walls, which meant Juanito would be spending all hours of the night wiping that shit down, not to mention disposing of the body. He had to do the exact same thing the other day, after Javier got carried away with a piece of barbed wire. The pigs he kept out back were getting fatter by the minute.

It wasn't that Este really felt bad for Juanito, it was more that it would steal his time away from *him*. After all, Este was having him do all sorts of things that in some ways were far worse. Juanito wasn't even gay. Not that Este was either, he just liked to get off and it usually didn't matter who was sucking his dick. It was more about the power. The control. And that need to humiliate someone the way he used to be humiliated himself, back when he was a little punk hanging on the corners of the *colonias* of Juarez. When he told Juanito to get on his knees and put his cock in his mouth, he felt like a king. The king he always should have been. The *patron* he'd dreamed about.

He'd bided his time long enough. Put up with Javier long enough. He had to act now, before Javier really went to the dark side. It wasn't that Javier would slip up. Este had told Luisa that her husband was getting sloppy, but that wasn't really the case. Ever since Alana's death, he'd become sharper, like a new knife. He'd become more focused on building his empire and taking the jagged pieces of what was once one federation of *narcos* and putting them back together again, with him at the helm.

Javier was lost, yes. Grieving, no doubt. But he wasn't letting go of the business. And if anything, he was becoming more dangerous. Unpredictable. Inhumane. Este had never, ever feared Javier before. He had no reason to. He knew Javier had always looked at him like a lackey, a joke, and that was something he purposely cultivated. Because who would ever suspect Este of really using his brain? He was smart enough for the techie stuff, but no one would expect him to be devious. Or calculating. In fact, Este grew tired of the surfer look a year ago but kept it up because appearances were everything in this place. He fucking *hated* wearing flip-flops.

But now, Este wasn't so sure that Javier wouldn't snap one day and have his own head chopped off, for no real reason at all. What Este had wanted to accomplish by offing Alana—(he had offed her, hadn't he? He wondered that sometimes at night, the image of the boat exploding in the background again and again. Were the female remains Alana's? The DNA findings on Alana were faked to bring certainty to Javier, but Este wasn't quite certain himself.)—was to bring Javier to his knees and make him vulnerable. In a sense, it had worked. But Este had to act fast now before it took a turn for the worse and Javier became harder to manage.

His grace was gone. His elegance was still there, but when Este looked into those golden eyes, he only saw rage, and behind that rage, madness. The old Javier would never have killed a whore without reason, and now he was just doing it out of this newfound bloodlust. The old Javier probably wouldn't have cheated on his wife (even though the old Javier did have a habit of cheating on *other* partners, and later, beheading them, so maybe this wasn't new). And the old Javier would *never* have been so ambitious as to kidnap a *federale* as a means to assassinate another cartel leader.

The first step was Luisa. He was almost there. Even though Javier's behavior surprised him, he wanted him to keep pushing his wife away. He wanted Javier to cheat on her. He wanted Luisa ruined and helpless and looking for love and affection anywhere.

Este wanted Luisa to come to him. He would show her what she was missing, how a real man fucked. He would give her everything that Javier couldn't. He would do this, in secret, for a long time, until the secret came out. He would then take her for his own, and when he was bored of her one day, kill her. Make sure Javier knew about that, too. Maybe give him a front row seat.

Of course, he would take the cartel as well. The plans were being set in motion for that. He could have kissed Javier for being so ballsy and ambitious.

It was all pretty much perfect.

But if he didn't act now, he could end up dead.

And death was something Este feared. Death before getting to show the world what a fool Javier Bernal was. Death before getting to show the world it had underestimated Esteban Mendoza.

Esteban left Javier's office and strode down the hall, down the stairs to the basement. This was where Juanito lived. He actually had it pretty good, at least in Este's mind he did. He had more money than he knew what to do with, but because he was under Este's command (and yes, Javier's, as he had so recently demonstrated), he couldn't have his own fancy house with fancy cars and fancy hookers. He was told he could have all that later. It was always later. Now, his job was just to do as they said, no matter what it was, and in time he would rise in the ranks.

What Javier didn't know, though, was that Juanito was loyal to Esteban and not to him. The minute that Juanito joined the cartel, Este had taken him under his wing. At first Este had explained everything as a bit of hazing. He'd had his own little torture session on Juanito—pulling off toenails with a clamp, waterboarding, using a heated hammer to make burns on his back. Things that Javier would never notice. But Juanito sure did. And fear of Este was built into him from the start.

It made him so much more compliant. The rape came later (though Juanito was willing to go through with it, Este liked to think of it as rape—it turned him on even more). More torture here and there. Pretty soon Juanito was willing to do whatever Este asked of him. And one of the first things he had asked was to help orchestrate the murder of Javier's sister.

If Juanito had any objections to that, he didn't dare voice them to Este. He went through with it. Took Alana's phone call for help and instead of patching her through to Javier, told her help was on the way.

Este picked up Alana, and the rest was history.

Now Este wanted Juanito's help with the next phase of the plan, and he knew he could get it. But just in case Juanito was starting to fear Javier like Este was, he needed to put that fear of himself back into him.

Este opened the door to Juanito's room without knocking. It was dark, so Este flicked on the lights. Juanito was in bed, sleeping, but sprang awake in a second. No one knew how to sleep through anything in this compound.

"What is it?" he asked, wiping the sleep from his eyes. Juanito was such a young kid. Este forgot at times until he saw that emptiness instead of youth in his eyes. But that loss of innocence was pretty much all his fault and he might as well take pride in it.

"I made a mess in Javier's office, hey," Este said. "I need you to take care of it. After you take care of me."

Este made an elegant gesture with his fingers for Juanito to turn around. A current of fear passed over his eyes, and it made Este immediately hard.

Juanito knew the drill. He shuffled out of his boxer shorts—a stupid pair with bananas on it—and got on all fours, his small, flabby ass facing Este.

Este didn't admire his body, didn't admire anything except his compliancy. He knew he was going to cause him a lot of pain and that helped with the hard-on.

Thank god the room was soundproof. Este slammed into him, his grip merciless on his hips. Juanito cried out in horror, in pain, a scream that would have made anyone's dick shrink in an instant, but it did the opposite to Esteban. Besides, now he wasn't even thinking about Juanito. His thoughts were all on Luisa. On what he would do to her. This same thing. She was going to go along willingly at first—that was part of the plan. Get her desire, her trust. But in time, that desire would turn to fear.

And when Este tired of the fear, he'd fuck her with his gun. He did that to a woman once, the only woman he remotely had feelings for. He would do it again. Luisa would love the danger of it all. He knew she liked fucked up shit like that.

And then Este would pull the trigger while it was deep inside her.

And then he would rule the world.

CHAPTER FIVE

Luisa

Sometimes, lately anyway, when I thought back to the day I had married Javier, my mind got all lost and jumbled. Confused. I brought up images of my wedding to Salvador Reyes. Perhaps because I was terribly nervous before both.

Of course I was nervous with Salvador, because I knew how powerful he was. I knew he had the capacity to hurt me, I knew I wasn't in love—or even "in like"—with him. And I was a virgin. But I hadn't expected to be nervous with Javier.

It was only a month after he killed Salvador and I joined Javier at his compound—this same compound—that Javier proposed to me.

We were in bed one Sunday morning. Sundays were the best days. We'd awake when the sun rose in the east and streamed in through the windows, then we'd spend a few hours under the covers. Sometimes we'd make love right away, other times we'd wait until coffee was delivered. But we never got out of bed unsatisfied.

That morning, Javier was in a quiet mood. This was nothing new—sometimes something dark and heavy would befall him. I could see it in his eyes. They didn't quite have that intensity anymore and he seemed to be tortured subtly by some inner demons. I knew he had a lot of them.

We made love slowly. He took his time, not in a sly, teasing way, but as if he were trying to memorize me, hold on to every second, every moment. It unnerved me because I wasn't used to it. I was used to dangerous, rough, wild sex, or a quick and passionate fuck. But not this forlorn, pensive emotion. Not from him.

After we both came with soft cries, he slid out of me from behind then flipped me over so that I was on my back. He climbed on top of me, his weight on his elbows on either side of my shoulders. He brushed my hair off my damp face, the sun and our sex heating up the room, and those wonderful eyes of his peered down at me.

They were searching, like a hawk, golden in the light, but they were sad. I didn't think I'd ever seen him sad. It made me hold my breath and I wrapped my hands around the small of his back, brushing gently against his skin, holding his body to me.

"Do you love me?" he asked, his voice low, almost hesitant.

I stared up at him in surprise. Of course I loved him. With everything I had. Didn't I tell him that all the time? Even though I had yet to hear it back, I still told him because I was unashamed of the truth.

"I love you," I told him.

"Do you want me to love you?" he asked, fainter now. He ran the tip of his fingers along my forehead, down my cheekbones, across my jaw, more gentle than a feather.

I didn't know how to answer that. Did he not love me?

Could he?

Would he?

So I said, "Yes."

He carefully licked his lips, brows furrowed slightly in thought.

"Do you want me to marry you?"

Now I was really surprised. I felt like the wind had been knocked out of me. My mouth dropped open and my brain and heart battled each other for a moment, wondering if my answer would set me up for some sort of humiliation.

But still, the truth. "Yes," I whispered.

"Good," he said, and only then did he give me the quietest of smiles. "Because I love you, Luisa. Even when I thought I didn't have it in me, I do. I love you. And I want you to be my wife. My queen. My everything. Rule with me." He leaned closer and kissed me delicately on the lips. "Marry me."

And I said yes. The room grew brighter. The sun filled my soul. And I thought I could never be happier.

We laughed, drunk on love, on the future, and we made love several times that morning. He wouldn't stop. He was insatiable. I couldn't stop either. I was just so taken with him that I wanted him to keep taking me. Forever.

The wedding happened a week later. Needless to say, there wasn't much planning. When most *narcos* get married, it turns into a nationwide celebration. Mayors and Sinaloan officials are supposed to show up, as well as the *narco* families whom Javier had good relations with. They are supposed to be huge feasts, real traditional parties. I should know—I had just that with Salvador.

But maybe because of my past, Javier opted for something quiet. In fact, it was just me, him, a minister, and Este as the witness. In a small, thick-walled church out in the middle of the hills. At least it had a beautiful view of the valley and Culiacán in the distance. A view of everything that would belong to me.

And yet I was nervous. Tapping my foot, picking at my simple white dress that was as delicate as a nightgown. I was nervous, because to me, this was it. Javier was it. If anything went wrong, if it all went south, there wouldn't be anyone else. I wanted him forever or I wanted nothing.

I had reason to be nervous, it turned out. Because now, as I sat alone at the kitchen table pouring myself another glass of wine, the evening breeze sweeping through the screened window and bringing with it the smell of rain and relief, I realized I had nothing.

The other night, when he finally succumbed to me, I knew I wouldn't get another chance again. I don't know how I knew it, but I did. I saw it in his face after we were done. I didn't care about the pain. I didn't care about the scarring or the blood. I didn't care if he hit me (which he didn't, and wouldn't, it wasn't his style). I knew that made me sound like a pathetic, lovesick woman, but it was the truth.

I just wanted something of him. His attention. Even if it meant his wrath. I wanted it. The feel of his body, his touch, his desire. And I got it. I knew he wanted to make people hurt, so I gave him the chance to hurt me. The conflict showed in his eyes, the slight hesitations he made. He was so afraid of really hurting me, but I wasn't, because I knew he wouldn't. He was more afraid of himself than I was of him.

But with whatever I got, it was even worse when it was taken away. Now I was aching for more and saddled with this uncomfortable feeling that there never would be. That it was over between us. And there would be nothing left for me.

Juanito strolled into the kitchen to get something from the fridge. Dinner had been served by our cook, Alberto, but I had eaten alone. Esteban ate elsewhere. I'm not sure the last time Javier had dinner with me, and Juanito seemed to fend for himself.

"Hungry again?" I asked him as he pulled a plate of leftovers out.

He looked sheepish. "I didn't eat earlier."

I'd never seen him have dinner with us. I wanted to ask Javier how he was being treated—lately his young face looked years older, gaunt and ashen, and his eyes were dull. But I didn't dare approach Javier with this stuff now. Before Alana, yes. But not after. Funny, I had started to think of life as Before AD and After AD (Alana's Death). Besides, Juanito was probably getting high on his own supply. Many of the *narcos* did, though the worst Javier did was drink. Even now, it was only booze that Javier occasionally dipped into.

That, and murder.

Juanito was in charge of our finances after Javier was through with them, just going over the boring stuff like an accountant. There's a price to dealing with large sums of money when you're trading in a billion dollar industry: you pay the *pisa* to plazas, dock handling charges, shipping costs, trucks, labor, equipment, security. Juanito was learning where the money went after it came to us. I knew that Javier had plans for him when he was ready, but I didn't know what they were. For now, he just did whatever Javier passed down to Esteban.

I patted the seat next to me. "Sit down." He stared at me, hesitant. I flashed him a smile, which I knew was relaxed and easy, maybe even sloppy, thanks to the wine. I'd already had three glasses.

"Okay," he said. He seemed jumpy. He sat down beside me, and it was then that I noticed he had rope burns around his wrists. I stared at them for a moment, trying to figure out what they could be from. He caught me looking and gave me a sheepish look. But he didn't explain.

"I don't think I've talked to you much lately," I said, trying to put him at ease. "How are you?"

"I'm good," he said flatly. He smiled and nodded, as if to convince himself. "Very good. Excited about the move."

"The move?" I asked, then remembered what Este had said about bringing us to a ranch somewhere when the *federale* was captured. I'd wanted to talk about it more with Javier but, well, that didn't happen.

"Oh," Juanito said slowly, reading my face. "I meant *our* move. You're staying here. Right?"

I frowned. "I don't see why I would."

He blinked, now unsure. "We're leaving *tomorrow*."

"What?!" I exclaimed, nearly knocking over my glass. I saved it just in time and swore under my breath.

"You don't know?" Juanito said, and now there was fear in his eyes. I was too angry to coddle him.

I got up, my chair sliding noisily across the tile floor. "Do I look like I know?"

"Please don't tell Este I told you," he pleaded to me, his eyes now filled with fear.

I pursed my lips for a moment. Why would I tell Este? Juanito should be fearing Javier. And I was sure he would after I was done with him.

"I'm talking to my husband. Your *patron*." *And your patron*, I thought to myself, *who wants to keep you in the dark for as long as he can.*

Not if I could help it.

I marched out of the kitchen, hearing Juanito curse to himself as I left. I went straight down the hall to my husband's office and nodded at Diego standing guard outside of it.

"I need to speak with him," I said, seething, my heart racing wildly in my throat.

I couldn't see Diego's eyes behind his dark aviator shades which he liked to wear, even inside. I only saw my reflection. I looked like a mess of a woman. I *was* a mess of a woman.

"He asked for no one to disturb him," Diego said calmly.

"Is he busy getting some *puta*?" I asked, and he balked slightly at that.

"I don't know what Javier does," he said, even though I bet he knew exactly what Javier did. Bet he handed out the condoms. "But I have my orders."

"And you realize I'm not going to obey them," I told him. "I pay your salary too."

He seemed to fall asleep on his feet before I realized he was probably staring at me and thinking. Then he took in a deep breath and knocked on the door.

Javier immediately barked, "I said fuck off!"

"He is in a bad mood, *senora*," Diego said to me in a low voice. "Things didn't quite go as he planned today."

I raised my brows. "Today?"

"With the *federale*."

I stared blankly at him. He tilted his head then nodded, realizing I didn't know anything.

To his credit, he continued. "Javier was adamant that no one get killed. One of the *federales* reached for his gun and our *sicario* reacted. The *federale* is dead. But we do have Evaristo Sanchez now, as planned. Javier will get over it."

"And me," I said. "Do you know what happens to me? Sanchez is in the desert somewhere, right?"

"Yes," he said simply. He didn't care that he was the one informing me. Perhaps because Diego didn't fear Javier. Diego certainly worked for him—for *us*—and was a man to be trusted, but Diego was at least twenty years his senior and had more experience in the cartels and in life, more than Javier had.

And Javier needed him.

He went on. "You will have to check with your husband about the details. But if I were you, it should wait."

"It can't wait. Juanito just said they are leaving tomorrow. You're going too?'

His lips came together in a thin line and he didn't answer, so I knocked on the door instead.

"Jesus Christ, Diego," Javier swore from the other side. "What part of *fuck* and *off* do you not understand?"

I knew that Diego was giving me an "it's your funeral" look under those glasses but I didn't care. I put my hand on the knob and opened the door.

I stormed into the room, slamming the door behind me.

Javier wasn't with another woman, not at the moment. He had just been standing at the window and staring out at the jungle and the craggy hills that rose above it in the distance, barely visible now in the dusk. An open bottle of tequila and a full highball glass were on the table.

He whirled around, ready to rage, his amber eyes flashing, but when he saw it was me, he stopped, stunned.

"Luisa," he said. Just the sound of his voice made me realize that I hadn't come to find him in a long time.

But I wasn't there to make nice, not now. He might have been mad over some dumb mistake one of our men had made, but I was even more so.

"Why didn't you tell me!?" I yelled at him, marching right over to the window.

He swallowed and took his time before he answered. "About what?"

I gestured to the room. "Everything. You already got the *federale?*"

He swallowed then raised his chin to look down on me. "What's your point?"

"My point?" I repeated, flabbergasted. I could feel my throat getting thick, my face growing hot. I prayed I wouldn't cry, wouldn't be weak. "My point is...is...Javier, I'm sick and tired of you pushing me away like this. Not telling me anything. We used to be a team."

His eyes didn't change. His face became expressionless, like stone. "There was a place for that. Things are different now."

"But I am still your wife!"

"And you knew what you were marrying when you agreed to become my wife," he said, an edge now in his voice. "And sometimes, you have to accept that. Accept this."

"Accept that you kidnapped a *federale* without telling me about it, and are now holding him in the desert somewhere, where you are going tomorrow, all while I'm supposed to stay here?!"

He raised a brow ever so slightly. "It is no place for a lady."

"Oh, we both know I am not and never will be a lady," I said, almost sneering. "You're just trying to get rid of me."

"So what if I am?"

I froze, caught off-guard. He'd said that far too easily. "Just like that...I'm suddenly someone to be thrown away. You used to *love* me!" I pressed my hand hard into his chest where his heart should have been.

With a slight narrowing of his eyes, he said, "This is for your own good. Don't try and twist it around with some feminine woe-is-me bullshit."

"Woe is me?" I repeated incredulously.

"There are bigger things going on here than just your *feelings*," he said, stepping back and away from my hand, like he couldn't stand for me to touch him at all. "Things that affect us all."

"Well how the fuck am I supposed to know that when you don't tell me anything?!"

He turned around, chewing on his lip briefly. "You want to know what's going on?" he asked, his smooth tone suggesting I shouldn't even be informed. "Our *sicarios* took Evaristo right out of his apartment outside Tijuana. He's now at one of our *fincas*, outside the shithole town of La Perla, where he will stay until he gives us the information we need. When I get that information, I will take control over the Tijuana plaza."

"It's too risky," I said.

"And that's why I never asked for your opinion," he stated. "Because I knew that's what you'd say."

"Kidnapping a *federale*, Javier..."

"It's already been done," he snapped. "And he will talk. And we will get what we want."

"But I won't get what I want." I let my words hang in the air. I wanted him to snap at them. He didn't, though. Because he knew.

He looked away. "Is that it?" he said softly. "You wanted to yell at me because I'm trying to keep you safe?"

"How is keeping me here safe? You think because Arturo and some of the guards will protect me? The only person who can really protect me is you." And what I didn't want to say was that I was afraid that if he left me here, he'd leave me to die. That it could all be part of some plan to get rid of me. Not the best thing to think about your husband, but I couldn't help it. I felt lost with rage and rejection, and everything seemed like a threat.

"The *federales* could come for Evaristo. They may track us. You would be safer here."

"I don't believe you for a second."

"Fine," he said. His voice was calm, but I could tell from the way he spun his watch around his wrist, the way the muscles in his neck looked strained, that he was close to erupting. "Don't believe me. All I ask of you, as my wife, is to stay out of my way."

I couldn't help but scoff. "That's all you ask of me?"

"Do you see me asking anything else?" His glare, his words, were knife sharp.

My head shook slightly as I folded my arms and took a deep breath through my nose to try and steady everything that was about to blurt out. "How about turning a blind eye on all the women—the prostitutes, whores, whatever they are—that you've been fucking behind my back?"

To his credit he kept his mask on, but his eyes flinched slightly. He didn't say anything.

"You think I didn't know?" I said, coming up to him until I was inches away. His spicy scent filled my nose, something that would normally turn me on or bring me peace, but now it was bringing me nothing at all. All my rage was making me feel hollow, like it was carving me out from the middle. Still, I wouldn't let it go. "You're practically doing it in public, flaunting it, as if you want to prove that you can get away with it, as if you can get away with anything! You don't care if it hurts me, or maybe it's that you *want* to hurt me. Well, you're doing it. It kills me, Javier. *Kills me* to know you've been unfaithful."

I watched him closely, my breath heavy, wanting to see something in his eyes, in his soul.

But he only swallowed and said, "You don't understand."

"Fuck you!" I yelled, my hands going against his hard chest and shoving him back. "I understand! What the fuck is there to understand?"

"Calm down," he said, putting his hands over my arms, but I swatted him away and pushed him back again. The fact that he was basically immovable made me angrier.

"At least admit it! Admit it!"

"Fine," he said, his hand coming over my wrist and holding it hard, the pain almost hard to bear. "I admit it. Is that what you want to hear? Does that make you feel better?"

"No," I practically spat at him.

"Does the fact that most of them don't walk out of here alive, does that make you feel better?"

"It makes it worse." I grimaced, shaking my head vigorously. "You're using your sister's death as an excuse to be an asshole, a monster."

That got his attention. His pupils turned to tiny pinpricks in the amber. I regretted it, but there was too much anger and adrenaline rushing through me to back down now. I would not cower to him.

"What did you just say?" he said through clenched teeth.

Of course, now he was mad. He was upset. I practically had to throw rocks at him to get him to feel something.

I straightened up and looked him dead in the eye. "Sometimes I wish your sister died long before I met you, at least then I could have had an idea what kind of husband you were going to be."

I didn't see the hit coming. There was just a crack across my cheek, then stars, then black swirls at the edges of my sight. But I didn't fall down. I think I was too stunned to. I just held my cheek, the skin throbbing, the bone screaming, and stared wide-eyed at Javier.

He had hit me.

It was a slap across the face and I probably should have expected it, but he'd never hit me before. For all the painful, twisted things he'd done to me—that we'd done to each other—he'd never done this. It wasn't his style to hit women, a slap or not.

I didn't know what his style was anymore. But now, now I feared it.

I feared him.

He stared at me in a rage, nostrils flaring, his chest heaving, and he jabbed his finger at me while I stood there, holding my cheek, trying to breathe through the shock of it all.

"You do not disrespect my sister like that," he growled, his voice rough and hard and frightening. "She is my family. She was my family. And that's the one thing you obviously are not, because families do not disrespect each other."

I had nothing to say to that. No protests. And the apology I had, because really, I meant Alana no disrespect, was caught in my chest, unable to come out. I just stared at him, wondering what this meant now that I was no longer family.

He watched me for a few moments, the two of us locked in our gazes, with so much anger that the air was electric between us. Then he winced as if pained, and turned away from me.

"Get out," he said quietly. "Please." He paused before screaming, "Go!"

I snapped to it and turned from him as quickly as I could, scuttling out of the room. I didn't even look at Diego as I passed him and ran down the hall, hot tears burning behind my eyes.

I couldn't stay inside, couldn't stand to feel the walls constricting around me. I rushed out of the house and into the dying light. Through the kitchen window I could see Esteban laughing, his hand on Juanito's shoulder, who was smiling. At the time I barely registered it, but I would go back to that image later and wonder why Juanito wasn't in trouble.

I'd wonder about a lot of things.

But as it was, I could only think about myself at that moment and how I was nothing more than a wounded animal. My cheek throbbed but the pain inside was far worse. It was debilitating, hindering my actual movement. I practically staggered all the way to the pond.

The minute I was behind the cover of the palms and reeds, I collapsed to the ground, just feet from my usual spot. The look in Javier's eyes, the sincerity in his words, kept flashing through my mind, stabbing me over and over again.

It wasn't that he wanted to hurt me. It's that he wanted me to hear the truth.

That horrible, bitter truth that seemed to be stuck in my throat, and I was unable to dislodge it no matter how hard I tried to fight.

The tears came, broken at first, just like me. Fragments of sobs. I felt like a little girl, curled up on the floor of the closet after a fight with my parents. My mind even wanted to hold on to the hope that Javier would feel bad for what he'd said, what he'd done, that he would show remorse, worry, that he would come out here looking for me. That he'd scoop me up in his arms and tell me that we would get through this. That we could survive.

That he loved me.

But I knew that wouldn't happen, because he was right. I knew what I was getting into when I married him. I knew he wasn't like most men; in fact, I'd never known anyone like him. So ruthless and cunning, but with tenderness, loyalty, and a twisted code of morals hidden deep inside him.

All the good in him vanished with Alana, and the Javier that was left was a walking ghost. And I had promised, for better or for worse, to stay by his side.

So I was stuck with a man who no longer wanted me to be a part of his life. But there was no way I could up and leave either. How do you leave one of the most powerful men in the country? You don't. You stay and you keep quiet.

And the worst part was, as much as I was falling out of love...I still loved him something terrible.

Love was a terrible thing.

I lay down in that grass, mosquitos buzzing at my ears that I didn't bother to swat away. Let them suck me dry, let them take the last of me.

"Luisa?" I heard Esteban's voice in the dark. Footsteps and his presence over me followed. I didn't want to move, didn't want to acknowledge him.

I felt him crouch beside me, and he put his hand on my arm. His skin was soft and warm, and the contact seemed to bring comfort. I would have taken anything as comfort at that point. I realized just then how starved for affection and attention I was.

Before I opened my eyes, I realized that Esteban had been the only person to offer me anything recently. I wasn't sure how I felt about that.

"Luisa," he said again, gently now. I looked up at him and saw nothing but concern in those green eyes of his. They stood out in such sharp contrast to the scar on his cheek. Like Javier, he was a man comprised of both good and bad, with the bad side often pushed to the extreme. But now, when I needed it most, he was offering me the good.

I was such a fool.

"Hey," I said softly.

"What happened?" he asked, hand now on my hand. I didn't brush him away.

"Marital problems," I managed to say. I sighed and slowly lifted myself so I was sitting up. Bats began to fly overheard, snatching up the evening's insects.

"I figured as much," he said, settling down to sit beside me. "I talked to Juanito, hey."

"Oh," I said, suddenly wary. "It wasn't his fault he told me. He thought I knew."

"As you should have. I thought Javier would have at least informed you on when we were leaving and that you would have to stay behind."

I swallowed hard, feeling the pinch again. The rejection.

"I'll talk to him though," he went on. "Let him know how ridiculous he's being. You're a team, you two. You're just as much in this business as he is. You've made some incredibly insightful moves, you know, and I know he needs to be reminded of all this. If it weren't for your own plans and ideas, we wouldn't have the cocaine pipeline from Columbia."

I nodded absently. It was true that I had been contributing to the organization, even finding ways for us to expand. But that was all past tense now. Still, it was nice that Esteban remembered.

"No need to talk to him," I told him. "He won't listen. He doesn't care. He says he's keeping me safe but...it's not just that. He doesn't consider me part of the family anymore."

"Then he's an idiot," Esteban said. "There's a time to grieve and there's a time to move on. He can't treat his own wife like she's no longer a part of him. He can't just kick you to the curb. Doesn't he see how wonderful you are?"

His words made my heart flip, just a little. It was jarring to hear anything nice about myself, especially coming from him.

"I don't think he cares if I'm wonderful or not. I'm just in the way."

Esteban shook his head and grabbed my hand again. "Luisa, I wasn't kidding when I told you that you deserve better than this. You do. And you know it. That's what pains me."

I eyed him. "I don't think you know anything about pain."

A stiff smile came across his lips. "No? Maybe you don't know much about me."

He was right about that. I actually knew very little about Esteban Mendoza. Maybe it was about time I started.

He seemed to lean in closer as he said, "You could let me in, hey? I'd like that. I would like you to get to know me. You might like what you find. You might find we have more in common than you think."

There was a glittering intensity in his eyes that I had a hard time looking away from. I tried to remind myself that this was Esteban, the man who decided it was fun to Taser me at one point. Granted, I had been trying to escape at the time. Perhaps now, in the position I was in, I couldn't say I'd do anything differently.

Maybe we were alike.

Finally I had to look away, my gaze directed at the base of the palm in front of us. In the grainy twilight I could barely make out tiny red ants scurrying up the tree. They had absolutely no interest in the brutality of our compound, the screams or the breaking hearts or the ending marriages or the lives full of bad choices in order to live selfishly. They didn't care. We were insignificant to them.

Suddenly, Esteban reached out and tucked a strand of hair behind my ear, a disarmingly tender gesture. I couldn't help but freeze, afraid for my eyes to meet his again, afraid that this weird electric current in the air was more than it should have been.

"I won't leave you behind," he said. "You're coming with me tomorrow."

With us, I wanted to say. But I didn't. Because at that moment, what he said sounded real.

I wanted real.

I just wasn't prepared for how real it was going to get.

CHAPTER SIX

Javier

I wouldn't admit many things to people, but I would admit a lot to myself. And when I hit Luisa, I knew I had done wrong. Taken it too far. That I'd become less of a man for doing that.

All my life, I thought I could operate under my own code of morals and ideals. It was no different than most, I supposed. The cop who had to shoot someone in self defense. The soldiers that go to war and raid villages in the name of freedom. Everyone made excuses for what they did, because they believed in it. Because they believed they were in the right.

I had always thought of myself as a somewhat civilized, almost classy, *narco*. I, at least, wanted to bring purpose and grace to what I did. I didn't believe in killing mercilessly. I believed in mercy, in forgiveness, in giving people second chances. I believed in letting people go after I got what I wanted from them.

I believed that to snitch was an outrage, even though we were dealing and fighting and killing each other to work in a billion dollar industry. I believed that religious celebrations were to be respected. I believed that family came first. I believed that women and children were not to be harmed.

I believed a lot of things. I also believed that I would never hit any woman. I knew that it didn't make sense, considering that I could carve up their backs without a sweat. But there was something elegant and sexual about knife play. Whips, chains, ropes? Sure. But to hit was ugly. Brutal. Unbecoming.

Cheap.

So when I found myself striking Luisa across the face, I thought for a moment that perhaps I had lost my mind. Never mind the needless, senseless deaths that were at my hands over the past few months. Never mind that I had broken promises to others and to myself. Dirty, filthy promises. It was then and only then that I knew I had lost who I was. That every moral fiber that I based myself on was threadbare, and I was close, oh so close, to losing all sense of myself forever.

It scared me. I watched her leave the room, and though I was reeling from her own words, the callous ones that reached deep inside me and left a scar, I knew I might have damaged her beyond repair. I could heal myself in time, but could she? Would we? I didn't think so.

I tried to tell myself that it was for the best. That things were so strained between us that we never had a chance of coming back. But the fact was, I didn't want her near me anymore. Not because I didn't love her, but because I didn't want to do that again. I didn't want to see that look in her eyes, the betrayal. Not just because of how I slapped her, but because the truth was, I was a terrible, horrible husband. Unfaithful, cruel, and cold.

I knew she wouldn't be in my bed that night; regardless, I decided to sleep on the small couch in the office. Perhaps a mistake, considering the big day I had ahead of myself. I needed as much sleep as possible.

But who was I kidding. I didn't even close my eyes for a second, and it had nothing to do with the couch. I kept seeing Luisa in the black and did what I could to absorb the guilt that was threatening to eat me from the inside out. So I did what I always did when it came to those kind of feelings—I blocked them out, shut them down, and told myself I didn't feel a thing.

The next morning there was a knock at the door. I'd just finished doing my morning exercises, push-ups and sit-ups to get the blood flowing, and a small part of me was hoping it was Luisa, perhaps here to apologize, maybe to spare me from apologizing to her.

But it was Este. He came in and gave me the once over.

"You look like shit, *esé*," he said, and though his tone was juvenile as always, he didn't smirk. In fact, he looked rather grave.

"Even on my worst days, I'd rather look like shit than you," I answered quickly, reaching for the hand towel and dabbing the last vestiges of sweat from my face. "What do you want? We don't have much time before we push off."

"It's about Luisa," he said. He was hesitant, probing.

I made sure I gave him nothing to go on. "What about her?"

"I don't think..." He paused then seemed to compose his thoughts. "It's not safe to leave her here, Javi. I know you trust Arturo and the others, and I do too, but I just don't think it sends the right message."

I eyed him curiously. "And what message is that?"

"That you're afraid to bring her along," he said. "Or that you just don't care for her anymore." He seemed to watch me closely. "That makes you both more vulnerable."

"She'll be fine here," I said, even though I was starting to doubt it myself. What if I came back and she was gone? I remembered everything I'd said to her last night but it all still scared me. I wanted to push her away, yet at the same time the thought of losing her entirely wasn't something I could handle at the moment.

"Will she?" He folded his arms across his chest. "How do you know that?"

"Because I would kill anyone who would let harm come to her."

"Be that as it may, she would be dead. And all you'd have is the chance to kill someone who fucked up, which isn't anything new. Listen...do you really want that blood on your hands?"

I cocked my head, appraising him, wondering what his angle was here. "Why do you care?"

"Because you're a lot easier to deal with when she's around," he said. "And you listen to her. At least, you used to. She might be a good person to have during the interrogations of Evaristo, just to keep you in check. You don't want to bring out your machete on him, not right away."

"Not ever," I said quickly, knowing we'd already done enough damage when one of the *sicarios*—who was lying in a dusty grave somewhere—took out a *federale* during the raid. "Look, what's been happening..." I ran my hand through my hair then shook it off, standing up straight. "I will stay true to my word with Sanchez. I want him because I want someone else. When I get the info, I'll let him go. I'm not stupid enough to anger the *federales*."

"Well, then I believe you," he said. He stepped closer to me and put his hand on my shoulder. I eyed it warily. "I don't often get hunches, Javi, but when I do I listen to them. Trust me when I say that leaving her here would be a big mistake. You need her still, even though you think you don't. She's more than just your wife—she's good for all of us."

Well, here was something fucking new. Esteban being sincere and somewhat emotional. I wasn't sure I liked it. In fact, I didn't like it at all. Emotions got you killed in this business. But he was making sense, and I knew that if something happened to Luisa, I'd never forgive myself. Besides, in the long run, the ranch was no less safe than here.

I just nodded and stepped away from his hand. "You go tell her, then. She needs to be packed up in twenty minutes."

He grinned at me like he'd won the lottery and quickly left the room. I stood there in the middle of my office for a good minute or two, my brain trying to focus on something in Este's smile. When I couldn't figure out what it was, I started packing.

...

Helicopter travel comes with some risks, but you can't beat the immediate payoff. I hopped into the craft with Diego, Esteban, Luisa, and our trusted pilot, and headed off to the *finca* in the Chihuahuan Desert, while the rest of the crew would come via a protected convoy of armed SUVs.

Luisa was sitting beside me, staring out the window at the scenery below with wide eyes as the landscape changed from the verdant mountains of Sinaloa into the fawn-colored desert as we headed deeper inland.

To me, there was nothing more beautiful than the desert. While others found it boring, I found it stark, rough, and relentless, filled with a million hidden things that wanted to kill you. The desert demanded our respect, and in return, it would clear your head and remind you how damn insignificant you really were.

I needed that sometimes. Sitting here in one of my nicest white linen suits, being chauffeured by one of the many helicopters that I owned, a whole world at my feet, sometimes it was good to humble me, just a bit. Humility only made me want to work harder.

Luisa shifted in her seat, trying to get a better look at one of the craggy canyons that opened wide and long below, rust, taupe, and coffee-colored sands stretching into the distance. She was wearing a short but simple black dress that lifted as she strained to see, and her perfect legs, toned and golden brown, were on display.

I felt my dick twitch in my pants and took a deep breath through my nose. Aside from the other night, I hadn't been this close to her in what felt like forever, and it was hard not to just flip her on her knees and maul her right here. It didn't matter that we weren't alone, the *patron* could get away with more than just murder.

Luisa wouldn't have allowed a public fuck under normal circumstances, but today she wasn't even looking me in the eye. I couldn't blame her. Even though she did a good job with her makeup, you could still see the puffy red mark on her cheek. She kept her hair on it, flowing dramatically over that side of her face, but I knew it was there. We all did.

Besides, it was still for the best to keep her as far away from me as possible. Even though she was coming to the ranch, she would be put in her own room, and I would be spending as much time with Evaristo as needed.

I wondered how long and what it would take to make him talk. Perhaps he'd be a pussy like so many agents and cough it up right away. After all, what was it to him if we nabbed Hernandez? One less *narco* to deal with—isn't that what they wanted? Though the thought of him giving in made the whole situation a little less fun.

I looked at the rest of the cabin and saw Esteban leering over Luisa in the same way that I had. I frowned, watching him carefully, waiting for him to remember where he was and that he wasn't supposed to ogle the *patron*'s wife.

Eventually, the corner of Este's mouth lifted slightly, as if he were smiling to himself. The expression in his eyes, though, was anything but happy. It was carnal, something I wasn't used to seeing from him. I swallowed the slight sense of unease I had, telling myself that I was prepared for anything.

It wasn't long until I spotted the ranch on the horizon. I nudged Luisa with my shoulder, and she glanced at me with hardened eyes.

I nodded at it. "There she is. Your new home for the next while."

She nodded, silent, and looked back.

The ranch was located down a five kilometer dirt road off the desolate highway sixty-seven. The closest town—La Perla—was nothing more than a few houses and dusty shops, a hard place where the locals would lean back against their adobe houses and squint into the sun, beer in hand, wondering where the years had gone.

We flew close to the sandy road, following it as it led to the compound, the dust whirring beneath the rotors. I'd picked out the spot myself last year when we snatched the property from a *narco* who wasn't following the rules. There were other *fincas*, properties to hide in, but I liked this one the best. It wasn't all harsh desert either. There was a wash that had some water trickling through it during the winter, and mesquite trees lined it, providing shade. The rest of the property sat beneath the rocky crag that hid a family of coyotes at its base and a golden eagle's nest at the top.

The chopper touched down on the landing pad, which was located between the long garage and the barn. The horses in the outer pasture ran away from the sound, their tails flying in the wind.

"Oh," Luisa said excitedly, and when she turned to look at me, I saw the woman I fell in love with. "I didn't know you had horses."

"*We* have horses," I told her, tempted to put my hand on her leg, but not willing to risk public rejection. "Evelyn takes care of them and she will take care of us."

Evelyn Aguilar was the mother of one of our *narcos* who was captured and tortured last year, probably by the Zetas. After he was found, I made a vow to keep his mother safe and employed. Evelyn lived by herself out here, looking after the ranch and the horses, and filling in as a housekeeper and cook whenever the ranch was being used. So far, I'd only come out here once and just for a few days, but her debt to me was deep, and she had waited on me hand and foot.

Luisa seemed to remember that she despised me, so her look became hard and she turned away, as if she was too stubborn to let herself get excited. I'd known she was that stubborn but I hoped later on when I told her she could go riding that the look would come back into her eyes again.

The chopper landed in a cloud of dust and was quickly approached by Borrero and Morales, two members of my security team and the top *sicarios* who carried out the kidnapping of Evaristo. Aside from Diego, they were the best of the best. It's too bad that *federale* had to die during the event, but I knew that hadn't been their fault. They were far too smart for that.

Borrero, tall and lanky with a skinny moustache and a penchant for wearing red, shook my hand as I got out of the helicopter. "You got here quicker than we expected."

"Is that bad?" I asked as I walked away from the whirling sand. I nodded at Morales who was standing with his arms folded and he nodded back. If Borrero was red, Morales was black. He'd grown up in the desert and then later spent his formative years as a chief instructor for the military training camps that took place out in places like this. His skin was dark and weather-beaten, and he always wore a black cowboy hat and leather boots. Like Diego, he had a sordid past I didn't care to know much about and was the kind of man you wanted—*needed*—on your side.

"Not bad," Borrero said, following me. "Sanchez is still unconscious though."

"I'm sure I'll find a way to wake him up." I looked over my shoulder to make sure Luisa was all right. Esteban had her hand

and was helping her out of the helicopter, her hair flying around her like a black cape as the rotors slowed. "Where is he?"

"In the tunnel," Morales said as he fished a cigarette out of his front pocket. "Thought it would be a more agreeable place for him to wake up. Especially for whatever you have planned."

All *fincas* have at least one escape route. This ranch had a tunnel leading out from behind the hot water tank in the basement that went all the way behind the mountain and into the wash. The other end opened up by a crop of prickly pear on the riverbank and under a camo net, shielded by *nopales* and tarbush, there was a black, bulletproof truck, tank full and ready to go the distance.

Remembering my manners, I stopped and waited for Luisa and the rest before approaching the house. There, on the long wraparound porch out front, was Evelyn, waving at us like an old frontier wife. Her greying hair was pulled back in braids and she wore a long peasant dress.

"Welcome," she said, clapping her hands together. She had to be excited that she had company for once. Living out here must be lonely, though the solitude was one of the reasons I liked it so much. Having an entourage around you twenty-four seven was exhausting and I wondered if I could ever truly be on my own without someone watching me, whether for my own protection or otherwise. A small price to pay for being the top *narco*, but a price nonetheless.

"You must be Luisa," she said to Luisa as she came forward, holding out her hand in politeness. Evelyn pulled her into a tight hug, and I had to chuckle at that. Evelyn was round and fluffy, like a stuffed pancake, and about sixty-four, though she looked much older. Nothing aged you as much as grief. Even now I was seeing more silver hairs at my temples and a line between my brows that hadn't been there before.

"The place looks great," I said to Evelyn respectfully. "I can tell we are in good hands."

She beamed at that, ever grateful to me, and then to my relief she took Luisa and started giving her a tour of the sprawling ranch house. Luisa didn't need to be a part of what would happen next.

After they'd gone, I looked to Borrero and Morales. "Show me to the *federale*." I glanced at Esteban and said, "You should get yourself settled."

He raised a brow but didn't say anything to that. Esteban wasn't new to the interrogation process, but still, I felt better not having him there.

I followed Borerro and Morales, with Diego behind me as always, down the hall and stairs to the basement. It was clean, dark, and cool down here, with a metal chair in the middle of the room and rope coiled underneath it. Two other chairs were stacked in the corner beside a sink and a storage chest. There was an arsenal of depravity in that chest; I had spent a full day here last time picking out the best means of torture and filling it up just so.

The closet that contained the hot water tank looked like any other, complete with a mop and bucket—crucial for washing away the blood—and you could barely fit inside it. But Borrero squeezed past the heater and pushed at the bricks on the wall behind it. A hidden door opened with a groan, the grating sound of bricks grinding against each other, and soon he disappeared.

We followed him—Diego grunting because his stomach could barely squeeze past the heater—and then we were in a long, dirt tunnel that stretched straight out for a few yards before curling around to the left. Faint lights lined the ceiling, and in the middle of the tunnel was Evaristo, hands and feet bound, tied with a metal leash to a chair. He had a ball-gag in his mouth, and his head was slumped over, his eyes closed.

In person he looked a lot younger than I had thought. Maybe everyone looked a bit younger when they had their eyes closed. Innocent, almost, though I knew the boy-man couldn't be where he was with the *federales* and still maintain his innocence. They might have been fighting on the other side, but they were still capable of being as twisted and immoral as the cartels were. At least we had a code of conduct. They pretended they had one and called it justice.

Beside Evaristo on the ground were two buckets of water and a large metal toolbox. I wondered what my *sicarios* had selected for me and what they'd already used themselves.

As Diego closed the brick wall behind us, I went over to Evaristo and looked him over closely. One of his eyes and the corresponding cheekbone was black and blue, and there was a trail of dried blood beneath his nose. His dark hair was matted down, maybe with sweat, maybe with blood. Other than that though, he didn't look half bad.

"He got a little frisky when we first took him," Morales explained. "I roughed him up a bit, knocked him out."

"He's been out ever since?"

He shook his head and puffed on his cigarette, the smoke wafting down the tunnel, trying to find fresh air. "He came to but we put him back under. The more disoriented he is, the better. It's been a few hours though since we last gave him a hit, so I'm sure you can wake him and get him talking."

I was sure about the first part but not the second.

Before I did anything to wake him, I crouched down and inspected the tool box. At the top was a small battery pack and rod. It was the typical *narco* route for interrogations, but it was a staple because it worked so damn well.

I picked it up then nodded at Borrero and the bucket. "Wake him."

Borrero came over and tipped the water over Evaristo's head. He immediately jerked in his seat, blue eyes wide and crazed, the gag sucked into his mouth as he inhaled hard. Now he looked older. This was good. I didn't like the idea of having to torture a boy, even though I would do it to get what I needed.

As Evaristo jerked against the metal leash and fought against the bonds, I stooped over in front of him and looked him in the eye.

"Welcome," I said to him. "I think you know who I am. And I know who you are. And we're going to play a little game, you and I. I think you're very good at playing games, aren't you *federale?*"

Water streamed down Evaristo's face. His eyes widened at first then narrowed as he seemed to recognize who I was. Of course he recognized me. I was their number one target, it had just been his rotten luck that he was dispatched to go after the Tijuana cartel instead. Too much pressure from the DEAs in

California. They wanted the drugs to stop appearing in their backyards but hadn't quite figured out that all the drugs came from somewhere.

"Ah, you do know me," I said, reaching out to brush his hair off his forehead. He flinched at my touch, as he should, and I was briefly, uncomfortably, reminded of Luisa. I swallowed that down and kept my focus on him. "So, the question is, how long do you want to play this game? You can make it really easy for yourself. You can talk right away and I won't even have to use this." I lifted the battery pack. He didn't seem affected in the slightest, which was admirable considering he *knew* what it could do. "I also give you my word, and you should know my word is good. If you give me what I want, I will let you go. I won't drive you up to the PFM building in Mexico City, but I will let you walk out of here alive. You understand?"

Evaristo didn't nod but I could see in his eyes that he did understand. And he didn't like it. He was already prepared to put up a front and he had no idea what I was going to ask of him.

"We're not interested in your organization," I told him. "We're interested in your information. I want everything you have on Angel Hernandez. I know you know where he is, but you haven't been given the bureaucratic authority to capture him yet. What a pain in the ass bureaucracy is, am I right? They couldn't even save your own sorry little ass. You wanted Hernandez and you got me instead." I put one hand on the ball gag and the other held the battery in view. "Are you ready to talk?"

He gave me nothing. I pulled down the gag and he gulped in air.

"Well?" I prodded.

When he caught his breath, his eyes sliced into mine. "Fuck you," he said, spittle flying.

I raised my brow. "They've trained you well." I sighed and straightened up, looking down at the battery pack. "I think I'll keep you ungagged. Screaming gets me off." I shot him a smile. "And you will scream. They can't train that out of you."

I looked over my shoulder at my security team. "Any of you bothered by screaming?" I asked them, knowing they didn't mind it at all. Morales grinned eerily.

Within minutes, Borrero and Morales stripped Evaristo naked, threw more water on him, and I had attached the *picana* prod to the battery pack. Diego held the pack, in charge of the voltage, and I waved the prod at Evaristo's neck. It was a good, sensitive place to start. "Let's see what you've got."

What Evaristo had was a huge capacity for pain and screaming. Can't say it didn't turn me on.

CHAPTER SEVEN

Luisa

"This is where you will be staying with Mr. Bernal," the kindly Evelyn Aguilar told me, opening a door to a very spacious master bedroom that seemed to take up the whole end of the house. I stepped in gingerly and looked at the rustic furniture and terracotta tile floors. It was simple, yet I knew that the furniture only looked shabby and probably had cost a fortune. The view was of the south and the crooked mountains rising from the desert floor. The windows were small and deep-set into the adobe walls, so the view was partially obscured. I knew it was that way for our protection, from intruders and from the desert sun.

I gave Evelyn a small smile. "It's lovely. But I'm afraid I require a room of my own."

Thankfully she just nodded and said, "Oh yes, come with me," and didn't question why I wouldn't be sleeping with my husband. Perhaps this was normal to her. Perhaps when Javier had stayed here before, he hadn't quite been alone.

My stomach clenched at the thought. Even though I had known about his callous infidelity before I confronted him, the fact that he fessed up to it so easily, and without any remorse, continued to make me sick. He knew he'd hurt me and he just didn't care.

Or perhaps he did. After all, he decided to allow me on the trip to the ranch in the end. But it had been Esteban who told me that this morning, not him, and I was starting to think it had been Esteban's idea as well.

I couldn't pretend that I hadn't noticed his roving eyes on me, either. Just this morning as I sat outside on the front bench and sipped my coffee, wearing just a camisole and shorts, he couldn't keep his eyes off me as he told me the news. Same with on the helicopter. Esteban had been ballsy to do it in front of my husband as well. Not that I felt bad about it—Javier deserved that and then some—but it made me a little uneasy about being around Esteban now. He'd been my closest companion over these last horrible months, but the sexually charged looks threatened to push our relationship in another direction.

It scared me. It also made my heart flip and my thighs clench, just a little bit. Enough that I noticed. Enough that I liked it. And that scared me even more. I wasn't in the right frame of mind to handle any sort of temptation like that.

I wasn't really in the right frame of mind to handle anything. And now I was in the middle of Mexico, in a hot, unyielding desert, wondering if it had been the right decision to come here, even though it's what I had wanted. I had felt trapped and isolated at home, but at least it was still my home. This place was a stranger to me and I felt like I was at its mercy.

"Here we go," Evelyn said, pushing open another door further down one of the halls. It was much smaller, but it had an en-suite bathroom, and the heavily locked French door looked like it opened to the wraparound porch. I could already see myself having my morning coffee here and watching the horses run in the distance. At least there was that.

"Thank you, it's perfect," I said and her face lit right up. Minutes later she returned with my bags—I didn't know how to pack light but she was surprisingly strong—and I shut the door behind her, collapsing onto the bed. The mattress was on the firm side but I found myself drifting off within minutes.

I'm not sure how long I was out but the screaming woke me up. I knew it had been coming—I'd learned to accept the screams as progress—but they still rattled me. I lay there, breathing hard, having a hard time seeing the progress in any of this. I felt like I was just spinning my wheels.

And the screaming didn't stop, no matter how long I tried to wait it out. I'd been filled in by Esteban about the man in the tunnel, *federale* agent Evaristo Sanchez, and I still thought the risk we were taking was too great. I didn't take any pleasure in this, because whatever horrible things Javier and his men were doing to the young agent, I knew that it would be used against us one day.

Finally, I'd had enough. I couldn't fall asleep, and my heart would not stop racing. I got up, slipping on a pair of suede, low-heeled boots and hat, and headed out into the hallway. I passed by the spacious kitchen with white-washed walls and exposed wood beams on the ceiling.

Evelyn was busy chopping vegetables and cheerfully humming a *corrida* tune to herself. I told her I was going for a walk, and she warned me to be careful about rattlesnakes. I merely pointed at my boots. The desert hills around San Jose del Cabo where I grew up were equally as dangerous and I knew how to handle myself.

The moment I stepped outside, the thick air blanketing me like an open oven, the screams began to fade. I headed straight over to the peeling wood fence that housed the horses. The fence seemed to go on forever, dipping over a low hill and fading off into the distance.

I leaned against it, careful not to get splinters on my arms, and a breeze swept off the hills, hot but smelling of hay. A dapple grey horse grazed on tufts of dry grass, its tail swishing. I smiled despite myself. For a moment, I imagined what it would be like to hop on its back and get the hell out of here. Just me and the horse and the desert, no fear, no constraints. Just freedom.

I knew I wouldn't get far. If I didn't succumb to the relentless heat and the fact that my cell phone didn't work out here and I had no idea where I was going, Javier and his men would find me in minutes.

Unless he didn't, I told myself, and before I knew what I was doing, I was stepping through the fence. *Unless he couldn't care less where you went. Don't be so naïve.*

I picked up some hay that was gathered near a shanty at the gate and headed across the paddock, hoping I wouldn't scare the horse. There were other horses here, spread out in small herds, maybe twenty in total, but this horse was the closest. And alone.

"You and me both," I said under my breath as I quietly approached him.

He kept his eye on me as I came close, but only raised his head at the last minute. I held out the hay, perhaps too fast, and the horse took off, spooked.

I sighed as I watched him gallop away until he disappeared over the hill. I looked behind me at the house and clenched the hay in my hand. I had nothing better to do.

I set off after the horse, determined to win over something in my life. I went over the hill and saw the land gently slope toward a dried up riverbed where mesquite and acacia grew. The horse had paused down there, grazing on yellow flowers that grew in the sparse shade.

I headed after it, watching my feet carefully as my boots navigated the loose rocks and hard sand. Scorpions scuttled away from my shadow.

It was cool down by the wash, even with the water all dried up. The horse had his head up, watching me, but I thought I saw some kind of understanding in his large dark eyes. I decided to stay put, holding the hay at my side.

"It's okay, boy," I told him softly. "I won't hurt you."

The horse watched me then slowly resumed chewing before it lowered its head again and went back to plucking the flowers off the shrub, its lips nipping them delicately.

I didn't know how long I stood there for, just watching the gorgeous animal. If I couldn't hop on his back and ride off into the sunset to start a new life, maybe I could convince Javier to bring him back home with us. We had the barn that had the pigs back on our compound, and we could easily use one of the stalls for him.

I was just about to come up with a name for him—*Bandito*—when he slowly took a few steps toward me, head down, seeming to hone in on the hay. I carefully held out my hand and he took the hay from me.

"Aren't you handsome?" I asked him, wondering if he'd run if I tried to pet him.

But before I had the answer, he suddenly raised his head, the whites of his eyes showing, and then turned on a dime, galloping off and leaving me in the dust again.

I coughed and turned around, wondering what had startled him.

Coming down the slope was Esteban, his eyes sharply fixed on me.

"What are you doing?" he asked, jogging the last little bit. I was having a hard time pretending not to notice that his shirt was off and slung over one shoulder. He was fit, all sculpted abs and a deep tan. I looked to his feet and saw that he had slip-on sneakers instead of flip-flops on for once.

"I was getting to know the horses," I told him as he stopped right in front of me. He smelled liked sweat. It wasn't a terrible smell, it was actually rather primal. His skin glistened and I looked up at his face, the brim of my hat shielding me from the intense sun.

"You shouldn't wander too far," he said. "The desert is no place for a woman like you."

My brows rose. "A woman like me? And what kind of woman am I?"

"One that shouldn't be so bold, not in places like this. There are many things out here that can kill you, hey."

I rolled my eyes and turned, heading down to the wash, seeking the shade. "Oh please, you think I didn't grow up with the desert in my backyard?"

"I'm sure you did," he said, and I could hear him trailing after me. "But you're not a little girl on the Baja anymore. You're a queen. And you need to treat yourself like one."

"Queen," I muttered, and sat down on a large, wide rock beneath a tall mesquite. "I doubt a queen would have contemplated escaping on a horse across the desert."

He sat down beside me, his arm pressing against mine. I stiffened, trying to relax with him so near but I couldn't.

"Oh, I bet many queens try to escape. Few make it. Didn't you ever see *Roman Holiday*?"

I gave him an incredulous look, trying not to smile. "With Audrey Hepburn? Badly dubbed in Spanish?"

"Yes," he said, grinning at me. "She was a princess, and she wanted nothing more to escape. I think it's very common." He leaned in closer, his gaze suddenly intensifying. "I could be your Gregory Peck, hey."

I managed a weak smile. "You're not handsome enough," I told him.

I thought he would have looked insulted at that, but instead he put his hand on the back of my neck, holding me there. "I may not be handsome, but I sure can fuck better than him."

I couldn't respond to that. I couldn't do anything as he leaned in and kissed me hard and wet on the mouth. His tongue slipped in through my lips, and I found myself opening my mouth to let him in.

This was so terribly wrong and I knew I had to stop it.

It was wrong.

It shouldn't happen.

It couldn't happen.

But for that one second, I kissed him back. The feel of his tongue against mine was slick, hot, and electrifying, and every nerve in my body was on fire, like the sun above the mesquite.

I couldn't remember the last time Javier had kissed me.

Just that thought made my heart knot up, bringing me back to reality. I put my hands on Esteban's shoulders and pushed him back, breaking off the kiss.

I wouldn't play this game with him.

I wouldn't give in to my urges, the same urges he was preying on, trying to get me to break, to offer me affection and attention when I'd had none.

His gaze was just as intense as before and he was breathing heavily. "Don't tell me that you didn't want that. That you haven't thought about it." He took my hand and placed it on the crotch of his shorts so I could feel how thick and hard he was.

I felt dizzy, out of breath. The sun, the heat; it was too much.

I couldn't let this happen.

I pulled my hand back and got to my feet, unsteady. "I have to go back."

He got up too, grasping my wrist tightly so I couldn't walk away without a fight.

"Let go or I'll scream," I said, wishing my voice didn't sound broken.

"We both know no one will hear you," he warned. "We also know that you won't. Because I'm not doing anything wrong. And neither are you."

"I'm married," I said feebly.

I took my vows under oath, under god.

If I didn't have my morals, what did I have at all?

"I *know*," he said. "And is this what you want for the rest of your married life? The lonesome queen who pines in her castle for someone she can't have—her husband? All while the king has his share of whoever he wants to fuck."

The truth hurt. And it didn't matter how many times I heard it, it still had that fatal sting, like the scorpions in the shadows.

But I couldn't do this. I had to be good. I had to honor my vows. Without them, I had nothing. Someone had to believe in love.

I had to believe.

Even if I was a fool.

"I have to go," I told him, but Esteban held tighter, till my wrist began to ache. Why were all the men around me so set on pain? Why did I always feel so powerless against them?

Why did they stir up trapped, dark feelings inside me, the ones I always wanted to bury?

"I wouldn't go back if I were you," he said, his look cautioning. "Not while Javier is occupied."

The mention of his name made me flinch a little, and I wished I couldn't still feel Esteban's rough lips on mine, taste his sweat. So much guilt already for so little.

"I can handle it," I told him. "Sadly, I'm used to torture."

"Oh no, Luisa," he said, tilting his head sympathetically. "He's done with Evaristo for today. It's the women..."

My throat felt like it was starting to close up. "Women? What women?"

"You didn't see the cars pull in?" he asked, and when I shook my head he sighed. "I guess it was good you were out here, then."

"What cars? From where?" I asked, alarmed.

"He had them brought in from Durango. Can't have a proper *finca* without the *putas* for everyone. Especially your husband. Don't take it too personally, though, I'm sure it's no reflection on you."

It was stupid and foolish to feel as devastated as I did, like my heart was being cut from my chest. I didn't even know I had a heart left after everything already.

I looked away and Esteban tugged me toward him. "Hey," he said softly, finally releasing my wrist and putting his hands on both sides of my face. It took everything I had not to break down. "I'm sorry. I shouldn't have told you. I didn't think this would bother you anymore. But your heart, Luisa. You have such a good, big heart. And it breaks me to know you wasted it all on him."

I couldn't meet Esteban's eyes. I didn't want to see my reflection in them.

"Javier is *patron* now," he said. "He's got everything he wants. And what do you have? What do you deserve? I've seen him around you. I know you sleep in separate rooms. He won't even touch you. It's like you disgust him."

"Esteban, please," I cried out, feeling my eyes fill with tears. "I'm hurting enough."

"I agree," he said. "And it's time to stop. Look at me."

I couldn't. I shook my head and the tears spilled.

"Look at me, Luisa." The pressure on my face increased, and finally I let my blurry vision meet his intense stare. "Javier is a changed man and he's not coming back. You're stuck in this marriage with him for the rest of your life, chained to a monster. His pride is too big to let you go, and if you go anyway, you won't last long."

I didn't want to believe any of that, but I knew it was true. I was sewn into this life now.

"And no other man is going to want to fuck you, to be with you, when you're married to one of the most powerful and dangerous men in the country. No other man but me."

My eyes widened and his gaze seared like the desert heat. "I can give you everything that he can't," he said. "I can give you more than he ever could."

He kissed me again, holding me in place, and this time I fought more, because to give in would be to believe all the horrible things he'd just said. But Esteban was relentless, his tongue fucking my mouth as he pressed his erection against my hip. One hand reached under and pulled up my dress, his fingers trying to slip between my legs.

But I couldn't, I couldn't.

"No," I told him, my words muffled against his lips, realizing we were in the damn desert of all places.

"There is no more *no* anymore," he said. Suddenly he shoved me down so I was on my knees, and I cried out in pain as the rocks cut into my skin. "Shut up," he said, and I raised my head to see him take his cock out of his pants. "Suck it. See what I taste like."

I was too stunned, my knees throbbing, but he made a fist in my hair and yanked me forward. Nearly powerless to protest, I took him in my hands and into my mouth. His salt hit my tongue, but he thrust his hips forward until he was as far in me as he could go. I nearly gagged.

"God, you're fucking beautiful," he said through a moan. "Such a queen. You suck so good but I'm going to fuck you so much better. So much better than him."

It was then that I realized how little choice I had. How little choice I'd always had. For my whole life I'd been stuck between a rock and a hard place. Working tirelessly for my parents—I'd had no choice in that, not really. I either did it or they died. Marrying Salvador, I'd had no choice either. He would have killed me and my parents if I had said no to him. Going off with Javier had been the best choice I'd ever had, because finally I had been in the position to go off on my own and live my own life.

But I was an idiot who fell in love.

Love turned on me and broke me. I lost the love of my husband along with his desire and respect.

And now I had another impossible choice. I could protest, I could try and walk away from this situation and pretend that I didn't want it, that I hadn't thought about it, that I didn't need what Esteban was offering me. I could walk away...if he let me.

Or I could give in. I could let that bad, dirty part of me come out to play and toss my morals out the door. My morals that had done nothing but keep me frozen in time, a loser of the heart. My morals were nothing more than a fucking cage.

My morals would hold me hostage for life.

You don't have a choice, I told myself, though deep down I knew I did, and I knew the one I was about to make was the bad one—the wrong one.

I thought about Javier and the women and the love I'd never have again.

That touch.

That intimacy.

I had something like that now.

To take it was my choice. Finally, *I* had a choice.

The guilt went and slithered off somewhere, like the snakes on the desert floor, taking my morals with it. My soul went on leave.

I took Esteban in, my hands pumping him, unsurely at first, but then my grip tightened as I shed all inhibition, filled with the perverse need to continue. I was getting off on this, despite how badly I needed to stop.

"Oh, so good," he went on, slamming in harder, my teeth razing him, but he only seemed to get thicker. "Is my big cock making your little cunt wet? Is it? Don't get too slick though, gorgeous, I want it to hurt a little. I want you to feel every single inch of me from the inside. I want you to scream."

Suddenly he pulled out of my mouth, and with his hand on my forehead, shoved me backward into the dirt. My head struck the edge of a rock and I cried out again, feeling wetness in my hair. As everything swung around me in a dizzying wave, I looked at the rock to see blood on it. I was bleeding from the head.

But Esteban didn't care. He was pushing up my dress around my waist and pushing my thong to the side, ready to enter me.

"Stop. I hit my head," I tried to say, but then he was on me and my head was pressed back into the rough sand.

"You won't care about that soon," he said, his lips on mine and kissing me feverishly as he guided himself into me. He was right; it did hurt. The friction was painful as he jammed himself inside to the hilt.

I gasped, trying to breathe through it, but he was merciless and thrust harder, the rocks digging into my back, my ass, everywhere. I was aching sharply and all over until he put his fingers in my mouth, getting them wet, and then placed them at my clit. Just the simple pressure made the pain melt into pleasure.

"I've wanted you for so long," he groaned against my neck, biting me. All I could think was that I was going to look like a real wreck after this, like a truck had hit me. I wondered what Javier would say. And then I realized how much I wanted him to say something; I wanted him to care.

My wants were very dangerous.

"So fucking long I've dreamed of this and all the things I wanted to do," he said, nipping my lower lip between his teeth. "You do realize this is just the beginning and not the end. I will own you, Luisa. And you will be mine."

I didn't know how to feel about that. I didn't know how to feel about anything until desire was throbbing through me, and all I knew was that I wanted it more, more, more. The sex, the wanting, the needing. I welcomed it through my veins, swept away by the passion, the delirious lust. It was making me feel something good for once. It was erasing all the pain on my skin and the pain deep inside.

I put my hands on Esteban's firm ass and drove my nails in, wanting him in deeper, wanting the feeling to never end. I felt wild and free and righteous. I had been owed this. The sweat poured off him and onto me, soaking my dress, the sun high in the sky behind him, waiting to dry it off.

Somewhere in the distance I think I heard a rattlesnake, but there wasn't even fear anymore. There was just this yearning that might never end, and I was lost, lost, lost in someone else as they were lost in me.

"Fuck," Esteban grunted, and I felt him strain as he came. "Fuck, fuck, fuck."

It was enough to set me off. I came hard, crying out a bunch of nonsense that seemed to soar up into the sky, feeling so much heat expand on me and in me. I was yanked into an undertow, not knowing which way was up and which way would have me drown.

I was so sated that I didn't care if I drowned or not. I just lay there, bleeding and broken and bruised on the ground, while Esteban lay on top of me, sweat pooling between us. We both tried to catch our breath, the air dusty and dry and filling our lungs. I felt like my heart would never slow down.

Finally Esteban raised his head and peered at me, a sloppy smile on his face. He tucked my hair behind my ear and said, "You certainly don't look like a queen right now."

I couldn't help but smile back. "Some queens like getting dirty."

"Dirty queen," he mused. "That's you all right. But from now on, you're my dirty queen. No one else's."

I swallowed hard, trying to figure out just what he was expecting. Was this not just a fuck, a heat of the moment thing? Or did Esteban expect this to continue? Was I to keep him as a lover just as Javier kept lovers of his own?

I wasn't prepared to entertain that just yet. Not now, when my emotions were high and my intentions were running away on me.

And then the guilt hit me straight on like a freight train.

I panicked and quickly got to my feet, pulling down my dress and wiping off the dust. I tried to get myself looking normal, but the dirt clung to me, as did the pebbles which were nearly embedded in my skin. I couldn't get it off, couldn't get clean. My hands whacked all over my limbs.

"Hey," Esteban said as he got to his feet. "Luisa."

I kept wiping at myself and everything started to spin.

He reached out and grabbed my arms.

"I can't get clean," I said, my voice shaking. "I can't get the dirt off."

"Calm down," he said. "Turn around, I'll help you."

I turned around, my eyes fixing on the bloodstained rock. What had I done? How would I explain the wound on my head? Javier would know, he'd *know*.

Este wiped down the back of me then said, "There. Some cuts and scrapes, but you can tell him you fell down, *if* he even notices."

"He'll notice," I said. He'd see the guilt on my face, the guilt that was pouring over me like thick black tar. "Esteban, we can never, ever tell him. We can never tell him what we did."

He zipped up his shorts and gave me a wry look. "You think he'd be hurt?"

I shook my head, even though I wasn't quite sure. "He can't know."

"I know," he said calmly. "If he knew, he would kill you."

I swallowed, wondering if that was the truth. "He'd kill you too," I pointed out.

But Esteban just smiled.

I reached behind my head and looked at the blood on my fingers.

He reached out and grabbed my hand, sticking my bloody fingers in his mouth. He slowly drew them out and said, "All clean. Shall we head back?"

Going back now sounded like the most dangerous prospect in the world. "I can't," I said. "I can't."

"You can, and you will. If he asks, if anyone asks, tell them you took a tumble." He jerked his chin to the hill. "You go back first. I'll follow later."

I took in a deep breath and wished the pain inside me, that knot in my heart, would have stayed away after the sex. But it was back. "Okay." I paused. "We won't ever tell."

"No, we won't," Esteban said. "Now go. And remember what I told you about him. Just go straight to your room and take a shower. It will be easier on you that way."

I nodded, staring at him for a moment before I turned and headed up the hill. It took me a while to head back to the ranch house, but then again it felt like I was sleepwalking or in a dream.

I couldn't believe what had just happened. How weak I had been to commit adultery, and with Esteban no less. How foolish and stupid I was to take such a dumb chance. I had a good life. Maybe I didn't have love anymore, or sex without having to practically beg for it, and maybe my husband was a totally different person. But I had money and security.

But it was amazing how little money and security mattered in the long run when your own heart wasn't being loved.

I had no illusions about Esteban loving me. I knew he didn't. I knew that he might hold some affection for me and that perhaps his attraction to me was based more on one-upping Javier, having what he had, that envy he felt for his boss.

I also had no illusions about loving Esteban. I didn't. I didn't even know if I liked him. But he had been there out in the desert, and he knew what I had needed before I did.

The fact was, I still loved Javier even though it was futile and painful to do so. I was also sure that a part of my own heart was breaking over what I had just done. But despite that, I also knew that I would eventually come to terms with it. And one day I'd be forced to make another choice: to make peace with my life the way it was.

Or to do it again.

I was too afraid of what my answer would be.

When I got closer to the house though, the guilt and dirt I felt on my soul waned a bit. Because there were cars parked outside, and from somewhere in the house I heard a girlish giggle.

I carefully walked down the porch, my footsteps heavy from the boots, and went into the kitchen. Evelyn looked up at me in concern.

"Luisa, what happened?" She quickly put a plate away then scurried over to me.

"It's fine," I said, surprised at how calm I suddenly felt. "I was following the horses and I slipped on the hill, tumbled for a bit. I'm okay. Just embarrassed."

She didn't seem to believe me so I deftly changed the subject. "Who came in the cars? I thought I heard a female laugh."

Evelyn looked grave. "You know how boys are," she said. "They wanted company."

I gave her a stiff smile. "I'm going to go shower. I might skip lunch if that's okay with you."

She nodded, seeming to understand.

As I went down the hall, I heard the laughter again. Two girls now. Thankfully they weren't coming from Javier's room but someone else's. I quickly went into my small bedroom, locked the door, and went into the bathroom. I avoided my reflection in the mirror and stripped, then got in the shower.

I couldn't get the water hot enough. I turned it hotter and hotter, until the air filled with steam and I was sure it was scalding me.

But still, I felt like I couldn't get clean.

CHAPTER EIGHT

Esteban

Esteban watched as Luisa climbed up the hill and out of his sight. Though she didn't know it yet, she really did look like she'd been ravaged. It pleased him to no end to know that it was all because of him. That he finally had done it. And even though fucking her was a means to an end, it wasn't half bad.

Actually, Luisa was better than he had expected. Sure, she wasn't wild, but he hadn't really given her much choice out here. And she protested, which he liked the most. In some ways he wanted her to really fight back. The fact that she hadn't meant that she'd been thinking about him, needing a good roll in the hay, something he'd only hoped for once.

In time, because they would do this again and again, it would become too much for her. It sickened him to think that Javier had probably screwed her six kinky ways from Sunday, with all his affinity for ropes and knives and asphyxiation. Because of that, Luisa was a hardened champ when it came to pushing boundaries and limits. But eventually Esteban would take it too far, and he relished the moment she became afraid of him, the moment she'd ask him to stop and he wouldn't.

That would be the moment Luisa realized how truly fucked she was. Because then he would hold all the power. She'd be his dirty queen and she'd get even dirtier, because he'd probably make her sleep with the pigs at that point. He saw it in her face, that former beauty queen, the girl who was a twenty-three-year-old virgin with loving parents and a moral outlook on life. She thought she was above scum like Esteban. Hell, she felt things like *guilt*. He didn't even know what guilt felt like.

He couldn't wait to wipe that smug, righteous look from her beautiful face and make her uglier, inside and out, day by day. It was what got him out of bed in the morning. That, and the look on Javier's face when he realized how much he had underestimated him. The look on his face when he saw how everything else had been taken away.

Oh, Luisa was playing into his plans so well. He hadn't counted on her still smarting over Javier's infidelities, but the woman felt far too much. In that respect alone, she would never cut it as a true *narco* queen. The real queens of the country knew to turn a blind eye to their husband's affairs. It was just the price you paid for being married to a *patron*. Their infidelity was inevitable. Everybody in the whole world knew it.

But Luisa, she hurt and bled over something so accepted. She had a soul and a heart that were so woefully out of place, but at least they made her gullible and easier to mold. She believed everything that Esteban told her about her own husband. She ate up every lie that came out of his mouth.

It was genius of him to mention the whores that had been driven in. The women weren't for Javier, though, not this time. They were for Borrero, Arturo, and whomever else. Maybe even Esteban, if he felt like it. But Javier had Evaristo now, and he was in his zone and wouldn't be distracted by women at this point. He was terribly single-minded at times.

Esteban had wanted Luisa to believe the opposite and so she did. And that led her right to him, aching and vulnerable.

The sound of hoof beats came from behind him, and Esteban turned around to see the dapple grey stallion that had enraptured Luisa so much. For no real reason other than an extremely misplaced sense of jealousy, Esteban hated that damn horse even though it had, in some ways, helped with the plan.

The horse stared at him cautiously, and Esteban fancied he could almost see the wheels turning in its head, trying to decide if he was friend or foe.

"If I had a knife on me, I'd slit your throat right now," Esteban said to the horse. He wasn't joking either. Killing animals meant nothing to him. It had probably all started when he was ten years old and tied his neighbor's beloved dog to their truck and watched as the owner, unaware, dragged the animal to its death. Esteban laughed at the horror of it all and felt thrilled that he, just a little boy, had the power to end a life so easily.

He would do it again and again.

Later, the puppies and cats and rabbits, they would become people. And it felt even better.

The horse seemed to decide Esteban was a foe after all. He snorted once and then took off at a trot, leaving Esteban behind. He had the brief fantasy of finding it later, slicing its head off, and delivering it to Luisa, blaming it on Javier. It was a little too *Godfather*-esque for Esteban's tastes but he thought it might be fitting.

He watched the horse go and then slowly headed back up the hill, toward the ranch. He knew he had to keep it casual between Luisa and himself for the next day or two, to give her space and time to realize that what she wanted was him. But he couldn't let it go too long. He had a schedule to keep, and it all depended on the man in the tunnel. The longer he could hold out, the better. He could only hope the agent was stubborn as all hell, and that Javier took his time. That was one thing he could count on. Javier didn't like to rush. He enjoyed the art of it all.

What a sick fuck.

...

Though it was hard to practice patience, a virtue Esteban never had in spades, he did what he could to keep Luisa at bay. It wasn't that hard. She was staying away from him. She wouldn't even look at him. He didn't know if it was out of guilt or the fear that Javier would see something in her eyes.

But of course Javier never saw anything because Javier was rarely seen above ground. He spent most of the day in the tunnel with Evaristo. Esteban only went down once or twice, to deliver news about a shipment to Javier or something else of importance—far from Evaristo's ears of course—and sometimes he caught Javier at breakfast before he went on his morning run across the desert.

Other than that though, Javier was caught up in his obsession. He didn't suspect a thing, and to Esteban's relief, he was taking things with Evaristo slowly. He was still using the battery pack, and Evaristo wasn't talking, but Javier was in no hurry to brutalize him beyond mercy. This was a day by day event that consumed the *patron*.

One evening after a dinner of Evelyn's heavenly *nopales* and chicken stew, Luisa got up and headed out into the desert on her evening walk. Esteban knew now was the time to strike.

He waited and then followed her out there as she climbed into the horse pasture. All the animals were out of sight so she kept going. He was glad he had brought his knife this time.

She went down into the wash but then headed up out of it and to a ridge, disappearing behind clumps of *yucca* and *agave*.

When he found her, she was sitting on a bunch of smooth boulders and staring off into the distance. If you squinted beyond the mirage of sun shimmer, you could see the faint line of the highway. Other than that, it was desolation.

She knew he had been following her. She didn't turn around or even flinch when she heard him call her name.

She knew and she had been waiting. This was what Esteban had wanted.

They didn't talk much. She held a world of sadness in her big eyes, but anger too, and it was the anger that fueled her. Esteban didn't even need to add anything to that fire.

He sat down on the rock and unzipped his shorts. He pulled her on top of him, and she was ready to go.

They fucked like that in the desert, the sun searing their shoulders and the wide open spaces around them swallowing their cries.

Esteban didn't think it was as good as last time, maybe because she wanted it and was wet and willing. There was no pain and no blood. But he saw the pain inside her, and that alone was enough to make him come.

Later, he'd pull Juanito into his room and inflict the pain on him that he couldn't inflict on her. Juanito took it like a champion and Esteban made false promises that he wouldn't do it again as long as Juanito behaved.

Then he was back to Luisa, hauling her out under the moon and pushing her to the dirt.

They carried on like that for a week.

One full week out in the middle of nowhere. Fucking in the dry earth, amidst the snakes and scorpions and other horrible, dangerous creatures, just like themselves. All the while, underneath that same earth, Javier worked away on Evaristo, wanting answers.

He'll get them soon enough, Esteban thought to himself.

The clock was ticking.

CHAPTER NINE

Javier

"Are you ready to talk?" I asked Evaristo calmly. I was sitting in my usual chair in the corner, running a file over my nails. They were getting awfully damaged over the work of last week. Torture would do that to you. Sometimes it was as hard on me as it was on them.

Not that I was being too hard on the *federale*. I had been taking it slow and easy, warming him up. But now, now I felt as if I had been far too nice to him. The agent wasn't talking, he wasn't even close to it, and I had to step it up a notch.

He'd been trained almost too well, and he was as stubborn as fuck. He could take the voltage and not talk, even when applied to the bottoms of his feet. His dick was a last resort, but there was something crude about shocking the genitals. Not to mention they often shit a brick after, and I sure as hell didn't want anything other than piss and blood around here.

I would prefer to remove a finger or toe with a thin, jagged saw rather than shock him there. But before I would even consider that, I'd apply some heat.

"Evaristo," I said, louder now. My voice echoed down the tunnel. I was starting to feel like a snake, like this was my burrow, my new home. The few times I had gone outside here I was almost blinded by the sun.

Evaristo, still naked, always naked, turned to look at me. He was always silent, too. I really admired him for that. He had no reason to put up such a front with me. After all, the information had nothing to do with him or his organization. I tried to reason with him, to tell him that my taking out Angel would only help them. One less *narco*. But he wouldn't have it. He didn't speak—at least, he didn't give me information—because his loyalty and sense of righteousness was that strong.

But he would break. I could see it in his eyes. He was tired. Weary. And I was starting to make the other side look good.

I eyed Diego who was leaning against the dirt wall. Borrero and Morales were elsewhere, perhaps partaking in the women in the house. I had no interest in that anymore. All my rage and violence was getting a daily outlet now.

"Let's see, what might give our young friend here some... motivation?" I said to Diego. "Do you have a lighter?"

He nodded and tossed one to me which I caught in one hand. Diego brought a small can of gasoline out from beside the toolbox and found the t-shirt Evaristo must have been wearing when he was brought in. He dumped the gas on the shirt, soaking it through.

"Why are you spending so much time with me?" Evaristo asked, his voice hoarse yet somehow strong.

I cocked my head at him. "Because you're being a pain in the ass. Do you really think you're going to win any favors with your peers because you held out long enough? Does it matter when you're going to give in, in the end?"

He shrugged even though the movement made him wince. I walked over to him, flicking the lighter as I went.

"I don't care what my peers think," he said.

"Oh, is that so? I totally would have pegged you for a brownnoser from the way you're holding out on me. I figured back at work you're nothing better than a dog with its nose up someone else's shithole, taking whatever comes your way."

"Then you don't know me at all."

"I think I know enough of you," I told him. "You want to be looked at as a hero. A self-righteous little prick and example for all the damned *federales*."

"Maybe," he said, eyeing me. "Maybe I don't give a flying fuck about them. Maybe I'm trying to see what *you* are made of."

I exchanged a look with Diego. He lifted up the soaked shirt, ready to follow through. We both knew it got dangerous when the captor got too personal. I couldn't help but be fascinated though. I subtly shook my head at Diego to keep him on standby.

"You should know what I'm made of," I told Evaristo as I crouched down beside him. I flicked the lighter on and pressed it into his thigh. "Sugar and spice and everything nice." He began to sweat and his skin started to burn beneath the flame. "Or is it worms and snails and puppy dog tails? Yes, I suppose the last one suits me better."

He clamped his eyes shut, face contorted in pain until I took the lighter away.

"So tell me, why do you want to know what I'm made of?" I asked him.

He didn't open his eyes. He breathed in and out harshly before he said, "You said you're going to let me go. I'm going to make sure that I know who I'm dealing with in the future."

I laughed. "I gave you my word and this is the thanks I get. Well, go ahead and tell your boss all about me, I'm sure he'll be impressed. More by me than the fact you got this information."

"Maybe it wouldn't be for my boss," Evaristo said. "And just for my own knowledge."

I really didn't know what this kid was getting at now, but I had a feeling he was just trying to waste my time. I nodded at Diego who came over and manhandled Evaristo, undoing the ties around his chest and pushing him down so that his head was between his knees. Evaristo struggled and Diego slammed his elbow into his cheekbone with a loud crack.

I winced at the brutality, knowing that it could make talking more difficult for the agent now, but didn't say anything. When Diego was done tying him in this new position, his bare back exposed, Evaristo spit out a tooth.

"You're merciless," he said, his words a thick jumble as blood pooled out of his mouth. "That's good. It would be even better if you didn't let me walk at the end."

I couldn't help but chew my lip for a second as I raised my brows at Diego. Was it our luck that we had kidnapped some sort of masochist? God, wouldn't that be just a fuck in the ass.

Diego wasted no time. He threw the wet, gasoline-soaked shirt across Evaristo's back and pressed it into his skin. I walked up and flicked on the lighter, holding it inches away.

"Tell us how to get Angel Hernandez and we won't have to do this."

"You will have to do this," he answered.

And so I did. I held the lighter to the shirt until it caught fire, then stepped back and watched as the flames spread along his back. Evaristo screamed and screamed and *screamed* until the fire naturally went out.

"That wasn't even the bad part," I told him as he gasped for breath, sweat dripping off his face and mixing with the blood on the ground. "Do you want to talk before that?"

He groaned, panting, but managed to say, "You think I don't know this game? You'll have to do it anyway."

He was right about that. Only a fool would think it was over at this point.

"Fair enough," I said. I grabbed the edge of the charred t-shirt that was now seared to his skin and ripped it right off. It took a layer of burned flesh with it.

Evaristo's screams were deafening and seemed to go on forever. I could feel them in my bones. I didn't feel anything but hope. Hope that when he calmed down, maybe he would finally talk. This was starting to become something of a chore, and if he was a masochist, that was going to take most of the fun out of it.

But every masochist has a breaking point. I wondered how much of a sadist I'd have to be to find it.

I didn't want to do the burn method again. The chance that he could go into shock was too high, and generally most people died after the third try. By then the internal organs are fried.

So Diego lifted his foot and very slowly I began to saw off his pinky toe.

Evaristo still didn't talk, despite the excruciating time I took to cut through the gristle and bone, and we had to inject him with adrenaline to keep him alert and conscious.

Finally—*finally*—as his toe rested on the ground in front of him, severed from his foot, and after Diego had taken off his own shirt to soak with gasoline, Evaristo muttered, "Please…"

I motioned for Diego to pause and pulled Evaristo back by the hair. "Please what?" I asked, staring down at his face, puffy, black and blue. He'd aged centuries at my hands, and I was shocked to find that the need to hurt, maim, and destroy was still inside me.

He opened his eyes and stared right at me. They were red, all his blood vessels having burst at some point. "You're worse than they say you are," he said slowly, painfully.

I tried not to smile. "Then you'll talk? Or do you want more?" My eyes slid to Diego and back.

Evaristo breathed in and out, thinking. I nodded at Diego who slapped the shirt down on his raw back.

I kept my fist in his hair as he cried out, screaming again. "No, no more. No more, please! Don't light it. Don't light it! I'll talk." He shut his eyes, and for a moment I thought he might cry, but when he opened them again he said, "If you keep your promise."

"That I let you go?" I asked. "I gave you my word and that's the truth." If Evaristo ended up dying in the desert, food for vultures, I didn't really care. But I *would* let him go.

"Okay," he said. "Okay. I want water."

"You'll get water after you talk. In fact, I'll have my wife take good care of you." That was one reason why I brought Luisa along—she was very good at tending to captives after they'd been tortured. It made them feel safe. Sometimes I had her do it during the whole process, as a way of playing good cop and bad cop. She probably didn't want to do it, but I knew she would. Her heart was too good to let someone suffer.

Evaristo slowly nodded and tried to breathe through what was left of his pain. Then he opened his mouth and began talking.

Half an hour later I had all the information I needed to successfully destroy Angel Hernandez, to do the things that Evaristo's very own agency wouldn't come right out and do because of bureaucratic tape and involvement in the DEA. He still didn't believe we were doing his organization a favor. In fact, he didn't seem to have much faith in them at all.

I couldn't blame him.

"Well," I said to him as Diego finished writing up everything in his notebook. "I'll go get Luisa and some water." I started to walk away but paused, looking at him over my shoulder. His eyes were drooping shut and I had an odd twinge of respect for the young man.

"Evaristo," I called out. He lifted his head and stared at me. "You proved yourself today, what you're made of. Your agency is lucky to have you. And you are far too smart and valuable to be a *federale*. If you ever want to fight for the other team, you have a place here. Just keep that in mind when you return. You may think you'll be in their good graces, but they will shun you. They will wonder what you told me and call you a snitch. And sooner or later, you'll be working a desk job in some office in Mexico City, because they won't trust you after everything you were put through. They won't show you any respect. All this pain will be for nothing. But you have my respect."

He watched me for a moment. Then he said, "Fuck you," and closed his eyes.

I shrugged. "As you wish."

I left the tunnel and went upstairs. I had totally lost track of time. I had lost track of days. It was almost dark outside, the light fading to a bruise, the color of Evaristo's cheek.

I found Luisa in the kitchen, sitting at the table with a cup of tea in front of her. She was alone.

I stopped in the doorframe and watched her for a moment. I couldn't tell if she was lost in her head or ignoring me. Her hair fell across her face as she stared out the windows at the darkening desert.

Something beat inside me quietly. And for once it wasn't rage.

It was regret.

"Luisa," I said softly.

She looked up at me, so startled that she spilled some of her tea on the table. Her eyes held something dangerous in them. It was fear of me. I couldn't blame her.

"Sorry," I apologized. I came over and sat down beside her. She seemed so small all of a sudden. I felt like I hadn't laid eyes on her for a week and that might have been true. "Are you okay?"

Now the fear changed into something that looked like guilt. I didn't like that look. It made my chest feel hollow. It made me feel like a million things were about to go very wrong.

She nodded and picked up a napkin from the middle of the country table, dabbing at the tea. I reached out and put my hand over hers. I half-expected her to snatch hers away but she held it there as if frozen. In fact, it appeared she was holding her breath.

"I mean here, on the ranch," I said, clearing my throat. "How have you been doing?"

She watched me for a few moments as if trying to gauge my sincerity.

"I'm fine," she finally said, her voice barely above a whisper. I licked my lips as I watched hers, so full and soft.

"Where is everyone else?" I asked.

She shrugged and slowly moved her hand out from under mine. "They went into La Perla. Evelyn is with the horses."

"She runs a tight ship around here. She's a good woman," I said. "So are you."

She flinched as if I'd hit her again. "Luisa," I said carefully. "Has something happened?"

She rubbed her lips together then looked me dead in the eye. "Why do you care about me all of a sudden?"

Now it was my turn to act like I'd been backhanded. But I couldn't get mad, even though I wanted to, because she had a right to say that. She had a right to say anything she wanted.

"Because you're my wife," I told her, wishing that meant something to her. "So, has something happened?"

She shook her head. "There is nothing."

She let that word hang in the air. Nothing.

Nothing at all.

Nothing between us.

The wave of shame came over me like a tidal wave. At one point she had been everything to me, and now, now I was realizing how close I'd come to losing her, if I hadn't already.

I had pushed her away and away and away, but I didn't want to do that anymore.

I just didn't think I could get her back.

The look in her eyes told me that she hated me. She was hard now, like a woman carved from stone, and I was afraid that no matter what I said or did, I could never bring her back to the way she had been before. I had broken her in too many pieces, and what had been pieced back together had no room for me.

"Are you happy?" I asked her despite myself. It was a stupid question.

She gave me a sharp look. "What do you think?"

I pressed my lips together and nodded. "I'm sorry."

But she didn't seem to understand that I was sincere or appreciate how sorry I was. I knew sorry meant nothing anymore. In fact, the words that came out of my mouth made her tense up even more.

Annoyed, she brushed her hair back from her face and looked down at her cup of tea before taking a sip.

Her neck was covered in small bruises.

My heart stilled but I made sure concern wasn't showing on my face. I stared at them for a moment, memorizing the shape, before she could catch me looking.

They looked like fucking hickeys. Or bite marks. They looked like what I used to do with her when I was feeling particularly bloodthirsty and crazed with lust.

My mind raced, trying to come up with an explanation. She also had bite marks on the backs of her hands, so it's possible something in the desert air had been biting her.

It was possible.

But unlikely.

I pushed it aside for now.

"I have good news," I said. She didn't look at me but I went on. "Evaristo talked. We'll keep him for a few more days." I paused. "I need a favor from you."

"Oh?" she said.

"He's pretty beat up," I explained. "It wasn't pretty, what I had to do down there."

"But I bet you enjoyed it," she muttered quickly.

I appraised her, the sharpness of her words, the burning in her eyes. "Yes, I did," I admitted slowly. "Does that still surprise you even now?"

She looked right at me. "He never did anything to you. He didn't deserve it, what you did. He was an innocent bystander. That used to be something you believed in."

"I used to believe in a lot of things, Luisa. Myself, included."

"That makes two of us."

Ouch. I managed a smile, as if it didn't sting. "Back to the favor though…can you tend to Evaristo?"

She rolled her eyes. "Play nurse again?"

My expression grew grim. "This isn't a game, Luisa. You know that. I'm not asking you to put on a nurse's uniform and give him a pity fuck." My eyes narrowed as I watched her freeze up again. "That's not something you're willing to do, is it?"

She got out of her chair abruptly, nearly spilling her tea again. "Of course not," she said, taking the cup to the sink. Her actions were entirely deflective.

"Good," I said, rising up. "Now you don't have to do anything you don't want to, but I thought it might appeal to your good side that there's a wounded, innocent man down there who needs your help."

"My good side?" she repeated, keeping her back to me.

"We both know you've got bad in you as well."

But just how much bad has come out to play lately? I wondered. *And with whom? I had an idea.*

"Fine," she said, turning around and walking past me. "I'll go help him."

I reached out and grabbed her arm. Her eyes widened as I pulled her close to me.

"You look different these days," I told her.

She held her ground. "Maybe it's the dry air."

I smirked at her. "Maybe it is. Maybe it's a lot of things."

Our eyes were locked intensely, another game to see who would look away first.

I chickened out first.

I leaned down and kissed her, hard and flush on the lips, my grip still firm on her arm. I'd forgotten how well my lips knew her. I realized how long it had been since I'd last kissed her. I realized how damn much I missed her.

She barely kissed me back. She made a sound of surprise and pulled back, and when she looked up at me, she looked more scared—and confused—than ever.

All she saw was a monster.

She swallowed, her eyebrows coming together, trying to process it. You'd think she had just been doused in acid.

"Don't worry," I told her gruffly. "I won't ask anything more of you."

I let go of her and she stepped back, still looking shocked, as if it hadn't been her husband at all that had kissed her. It took all of me to not feel even remotely humiliated.

With her head down, she slowly turned away, as if to run.

"Oh," I said lightly before she could leave the kitchen. "I'd appreciate it if you didn't say anything to Esteban about the interrogation process."

"Why...why Esteban?" she asked, slowly turning around, hand at her chest.

I frowned, not liking her reaction. "Because I know you two are close. And I also know he thinks he has a right to know my business. *Our* business. He doesn't. So as far as you know now, I'm still interrogating Evaristo and he hasn't said anything. Can you do that? Can you *lie*?"

I swear I saw relief wash over her. She nodded quickly and left the room, leaving me alone.

Of course she could lie. I knew she was lying to me already.

I just didn't know about what.

But I knew I'd get it out of her.

And that it was going to hurt.

CHAPTER TEN

Esteban

That night, Luisa didn't come out to see Esteban. He sat on the fencepost for a while, then thinking perhaps he was being too bold, he headed along the rails until they dipped over the hill. He waited in the wash, at the base of the acacia. He went over the ridge and waited on the boulders until the moon was halfway across the night sky.

She never came.

This didn't worry him. It angered him. How fucking dare she stand up their tryst already, leaving him hanging out to dry? If Javier weren't around, he'd give her a black eye to teach her a lesson, and that would be getting off easily. Hell, he thought he should give her a black eye anyway. How would she explain it? That Esteban hit her for no reason? Not damn likely.

It didn't really matter now. Tomorrow he was making the call. Tomorrow he would set everything in motion and things would change, for the better. For him and Luisa, at first. And then just for him.

He dusted his hands off on his shorts and headed back to the house. Maybe he could sneak into her room and have a quick fuck there before escaping out the door to the patio. Maybe that's what she was waiting for.

He had to admit, he was starting to look forward to their escapades. Sure, she didn't respond in the same way that Juanito did. She didn't have that fear of him. She didn't mind pain so much. But he knew she would in time, and just picturing that was enough to get him going.

Besides, Luisa really was beautiful. In any other life and at any other time, he could imagine himself being with her. Not forever. Not really for any length of time. And he certainly wouldn't love her because he could never feel that emotion, let alone be that selfless.

But he would have a good time with her. She would fulfill his needs. She was stunning to look at, beautiful to feel, and he'd enjoyed corrupting her once pure soul bit by bit. He would have shown Luisa proudly on his arm to anyone who looked his way, and he would feel like the king of the world to have such a rare creature in his possession—smart, funny, gorgeous. She was beautiful and yet he hated it at the same time.

And then in the end, he would say goodbye and move on. He probably wouldn't even kill her. He'd just let her leave and that would be the end of it. It was almost noble of him in this imaginary future.

But that's not the way his world worked, and it wasn't the hand he had been dealt. This Luisa wasn't really his. She didn't really care for him at all—he was just a cock and an excuse to exact her own brand of revenge on Javier. He didn't care one way or another what her feelings were because the damage had already been done.

Soon Javier would find out, when Esteban allowed it. The day after tomorrow. When everything else in the *patron's* life went to shit. He would know and Esteban would become king.

Smiling to himself, he walked down the hallway and stopped at Luisa's door, about to knock.

"What are you doing?" Javier asked, voice cold as steel in the dark.

Esteban turned to see Javier at the end. He had blended in with the shadows a little too well, the light from the kitchen failing to illuminate him until he walked forward and stopped just as the light hit his eyes.

God, his eyes were some scary ass shit at times, Esteban thought. *Like a snake's.*

"I was seeing if Luisa was awake," Esteban said, knowing it would only make Javier suspicious if he tried to cover it up.

"Why?" Javier's eyes locked on him in that very predatory-like way. They burned amber under his black brows while the shadows played up his high cheekbones and wide mouth.

Esteban shrugged and gave him his trademark stupid grin. "Bored, I guess. You're not around much."

Javier's jaw tensed. "I've been busy."

"Has the fed talked yet?"

He shook his head. "Soon though."

It better not be until the day after tomorrow, Esteban thought. *I need Evaristo here.*

"And what's the plan after that?" he asked, just to keep him talking, to get him to forget that he was ever about to knock on Luisa's door because he was "bored."

"You'll see," Javier said. He eyed his wife's door and said, "If I were you, I'd let her sleep. She's had a long day. Goodnight."

As Javier turned around and disappeared into the dark hall, Esteban frowned. Had Javier been with Luisa today? When? And why?

Had she talked?

He was tempted now more than ever to go inside and wake her up, if she was asleep at all, but he had a feeling Javier would be watching.

Always watching.

Esteban would just have to be a bit more careful.

One more day, he told himself as he strolled toward his room. One more day.

CHAPTER ELEVEN

Luisa

Despite my better judgement, I couldn't help but be captivated by Evaristo Sanchez. Of course, it was my first time laying eyes on him in the flesh, and I knew there was a handsome man beneath the bruises and blood. Javier and Diego had really worked him over.

But he still had this quiet charm and tenacity you rarely found in these situations. When I first introduced myself, he looked at me through slits for eyes and said, "You must be an angel. I must be dead."

I told him if I was an angel, I was a dirty one and he certainly wasn't in heaven. He said he wasn't in hell anymore, and we agreed he was in a kind of limbo, that though the torture was over, it didn't change the fact that his back had been brutally burned and he was missing his pinky toe.

I had played nurse before so I did what I could without acting too squeamish about it. I anointed his wounds with antiseptic and wrapped his toe and foot. I gave him antibiotics that were always lying around, along with a small dose of morphine for the pain.

Evaristo didn't do or say much else, but he watched me closely. There was a cot set up in the basement so Borrero and I helped him squeeze past the hot water heater and into the room.

"Your husband is an interesting man," Evaristo said as he eased himself down onto the cot. His blue eyes were bloodshot and glazed from the drugs, and I knew he wasn't feeling any agony at this point. I'm not sure if I'd be so stoic after a week-long torture session, especially if I didn't have my toe by the end of it.

I also wouldn't be using the word *interesting* to describe Javier.

I stared at him for a moment. "Interesting? You should be calling him a monster."

"Oh, I'm sure I did for a moment there. But he can't be so bad, if you're married to him."

That felt like a gut punch, and I instinctively wrapped my arms around myself, aware that Borrero was watching our exchange. "I'm not as good as you think," I said quietly.

"No?" he asked. "And is your husband as bad as I think? As the world thinks? You survived Salvador Reyes before, didn't you? I guess this is just a lesser of two evils."

"It depends if you believe evil is absolute or not."

"And do you believe that? You were raised Catholic, weren't you?"

So many questions. So personal. I straightened up, not wanting to get into religious beliefs with him. I didn't want to think God had been looking over my shoulder for the past week, watching me commit sin after sin.

And in some ways, loving it.

In some ways, hating myself even more.

The way Javier kissed me today...I didn't know what to do. It was so unexpected. It bruised my heart and soul and left me reeling, aching. Because he was giving me what I'd been craving, what I'd been looking for in Esteban.

And in that kiss, I realized the horror of what I had done.

Yes, I also knew the horror of what he had done. The women he'd been with. The innocent lives he'd taken. But even though I wasn't willing to forgive him, I could at least understand what was happening to him.

I couldn't understand what was happening to me. I had sex with Esteban over and over again while my husband was down here, torturing this poor man for information.

We were both so fucking dirty.

And today, today was the first I'd seen Javier try and pick himself up out of it. He hadn't killed Evaristo. He was letting him walk when any other *patron* would have offed him. And he had reached out to me. Kissed me. Made me feel useful for once, even if it was just to come down here and take care of a tortured man.

I wanted Javier to try again. To keep trying.

I wanted to forget all the bad that I had done. I wanted to remove it from my heart.

"Are you crying?" Evaristo asked.

I ran my fingers under my eyes and saw that I was. Borrero stepped away from the wall, concerned, but I just waved him off. "Oh, I guess it's the air here. So dry."

Evaristo nodded though I knew he didn't believe me.

"I'd say you could do better than him," he said softly. "But that's none of my business, what goes into a marriage. Or a business. Just tell me...do you believe in him?"

He watched me with open curiosity.

"Do I believe in him?"

"Yes. Do you think he'll take over the Tijuana cartel and then proceed to take over whatever is left?"

"Javier is very ambitious," I stated.

"I'm not talking ambition. I know he's ambitious. Everyone in the world knows that. Do you think he—you all—will succeed in the end? That you will rule absolute. Does he have what it takes to take this as far as it can go?"

"Yes," I said, without hesitating. "Unless he gets killed, I think he will go as far as he possibly can."

He nodded, seemingly satisfied. "Then there isn't much the *federales* can do to stop him. Except kill him."

I blinked and quickly exchanged a look with Borrero, who was standing at attention. Was that a threat?

"They won't kill him," I said, raising my chin.

His eyes managed to stay kind. "Let's hope they don't." He let out a long breath and closed his eyes. "Thank you for being an angel." Then he seemed to drift off to sleep.

I watched him, puzzled at our exchange, until Borrero came over and laid his hand on my shoulder.

"Let's go, Luisa. You've done enough," he said, and led me up the stairs.

After that, I went straight to the kitchen to down what was left of a bottle of merlot, then I went to my room. I rested there for a while, tossing and turning under the covers. It was a cold night and I felt even colder inside. I was supposed to go meet Esteban for our nightly tryst but I wasn't in the mood.

I wouldn't be in the mood again. With a simple, impulsive kiss, Javier had sealed himself as mine again. I had done something terrible, but I was ready to put that behind me now. Hope was so very dangerous, but at the moment it was blooming inside me, like the desert wildflowers after a rain.

I was almost asleep when I heard voices outside my door.

Javier.

Esteban.

They didn't sound like they were fighting. In fact, they sounded as they usually did. Javier, hard and calm, Esteban, easygoing, like everything in life was one big joke.

Except Esteban wasn't easygoing at all. In fact, the more time I spent with him, the more I started to realize there was more to him than what met the eye. For one, he was pushy and violent. Enough that I could see him going to a dark place very quickly, a place where no rules applied. The attitude he had most of the time was just a front, covering up something darker. The only problem was, I didn't know if this was common knowledge and I was just slow to catch on to it, or if he was someone I needed to watch closely.

Of course, now he was. I had made it that way.

It grew silent, and I heard footsteps disappearing down the hall.

I sat up in my bed and listened, trying to make sure he was truly gone. The last thing I wanted was for Esteban to come and find me tonight.

I got out of bed, just wearing a camisole and my underwear, and crept over to the door. I opened it a crack and looked up and down the hall. It was dark and empty.

I took in a deep breath and silently closed the door behind me before I tiptoed down the hall. From one room I heard manly grunts, from another I heard a woman's giggle. I didn't know where Esteban was.

But I knew where my husband should have been.

I stopped at his door, noting that Diego wasn't on duty. This house was half the size of the mansion back at home, so either Diego or Arturo was probably patrolling the perimeter of the building.

I tried the knob but of course it was locked. He would never leave his bedroom door unlocked unless Diego was there.

I knocked as quietly as possible, not wanting to draw attention to myself to anyone but him.

The door opened slightly and Javier stared at me through the gap, backlit by the lamp in his room. His eyes were shadowy but I could tell they were surprised.

"Is everything okay?" he asked, looking over my shoulder with concern.

I nodded, feeling almost nervous, like a girl on her first date. "I'm fine. Can I come in?"

"Sure," he said, holding the door open for me. I brushed past him, feeling the air between us intensify as he quickly looked out the door, checking again for who knows what, before closing and locking it.

I stood in the middle of the room and looked around, as if I hadn't seen it before. The truth was, I didn't know where to look or what to say or why I was really here.

"What is it?" he asked. His voice was lower now and smoother than scotch.

I turned to face him. He stood by the door, his hands at his sides, though his fingers were twitching slightly as if he didn't quite know what to do with them. He was shirtless, wearing loose black pajama pants, this very thin material that left nothing to the imagination if he got a little excited, and he often did. His shaggy hair was messy for once, across his forehead, making him look years younger. But his eyes burned the same. His eyes never lied.

Did mine? I wondered what he had seen in them early.

Had he seen the truth?

I chewed on my lip but didn't answer him.

He frowned, a deep line between his brows.

His nostrils flared slightly. His shoulders tensed up.

Eyes blazed like the sun.

Then he strode toward me and took me in his arms.

His lips found mine, hot and feverish, and one of his hands was in my hair and the other was wrapped around my waist. His strong fingers dug into me like he was incapable of letting go.

I wished he never would.

I whimpered in his grasp, at the desperation as his body strained against mine. He was kissing me so deeply that I could feel it in my toes, and my nerves were razed and raring, filling me with a need so strong it was almost violent.

"Luisa," he said, breathing hard as he pulled his lips off of mine and licked down my neck, behind my ear. Just the sound of my name was making my knees liquefy. "I need to fuck you, claim you. My wife."

His wife. I was so close to drowning in my guilt.

I decided to drown in him instead.

"I'm all yours," I said breathlessly.

He grunted at that and wrapped his hands under my ass, picking me up and ravaging my neck as we moved backward toward the bed. He threw me down on it, immediately ripping my thin camisole in two while I slid out of my shorts.

While one hand slipped between my legs, the movement silky smooth, his other arm pressed down on my windpipe. With less air coming in, every sensation was heightened. The feel of his stubble as his chin raked against my skin, his large tongue lapping around my breasts, the hardness of his erection as it pressed against my legs, the blissful intrusion of his long fingers finding purchase inside me.

I moaned, lost in lust, and the pressure on my neck increased. I couldn't tell if it was the lack of oxygen or my desire for Javier that was making the world seem smaller.

Finally I had to put my fingers on his arm to try and release some of the pressure. He pressed harder for a second, then raised his head to look at me. I couldn't speak, I had to tell him with my eyes that it was too much and I couldn't breathe.

For one frightening second there was a look in him that told me this was his intention, but just like that, it melted away and there was softness instead. He took his arm off of me and gently kissed down my windpipe before coming up to my ear.

"I don't wish to hurt you anymore," he whispered.

I inhaled deeply, letting it expand in my lungs, and nodded.

He kissed me long and hard, and I felt myself stealing his breath. His tongue was wet and probing, and I suddenly needed that tongue elsewhere.

He knew this. He knew me too well. He moved down and off the bed until his head was between my legs. His lips found me, his tongue slow and teasing. He moaned into me. This was his favorite thing, my taste, my very essence. It fired Javier up like nothing else, and I knew he was stroking himself as he did so. I could make his cock harder than cement.

"Oh god," I whimpered, my back arched and my hands gripping his silky hair as I pulled his mouth deeper into me. His tongue thrust inside and I automatically clenched around him as he pushed it back and forth, revving me into a frenzy. I ground my hips, wanting more, more, more.

"What did I tell you about being greedy?" he murmured into me, taking the chance to lick up the insides of my thighs.

"Something about how I could be as greedy as I wanted," I said through a moan.

"You're right. You want it all and I will give it to you."

He razed his teeth over my clit then plunged his tongue inside me again while two fingers dipped into my tight ass.

I came immediately, hard and wild, my body bucking like a runaway horse. I shouted out his name, moaning like a woman possessed.

"How many times can I make my queen come?" he challenged, his voice sounding far away as I rode through the orgasm, my soul splintering out into shards of light. It threatened to let loose a million emotions I was trying so hard to cage.

Luckily Javier was fast. He stood up, completely naked now, his gorgeous cock jutting out, and yanked my thighs toward him and up, so my hips were raised and my legs were hooked over his shoulders.

He thrust into me, grinding his teeth, the muscles in his neck corded.

"Fuck," he muttered, closing his eyes as he slowly pulled out. Achingly, teasingly. Then he pushed in again to the hilt.

My breath hitched as he sunk in deeper, and I was enraptured by the intensity on his face, the desire and lust that seemed to smolder throughout him. His eyes lifted to meet mine and held me there. I was his hostage, his captive, all over again.

I wouldn't have it any other way.

I gave myself to him as he pounded in and out. Open, vulnerable, exposed, he could have all of me if I could even get a taste of all of him.

Just when the strain seemed too much and his eyes pinched shut, about to come, he somehow had the nerve to stop. He pulled out and I was suddenly bereft without him inside me.

"I need you closer," he said, and he got on the bed so that he was sitting up, and then pulled me on top so that I was straddling him. "Much closer."

I eased onto his cock, reveling in how full he made me feel, and while one arm went around my waist, holding me close to his own sweaty, hard chest, the other disappeared into my hair. He held me softly but firmly in place, our bodies fused.

He kissed me, mouth open and insatiable, then stared deep into my eyes. There was so much I wanted to see in them.

"Luisa," he murmured.

"Yes?" I asked as I fell deeper and deeper.

Javier started nibbling across my jaw and I closed my eyes to take it all in.

"I want a son," he whispered, voice ragged against my neck.

I pulled back and faced him, stunned. "What?"

It was the way of life here in Mexico, and that was no less important in the cartels. Family was everything, and the *patrons* always wanted big families with sons who would eventually take over the family business.

When it came to children though, it was something that Javier and I discussed only once. While I wanted a family at some point, he was hesitant. He had once confessed to me in the middle of the night that he feared he would be just like his own father, deadbeat and horrible. I couldn't convince him otherwise.

I didn't have a womb that demanded kids or ached for them. I ached for him. But I also knew that Javier was talking nonsense when it came to his fears. Though there was no denying that he, at times, was not a good person and could very well be the monster that everyone feared, I knew he would make a wonderful father. He was fiercely loyal and protective, and our baby would grow up to be the most spoiled brat in the land.

But I never pushed the issue with him, because I wanted what he wanted, at least for now, and if I ever started feeling the urge, that ticking clock that enslaved women, then I would let him know. I would stop taking the pill and we would start trying.

I never dreamed he would let me know first.

But now I could hear it in his voice, raw and choked, that desire.

I stared up at him, locked in the intensity of his gaze. "You want a baby?"

He swallowed and brushed the hair off my forehead. "Yes, Luisa. I do. For us. For the future." He paused, seeming to get lost in himself, his face contorting slightly with want and need. "I love you. And I am so, so sorry that I haven't been there. I am so sorry for what I've done to you."

"No." I spoke softly, unable to handle this.

"Yes," he said. "It is the truth. And I know the truth doesn't mean much from me. But..." He closed his eyes and rested his forehead against mine, "I want it to matter. I want to start over. All of this, all of us. Will you do that with me? Will you love me again?"

My heart shattered beautifully, shards flying everywhere inside, landing soft, and I was filled with nothing but warmth.

I ran my hands through his thick, soft hair. "Of course I will. I never stopped, Javier. It didn't matter what you did. I tried, but I couldn't. You're embedded in my skin."

"And you're embedded in mine," he said. "Deeper than you will ever know."

At that, he moved his hips, pushing himself deeper inside. I welcomed him with a greedy groan.

CHAPTER TWELVE

Luisa

The next morning I woke up in Javier's bed. I was alone—I had prepared myself for that. But the space next to me was still warm and I could hear his shower running.

I sighed happily and rolled over as the bright sunshine streamed in through the deep-set windows. Everything looked white-washed and clean. I felt clean too, as if I'd been stripped of everything dark and toxic, and all that was left was a new me.

I knew it was naïve and wishful thinking but I didn't care. I needed to cling to the belief that we could start fresh, start anew. I needed to believe that our love was strong enough to survive anything.

The shower turned off and Javier strode out of the bathroom, towel wrapped around his waist, his athletic and toned upper body showcased in the morning glow. He gave me a quick smile as he walked over to the closet, completely in business mode.

It was his demeanor that reminded me of exactly what was going on and what was at stake. Last night may have been everything I'd needed and wanted, and it could have been the same for him. But he was a man with a job to do and that was the kind of thing that couldn't take a backseat.

"Big day?" I commented. I realized I was just trying to make conversation, and that in turn made me see that despite everything that had happened, nothing was back to normal.

"It is," he said, slipping on a black dress shirt and facing the mirror. "Another day of fixing up our *federale*, if you don't mind so much."

I shook my head. "It's fine. I kind of like him."

"Well, don't get too attached," he warned. "Tomorrow he's out of here."

"What exactly do you plan on doing with him?"

He shrugged. "Not sure yet. We'll play it by ear. Diego thinks that we should kick him out of the chopper in the middle of the desert. I'm more inclined to get Juanito or someone to drop him off in Monterey. The city has always been so neutral anyway."

"Sounds like you've got it all figured out," I said, running my hands over the soft sheets.

"I've got that figured out," he said as he pulled on white linen pants. Always commando. "What I've really got to focus on is what to do with the intel on Hernandez. We can't screw this up. We get one shot to get him, and anything after that we are fucked."

I nodded, feeling privileged to be let in on this information again, feeling a part of his life, like a true partner. "Well, other than making sure Evaristo is comfortable, whatever you need from me, just ask."

He smiled at me in the mirror's reflection. "I'm glad you asked that. Because there is something I would like to ask you."

"Yeah?"

"And Esteban."

My blood turned to ice. My lungs froze right over.

Oh fuck.

"Oh?" I said, and Javier slowly walked over to me as he slipped on a belt through the loops on his pants.

"Yeah. I would like to ask something of the two of you."

I plastered the fakest damn smile on my face. "What is it?"

He smiled right back but I couldn't be sure if it was fake or malicious, or what it was. I was so paranoid that my heart was threatening to fly right out of my chest.

He knows. He knows.

He hads to know.

"It's something that can wait for now," Javier said, putting his hand on my shoulder. He leaned down and kissed me lightly on the lips. I had to force my body to break the freeze and kiss him back as I normally would.

I wondered if he could taste the fear on me.

"I've got a busy day," he said, turning around and walking back to his dresser to slip on his watch. "I think I'm going to head with Diego to La Perla or maybe Durango and see if we can get some work done. It's better to do the work in the car and pilfer someone's wifi. It won't leave a trace, just in case our systems are being watched."

I nodded absently. "Is that possible?" I asked, just wanting him to keep talking.

"Anything is possible, my queen," he said, shooting me a wicked smile. "You should know that more than anyone."

I couldn't swallow the brick in my throat. I smiled again and slowly got out of bed. "I should get dressed," I said, willing my voice to remain steady.

"I'll see you later. Bring Esteban back here around nine tonight," he said before he strode out the door and into the hall, closing it behind him and barking at Diego who must have been outside.

Oh shit.

SHIT.

What the hell did this mean?

I felt like I was about to have a full-blown meltdown. Panic was creeping up my body, worming its way into my chest. I had to remind myself to breathe in and out, to not let my guilt get the best of me. The fact that he wanted to talk to both of us didn't have to mean the worst. It didn't mean he knew.

It didn't, it couldn't.

I had to find Esteban right away, but I had to wait until Javier and Diego were gone, so I practically forced myself to shower and spend time getting ready before I went out to look for him.

I didn't have to look far. Esteban was on the porch, staring off into the distance, a cup of coffee in his hand. It was a lovely beautiful morning, the sky saturated blue and stretching as far as the eye could see. There wasn't a single cloud.

It's too bad I couldn't take the time to fully appreciate it.

"Esteban," I said warily as I walked across the porch to him. He didn't turn to look at me. He was probably mad about me standing him up last night.

I stood beside him, watching his gaze. That favorite horse of mine was in the distance. Esteban seemed so focused on him, and not in a good way.

"Where were you last night?" he asked me, voice hard. He still wouldn't look at me.

"Sorry about that," I said.

"But where were you?"

I hesitated. "With Javier."

He nodded. "I see. In what way were you with him?"

"Esteban, I think he knows," I said, skirting the issue.

Finally he looked at me, and his eyes were smoldering with hate. "What did you do?"

My chin jerked back, surprised that he would blame me so fast. "I didn't do anything!" His look intensified. I shook my head. "I swear to god, I didn't do anything or say anything."

"Then why do you think he knows?"

"He asked if the both of us would come to his room tonight. At nine. That there was something he needed to ask us."

He stared at me for a moment. "Did you fuck him last night?"

"Esteban," I warned, stepping away from him. "That's none of your business."

"You're wrong," he sniped, and reached out to grab the back of my neck, his fingers squeezing the skin as he yanked me to him. "Everything you do is my business now. You're not his anymore, you got that? You're mine. And there's nothing you can do to change it. It's happening."

What was happening? I wanted to ask, but he squeezed my neck harder and I winced from the pain.

"Hey," I heard Borrero say as he stepped out from the kitchen to the porch. "What's going on here?"

Esteban immediately let go of my neck, and my hand flew back there to press on the pain. "Nothing you should worry your pretty little head about," Esteban said to Borrero.

Borrero glared at him and walked over to me. "You all right, Luisa?" he asked as Esteban stomped off the porch and headed toward the barn.

I nodded, trying to catch my breath. "I guess I said the wrong thing."

Borrero watched me curiously for a moment before his eyes drifted off to Esteban in the distance. "You know I'm supposed to keep you safe. If Javier had seen what I had just seen..."

Javier would have probably chopped Esteban's arm off.

"I know," I told him, trying to smile. "It's fine."

"I'll be watching you, you know," he said, and now I couldn't figure out if it was for my own protection or because Javier might have told him about his own suspicions.

"I'll be staying out of trouble, don't worry," I said to the *sicario* before heading back inside the house.

...

I stayed out of trouble by staying near Evelyn the entire day and helping her with her chores. The more we talked, the more I realized that she was far smarter than I had initially thought, and we had a lot in common. We both had to hide behind a mask. I wore a beauty queen one and she wore one of an old maid, but we both were so much more than we appeared to be.

Evelyn told me that the ranch had been used a lot recently for the sole purpose of training. While I knew that Javier was trying to set up his own army to battle against those crazy Zetas, I didn't realize so many of the camps took place here. It was good to know that we were improving the army we already had, the ones who could battle it out against the Gulf Cartel and whomever else declared us their enemy.

Speaking of enemies, the only time I was away from Evelyn was when I was with Evaristo in the basement. He looked only marginally better than he did yesterday and he wasn't as talkative, but he still watched me with almost reverence as I applied the ointments and fed him his pills.

It was around eight o'clock when Diego and Javier returned home from wherever they had gone. They quickly corralled

Morales and went walking around the property as the sun was dying in the west. I guessed they were discussing whatever it was they had learned that day, the next steps in the plan to get Hernandez.

When it was close to nine, I quickly finished the wine I was having with Evelyn—I'd had more than I meant to, my nerves getting the best of me—and headed to Javier's room, hoping to find Esteban.

I didn't. It was empty. I wondered if I should go looking for him or if Javier would.

But before I could answer that question, Javier walked through the door, Esteban in tow.

"Please sit down. Both of you," Javier said, gesturing to the bed with an open palm. His tone was light and I started to have some hope that he wasn't about to kill us.

That was until he went and locked the door.

"What's this about, Javi?" Esteban asked, seeming more bored than intrigued. He was good at pretending. I knew he had to be at least shitting himself a little bit. Even sitting next to Esteban felt electric and dangerous.

Javier eyed us coolly. "I'll get to that. You're not armed, are you Este?"

Esteban exchanged a quick glance with me then shrugged. "I'm always armed."

Javier held out his hand. "Give it to me."

Esteban didn't move. "Why?"

"Because we're all friends here, aren't we? And friends—real friends—shouldn't need to arm themselves when they're with each other. We are real friends, the three of us, right? Don't you dare prove me wrong."

I swallowed and watched with bated breath as Esteban nodded and slowly pulled out his pistol from the back of his shorts. Javier snatched it out of his grasp and walked over to the dresser, placing it on top.

"Doesn't that mean you need to disarm yourself too?" Esteban asked.

Javier smiled like a snake. That panic in the pit of my stomach started to squirm.

"Of course," he said, and he brought his gun out, putting it beside Esteban's. I didn't dare mention that I knew Javier had a small pistol strapped to his leg and a knife on the other. I saw him strap them on before he pulled on his pants that morning, like he always did. *Patrons* believed in extra protection.

"So why exactly are we all gunless pussies now?" Esteban asked.

Javier leaned against the dresser. "I didn't want anyone to freak out from what I'm about to ask you. A favor."

A favor?

"What is it?" I said, trying not to sound scared.

He cocked his head slightly and appraised me for a moment. "A little fantasy of mine."

I frowned, not sure what he was getting at.

"Esteban," Javier said to him, "as I'm sure you are aware, I've been having some issues lately. Alana's death…hasn't been easy on me. And I've been taking it out on the wrong people. You, I'm sure, plus others. Many, many others. But mostly my poor wife." Javier gave me a quick smile. "I've been unfaithful to her. I've been rude and rough and disrespectful. I have failed as her husband."

The fact that Javier was admitting this troubled me. I knew he had a hard enough time admitting his faults to me in general, but to Esteban? He was the last person he wanted to look weak in front of, but that's just what he was doing here.

I glanced at Esteban out of the corner of my eye. He was sitting rigid, looking about as worried as I felt.

Javier went on, hands behind his back. "But I don't want to be that to her anymore. I want to be a better man, so to speak. We're going to start a family."

Esteban's eyes widened and he swallowed hard. "Congratulations."

"Thank you," Javier said simply. "Of course, she's not pregnant yet. At least, I don't think so. We made love last night but these things can take time."

I didn't know where this was going, but it was wrong. Everything that Javier was saying, even though it was the truth, was wrong. He wasn't acting like himself. He had some ulterior motive, some purpose, and I didn't know what it was.

"But an heir, particularly a son, will do wonders for us and the organization. Don't you think?"

Esteban shrugged again though this time it seemed forced. "I guess. It's the way."

"It is the way," Javier said with a sharp nod. "And the way is about family and responsibility and doing what's right to protect that unit. It's not for frivolous acts. It's not for degenerates. There is no place in the family unit for…uncouth urges." He eyed both of us. "I guess I'm not being very clear. I admit I'm having a hell of a time just coming out and saying it. I've done this many times before, sorry Luisa, just not with you both."

I stared at Javier, waiting for him to put an end to my confusion.

He smiled something wicked. "Before I become a father, I want one last fantasy out of my system. One last *rotten* immoral urge." He paused. "I want the both of you tonight. Together. Right here."

I blinked. Did I hear that right? I glanced at Esteban who was staring back at me with matching confusion.

He couldn't mean what I thought he meant.

"Uh," Esteban said, scratching at the scar on his cheek. "Correct me if I'm wrong, *patron*, but…are you asking for a threesome?"

My brows raised and I looked anxiously at Javier for his answer.

"It sounds so juvenile, doesn't it?" Javier said. "But yes, that is exactly what I'm asking for. As a favor to me. Do you have any objections?"

"Yes," I said at the same time Este did.

Javier clapped his hands together and stood right over us, peering down. "I thought you would. But you're going to be a part of this regardless. There is no saying no to me, you should know that by now."

I knew that, but it didn't mean I wouldn't try. Because nothing good could come of this. And I think that's exactly what Javier had in mind.

Esteban cleared his throat. "I didn't think you were the kind of guy who would easily share his woman."

Javier gave him a cutting look. "Oh, I assure you I am not. But because I'll be having a piece of you as well, I think it evens out. Now, strip."

There was no way this was about to happen. Esteban wouldn't allow it. Forget about the affair, he still wouldn't allow it. Esteban seemed to spend his days fighting the authority that Javier had over him. He wouldn't just let Javier call the shots now, especially in a sexual manner. It would humiliate him.

Which was the whole point. Now I knew what Javier was doing.

But why I was involved, I didn't know.

To my complete surprise, Esteban stood up, and with his eyes on Javier, pulled his shirt over his head and threw it to the ground. Then he undid his shorts, sliding them down until his bare ass was right beside me.

No. No, no, no.

No.

I looked away. I couldn't do this. It should have been a million girls' fantasies but there was something so inherently wrong about this. If this had come from a genuine, organic place, then maybe I would have been more than up for it. But was no way in hell this was ever one of Javier's fantasies and I was completely on edge.

Javier barely gave Esteban the once over—he didn't look too impressed—and then fixed his gaze on me.

"My queen," he said, and I wished I could see the glimmer of tenderness in his eyes, what I had seen last night when we made love. But I didn't see anything there except something wicked.

Devious.

He smiled at me and jerked his chin to Esteban. "Isn't this what you want?"

I shook my head, my hands gripping the edge of the bed.

"No?" Javier asked, leaning over and putting his hand into my hair, making a fist. I stiffened, my eyes locked with his as

I silently pleaded for this not to happen. "You never fancied having a fuck with your friend Este here?"

Oh Jesus. He knows.

He knows.

He grinned at me. It was beautiful. It was terrifying.

"Well, if you've never fancied Este, I know he sure as hell has fancied you." He looked to Esteban briefly. "Isn't that right, you little shit?"

Esteban, stark naked, just shrugged.

The bastard just shrugged.

"Of course," Esteban said, so carefree that it grated on me. "Who wouldn't want Luisa? I mean, look at her."

Javier nodded, seemingly satisfied. "See, Luisa, he wants you. And if you say you don't want him, well I guess you'll just have to pretend. Now, take off your clothes before I make Este do it for you."

I kept staring at Javier.

"Why are you doing this?" I whispered.

He yanked my head forward and put his lips to my ear.

"Because," he said softly, drawing out the word before biting my earlobe.

A shiver rocked through me.

He pulled back and released my hair. His fingers curled around the hem of my dress and started tugging it up my legs. I understood that this was for my own humiliation now. He was looking for guilt. He was searching for truth.

I had to pretend, just as Esteban was, that this was okay.

My life depended on it.

I took in a deep breath, managed a small smile that gave Javier a bit of pause, then I raised my arms over my head to help him. Javier pulled the dress off, and then I was just sitting on the edge of the bed in my bra and underwear. The set was black and lacy, and the minute I felt the eyes of both men on me, taking me in like a feast, I couldn't say I wasn't turned on. Maybe I wouldn't have to pretend in the end.

Maybe I could get out of this alive.

"Stand on the bed," Javier commanded. "Then take the rest off. Slowly."

I took in a deep breath then stood up, going to the middle of the bed in a few shaky steps. I faced them while I slowly unhooked my bra, my breasts bouncing free. The air felt cool against my nipples, but they were already hard. The more they stared at me—my husband and my lover—the more turned on I became. I knew that Javier wanted all the control, but the more I owned it, the more that control belonged to me.

I eased my panties down my legs and stepped out of them. Now I was completely nude and on display. I kept my eyes on Javier, not wanting to look at Esteban, too afraid to give anything away.

"Get on your knees," Javier said. "Come to the edge of the bed." He jerked his head at Esteban. "Get him off."

I swallowed hard and tried to play it cool. Esteban certainly was. He was grinning like a fool as he came to the edge of the bed, his cock already hard and upright.

I didn't move, not yet. "And what will you do?"

Javier, still in his clothes, said, "Watch." He paused and gave me a tight smile. "For now." He moved over to the dresser, the guns still on top, and leaned against it casually, folding his arms. "No more stalling, my queen. Do it."

And so I did. I dropped to my knees and crawled to the end of the bed. With one shaking hand, I wrapped it around Esteban's hard length and prepared to put it in my mouth.

"Make sure you watch him," said Javier.

I was hoping I wouldn't have to look at Esteban at all. I took his cock in and met his eyes. I was hoping I could go out of focus and not really look at him, at the smug intensity, but Javier barked, "Act like you're enjoying it!"

I tried. But Javier wasn't buying it, I could tell. He let out an aggrieved sigh.

Suddenly he was climbing on the bed behind me, his hands grabbing my ass and squeezing it, kneading it. I began to melt into the motion and I started sucking Esteban with more passion. I was starting to become insatiable.

Javier spread my cheeks apart and I briefly tensed as I felt his tongue slowly, laboriously, licking around the pucker before trailing down my crack.

"You're wet as sin," Javier murmured into me, and the vibration of his low voice alone made my head spin. He rubbed his fingers along my slick folds, teasing my opening, my body begging for his penetration. "Maybe you like this after all."

He pushed two fingers, three fingers, four inside me, deep as he could go, while his mouth and tongue ravished me over and over again. I gasped, losing my concentration on Esteban, his shiny, hard cock bobbing in front of me. Javier then pressed his thumb into my ass, past the joint and I lost all control of my body.

The orgasm ripped through me like a tidal wave. I cried out as every part of me quaked and shuddered. Javier barely slowed down, forcing me to come again quickly.

The bliss was nearly unbearable. It took all that I had to keep tending to Esteban, who was now holding my head and pulling me back to him, forcing his cock into my mouth again.

Javier brought his face and hands away and then I heard his fly unzip. Next thing I knew he was rubbing wet fingers around me before his cock slowly eased into my ass and I expanded around his hard width.

With his hands tight, gripping my hips like he was trying to break me, he pushed himself in to the hilt and groaned.

"So fucking tight, my queen. Dirty fucking queen," he said between gasps as he began his rhythmic pumping.

I felt like I was on some kind of drug, some kind of trip. Every nerve was a live wire, and I was drowning in this symphony of flesh, sandwiched between two crazed, possessive men that would normally never share me.

I only belonged to one of them. Even though Esteban's cock felt good in my mouth, in this wild, hedonistic heat of the moment, it was Javier as he thrust himself deep inside, who was mine.

My king.

And the man in control.

As I was on the verge of coming again, Javier fingers stroking me now, Esteban began to tense up. He grabbed a fist of my hair, pulling sharply, and I could feel his ass muscles squeezing.

"Fuck me, fuck, fuck," he cried out softly as he came into my mouth, his hot cum dripping down my throat and out the corner of my lips.

"You come like a girl," Javier remarked to Esteban as he continued to fuck me from behind, my breasts swinging. I didn't know if Esteban took offense to that jibe or not, because I was coming all over again, an explosion of stars that took me somewhere very far away.

I could barely catch my breath. Letting go of Esteban, I collapsed onto the mattress, trying to muster reality from a lustful high. Javier slowly pulled himself out, still hard. For whatever reason, he hadn't come yet. That wasn't his style.

"Now we're just getting started," Javier said. He climbed off the bed, walking around to where Esteban was. His hard cock was in his tightly fisted hand, but otherwise he was still dressed. He gestured at Esteban who was still reeling from his orgasm.

"You, get on the bed and fuck her," Javier commanded.

I blinked. We weren't done?

Esteban seemed to hesitate as well. He'd just come after all, though he'd proved to me before that he was something of a machine. It wasn't sex that turned him, it was the violence and danger of it all and there wasn't anything more dangerous than what we were doing now.

"Take her on her back, edge of the bed, right here." Javier was determined, his tone flinty. "Be rough with her, I don't mind. I'm sure she doesn't either."

"Do you want to give me a minute," Esteban muttered. "I don't really get a fucking boner on command." He started stroking his cock while Javier watched him with cold eyes.

As I'd thought, it didn't take Esteban long to get somewhat hard again.

"Get on with it," Javier commanded.

"What's the hurry?" Esteban said but obeyed nonetheless. He reached for me and flipped me over so that I was on my back, and even though he'd just come, the man was ready for me all over again. He climbed on top of me, and while taking a rough grip of my hips, thrust his cock inside me. I had barely recovered, my body still throbbing.

"That's right," Javier said, now standing right above me, his own cock poised straight out. "Just like that."

Esteban's expression intensified as he pinned me to the mattress, smoothly grinding his hips into mine, his cock diving in and out between my legs.

Then Javier said something I'd never expected him to say.

CHAPTER THIRTEEN

Javier

Esteban gave the whole show away. He was just a little too into it, too much acting. Then there was Luisa who was trying not to meet his eyes, looking guilty as hell. They both thought they were acting, but their actions didn't match. It shouldn't have been this way. It shouldn't have been the truth.

It wasn't easy having to watch it all unfold. Seeing her with him and having all my darkest, most destructive suspicions confirmed.

But it had to be done. If I had called either of them out on their affair, they would have denied it anyway. Here, here, in front of my goddamn fucking face, I could see their connection. Her guilt. And his smug smile, the one that silently told me he'd had his way with her before. That this was just the icing on the cake. That he thought he had pulled a fast one on me.

I tried not to think about the timeline, the logistics, when this had started between them. Was it before Alana's death? The beginning of our marriage? Or had it started here at the ranch? Maybe it was somewhere in between.

Regardless, by the way they worked each other's bodies, they knew each other very, very well.

I wanted nothing more than to let the rage enslave me. I wanted to kill the both of them, right here, right now.

And on top of it all, on top of the anger that was choking me, causing my lungs to burn and my vision to swirl, there was hurt.

Stupid, foolish fucking hurt. I didn't think I had it in me anymore. To feel. To bleed. More than that, I deserved this hurt. I knew I did. But it didn't change a thing. It didn't stop my heart from plummeting to its death.

But I couldn't do it now. Couldn't kill them now. I wasn't ready yet. I wasn't done.

"Esteban," I croaked out while he continued to fuck my wife just inches away. Luisa peered up at me as I stood right above. "It's my turn."

Esteban slowed his thrusting, the sweat building on his back, and then looked up at me. His eyes were feverish with lust, and he was annoyed I was interrupting his little fuckfest. Luisa giving him head wasn't good enough for him—he wanted to be deep inside of her. He wanted his claim.

He wouldn't get it.

I stroked my cock, my eyes locked on Este's in challenge, and I smiled.

"Suck me off. Return the favor."

Now I had his attention. He looked like he wanted to murder me, which made my smile wider. He thought he was in control here? He was wrong. In this play, I had all the power. I always did.

"Didn't know your gate hinged that way," Esteban said, trying to sound cool, but I could see the disgust in his eyes. He wasn't disgusted by the fact that I was a man and he was a man, but because submitting to me was the last thing he was prepared to do. But he would do it.

"It doesn't," I told him. "But you seem like you were born to suck my dick. I'm just giving you the chance to live up to your potential."

His glare deepened, his face growing red.

I was enjoying this far too much. He should have been glad I wasn't flipping him over and fucking him in his hairy ass. Maybe he was too afraid he'd enjoy it. At least this way I could watch every agonized moment on his face.

I quickly reached down, shoving up my pant leg and pulling out my gun. Luisa gasped and Esteban froze, mid-thrust, as I waved it in front of their faces. I cocked the hammer for impact, the sound sweet.

"I don't have all night," I told him, and I pressed my cock in his face. "Don't make me ask you again, or I'll be putting this gun in your mouth instead."

"Javier..." Luisa protested softly.

I gave her a wry look. "Shut the fuck up. You want to play the game, just take what he's giving you, and I'll take what he's going to give me." I looked back to Esteban. "Now, open up, sunshine."

If looks could kill, I'd have been a dead man twice over. But I was the man with the gun, not him.

With great reluctance, Esteban opened his mouth and took me in. I'd be lying if I said it didn't feel good, but the humiliation on his face made it so much better.

"You suck dick like a girl too," I told him with a grin. "Where'd you learn to do that, hmmm?"

He paused and I pressed the gun against his forehead, trying to make a mark. "Keep going, you fuck, and act like you like it."

He went back to it and somehow managed to keep fucking Luisa at the same time. But of course he managed, because the two of them had an ease with each other that made me physically sick. That was all I really needed to know the truth. It's all I needed to see.

"All right," I said after a minute, grabbing him by the hair. "I've had enough. You're so good at sucking cock, Este, it's a bit concerning. And while I really would enjoy coming all over your goddamn ugly face, I think you've gotten my point." I pulled out of his mouth, gripped my gun, and pistol-whipped him across the face.

Luisa screamed and Este fell on top of her, blood spraying everywhere.

"And that's just in case you didn't."

He looked up at me, moaning and holding the side of his cheek where the blood rained down.

"You think I don't know," I said, trying to stay in control, to keep my voice from shaking. All I could feel was the tar-black rage threatening to consume me. "You think I can't see it?"

Luisa quickly crawled out from under Esteban, but I caught her arm before she could run to the door. I whipped her backward onto the bed, keeping the gun trained on her.

"Don't think I wouldn't put a bullet in your brain, you lying fucking bitch." I gritted my teeth and black dots filled my vision, pulsing with the spreading anger. Though I had told myself I wouldn't harm her, seeing the truth in their eyes hurt more than I thought possible. It didn't matter what I had done before, or that this was some sick karma.

Because, beneath it all, I *knew* I deserved this and worse.

But knowing didn't stop the rage. It only fueled it.

"Javier, please," she said. She didn't say more than that. There was nothing else she really could say, and she knew it.

I shook my head. "And with him. God, Esteban, you must have thought you were so fucking smart doing that. Trying to one-up your *patron* again." He sat beside Luisa, naked and pathetic, holding his face while his eyes danced between agony and fear. "But you know you're not leaving this room alive. You know it. How does that make you feel?"

"Okay, knowing I'll die with a bigger dick than you," he answered.

I shrugged and aimed the gun at him. "Whatever makes you feel better." Then I paused and aimed it at his dick. "On second thought, I don't want you to feel better at all. And what could feel worse than having your dick shot off, *hey*?"

My finger touched the trigger, about to pull.

And suddenly the room shifted to the left as an enormous roar filled my ears and everything was aglow, shrapnel flying everywhere. I hit the ground as parts of the roof rained down on me. There were screams, I could smell smoke, and I didn't know which way was up until I heard Diego's voice, so small and tinny, and then his hands on my shoulders, pulling me up.

"Come on," he said. Maybe he was shouting, I didn't even know where I was for a second. As he hauled me out of the room, I looked back to see Luisa and Esteban gone and embers falling down from the ceiling like snow.

"Luisa," I said, and erupted into a coughing fit.

"Borrero is on it," Diego said. He brought me into the hallway, shielding me as we went. Blasts of gunfire came from the kitchen, but there was no time to dwell on it as we headed for the basement door. Between staccato shots, a man screamed in agony. I had no idea who it belonged to.

We quickly ran down the dark staircase and into the basement. The single bulb swung from the commotion, casting the room with an eerie glow, and beneath it all was Evaristo, bound to the cot and looking at us with wide eyes.

"Get him!" I yelled at Diego, my voice struggling to be heard above the gunfire upstairs. "We can't afford to leave him behind."

Not because I had any sentiment for the man, but because he knew too much about my escape route. If he was questioned by anyone for a second, he would give it all up. After all, I was the monster that had tortured him.

Diego gave me a wary look then pushed me forward so I was in the closet. I squeezed past the hot water heater and pushed on the brick wall as I heard him untie Evaristo, and they quickly followed.

Once on the other side, Diego closed the door behind him. There was only the tunnel in front of us, leading to freedom.

"What the fuck is going on?" I asked them. Diego had Evaristo by the scruff of his shirt, and I noted with a strange pang of sympathy that the man could barely walk.

"I'd ask you the same thing," Diego said, nodding down at my crotch. My fly was unzipped, the tip of my cock poking out.

I grimaced and quickly did it up. I eyed Evaristo. "Is this the *federales*?" I asked him.

He didn't say anything at first, and Diego pulled him along as we hurried down the tunnel.

"Could be Tijuana," Diego said, "if they got wind of what you were after."

"Could be the Zetas too," I said.

"Could also be my guys," Evaristo managed to say, struggling to keep up. "Bomb blast to get you running. Not uncommon."

I eyed him sharply. "Seems like you could lose innocent lives that way."

He smiled, his lips still puffy from the beating, his cheeks black and blue. "No one is innocent in Mexico, *patron.*"

Unfortunately, he was right about that.

"And you didn't see this coming?" I asked him.

He shook his head then winced, a piece of matted hair falling over his forehead. "I've been with you. And even if I did know something, I wouldn't tell you. You're not torturing me anymore."

The tunnel curved to the right, the thick dirt walls blotting the view in front of us, and for a moment I feared that perhaps there was no way out. I'd never actually done a test in this *finca*, let alone any of the others.

But then it straightened and you could see the end, a rough wooden ladder leading up out of the ground. The lights above flickered as the ground shook from another blast, albeit further away, and then went out.

Diego's flashlight went on in a second.

"Almost there," he said, and I thought back to Luisa. Even though I had threatened to kill her moments earlier, now that I was faced with the possibility that she might be back there, that she might be hurt, I couldn't even bear it.

"Are you sure Borerro has Luisa?" I asked Diego as we came to the ladder.

He nodded. "I saw her run with Esteban out the door before I got there. Borrero was right behind me. He and Morales, it's their job to keep her safe."

I tried not to grit my teeth at the mention of Esteban. Just the fact that the two of them ran out of the room before I could even get out added insult to injury.

Had this been their doing somehow?

"Did it…" I tried to think of a way to phrase my fears without losing face. "Did it seem like Esteban was taking her?"

"I'm sorry, Javier. I do not know," he said. "But what I do know is that *you* are safe. This ladder here will lead you to safety. That is *my* job."

I nodded and gripped the ladder for a moment before climbing up.

The top of the hole was covered in planks of wood. I pushed them up and to the side as the cool desert night assaulted my face and stars gazed down.

I slowly climbed out, seeing silhouettes of trees. We were on the other side of the small hill, the *finca* obscured from view, even though the hill's outline lit up with another bomb blast or gunfire fight.

There was no time to panic. To worry about my empire. To be concerned about my wife.

There was no time at all because the heavy, clattering sound of many AKs being pointed at you seemed to make time *slow*.

"Put your hands above your head, Bernal." A deep voice came from the direction of the trees. But they weren't just trees. They were people.

The blinding red dot of a sniper's rifle shone in my face.

I was surrounded by masked *federales*, each of them with a weapon trained on me.

I couldn't move, couldn't even think.

I heard Diego swear from beneath me on the ladder, still in the tunnel, and I knew he was running the other way, back to the *finca*. Maybe with Evaristo, maybe alone. He wasn't abandoning me. He knew he wouldn't have a chance of protecting me now.

He knew I still needed him.

"Javier Bernal." That deep voice came again and footsteps seemed to echo through the earth. A large man stopped feet away from me, his gun taking the stage. "You're under arrest by the PFM. Surrender or we will take you in dead. We will gladly do so."

I swallowed and slowly put my hands up in the air, knowing I was caught and there was no way out of it.

"Ah, the *federales*," I said. "I finally get to meet Mexico's finest *putas*."

The next thing I saw was the butt of a rifle.

Heard the crack of my nose.

And everything went black.

...

When I came to, I was being brought to my feet by a man who had horrible B.O., and being forced into a helicopter.

"Get him in," someone yelled, and it was then that I felt the heat of the fire. I raised my head, my vision swimming, and saw the ranch burning down. *Federales* were everywhere, and everyone that belonged to me was gone.

Everyone except Esteban and Luisa.

They were a few yards away, beside a convoy of SUVs, their faces lit by flames.

For one beautiful instant I was so damned grateful that Luisa was alive.

But then I became aware of what I was really looking at.

I was in handcuffs, being hauled into the helicopter, *federales* and their guns trained on me.

But Esteban and Luisa were uncuffed. They were free. They were wrapped in rescue blankets, as if the *federales* had tended to them, kissed their fucking boo-boos, and put Band-Aids on them. They weren't even being watched, except for an agent who walked past Esteban and put his hand on his shoulder, whispering something into his ear.

Esteban kept his eyes on me, ablaze in the flames. His mouth curled into a slight smile.

He wore a look I'd hoped to never see.

A look that said, "I win."

Then he turned and walked away toward the SUVs, pulling Luisa with him.

She was staring at me in utter horror, throwing looks over her shoulder as if she couldn't quite believe it all.

I'm not sure if the horror was meant for me and my fate in prison, or for what she'd just done.

It wasn't enough that they'd had an affair. The two of them had set me up.

They'd turned me in.

And they'd rule the empire—my empire—together.

The chopper rose up, and as I stared blankly at the ground below, the two of them got smaller, along with the blazing ranch and the desert hills. It didn't feel like I was flying though.

It felt like I was falling.

I was heading for rock bottom.

And if the impact didn't kill me, it was going to fucking hurt like hell.

After everything I'd worked so hard for, in the end, love would be my ruin.

CHAPTER FOURTEEN

Luisa

It had all happened in the blink of an eye. My world shifted from one horrific scene to the next. One moment it looked as if Javier was going to kill the both of us, the next moment the whole world exploded.

I didn't even have time to react. Even though Esteban seemed shocked, he acted right away, scooping me up and throwing me over his shoulder as we headed for the door. I screamed for Javier. I knew he'd gone down, but I couldn't see him in the darkness, the only light coming from the flames licking a hole in the side of the room.

But Esteban didn't stop. He kept running until we were in the kitchen. Even though it was late, Evelyn was there with a rifle in her hands, telling us we were under attack and to get to safety. She didn't even blink at the fact that we were both naked and together.

Esteban pulled me outside to the porch, and I looked inside just in time to see Evelyn firing at men in black, masks on their faces.

The *federales*.

Many of them, one of her.

I turned away before I could see the result.

Esteban still had a stronghold on me, and he led me out to the dirt road that would take you to La Perla. In the distance, headlights and flashing sirens lit up the sand, coming our way.

"What are we going to do?" I asked him. "We have to get Javier."

"Javier is gone," he said, coming to a stop but still holding on. "He's going to try and escape out the tunnel. Notice that you weren't included."

"We left him on the floor!" I yelled, and suddenly reality hit me, that he could have been hurt or dead. I tried to run back, but Esteban swung me around until I went flying into the dirt.

"I just saved your fucking life," he yelled, nearly spitting at me. "You think he wouldn't have killed us both in there?"

I got to my knees just as the cars pulled up, their headlights illuminating our naked bodies. "We need to run!" I told him, trying to flee, but he was fast and pulled me up by my hair.

"There's no running, Luisa. Not anymore," he said.

I gasped from the pain, my eyes wild as I looked over at the masked *federales* getting out of the cars, their guns trained on us. I felt like it was all going to end in a second.

Javier Bernal's wife and right-hand man in custody?

Game over.

The *federales* yelled at us to get our hands in the air, and we complied, even though the darkness and the distance were calling my name. I could run. Find Javier, make sure he was okay. I could save myself at least.

But to move would mean death.

A man stepped out of the first car, tall and extra forbidding with his bulletproof vest, black helmet, and mask.

"Esteban," he said.

Esteban nodded. "If he's anywhere, he's in the tunnel."

My mouth dropped open. How quickly he had sold him out!

"We already have our guys on the other end," the soldier said. "It should be a clean capture." He turned his sharp eyes to me. "Luisa. I'm Adan Garcia Ruiz. We're sorry it had to come to this. But you'll be better off this way. We've promised Esteban his protection and yours."

I stared at them for a moment while one of the soldiers approached us, holding out silver emergency blankets.

"Protection? Why?" I asked as I snatched the blanket, taking a step away from them and quickly wrapping myself up.

Ruiz and Esteban exchanged a look. "We made a deal," Ruiz explained. "We didn't want to, but we saw an opportunity. Your husband for your freedom."

I stared at Esteban, my heart picking up speed. "You set this up? You sold us out!?"

"I sold out Javier," he said calmly, wrapping the blanket around his waist, like it was a towel and he was just stepping out of the spa. "It was the right thing to do. He had too much power and the cartel was bound to collapse in time. I just sped it up." He gave me a wry smile. "I was tired of the business. Figured this was the only way I could retire and live the simple life on a beach somewhere. Spend my days surfing."

I couldn't believe it. I just shook my head, hand at my chest, fingers curling over my heart.

Javier.

All this time, Esteban had been setting him up.

"That's bullshit," I sneered at him. "You just want to take over."

"We'll be watching him. And you," Ruiz said, "to make sure that doesn't happen. But at the same time, we're grateful. Let's just hope that Evaristo is still alive."

"He is," I said feebly. "Javier only wanted information on Hernandez and the Tijuana cartel. He kept his word and let him go."

God, at least I hoped he let him go. If the *federales* captured Javier, it could be the difference between life in prison and killing him on the spot.

And still, I couldn't believe any of this. I closed my eyes and prayed that Javier would somehow escape, that maybe Diego saw the tunnel had been compromised, that he got wind of a snitch. Javier had already done prison once in America, before I had met him, but now if he were caught, he'd be put in Puente Grande. Where the worst of Mexico's worst would go.

And with so many *narcos* in there already, families torn apart and lives shattered by the drug trade, by our cartel, Javier could be fair game.

He would get no special treatment, the *federales* would make sure of that.

He was in for many years of hell.

And me, I was free.

For the first time in my life, it wasn't what I wanted.

I wanted to collapse to the ground. I guess the soldier closest to me saw that because he put his arm out and led me over to the SUV, placing me inside and giving me a bottle of water. He was saying something to me, but I didn't remember what it was because all I could think about was Javier.

After everything, he was still everything.

I didn't know how long I was sitting there for. The ranch house was consumed byflames. I never saw Evelyn, Borrero, Morales, Diego, or Juanito again. Javier. It was like Esteban and I were the only ones who got out alive.

Then there was a roar of crunching tires, and headlights appeared around the small hill behind the blazing house. They pulled right up next to a helicopter, the blades slowly starting to rotate.

The doors of one of the SUVs opened, and that's when I saw Javier. Seemingly unconscious and being dragged by two beefy soldiers, but he was there and he was alive.

He was alive.

And he was about to be taken from me forever.

Without thinking, I suddenly jumped up and out of the car, running toward him, my blanket trailing behind me. The sharp rocks and cacti pierced my bare feet, but I couldn't feel them.

"Javier!" I yelled, but he didn't stir and I could hear soldiers running after me. Esteban was the first to catch up.

He put his hand on my shoulder, nails digging in and pulling me back. One of the other soldiers stepped in front of my vision briefly, yelling at me to forget it, to turn around and head to the cars.

I stopped and watched, hoping that Javier would wake up and see me. The soldier backed off and I shrugged off Esteban's hand.

Look at me, Javier. Look at me, I thought. *Please be all right.*

But when he did come to, just as he was being put into the chopper, I realized my wish had been dangerous. His gaze sharpened and he saw me. He saw us.

We were free. He was captured.

His eyes broke my damn heart.

His eyes that told me he knew what I had done and that he would never be the same. His eyes that told me I had ruined him to the very ground.

As the chopper lifted up, I knew I was dead to him.

And I would most likely never see my husband alive again.

...

I didn't remember much after the *federales'* raid. Three days passed in a blur and I was high as a kite on some kind of pills that the *federales* kept giving me. Every moment that I was coherent, I collapsed into rage or a sobbing fit, unable to get it all out, everything that was killing me inside.

I couldn't stop blaming myself. I couldn't stop bleeding over Javier.

After a while, I welcomed the pills.

Though Evaristo had been tortured and damaged, the fact that he was alive seemed to soften the *federales'* attitudes toward us. Then again, Esteban told them that Javier had wanted to kill him and Esteban went out of his way to ensure that wouldn't happen.

It was a lie that did my head in, but in my drugged state, I couldn't do much but sleep and cry.

Esteban and I had been taken to an unmarked facility in Culiacán that seemed to be half medical facility, half intelligence offices. I spent my days in a small room with a nurse, and I only saw Esteban on occasion or sometimes Ruiz. On my last day, I saw Evaristo. He had been recovering nicely, and he backed up Esteban's story—that he was the reason Evaristo was alive.

"Why are you lying?" I asked him, slurring my words as I tried to sit up.

Evaristo put his hands on my shoulders, holding me steady. "Because it doesn't make any difference to your husband now. And believe it or not, Esteban's lie is saving your life. You'll walk out of here soon a free woman."

"The *federales* never would have killed me," I told him.

He smiled but didn't say anything more.

Finally I was allowed to leave with Esteban. We were set loose on the streets, and though it didn't take long for Esteban to quickly wrangle a car for us, I couldn't help but feel that we were being watched with every step we took. Esteban might have traded Javier for our freedom, but what kind of freedom would it be? I needed to escape somewhere far away, to get out from under the shadow of the *federales* and the cartels.

But I couldn't even do that. Because I was a useless mess.

For the first time since I had left Cabo and walked off with Salvador Reyes, I knew I was nothing more than a lost little girl, powerless at the hands of men.

An SUV pulled up on the busy street, and for a moment I thought Esteban would just let me walk away. Maybe I could disappear into the crowds and start my life over again. It wouldn't be easy, but it would be real, and it would be mine.

As if he knew what I was thinking, Esteban quickly grabbed my arm then opened the back door to the SUV, roughly shoving me inside. The doors immediately locked, and I was surprised to see Juanito in the driver's seat.

He didn't seem ashamed in the slightest. In fact, he looked proud as he glanced at me in the rear view mirror, his posture straight and chin high.

As we drove through the city and toward the hills, I couldn't figure out if Juanito was acting for me or Esteban. After all, though Javier was in prison and none of us would probably see him again, as long as he was alive he would still run his business. That's just how it worked and why so many government agents from both Mexico and America would rather the kingpins be dead. Dead was dead, but prison hardly hampered their career.

It wasn't until we arrived at the compound—my home—that I knew the stone cold truth.

This was no longer my home. It was no longer my compound.

I was no longer queen.

On the fence at the entrance, the gardener Carlos's severed head was stuck roughly on a post. He had been decapitated, blood dripping from his sawn neck, his once genial face frozen in fear, in anguish, a warning of what would happen to me.

I could only watch as we passed by, my stomach sinking as six or seven men with AKs swarmed the vehicle, following us down the driveway. When we came to a stop, Esteban opened his door then reached across for me, grabbing me by the hair. I yelped as he dragged me out of the car and threw me down on the cement.

The ground cut my knees and elbows, and I tried to get to my feet but Esteban kicked me squarely in the shoulder. Pain radiated from my bones as I fell backward on the pavement.

"You're home, Luisa," Esteban sneered. I brushed my hair away from my face, feeling like a panicked, cornered animal as the men gathered around me, Esteban standing in the middle of them all and staring down at me with a look of such utter superiority that it made me sick.

There was no way he could just take over the cartel like this, not with Javier in prison. My husband had far too many people loyal to him to let this happen.

Yet, as I looked around wildly I couldn't see a single familiar face. Only Juanito, and from his eager, completely unapologetic expression I knew he wasn't the Juanito I had known.

Everyone was a stranger, and I was in a hell of a lot of trouble.

I didn't know what to do or say. I tried to scramble to my feet, but Esteban was quick and kicked out again, this time the tip of his shoe catching my chin. My teeth slammed together and more stars began to spin outward from my vision. Somehow I didn't collapse to the ground, though blood immediately filled my mouth. I had a few seconds to make a decision as the men seemed to close in on me, Esteban laughing now, everything sounding like I was underwater.

I could plead for my life, for my place here. I could try and reason with Esteban.

Or I could fight.

I knew either choice would end more or less the same way, and even though "more or less" sometimes meant the difference between life and death in our world, both options were bleak.

So I chose to fight.

I got to my feet, unsteady and lilting to the right a little, but I did it. Holding my jaw, I raised my chin and looked Esteban right in the eyes.

"I am still queen," I said, though it was more of a mumble, as moving my mouth made me nauseous. I said it as proudly as I could, looking at the depraved and ugly faces of the men around me. "And by law, this is my land, my home, and you are all still employees of my cartel."

There was a pause before the men all glanced at each other and started laughing, as if it were the funniest thing they had ever heard. So much machoism in this country. It didn't matter if I was in power of a cartel or just a simple woman wanting a job. The men always treated you like a joke if you were anything more than a whore or a mother.

Esteban wasn't laughing though. He was glaring at me as if he couldn't believe I had the nerve to stand up to him. He didn't want to hear the truth—that by my marriage to Javier, everything was really and truly mine.

The truth hurt. And now I knew he was going to make me pay for it.

"Is that so?" Esteban finally said, unable to hide the irritation in his voice. "You must think you're in the wrong country, hey. There are no laws here. You should know that more than any of us, beauty queen." He eyed the men and jerked his chin at me. "Get her."

My body turned on instinct, and I immediately began running for the house, the front door just twenty feet away. But before I could, someone reached out and tackled me from behind, sending me flying into the gardenia that lined the edge of the wall.

I screamed, but it was futile. Hands, so many hands, grabbing my body, pulling me up, then seeming to pull me apart.

One of the men, the biggest one, lifted me up by the throat, his fat, thick fingers pressing into my jaw. The pain was so intense I prayed I'd pass out but didn't. By some sick, cruel joke, I didn't.

"We don't bow to no queen," the man said, his nose swollen with purplish veins, his breath so sour I could have gagged if I wasn't being choked already. His grip tightened until I was sure my windpipe had been crushed. Light danced before my eyes.

"Don't kill her," I heard Esteban calmly say in the background. "Just teach her a thing or two."

The man grunted then marched forward, still holding me by the throat, until I was pressed up against one of the white pillars by the door. He banged my head against it, hard, the pain shooting down my spine, while my arms were yanked behind the pillar by someone else and handcuffs were placed around my wrists. Two men grabbed hold of my legs so I couldn't move.

He pulled a knife out from a holster around his waist, the sun glinting off the sharp, narrow blade, and placed the tip at the neckline of the cotton dress the *federales* had given me to wear. Pressing the blade in until I felt it lightly puncture my skin, he began to drag it down slowly. I stared as blood spilled down my chest, the dress ripping down the middle as he went.

The pain was intense, almost sickly. I sucked in my breath, trying not to scream, trying so hard to hide my fear, but when he got to the soft part of my stomach and pressed the blade further in, I couldn't hold back.

I cried out, turning my face away from the sight as he quickly brought the knife down, ripping the rest of my dress. Without undergarments, I was completely exposed, naked and bleeding before them like I was about to be burned at the stake. My knife wounds stung from the air, causing tears to well in my eyes.

"Spread her legs," the man ordered to the others.

I wouldn't plead. I wouldn't ask them to spare me. I would take it like I had taken it from Salvador, from his men, once upon a time when I thought life was worse than this.

I'd been wrong.

Nothing had been as bad as this.

My legs were wrenched apart. The man undid his fly and took his disgusting appendage out and started stroking it in front of me. I looked away. The other men started hooting and hollering, and I shut my eyes, praying that Esteban wouldn't want to share me this way, that he would have a change of heart. But I knew my wishes were useless. Esteban wanted this, and I had brought this all upon myself when I had believed he was a better person than he was.

"Look at me bitch," the man said, grabbing my face with one hand and sending me into a vortex of pain. He forced me to face him as he grinned at me and his grubby fingers thrust between my legs, dry and intruding, making way. With an angry push of his cock, he entered me, and I felt as if my body were being torn apart. More than that, I felt my soul was, too, and that I might never be able to piece it together again. I felt stolen. My insides were nothing but dirt.

The man licked up my face with his sour, wet tongue as he thrust hard into me, the pain almost splintering, like it was breaking off into slivers that dug deeper and deeper. I closed my eyes tightly and did what I could to go off into another place, like I had done before. But that place felt out of reach. As he jabbed himself inside me over and over again, like a sweating, fat pig, his greasy hands clawing painfully at my breasts, only then did I hear Esteban.

"That's enough," he said loudly from behind me. "Pull out of her, you fuck. She's not getting fucking pregnant by someone like you."

The man sneered at me, on the verge of coming, but did as he was told. He then proceeded to jack off until he came all over my body, his semen mixing with the blood. After a satisfied grunt, he leaned in close to me, snorted up something deep from his throat, and spit it directly into my face.

I flinched and he laughed loudly in my face. He muttered "fucking *puta*" before walking away.

"Have you learned your lesson yet, Luisa?" Esteban asked then appeared in front of me. His shaggy, highlighted hair fell across his face, making him look younger, something I hated. I hated that a monster could walk around in this disguise, pretending to be human when he was anything but.

I didn't say anything. I could barely breathe from the pain.

Esteban reached over and wiped the spit from my face. He looked at it dripping from his hand, then put it between my legs, roughly pushing his fingers inside me.

"You're still not wet," he said, his mouth close to mine, eyes watching me like I was his to eat, to destroy. "I thought a whore like you was always ready."

I turned my face away.

"You think I'm disgusting now, don't you?" he went on, voice amused but with an edge, like he would snap at any minute. "You didn't before. All those times we fucked, but I guess I was just fucking you. You're such a fucking cunt, you know that? A goddamn stupid little twat who thought she could cheat on her husband and get away with it. Did you actually trust me? Could you actually have been that dumb?"

Suddenly he grabbed me by the crown of my hair and shoved my head back into the pillar, my skull nearly splitting. "Are you that fucking stupid!?" he screamed in my face. He thrust his fingers further inside me, but the pain from my head was still washing over me like thick, hot sauce. "I was such a waste of your time! You thought I actually liked you. You thought I was actually attracted to you! You're nothing but a fucking cunt!" He curled his fingers inside me, and with great force, dragged them out of me, his fingernails scraping down my inner walls until I screamed.

I screamed and screamed and screamed until he head-butted me, and then unconsciousness came for me like a dark, welcome blanket. Esteban ordered the next guy to take me, but by the time the man came up, his dick in one hand, a belt wrapped around his other, I went under, to a place I hoped I would never arise from again.

CHAPTER FIFTEEN

Esteban

Even though the *federales* upheld heir end of the bargain and had let Esteban (and Luisa, begrudgingly) walk free, Esteban still couldn't help but feel uneasy the moment he left their institution in Culiacán. He didn't trust them—obviously he trusted no one but himself, so he wouldn't have been surprised if they suddenly showed up at his door wanting his arrest.

They hadn't though—not so far. Esteban wasn't really sure if they knew where Javier's compound was. They hadn't asked for any of that information the whole time he'd been in contact with them. He was sure they knew, but all they seemed to focus on was the capture and arrest (and maybe the body, depending on how much "justice" they felt needed to be served) of Javier Bernal. He was all they ever wanted, all they ever needed.

In fact, it annoyed Esteban a little that they weren't at all concerned about what he did. *They should be following me. Watching me*, Esteban thought to himself as he stood in his new office, staring out the window and unconsciously imitating his old boss. *They should fear me.*

But they gave him something akin to a slap on the wrist, and he and Luisa were let go. Of course, Esteban was already annoyed that the raid hadn't exactly gone as planned. They were supposed to show up in the early hours of the morning instead of at night. He had planned for them to get Javier when he was sleeping and vulnerable. Instead, it all happened when Javier was on his A-game, ensuring he had a chance to try and escape.

What Esteban had really hoped for was for them to kill Javier, accidental or not, and take him out of the picture. Instead, they had botched it. He knew he should have been somewhat grateful they had interrupted Javier when they did, otherwise he would have one less appendage, his weapon of choice, and the symbol of everything he was, but at the moment he couldn't quite muster any gratefulness up.

There was one plus to having Javier alive and in prison, though. Instead of doing away with Luisa like he had originally planned, he had reason now to keep her alive. Not just alive, but alive and ruined and ravaged. She'd become his new punching bag instead of Juanito, and he made sure that every brutal thing he was doing to her would eventually get back to Javier and Sinaloa. He wanted them all to know that he was the one with the power now—he had the control, and Javier had nothing. Javier couldn't even protect his own wife.

He hoped the message was getting across. His team was still small, though they were fiercely loyal. He had been building them up in secret for a year now, which was easier said than done. Most *narcos* wanted to serve Javier, not him, so he had to prey on ones just like Juanito—the weak-minded, the hopeless, the poor and desperate. Perhaps they weren't the most intelligent or quick soldiers, but at least they didn't possess any morals whatsoever and they would do whatever Esteban asked of them.

Esteban had made sure of that last part. Taking a page from the initiation tactics of the Zetas and the Juarez cartel, when he rounded up his troops, one by one, he'd made them do a slew of horrid things, from slaughtering live animals to working their way up to slaughtering live people. The last initiation they had to pass through to make it into Esteban's good graces was to pick an elderly couple up off the street and decapitate one in front of the other before burning the other alive in a barrel. Very few were able to do it, and those who chickened out were decapitated by the others who did make it through the last test.

Those who passed though, they became part of Esteban's team. The moment that Javier had been captured they quickly infiltrated his compound and killed everyone loyal to Javier, even those who said they weren't, that they would be willing to switch.

Esteban had taken no chances. By the time he and Luisa arrived, it all belonged to him. And so did she.

Now, Luisa was locked in her room and given no freedom. She was tended to by Juanito because Esteban couldn't stand to look at her beautiful face half the time, bothered by her strength and still apparent devotion to Javier. Juanito was a good choice anyway. He was starting to come into his own and seemed to enjoy exacting the same pain on Luisa that Esteban had acted on him. Funny how the cycle always worked. So damn predictable.

And Luisa herself would cycle into a new life of horror and depravity. There would be no Javier now to rescue her, and even if there was, Esteban knew he wouldn't want her cheating, double-crossing ass anyway.

The circle will go on.

Esteban smiled at that thought then looked around Javier's office. He sat down at Javier's chair, took a deep swig from his bottle of tequila, and put his dirty bare feet up on the desk.

He was home.

CHAPTER SIXTEEN

Javier

"They're going to eat you alive in there, *patron*," one of the prison guards said to me as I was led down the darkened hall. The guards always had that look to them, like their acne-scarred faces and missing teeth were part of the starchy uniform. Of course, most of the guards were no less criminal than the prisoners, it's just that they knew how to suck all the right dicks. Prisoners did too, but that was just to survive, not to get ahead in some shitty job so they could continue living their shitty lives.

I nodded at the guard with a tense smile, making a mental note to take his head off the first chance I got. I was counting on having more than a few chances, and I was sure I'd have more than a few people I wouldn't mind decapitating before my time here was served.

But that would all wait. Puente Grande was no joke. The biggest and baddest prison in Mexico, it held the worst of the worst. I wasn't even the only kingpin in the joint—Almorez Fuente, who used to head up the Juarez Cartel before I had his local police force – *La Linea* – corrupted, was serving a long sentence somewhere in the building. I made another mental note not to be near him anytime in the future. He'd be out for revenge, though I knew a lot about that by now.

I was making a lot of mental notes. The minute the helicopter lifted away from my burning *finca*, I knew I had to track down Este and Luisa and kill the both of them for what they had done to me. More mental notes followed after that. It was the only way I knew how to compartmentalize exactly what had happened to me. It was the only way to know what to do next.

I was extra nice to the two prison guards who were leading me down the hall and past the assholes. They had done such a good job explaining to the other guards what exactly was going to go down. That I was going to be placed in a cell in the worst block of the prison, after being in solitary confinement for a few days. That I was going to have to shit in front of people and possibly eat it. That I was going to be fed oats mixed with rat droppings and rotten milk. That my tight little ass was going to be brutalized every hour, on the hour, until I was shitting out blood.

Not exactly the most politically correct talk from the guards, but it was enough to get all the prison workers to feel sorry for me.

Well, not all of them. Not the one guiding me on the left, Heriberto, with his tall, lean build and shaved head, and not the one on the right, Emilio, with his crooked smile and beer gut. They didn't feel sorry for me. They loved me, just as the warden did, just as the sniper on the roof, the cook in the kitchen, the administrator, and about ten of the forty guards working here did.

They loved me because I was a wonderful boss.

Heriberto and Emilio continued to lead me down the hallway until we entered the middle of the prison block. Then it became more of a parade and I was on display. The whole place—this dank, cold, cement, piss-scented hellhole, erupted into a volcano of lewd language. Some of the inmates, the more crazed ones, were yelling things at me that I think could have been complimentary. It was hard to tell since half of them didn't seem to know how to speak. The other half, the quieter ones with the bitter eyes, hissed shit at me. One actually threw legitimate shit, but I dodged that quick.

I was a man who either made them a lot of money at one point, or I was a man who ruined their lives. And I was in the middle of them all, wearing an orange jumpsuit. I was now one of them.

Javier Bernal, captured at last.

But we didn't stop in that block. This was more for show, so that the prisoners, that everyone, knew I was here and this was my new home.

They led me up to the third level and down another long hall with the occasional metal door here and there. I knew there was nothing behind those doors but a bucket in the corner and a blanket. There were no windows. No furniture. Nothing.

That's where I had been ordered to be placed. That was to be my home for the next fifty years, or until I croaked, whatever came first. A cement cell that would drive any man to madness.

But instead, I was placed in the cell at the end of the hall. The door looked exactly like the others. Thick steel with a tiny sliding window in the middle, operable only from the outside.

Inside, though, was a whole other situation.

It was about three times the size of a normal cell. There was a toilet in the corner with a slight partition around it. A large, clean queen bed was in the middle, as was a small table and two chairs, a bookshelf filled with books, and an MP3 player with earphones and speaker. There was a large window you could open, and though there were bars on it, it had a nice view of a dried up river and the rolling brown hills in the distance. If you squinted past the parking lot of the prison, you could pretend you were in the middle of the country on vacation.

But this wasn't a vacation. I didn't take vacations, even if I was in prison. I had work to do. A lot of it. I had an empire I had to hold on to. It was all I had left.

"I hope this is comfortable," Heriberto said as they ushered me in. I stuck my hands in front of me, and he quickly undid the handcuffs.

I looked around and shrugged. "It will do. Do I at least get my suits?"

He gave me an apologetic smile. "Sorry, *patron*. You must wear the jumpsuit, just in case someone shows up."

Someone that wasn't on my payroll.

I nodded, understanding. Orange flattered me anyway.

They removed the cuffs and headed back to the door. Emilio said over his shoulder, "We'll be by soon to bring you dinner. What type of wine would you like?"

"No wine," I told him with a shake of my wrist. "Espresso afterward will do." I needed to stay sharp.

After they left, I walked to the window and stared out at the horizon, blue sky melting into the haze of earth. I took a deep breath in through my nose and tried to pretend that everything was okay.

Everything wasn't okay, of course. Everything was absolutely horrible. But at least Este and Luisa's betrayal, though a surprise, hadn't left me ruined. Not on the outside, which was what they wanted.

I wasn't stupid. I had never completely trusted Esteban. He was good for some things, lousy for others, but I never in a million years thought he was loyal. After all, I could pick up on that bitterness, that desperation that swam behind his eyes and laced his every word. He wanted everything I had—he was always that way. When you combined that with the fact that I had been screwed by my partners and co-workers before in this business, I knew I always had to keep Este at arm's length.

I always knew he would try and fuck me over.

So, like any good king, I had a back-up plan. You had to prepare for the worst if you wanted to stay at the top. You had to expect it, and in some ways, welcome it.

I knew that if I were ever captured by the *federales*, I would be put into Puente Grande. That's just the way it was. Of course if I were captured by the Americans, that would be different, but I had good lawyers and I always had a chip to bargain with. Plus American prisons weren't as bad as shitholes like this, where prisoners died every damn day, beaten to death in their cells over nothing, and no one batted an eye.

Knowing my eventual fate, for the last year I'd had my men round up the best in the prison system. They were all paid an extra salary from me: $75,000 for the guards, $100,000 for the warden and director. There were twenty in total that called me their boss and would do whatever they could to not only ensure that I had a pleasant stay here and would be fully protected, but would help me escape as well.

Of course, the government and other officials couldn't know of this. They blindly thought their workers couldn't be corrupted. But I was oh so good at corruption.

I owned them now, and it was just a matter of time before I would be smuggled out of here, unbeknownst to the world. By the time that anyone of importance caught on that I wasn't in prison anymore, I would be long gone. I would be reclaiming my throne.

That was the main problem now. That while prison couldn't hold me, I worried I couldn't hold on to my cartel. It was one thing to be captured. Most kingpins ran their business behind bars. But it was another thing to be captured and set up by a man who aimed to take everything you had, wife included. He would try and ruin everything I had worked so hard for. All that bloodshed over the years and the sacrifices I'd made, just for him to take the reins.

Luckily, I had prepared for that, too. I had a good number of men from different cities and plazas that Esteban hardly knew about. They hadn't been at the compound with me for that very reason, but they were also very big, very bad, and very dangerous. My reach stretched further than Esteban's ever could. So while I knew he was probably settling down in my old house with my old wife, with his own crew of whatever fucking delinquents he could have mustered up, he wouldn't stay that way.

Problem was though, he was going to try. I didn't have a TV in my room but I was sure I'd get the newspaper. I knew that Esteban would make an announcement soon, and it would reach my ears—news to the people of Mexico that he was now in charge and running the show, probably on my behalf.

I would lose face a little from that, at least to the public, that I needed him to continue it for me. I hated losing face.

I took in another deep breath, feeling the rage beginning to boil. I needed to keep thinking analytically and without emotion. I needed to put my plan in motion to get out of here, and then put an end to Esteban, to get my revenge.

The minute my anger took over, the minute I thought about what I had really lost, then I would lose focus. I would become a slave to feelings, and that was a very dangerous thing for a person in my position.

I wanted to talk to Diego, so when Emilio brought me dinner—filet mignon in a mushroom cabernet sauce prepared by a private chef—I asked for Emilio to track Diego down somehow and as soon as possible. I wasn't even sure if the man was alive.

They promised me they would pass the word on, and after flipping through a worn copy of Moby Dick, I lay down in my bed to sleep.

But sleep wouldn't come. Though the mattress was soft and the sheets were smooth, I kept seeing images flash behind my eyes.

Images of Luisa.

Her with Esteban. The guilt on her face. Her body as Esteban fucked her. In and out. Him with her. My woman, defiled.

Looking back, I don't even know how I got through that. I supposed that was one of the benefits of being so angry—you go blind to everything. But now it was seeping back in, invading my addled mind. Her lips around his cock, how small and vulnerable she looked beneath him, his hands moving up and down her body like she was an afterthought, because he knew it so damn well.

As I lay there, my mind volleyed between being ashamed for making her go through with it all, to feeling righteous because she deserved it. I hated her, yet I still loved her. And if I dwelled on it anymore, it was going to tear me apart. But maybe I needed to be torn apart, just for a minute, because I deserved shit just as much as she did.

I had failed as a husband because of my own damn grief. And I failed at grief because I hated her so. And I hated her so because I loved her more than anything.

And that's how everything was going to end. In a big fucking mess. Because we were terrible people who did terrible things to each other. We were slaves to hate because hate was strong, and we sacrificed love to fuel it.

...

The next day when Emilio brought me my breakfast, I was informed that while Diego was alive and well, he was a slippery snake to get a hold of. I'd say I taught him well, but sometimes I thought Diego knew far more than I did.

Needless to say, that didn't put me at ease. And when Heriberto brought me the newspaper, I cringed when I saw the headline "I'm the new boss," followed by a story about Esteban taking over the cartel. In fact, judging by the childish writing and his goddamn spelling errors, I was pretty sure Esteban wrote the whole article himself and passed it on to a journalist who had no choice but to publish it.

So that didn't help. I spent the rest of the day stewing, trying to get in contact with Morales or Borrero. No luck there. They were both dead. Finally, I was able to get a message to "Bandito" Bardem, a *narco* in Juarez, who promised to come and fill me in on what was going on.

Three days passed before he showed up, and by then I was ready to bite his fucking head off.

I hadn't seen Bandito in months. Short and stocky, he had a face like a piece of ham, and a mustache that always seemed dipped in some kind of oil. Probably bacon grease. His shirts, though expensive, always had sweat stains, and he was a slave to that *narco* look that all the boys in Juarez had—cowboy boots, lariat necklaces, and giant hats. He looked like Speedy Gonzalez from the cartoons I had watched growing up.

But despite his godawful taste in clothes and mustache wax, he was a good man. A mean man. To be mean was usually good, and Bandito could be as vicious as a viper. When he wasn't eating, of course. Which he was doing when he walked in the door, salsa verde dripping through his hands and onto the floor.

I raised my brow and breathed in deep, knowing if I blew up at him now there was nothing to stop him from walking out. I needed intel, and I needed it from someone like him who had power and knew what he was doing, even if he looked like a piece of pork with boots attached.

"Javier," he said through a mumble of food. "Nice outfit."

"Same to you," I said as I sat down in the chair, motioning for him to take the other one.

He grinned at me and took a seat, finishing off the rest of the taco and wiping his face with his hands. I shuddered but he didn't seem to notice.

"Where is Diego?" I asked him.

He shrugged. "I don't know. He's alive."

"I know that," I snapped. "I need him here. There is unfinished business I need to attend to with him."

"Does this involve taking down Esteban?"

"Of course it does."

He nodded. "Well, I can help you with that. It can't be easy for a man like you to be made a fool of. And to know what's happening to your own wife."

I froze. I swallowed slowly. "What?" My voice was quiet, but my heart thumped loudly.

He frowned. "You don't know much, do you? Don't they keep you informed in here? Shit, this cell is nicer than my house."

That wasn't true since he lived in a McMansion in El Paso, but still.

"No," I said. "Nothing to do with Luisa."

"Oh." He wiped his lips again, nervous now. "Well, I don't know how to tell you this, or even if you care, but your wife... she's not doing well."

Everything inside me flinched. "What do you mean?" I asked, even though I didn't want to know. I wanted to pretend that I didn't care, to save face again, but I knew that was impossible.

"Well, she's with Esteban now, so what do you think?"

"I think she wanted to be with Este," I told him.

"If that was true then, it can't be true now. He's a sick fuck, did you know that?"

I had my suspicions. Then again, how could he be any worse than me? Suddenly, images of what I had done, the barbed wire, the machete, came at me, and I realized if I had the power and nerve and rage to do that to them, he had the same ammo to do it to my wife.

"Is she alive?" I was barely audible.

"I said she wasn't doing well. If she was dead, she would be doing better, my friend. Esteban is trying to prove how tough he is, and well, unfortunately he's using her to do it. There are pictures...on the internet. He leaked them or someone from the cartel—well, his followers—did. I wouldn't look if I were you."

"I won't," I said. I didn't want to. I couldn't bear it. Just knowing what was happening, the humiliation, the retaliation, was enough to cloud my judgement. I cleared my throat, trying to shake it all away. I needed a drink badly. "Listen," I said. "I need Diego."

"I see that. I'll see what I can do for you. And you better hurry too, or there won't be much left of her."

"She's pretty much dead to me as it is," I said. "She wasn't faithful. She brought this on herself."

"I know," he said, and leaned forward to look me square in the eye. "But would you rather inflict your own revenge on her, or let Esteban do it for you?"

I let his words sink in. There was no way I would let Esteban take away what was still mine.

CHAPTER SEVENTEEN

Javier

A week passed in the prison without word from the outside world, and for the first time since I was brought in here, I was starting to fear that I might never get out. I was still treated like a king, but even though Heriberto, Emilio, and the warden were all on my payroll and under my control, they weren't really part of the cartel. That wasn't their trade. They helped me the best they could, but getting intelligence in and out was harder than it seemed. It was akin to sending a flea-ridden passenger pigeon into the sky and hoping for the best.

I had no doubts, of course, that they would help me escape, but I also knew it had to be planned just so. I didn't want to leave the safety of the prison before I knew that a plan was in place. Everything had to be just right this time.

Finally though, on a hot humid night that sent moths to my window, right before I fell asleep, there was a knock at my door. I shuffled over to it in the dark and opened it.

Diego was in the hallway, backlit by a dim light. Emilio was behind him and gave me a quick nod before shuffling back down the hall.

"Javier," Diego said, his voice gruff. "I came as soon as I was able to."

"I have a hard time believing that. Did you expect me to shit where I sleep forever?"

His expression didn't change. He wasn't in a humorous mood, but then again, when was he?

I gestured him inside the room and flicked on the lights. He looked around, nodding at the set-up.

"It's not half bad."

I closed the door behind us. "For an ape, perhaps. What the fuck happened to you?"

He shook his head and sat down on the bed. "It's a long story," he said, almost sighing. "I managed to escape when the *federales* came."

"What about Evaristo?"

"He went with them," he said hesitantly.

"And then?"

"And then when I was headed over here, I was apprehended."

"By whom?"

"Evaristo."

Fuck. So then what the hell did this mean? Diego had been compromised? I mean, he was here wasn't he?

"You wearing a wire?" I asked him. "Because I'm already in prison. I have no problem with slicing your clothes open and finding out. If I hit an artery, it will be an accident."

He glared at me. "Calm down. What kind of idiot do you think I take you for?"

I shrugged. "Everyone seems to think I'm an idiot lately. Take off your clothes."

The expression on his face was almost comical. "You want me to do what?"

"I'm not stupid, and I have to make sure, so take them off. I won't stare too long, I promise."

Diego grunted and got up, shucking off his denim shirt. "I don't know what fucking games you were playing in your bedroom when this all went to shit, but you better not have anything kinky in mind."

"I was only playing mind games, the best kind."

Reluctantly Diego got down to his tighty whities, and when I was satisfied that there was no wire on him, he redressed.

"All right then, get me up to speed then get me out of here," I said impatiently.

He slowly belted his pants and gave me a dry look. "You really are the love 'em and leave 'em type, aren't you?"

"So now you're trying to be funny, after all this time?"

Diego sat back down on the bed, lips pursed, hands folded in front of him. "Here's the thing. Evaristo is with us."

"*With us?*"

"Yes," he said with a nod. "With us. He switched."

"You don't just switch."

"In this land, in this work, you do. You know that. Este switched."

I curled my fists together, trying to breathe out my annoyance. "Este never switched. He was always planning on doing this. We both knew he would try something."

"But he still switched. He turned on you."

"Well, so did a lot of people."

"Not Luisa," he said.

I raised my hand. "I don't even want you to mention her name," I snapped. "She has nothing to do with this anymore. She can't. This is about revenge, Diego. That's all I want. I want everything back the way it was, and I want dead bodies at my feet, do you understand that? And I don't want no fucking *federale* agent standing in my way, regardless if he switched or not."

"He won't. He's here to help us, to be part of us."

"He's lying. We can't trust him."

"I think we can. And we need someone like him. Young and bright and determined. You know the story of how he grew up—he was never meant to be part of the *federales* and those damn politicians. They turned on him right away, demoted him. You were right about that, they were too afraid he snitched."

"He did snitch," I said. "He gave us the info. Just too fucking bad that has to take the backseat until I'm out of here and done with Esteban."

"He'll help us," he said imploringly. "And you'll want his help."

"Why?"

"Because he made a bargain with Esteban. He's got surveillance on him."

"So do we," I said.

"But not like the *federales* do. And yes, we know he's at the compound, but we have to make sure. And if we don't get Este there, we have to be able to track him. We have no idea what he's been doing on the side all this time."

I shook my head and sat down. "I don't like this. Adding people in, it's too complicated."

"I know, *patron*. But he's here now, downstairs, and setting something up that will get you out of here immediately."

I looked at him sharply. "What? I don't need help getting out. I paid for this."

"He's going to make a statement after, saying you are still in your cell and unharmed. It will let us do everything we need to without anyone thinking you're loose—that you're a threat. Este will be caught off-guard."

"Wait," I said, my mind struggling to catch up. "Make a statement after? After what?"

"You need your own brand of crazy to fight his crazies," Diego said, standing up.

Suddenly an alarm went off from somewhere in the building.

"What the fuck is going on?" I asked. Outside the window, red lights flashed and spotlights were searching the hills.

"Prison riot," Diego said. "They're all being let out of their cages, and whoever is left standing is coming with us."

"That's a bit unnecessary," I said. "Not to mention morbid. A fight to the death, the winners join us? Are we savages?"

"You have no idea what's going on with Este, do you?" he asked, and I saw a glimmer of sorrow in his eyes. It made my palms sweat. "After I tell you, you're going to want to create as much fucking mayhem as possible."

"It's Luisa," I said. "I heard."

He gave me a terse smile. "It's not just Luisa, Javier. It's about your sister. Alana."

Even with the flashing lights and the godawful siren blaring in my ears, everything in the room seemed to still.

Alana.

I could barely speak. "What about her? She's dead."

"I know." He breathed out deeply. "But it was Esteban who killed her."

Funny how some words could render you immobile. I could only blink at Diego, trying to comprehend what he was saying.

"Excuse me?" I finally said, my hands balling up into fists again, nails digging into my palms. I absently noted I needed a manicure, as if that was something normal and safe I could focus on.

"Perhaps you should sit down," Diego said, carefully resting his hand on my shoulder.

I shrugged him off. "Esteban killed Alana?" I repeated slowly.

"It was printed today in one of the papers," he said. "I'm guessing you didn't see."

I shook my head once, my mouth open, fumbling for words, for anything.

Sympathy looked strange on Diego's rough face. "I'm sorry. He announced to the world that it was he who stole the boat, kidnapped your sister, then blew it all to hell with her on it on the way to Cabo San Lucas. He even went on to say that he hired an American *sicario* to do the job, and when he couldn't, he killed him, too."

An American assassin. Somewhere in the back of my fading mind I knew he was talking about Derek Conway, a man who used to work for me then disappeared. Fragments of the last conversation I had with Alana came floating back, like a puzzle rebuilding itself in my head, piece by piece.

The only thing I could say was, "Why?" But even then I knew it was a stupid question. The only answer was because.

Because she was my sister.

One of the last of my family left.

Because he knew personally how much family meant to me, even if my own family didn't know it themselves.

He killed her to send me into a tailspin.

My beautiful, darling young sister.

Then he moved on to Luisa. Seduced her when she was lost and vulnerable, and I was taking out my rage on the rest of the world, purposefully pushing her away, wanting her out of my life, wanting to drown in grief and violence and madness.

He took advantage of every part of me.

Now I was in jail, and he wasn't going to stop until my cartel was in his hands, until he'd wrung every lost drop of blood from my body.

It takes a monster to know a monster.

He was the worst of us all.

And I was going to rip him from limb to limb, tear him from ass to mouth, skin him alive and piss on his broken bones until I lost all traces of whatever humanity I had left.

I was living, breathing wrath, and I was never going to stop.

I don't really remember what happened next. Everything went black, but it could have been my rage, or it could have been the prison's power system failing.

The door to my cell opened and Diego and I walked out, into a land of screams and anguish. I would fit in here just fine.

Heriberto, Emilio and the tall, rangy warden were there, armed to the teeth with guns, knives and batons. If they were nervous or excited, I couldn't tell.

One of them handed me a machete and "thank you" was the last thing I said until the slaughter was over.

I don't know how many people I killed. It didn't matter. At some point Diego had to stop me from chopping up an inmate into even smaller bits. I let the hate and anger fuel me until I was some sort of machine.

Naturally, my first stop was the ugly guard who had teased me when I walked in. I did as I told myself I would. But before I slowly sliced the machete across his throat and took off his head, I hacked off his hands and feet then shoved his foot in his mouth. I thought it would be ironic. Maybe it was barbaric.

After that I just went crazy, adding to the mayhem while the two guards, warden, and Diego stood by my side for protection, and sometimes taking part. I wasn't going to walk around here without them. They kept the fuckers out for blood at bay while I was able to let my lucid fire unleash.

By the end of it, the whole prison block, inhabited by the worst of the worst, was filled with dead bodies. There was more blood underfoot than floor. The twelve that remained standing looked like the walking dead, chains and steel bars and knives in their hands.

But they knew who I was, they had fought well, and they were willing to walk out of this place with me while I exacted my revenge. Esteban might have been building an army of depravity, but now I had mine and then some. I had everything except my boot on his throat and I was going to get that next.

I marched out of the prison with blood on my hands, under a dark and empty sky. I was a free man. While the prisoners were taken into waiting SUVs, Diego walked me out to Evaristo, who was standing in an ill-fitting suit that could have only been a product of a government agency.

"Congratulations, you made it out alive," he said to me, holding out his hand. He didn't seem the slightest bit disturbed that when I half-heartedly shook it, I left his palm sticky with blood.

"That was always the plan," I said wryly while I eyed Diego for support, just in case. Diego only nodded, giving me his okay once again that Evaristo was to be trusted. I couldn't be sure about that, even though so far he had let me walk out of prison, the very prison that his company had put me into. Not to mention that he had just let a slew of other inmates go. And the other half had been brutally murdered.

"And I know I'm a new addition to your plan," he said with a quick smile. Though the torture had happened weeks earlier, his face was still puffy in places. It made him look older, more respectable. "But I can help you."

"And what do you want in return?' I asked. There was always a catch. In the distance I could hear choppers, and some of the men looked toward the sky in fear.

"To have opportunity," he simply said. "To have respect. A chance to go further than I ever thought possible." He nodded at a man who had been standing silently next to him. "Get them wherever they need to go. I'll take care of this. As far as the country will know, a prison riot broke out, decimating all of the most heinous criminals. Javier Bernal remains in his cell unharmed, and Puente Grande remains the unescapable prison that the world thinks it is." He looked at me again with a smirk. "They're all yours, every one of them. You'll be taken to a safe house and I'll be in touch later tonight."

He strode off toward the building, the sirens still going, the choppers coming closer. If we didn't move now, we'd be on national news.

We quickly hurried off into the waiting SUV and drove off into the night.

...

I didn't know where the safe house was—somewhere between Guadalajara and Mexico City, but it was remote and more secure than I could have ever imagined. It was pretty much a bunker cut into a swath of jungle. Even if it were daylight, there was no way you'd see it until you were literally right on top of it.

It was also surprisingly spacious inside the bunker. The whole underground structure must have been the size of a mansion, simply decorated but still more than just a hole in the ground. There was a kitchen, bathrooms, dining and living rooms, plus various bedrooms with bunks and offices. Many of the doors were closed. The crazy escapees, who I guessed were "mine" as Evaristo had put it, were led down the hall to the bunks. I didn't know how any of them could sleep next to each other after such a violent storm at the prison.

There was something entirely unnerving about being underground, trapped like a gopher. I kept expecting for someone to point a gun in my face and demand my return to Puente Grande, or at the very least, kill me.

But that didn't happen, and as the night wore on, the more I realized I needed places just like this. Yes, mansions and spacious grounds and all the beautiful things I cultivated were something I wanted in my daily life, but I also needed to feel safe. After everything that had happened, I knew being safe and feeling safe were two different things.

I didn't sleep that night. The adrenaline from the slaughter, from the escape, was still coursing through my veins. I changed into a spare set of clothes that Evaristo's man had brought out for me—black pants and a linen dress shirt—and stayed up in the living area with Diego, drinking the few beers we found in the safe house's fridge, trying to calm down. For all my impatience, I knew we had to wait here for Evaristo before we did anything else. If I acted on instinct alone, I would have stolen an SUV and driven right up to the compound near Culiacán, ambushed the house, and hoped Esteban was home.

I still didn't know what to do about Luisa. The more I thought about her, the more disquieted I felt.

After I had lapsed into silence for a long time, Diego nudged my beer with his. In the dead air of the bunker, the sound fell flat.

"What are you going to do about Luisa?" Diego asked, reading me so well.

I exhaled out my nose then shook my head and leaned back in my seat. "I don't know."

"Will you kill her?"

I closed my eyes and tried to find the truth. The truth could hurt me, but at least it was real.

"I want to kill her," I said, and then corrected myself as I imagined her dead in my hands. "I need to kill her. For what she has done to me."

"Javier, I don't mean to play devil's advocate here, but I don't think Luisa had anything to do with putting you in jail."

My throat felt thick. I looked at my hands, the blood still in my cuticles. "She was fucking Esteban. Isn't that enough?"

"That's up to you, my friend. But if you want revenge on her, you will have to wait your turn. Esteban comes first. He must be dealt with."

"I'll deal with him," I said, my eyes hard as I stared at him. "I'm more than ready to."

"I know. I just don't want things to go to shit when we find him."

"If anyone finds him, they aren't to kill him. They are to bring him to me."

"I think everyone knows that. The whole country is awaiting your revenge, you know. Esteban has set himself up to be the villain here, not you. In some ways, you've got more of your people's respect. Being in prison while he walks free with your wife, the same woman he publicly tortures, has made you out to be a martyr. And when you finally do get your revenge, they'll revere you more for it. Without meaning to, Esteban has led a whole new victory into your hands."

"But at what cost?" I asked quietly.

He'd killed my sister. He'd stolen my wife. Those were things that could never be made up for, no matter how much the country believed in me or set me up to be a demi-god, like so many *narcos* before me.

Diego nodded grimly. "You tell me what to do and I'll do it. If you decide to kill Luisa, I'll look away, but I won't help you. If you tell me to protect Luisa and save her from him, I will. I have your back, Javier."

I gave him a wry look. "She has a way of worming into your heart, doesn't she?"

His smile was grave, and I knew then how much he actually respected my wife. I wondered if Diego had ever fallen in love, ever married, ever had children. He never talked about his past like that, but so many people wiped their past clean when they became a *narco* or *sicario*. They couldn't hold on to memories because memories were just fire and would burn in their hands. You couldn't hold a gun if your hands were ruined

Mine were only bloody.

It was almost morning when Evaristo appeared in the bunker, coming down the narrow staircase from the world up top.

"Didn't get any sleep?" he asked, peering down at Diego and me as we sat on the couches, tapping our fingers and feet from boredom and anticipation. It was odd to see him now with that authoritative slant, after everything I'd done to him.

"We've been waiting for you," I said, suddenly exhausted. "Like little bitches."

He smiled and shoved his hands into his pants pockets. "You know, I'm the one who should have the problem with you."

"Is that right?" I asked carefully, sliding my tongue over my teeth.

"I'm the one who is still missing a toe."

I shrugged. "And I had to wear the same orange jumpsuit for a few weeks, all while you made a deal with Esteban, the actual devil."

He sighed and sat on the arm of the opposite couch, rubbing his hand on the back of his neck. "Normally I would argue that. Javier, I know a lot more about you than you can ever imagine. About your rise within the ranks of Travis Raines, the *gringo*, all the way to your takeover. About your little scuffle with the Americans in California, which then had you thrown into a US prison, then your release and the kidnapping of Luisa Reyes. The fall of Salvador. The Sinaloa cartel that you took." He paused. "But despite all you've done, I know you're not Esteban Mendoza. There is a line between ambition and lunacy, between, well, evil and pure evil, if you want to be dramatic."

"Are you sure you don't want to be on the more dramatic side?" I asked.

He shook his head. "You know, I had a brief talk with your wife." I stiffened. "When you sent her to look after me. She's a good, kind woman, you know. But full of spikes, as my grandmother would say. She told me you would go far, all the way to the top. That you would not fail. And I believed her. I wanted in on that. Esteban is just a rabid dog. He's dangerous and deranged, and getting more psychotic as this goes on. I haven't just been studying you, I've been studying him. But he doesn't have your intelligence, your charm, or your connections. He is the losing side. You are not. You will take it all back, and for once I will be on the side that wins."

After a moment I said, "That's a nice speech. But you probably should have arrested Esteban while you had the chance."

"There was no chance with the *federales*. Contrary to your belief, they do things by the book. And that's why they always lose and will continue to lose in the end. Being good just doesn't guarantee success. If anything, it means failure."

I exchanged a glance with Diego. "A pessimist," he remarked.

"A realist," Evaristo countered.

"And so young at that," I added.

"It's in our blood, what can I say." He got up off the couch. "Unless you have any objections, tomorrow we strike your residence near Culiacán."

"My objection is that I'd rather strike it right now, while they are both there and are both alive."

"And you're too smart to know that we aren't about to rush into anything. Try and get some rest," he said, undoing his tie and walking into the kitchen.

Sleep would be unlikely. But I found myself drifting away on that couch for a few hours, despite my own objections.

CHAPTER EIGHTEEN

Luisa

Javier always told me he didn't think he had a soul, and if he did, he was sure it was a dirty one. I was more inclined to believe he did, despite the way he ruled his life. I used to believe that everyone had a soul, somewhere deep in their body, and it was up to them to let their real spirit free. Even those deemed bad, corrupt, and immoral had light shining through them from time to time. In Javier's case, I likened his soul to a dirty window. The glow was muddled, and what did come through was in little cracks and smudges.

But those little cracks held the brightest light, piercing through the darkness and shining a spotlight in some of the blackest places of the heart. Javier had those cracks, that sharp light, and it was blinding sometimes. I felt I was special just to witness it.

That was just a memory now. I'd met men that had no soul, men like Salvador who proved my theory wrong. And now I was with Esteban, a man who was far, far worse than my ex-husband and abuser. Salvador was rough and wicked, but for all the bad that he was, it wasn't unusual. Men like him thrived in the cartels; they were born to be *narcos*. You knew who he was from the start. He made no apologies; he wanted to frighten the world.

But Esteban Mendoza was pure evil. He wasn't even human—I knew that. If you believed in absolute evil, he was evil absolute. He hid under the persona of being young, dumb, and careless, and even though he certainly wasn't smart, his capacity for inflicting pain and suffering was beyond my understanding.

And what I couldn't understand, I had no choice but to fear. This was a man beyond reasoning and help, and what hurt most of all, what made me feel like I was too stupid to live—that I almost deserved his cruelty, was that I had never seen it coming. I had fallen for him. Not the real thing, but at least a tempered version of it. I fell for the illusion of someone that was bad, but not *that* bad. I was lured in by a man who said all the right things and was there when my husband wasn't. He made me feel like I was someone worth loving, if not liking. If not respecting.

I never dreamed that beneath the easy smile and jealous tendencies, the devil incarnate was lurking.

He was a living nightmare.

And I couldn't wake up.

Esteban kept me locked in my room most of the time. The irony was that this used to be the very room that Javier had held me captive in, the one with the windows that didn't open and wouldn't break. Looking back, I would have given anything to have been under Javier's wrath instead of this. I held strong with Javier during that time because somehow, somewhere, I knew that I could get through to him.

Instead, Javier had gotten through to me.

But now it was different. It wasn't even a place. It was this black, nebulous hole of pain and humiliation. Sometimes it was Esteban who had his way with me, other times it was Juanito. At least he was someone I could appeal to. My tears seemed to keep his violence at bay, because Juanito's violence was only taught through Esteban. It wasn't in his nature, like it wasn't in so many people's nature. He wasn't born this way. It was thrust upon him, and he was molded by the bad and the wicked. We were a nation of people under this heavy hand.

But Esteban's nature was evil from the moment he came out of the womb. He disguised it from day one from the rest of the world, fooling us all. The minute his plan went into effect was the moment he let it blossom and flourish, transforming himself from someone bad into someone straight from hell. And when he dealt with me, I could feel it.

It was all I could feel. Nothing but evil. I was sleeping near my own feces and urine, forced to drink the same water the hogs drank. Sometimes live chickens would be placed in my room—chickens who were angry and starved, and they would peck at me over and over again until I had no choice but to kill them. I was given no food at all, and when I asked for some, Esteban shoved their rotting carcasses in my face, telling me that was my food.

By day five, I stripped the chickens of their feathers and was forced to eat them raw. It was either do that or starve, and I needed every ounce of strength I could get.

Because despite everything that was happening to me and the brutality that I kept witnessing, I needed to fight back. It didn't matter if the room was covered in feathers and I was cowering in the corner naked, bruised, and beaten, with matted hair, tearing into a putrid chicken with blood-stained teeth. I had plans to get out of here.

Or I was going to die trying.

And if I was going to die, I was going to try and inflict as much pain and bloodshed as I could as I went out.

Maybe then I'd die with a smile on my face.

I might have underestimated Esteban.

But I would make sure he underestimated me.

The days and nights passed slowly in this house. I had no way of keeping track because sleep rarely came for me, and I kept the curtains closed all the time, wanting to forget where I was, what was out there. I lived in darkness, and in that darkness, I grew something sharp and ragged in my heart. It was strength and it was vengeance and it was enough to keep it beating, to keep me alive.

It must have been the night because the room was dense black and deader than usual. I was sitting back against the wall, trailing a chicken feather up and down my bare body, trying to pretend I was somewhere else. That the feather was a soft caress, skin on skin—a lover's touch. Something nice, something sweet, something hopeful. Even though Javier could be rough with me at times and I liked it, he could also be gentle, tender, and passionate. I wanted to pretend the feather was him—his lips, forgiveness for all my sins.

I sat there, just letting myself believe each stroke was full of hope, the tickle on my scratched arms, a balm on my cuts and wounds.

The door opened abruptly, light from the hall cutting abrasively into the room. Esteban strode inside, his shadow menacing and seeming to hold more depth than it should have. In his hands was a toolbox, which he carefully placed on the floor before locking the door behind him.

We were engulfed in blackness again. I told myself to not be afraid, that he couldn't do anything worse to me, that I was strong enough to get through this, but I couldn't help sucking in my breath, holding it in like it was too precious to spare in the same room as him.

"Sitting in the dark," he said, always so jovial. It made everything that much more disturbing. "It's not healthy for you."

I heard him open the box and fish around for something. Metal clinked against glass, things that sounded sharp. I suppressed a shiver and wondered if now was the time to act. If this would be my chance.

As he searched for something, I slowly, quietly got to my feet, staying hunched over, and walked sideways along the wall. I knew the room inside out by now, knew where the bed was, the small armchair, the bedside table. If I could get to the door without him noticing, then I could attack, as long as he didn't attack me first.

I didn't have much in the way of weapons, but I did have the chicken bones that I'd broken apart until I found the sharpest, hardest shards. I'd wrapped them all together into a short knife with torn strips of my old nightgown.

It wasn't much, but I also had rage and the basic human need for survival.

He wasn't human, so he couldn't have that. And I wouldn't let him take it from me.

"Quiet these days, aren't we?" Esteban asked. The sound of the box slammed shut. I paused near the bed, my hands guiding me along it. I could almost hear him fiddling with something in his hands, though I had no idea what it could be. A knife, but more complicated than that.

There wasn't much else to my plan other than fighting my way out by either killing or maiming him then hoping I could have an easy escape. It was just as likely that I'd die out there, by the hands of his crew that enjoyed torturing me and defiling me just as much as he did.

But there was a small chance that I could get out alive and after everything was said and done, I would do what I could to get back to Javier. I would go to Puente Grande and beg to see him, just for a moment, knowing full well he would hate me. Possibly even kill me. But even though I was sure he wouldn't believe me when I told him I never wanted any of this, I at least had to let him know. He was still everything I had, and I never did any of the horrible things I did because I stopped loving him.

How fucking pathetic was I? I was hiding in the dark from a psychotic torturer, plotting my escape, and my heart kept clinging to love.

Javier would have been so disappointed in me.

"You know, Luisa," Esteban went on, slowly. Though his tone was edgier now, his voice was still aimed at the spot where I used to be. He thought I was still sitting there in the dark. I wondered how long it would take for his eyes to adjust, or if he'd mistaken the dark shadows for me. "Every good thing must come to an end. You must think of yourself as a good thing, don't you? After all, you were the beauty queen. That must have done wonders for your self-esteem, for your impression of your own life. Didn't it?"

I kept my breathing as quiet as possible and started along the bed again. It was agonizing moving so slowly, but I knew I couldn't mess it up by being impatient.

"They must have called you a beauty," he said. I heard his footsteps, now right across from me but heading toward the wall. "That's how you caught the eye of Salvador Reyes, isn't it? You were so damn fucking pretty that he had to make you his wife." His voice become lower, almost a conspiratorial whisper. "Don't you know that if you didn't have your beauty, you wouldn't be worth anything to anyone at all? Do you think Javier would have been so enraptured by you if you were fat and ugly, if your body at all reflected the kind of person you really are? No, of course not. But you got another free pass in your life's ride, while everyone else in this country suffers."

He was baiting me, getting me to snap back, to say something that would give him an excuse to beat me, even though he could find an excuse in anything. I had to literally bite my tongue, thick and swollen from lack of water, to prevent myself from saying what I really wanted to. Esteban must have grown up so damn jealous of everyone around him that it didn't matter what sex you were, he wanted what you had and he felt entitled to take it.

"It's not fair, Luisa," he said, and now his voice was cracking with anger. "It's not fair that you got to have everything you did. And loving parents, too? How fucking dare you!" He paused then took in a deep breath. When he spoke again, he was calmer. Ice. "I took Javier away from you. I took your cartel, your purpose. I'll take your parents soon, too. But now, tonight, I'm taking away something you never deserved to have. Your beauty."

My eyes widened as I heard the sharp scrape of rusty scissors being yanked open.

"Now are you going to be a good little girl or what?" he asked as he ran blindly forward, his footsteps echoing loudly.

I moved as quickly and quietly as I could, willing myself not to panic, to make noise, but it was hard when he yelled, "Where are you, you little bitch!?" and began to run around the edge of the room.

I heard him bump into the bed, swearing and grunting angrily, too close now for comfort. I had to run for it.

I started for the door, guided by the light underneath it, and went for the lock. My hands groped for it, my heart on fire and nerves alight as panic threatened to consume me. I clumsily found the handle, then tried to place where the lock would be, but by the time my fingers closed over it, it was too late.

Esteban was behind me and stabbed the scissors down into my shoulder, slicing through flesh, muscle, and bone. An image of the chicken I ate flashed in my eyes, the way their bones could break, but it also reminded me of what I had in my hands.

Instead of screaming, I took that energy in and whirled around, stabbing wildly with my knife of bones hoping to get him in the face. The end of it went into a soft spot of skin, maybe the lower throat, and he let out an enraged yelp as it stuck fast.

Before I could do anymore damage, he decked me in the face until I flew back against the wall, my face exploding in stars of pain.

I wouldn't let it keep me down. I scrambled to all fours, staying low, and charged at him, going for where his legs should be. One knee grazed my chin, but I was able to wrap my hands around the other one, my nails turning into makeshift claws as I dug them into his skin as deep as possible. He screamed and tried to shake me off, but not before I jerked my head down and bit into the back of his calf, tearing my teeth in, wanting to take out a chunk.

I had become a feral, wild beast.

I would do anything to survive.

I felt the blood run down my chin; I tasted his tainted flesh. I was holding on tight, digging my incisors in, more, more, more, but then his hand was in my hair and he was tossing me away from him until I was on my back and on the floor.

Everything spun, but I knew I couldn't let it stop me. I tried to get back up, but then his elbow was driving down into my collarbone, trying to break it, and his other hand was repeatedly banging my head into the floor.

"You fucking bitch, you fucking bitch!" he kept shouting over and over again like a man possessed, until finally he stopped. I couldn't even move. I felt completely paralyzed from the head down, a sitting fucking duck who was about to have her own feathers plucked.

He briefly crawled off of me, heading across the room, and that's when I knew I had to run again. I could try to escape, and if I got to the unlocked door, I would make it out.

I was so close.

But I couldn't. I didn't know what he had done to me, but I just couldn't move a muscle. No matter how hard I fought past the haze, no matter how hard I concentrated, willing my body to respond, it felt as dead as the rest of me.

I'd never been more frightened, more helpless, more alone, in all my sorry life.

I hadn't wanted to cry around Esteban at all. I told myself I wouldn't shed one tear in front of him. I wouldn't give him the pleasure of what he was doing to me.

But now, now the fear was so real as I lay there, naked and broken in the darkness, bleeding and paralyzed. It came for me at once, and the tears fell from my eyes, sliding down the sides of my face to the floor.

I was so sad. So damn sad.

This was how I was going to die, and I was going to suffer for a long time before I did.

At least I tried.

I tried.

I fucking tried to live, I tried my damned hardest.

I made a million and one mistakes, but I still tried.

God, I wished I didn't have to die alone and in pain.

I wished Javier was here with me.

I tried to bring the image of him into my vision. Like the feather against my skin, I hoped it would trick me enough to bring me the strength to die with dignity, to endure what horror was to come. I hoped it would erase the fear. The sorrow that filled me up, a well of seeping black drops.

Then a light went on in my face, my eyes squeezed shut in response, and Esteban chuckled.

"You're crying?" he said mockingly as he came back over to me. "The little girl is crying? You fucking pathetic little cunt. I haven't even given you anything to cry about yet."

I heard him pick up the scissors, and he kneeled beside me. He grabbed my hair and began slicing through my strands. His movements were rough, the scissors dull even though they razed my skull in places, and I felt the blood spill down my face and neck.

"You won't look pretty after this," he said, going around my head until he was apparently satisfied. My head felt lighter, colder, without all my hair which now lay on the ground around me. I felt like I should have lost a part of myself, if only I hadn't lost myself already.

Please move. Move! I yelled at myself, at my body. *Please, please, please. Try!*

"Hmmm," Esteban mused. I didn't have to open my eyes to know he was looking me over. "You're not as ugly as you should be. Hair can grow back, can't it? I should know, mine comes in quite fast. I have to get it trimmed every few months."

His blasé words floated over me, having no bearing. I was lost inside my head, in a life or death battle for control of my body.

Almost, almost, almost. I willed every muscle to react. I tried to imagine every nerve coming alive. I couldn't be paralyzed; I had to be stunned. But my body was stubborn. It didn't seem to understand what was happening, and it wasn't connecting with the adrenaline that could save me.

Esteban took the scissors, trailing them from my collarbone and down the scar his men had left last week when they gang raped me, and over to my breast.

"I could cut this off," he said softly as he scraped the blade over my nipple.

Move, move, move.

"No man would want you after that," he said, bringing the blade back over again until I could feel it cut. It was shallow, but it was a warning of what was to come.

Please, please, move.

"Or I could take a chunk out myself with my own teeth. Chew up your fat. Spit it back at you."

He was more than depraved now. He'd officially gone mad with his own brutality. He'd gone insane.

He continued, "It's only fair. You got my leg pretty good. Luckily I'm used to scars. But you don't have enough. Just the one on your back."

The one that said Javier.

Javier.

Javier would be so angry at me for giving up like this, for letting Esteban win.

"But men would have to get you naked in order to be repulsed. You could live your life a beauty as long as that didn't happen, as long as you stayed an untouchable queen. And I can't let that happen. We've come so far, and what sort of *patron* would I be if I didn't do my worst? What kind of message would that send to everyone else?"

I felt him lift away from me slightly, taking the scissors with him. I didn't dare breathe out in relief. There would be no relief here.

I opened my eyes and looked at him, lit up in a cold glow by the screen of his phone which lay on the floor. He was reaching beside him and bringing up a glass bottle with a peeling label.

Acid.

Sulfuric acid.

No, no, no.

But his eyes said yes and he quickly unscrewed the bottle, holding it out above my stomach. He tipped it slightly. The liquid fell out in a single splash.

For a moment it was like I didn't feel anything—for a moment I thought I was free, but that's only because the pain was too much for my senses to bear.

Then it hit like a freight train of fire.

I screamed until my throat felt like it was being ripped raw as the acid ate away at my skin, a small but deadly puddle on my stomach.

"I'm sorry," Esteban said loudly, trying to be heard above my anguished cries. "But you know you deserve this. Luisa, you really do."

He moved the bottle up to my face. "And this is where it's really going to hurt. Your beauty, your lazy power—gone. Forever."

I watched his cold green eyes in horror. I watched the small smile on his lips. I watched as his hand moved slightly and the bottle tipped, the acid running to the edge of the rim.

I turned my head, pinching my eyes shut in time for the acid to hit my left cheekbone. I cried out again as my whole head felt like it had erupted in flames. It was as if the acid was burning a black hole in my head, in my heart, in my soul.

And somewhere deep inside me, deeper than the acid could go, my mind and body connected. The adrenaline pumped through me in one hard burst, kicking in like a jumpstart.

I moved before I could even think. I reached out, knocking the acid out of his hands while pushing him back. With strength I didn't even know existed in me, I managed to leap on top of him, pressing his head back into the acid on the ground. He yelped as the acid made contact, burning through his hair, and I knew I had no more than a split second before he threw me off of him.

I swiped the scissors from the ground beside me, making a fist around the handle, and plunged them straight down into his left eyeball.

It didn't even make me squeamish, not even as the eyeball bulged around the blades as they pierced through it. I just yelled a crazed battle cry in his face as I stabbed him.

Unfortunately I didn't have enough strength or time to push it all the way into his skull and brain.

My time had run out.

Esteban screamed in horrific agony and threw me off of him. I did what I could to crawl away and look for something else to use in defense, my face and body burning as the acid ate at the nerves. Over by the box of tools he struggled to get to his feet, knocking them over, and in the glow of the phone I saw him place both his hands over the scissor handle and pull it out with one quick tug.

His eye came out with it, stuck on the scissors' end.

The scream that followed was animalistic, the sound of a creature dying filling the room, yet it was quickly buried by the sound of gunfire outside the window. Esteban howled and staggered over to the door, flinging it open and running out into the hallway which was filled with more gunfire and shouting.

He took the scissors, and his eye, with him.

I was left behind.

To die or to live.

Mustering what strength I could, I started to crawl across the floor. My shoulder and breast gashed and bleeding, my hair shorn, my collarbone smashed in, my face and stomach burning away. I had to survive. After all this, I had to live.

I almost made it to the door before the last of the adrenaline was depleted from my veins. Then I stopped, collapsing on the floor, and the last tear fell from my eyes.

I had tried.

CHAPTER NINETEEN

Javier

We left just before dusk, three SUVs filled with some of Mexico's most wanted. Me, Evaristo, and Diego were in the middle car, with one of Evaristo's men at the wheel. He didn't talk much, which I appreciated.

In fact, not many of us did as we rolled along the highways and backroads, heading up toward the capitol of Sinaloa, and my home.

My home. It had started to sound foreign ever since I was put away. It was as if I had believed Esteban and his attempts to take over.

I wouldn't believe that anymore. It was my home, and I was going to take back everything that was rightfully mine. I had no choice but to rise like a phoenix from the ashes and rule again once more.

Around a kilometer away from the compound, we took a sharp left turn down an even rougher dirt road, one that used to lead to a poppy farm once upon a time before the DEA razed it down all those years ago. We rolled in and out of potholes that would have swallowed a smaller car, until we came to a small clearing among the leafy ceiba trees.

We parked and Evaristo turned to face Diego and me in the back seat.

"Isn't this where your tunnel leads?"

Shit. He was good. He was able to lead us right here without me saying anything. The tunnel—built by the previous *narco* owner—led from the house to an area beyond the hog's barn, then had another entrance point here, the old poppy field far beyond the rugged brush that surrounded the compound.

I studied Evaristo for a moment. "All this intel you had on me and you couldn't make a move. Why?"

He shrugged. "Same reason why we didn't go after Hernandez when we had him. We've been trying to borrow the book from the North Americans and give warrant and reason to our arrests. A waste of time, as you know. We had you. Have you. We have everyone, almost, except the ones who are really on the run, as you may have to be if and when word gets out. But we are not allowed to make a move until all the boxes have been checked. I think it has a lot to do with the North Americans meddling in our jobs, even though the *federales* would never admit it. There has been far too much money put into our force."

"I guess they're hoping you won't be so corrupt this time around."

He smiled. "And you can see they were wrong about that."

We got out of the cars and gathered around while Evaristo and some of his men opened the trunk and started handing out ammo. They had been briefed over and over again during the day on what was going to take place, and unsurprisingly there were no objections. The whole lot of them were primed for more bloodshed. You could practically see them salivating at the mouth.

It didn't help that when morning came around, one of the men was found strangled to death. Apparently he had been a child molester, and that's why he had been behind bars. Even the country's worst criminals had a limit to how much they would tolerate.

Me, Diego, and one of Evaristo's men were to go in through the tunnel—this was my decision, of course. It was my home, and I should be the first one to step foot in it and reclaim my property. I knew the tunnel would take us to a space behind the pantry in the kitchen. I had no idea if our entry was going to be quiet and undetected, but the kitchen was as good a place as any. We were also armed to the teeth which helped. I alone had a grenade, two pistols, and a hunter's knife, while Diego was armed with an AK and who knows what else up his sleeves.

While we were coming up from the inside, Evaristo would be leading the other men to approach the house from three different sides. Everyone inside would scramble, and I would catch Este, hopefully while he was heading toward the very tunnel I had just come from.

Now that we knew for sure he was inside—Evaristo had been monitoring the site through government satellite images this morning—I could feel the same anger from earlier simmering deep within me.

I was going to take him down. I was going to make him pay.

Evaristo gave us the go ahead.

Diego and I hoisted up the flat board that had been covered in giant waxy leaves, and peered down into the tunnel. We pulled down the agency-issued night vision glasses Evaristo had given us and proceeded to climb down the metal ladder and onto the dirt floor below. The tunnel had no lights and was far cruder than the one at the *finca*, but at least this way we could see without drawing attention to ourselves. Our communication between each other was kept to a minimum as well—we all had earpieces but weren't allowed to use them until the time was right, just in case Esteban and all his high-tech glory were monitoring the place for frequencies.

Diego and I stared up at Evaristo through the tunnel hole, backlit by a vibrant night sky. He held up his phone. "I'm tracking you. When I see you get into the house, we will ambush. After that, you're free to use your radio transmitters."

I didn't care how efficient he was being, I didn't like being bossed around.

"Remember, I want Esteban alive," I told him.

He saluted me. "Yes, *patron*."

At least he still knew his place.

He turned back to my new army, an army of depravity, and Diego and I started jogging down the long tunnel. It wasn't a quick journey, but luckily I'd been keeping in shape during the Puente Grande stint. The only reason the 1.5 kilometer run felt longer was because with each second that passed by, I was gearing myself up to unleash utter destruction.

With every breath I took, I thought of Alana.

With every footfall, I thought of Luisa.

Back and forth, the two of them, until there was nothing but ugliness inside me.

It was the perfect insurance to ensure that I wouldn't hold back tonight.

Finally the tunnel started to slope upward and curve sharply to the right, and I knew we were under the house now. We paused before the ladder to listen. There was nothing but dead air and the sound of our own breathing.

I jerked my chin at him to say, *You first this time.*

He nodded and climbed up, his hefty weight making the ladder wobble slightly, shaking dirt loose from the tunnel wall. This was where we had nothing but a hope and a prayer that there wasn't anything stacked on top of the cover.

Diego slowly began to push up. I held my breath as he struggled for a moment, so sure that something was going to immediately crash in the pantry.

But he kept pushing, and he was able to slowly slide the cover over, air smelling of flour and tin wafting down toward us. There was a slight clank as it knocked into something solid but other than that we were as quiet as possible.

Diego eased himself up the ladder and looked around once he was fully out. I quickly climbed up after him, and together we squeezed into the narrow space. If I hadn't been so strung out, I would have made a joke about his breath, but as it was, nothing was funny at the moment.

My gun began to feel heavy in my hands. I needed to use it, and soon.

Light was seeping in underneath the door, so I pushed my goggles up on my head and slowly pushed it open.

The kitchen was empty, and the only light came from above the stove. The fridge hummed and the house was silent except for muffled laughter coming from down the hall.

A terrible scream splintered the room.

A man's scream.

Had the ambush already begun?

I exchanged a worried glance with Diego as we heard doors further down the hall being flung open. Footsteps.

People ran past the kitchen, heading up the stairs toward the scream, not bothering to look our way.

All of them except for Juanito, that was.

He stopped dead in his tracks at the archway, staring at us like we were ghosts. I couldn't help but grin.

He snapped out of it, reaching for his gun, but mine was already aimed at him. I shot him in the kneecaps, both of them, just as his gun fired, bullets cracking the ceiling.

Then, as if on cue, all of the outside erupted in gunfire. The sound shook the walls, and through the rattling windows bursts of light filled the sky. My army was here.

I ran over to Juanito who was screaming in pain, and picked him up by the collar, shaking him.

"All right you little fuckface," I sneered at him, trying to fight the urge to strangle the fucking life out of him. "Tell me where Esteban is and I'll make your death painless. Don't tell me and I'll break your bones with a hammer. Which one is it?"

His screaming wouldn't stop. I shook him again. "You can't protect him now. You'll never fucking walk again and he sure as hell won't give two fucks about a pathetic piece of garbage like you. So talk."

But before he could, Diego was calling out my name. I let go of Juanito, rolling over him just in time as the air above me burned with bullets. Diego fired back at the assailants, and I kept rolling until I was behind the kitchen island. I quickly reached for the grenade which I knew could take out enough of them without damaging the structural integrity of the house, and tossed it out of the kitchen. It rolled down the hallway.

They yelled at each other to move but it was too late. I pressed my hands over my ears as the blast went off.

"Jesus, Javi," Diego swore as pieces of plaster rained down on him. "You haven't even moved back in yet."

I didn't care if it was sloppier than my usual methods—it was efficient. I scrambled to my feet and stared at the wreckage. There was a ragged hole in the wall, smoke and flames licking the edge.

I shrugged. "I wanted to open up that room anyway."

Miraculously, or something of that nature, Juanito was still alive, holding on to his bleeding and blasted knees as he writhed on the floor.

He was missing half his face though, so it wasn't like he escaped the explosion unscathed. He was *very* scathed and crawling for freedom.

I covered my nose and mouth with the crook of my elbow and walked into the smoke, letting it wash over me. Juanito looked up at me with what was left of him, begging for mercy with an outstretched hand.

I stepped on his hand instead, crunching the bones beneath my boot.

"That was for my sister," I seethed. "I know you intercepted her call when she was calling me for help."

"Javier, we have to go," Diego said, coughing and coming over to stop me. A war was raging around me, but none of it mattered. All that mattered was an eye for an eye.

This time I stomped on Juanito's arm, driving it in with all my might, like I was squashing a cockroach, until I felt it break beneath me.

He screamed.

I smiled.

But I was the furthest thing from happy.

And Juanito couldn't even speak at this point. His mouth was a flap of burning skin, covering a gaping hole. He was useless.

I slid the hunter's knife out of its sheath, and with one swift motion, stabbed it downward into the top of his skull.

The screaming stopped.

"Javier," Diego warned again, pulling at me. "That earlier scream was Esteban's scream. He's upstairs."

I nodded, trying to keep focus, and yanked the knife back out, wiping the brain and blood on my pants. They weren't my pants anyway.

Diego led the way into the smoldering hallway, stepping over the dead bodies of Esteban's fuckheads. Some of them were missing body parts—a foot here, a torso there—others were just a splash of guts on what was left of the wall.

We made our way up the stairs, using the cover of smoke to our advantage, and firing at anyone who came at us. We kicked open doors, checked the rooms, searching for Esteban.

It wasn't until we came to the last room, what had once been Luisa's prison, that I realized what I was going to find.

Of course this would be her prison again.

Of course she would be in there.

With my heart already in a vise, I paused before looking in the room.

The door was already open. With what little light was left in the hallway, it illuminated Luisa lying inside on the floor.

I didn't recognize her at first.

She was nothing more than a pile of blood-splashed limbs—a corpse.

Her hair was all gone, shorn off in clumps around her. She was bleeding and cut, mangled and bruised.

Naked and burned.

I immediately lost my breath, like someone had thrown a brick at my gut, and I grabbed the doorframe to steady myself. I couldn't feel my knees.

My angel.

My queen.

Ravaged.

Ruined.

I'd never wipe the sight of her from my mind, never forget the horror.

A sob caught in my throat, but I didn't know if I was going to vomit right here, or cry.

Diego dropped to his knees beside her, his hands hovering over her body, but he couldn't bring himself to touch her, as if touching her would break her into a million pieces.

"Javier," he said without looking at me. He didn't say anything else. I could only hold on as if that doorframe was the one thing keeping me from descending into complete madness.

She was so beaten, so broken. By life, by everything.

My queen.

My queen.

"Javier," Diego said again, clearing his throat. He finally lay his finger underneath her purple and black chin. "She's alive. Barely. But she is alive."

He looked at me and I saw my own hate reflected in his eyes. "I'll take care of her," he said. "You get Esteban. He's the one who did this."

He didn't have to tell me that. I already knew. He'd done this and who knows what else to my wife, showing off for the world to see. He'd discarded her here, alone in the dark, to die.

I wasn't put away in Puente Grande just so that he could try and take over the cartel. I was put there so I couldn't protect the one thing that mattered to me. I was put there so I and the whole world would see just how far he would go.

And he'd succeeded.

I couldn't protect her.

I had failed.

But I would do what I could now, while I could.

I gathered up strength, burying my sorrow and shock in some cold, hard place inside me. I knew Diego would keep his word.

I turned and ran back down the hall, slamming on my earpiece as I went.

"Where are you?" I yelled into it, shooting at someone just as they ran out of the burning hallway at the bottom of the stairs. The man fell with a yell and I ran past, heading for the back of the house.

I heard Evaristo's voice crackle in my ear. "Front lawn. Be careful, your own men are around the corner and they shoot first, ask questions later."

I'd forgotten he was tracking me. I shoved the back door open and ran across the grass, heading toward the koi pond and staying low so that neither friend nor foe could get a shot off.

"I found Luisa," I said, surprised that I could say her name without my voice cracking. "Diego is with her. I want Este."

"I want him, too," Evaristo said. "But he's not here."

"That's not fucking good enough!" I yelled just as someone took a shot at me from the roof, the bullet missing me by a few feet and going into the pond.

What a terrible shot, I thought as I turned to look.

And there he fucking was.

Esteban was standing on the roof, alone, gun in one hand, his body lit by the lights below.

His other hand was over his eye. No wonder he missed—the fuck could barely see.

I didn't have to tell myself to shoot back. I was already pulling the trigger. A deafening roar filled my ears, and I was shoved to the grass by a gust of whirring wind that whipped my shirttails.

I rolled onto my back, gun raised in time to see a Lama helicopter slowly rising from the other side of the pond, hidden behind a clump of trees where Luisa used to hide.

Luisa.

The image of her was burned into my brain.

The vicious, ugly burn on her delicate skin.

I bellowed in anger and tried to get to my feet, to get a clear shot at Esteban, but he was already running to the edge of the roof, ready to hitch a ride. The chopper was now fully warmed up and flying toward me, the guns of the men on board taking fire.

"He's on the roof!" I managed to yell to Evaristo before I rolled away. I went right into the pond, swimming deep into the reeds and lily pads that would provide cover. Bullets plunged into the water alongside me.

My leg exploded in a bright burst of pain, and that's when I knew I'd been hit. I stayed under, staring up through the murky water at the lights of the chopper as it continued on its way, stirring the pond into waves, heading for the house.

I burst up through the water, gasping for breath, and wasted no time in climbing out of the pond. Esteban was so close to getting on the helicopter. I ran as fast as I could with my damaged leg, trying to get a shot in, but they only hit the rotors.

Esteban leaped, making it on board, and the chopper quickly pulled away into the night.

"Motherfucker!" I screamed.

I tapped my earpiece, but the water had ruined it. I tossed it away in anger and limped around to the front of the house.

Thankfully, the battle had been in our favor, and while many of our men were dead, we were still the last ones standing. The gunfire and mayhem was over.

"I saw him get away," Evaristo said gruffly as he saw me staggering around the corner. "We had a rocket launcher ready, but it stuffed up at the last fucking minute. Piece of fucking shit."

He was mad. Really mad. And that's when I knew he was legit. He wanted Esteban as much as the rest of us did. He was the one who had been making him look like a fool, ever since I was put away and now he really knew that if my side were to thrive, and he were to thrive in it, Esteban must be killed.

I shook my head. "It doesn't matter. We're getting him. Now. Every day after this. For the rest of my life, we are getting him. I want his head on a fucking plate."

Evaristo exhaled angrily then eyed my leg. "You're shot."

"It happens," I said, not willing to dwell on it, not now. With the adrenaline still running through me, I could ignore the pain. "We need to deal with Luisa first."

He snapped his fingers, and his main man, Paolo, came over. "Get this place cleaned up," Evaristo ordered him. "Find a place to burn all the bodies."

"We usually just feed them to the pigs," I pointed out. "But who knows what they've been eating lately."

Paolo went and gathered the rest of the men for the dirty work while Evaristo and I went back inside the house, hurrying now to get to Luisa.

"We'll get you both taken care of as much as I can," he said as we made our way upstairs. "There are a lot of clinics, even out of the country where no one can watch you."

I nodded absently, unable to ignore the uneasiness in my chest. Diego was at the end of the hall, holding Luisa in his arms like some sort of action hero. He'd taken off his jacket and wrapped her in it. Her head was back, her arm swinging limply beneath her.

But he didn't need to be a hero right now. I did. Even though I was the opposite of one. An anti-hero was still a hero in the end, but I would never be more than a villain.

"Shit," Evaristo swore under his breath as we got closer. "You sure she's alive?"

I couldn't take my eyes off of her. Smoke billowed down the hall, enveloping us, and I could see her through the haze, clear as day. Her beautiful skin, broken down like a bruised peach.

"She's barely holding on," Diego said, and the tremor of worry in his voice told me we didn't have much time. I also could have hugged the damn man for taking care of her like that.

"Give her to me," I said, reaching for her.

"Your leg, Javier," Evaristo reminded me.

"Fuck my leg," I snapped as Diego handed her over, placing my wife in my arms. She was lighter than usual, and beneath the blood I could see her ribs jutting out. She'd been starved on top of everything else. I should have never expected anything less from Esteban.

The more I stared down at her in my arms, the more that empty space inside of me increased, spinning outward, invading every corner of which I was alive. She'd undone me many times in the past, but I wasn't sure I could piece myself together again. Not now. I was ruined over what she'd done to me, and I was ruined over what had been done to her.

Our marriage had been obliterated, and this was all that was left.

I was going to hold on to that until my fingers were raw.

"We have to go," Diego said to me, and I managed to say something back—I don't know what, but somehow I put one bad leg in front of the other. We walked down the hallway of what used to be our house, of what used to be a pretty good life, and I could almost hear her bubbly laughter, her intoxicating grin, from memories past. Fire, smoke, and the stench of burning bodies filled the air, while my wife's birdlike body, her fragile life, was in my hands. I could have given into the thick rage that had gotten me here; I could have killed her—put her out of her misery, even—and had my revenge on her. It would have been so easy and the others would have looked away.

I just couldn't.

Maybe that made me weak. Maybe it made me strong. I didn't know and I didn't really care.

All of my vengeance was for Esteban now. He took everything away from me and made my loved ones suffer. Luisa never took anything from me. Instead, in her devastation here, she gave me something instead. And as I held her, I knew I had a piece of myself back, a part that I had lost along the way, a part I never thought I'd find again.

It didn't make me whole. I didn't think anything ever could. Some people weren't meant to be whole, to have a soul.

But it was something.

I would not harm my wife. Not anymore, and not in any way. I didn't know if she would pull through and if we could ever have what we once had, no matter how fleeting it had been, but I knew I'd have to learn to let go of that suffocating hate and start all over again. Learning to forgive her would be the toughest thing I'd ever have to do.

If she pulls through, I thought.

I had a hard time believing I wasn't carrying a dead woman in my arms.

CHAPTER TWENTY

Luisa

When I was a young girl, maybe eight or so, my father once took me to the dry bluffs above the ocean to see if we could catch a glimpse of the migratory humpback whales. Even though they were common during the winter months, I'd never seen them, so papa took me to the best viewing area he could find.

Unfortunately it happened to be part of one of the fancier resorts that dotted the beaches between San Jose del Cabo and Cabo San Lucas. He told me to dress up in my Sunday best, a white cotton dress with red embroidered flowers that I thought made me look like a princess, and he donned his straw fedora.

He drove us there in the afternoon, parking in the lot, and then we walked in through the hotel like we belonged there. I'd felt so special, so much like royalty, walking across that white marble floor of the lobby, so shiny I could see my own reflection. I remembered the sound of my Mary Janes hitting the floor and hoping that no one would see the layer of dust on my shoes. They'd know we were imposters for sure.

Once we made it outside, papa led me along the pool area as I tried not to gawk at the vacationing gringos, impossibly pretty people reading, laughing, and splashing without a care in the world. We stopped at the bluffs, leaning over the fence and watching for the whales.

I remembered how bright it was, that sun shimmering off the water. There were other people there too, guests watching for them and talking excitedly in English. I wanted nothing more than to see these beautiful mammals break the ocean surface.

The whales had always been a symbol of everything graceful and wild and free.

Everything I wanted to be.

We were watching for only a few minutes though, scanning the waves, hoping beyond hope to see them, when a woman in a white pantsuit approached us. Her nametag said Gloria. She was Mexican, too, but at that moment she pretended she wasn't.

She didn't even ask if we were staying there. I guessed it was too obvious that we weren't. She just told us we had to leave.

My papa nodded, not wanting to cause a scene, but I stomped my foot and held on to that railing.

"I want to see the whales. The whales are for everyone to see."

"Not from here, they aren't," Gloria said snidely. "You must leave."

"But why? We are not harming anyone. We just want to watch."

"This hotel is for guests only. You are not a guest."

"Let's go, Luisa." Papa grabbed my arm, and I saw so much sadness and disappointment in his eyes that it only made me madder. Here he was, trying to do something nice for me, something free that we could afford, and we weren't even allowed to lay our eyes on the ocean that belonged to all of us equally.

"I will have to call security if you don't leave," Gloria said.

"So you can throw us in jail?" I cried out, and now other guests were looking at us.

Then some older gentleman, white skinned with a crippling sunburn on his nose, approached us and said to Gloria, "It's okay. They can stay on account of me. They can be my guests."

I could have hugged that man, a vacationer with a good soul, but Gloria was having none of it. "They have to leave, sir," she said to him, blowing him off. "They don't belong here."

And though I'd grown up knowing how unfair life was, that was the first time I'd felt the pinch. Mexicans like Gloria and rich white people had rights that we did not. They had access to land and sights that should have been for everyone. They were privileged. They had power. They were the true royalty of the country.

I would realize, later, that they weren't even at the top of our food chain. The *narcos* were the true royalty, more than them, more than the government.

If you wanted to be queen, that's where you had to be.

I finally saw the whales one day when I was nineteen and driving to my waitressing job in Cabo San Lucas. But by then, the magic and everything they had meant to me had long since disappeared.

And now, as I lay here in some bed, in a clinical, silent room, tethered between life and death, I saw the whales behind my eyes. Swimming, singing. They gave me comfort and kept me cool. They beckoned for me to go under, to feel that silky water slide past my skin, to feel free and wild. They dove deeper and deeper, but as they disappeared into the cobalt depths, I knew I couldn't follow them. Not now. Not yet.

I raised my palm in the water to say goodbye, watching their flukes dissolve into the great blue, then slowly I made my way to the surface and opened my eyes.

Evaristo was standing over me, observing me closely.

"Luisa," he said. "Welcome back."

I tried to speak, to ask where I was.

If Evaristo was here, then it meant the *federales* had me.

A landslide of horrors came flooding back.

Esteban.

The look in his atrocious eyes.

The torture.

The endless pain.

My mind shut down. I was pulled under again after that, back to the deep, deep blue.

I don't know how much time passed before I felt myself coming out of it again. I blinked slowly, expecting to see ocean, but only saw a white ceiling above me. The flecks of paint came in and out of focus. They reminded me of when I was young and in school, staring at the cheaply made walls to pass the time. I tried to feel my body from the inside out and worked on moving my toes, my fingers, carefully. Everything felt tight like a rubber band, especially my face and stomach where I knew I had been badly burned.

Horribly disfigured and scarred for life.

I closed my eyes and took a deep breath, letting the air fill me, bringing me life and strength. I had been ruined, but I would survive. I would learn to live again anew.

I heard someone shift beside me. I remembered seeing Evaristo. He must have rescued me from the house. Perhaps the agency went back on their word and took Esteban down. Maybe he was in prison.

Maybe he was dead, killed in a gruesome, painful death.

I could only hope.

"Who is there?" I asked weakly, too afraid to turn my head, that the pain would be too much.

The person stood up, casting a shadow in the corner of my eye. Someone took my hand. I knew the grip better than I knew myself.

Javier's face came into view, peering down at me with those golden eyes that seemed almost soulful. "You don't need to talk," he told me, voice soothing me like that feather on my skin.

It was too much. Tears welled in my eyes.

"Don't you dare cry on me," he said sternly, gripping my hand harder. "Don't." He swallowed hard.

I sucked in my breath, trying to steady the emotions that were flying all over the place.

"Where am I?" I asked.

"In a private clinic in San Salvador."

"We're in El Salvador?" My mind raced. "Are you really here?"

He nodded, smiling only slightly. He looked older somehow, greyer at his temples, his features strained. It made me realize how horrible I must have looked, the burns, my face, my hair chopped off.

I closed my eyes and turned my head, pain ripping through me in nauseating spasms. "I don't want you to see me like this," I said, voice choked in my throat, even though I realized how petty it sounded.

"I want to see you like this," he said.

"Because I deserve it."

"Because you're *alive*. When we first found you, I was certain you were anything but." He paused and I felt soft fingers on my scalp. "No one deserves this. Especially not you."

But I did. I did. And I didn't deserve to have him by my side right now being tender with me. I needed his wrath, his punishment, his torture. I couldn't have been anything more than trash to him after all the terrible things I had done.

My heart wept for a million bad choices.

Then I started to weep myself.

"Luisa," Javier said, leaning over further. "Look at me."

I opened my eyes and the tears spilled down the sides of my cheeks. I expected my face to sting, but I felt nothing at all. All the nerves had been burned away.

"You're going to be okay." His gaze was deep and intense—I felt it in my bones.

I could barely shake my head.

"Yes," he said angrily. "You will be. You're my wife, my queen, and this is something you'll get over. We both will."

"How?" I cried out. "How can I get over this? Look at me! I'm destroyed. I'm barely even a woman anymore, barely even a human being. I'm mangled garbage. Look at us! How could you ever, ever forgive me? How can I ever get back the husband and the marriage I had? Why would I ever be allowed that?"

His jaw tensed. He closed his eyes briefly, breathing out slowly through his nose. "I don't know," he said. When his eyes opened, they were lost. "I don't know how we can move past this, if I can forgive you, if we even deserve a fresh start. All I know is that I'll try. *We'll* try."

It wouldn't be enough. I knew that. We had hurt each other too much.

"I want Esteban dead," I told him, surprised at the strength in my voice. "I want him to pay."

The corner of Javier's mouth curled up now, his eyes glinting wickedly, like a million amber knives. "He will pay. I will make sure of that. He will pay over and over again, I promise you."

"No," I said. "I want to be the one that makes him suffer."

He shook his head. "You're far too hurt for that."

"I don't care."

"Luisa, your collarbone is broken. You're burned—"

"I. Will. Make. Him. Pay," I ground out, squeezing Javier's hand with the same kind of ferocity.

He studied me for a moment, almost amused. "You really are the woman for me, aren't you? Have I ever told you that there's nothing sexier than seeing bloodlust in your eyes?"

"Javier," I pleaded.

He sighed impatiently. "Look. We've tracked him as far as El Salvador. Evaristo is using the agency's satellites to get readings on known safe houses. I'm using my men across Central America to spot him. We—"

"Evaristo?"

He smirked. "Right, you don't know. I escaped from prison with his help. He switched teams."

I frowned.

"He's not gay," Javier added. "Not that I'd blame him with a hot piece of ass like me around. He's just one of us now."

"You corrupted a fed."

"He corrupted himself. He wanted to be on the winning side for once. His intel got us to you. We knew Esteban had you and was in the compound when we ambushed it. Unfortunately, that fuck got away."

"How did he look?" I asked, remembering our vicious, bloody battle.

He cocked his head. "Not good. Somewhat blind. Why? Please tell me you fucked him up."

I could only manage a small, tight smile. "He cut off my hair. I put the scissors in his eye."

Javier broke into a wide grin and leaned down to kiss my forehead. "That's my woman," he said proudly, and I tried not to wince at the feeling of his lips on my skin.

"I think the acid burned away some of his hair too," I added. "But that's not enough. I want more. I want to rip his head off with my own fucking teeth."

He raised his eyebrows. "My god, if you weren't so damn injured, you wouldn't be able to keep me off you right now."

At the thought of that, my heart sank and the smile fell from my face.

"What?" he asked quickly.

I turned my head away, staring at the wall, feeling everything. The shame. The knowledge that nothing would be the same. "How could you want me after everything?"

"Because," he said, sounding confused. "You're you."

"I'm not." I let out a small, sad little sob. "I don't know what I am now. A monster."

His eyes narrowed into slits. "We both know who the real monster is here," he said sharply.

"Please. You know it. I'm ugly. I'll never be the same. Even if I can get your forgiveness, I won't look the same to you again."

"Luisa, stop talking like an idiot. Give me time. Give us time."

"My looks won't change with time."

"Your looks?" He trailed his fingers down my arm. "What about your looks?"

"My hair, my scars, my burns." I could almost feel the same acid eating away at my soul.

"Hey now," Javier said, putting his hand under my chin and gently tipping my face toward him. He appraised me coolly, taking me all in. Finally, he nodded and said, "You're better now."

"What?"

He shrugged casually. "What can I say? I think you look better. With your hair short like that, you can see more of your gorgeous face. And the burns only make you look stronger. Like a warrior. Like the queen that you are. Like nothing will hurt you ever again, because you've lived through it already. What could be more beautiful than that?" He leaned over and kissed me gently on the lips. "You know now that you could never be ugly to me," he murmured.

My heart wanted to swell with his words, so terribly honest that it took my breath away. When Javier was cruel, he was brutal, but when he was tender, it was almost more disarming.

Yet, at the same time I knew he wouldn't be quick to forgive me. We had so much distance between us we needed to gap. He might have implied that he was still physically attracted to me, a fact that brought with it a whole mess of other issues, but I didn't know when he would let me in again.

"Sorry to disturb you," Evaristo said, opening the door to the room while lightly knocking on it at the same time.

Javier glared at him. "She finally comes to and there you are. Can't even give us a damn minute."

He smiled at me brightly, looking so different in a suit and not the tortured man in the basement. "Luisa, I'm glad you're awake. You've been out of it for the last few days."

"How long have I been here?"

"A week," he said.

"And you still haven't found Esteban?" I asked.

"Actually," Evaristo said quickly, coming over to us. He turned to Javier excitedly. "We have. We just spotted him on the satellite footage, in a village in the mountains in Southeast Guatemala."

"Well, fuck," Javier said, gesturing wildly, his eyes wide and bright. "What the hell are you doing waltzing in here like this? Let's go!"

"I want to go," I said quickly.

Both men looked at me as if I were insane. I probably was. But I couldn't rest here, not without finding Esteban with them and taking out his other eye.

"You're in no shape to move," Evaristo said. "Stay here. We will have people taking good care of you. You'll be protected around the clock."

"Leave Diego here," Javier said, which surprised me. "He can guard her."

It seemed to surprise Evaristo too. "You sure? We might need him."

He shook his head. "I'm not leaving her in the hands of someone I don't know or trust."

"Forget trust," I told them. "I'm not afraid. I just want him dead." I tried to get up but the pain was so great, and it spread like fire. I cried out and Javier gently pushed me back onto the bed.

"No, Luisa," he told me. "We will get Esteban alive. And I will bring him back here for you. You can do whatever you want with him. I promise."

"Please."

"I promise," he repeated. He jerked his chin at Evaristo. "Come on. Let's find Diego and get going."

The two of them stalked off. For a moment, I thought if I just tried hard enough I could move, but my whole upper body failed on me. The agony was just too great. I lay back, breathing hard, wishing my anger could fool me into thinking I was okay. But all it did was tire me.

My last thoughts before I fell asleep were of all the terrible things I would do if Javier brought Esteban back here.

For the first time in a long time, I smiled.

CHAPTER TWENTY-ONE

Javier

It wasn't easy leaving Luisa behind in her condition, but there was no fucking way I was going to let this go. My mind was on a single track and that track led to blood and bone.

It wasn't easy leaving Diego behind either, but it had to be done. I didn't trust anyone but him at this point. He understood, vowing to watch over her as he had done before, though I read it on his face that he wanted to join the massacre.

Keeping true to my word, if we did manage to capture Esteban alive, I would bring him back to Luisa and Diego. Then we could all fucking take turns doing whatever it was our hearts desired.

I'd never seen such thirst for blood and violence in Luisa before.

I had to say it unnerved me in the best possible way. I saw in her what I saw in myself, something dark and frightening and unstoppable. The fact that she actually drove a pair of scissors through Esteban's eye stirred up something deeper inside me—not just my cock.

It was wrong of me to want to encourage that bloodlust, but I couldn't help it. They say a marriage only works if it's an equal partnership, and this would establish her as a real cartel queen. Not just having a say in the business and giving her opinions, but actually getting her hands dirty. Bloody. That said *narco* royalty like nothing else did.

"Remember we want him alive," I said to Evaristo, raising my voice to be heard over the churning rotors.

We were en route to Las Aguas, a tiny village outside the town of Nueva Santa Rosa. The two of us were in one chopper with some of the best backup men I had. There were another two choppers carrying the derelicts of my new army, the ones who fought the hardest and craziest at the compound. Even I was a little afraid of them. Nothing was more dangerous than a meathead with a machete, but at least they got the job done.

"No promises," Evaristo said. "If it's a choice of killing him or letting him get away, you can guess which one I'll be taking."

We didn't fly directly to the village. That would have been too risky. Instead, the choppers landed in the next valley over then we piled into the SUVs I had arranged earlier. They took us high into the mountains, climbing the steep road at night so we could remain unseen. The next morning, when the haze cleared, I could see we were settled on a ridge that looked down over the tiny village of stucco houses nestled along a narrow river.

The village couldn't have more than a hundred people in it. Evaristo estimated there were about fifty. The only reason we had an inkling that Este was here was because one of the Guatemalan ops visually identified him in Santa Rosa. Some digging around later not only confirmed that it was him, but that he was headed over the mountains. Using the *federales* fancy tracking system, they were able to intercept a phone call made from someone named Fez who was asking about my whereabouts. Voice recognition confirmed it was Esteban and triangulated the signal to somewhere in this valley.

I could feel him close by anyway. I could barely sleep, and not because I was on a sleeping bag on the cold ground, but because I could taste the blood.

"He's there," Evaristo said that morning, handing me a cup of instant coffee. It wasn't much better than gas station runoff, but it would have to do. I never understood why roughing it had to be "rough." Even a French press and some good local beans would go a long way out here.

"You know for sure?"

He nodded. "Just got off the phone with the agency. The satellite images are being printed on the computer right now, but I already got a look at them. There's only one structure down there big enough and nice enough for Esteban and his men. A barn and a neighboring house."

"Makes sense," I said, my palms itching to go as I took another sip of the godawful brew. "They are animals after all."

"I'm not sure ours are much different," he noted, nodding at one criminal who was busy taking a piss on a sleeping man's head.

I rolled my eyes. When this was all said and done, I'd be a lot better off if I could just kill them all. They might have been good for getting this job done, but they were far too stupid, not to mention uncouth, to be associated with the name Javier Bernal.

I leaned in closer to Evaristo. In the harsh light of dawn I was aware of how young this kid really was. "Let me ask you, how long do you think you'll play the loyal *federale* for?"

He grinned at me sheepishly. "For as long as they think you're still in prison. As good as those guards and the warden are, the cover-up only lasts for so long. Even with the prison director under your thumb, the truth will come out. And when it does, all fingers will point to me."

"You'll be on the run then," I told him. "You'll have to change your name. Your appearance."

"That's if I live that long, *patron*." He shrugged. "I will use them while I can, like they have used me. And they *have* used me. They prey on the weak, that's the difference between you and them. You, Javier, prey on the strong. The government preys on the weak, the ones without much choice. The ones like me. Then they mold you to be their little toy soldier. You live your short life fighting their battles without really knowing what you're fighting for." His eyes scanned the distant peaks as the mist lifted. "The cartels have caused so much violence in this country, but that's nothing new. Mexico is a country built on violence and corruption. You know how Cortes founded the country?"

I nodded. I didn't remember much from school. I dropped out when I was young, after my father died, having to work in his business and take care of my mother and sisters. But that didn't stop me from seeking knowledge on my own, and the inception of Mexico was something larger than life.

"Well," Evaristo went on, "then you know that barbaric violence and a shitty class system has been our way from the very start. Those at the top feed off of each other. Those at the bottom suffer endlessly. The cartels rule because the government allows them to. Because it benefits them both."

"And thank god for that," I added.

"Yes, thank god. Or the devil. Whichever one you choose."

Paolo came over to Evaristo. "Sir, we have confirmation that Esteban Mendoza is there right now."

One hell of a wicked grin spread across my face. I'm pretty sure it stayed there the whole time as we quickly loaded into the SUVs and drove down the rocky, steep road, which was nothing more than a deer trail all the way down into the valley. It was still so early that we hoped we wouldn't be detected.

We eventually reached the bottom in one piece and raced down the one dirt road through the middle of the village.

The few villagers that were awake saw us and started yelling, but we zoomed past them, heading all the way to the house and the barn. We piled out, weapons in our hands as the dust rose above us. The bigger men went in through the front door, kicking it down with their heavy boots and breaking windows.

Evaristo and I went around the back, pistols drawn, ready to shoot. I had to remind myself over and over again that I wasn't shooting to kill, just to maim. From the way I was gripping my gun, I was afraid that I might just kill him on the spot.

Suddenly the promise I made to Luisa was gone and all I could think about was putting the bullets through his head repeatedly. It would take away the fun, but it would feel oh so fucking good just to see him caught. To see the fear of death. I wanted to smell it on him.

At the last minute, I shoved Evaristo out of the way and entered the back of the house first, not giving a damn if he was the one properly trained for this or not. I'd done okay so far.

The house was empty though. There was no one inside and not a single sign of them having been there at all. Floorboards were ripped up looking for tunnels that were never found, and the place was swept for leftover communication, anything to point to Esteban, but there was nothing.

But I knew he had been here. I knew we had been close.

Too close.

I turned to Evaristo. "Burn the place down," I said.

"The house?"

"The village. They know he was here. They know he left. Interrogate them all. If they can't give us answer, then we burn it."

Evaristo frowned, hesitating. The good and evil we were just discussing was now battling in his head. "This isn't even Mexico, Javier."

"So," I said simply. "Word will still get back to him. Burn it all."

He put his hand on my shoulder. "Listen, there is a fine line between revenge and lunacy. Concentrate on him, not on those he may or may not have involved."

"Burn it to the fucking ground!" I screamed in his face, my skin growing red hot, spittle flying out of my mouth and onto his cheek.

He slowly wiped it away and nodded. "Yes, *patron*."

Evaristo still gave the frightened villagers a chance to live. They walked into the mountains, staring back at their homes as they burned and burned, the smoking rise high above the valley floor.

I felt absolutely nothing as I watched it all disappear behind us, the SUV climbing into the hills. I thought the destruction and the flames would at least burn off some of the debilitating frustration I felt at having lost him once again, but it didn't.

It just made things worse.

And with the way things were, I wasn't sure how much worse it would get before it finally got better.

CHAPTER TWENTY-TWO

Luisa

It took five days for Javier to return to San Salvador. Diego hadn't had much contact with him, and the last we heard before they went to radio silence was that he was in the mountains without a signal except for the satellite phones. The two of us waited day in and day out, anxiously trying to pass the time.

Not that Diego would ever show any anxiety. The big beast of a man was as cool as a cucumber, reminding me of how Javier could be on his good days. Or maybe those were his bad days. It was hard to tell when both fire and ice could burn you.

By day four, I was doing a lot better. I was in a sling now and could walk around, though moving my shoulder hurt like hell, even with low doses of morphine. Sometimes it felt like there was a grinder inside me, working to the bone.

The morphine was more for the burns anyway. Thankfully the one on my face was healing faster and didn't need a bandage, even though I wanted it covered up more than anything. The one on my stomach was trickier and sometimes the pain got so bad I would break down and cry.

Diego wanted the nurses to give me more drugs, but I was adamant against it. I wanted to be as clear-headed as possible these days, even if it hurt me to do so. I played one-handed cards with him instead, determined to pull through and save face.

When Javier walked into the room on the fifth day, I knew it was bad news. Not just because he didn't have Esteban with him, but because I was certain he would have notified us along the way if he was successful. No one likes to broadcast their failures.

Needless to say, I was glad to see him. Even though I felt like an absolute wreck with my beaten looks and pain that half-straddled the morphine cloud, the sight of him, defeated or not, warmed my bitter heart.

"No good, huh?" Diego asked while Javier strode across the room and collapsed into one of the stiff metal chairs by the wall.

Javier leaned forward, brows pinched between his fingers, but didn't say a word.

Diego looked at me. "Perhaps I should leave you two alone." When Javier didn't move nor utter his protest, Diego got up and left, closing the door behind him.

I leaned back against the wall and started gathering up the cards, leftovers from our simple game of *Burro Castigado*. "Do you want to talk about it?"

Javier shook his head, his eyes still closed.

"That's fine," I said. "I'm doing better, by the way. I can leave here tomorrow they said."

Finally he looked at me. "Good." He sighed heavily. "Sorry, I didn't mean to...you look a lot better."

I smiled softly. "I thought you said I already looked better." I gently touched the burn on my face for emphasis. It had stopped being numb, a good sign even though the outer damage wouldn't go away.

"I meant it," he said. But he still didn't get up. I was acutely aware that whatever exchange we had shared when he first saw me here wasn't about to happen again. Not now.

"Do I dare ask what happened?" I said cautiously, worried that the question would press all the wrong buttons. He was tense, stressed, and if he hadn't unleashed his fury on Esteban there was always the chance he would unleash it on me.

But he didn't. He sighed and leaned back in his chair, legs stretched out in front of him. His dark jeans were coated with a layer of dust, and only then did I note how uncharacteristically messy he was. Even his longish hair was out of place.

It actually made him look a bit boyish. Not quite vulnerable because Javier was anything but, but...younger.

"He was there, Luisa." He wiped his hand over his face and stared out the window. "He was there. We were so close. We missed him by a matter of ten minutes, I'm guessing. If we had known that to begin with, we could have gotten him. We wasted too much time in his house. We've wasted too much time already."

"But," I said, running my hand over the cards and flipping them up one by one. "There is no time limit on revenge. Don't they say it's a dish best served cold?"

"The Americans say that," Javier said, eyes hard. "The longer he's out there, the longer he's allowed to think he has won. He has *not* won."

"No," I said. "I'm still alive. And you're here with me." I swallowed hard, afraid to go on. But I had to. "Aren't you?"

He looked at me sharply. "Of course I am."

"And so he knows that. He knows we're coming for him. That's why it's best to wait a while. Wait for him to relax. Let his guard down."

He got out of his chair and stormed over to me, eyes blazing. "You're telling me," he said, waving his hand over my body, "that you're okay with just letting him getting away with this, with what he did to you? Can you honestly say that you can wait to catch him one day when he's not expecting it? Is that what you can do? Fuck." He turned around, his back to me, and shook his head. "Well I can't do that. I can't live my life knowing he's out there and that he's ruined us."

My heart grew heavy. "Don't forget I had my hand in that, too."

He whirled around. "Oh, I haven't forgotten," he snapped. He closed his eyes and ran his hand through his hair, trying to compose himself. When he opened them again, his gaze was directed at the floor. "The sooner he's dead, the better it is for us. The sooner we can move on and pick up the pieces."

And what makes you think we can do that anyway, I wanted to ask. But I didn't dare. I was too afraid of the truth. The truth that, despite everything, forgiving me was the last thing on his mind.

My body would heal before we ever did.

I flipped over the last card. Queen of spades.

Unlucky.

...

The next day I was able to leave the clinic as promised. I said goodbye to the nurses and doctors who took care of me, but to them I was just another anonymous person coming in from the endless violence. Diego and I had theorized that they didn't just work for the agencies in the area but for whatever cartels were willing to pay the highest price. With that in mind, I was glad that Diego was there to guard me. Any doctor would have sold me out to someone willing to pay for it.

I went with Evaristo, his second-in-command, Paolo, Diego, and Javier in a small convoy of cars out toward the western coast of El Salvador. There was one humble safe house on a golden beach, and another a few yards away, nestled in the jungle.

Javier and I commandeered the beach house with Diego, while Evaristo and Paolo watched over Javier's army in the other.

It was strange being in such a small space with just the three of us. Javier and I had one bedroom to ourselves overlooking the ocean, while Diego was stationed near the front. Though we couldn't see them, there were other guards patrolling the grounds, making sure we were safe. It was hot here so close to the equator, and there was never a moment when I wasn't coated in a thin sheen of sweat.

The whole set-up reminded me of when I first married Salvador. Our honeymoon had been at a similar place, with similar protection. And I had been similarly nervous.

Despite everything that had changed between Javier and I, what had done the most damage had nothing to do with him or me.

It was Esteban.

Because of him and his men, I'd grown averse to Javier's touch. Anyone's touch, really, but especially his.

That night, when we arrived at the house, we settled into our new room. It was clean and comfortable. Nothing fancy. Teak wood on the mirrors and doors, a ceiling fan, terracotta tiled floors. The kind of place vacationers would rent for a taste of Latin America.

There was one queen size bed in the middle of the room, and the sight of it made my heart jump.

I carefully got ready for bed, taking my time to change into my nightgown in the washroom. Everything took longer with my shoulder incapacitated. Javier had offered to help me a few times but there was no way I'd let him see me naked.

I didn't want him to be repulsed.

And I feared what would happen if he were turned on.

When I finally emerged, he was in bed, the sheet pulled up to his abdomen. I knew he was naked underneath.

He wasn't smiling though. He was reading me, almost desperately, as I stepped out of the bathroom. I was a bit unsteady on my feet, a side effect from the massive amounts of codeine I'd been prescribed for pain, even though it hadn't done much so far.

Javier made a move to help me. I tried to shoo him away but he was adamant. And naked. And had a formidable erection as he led me over to my side of the bed.

"You're still in pain," he noted, lowering me down.

"I'm fine."

He gave me a half smile. "You know, my dear, we do own most of the drugs in the world. I'm sure I can get you something stronger than fucking codeine."

"It's fine," I said again. Javier didn't get high on his own supply, and neither did I.

He came around to his side of the bed and turned on his side, facing me. I had no choice but to sleep on my back. My shoulder wouldn't allow anything else.

The tension between us was hard to ignore. It was physical—you could almost see it hanging in the air. Even the creaking ceiling fan couldn't blow it away. So many things that hadn't been said. So many things that begged to be said again.

And I was caught between a rock and a hard place.

The need to feel beautiful.

The need to never feel beautiful, because I was afraid of what that beauty would do.

"Luisa," Javier said quietly. His gaze held mine even when I wanted to look away. "You know I don't care."

I anxiously rubbed my lips together before saying, "About what?"

"What you're worried about."

He reached out and ran the tip of his finger along the scar that one of Esteban's men had left on my chest, the one that led all the way to my stomach. The scar he left before he had raped me. Before they all did.

I could still see them, could still smell them, even when I didn't close my eyes. They were always there. They had permeated my soul.

I shuddered and Javier abruptly took his hand away. A few heavy beats passed between us.

He swallowed. "We can get past this," he said thickly.

I couldn't answer because I didn't know what he meant. There was so fucking much to get past now. How would we ever get ahead?

"It's just skin," he added.

"No." I stared up at the ceiling fan. "It's not just skin. It's a memory. My skin remembers."

He breathed in sharply. "Does it remember me at all?"

I turned my head to look at him, taken aback by the rawness in his voice.

"I hope it will," I said.

I hope that more than anything.

He held my gaze, and I could see that frustration and impatience mount. He was thinking that Esteban was out there still and all the damage was in here.

...

"Here you are." Javier's voice rose above the crashing waves.

I turned my head, hugging my shawl close as he walked out onto the beach, barefoot and in linen pants and a dress shirt. He was holding two glasses of red wine. It was hard to get the good stuff in El Salvador, let alone the reserves that we owned back in Mexico, but it would do for now.

At the moment, it seemed like everything would do for now.

We'd been at the safe house on the beach for just over two weeks. Everyone was well-fed, well taken care of, but tensions were high.

With no action at all, the criminals needed an outlet, and one was found wandering around the bedroom while I was trying to take a shower. Needless to say, Javier showed up and shot him on the spot. Diego was berated for letting his guard down for one second, though I wouldn't and couldn't blame the man. He'd done so much for me, for all of us already.

I felt myself spin the other way, toward fear, sucked in a big black hole I couldn't quite crawl out of. I shut down and closed myself off from everyone, including my husband. It just wasn't worth the risk.

Meanwhile, word had gotten out that Javier was no longer in Puente Grande. The prison director was sacked, the warden was found beheaded in a ditch, and a handful of guards went missing.

As predicted, Evaristo was on the chopping block for that fiasco. He promptly disappeared from the agency, having already prepared a new life for himself. Javier found it grossly amusing that Evaristo had taken on the identity of a priest, Father Armando, but desperate times seemed to call for desperate measures. At the house he was still Evaristo, but when he went out into the nearest towns for supplies or recon, he was Father Armando, complete with the whole black-robed garments.

No one here seemed to be living anymore. We were just existing. Waiting. It's funny how far revenge can drive a person. I was willing to give up so much for just one sweet taste.

I still wanted mine. It's all I ever thought about. The more Javier, Evaristo, and Diego scanned networks and emails and plotted and mapped, the more despondent they got. But all I could think about was murdering the man who put us all here. After a while, even my guilt seemed to abate, just long enough for me to believe I had the right to kill him as I saw fit. After that was done, then I would deal with everything else I had shoved aside.

Including my husband.

Javier handed me the glass of wine, reaching out to me when I'd been anything but receptive.

I took the glass from him, thanking him quietly.

He eased himself down on the log beside me.

"How is your shoulder?" he asked. Normally I'd say he was making conversation, but I'd barely seen him lately. Most of the time I slept. Dreamed of blood.

I pressed the small bump on my collarbone where it had broken. I didn't need a sling anymore, which was good.

"It's fine. I can't lift my arm over my head or far out to the side, but at least I can use it now."

He nodded and brought his attention to the waves. They pounded against the shore, sending ocean spray into the air which only seemed to add to the heat.

"It's been dead end after dead end." He sighed angrily. "I know you said revenge is a dish best served cold but the longer this takes, the more I fear we'll never get him."

That doesn't sound like you, I wanted to say. Javier's determination usually knew no bounds. Strangely enough, he was an eternal optimist in such a negative business, always believing he would get his way in the end.

Then again, I didn't feel like myself either. I didn't know who I felt like. Everything was different. Our location, our team, our relationship. Even the face that looked back at me in the mirror wasn't Luisa Bernal. She was no queen. She was a scarred, broken woman.

"Talk to me," Javier said imploringly.

I slowly met his gaze. "I don't know what to say."

He studied me for a moment. "Did Esteban ever say anything to you about his plans, about safe houses, about where he might go in an emergency?"

I shook my head. "I don't know."

"Think!" He smacked his hand against his thigh.

I balked, gripping the stem of the wine glass. "You seriously think I want to remember? Do you want me to pull up the memories of what happened there? I'm trying to block it out, Javier! Don't you know what he did to me?"

"Of course I know what he did to you," he said sharply. "You won't even let me touch you. I'm your fucking husband."

"You're also a fucking liar and a cheat!" I yelled, overwhelmed by the anger blanketing me. I got to my feet, the wine splashing around the glass.

Javier got to his feet too, eyes blazing, nostrils flaring. "You were the one fucking him to begin with!"

"Only because you did it first. Only because you pushed me away! You treated me like garbage. I thought our marriage was over and he was the only one who showed any interest in me. And yeah, I regret it a million times over and over and over because I was an idiot who slept with the devil and invited him in to fuck up my life—our life. I was so, so, *stupid,* and this all happened because of me. But I can't forget…" I sucked in my breath, trying to calm down. This was the first outburst I'd had since being in the clinic.

He reached out and put his hand behind my neck, holding me. "I am sorry," he said.

I looked away but he squeezed me harder. "I am sorry," he repeated. "I'm not going to make excuses. I was just looking for reasons to hurt you, to hurt myself, and I don't know why. But it happened and there is nothing I can do about it."

I stared at him with sadness. "You'll do it again."

"No," he said adamantly, shaking his head. "I will not."

"You will. Because when you touch me, I remember them. I can't be with you like that. And I know there's only so much you can take. You'll go elsewhere. It will happen again, and I'll have no choice but to watch."

"You will not remember them," he said, pulling me to him, wine spilling everywhere. "I will make you forget."

"It doesn't work that way," I protested.

He kissed me anyway. I froze but his lips were persistent, drawing out a deep, hard kiss. His tongue was wet, warm, feverish against mine, desperate to unleash something in me. I wanted to give in right there. I wanted to succumb to the lust, to the love, to his wildness. He moaned into me which only shot vibrations right to my core, making me swell with need and want.

I had to have my husband back.

He threw the wine glass to the sand while I barely held on to mine. He put one palm on my head, where if I had long hair he would have made a fist, and his other hand on my waist, pulling me close to him. He pressed me into him, his dick hard and straining against me, while he slid his fingers down over my ass, taking a hefty squeeze that normally would have sent me into overdrive.

But I couldn't do it.

"No," I mumbled against him, pushing him away.

"No?" he repeated, breathing hard, trying to come closer again, but I shoved him off as much as I could.

"I can't do it," I cried out softly. "I can't do it, I'm sorry." It hadn't been his hand on my ass, it had been Esteban's. And it hadn't been his cock vying for me, it had been one of my rapists. That vile look, the sour breath, the humiliation, the pain. I closed my eyes and opened them again, hoping Javier's face would set me right.

The man was hurt. Angry. Frustrated. He stared at me so intently I thought he might be able to see all the ugliness inside, the traces they had left behind. Maybe he did see that, because he stepped back and turned away from me, running his hands through his hair, exhaling through his nose.

"I'm sorry," I called out softly. "When you touch me, it's not you."

He stopped a few feet away, his hands balling at his sides. He leaned his head back, seeming to ask something of the fading sky. Finally he turned to face me.

"Don't you think I need this too?" he asked, voice breaking. "That I need to do this? This isn't about fucking you, Luisa. This is about erasing him."

There was a bitter taste in my mouth. As hard of a time as I was having with this, so was Javier. He was a possessive man through and through, and he needed to own me, both body and soul.

Esteban was a tar-black cloud hanging over every inch of us, never letting go.

"I know," I told him, suddenly just so empty and weak with everything. "I'm sorry."

We stood there on the beach staring at each other for a moment, the wind picking up and brushing his hair across his face. There was so much space between us now, space I didn't know if we'd ever bridge.

"I'm sorry too," he eventually said. He opened his mouth to add something else then closed it and walked off toward the house, leaving me to the early stars and dark waves.

Later that night, I dreamed of Esteban.

This wasn't new. I had nightmares nearly every night. He would douse me with acid again and again or tie me to the bed and let the chickens peck me to death.

But this dream wasn't frightening. I was in it like an apparition, floating past him and Juanito as they planned at the kitchen table. Discussing a map. A place that Esteban wanted to go, a place he'd been before.

The dream ended.

But it was enough to jog my memory.

I woke up in the middle of the night and reached for Javier, shaking him.

"What is it?" he asked, immediately awake. I could see his eyes shining in the dark as he sat up beside me.

I put my hand over his and squeezed it.

"I know where Esteban is."

CHAPTER TWENTY-THREE

Esteban

"Are we there yet?"

Esteban wasn't sure which one of his idiots had asked that question. Though there weren't many of them left, they were all starting to look and act the same, like monkeys who'd been given Kool-Aid and AK-47s. Esteban had thought he was being smart by recruiting such derelict soldiers, but that was just another thing that wasn't going his way at the moment.

Now they were hiking through the jungle outside of Catacamas in Honduras. His lone helicopter ate shit weeks ago, just before the PFM raid in Guatemala, and he'd been on the run ever since with no time to get new supplies.

Yeah, things really weren't going as planned.

Javier had become a thorn in his side once again. The prick had escaped from prison without anyone noticing, and the next thing Esteban knew, his compound was under attack from Javier and that bootlicking fed, Evaristo Sanchez, who was obviously no longer working for the *federales* and had cut some sort of deal with Javier.

Esteban hated the fact that he hadn't seen that one coming. If only he'd used his brain he could have brought Evaristo over to his side before all this happened. He'd been too cocky and that was his downfall, as usual.

But Esteban was having a hard time thinking properly these days. He was dipping into the cocaine too much. It made him feel smart and invincible, but it was really doing the opposite. In the past, Este would take it just to get through the day, even though it had a tendency to make him more violent. The more coke Este did, the more his logic was derailed, the more that he acted without thinking..

He was on the brink of insanity, if not over it. He was doing things that even he thought he'd never do, and had reached a new point of depravity. And it was costing him. If he had been thinking a little clearer, perhaps Luisa wouldn't have been able to drive those scissors into his eye.

He didn't even miss his eye. Sure it fucked up his depth perception and he was pretty much useless with a weapon of any kind, but he thought it made him look cool. He refused to wear an eye patch, preferring for others to stare into the ugly, gaping hole in his face that complemented his facial scar so well. "Eyeless Este," his men had started to call him.

He liked the nickname. It was better than "Erectionless Este," which some *puta* had called him when he was a teenager. It was because of her that he discovered he could get an erection after all, but it was only when violence or the thought of violence was involved, at least at the beginning. He didn't kill the little bitch, but he sure did make her scream. After that, she never uttered anything towards him again. None of the girls did.

What he didn't like about this whole situation was that half of the hair at the back of his head had fallen out in clumps because of the acid. He'd started to wear a baseball cap after that, cursing Luisa for being such a crazy cunt.

So with Evaritso and Javier now working together, Esteban needed to stay one step ahead. There had been too many casualties though, and now that it was common knowledge that Javier Bernal was alive and well, Esteban was losing his people to Javier.

That was a hard pill to swallow. To know that after all he'd done, Javier was still on top and calling the shots. It didn't even bring him any pleasure to know that he'd made his beauty queen less of a beauty. She was still with him, still his queen, her crown tarnished but wearable.

The drugs made things better. They always did. It's too bad his crew were starting to dip into it as well, making them even more apelike than normal.

But Esteban had one last card up his sleeve, one last place to go. A place he'd discussed at length with Juanito, poor naïve Juanito, just in case something ever were to happen.

At least he was smart enough to have a back-up plan.

They would journey up the thick, unyielding jungle to the compound in the trees. He at least knew from the last time it was used that there were more guns, more ammo, and even a helicopter, if they were lucky. In that fortress where so much blood had once been spilled and so much drama had taken place, Esteban would recoup. He would re-plan. Then he would do whatever it took to rule again.

There were hostages he could take. Javier still had a sister in New York, did he not? Luisa had her parents in San Diego—and there were enemies of Javier's he could convince to join his side. Hell, the *federales* might even want to strike another deal. If Javier was put away again, there was no way he'd be walking out of there alive.

Esteban smiled at all the possibilities. He just needed to get to his new castle and wait.

CHAPTER TWENTY-FOUR

Javier

I stared at Luisa for a moment, trying to see her features in the dark. She squeezed my hand, a simple gesture that shot fire up my arm.

"You know where Esteban is?" I asked, trying to not get my hopes up even though my pulse had already kicked up a few notches.

She nodded. "Yes. I had a dream just now. But it wasn't a dream. I was remembering something I'd heard. He and Juanito were discussing the *fincas* and safe houses that they knew of. Esteban said there was one in Honduras, inside a national park. He said you'd never go back because of what happened there. I think that's where he is, where he thinks you'll never go."

All at once, I knew she was right. The place she was talking about could only be the former compound of Travis Raines. It was a place where a lot of shit went down a few years ago, even though it felt like another lifetime. It *had* been another lifetime, back when Raines was still alive and I was caught up with enemies and ex-lovers. I left that place the leader of Raines' cartel, even though I'd lost something, someone else, in the process.

I'd never done well with humiliation. Esteban knew that.

"It's not easy to get to," I told her, even though I knew I'd go through hell and high water to take that man's life.

"I don't care," she said. "And I'm going with you."

I knew she'd say that. "Am I bad a husband if I don't object?"

She shook her head vigorously. "I wouldn't expect anything less from you."

Honestly, I didn't like the idea of her coming along. I wasn't kidding when I said it wouldn't be easy to get to. To attack Este undetected meant we could only drive to a certain point. Then we'd have to hike the rest of the way. We couldn't bring helicopters—they'd give him too much warning. The journey would take at least a day and a half, and I wasn't sure if she could handle it in her condition, even if she was healing nicely. And I sure as hell didn't know if she could handle the actual ambush. It was risky to have her there.

But I also knew it was riskier to leave her behind. I needed Diego for this one. Besides, I owed it to her. I promised her she could get her hands dirty and I needed to keep my promises again. I wanted to see what she'd do to Esteban if she had half the chance. So even though I was purposely putting my wife in harm's way by letting her come along, it was still the right thing to do.

Only in our fucked up little world would *that* be the right thing to do.

I couldn't sleep after that, and neither could she. We decided to wait until morning to wake up Diego and Evaristo and fill them in, so the two of us went into the kitchen, brewed a giant pot of coffee—*good* coffee—and sat at the kitchen table, going over maps and Google Earth images. It was all we could do now that we didn't have access to the *federales* information, but it helped.

I had to admit, it was kind of romantic. She and I drinking coffee, the waves crashing outside, the world dark and sleeping, while we planned the murder and torture of Esteban Mendoza. I might have been falling in love with her all over again. There was something about that relentless fire in her eyes.

Of course the more we talked, the more I stared at her and fell for her, the more I needed to be inside her again to claim her as mine once more. I understood why she couldn't stand for me to touch her that way and it crippled me to the bone. Because she was mine. Just mine. Always mine.

I hadn't been denied much in my life, but Esteban was still denying her from fully belonging to me. I had no choice but to suck up that rage, let it fester bitterly inside me, and unleash it on him later. Our plans got more and more in-depth as the night slinked off into morning.

When Diego stirred and Evaristo came by for his morning debrief, the both of us were pumped up with bloodlust. Our bags were packed, knives were sharp, and we were ready to go fuck shit up.

It didn't take long before we got the army up to speed. They were like a bunch of caged animals, nearly foaming at the mouth once they realized they finally had the chance to run free again. After seeing them in action before, I had no doubt that they were going to lose their minds during the ambush, but my only rule again and again was that no one was to touch Esteban except for me or Luisa.

The drive to the park took seven hours, our convoys crossing the border into Honduras with no problems. With a fake priest—Father fucking Armando—in the car, and our false passports, we went undetected. I did a lot of business in Honduras, but with me on the most wanted list all over again, you never knew where the *federales,* or even the DEA were, or who was on what payroll.

"Did you know there's a town called San Esteban near where we're going?" Luisa asked from beside me, studying a map.

"Must be fate," I remarked, adjusting my bulletproof vest. I'd made sure we all had them on. It saved my life last time I was here.

We didn't end up going as far as San Esteban, but we did drive into a rural town that was bordered by steep terrain and laced with thick vegetation. Just on the outskirts was an abandoned barn that I had used once before to hide our vehicles. The field around also made for a great helicopter landing site, if we were lucky enough to return that way. If we didn't, then it would be a long hike back, though at least we'd be heading downhill.

After we parked the SUVs in the barn, I gave everyone a rundown about the trail, the property, and what to expect. We were a motley crew, but at least we all had blood and vengeance on our minds. While the dust motes danced around the barn, lit up by the setting sun, I had flashbacks to the last time I was here, when I had another motley crew of my own, bound by another form of revenge. Funny how life could come full circle like that.

Thank god I didn't have to deal with any *gringos* this time around. They were only good for ruining things and maybe a good fuck.

When we were ready, armed with packs and ammo, we set off down the long dirt road toward the outskirts of the Sierra de Agalta national park. I led them into the forest. Diego was behind me, then Luisa and Evaristo, and Paolo was at the end with all the crazy fuckers in between.

It was a long, laborious climb into the night, with only small flashlights shining the way. Even without the sun, it was hot as fuck, the thick canopy seeming to seal in the heat. Sweat poured down my face and I didn't bother to wipe it away. Every so often I would ask Luisa if she was okay, and she always said she was. She wouldn't let me think for a second that she was tired or needed a rest.

Still, I knew she was stubborn and made sure we stopped often enough, even though it made everyone more restless and anxious, including me.

Finally, at around one am, we came across a small clearing beneath a few banyan trees and decided we should rest for a few hours. None of us would be able to perform our best if we didn't have some sleep.

There was only one sleeping bag between Luisa and me, and even though I had so much anticipation thrumming through my veins and needed to get off something fierce, I knew it was best if I didn't share it with her. She would balk at my touch, and I wouldn't be able to stop touching her once I started.

"Take it," I told her, leaning against the tree while she spread it out on the leaf-covered forest floor.

She didn't argue. "Are you sure you're all right sleeping like that?"

I nodded. "I probably won't sleep anyway. I'll be watching over you."

She gave me a small smile and crawled into the bag. True to my word, I did stay up most of the night, sharpening my knives and stabbing any large bugs or reptiles that came our way. It was satisfying to pin the snakes to the ground, even more so when I pretended they were Este.

We set out again just before dawn, walking faster and faster the closer we got. Finally the jungle seemed to glow, the trees opened up, and the outer wall of the compound appeared, spotlights shining from the top of the wall.

"You must rack up quite the power bill out here," Luisa said, but I immediately put my finger to my mouth to shush her. This was the last chance we had to go over everything before we were too close to the house and within earshot. I didn't know who was here, let alone if Esteban was here at all, but we couldn't be too careful, not now.

I quickly went over the plan again. Similar to the raid on the compound in Sinaloa, we would all split up, with Diego, Luisa, and I going in from the back while the rest flushed Esteban out. There were no tunnels here, so there was no place for him to go but the jungle.

That's where we would be waiting.

"Good luck," Evaristo said, shaking my hand.

I grinned at him. "Thanks, *father*."

He rolled his eyes then took off with the rest of them along the wall, heading north. Luisa, Diego, and I turned and ran along to the south. Once we got to a tree that was easy to climb, I swung myself up there until I dropped to the wall, Diego and Luisa staying below.

Flattening myself, I brought out my binoculars and took everything in.

Travis's old complex was larger than I remembered. The pretentious asshole had it built in the same style as a French estate, and it had been terribly out of place at the time. Now, since the property was mine and I hadn't been here in many years, it was looking more natural, like it belonged. The jungle had reclaimed it, and vines had begun to grow up the sides of the sprawling house, resembling an ancient relic instead of the palace it once was.

The pool was black with stagnant water and leaves. The pool house was gone, collapsed under the weight of vines. A helicopter sat on the landing pad, but I couldn't be sure if it would start or not. After I'd taken over Travis's cartel—albeit briefly, before his loyalists splintered off and formed a new version of the Zetas—I'd only stayed up here for a few months. It was the only place I felt secure enough to start building a new empire.

Everything was pretty much as I had left it, which made me smile because if the outside looked this bad, the inside had to be pretty disgusting. I wondered how Esteban liked it, holing up inside a rotting palace filled with shit, mold, and snakes.

I knew for sure he was here. In fact, I could see him right through my binoculars. He was in the kitchen, staring out the window at nothing, a cup of something, coffee maybe, in his hand. For a moment he almost looked human, but I knew I shouldn't be fooled. That was the man who betrayed me. The man who killed my sister. The man who made my own wife flinch whenever I touched her.

That was the man I was finally going to kill.

I gripped the binoculars hard in my hands, trying to calm my heart and stop myself from just rolling off the wall and sprinting toward him, guns blazing. But I was too far away, and I knew one of his men would try and pick me off before then. I could already see two of them patrolling the outside, one with an AK in his hands, the other with what looked like a sledgehammer. I had no idea what he expected to do with that if someone approached (throw it?) but I knew if I could get my hands on it, I would have a lot of fun, especially if it were between me and Esteban.

I jumped down, landing between Diego and Luisa. "He's there," I told them. "We need to keep moving and come up the back. He's got a patrol set up."

Luisa's eyes flashed beautifully. "Did you really see him?"

I gave her a nod. "In the ugly flesh."

She gave me a vicious little grin but didn't say anything else. She didn't need to.

We ran along the wall until it curved to the west then used another tree to get ourselves over the wall. Luisa was more difficult because of her shoulder, but she managed to do it, grinding her teeth through the pain.

The back of the property provided the most coverage and was pretty much a tangled forest between the wall and the pool. We slid through it, going from tree to tree as we moved forward, making sure to stay as hidden as possible. We all had guns, which was a good and bad thing. Good because we were protected, bad because the sight of Luisa holding one always made my cock as hard as concrete. She knew this too, which was probably why she was avoiding looking at me. It was as distracting as sin during a time I didn't need any distractions.

When we got to the last shrub that offered a bit of coverage between us and the house, I told Diego that as soon as we heard the ambush begin, he should run straight ahead and start picking off any of the patrollers. Meanwhile, Luisa and I would head for the helicopter.

"How do you know if it even works? It's a pile of rust," Luisa whispered as we all stayed down in a crouch.

"It doesn't matter if it works or not. Esteban is a chicken shit. That's the first place he will go. And that's where we'll be waiting."

Suddenly the air erupted with gunfire. In an instant it was bedlam at the house, explosions and bullets ripping through the air.

It was time to go.

Diego nodded at me then leaped out from around the bush and took off toward the mansion. I cautiously poked my head over the foliage and watched him go, shooting as he ran at a few of Esteban's soldiers who were spraying bullets into the air. Diego was one of the best marksmen I knew, and he took them down without missing a stride.

"Okay, now!" I told Luisa, grabbing her by her good arm and hauling her up. We ran alongside the filthy pool, curving toward the helicopter, while the house lit up like sparklers, a cacophony of gunfire and screams. I knew Evaristo and my army were doing their job, I just hoped it would be enough to drive Esteban out of the house and to supposed safety.

Then Luisa tripped and fell, nearly taking me down with her as she landed on the grass. She cried out and I went back for her, yanking her to her feet.

Just in time to hear something land with a dull thump and roll toward us.

I whipped around to see a grenade at our feet.

No pin.

"Run!" I yelled to Luisa, covering her with my body and turning us away. We ran for the trees but didn't get far enough.

The grenade went off, a blast that tore through my ears, filling my vision with fire and stars. It ripped Luisa out of my grip, sending me flying forward in the air until I landed in a heap at the base of the same bush we hid behind.

I lay there for a few moments, unsure if I was alive or dead. I couldn't hear. I tried to get to my feet, wondering if I even had feet anymore. I did, but they didn't work. I fell back down.

Luisa.

Luisa.

I managed to roll over and lift myself onto my elbows.

The world was spinning and I couldn't see her anywhere. Smoke and flames licked the grass over where the grenade had gone off. My head felt like a million of them were still exploding inside it.

Luisa!

But I couldn't scream. I staggered to my feet, weaving forward, until I saw her.

She was floating face down in the pool.

I didn't know where that grenade had come from, who threw it, and if there were any more, but I didn't care. I jumped right into the thick, black water and swam for her. Halfway across the pond, just out of arm's reach, my feet tangled in weeds and branches, trying to pull me down. My body, so tired, so nearly decimated by the blast, wanted me to just give up.

I couldn't protect her before, but I would die trying to protect her now.

I started kicking, propelling myself forward until I was free. I reached Luisa, quickly turning her over and trying to clear the leaves from her mouth.

"Luisa," I croaked quietly, my voice almost absent.

She didn't stir.

Bullets rained from above.

Son of a *bitch*.

I grabbed Luisa and swam to the edge, hauling us out of the pool with what strength I had left. Every now and then I'd aim my gun and shoot at the dark figures in the distance, not caring anymore whose side they were on.

Once out of the pool, I threw her over my shoulder, her body heavy from the water, and ran for the chopper. Inside, the helicopter body rusty and covered with weeds, I brought her to the backseats, placed her on them, and started giving her CPR.

"Come on," I said to her, tapping her cheek quickly, listening for breathing. "Come on, my queen. Don't die on me now, not after all of this. You're so close." I breathed into her again then tore off her bulletproof vest and started pumping at her heart. "You're so close."

"Not close enough," a voice said.

I closed my eyes, trying to absorb the fucking fury of it all.

I slowly turned around to see Esteban pointing a gun at me.

"Jesus," I exclaimed, unable to help myself. "You look like fucking ass."

He had no eyeball. Luisa really fucked him up that way. It was just a bloody hole of pink and black tissue. His hair was falling out, with huge bald patches everywhere. He was the ugliest motherfucker I'd ever seen, inside and out.

Part of me wanted to laugh, but I wasn't about to provoke him, not with Luisa not breathing beside me. Also, there really was nothing funny about the situation whatsoever.

Still, he wasn't easy to look at.

"Put your hands up," he said, gesturing with the gun.

I frowned at him. "Put your hands up? You've been watching too many American cop shows, *puta*."

He stepped forward so the gun was just inches from my face. I stared down the barrel then raised a brow. He wasn't going to shoot me, not yet. He had a speech prepared—he wouldn't let me die without me hearing about all the different ways I was about to die. I knew this because I had planned on doing the same with him.

But I needed to get Luisa to start breathing again. Time was running out to a point where I wouldn't be able to bring her back.

Don't think about it, I told myself. *Get around the situation.*

But the situation said the two of us were fucked right up the ass, which was usually my favorite thing, but not this time. Definitely not this time.

I took a deep breath through my nose. "So let's hear it then," I said. "Or can I at least save my wife so she can hear whatever bullshit it is you're about to spew."

"I don't have much to say, so let her stay dead," he said with a nasty smirk. He quickly rubbed underneath his nose and stared down at me with one bloodshot eye. "She was a feisty little cunt, I'll tell you that. But nowhere near the finest pussy I've ever had. Maybe even overrated. Gave it up a little too easily. A little too loose, to be honest. I hope you've been keeping that whore on a leash because there's no way your small dick could have stretched her out like that."

I swallowed the bile in my throat, every nerve inside me rattling like a beast in a cage, wanting to unleash my fury. But the gun was pressed against my nose, and even though I knew he'd lost some depth perception with that missing eye, he wouldn't miss blowing my brains out if he pulled the trigger.

"But no," he said, "other than that, I don't have much to say. I don't believe in buying you any more time. You got this far, Javier, but you didn't get all the way to the end."

"You're not going to torture me at all?" I asked, my eyes boring into his. "That doesn't sound like you."

He shrugged. "I'm a busy man, hey. Seeing you finally fucking die will be good enough for me. Seeing your ugly *puta* already dead beside you is just icing on the cake." He sniffed hard through his nose. The guy was high as a kite. No wonder he just wanted to get this over with.

"So you're saying you don't want me to suck your dick?" I asked.

He blinked at me. "What?"

Suddenly Luisa wheezed loudly from beside me, taking in air, coming alive.

It was enough to startle Esteban.

It was enough for me to take advantage and knock his hand out of my face.

He pulled the trigger, but it was too late for him. The bullet went whizzing into the side of the chopper, and I leaped onto him, forcing us both to the floor. We rolled toward the doors, and for a moment he was on top, then I was on top trying to hold him down and keep the gun from firing again. I was strong, but he was on one hell of a cocaine high.

Then Luisa was above us both, gun in her hand, trained on Esteban's face.

"Do it!" I yelled at her, my arms fighting to keep him down, sweat dripping off my face and onto his.

"We're doing it my way," she said, voice hoarse. She aimed the gun at his legs. "Get out of the way, Javi."

I briefly slid my legs off of him, and that was enough for her to take the shot at his knee, blood splattering all over us.

Esteban screamed in agony, momentarily losing grip on his gun. I knocked it out of his hand. Luisa quickly ran over to scoop it up then immediately turned it around and shot a hole through his palm.

Este bellowed like an animal, weakening beneath me, and I raised my head to look at Luisa. She was grinning wildly, like she'd just received the best Christmas present ever.

"Hey," I said to her. "I told you we were going to share him. Don't hog all the fun."

She looked somewhat bashful. "Sorry."

I quickly got to my feet and flipped him over onto his back, his blood spreading on the floor. I pulled out a pair of handcuffs and slapped them over his wrists, even though there wasn't much left of one hand.

"The seats," I told Luisa.

She ran over and straightened out all the seatbelts while I hauled Esteban over.

"Fuck you, fuck you," he kept saying, even though his body was starting to shake from the shock.

"No, I fucked you, remember," I reminded him, shoving him on the seat horizontally while Luisa quickly tied the belts around his legs and waist, keeping him in place. "You better not go into shock on me."

I looked at Luisa. "Do you have the vial or did we lose it in the blast?"

She reached down and patted her soaking cargo pants pockets. She undid the button on one and brought out a small wet box that contained a syringe full of adrenaline. I didn't want to give it to him yet, not until he was on the verge of unconsciousness, but I was glad we had it.

"How are you?" I asked her while Esteban moaned and thrashed on the seats.

"I feel like I drank a pool full of shit and my head won't stop pounding and everything sounds like it's coming from underwater. But other than that, I'm great." She smiled brightly. Well, as brightly as one could when about to torture the living hell out of someone.

She looked fucking fantastic.

I wrapped the last of the belts across Este's chest, buckling them, then I straightened up, looming over him.

"Este, Este, Este," I said to him.

"Fuck you!" he screamed. He sniffed deep then spit forcefully in my face. "You fucking shit!"

I rolled my eyes and wiped it away.

"Well, that's just rude," I chided him. I looked at Luisa. "Get your knife out. Cut out his tongue."

"No!" he screamed, but I quickly drove my elbow into his mouth, shattering his teeth and jaw. It would help.

His head rolled to the side, his moaning never stopping, and he spit out his teeth in a pile of blood. "That's for being a traitor," I told him. "For killing my sister. For hurting my wife. There's plenty more where that came from."

I reached down with my hands, forcing his broken jaw wide open. He gurgled on his teeth and blood, choked on his own screams. "You better hurry, my dear, I don't want him to die just yet."

Luisa came up beside me and I moved out of the way so she could have easier access. "Take my knife from my boot," I told her, shaking my leg at her. "Stick the end of the knife through the tip of his tongue, otherwise you'll never get a good grip. Then use the other knife to saw it in half."

She didn't even grimace. "You seem to know your stuff."

I shrugged in assent. "Normally I'd use clamps but we have to improvise here. At least he won't be able to talk anymore."

And so Luisa did as I suggested. It was easier to get Esteban's mouth wider without so many teeth; plus he wasn't able to move it to offer resistance, so there's that. She stabbed the tip of his tongue with the knife, and as she held it in place, blood drowning the blade, she sawed it off.

The sounds coming from Este were inhuman, but then again so was he. I didn't feel anything except the need to cause more suffering, to finally get even.

I quickly turned him over so he'd bleed out of his mouth and not fill his lungs up with blood.

I leaned in close to his ear, his gurgles sounding like music.

"You know what Este?" I said. "At one point, I actually liked you. You with your fucking flip-flops and your Jennifer Aniston highlights. I really did. You were annoying as fuck and extremely stupid, but I thought there was something, I don't know, *endearing* about you. Then the more I got to know you, worked with you, the more I realized that you just had one big epic hard-on for me and my life. That you wanted to be me more than anything. You wanted to be me so much that it actually drove you insane. That's when I realized you were nothing more than a pathetic piece of shit—an ugly fucking dog that wouldn't stop following me around, sniffing the alpha for scraps, licking my balls to win favors. And that's what you still are. Only now you've had a taste of what you could have become. And now you'll know what it's like to die a complete failure with the taste of my balls still in your mouth."

I looked at Luisa, who was staring down at him with a hatred I'd never seen before. "Hey," I said to her. "You do what you need to do. That will be enough for me."

She swallowed, taking in a deep breath, as if trying to compose herself. "Unzip his pants."

I smirked. I had a feeling it would come to this.

Este was too weak to fight back. I unzipped his pants, bringing them down to mid-hip, until his dick flipped out.

I laughed. "Not so impressive now, are you?" Este could only twitch in response.

I moved over and pressed down on his hips to hold him in place.

"You do the honors, Luisa," I said, but turned myself away so I wouldn't have to watch. I may have done far worse to others in my life, but there were still some things that made me squeamish. I'd like to say it kept me humble.

"I haven't forgot what you did to me," Luisa said to Esteban, her voice hushed, strained, almost confessional. In some ways it felt like a private moment, like I shouldn't be here to listen. "I lived with it day after day. I'm sure I will live with it for many days more. But I've gone through it before and came out stronger, and I will do the same after you. It will be even better because I know that after this, you won't be able to hurt me anymore. I know that you'll die suffering, just as I suffered. Right now, you are Esteban, you are my old boss, you are Salvador and every other man who tried to have their way with me." She paused and I could feel her adjust beside me, poised to make the cut. "And me, I'm every woman that you all ever hurt, ever touched, ever raped. I wish I could say I will take no pleasure in this, but if my husband has taught me anything, it's to be unapologetic. So, I'm not sorry. You deserve this. Then you deserve to die."

The air filled with sounds that even I hoped I would never hear again. Knife. Flesh. Blood. Esteban's guttural, wet howls of agony.

By the time Luisa was done dismembering him, he was twitching uncontrollably. I knew he was close to going into shock. I avoided the bloodbath by his crotch and looked her dead in the eye. To my surprise, even though she was breathing hard and her eyes were wide, she didn't look upset, mad, or anything other than calm. Peaceful, almost.

"Should I get the adrenaline?" she asked. "I think he's going into shock."

I shook my head, suddenly exhausted. "Let him go. I think we're done here."

She seemed to think that over, squeezing the knife handle, wondering what else she could do to him. She impressed me more with each passing second.

I put my red right hand on her shoulder, marveling at how much of Esteban's blood had spilled on us. I was going to suggest that we watch him die then go back to find the others. The gunfire had stopped, and I think I knew which side had won.

But she walked over to him and looked down at his face.

His one good eye was fixed on her, seeming to beg for mercy.

She lifted the knife above him.

In one swift motion, she plunged it into his eye, into his brain, right to the hilt.

Crunch.

She twisted the blade to the right, to the left, breaking bone and sinew.

Esteban Mendoza jerked once, twice, then finally stilled.

He was dead.

He was *very* dead.

I watched her carefully, not sure how she would react now that it was all over and the adrenaline would be wearing off soon. I was used to this—I had ways of separating the act from myself. I had ways of enjoying it, too.

But she wasn't used to being a party to torture except for the torture done to her.

"Luisa," I said softly, coming up behind her. I placed my hand on her arm, sliding it down over her grip on the knife, and pried her fingers loose. I slowly pulled her back, leading her away from his disfigured corpse.

"Talk to me," I whispered, turning her around to face me. I placed my hands on her cheeks, leaving sticky red handprints underneath.

She closed her eyes for a moment, breathing in deep.

She opened them. They burned for me. "I love you," she said.

My heart expanded, building with an internal fire.

"I love you too," I murmured. "My beautiful queen."

I kissed her sweetly, softly, not wanting to scare her off as I had before, unsure how she would take me.

But she kissed me back.

It might have been the best kiss I'd ever had.

CHAPTER TWENTY-FIVE

Luisa

I didn't know how I would feel when I finally got my revenge. When Esteban was finally dead by my own hands. I assumed I would feel guilt, maybe regret. The old lesson that revenge isn't always so sweet, that it can cause you to lose your very soul.

But the moment I sawed off his tongue, cut off his dick, and stabbed that knife right into his degenerate brain, I didn't feel any of those things.

Instead of losing my soul in the process, I felt like I'd gained one. That whatever part of me I'd lost, the part he'd *stolen* from me, came right back.

I felt full, whole.

And I felt momentous relief. It was wave after wave of cool, freeing reprieve, soaking me to the bone, giving my tired spirit wings again.

No, I didn't regret a goddamn thing.

Javier was there for me through it all. It was his sister that died, his friend that screwed him, screwed me, hurt me. But he let me do what I needed to do, even though I knew he was dying to do it himself.

He gave me the knife and set me free.

I couldn't thank him enough.

Or maybe I could.

He pulled me away from Esteban's dead, disgusting body and held my face in his bloody hands. I felt nothing but pure, complete love for him.

I'd been reborn. I'd never wanted him more.

So when he kissed me, soft and sweet, I answered with all the passion that had been buried away for far too long.

He moaned into my mouth, his hands touching my sides, so careful, so cautious.

"I need you," I told him, breaking away as his lips went for my neck—a wet, warm caress. I placed my hands over his, pressing them into my body, no longer afraid of him, no longer afraid of anyone. "I need you now. All of you. All of you, Javier."

He pulled back, searching my eyes. "Are you sure?"

I knew that he wasn't talking about the location.

I rubbed my red-stained hand over his crotch, feeling his hardness, his life pulse beneath me. "Fuck yes."

Something ignited in his eyes, as if he were finally seeing me for *me* for the very first time. His lips crashed against mine again, mouth so hungry as if he needed to consume me to live. I gave it right back. This was a wild, unrestrained need, and I thought I might die right then and there if I didn't get enough of him. The passion crackled between us—electric—a million fuses waiting to be blown.

I wanted to set them all off.

His hands were all over me, clawing and desperate, and I clung to him like a crazed animal, our clothes half torn, while the causality of our depravity and sweet revenge was just a few feet away. But I couldn't see that, couldn't see anything but Javier—didn't need anything but him.

We were down on the floor, one way, then the other, blood sticking beneath us. I got on my knees and grabbed the back of the pilot's chair while he yanked down my pants and thong. His fingers, feather soft like ghosts, trailed up and down my legs and over my inner thighs, making my skin quiver. But I needed more than that, I needed to be taken and claimed, devoured whole.

"Stop torturing me," I cried out.

He gave me a wicked chuckle in response. "Oh, but what beautiful torture this is," he murmured, licking a path down my spine, his fingers still teasing like angel wings. His head lowered, tongue snaking over my skin. I was desperate, straining for him, pressing myself back.

His tongue slid between my cheeks, dipping down, and I was greedy as hell, unable to stop the moans as they reverberated through my body.

"Fuck," Javier said, voice rough. "I've forgotten how good you taste. Nectar from the fucking gods. And mine, all mine."

Suddenly his grip on my thighs became hard, fingers digging in, and I knew he was giving in to his uncontrollable lust. He had patience in spades, but not this time, not now, not after everything we'd just gone through. He pulled back and I heard his pants unzip. I began to whimper quietly with mounting anticipation. I needed him to fill me, I needed more sweet release.

The desire was so acute, it hurt.

The tip of his hard cock pressed into me, just enough to tease, to get wet, and he took a firm hold of my hips. For one moment there was stillness, silence, and I thought I'd never breathe again. I thought the want and need would splinter my body into a million pieces.

Then he pushed in, so fucking deep, so damn thorough, groaning with insatiable lust—the same lust that made my knees shake, that threatened to undo my grip on the chair. His hand slid up between my breasts, cupping them, flicking over my hardened nipples, causing my nerves to ricochet until my whole body became electric. I was feeling what I thought I would never feel again.

"You're mine," he said huskily as he thrust forward. His balls hit my inner thighs as he rhythmically pounded me from behind, in and out, so deep, so thick. "Tell me you're mine."

I groaned, nearly unable to speak. "I'm yours."

"All of you, all of you," he said. Breathless, desperate.

"I'm yours."

"Your pussy is mine, your soul is mine." He leaned forward, biting the side of my neck, voice ragged with lust. "Your heart is mine. You're all mine. Every part of you, Luisa, every part."

"I'm yours," I said louder, moaning again as his fingers swirled over my clit. I was swelling with desire, dripping wet, a hair trigger. I wouldn't be able to hold back for much longer. I couldn't.

We were uncontrollable animals, primal, basic and so fucking dirty, and there wasn't anything we could do about that.

"You're my queen." His sweat dripped onto my back, his breathing hard. Everything was slippery and we were barely holding on, but he was tireless, wouldn't stop his frenzied thrusts. The whole helicopter started to shake. "I'm your king."

"You're my king," I managed to say before my eyes rolled back and I was lost in the delirium, his delicious thickness, the way he filled me whole. I couldn't imagine life without him, couldn't belong to anyone but him.

My king, my king, my king.

I went over the edge, in a rush of stars and colors and waves.

I was unbreakable now, unstoppable.

I was his.

I came so hard that I thought my body might never stop, the spasms rocking through me like I was the epicenter of a violent quake. I was flooded, with dark, hidden parts of me rising to the surface and rushing away, leaving me raw and bare to the bone.

It was only him and it was only me. King and Queen. That's all that existed in this rusty, bloody space, between these two tortured, filthy souls.

Tears spilled down my cheeks, a deluge of emotion no longer under wraps. All the death and pain had bloomed into something wild and beautiful. Something real.

He held me close to him, my back pressed against his slick chest, his pumping slowing as he poured himself inside me. His moans were intoxicating, the sound of the pleasure that he was getting from me and only me. Then he was gasping for air, almost as if he was in disbelief that he had finally claimed me once more.

"Luisa," he whispered, kissing my neck. "Luisa." But he didn't say anything else. He rested his head on my back and tried to regain his breath, his chest heaving against me.

We must have stayed like that for a few moments until I felt him slide out. When I managed to turn around, my limbs shaking from the strain of our lovemaking, I realized what a massacre this had been.

We were both a wreck, covered in blood and sweat. Javier's hair was messy, damp, and stuck to his forehead, his eyes glazed with peace and wonder. He held out his hand and helped me to my feet, holding on tight as I slid slightly on the wet floor.

He ran his fingers over my cheek and smiled. "Well, I've never done that before."

I raised a brow, pressing my hands to his chest. "You've never had sex next to a corpse? I have a hard time believing that."

"First time for everything, my dear," he said, kissing my forehead. He exhaled and looked around the helicopter, at the blood, guns, and body parts, then shrugged. "I guess we should go and make sure Diego and Evaristo are still alive."

I could tell I wasn't the only one who had forgotten about the war that had been waged out there. He held my hand, giving it a squeeze, and led me out the helicopter doors. We walked together across the overgrown lawn, my hand in his, past the dead bodies and the smoldering smoke. Diego, Evaristo, and a few others were conversing by the house.

They looked at us in surprise and waved.

We waved back at them.

King and queen.

EPILOGUE

Javier

"I've decided on a name," I said, walking out to the balcony where I knew Luisa was relaxing.

She was lying down on the chaise, reading a spy thriller, which she then put down on her chest and turned to face me. She peered over her large sunglasses expectantly.

"Oh?" she said, amused. We'd been doing this for a few weeks now, and every time she had a name, I disagreed, and every time I had one, she'd do the same. Normally a game like that would drive me insane with impatience, but this was actually somewhat fun.

"Yes," I said, coming over to the railing and leaning against it. The Pacific crashed just a few feet from the house, though the surf wasn't as angry today, and all the surfers who bobbed in the distance looked disappointed. I relished the fact that Esteban would have been rolling in his grave had he known Luisa and I would end up by his favorite surf spot. I even considered taking up the sport out of spite, but the idea of all that salt water drying my hair was too off-putting. Besides, Esteban was deader than dead, and the two of us were very much alive.

Two, plus one on the way.

"Well, what is it?" she prodded, running her hands over her stomach. It was absolutely huge now. It made her look monstrous, which I'd found wildly attractive for some reason. Six weeks to go and our son would be born.

Son.

Some days I couldn't even fathom it. Couldn't even wrap my head around it. But it's what we needed, not just for us, for our marriage, and our souls, but for the business. The moment I found out Luisa was pregnant with my child (and yes, I made sure it was in fact *my* child), I was over the moon with fear and relief, the two feelings in a constant battle. Fear that I would fuck things up as I had been known to do with every human being I'd ever come into contact with. Relief that finally I had an heir to take over the cartel. My blood. Someone I could truly trust, someone that I would raise to be just like me.

I mean, why not? Another version of myself couldn't hurt. He'd be wicked, intelligent, unapologetic, handsome, and if he were really lucky, taller than I was.

Up until now though, we couldn't decide on a damn name. If it had been a girl, I would have honored Alana by bestowing her with that name. But the sonogram proved it was a boy, and for that I was grateful.

I was certain we'd have a brood of kids in the future regardless, and if we had a girl, she'd need an older brother not only to protect her, but to look up to. Sure, there was risk in having a family. I knew that for a man in my position having loved ones increased the chances of loss and pain. But it didn't matter anymore. It would be worth it. It already was.

I sat beside Luisa and put my hands on her stomach, gently tracing over the side where the acid burn still remained, albeit fading away. "He's Vincente," I told her. "Vincente Bernal."

"Vincente," she repeated. "Vincente Bernal." She smiled. "I like it. No, I love it. Does it mean anything to you?"

I shook my head. It didn't mean anything. It just came to me that morning. "It just means our son."

I leaned forward and kissed her, putting my hands into her hair, which was now chin length and glossy black. The scars on her face were fading and barely visible when she covered them with makeup, but I still liked her bare-skinned. She looked more like a warrior that way. She looked more like Mrs. Bernal.

"Ahem." I heard Diego's voice.

I pulled away from Luisa to see him standing by the French doors.

"You and your timing," I said to him.

He gave me a vaguely apologetic look. "Sorry, *patron*, Luisa. I just wanted to make sure that everything was on for tomorrow, for the meeting."

I nodded and waved him away with my hand. "It's fine. Go and enjoy the beach or something."

"Yes sir," he said, even though I knew he was going right back inside to guard our bedroom door.

Luisa tugged on my arm. "I wish you didn't have to go to Tijuana."

"It's just for the night," I told her. It had taken a while, but a few months ago we were finally able to kill Angel Hernandez, the leader of the Tijuana Cartel, and I'd promptly taken over the plaza.

Naturally, I couldn't have done it without torturing Evaristo to begin with, but that was now water under the bridge. He was living in the nearby town of Todos Santos, acting as a priest for a tiny Catholic church which was a bit of a riot in itself, since the man wasn't holy whatsoever. Considering the church was so small to begin with, we all thought it would be the perfect cover now that Evaristo Sanchez was a wanted man across the country. The *federales* really hated a snitch—after all they'd tried so hard to prove to the government and the DEA that there was at least one official organization that could not be corrupted by the cartels.

Well, that didn't go so well for them. It just proved that no one was above corruption in this country, and if there had to be any changes made in Mexico, it had to start with the government. If they weren't paid so poorly, they probably wouldn't have to take bribes from people like me anyway.

But in the end, the way the country worked was better for us, although I'm not so sure about Evaristo. Though he'd become somewhat of a right-hand man to me, a lot of his time was taken up at the church. Father Armando, as he was known, was a handsome devil, and after he took his place as priest, suddenly the congregation doubled. Mainly women who were fawning over him, though there were a few husbands dragged along.

Still, there was a lot of business to conduct in Tijuana as the plazas and power shifted, and I was becoming something more of a business man again, constantly going back and forth. It was one of the reasons why we settled along the Baja Peninsula, so I could be closer to the new expansion and one of the busiest drug lines into America. It was worth it though—we were now more powerful than ever.

"Look," I told her, straightening up. "Next time I'm up there, you can come with me and we'll get you across the border. I'm sure your parents want to see you one more time before you give birth. It must be good luck or something."

"I don't think we need any more luck," she said, even though we both knew that wasn't true. We might be at the top, but that didn't mean we would stay there. There was no security in this business, just survival of the fittest. Luck could go either way, but as long as you had your own moral code and were willing to fight to the death to protect what was yours, you would go far.

And I still felt I had further to go.

"Oh," she said quickly, reaching down beside her and picking up a tote bag that carried a stack of magazines. "I found something weird today when I came back from town." She pulled out a postcard. "It was at our front door. I thought maybe they got the wrong house but...I don't know."

I took the postcard from her hands, staring at the glossy surface. It said *Utila, Honduras* on it and had a picture of a white sand beach.

I immediately felt uneasy.

I quickly turned it over and read the back.

There was no return address and no address to us. How could there be when this house didn't even officially exist.

The postcard just had a simple sentence scrawled on it, in familiar handwriting that knocked the wind out of me.

Pepito,
I'm doing okay.

Everything stilled around me, except for the postcard which began shaking in my tremoring hand.

Luisa placed her sunglasses on top of her head, staring up at me curiously. "Pepito," she said. "Alana called you that a few times."

I swallowed hard. "My nickname when we were young." I stared at her, waving the card vigorously. "This is Alana!"

She smiled. "I was hoping it was."

She was alive. All this time, my sister was alive. And apparently living on the island of Utila, so close but so far.

So alive.

All the grief, guilt, and sorrow that once pulled me under and made me sink to the greatest depths of violence and depression I had ever known all bubbled up at once, overtaking me.

I collapsed on my knees beside Luisa and cried.

I cried because I couldn't remember the last time I had cried. *If* I ever had.

She sank her fingers into my hair and held me as I got it all out, all the years of fucking up, all the terrible things I'd done to the people I loved. I would make no apologies for who I was, but I would to the ones I cared about the most. I had been a terrible brother, and for that I was sorry. I didn't deserve to have Alana back in my life. But she more than deserved to live.

When I was done, I'd felt cleansed. Definitely not pure, just...refreshed. Somewhat similar to when I would go on a violent rampage, but at least my hands weren't dirty this time. I was bloodless. I was clean.

"How did she find me?" I asked her.

She shrugged. "She's a Bernal. She's resourceful."

"She must be with Derrick," I said, remembering what Diego had told me. As a first-class assassin, Derrick was infinitely resourceful, but if he was keeping my sister alive, keeping her happy, then he could spy on me all he wanted. I owed him the world.

I took in a deep, steadying breath, composing myself. "What do I do next?"

Luisa kissed me softly on the forehead. "Javier, my love. Go to Tijuana. Do the right deals. Kill the right people. Then come back here and fuck me." She ran her hand down the side of my face, smiling wickedly. "This is your empire. Go build it."

And so I did.

THE END

ACKNOWLEDGEMENTS

This book could not have been made possible if it weren't for other books already in existence. Author Don Winslow's crime novels have always been a driving force in this entire trilogy, not only providing me with twisted, stunningly-written entertainment but with stone-cold fact. *The Cartel* as well as *The Power of the Dog* and *Savages* are among my favorite books ever and without them, Javier and his cartel wouldn't have the truth that they carry. (Also, thank you to Judy Morales for going to Don's Santa Barbara signing and getting *Cartel* and *Power of the Dog* personalized for me, I owe you the world, and to Sandy Borrero Romano for setting it all up! I legit have the best readers EVER).

El Sicario – The Autobiography of a Mexican Assassin by Molly Molloy and Charles Bowden, *Midnight in Mexico* by Alfredo Corchado, *The Devil's Highway* by Luisa Alberto Urrea (not particularly about cartels, but fascinating nonetheless) and *The Last Narco: Inside the Hunt for El Chapo, the World's Most Wanted Drug Lord* by Malcolm Beith were the books I consulted and read every moment of every day, during the writing of this book as well as the others in the trilogy. Without them, my words, characters and scenes would have fallen flat.

I'd also like to thank Ali Hymer for letting me bounce ideas off of her while we wine-toured in Napa (mmm, talking about zinfandels and decapitated penises), Sandra Cortez, Amanda Cantu, Jay Crownover for your honesty and wonderful reactions as you read and I wrote, Lisa Wilson, Luna Sol, MG Herrera, Kim Bailey, Tiffany Vitale-Corillo, Amy Fox, Rebecca Hughes, Arabella Brai, Nina Decker, Melissa Cooper, Pavlina Michou,

Courtney Epperson and Paula Novack for your enthusiasm in all things Javier Bernal, all the Anti-Heroes out there, my IG peeps, those damn wonderful WHORES and all they do, Dani Sanchez for her promotion, Laura Helseth for her proofing (and Javi squealing), Kara Malinczak for being an awesome editor as always and fully embracing this book in all its ugliness, nastiness and *brow raising*, and Naj Qamber for her last-minute overhaul of the cover, which really captures Luisa in all her cunningness.

And of course the biggest thank you goes to my husband, Scott, who had to put up with me while I wrote this book and I pretty much became Javier Bernal. He's going to be happy when I write contemporary romance again...I'm a LOT nicer to be around.

Oh, and I guess I should mention here that this won't be the last you'll ever see of Javier Bernal – I love the bastard too much. Evaristo Sanchez, the false priest, deserves something of his own. Also, there's a story I've been waiting to write until after Dirty Promises was finished. The thought of it makes me giddy like a fool. I'm not sure if it will be two books or one, if it will be self-published or go to a publisher. If the title(s) will be *Black Hearts, Dirty Souls*, or not.

If it will come in 2017.

But I will tell you it involves a love story between Vincente Bernal...and Violet McQueen. If you don't know who Violet McQueen is, I suggest you learn about Ellie and Camden in The Artists Trilogy...and that's all you need to know. Forbidden love at its absolute worst and finest. Bernals VS McQueens. It's going to be epic.

Thanks for coming on this cruel adventure with me! Feel free to follow me on Instagram (@authorhalle) for book news, giveaways, teasers and, of course, my daily adventures.